*A fascinating story, very well written. This is must reading.*

··· Sheilah Graham, United Features Syndicate

*By some mysterious alchemy, Mr. Berkman has caught both man and artist, pinned them down like the butterfly which was Whistler's signature.*

··· Sallie C. Lampee, Sacramento Union

*Wonderfully written, the type of book you do not wish to put down. Ted Berkman has convincingly captured the era, the styles of the individuals portrayed, and while it is obviously largely a fictional reconstruction, it reads like a very convincing observation.*

··· Richard H. Randall, Jr., Director
the Walters Art Gallery, Baltimore, MD

*Mr. Berkman has created a triumph. He sets the stage brilliantly in his Prologue. The complexities of Whistler's life are richly handled. The man behind the public mask emerges through Berkman's careful detailing and truly brilliant characterization. So few fictionalized biographies success- fully wed fact with believable dialogue. Mr. Berkman's years of research have paid off.*

··· Pomona (CA) Progress-Bulletin

**Books by Ted Berkman:**

Cast A Giant Shadow

Sabra

To Seize the Passing Dream

The Lady and the Law

My Prisoner

Around the World in 80 Years

# To SEIZE The PASSING DREAM

## A NOVEL OF WHISTLER, HIS WOMEN AND HIS WORLD

## Ted Berkman

Manifest Publications
Carpinteria, California
2000

# To Seize the Passing Dream

## A Story of Whistler, His Women and His World

### by Ted Berkman

Published by:
Manifest Publications
P.O. Box 429
Carpinteria, CA 93014-0429 U.S. A.

Library of Congress Catalog Card Number 99-65184

Cover Art: *Note en Rouge: L'Eventail (1884)*, F1913.91, and butterfly detail from *A Chinese Porcelain Covered Vase*, F1893.18; Courtesy of the Freer Gallery of Art, Smithsonian Institution Washington, D.C.

Cover Design by Valentina Laurence Pfeil

To Seize the Passing Dream

# Author's Note

The writing of *To Seize the Passing Dream* took some four years, divided about evenly between research and the typewriter. The Butterfly, as Whistler signed himself, wandered a good deal; and he was the subject of more words—if less understanding—than any other artist of his era. The book entailed thousands of miles of travel, climbing the equivalent of what seemed like the Himalayas in museum and library steps, and foraging through reams of reading matter, much of it in French or faded handscript.

Wherever Whistler walked—along the Hudson and the Thames, through the crumbling palaces of Venice and the cobbled streets of Montparnasse—I have walked in his footsteps, down to the cemetery at Chiswick where he buried his wife near Hogarth's grave and on July 22, 1903, himself went to his rest. My itinerary touched virtually all of his dwelling places and battlegrounds: the cadet barracks at West Point, rooftop garrets in Paris, the London Court of Exchequer. I would have been happy to dance at the Bal Bullier or Cremorne Gardens, but the former has been annihilated by a railroad cut and the once-golden gardens have yielded to a power station.

On the whole, Whistler's world of London and Paris remains a century later remarkably intact, if one makes allowance for remodeling (his brother-in-law's massive town house has become a warren of small apartments) and for altered street signs (the original Passage Stanislas peers out under new lettering in Montparnasse). In our swinging seventies, King's Road in Chelsea is still a magnet for rebels and individualists. Even by day, the quiet side streets enclose the Rossetti Garden Mansions and Godwin Court; by night the clock rolls back, and in the ghostly silence that follows the slamming of the last pub doors one can evoke the Victorian clatter of hoofs along the pavement.

To penetrate Whistler's world in a more personal sense, I have had the privilege of examining the Birnie Philip Bequest of Whistleriana at the University of Glasgow. This largest of Whistler treasure-troves, gift of the painter's heir, contains innumerable letters, catalogues and other memorabilia dealing with Whistler and his family, as well as many paintings rarely seen. While by agreement none of this documentation is quoted directly, the opportunity to explore it along with such items as Whistler's spectacles, his paint-encrusted palette and his private library yielded insights into character, circumstance, and relationships not available elsewhere.

Data of nearly comparable bulk originally assembled by Whistler's first biographers, Joseph and Elizabeth Pennell, but now owned by Glasgow University has been similarly scrutinized for background at the Library of Congress in Washington. This material includes correspondence, menus, canceled bills (and others not so canceled), and pounds of papers dealing with the painter's libel suit against John Ruskin and with Whistler's subsequent bankruptcy.

Since the best of what a great painter does usually finds an ultimate home in museums, I have tramped through many: French, English, Scottish, Spanish, Dutch, and American. Most important, of course, was the Louvre, where I disturbed musty storage racks and remote attics in search of early work of "the Master" and his Impressionist friends. At the Freer Gallery in Washington, D.C., which houses America's best Whistler collection, I was overwhelmed by the Peacock Room; twice I visited Madrid to see Whistler's beloved Velázquez portraits at El Prado. The better to comprehend what I was looking at, I studied drawing, oil painting, and pastels during 1969 at the Bercone Studio in New York, and the following year worked with etchers at the MacDowell Colony in Peterborough, New Hampshire.

There are a score of books dealing with Whistler's life and works, and more than a hundred long articles in magazines ranging from the *Journal of Military Service Institutions* to *The Studio*. His contemporaries were also keen diarists and much given to memoirs; I have read everybody's reminiscences of everybody else, as well as the newspaper files of the period stored in the Collindale Annex of London's British Museum.

*To Seize the Passing Dream* is a novel in that it includes not only invented dialogue, but the imagined thoughts of its central character. I chose this form because Whistler took great pains to camouflage and conceal himself, and a life of masquerade, by its very nature, can be illuminated only from the inside. Nonetheless, the book is rooted firmly in documentary evidence; my fiction begins where the trail of ascertainable fact ends. Wherever possible, I have worked from verbatim contemporary accounts. Some of what James McNeill Whistler says in *To Seize the Passing Dream* is his; more of it is mine; and I would hope that, apart from certain world-famous mots, the reader will be unable to say which is which.

I have violated no fact of consequence to accommodate my story-telling convenience, nor introduced any fictional people beyond the occasional waiter or concierge. Whistler's life was a full one; the problem has been to pick from the wealth of facts, then flesh out those involvements and episodes which seemed of particular interest, sometimes building them into dialogues as faithful to character, time and place as research could make them.

No liberties have been taken with basic relationships. The attitudes toward Whistler of, for example, Colonel Robert E. Lee at one end of the artist's life and Toulouse-Lautrec at the other, are extrapolated from concrete evidence. So are the invented scenes, such as Whistler's act of volunteering for military service in Chile; something very much like it must have happened to get him from one recorded point in his life to the next.

The standard source on Whistler has long been the 1911 Pennell biography, which for all of its formidable array of names and dates is essentially an account dictated by the painter himself toward the end of his life, highly flavored by vanity and forgetfulness. The Pennells had no knowledge of their subject's crucial early years, and were prohibited by Victorian discretion as well as hero-worship from exploring his most vital relationships, those with his mistress Jo Heffernan and his mother. Nor were they meticulous reporters. For instance, their supplementary Whistler Journal asserts baldly and without amplification that the painter disliked Jews—a charge not supported by his personal associations, his letters, or his conduct during the Dreyfus affair.

Although I make no pretense of definitive scholarship, I can claim thoroughness in the areas of my special focus. For instance, because the English-language texts of Whistler's letters to his artist friend Fantin-Latour seemed to me unidiomatic, I went back to the French originals in the Gazette des Beaux Arts and did my own translations. When I cite the price of a size-C picture frame in Louis Napoleon's Paris, or the steamship routes in 1866 between Southampton and Valparaiso, I am not guessing.

Some of this investigation brought unexpected dividends. The first hint of a close bond between Whistler and Toulouse-Lautrec came in Glasgow, when I found on the back of one of Trixie Godwin Whistler's letters a whimsical sketch of the Count.

Similarly, the Degas-Whistler story sprang from the discovery in the Louvre archives of the original copy-register in which the young anti-Salon rebels were required to inscribe their names, the date, and the titles of the canvases before which they wanted to set up their easels.

I found that at the time Degas was studying Whistler sketches, the only other painters he had thought worth emulating were Rembrandt, Veronese, and Ingres.

The re-creation of Jo Heffernan, of whom previously there had been only tantalizing traces, began with the ascertaining at London's Irish Embassy of her distinguished lineage . . . fully borne out by a letter uncovered in Washington from Jo to Whistler's lawyer. That Jo raised the child of Whistler's "infidelity" is established by a half-dozen references, although confusion persists about the boy's precise name and age.

Research into Whistler's mother—both the woman and the portrait —led to some surprises; who would have associated Clemenceau with the picture? The angry scene between mother and son over Jo is based on a letter from Anna Whistler to a friend in North Carolina, described at some length by Elizabeth Mumford in her biographical *Whistler's Mother*.

It would be ponderous to list all those who have been helpful. But I must make grateful mention at least of Professor Andrew McLaren Young, curator of the Birnie Philip Bequest at Glasgow University and his assistant, Robin Spencer; John Yeoman of the Chelsea Arts Club; Mmes. Sylvie Beguin and Yvonne Contin of the Louvre; Professor Jean Chennebenoist of the Lycée at Tourgéville-Deauville; Professor Steven Marcus of Columbia University; Frank A. Haentschke of the Freer Gallery; and Joel Blau. Valuable consultation was provided by Dr. Stephen Nordlicht and Dr. Reuben Fine.

I have also had the aid of many painters. Joel Goldblatt was kind enough to read my manuscript. Aaron Berkman, Ethelyn Honig, and the late Mark Rothko dealt patiently with innumerable questions; Larry Calcagno, Deanne Conner, Giselle Held, and the Spanish sculptor Juan Palá gave me a greater understanding of the thoughts and feelings of the working artist.

Of the institutions on whose resources I have repeatedly drawn, I should mention in New York first the Public Library, especially its Art-Architecture Division and the Donnell Branch, as well as the Thomas Watson Library of the Metropolitan Museum of Art, the New York Society Library, the British Information Service, the Cultural Services of the French Embassy, and the American-Irish Historical Society; in London the British Museum, Victoria and Albert Museum, Royal Academy of Arts, and King's Road Branch of the Kensington-Chelsea Public Library.

Finally, I thank Lee Barker, whose editorial verve has never been dulled by decades of providing authors with wise counsel.

*Prologue*
# Thames Nocturne

# Chapter One

He sat on a tavern balcony overlooking the Thames, blue-gray eyes scanning the riverside squalor of London's East End. In the rapidly fading light, he swept a stub of charcoal with quick, loose movements across the sketch pad in his lap. The artist sang softly to himself, his voice high and reedy against the din of steamboat whistles and dockside hammers: "Yankee Doodle went to London, ridin' on a ponee . . ."

A mile to the west, the first lights of the Tower Bridge winked on with voluptuous leisureliness. The year was 1875, and each lamp in turn glowed into life with the arrival of the lamplighter. Behind the bridge, the sky was a mass of whirling color . . . the late-autumn splendor of southern England.

"Damn!" Directly across the artist's line of vision, a gaggle of women were scrambling over the gravel-pocked flats. The tide was falling back, leaving chunks of coal, copper nails and other treasures for the poor of London half-buried in the river bed. The mudlarks, skirts hoisted high, shrieked as they waded into the brackish water, brandishing kettles and baskets overhead.

The man on the balcony was himself an arresting figure. From the fierce foxlike triangle of his face down to the astonishing pink bows on his shoes, everything about him crackled defiance. The militant air was not misleading. He was at forty-one the most controversial painter in England, widely hated and as widely feared. A self-avowed "artistic pirate," he had lately been forced to the very edge of the gangplank, with a dozen hands struggling for the honor of tossing him to the sharks.

The door behind him opened, and a slender girl of about twenty appeared. She wore a faded apron over a red-and-white checked gingham dress. "It's half after seven, Mr. Whistler."

The artist did not look up. "Of what possible interest could that be to me?" He spoke in a quiet drawl, tinged with the accents of the Old South.

"Well—for one thing—Mr. Greaves has been waiting for you down at the dock since six. And for another, I'm going off duty. My man'll be wanting his dinner."

"Ah, the sturdy Briton and his sordid beef." The well-poised head turned around, thick black curls swinging like silent bells. Slight but gracefully proportioned, he had been described publicly as a "pocket Apollo"; for once he had not challenged the popular judgment. "It amazes me," he went on, "that a people with so little talent for preparing food should be so obsessive about consuming it on a regular schedule."

"Yes, sir. Is there anything more I can do for you?"

"No, thank you, Daisy. Unless you could arrange to hold the light for another ten minutes?"

"Not even you can do that, sir."

The painter's brows, dark and satanic, converged in a frown. "Don't bet on it."

"Dai-sy!" a voice bawled from inside.

The girl turned, annoyed. "Be back in half a mo', sir."

The light was dimming now in swift, decisive stages. With kaleidoscopic suddenness the river was being transformed. The clamor subsided. What had been a nostalgic sunset scene, blazing with color, gave way to a muted twilight, carving new patterns of cloud shadows on the water. Within minutes this in turn was yielding to the subtle envelopment of night. A barge slipped silently upstream, its outlines receding to ghostly dimness. Oars splashed somewhere nearby, from a boat already half-lost in the gathering offshore mist. A skiff riding at anchor in the middle of the river bobbed abruptly into view, illuminated by the lanterns from a passing freighter, then vanished like a fragment of dream. Behind the freighter rippled a trail of reflected light, silent, shimmering, pregnant with mystery . . .

Whistler stared intently, his eyes vivid against a skin whose warm coloring hinted of olive trees and sandy Mediterranean shores. That such radiant vessels should also be myopic seemed an impertinence on the part of nature; yet there was no mistaking their squint as the artist strained forward in his chair.

The strain was not reflected in the sketch taking shape under his hand. With a few strong lines, some deftly-shaded masses, and a most eloquent use of space, he had created something beyond the recognizable shape of piers and afterdecks: an atmosphere. Now instinct took over the finishing touches. The charcoal, propelled by long nervous fingers that seemed to leap with a life of their own, flew over the paper.

The girl was back. "Things is a bit thick with Mr. Riley," she announced.

"Your estimable employer? The proprietor of the Angel?"

"He's been giving me what for about your bill, sir. Says you been drinking his whisky on tick for a month."

"And I've been wearing this blazer for three! Why should he expect to be paid ahead of my tailor?" Beneath his insouciance, the painter's eyes flicked restlessly.

"Ow now, Mr. Whistler. You're not telling me you ain't got the ready? That you're out of tin? In the lum?"

"I could never have hoped to put it so elegantly—but yes."

"Blimey!" Daisy stared at the rakish yellow straw, the impeccable white linen ducks matched to the navy blazer. "With all them bloomin' lovely things!"

"Just between us, Daisy—I'm afraid there's rather less than meets the eye." The painter turned up one of his square-toed dancing pumps, disclosing a neat round hole near the toe.

"What are we to do, sir? Mr. Riley says he don't believe in carrying bills above five quid."

"And quite right he is. At that point, the sporting thing to do is to wipe out the account and start all over." Whistler smiled, softening the jut of his jaw, the pugnacious tilt of his nose. It was a face to which men reacted equivocally, women less so. For them the combination of Puck and Mephistopheles aroused an impulse to fondle or spank—but either way, to touch.

Daisy leaned over his shoulder, peering at the sketch. "Why don't you finish up tomorrow, by daylight? A body can't see a thing now."

"That depends on who the body is. And what he's lookin' for, doncher know?"

The sudden Anglicism, mixed with the dropped "g," was disconcerting. The girl pointed to the drawing. "Is that supposed to be a buoy, on the right?"

"It's whatever you choose it to be. For me, it's a particular tone of gray, essential to the ultimate composition."

"But I don't see no buoy out there."

"An oversight of nature, my dear. It happens constantly."

"Coo!" The girl shook her head. "I wisht I could draw."

"But you do, my dear!" The artist stood up, placing the sketch carefully in a folder near the railing. "You draw a pint of ale from the tap as prettily as any barmaid in all of Limeyland."

Appreciative laughter. "Limeyland! You're not English yourself, are you, Mr. Whistler?"

Whistler stared at her. He drew a monocle from his waistcoat pocket and, screwing up his right eye, inserted it before delivering the imperious reply: "By the grace of the Lord—and His excellent good judgment—no!"

"Don't you like this country?"

"You have the finest fogs in the world. Unfortunately, they are not confined to the landscape."

Her hand on the doorknob, the girl lingered. "Where were you born, sir?"

"I wasn't. I descended from on high."

Flirtatiously, "I should have said from below."

"Ha-ha!" Whistler's laugh was short, hard—and ambiguous. It could signal either merriment, or—when rasped out with a faint cutting edge —imminent danger. This time, as nearly always with servants, children, and others lacking either the power or the instinct to hurt him, it was friendly. "You're an amusing tyke, Daisy."

Still the girl did not leave. She arched her back provocatively against the door. "When are you going to take my portrait, Mr. Whistler?"

The painter stroked his upcurled mustache, then dropped his hand to the Kentucky cavalry imperial adorning his chin. A mischievous glance came into the darting eyes. "Would you pose in the, ah—?" The long supple fingers made a swift gesture of undressing.

She met his gaze boldly. "For you, yes."

"Well, we shall see"—the full lips pursed wickedly—"what we shall see. Meantime, could you keep these in a safe place for me?" He indicated a few sticks of charcoal, a chamois cloth, an eraser, and a pad of sketching paper.

"Of course." Daisy gathered them up. "Can anybody learn to make pictures, Mr. Whistler? Or is it something that just runs in a family—?"

"You mean, is genius hereditary?" The painter adjusted his fluttering bow tie. "I can't say, my dear. Heaven has granted me no offspring."

This was not strictly true. As the painter was fully aware, at least one of his informal liaisons had left its mark.

Whistler fumbled in his jacket pocket. "Damnation. No silver." He looked up. "Would you by chance have a half-crown, Daisy?"

The girl fished in her apron and came up with a coin. Whistler accepted it gravely; then returned it with a ceremonious bow: "My compliments for your many courtesies." He turned on his heel and started toward the stairs.

Behind him, a final flutter from the bemused barmaid. "We don't see many artist fellows in the East End. Are they all like you, Mr. Whistler?"

Whistler did not look back. "Unfortunately for British painting, no."

Clattering down the weather-worn stairs, he had the light, perky step of a Viennese riding-master; one half-expected to see him flick an imperious whip, and spring into the saddle. At the bottom of the flight, he paused to fill his lungs. The riverfront air was an appalling but bracing mixture of rotting fish, tar, turpentine, and fresh brine; of curing sheds, empty whisky kegs, and Chinese fried chicken, all overlaid with a pungent blanket of soft coal smoke. There was a vitality here, long since drained from the manicured squares of Mayfair.

Still sniffing, he turned briskly onto Elephant Lane, the rough dirt path leading to the public dock some two hundred yards away. There was a better road inland, but he preferred to follow the river bank. Water had always fascinated him. It was loose, yielding, free; constantly shifting form, endlessly reborn. Its depths might enclose everything—or nothing. A river beckoned softly to the imagination, a woman inviting her lover to plumb her secrets. How typically perceptive of the French to give all rivers the feminine gender; and how much more delicate and languorous was "La Tamise" than "the Thames."

This in particular was his favorite moment, when the world hung suspended between day and night, drenched in mystery and enchantment. It was an hour that the native Briton, bent on hurrying to his hearth, tended to ignore; but for James McNeill Whistler, outlander from across the sea, it alone made exile endurable. In all the world— and he had seen much of it, from semi-Asiatic Russia to the Andes— there was nothing to match this mellow blue-gray silence. The evening mist, slowly rising from the somber Thames, was like a veil over the riverside, clothing it with poetry. In the harsh light of midday, the Thames might be a blowzy harridan, her colors faded and her rouge misplaced; but by night she was a veiled houri, promising unimaginable delights . . .

It was this twilight landscape, of factory chimneys transformed to campaniles, and shabby warehouses touched with lantern beams to become fairy palaces in the night, that he had determined to capture on canvas; an absurd gamble, said the critics, on which he was throwing away his last hope of a respectable future. But these diagrams in dots of yellow, this memory of a memory in dusky blue, were the stuff of his Nocturnes. Let others trumpet the sunlit pomp of Empire; he would be content to seize the passing dream.

"Over here, Jimmy."

The voice came from his right. He had reached the public dock. A few yards away, two figures were silhouetted against a rowboat rocking lightly on the tide.

The Greaves brothers, Walter and Harry, were youngish neighbors of Whistler on the Chelsea waterfront some seven nautical miles away. Their father ran a shipyard. Amateur artists, they were glad to provide ferry service across the face of London for the privilege of addressing "the Master" on terms of intimacy.

As Whistler reached the boat, he suddenly threw up his arm as if to shield his eyes. "Good God, Harry, are you trying to blind me? Take it off, man, take it off!"

"What's the matter, Jimmy?"

His head turned away, Whistler pointed. "That waistcoat. It's lighting up the entire river!"

Harry looked down at the offending garment, barely visible in the gloom.

"Those tones!" Whistler went on. "Outrageous orange on repulsive red. It's a Turner sunset, all glare and bombast. Not to be believed—painted—or worn!"

"I'm sorry, Jimmy." Humbly, "You can sit with your back to me."

Lowering his arm, Whistler shook his head. "This is a bad business, Harry. Two demerits, sir!"

Harry looked over appealingly at his older brother in the stern of the boat. Walter made a gesture as of puffing on a cigarette.

Picking up the cue, Harry pulled a small pouch from his pocket and held it out. "Brought some fresh tobacco for you, Jimmy. Turkish."

"Oh? Oh?" The eyebrows escalated. This was Whistlerian code for surprise, mingled with a certain skepticism. He sniffed the pouch. "So it is," he decreed. "Demerits canceled." He stepped nimbly into the boat and crossed to the empty slat in the center, facing Walter. "Cast off," he ordered. Harry's oars dipped into the water and the boat moved swiftly toward midstream.

Whistler took a leaf of paper from his pocket and started to roll it with his fingers. "What news, Walter?"

"Your friend George Boughton stopped by. Said he'd taken care of your dues at the Arts Club—"

"Good. Their 'little reminders' were getting tiresome."

"—and that it wasn't too soon to start planning for next year's Royal Academy. He thought you ought to consider sending one of your new Thames things."

"After the way they treated the portrait of my mother? Never!"

"But Jimmy—the Nocturnes are different."

"Much *too* different, I'm afraid."

Walter's plain, honest face showed bafflement. "What do you have to lose?"

"Nothing—unless you count dignity, honor, self-respect. They have shown themselves unworthy. So Whistler will continue to fly the black banner of the pirate, and leave it to the Academy to run up the white flag of surrender—if they can develop sufficient color sense to distinguish between the two!"

The fire retreated from the painter's eyes, and he tapped some tobacco from the pouch. "Was Boughton the only visitor?"

Walter shook his head. "Chap came three or four times in the afternoon, knocking at your door. Tradesman, from the look of him."

The painter leaned forward alertly, assuming a professional-detective air. "The knocks," he said. "Were they *thump-thump*? Or"—lowering his voice gently—"*rap rap*?"

"Oh, they were very soft and polite, Jimmy," Walter assured him. "That's bad."

Walter looked startled. "You see," Jimmy continued, "you can measure the amount of the debt by the severity of the knock. A loud, reckless bang on the door means a minor debt; the man isn't too concerned about collecting. Where larger sums are involved, however, the tradesman is more nervous—and therefore more respectful. This might have been the wine dealer, Lennert. Or even the poultryman."

"He looked more like wine. Reddish whiskers. Anyway, we told him you were away. On a long trip. Amsterdam, or Venice. Maybe even America."

"Ha ha!" The painter's laughter was high, almost a cackle, and glinting with malice. "That's good!" He fingered his imperial reflectively. "Ah, the blessed America. I really must go home for a visit one of these days. One can't keep disappointing a continent forever."

"He said that when you came back, you'd probably find a bailiff in possession."

Jimmy looked hurt. He had expected better things of Lennert. After all, as he pointed out to the Greaveses, the wine merchant was being honored by the appearance of his wares on the table of a noted artist. It was an unpurchasable form of advertising. To think that, merely over a technical delay in payment, Lennert should make this vulgar display at the very door of his benefactor's manor! "Shocking. I shall have to cross the man off my list."

Jimmy finished rolling his cigarette. He stretched his legs in the boat, crossing one pink bowed pump carefully over the other. "Any further tidings of a funereal nature?"

Walter hesitated. "Well—there was a messenger from Mr. Mintwood."

Jimmy's hand, about to strike a match, froze in midair. "Yes?"

"He won't be keeping his appointment for a sitting tomorrow. Or next week, either."

"Damn!" Jimmy flipped the match, unused, into the river.

Mintwood was a furniture manufacturer, a roly-poly little man with a large family and an even larger bankroll. Inexplicably, he had been much impressed by the recent one-man Whistler show at the Pall Mall

Galleries, and had commissioned a portrait. There were hints of plans for each of his five sons to follow their father to the Whistler posing platform and immortality.

Jimmy had been skeptical of the scheme from the outset. He would be bored with assorted Mintwoods, he knew, by the second or third son at the most.

As things turned out, he had been overoptimistic. The tycoon himself was fidgety from the first sitting, and resented being called back for more. A few days before, had come the inevitable explosion. Stepping down from the sitter's platform, Mintwood had waddled up to the still-wet canvas. He wrinkled his ample nose. "Do you call that, sir, an outstanding work of art?"

The painter laid down his brushes. "Do you call yourself, sir, an outstanding work of nature?"

Evidently Mintwood had not been amused. And now Jimmy was faced with the rich man's reprisal: no more commissions.

The painter blinked rapidly, dimly aware of an incipient tear. Despite his forty-odd years and a formidable record as a street brawler and international sophisticate, he still cried easily.

Well, he could live without Mintwood. The man was just another *nouveau riche* seeking a ride to notoriety on the coattails of a public figure.

Living without Mintwood's pound sterling was another matter. The Whistler exchequer was at low tide indeed. His two outstanding portrait canvases, of his mother and the philosopher-historian Thomas Carlyle, were leading a precarious existence, shuttling between pawnshops and dealers as collateral for the loans that kept him afloat.

Jimmy struck another match and lighted up. It was dark now. He gazed at the current, racing outward against them, rippling like muscles under the brown skin of the river. London Bridge loomed ahead, its gas lamps creating shimmering ladders of gold stretched across the water.

A damp wind stirred, and he shivered slightly. His British contemporaries were dining in their drapery-hung eighteen-room mansions, surrounded by priceless statuary, basking in knighthoods and a public acclaim that would not survive the decade. In all England, no other artist of his stature—the acknowledged peer and companion of Courbet, Degas, Manet—was paddling down a chilly river in pursuit of a private dream.

For two long decades he had been abroad, and what did he have to show for it? A collection of press cuttings, most of them frivolous, condescending or worse; a studio full of unsold and in many cases uncompleted paintings (the handful of successes seemed to shrink as the years went by); an upward-creeping mountain of debts. Only as an etcher had he been accepted at all, and his sets of Alsatian and Thames plates were long behind him.

Even on his own terms, he had failed as often as not. He could have visions like Michelangelo, and paint river scenes no other man could even approach; but he could not draw a leg like the comrades of his Paris student days, Degas and Fantin-Latour.

Nor was his personal life more satisfactory: a succession of more or less disreputable love affairs with women often beautiful, but rarely of his own social class. Until recently he had been uneasy host to his seventy-one-year-old mother, now visibly fading in retirement at Hastings.

He had come to London from Paris some fifteen years before, attracted by the presence of a married half sister . . . and the Thames. In retrospect, the move probably had been a mistake. He had arrived fresh from the ateliers of the Left Bank, bubbling over with the excitement of the realist-impressionist revolution, only to encounter the frozen conservatism of Britain's Royal Academy. England was overflowing with the riches of empire, and her artists were dedicated to keeping her newly prosperous merchants happy. The late Sir David Wilkie, a respected Academician, had summed up the matter briskly: "To know the taste of the public is to an artist the most valuable of all knowledge."

Saints, babies, and puppies were certifiably effective. So were innocent maidens subjected to—but rising above—temptation; a proper moral outlook was far more important than competent draftsmanship.

Against the torrent of pious platitudes, the young American had first offered the etched reality of the Thames dockside, thereby committing the crime of discovering beauty where it did not officially exist. He had gone on to do portraits that did not flatter—and were frankly unconcerned with—the sitter, then to wraithlike mood-paintings with no didactic purpose whatever. Most unpardonable of all, in British eyes, he had defended these outrages coolly, in person and in print.

The guardians of public taste, as suspicious of an unfamiliar accent in painting as in anything else, had reacted predictably. The American interloper was "vague," "slovenly," a "vulgar mountebank."

Certainly he had struck back; he was a Whistler and a McNeill, with generations of soldiering in his blood. He had prinked many a prying nose, laid about him with *epée* and broadsword like a beleaguered Cyrano. But their numbers were overwhelming; and although he had never been brought down, neither had he been able to cut a path through their tightly clustered ranks.

When jester's bells were thrust upon him—"another crop of Mr. Whistler's little jokes"—he had bowed with a suitable comic grimace and donned the jaunty cap as well. There were terrible moments, when he stormed and wept at his own incapacities. But only he knew that. Only he would ever know. By daring gesture and dazzling display, by skewering his enemies and bewildering his friends, he had kept the world at arm's length.

Every clown, according to theatrical legend, was a frustrated tragedian, a would-be Hamlet. Here, as in so many other things, he had turned the convention upside down; he was Hamlet in the garb of Harlequin. He took a small private pleasure in the knowledge. But it was one joke—perhaps the only one—that he kept to himself.

Now they were more than halfway home, in the middle of the long southward loop that began after Waterloo Bridge. They were skimming past the Houses of Parliament, great dim towers in the night, awesome reminders of the Anglo-Saxon solidity—and stolidity—that survived where more picturesque and volatile people went under. How many lances before his own had splintered against the heedless gates of the Royal Academy?

He straightened up. Enough of inner colloquy; he was in this fight to the finish.

Meanwhile, a bit of respite was in order. He sensed that, aboard the rowboat, spirits were flagging all around. The Mintwoods of the world must not be allowed to call the tune for their betters. "Walter!"

Walter Greaves looked up.

"We're celebrating tonight. You and Harry will be my guests at Cremorne. We'll send a messenger for Albert Moore, and make it dinner for four."

"But you don't have any tin, Jimmy. And they've cut off your credit at Cremorne."

"Ah, but not your cash, n'est-ce pas?" Whistler extended his open palm. "I'll only need a couple of quid. You'll have it back next week."

Walter nodded. He knew that the loan, like dozens before it, would be repaid. Whatever Jimmy's shortcomings as a credit risk for tradesmen, he was scrupulous about honoring personal obligations. And Walter admired the resilient optimism that seemed to burgeon in the face of mounting disasters.

The painter was standing up in the boat. "At ease, Harry. I'll have a go at the oars."

"Whatever you say, Jimmy. But you'll be rowing against a strong tide."

Jimmy smiled. "It won't be the first time." He settled into the bow seat and dug his oars powerfully into the water. His high, thin tenor floated defiantly toward the shore:

> "We don't want to fight,
> But by jingo! if we do
> We've got the ships,
> We've got the men,
> And got the money too–oo–oo!"

It was a little after eleven when the travelers, having docked in Chelsea, set out again from Cadogan Pier a few steps from Jimmy's house. Their rowboat slipped past the Old Battersea Bridge, its bony jumble of crisscrossed timbers softened to a long smooth curve by the moonless night. There were four men in the party now; the newcomer, like Whistler, was in evening clothes. He was Albert Moore, a slight, narrow-shouldered man with the remote air of an undergraduate poet. A full beard and mustache virtually covered his face, so that he seemed to be peering out wistfully at the world from behind a clump of bushes.

Actually, Moore was a stubborn and raffish-minded fellow, of whom a versifying Arts Club colleague had written:

> Comes brother Albert with a footstep fainter
> The delicate but disputatious painter

A specialist in neoclassic nudes, Moore composed his canvases brilliantly. But what really endeared him to Jimmy was his refusal to curry Academy favor by the usual patron-swapping and fake bonhomie.

Harry Greaves swung the boat westward, where the myriad gaslights of Cremorne gleamed on the north shore less than a mile away. Cremorne—officially the Royal Cremorne Pleasure Gardens—was a nocturnal playground of mild notoriety, spread over a rambling estate covered with elms, ash and oak trees. By day, when the one-shilling admission fee brought thousands of innocents to frolic among its lawns, kiosks, concert groves, and banquet halls, Cremorne was decorous enough. But at sundown the calico customers went east with the penny steamer, and silken ladies began to arrive with top-hatted gentlemen in quick pursuit.

Cremorne by night was a place for liaisons and flirtations, where a shopkeeping family man could sup behind discreet lattices with a female friend from the music halls . . . or, for a "present," extend his amorous acquaintance.

As Harry turned the boat northward toward shore, a circle of flame suddenly spurted out of a dark grove to their left. "Firewheel!"

shouted Walter Greaves. Moore stood up to look past him. "Magnificent, Jimmy," he murmured.

More streaks of light crackled and flared around the grounds; then, with a swish and a roar, a giant rocket streaked up over the trees into the blue-black sky, to burst in a brilliant corona, then fall away in a shower of golden petals.

Jimmy was on his feet. "Pull in your oars, Harry!" He turned to Walter. "Of course, you brought sketch paper."

Of course, Walter had. Too many expeditions in the past had had similar endings. He reached into an oilskin pouch—security against rain and mist—and drew out a drawing board pinned with rectangles of brown paper, along with sticks of black and white chalk. Jimmy sat down in the prow and waited. There would be another rocket soon. He would trace the silhouette of his design with the black chalk, indicating areas of shade; with the white he would touch in the streaks and dots of light. Then he could concentrate on the color values, in his own fashion.

Minutes passed in silence, the boat bobbing gently on the tide. Finally Moore spoke: "That was probably the last batch, Jimmy. It's nearly midnight."

"And I haven't et anything since noon," added Harry Greaves.

"Very naughty of you," observed Jimmy, eyes on the shore.

"Me neither," put in Walter.

"Munch on your memories, boys."

He did not intend to be callous. When Jimmy was working, human needs did not exist—his own or anyone else's.

The shoreline sputtered and blazed into action again, and Jimmy bent over his board. This and this alone was real for him: to see, to feel, and to give the feelings two-dimensional expression.

The scene before them would never be precisely the same again—in its blend of darkness and brilliance, of velvet sky and rough-dappled water, of silent trees and spiraling rockets. Or, if nature did so shape it again, he almost certainly would not be there to absorb and transmute its impact onto canvas. The meeting of a special moment in time and of a particular, infinitely sensitized set of human nerve endings was a one-time thing, the delicious challenge as well as the desperate hazard of art. Every resource accumulated in decades of training had to be summoned up and focused on this not-to-be-repeated instant which might at any second fade or be shattered. It was like transfixing a butterfly on the wing.

What he sought was to distill the magic at the heart of the moment . . . a magic to which even the dullest eye would not be insensible, but which only the artist could penetrate and record. Like the Japanese masters, who had also painted fireworks, he hoped to project the infinite and eternal cloaked in the guise of the present.

He would have to work fast, imprison the picture in his mind before it disappeared. His eye swept over the scene for a few seconds with fierce intensity, as if seeking to swallow it whole. Then he closed his lids: "Check me, would you, Alfred?"

Like a relay runner picking up a baton, Moore took over the concentrated scrutiny.

"At extreme left," Jimmy began, "clump of trees reaching almost to top of canvas, sloping down at angle of about forty-five degrees—no, make that sixty. Trees are dark brown mixed with green, quite opaque.

"Sky occupies most of remaining upper half of canvas: transparent cobalt blue and gray, areas of reflected green. In center, very dim outline of tall slender structure. To its right, a cluster of rocket fragments: irregular globes and triangles in tones of pink and vermilion.

"Below and to the right are main feature of composition: two twisting columns of falling sparks, like a spray of gold coins flung down from heaven.

"At bottom of trees, far left, a patch of gold balanced by pink, possibly a group around a table . . . Did I forget anything?"

"What about the foreground, Jimmy?"

"Didn't I mention that? A section of beach curving up to left, in tones of beige and yellow ochre, with one or two indistinct figures on shore. Stretch of ivory-black water, melting into dark green closer to shore. The basic color harmony is black, against the embroidery of gold scattered through the picture."

Harry Greaves picked up his oars. "The Gardens will be closing. I think we'd best go back and have some cold beef."

Jimmy nodded. "My apologies, gentlemen." He settled back in his seat. "But I suspect we shall have some fireworks of our own from this picture. Dark brown and green against ivory black: wait till the man from *The Times* sees that."

"Or *can't* see it," amended Moore.

"Ah, the howls of rage it will raise at the Royal Academy. 'Whistler has broken the rules again. One does not paint the night.'"

"With rockets, to boot," grinned Walter Greaves.

"A rocket," said Jimmy, "is exactly what the Academy needs."

"Aye," put in Harry Greaves from the bow, "and I can tell you just where they need it."

Moore's pale oval face came alive with merriment.

"Gentlemen, gentlemen!" Jimmy cried. "Let us leave vulgarity to its professionals, the Academicians."

But he was smiling. His sketch was completed and safely tucked away, an excellent prospect for raising new critical hackles. No steak or champagne could have done as much for his spirits.

As the boat sped eastward, he raised his voice again in the popular air celebrating the combative foreign policy of the British Prime Minister, Benjamin Disraeli:

> "We don't want to fight
> But by jingo! if we do—"

On arrival at Cadogan Pier, they started exuberantly down the dock, four abreast. Jimmy noticed that Harry Greaves was lagging a little behind.

"Pick up your heels, Harry," he bawled. "You're out of step with the squad."

Greaves made a hasty hop to adjust his stride.

"That's better. All together now, men . . . Left . . . Left . . ."

They crossed the dirt road in unison. As they reached a street lamp and swung left, Jimmy fell back to inspect the march. Head erect, shoulders squared, mustache bristling with authority, he suddenly looked less the artist than the regimental commander.

Which is what he might well have become, if not for silicon and Colonel Robert E. Lee.

# *Book One*
# Breaking Free

# Chapter Two

At midpoint in the nineteenth century, contrary to all logic and the natural inclinations of both parties, James Whistler and the United States Military Academy embarked on an uneasy love affair.

West Point had been understandably reluctant from the first. Jimmy at seventeen was scarcely the sort of strapping juvenile Hercules on whom his country was pinning its hopes for future field commanders. He stood a slender five feet six. His health record was dubious, his academic standing and conduct report worse. On the total picture, how could they accept him?

But in the face of his family background, how could they keep him out? He was the eldest son of an Army widow. His late father, Major George Washington Whistler, was one of the Academy's most distinguished graduates, a leading railroad engineer in America who later built the St. Petersburg–Moscow line under private contract to Czar Nicholas I. Furthermore, his grandfather was a pioneer American officer, his maternal Uncle Bill and Cousin Joe were West Pointers, and other forebears had been carrying arms or directing field hospitals for generations.

Grandfather John Whistler, founder of the family in America, was a peppery thick-chested Anglo-Irishman who first saw the New World as a redcoat under General Burgoyne, arriving at Saratoga just in time to take part in the British surrender there. Freed in a prisoner exchange, he returned to England long enough to elope with the daughter of a baronet neighbor, then came back to settle in Baltimore.

Within weeks John Whistler was shouldering a musket again, this time in the army of the Republic. He fought against his British ex-comrades, and later in the Midwest against the Shawnees, winding up as a major in command of Fort Dearborn (later to become Chicago). Of his fifteen children, six spent their lives on military posts as soldiers or Army wives.

The McNeills of North Carolina, descendants of a fierce Scottish clan, followed an even more martial pattern: except for a few who became doctors, McNeill men went into the Army, often via West Point. Jimmy's maternal grandfather had combined the family's two traditions by serving as an Army doctor.

The weight of all these influences—relatives and guardians, surgeons and colonels—was thrown behind Jimmy's application. When to this was added the recommendation of U. S. Senator Daniel Webster, the renowned orator, the authorities at the Academy gave up.

Their mixed feelings were fully shared by the candidate himself. True, the dashing military life had been one of his intermittent fancies since the gorgeous military pageants of St. Petersburg, where he had lived from the age of nine to fourteen while his father was hammering out a railroad; often he had amused the Czar's officers by prattling of one day commanding troops for the Republic. Even in more sophisticated adolescence, the prospect of smart uniforms, courtly dances, and similar appurtenances of the Southern aristocratic legend delighted him.

But the West Point reputation for discipline did not. And although he enjoyed rowing, swimming, and skating, he had never held a weapon more lethal than a popgun, and felt no desire to point a rifle in the direction of an animal, much less a fellow human.

However, there was not an infinity of choices open to the scion of a genteel but landless Maryland-North Carolina family. He was expected to enter either medicine, law, the clergy (his mother's fondest hope), or the Army. With the death of his father two years before, and the slashing of the family income from the twelve thousand dollars annually paid by the Czar to one-eighth that amount, free tuition had become a consideration.

So, the Military Academy and young Mr. Whistler embraced each other tentatively and hoped for the best.

Their mutual misgivings were promptly borne out. In their first extended contact—the plebe summer of 1851—Jimmy took exception to practically everything: the hard cots, rasping bugle call, close-order drill under a broiling sun, and night sentry duty, where the briefest catnap constituted a crime. And the food! To an incipient gourmet raised on Anna Whistler's subtle salads and flavorsome plum puddings, the rations on field maneuvers were inexcusable.

To register his discontent and revive his drooping spirits, Jimmy took refuge in the pastime that had been his chief pleasure since childhood: sketching. On tent flaps and artillery wagons he cartooned his impressions of camp life, including the physiognomies of various instructors. By fall, he had acquired a reputation as a droll fellow . . . along with a tidy stack of demerits.

The demerits mounted rapidly when, with the beginning of the school term, Jimmy moved into the North Barracks at West Point. He liked the *idea* of the Academy—the endless changes of spotless uniform, the formal dances where the Commandant "walked out" first, the proud gentleman's code of Duty, Honor, Country. It was the details that he kept tripping over: the remorseless routines of reveille, inspection, and lights-out. The Academy did not provide midnight snacks, so Jimmy undertook to remedy the oversight by smuggling oysters into his room, and heating biscuits over a gas jet. When supplies ran out, he led forbidden after-taps expeditions into town, for wheat-cakes and ice-cream sodas at Joe's, or steaks and beer at Benny Haven's. Conspicuous for his dark curls and lively "Frenchy manners," he was often caught.

He also had problems in class. His History professor, exasperated at Jimmy's inattention, once flung down a challenge: "Suppose you were at a dinner party, Mr. Whistler, and the conversation turned to the Mexican War. You, as a West Pointer, were asked to give the date of the Battle of Buena Vista. What would you do?"

"Do? Why, I should refuse to associate with people who could talk of such things at dinner!"

In the winter term, cadets in the 7:00 A.M. Surveying class were obliged to scramble with their transits and measuring chains along the gale-swept bluffs fringing the Hudson. Jimmy developed a technique of rolling out of bed half-dressed under his greatcoat to report "present," then slipping quietly back to his warm blankets. Discovered and duly penalized, he entered a spirited if highly technical protest to the instructor: "If I was absent without your knowledge or permission, how did you know I was absent?"

But his main torment was horses. In a day when the plane and the tank were unknown, the cavalry was the elite branch of Army service, and horsemanship the symbol of command status. A West Point officer was expected as a matter of course to ride superbly; anything less would be an embarrassment. Jimmy's father, typically, had all but lived in the saddle during years of building canals and railroads; Major Whistler never looked more impressive than when mounted on a 16-hand stallion.

His son, unfortunately, never looked less so. It wasn't Jimmy's stature—professional jockeys are small men—but rather a basic incompatibility. On his first outing, Jimmy was assigned a large, broad-rumped sorrel with what struck the cadet as a baleful eye. "What's his name"? Jimmy demanded of the dragoon in charge.

"Quaker."

"Hm . . . I have a feeling he's no Friend."

Hoisted aboard, Jimmy walked Quaker for a few paces, then began careening wildly around the ring. He made several bumpy journeys from withers to croup and back again until Quaker, wearying of the sport, came to an abrupt stop and deposited his rider in a handy tanbark. Jimmy lay quite still for a moment, as the instructor cantered up. "Mr. Whistler, are you hurt?"

Jimmy pulled himself to his feet, drawing off his gloves to brush the tanbark from his breeches. "No, sir. But I shall never understand how any man could wish to keep a horse for amusement."

In subsequent first-year drills, Jimmy rarely ended up holding his seat; the question was not whether he and his horse would part company, but when. On one occasion, riding in squad formation, he slid straight forward over the mount's head, prompting his instructor to observe, "Ah, Mr. Whistler, for once at the head of the squad!"

Scholastically, Jimmy's plebe year was tolerable. He wound up at around the middle of his class of sixty men, with superior grades in French. But, for one infraction or another, he had rung up a dozen punishment tours and some 190 demerits . . . against a ceiling of 200 that would cause automatic dismissal. He stood 212th in conduct out of a total Academy enrollment of 224.

His second year went better—only 168 demerits—but that was because he had less time: he was home nearly two months on sick leave for treatment of a chest ailment. More astonishing was an academic coup of sorts: he actually finished at the top of one of his classes. Admittedly the subject was not among the most martial: Drawing.

Robert Weir, professor of Drawing at West Point, was a tall rugged Scot with a dignified but humorous eye; in his youth he had swapped yarns with Washington Irving. An experienced professional, he had contributed the *Departure of the Pilgrims* panel to the rotunda of the U. S. Capitol.

Most of his cadet charges gave the civilian professor little to cheer about. He was therefore doubly enchanted when young Whistler, in what was supposed to be a dry topographical study, turned in a pen-and-ink landscape far surpassing the original model. From that moment, Jimmy could do no wrong. Weir excused him from routine exercises and gave him classical models to copy.

Weir's assistant, Lieutenant Martin Schmidt, was less indulgent. Thin and ramrod-stiff, Schmidt didn't like little Whistler's offhand ways, his dark foreign looks—or, particularly, the way Weir was constantly humoring him. One afternoon, making the rounds of the student desks, Schmidt saw his chance. Jimmy was crouched as usual over his work, nearsighted eyes all but brushing the paper. He was painting a water color of a church interior. Behind the head of a kneeling monk was a clearly indicated shadow.

Schmidt paused and raised his voice for the benefit of the class: "Your work, Mr. Whistler, is faulty in principle. What is the meaning of that shadow? There is none in the original oil model. And there can be none, by the laws of light and shade, since there is nothing to cast it. Really, Mr. Whistler, you should know better."

Jimmy made no answer. He merely flickered his blue-gray eyes in mild surprise, filled his brush and with a single graceful sweep threw a cowl over the head of the monk. The cowl, shadow, and entire composition had been in his mind's eye from the first; capriciously, in the mosaic manner that was his habit at the time, he had painted in the shadow first.

Lieutenant Schmidt flushed and moved silently down the aisle.

With Weir's backing, Jimmy was assigned to do sports posters, program jackets, and other official art at the Academy, taking over a role that his father—likewise number one in Drawing—had filled before him. Typical was his cover design for the 1852 Graduation Song, showing two impossibly slim but irresistibly graceful young men in parade uniform, facing each other at "order arms."

Less officially, he turned out ironic little sketches for his own amusement. One, entitled *Position of a Soldier: Annihilation of the Bowels,* showed a startled civilian reeling back before a stern cadet with *epée* extended; the comic dismay on the victim's face was worthy of a Daumier. Another portrayed a minuscule Cadet Whistler, chest puffed out to the bursting point, marching briskly across a field, trailed by a trio of brawny six-footers. It was captioned, "Merit its own Reward, or The best man leads off the Squad."

A chronic doodler—at the age of twelve, he had filled his Russian grammar text in St. Petersburg with drawings—Jimmy continued to spread his output over math notebooks, blueprints, and anything else that offered tempting blank spaces for decoration. This included examination papers, where his subjects were usually the instructors who would do the marking. Naturally, his demerit collection was reinforced.

On the whole, however, by his third year Jimmy had made a remarkable accommodation to the Academy, without substantial surrender of his idiosyncrasies. Reprimanded for wearing on one of his nocturnal jaunts a pair of forbidden snow boots, he addressed a lengthy essay to the Commandant on the uses of footgear, noting in passing the sad fact of his three new demerits: "But since it is adding but little to the whole, *what boots it?*" He had developed into a reasonably hardy physical specimen, able at long last to stay aboard a horse; had acquired, in the West Point fashion, a small inverted-V of a black mustache; and under the sobriquet of "Curly" or "Frenchy" was exceedingly popular among his classmates, so voluble that someone jocularly noted the verb formed by his initials as James Abbott Whistler. Within the week he inserted a "McNeill" ahead of the Whistler, there to remain forever.

His improvisations extended beyond the barracks, to a boarding-house on the post where a handful of cadets were able to get luxuries unavailable at the general mess. Jimmy wangled his way to this privileged table—and also into the affections of the landlady's French maid, Colette. When a mash note from Colette was relayed to Jimmy in chemistry class, and the instructor demanded to know what he was reading, the resourceful Whistler replied that it was an official advice from the Quartermaster's office. "Would you like to hear it, sir?" Without waiting for an answer, Jimmy went on "reading": " 'Dear Mr. Whistler: Your request for a new issue of field canteens has been referred, under Article 532 of regulations governing—' "

"That will do, Mr. Whistler," interrupted the instructor.

"Yes, sir. Thank you, sir." Jimmy folded the note—which proposed an after-hours rendezvous behind the mess hall—and put it in his pocket.

Seemingly there was nothing he could not talk his way out of, or into. It was therefore quite a shock when, on the afternoon of May 25, 1854, he found an envelope in his mailbox bearing the austere letterhead of the Commandant of the United States Military Academy. Colonel Robert E. Lee, hero of the Mexican War, future military leader of the Confederacy, and momentarily head of West Point, requested the presence of Cadet Whistler on "a matter of the utmost urgency."

Cadet interviews were held in the morning between seven and eight at the Superintendent's office in the old Library Building. This was an imposing pile of gray Gothic at the southeast corner of the Academy grounds, flanking the chapel and only a short walk from the North Barracks.

At ten minutes of seven, Jimmy was hustled across the intervening greensward by a three-man committee of volunteers determined to ensure that for once in his life, he arrived on time. The brass buttons on his full dress coat sparkled in the sun; his chin strap was drum-tight.

The committee deposited him on the library steps with the admonition to, for heaven's sake, "let the colonel get in a word here and there"; perhaps there would only be a reprimand. Then he was left alone.

He entered the building and walked through a cool, high-ceilinged corridor to the anteroom of the Superintendent's office. A snub-nosed Regular Army sergeant with hair bristly as a nail-brush motioned him to a bench.

Jimmy sat down. He would have a few minutes to reflect on the catalogue of his sins. "Fools make a mock at sin," as his mother was fond of noting from the Old Testament. On the other hand—he had been equally drilled in the maxims of St. Peter—"Charity shall cover the multitude of sins." Perhaps Colonel Lee was a New Testament man.

Thirty feet away, on the other side of the heavy oak door, Colonel Lee sat frowning at a pile of papers on his desk. The colonel was not looking forward to this interview, much as he had enjoyed two previous jousts with young Whistler. The lad had a mind flashing as quicksilver; but he was also obviously sensitive, and the colonel faced a duty that was not pleasant.

Lee stood up and strolled to the window, looking out over Kosciusko's Garden eastward to the Hudson. Known as the "Marble Model" in his cadet days because of his clear skin, broad forehead, and the sculptured dignity of his bearing, he was at forty-six a conspicuously handsome man, the prototype of the Southern cavalier. He stood just under six feet, with the fine nose and long jawline befitting a member of Virginia's "first family." Although his once-jet hair was flecked with gray, his dark brown eyes were as intense as ever, his gaze unwavering and serene.

Lee was celebrated for the concern he bore toward his cadets. Despite his own graduation standing as number two in the class of 1829, without a single demerit in four years, he did not expect similar miracles from all his charges. He followed their records sympathetically, and with "problem boys" in particular looked for strengths that would give him an excuse to overlook defects.

Yet he could never forget that he had been appointed Superintendent of the Academy to counteract charges of politically influenced laxity; that future officers were unlikely to serve their country well if they could not first master themselves; and that his own father, the famous Light-Horse Harry Lee, had fallen into tragedy for lack of personal discipline. Certain yardsticks had to be met, in the interests of the Army as well as of the cadets themselves . . . He went back to his desk and rang for the sergeant.

Within seconds Jimmy was saluting smartly from the threshold.

"At ease, Mr. Whistler." The colonel indicated a chair. "I suppose you realize why you're here?"

"If I didn't, sir, I should be even more stupid than those grades in front of you indicate."

Lee permitted himself a faint smile. There was really a good deal to respect in this youngster, even if he had not felt so much in common with the boy. Both had been admitted to the Academy largely on the strength of services rendered to the nation by their fathers; both had lost their illustrious predecessors in adolescence, and had become the mainstays of impoverished widows.

"The issue is somewhat more than grades, Mr. Whistler. As you know, two hundred demerits is considered the outside limit for an academic year. Your total now stands at two hundred eighteen, with the term not yet over."

Jimmy bit at his mustache. Obviously he had lost count. "Rather a staggering sum, sir, I must admit."

"Reflecting a staggering performance." Lee flipped open a page, although he was all too familiar with the file, having reviewed it after his four o'clock canter of the day before. "I note here negative citations for untied shoestrings, absence from the post without leave, improperly cleaned arms, failure to salute a superior officer, card-playing after taps, smoking in the mess . . . I doubt if any cadet in the history of the Academy has committed such a wide range of infractions."

The lively eyes danced in the expressive face. "I suppose that constitutes a distinction of sorts."

The boy is absolutely impenitent, Lee thought. Why do I find him so engaging? "You seem also," he went on, "to have found our classroom hours inconvenient."

"I presume you refer to my tardinesses?"

"And absences."

"Sir, I have merely exercised initiative—as befits an officer and leader of men. I ascertained that in the case of certain classes, I gained nothing by personal attendance that I could not obtain equally well, and in much shorter time, by consulting my colleagues afterward. In turn, I was able to assist them in drawing and French—a much more productive use of time all around. And since they enjoyed early rising and cold showers as I did not—what harm to anyone?"

*Touché*, thought the colonel admiringly. And what a pity to have to cut you down!

He leaned forward. "An interesting theory, Mr. Whistler—if only it had functioned more efficiently in, say, chemistry." Jimmy's face fell. "I have here your description before the Academic Board last week of the non-metallic element silicon, which is found in the combined state in minerals and rocks. You defined it as a 'saponifiable fat' or an 'elastic gas.' Not elastic enough, Mr. Whistler. Between the chemistry failure and the two hundred eighteen demerits"—the steady, compassionate gaze held firmly on the cadet's restless blue eyes—"you leave me no option but to recommend dismissal."

Jimmy sat for a moment in stunned silence, then slowly got to his feet. The jutting jaw quivered slightly, and he broke into a little laugh. Lee raised his head questioningly.

"I was just thinking, sir, I'd be able to tell my children—if silicon weren't found in rocks, your papa would be a major general."

Lee stood up. "I greatly doubt it, Mr. Whistler. Even if helium had the solid gravity of iron, and the world were suspended from the heavens by a pair of bedposts—that is, if all of modern science were abrogated overnight—you would still be a dubious candidate for major general. The enemy might well tremble at your approach—but so would our side."

Jimmy looked hurt. "My record is not so totally without merit, sir."

"No. But it does demonstrate an ingrained resistance to discipline, to taking orders from a superior."

"What if my superior is clearly inferior?"

"That is not for you, as a soldier, to judge. The rank on his shoulder defines your relationship. The rest is temperament."

Jimmy knew the interview was over, but he had to rush on. "I understood spirit was desirable in an officer!"

"Zeal, yes; excessive individualism, no."

"You ask me not to be myself, sir!"

"On the contrary. I think it best for all parties if you are. I merely suggest you would do better to be yourself elsewhere . . . in a more suitable milieu."

Jimmy nodded, crushed. In other words, it was what critics at home had been telling him for years: he lacked character. His fingers tightened around the braid of his cap, and he started slowly toward the door.

"Sit down, Mr. Whistler." The Superintendent's voice was not that of the parade ground, or even the classroom. "I understand from Professor Weir that you have considerable gifts as an artist." Bob Weir was an old friend of the colonel, had even done a portrait of him. Although Lee was not happy with the portrait, he still respected Weir's judgment.

Jimmy bowed slightly. "Professor Weir has been very kind."

"Talent is no commonplace thing, Mr. Whistler. Indeed, it is very possible that the paint brush is mightier than the sword—but our main responsibility here is to teach the sword. That you, and we, have different areas of interest is no reflection on either of us. Closer to my own day, a cadet named Edgar Allan Poe also failed to graduate. He is nonetheless, I dare say, remembered."

Jimmy managed a half-smile. "If I could just have one more chance, sir . . ."

"Why prolong the mutual agony? A good officer doesn't repeat his mistakes; he examines them. How long have you been drawing, Mr. Whistler?"

"Since the age of one or two, I've been told."

"Exactly. Whereas a West Point commission, I suspect, is essentially a family notion."

"It means a great deal to my mother, sir. And she means a great deal to me."

"I appreciate that. And value it. But unless we honor ourselves, Mr. Whistler, our own inner convictions, we honor nobody." The colonel paused, then continued slowly. "It is most unfortunate that Major Whistler, too, is not here to guide you. From all I have heard of him, I feel sure he would understand your situation."

At mention of Jimmy's father, the dam broke. A tear, beyond controlling, trickled down the cadet's cheek. Colonel Lee crossed quickly to the window and pulled down the blind. "That morning sun is hard on the eyes."

He turned and held out his hand. "I wish you good luck, Mr. Whistler. Not all the battlefields are lined with cannon. If I may make one suggestion: cultivate a certain minimum of self-discipline. Even talent requires shaping."

"Thank you, sir. I shall miss the Academy."

"You'll be taking some part of it with you, wherever you go."

"And leaving some part of me here, sir."

Outside, Jimmy was struck by the full weight of the disaster. For a moment he stood blinking on the library steps, split off from the Gothic towers of the campus and the robins chirping amiably overhead. Not that he had really intended to make a career of soldiering; it was a profession, as he put it to a fellow painter years later, "Only one remove from Jack Ketch who hangs men and then salves his conscience with the plea that someone told him to do it." But it would have been one thing to serve briefly, then retire with a flourish at a moment of his own choosing; it was quite another to be booted out in disgrace.

By degrees he became aware of the column of under classmen swinging past, the crisp rhythmic commands of the cadet corporal: "*Harch*, two, three, four . . . *Harch!*" Automatically he returned their salutes.

Hail . . . and farewell. No more morning drills for him; no gay graduation ball next summer; no neat little cards presenting *Second Lieutenant James Abbott McNeill Whistler*.

The column turned left past the chapel and disappeared toward the South Gate. Jimmy started down the steps. This time he had really done it; let down the loyalty of his friends, his father's memory, his mother's hopes. In spite of—could it possibly be because of?—the endless warnings, he had fulfilled the worst prophecies of his detractors. Like a foredoomed hero in Greek tragedy, he had arrived precisely at the outcome predicted by all the oracles of ruin. What on earth was wrong with him?

Without noticing, he had turned right and was walking north along a footpath overlooking the Hudson. The wide gleaming river was alive with billowing sails. Directly below, a paddle steamer poked its stately, leisurely way among the scurry of smaller vessels. Off Gee's Point, where the river made an abrupt elbow westward and the famous Revolutionary War chain had stretched across to Constitution Island, a tiny boat skimmed around the bend. Beyond, above green foothills covered with luxuriant pine forests, a great chain of mountains swept back in receding arcs.

As ever, it was the water that engrossed him. He pulled a stub of pencil from his pocket, and fished for the odd scrap of paper that was always there. Some day, somewhere, he would capture a river properly, as he had never been able to capture the Neva or the Hudson . . .

A tree stump stood near the path, with a board across it. He sat down on the stump, cradled the board in his lap, and went to work.

The clouds were good: cleanly modeled white masses hanging in a brisk west wind. Cumulus? Or were they nimbus? He was always getting the two mixed up in meteorology class.

A pleasant thought crossed his mind. Science 4A, Principles of Meteorology, no longer mattered. From now on, clouds would simply be clouds.

# Chapter Three

The immediate issue was his mother. Home again in the family's rented cottage at Stonington, Connecticut, he was acutely conscious of her distress.

Outwardly, she had borne up under his expulsion coolly enough; she even found excuses in his erratic health and the frequent interruptions to his early schooling. Yet he knew that her grief went deep; its expression would be reserved for church masses and her many hours of private prayer.

All through the Academy years, her admonitions had been insistent: about his careless ways, his indifference to salutary sleep habits and to letter writing. Once she even recounted a gloomy dream in which she saw him barely reprieved from death, only to resume more vigorously than ever his course of wickedness.

Now the day of reckoning had arrived. Her son was no longer the "strayed lamb" of her many warnings, but a lost soul on the road to perdition. He knew that in her mind, his failure would be interpreted as her own, as a rebuke from Heaven for some personal shortcoming; and the knowledge pained him. In spite of all their clashes, Jimmy was uncannily close to his mother. Her sorrow was his, and even less bearable because so rigidly enclosed.

The world of Anna McNeill Whistler was bounded by family and church, not necessarily in that order. Her fierce devotional bent came from her mother, daughter of a Sea Island cotton planter, who campaigned with evangelical fervor for the souls of her heathen black slaves. Anna, a round-faced reflective child with little personal sparkle, responded early and strongly to the call of Christ. Sundays found her in day-long attendance at the local Episcopal Church, reveling in services of Puritan intensity (all her life she was to compare, with the analytic precision of a racing handicapper, the oratorical merits of various fire-and-brimstone preachers).

Anna dressed primly, clinging despite the complaints of her friends to a tight, severe hair-do that reinforced her plain, open features and gave her a middle-aged look before she was twenty. She showed little interest in matters terrestrial until one day her brother Bill, a cadet at West Point, brought home his classmate "Pipes" Whistler, flutist of the Academy marching band, during a vacation furlough. Anna was smitten instantly. More than the long curly locks, the smooth white skin, and the soldierly bearing of George Washington Whistler, what attracted her was the uncommon poise of her brother's friend. Young Whistler had been born at Fort Wayne, Indiana, and raised in the wilderness; he had the manly self-sufficiency of the pioneer. If he was not quite as ardent a churchgoer as she might wish, that could be dealt with later; meanwhile there were the compensations of his agile flute and lively wit.

Unhappily but understandably, "Pipes" did not respond with equal enthusiasm to the shy, wispy little sister of Bill McNeill. "Pipes," along with half the cadet corps, was in hot pursuit of Mary Swift, the school surgeon's baby-faced blond daughter. Mary was a classic campus belle more addicted to the polka and the novels of Sir Walter Scott than to dusty sermons in the chapel.

Young Whistler, with his ready smile and his charming serenades, won the competition. In 1821, two years after graduation from the Point, he eloped with Mary Swift. To underline the irony for Anna McNeill, she and Mary—both daughters of Army doctors—had been close friends since grade school days.

Anna took her defeat stoically, continuing to see the happy couple while both their household and the young officer's career burgeoned. Then the impossible happened. In 1827 Mary Swift, after providing her husband with three children, fell gravely ill. Perhaps sensitive to Anna's secret, Mary extracted a deathbed promise from Whistler: if he married again, it would be to her friend Anna McNeill.

Anna did not press the young widower. His situation, and the dictates of nature, would work for her. For several years, during his frequent visits to the McNeill home in Baltimore, she listened to his engineering adventures and made sympathetic inquiries about his two boys and baby girl. The milestones of their courtship, unlike the whirlwind wooing of Mary Swift, were prosaic: a button sewed on "brother George's" coat; a few letters; a discreet exchange of gifts.

In 1831, Whistler proposed. Although quiet in her acceptance, Anna was happy beyond measure. Her prayers had been answered, her patient faith rewarded. So great was her joy that she had to warn herself against being carried away by worldly considerations; an angry Heaven might reach down in punishment.

Besides, there was a difficult task ahead. Anna, slow to smile, slight and thin-lipped although pink of cheek, had no illusions about "replacing" the buxom glamorous Mary Swift, or about the probable mixture of motives that had driven the major into her arms. He was a man alone, struggling to raise three young children. Between her and her husband was the unspoken awareness that, for the moment at least, she was part-housekeeper. But she was determined to be more than that to George Washington Whistler . . . much more.

For three years she kept to the unenviable role of stepmother, using the skills she had acquired in her father's surgical rooms to nurse a trio of far-from-robust children: George William, Joseph, and tiny Deborah (known in the family from infancy as "Debo").

Then, on July 10, 1843, she presented the major with a child of her own. James Abbott Whistler—silky-haired, fine of feature, with dainty well-made hands—was all a mother could desire in a first-born. When Major Whistler, bending over the sleeping infant's cradle, cried out "It's enough to make Sir Joshua Reynolds come out of his grave to paint him," Anna knew she had forged an important new link with her husband. Unlike graceful little Debo, whose every gesture achingly recalled Mary Swift, the latest Whistler would not be clouded by the shadow of an earlier love.

Jimmy—known also as Jemmie, Jamie, Jim, and Jem (but only on state occasions as James)—was followed two years later by Willie. But Anna's dreams of biblical fruitfulness were thereafter repeatedly thwarted; between 1842 and 1846, three sons in succession died before reaching the age of four, one of them during the long cruel sea voyage from New England to join father George in Russia. Added to the earlier loss of her stepson Joseph, this left Anna with only stepchildren George William and Debo, and her own two boys.

Anna McNeill had been raised with the cadences of the Bible ringing in her ears, and she was resolved that no shred of its benefits would escape her sons. Had more of her boys survived, the weight of her attentions would have been scattered; as it was, the concentrated force of her reformist urge fell upon Jimmy and Willie. They, at least, could be shaped in the manly image of their father, with an added measure of the godliness that had been necessarily shortchanged in the frontier upbringing of "Brother George." One or both boys, she hoped, would grow up to serve Christ.

Like the soldier of the Lord she considered herself to be, she mapped out her campaign along strict unsparing lines. Prayers, readings, and church attendance (three times every Sunday, in Russia) were pressed to the saturation point. The day began—before breakfast, of course—with the reading of a verse from the Psalms. Thereafter, every hour had its allocated purpose; even "Recreation," under such pitiless scheduling, became grim duty. Exhortations toward self-improvement were mingled with fearful forecasts of the doom that awaited violators of God's (or, interchangeably, Mummy's) will. When a German neighbor was dying of tuberculosis, Anna deliberately took the boys to his bedside, that they might be reminded of man's fragile grip on mortality. Frivolity—the definition of which extended to dancing, games, lace finery, and secular music—was painted in the most horrendous (and therefore to Jimmy, tempting) terms.

Sabbath was observed with a ferocity that would have delighted Oliver Cromwell. Even chess was banned on Sunday; likewise, to the major's dismay, visits by friends. The day belonged to the Lord, for meditation only; earthly concerns were not to intrude upon it . . . and no Orthodox Old Testament Jew in the ancient walled city of Jerusalem took more soberly than Anna McNeill Whistler the injunction to "keep it holy."

In practice, Saturday too was regularly sacrificed. Anna needed the day to set her house in order and prepare her lambs that they might be worthy of the Lord's inspection. Jimmy in particular, with his penchant for dirt-gathering mischief, had to be combed and scrubbed (an operation that she supervised personally until at seventeen he went off to West Point). Except for the Bible and religious texts, books were locked away for the weekend along with the marbles and toy trains of youth.

All this was tempered with bursts of quite human affection and even indulgence. There were good-night embraces, holiday gifts. And although Anna disapproved of fireworks, fearing that "our immortal interests" were imperiled by "turning night into day," she occasionally sanctioned a past-bedtime visit to a dazzling display of rockets on St. Petersburg's riverside promenade, the Nevsky Prospect.

Nonetheless, the prevailing atmosphere in the Whistlers' St. Petersburg household was gloom-and-doom, and it created a certain strain. Sinners can be forgiven; they often evoke a magnanimity we are pleased to exercise. Saints are something else; their living example of undiluted virtue is an implied reproof to the rest of us, a reminder of our own inadequacies. From this point of view, Anna Whistler stretched the tolerance of her fondest admirers.

The major, like his eldest son George William who had remained behind in the United States, was insulated in part by physical distance. For weeks at a time he was kept away from home by the endless task of constructing his railroad in the face of Arctic winds, pervasive corruption and an untrained work force. Slender Debo, who had inherited her father's musical gifts, took refuge in the piano and the attentions of the younger diplomatic set. Willie, plump and placid, a mother's boy from the outset, was quite content to trade his freedom for maternal approval.

Jimmy alone rebelled. The son of "Pipes" simply could not fall in line behind the daughter of Piety. Like Anna herself, who refused to modify her coiffure in her youth, he cherished the exercise of his individuality. Once, amid the sparkling fountains of the Czar's Winter Palace, he was asked if he would not like to be a Duke. Instantly he rejected the idea: "Who could be free with a pack of servants dogging his heels?"

For a boy of such spirit, Anna's constant strictures were anathema, automatically to be circumvented or defied. Anna, vexed and puzzled by this resistance to her labors, found her older boy "mulish and crossgrained"; he made her positively ill, she complained to friends, with his eternal questions and challenges.

Things were better whenever George Whistler came home, looming large in the doorway under his furry shuba and snow-covered sealskin cap. Then there would be long evenings before the fire, listening to Father's wonderful stories of how as a young Army engineer he had helped stake out the Northwest Territory, tramping five miles a day in 50-below cold, living in the wilderness on parched corn, sleeping in snow banks under buffalo skins. Sometimes, upon shouted request, the major would coax the skirl and blare of bagpipes out of his ever-obliging flute; or he might conduct a comical drill in ballroom etiquette for his sons, himself portraying the shy maiden who was to be put at her ease by a courtly bow.

There were also other paternal lessons, more abstract, in patriotism ("Wherever you are; observe July 4; ours is the only country worth living in") and in fair play (Anna Whistler noted sharply in her diary that her husband would not condemn a servant without proof even though every piece of silver in the house was missing). Yankee independence was to be treasured: when Anna Whistler rhapsodized over a superbly drilled Russian boy choir, her husband wondered aloud what the price had been in the cramping of free young souls. Throughout the major's talk ran a thread of dry humor. Decorated by Czar Nicholas with the Order of St. Anne, he observed that his family had "all enjoyed the Order of Saint Anne ever since the neatest of housekeepers became Mrs. Whistler"; and Jimmy had the distinct impression of a lightning wink in his own direction.

Yes, the major was a splendid buffer against the loving tyranny of Jimmy's mother; unfortunately, he was not often on the scene. And so, in the isolation of St. Petersburg, Anna Whistler was indispensable to Jimmy. Resented or not, she was nurse and comforter in his bouts with rheumatic fever; superintendent of his school lessons and his piano practice; source of hot buttered rolls, scrambled eggs, guidance, and approval. Harsh or forgiving, tender or distant or severe (and he could never be sure what reaction would come next), Anna Whistler was inevitably the center of Jimmy's universe.

It was a center he had to share with docile Willie, the "good boy" who was his mother's preferred companion on her shopping tours. Although Willie openly adored his big brother, Jimmy's feelings were more mixed. He envied the younger boy's secure status in their mother's affections, and often wished that he too could measure up to Anna Whistler's ideals in scholarliness, obedience, neatness, and religious devotion.

Two episodes from childhood lingered particularly in his mind. On his tenth birthday, after a period of rather tense wrangling, he had surprised his mother by slipping under her plate a poem he had found in a magazine. It spoke of a legendary "Indian tree" that, however tempted to spread its shoots afar, preferred always to incline downward to its life-giving Mother Earth:

> " 'Tis thus, though woo'd by flattering friends
> And fed with fame (if fame it be),
> This heart, my own dear mother, bends
> With love's true instinct back to thee."

As Jimmy read the poem aloud, Anna's gray eyes moistened, and for a brief, ecstatic moment Jimmy thought she would fling her arms around him. But Anna in her prudence—and folly—held back; and Jimmy never forgot. He was still the "bad boy."

Several years later, the two brothers were enrolled for a time in a French boarding school. On their first weekend at home, Willie confessed to his mother that he had been hideously homesick; at the prospect of leaving her again, he broke down and wept.

Anna went into her other boy's room, where Jimmy was sketching at his desk. "You really should show more consideration for your little brother," she began.

"But I do, Mother! One of the German boys at school tried to take Willie's bread and kvass. You should have seen the thrashing I gave him!"

"Indeed! I'm very glad I didn't. We're not paying Monsieur Jourdan's fancy fees so you may learn to be a ruffian!"

"I was only doing it to protect my brother."

"What he needs is your affection, Jemie. Your sympathy. You must understand: Willie is only twelve years old. He's lonely"—Anna loved to quote the Good Book—"'a stranger in a strange land.' He's not as strong and rough as you."

Jimmy scowled; what did his mother want of him? Anna rushed on: *"You do not know what he feels!"*

At this intimation of filial indifference, tears gushed to Jimmy's eyes. "Oh, Mother, you think I don't mind being away from home!" And he ran from the room.

Thereafter, his uncertainty about Anna Whistler's affections grew, and with it the battle of wills between two stubborn people who needed each other badly but needed their sense of independence more. When Jimmy was stricken with influenza a few months later, with his father and Willie away on a trip, he begged his mother not to leave his sickroom even for meals. But once on his feet again, he was as rebellious as ever.

In 1848, as a safeguard against the treacherous St. Petersburg winter, Jimmy was sent to London to stay with his half sister Debo, who had recently married the British surgeon Seymour Haden. At long range, Anna redoubled her exertions to force him onto the "straight and narrow way." From Russia, she deluged him with accounts of Willie's progress at school and church, mingled with lectures against succumbing to the gay social life of the British capital. Earthly existence, she reminded him, was no more than a preparatory school where God's children were disciplined for the long voyage in Eternity. He was not to dance, unless needed as a partner to fill out a quadrille; and under no circumstances was he to act in theatricals for mere entertainment.

Yet even among the reproofs were scattered notes of affection and apology. She was sending him a copy of *Don Quixote;* she personally saw no merit in it, but he might be amused. She hoped he would not be put off by her dry sermonizing, which was no doubt less agreeable reading than *Punch*. More than once, in an apparent access of self-questioning, she urged him to keep her letters from the eyes of strangers, or to destroy them. He never did.

Anna's oscillations were evident. She wanted Jimmy's love, but she was not ready to compromise lifelong principle for it. Instead, she employed every tactic that came to hand. She told the fourteen-year-old boy that he alone held the key to his parents' happiness; with the dismaying implied corollary that if he failed to meet her standards, he would forfeit her love.

No doubt Anna Whistler would have been shocked at the suggestion that her son had contrived to fail at college as a desperate gesture of reprisal. Nor could she have imagined that her repeated criticisms would all but erode a skin that was never very thick, leaving in effect exposed nerve endings that would be a hazard to their owner and a scourge to those who ran afoul of him for the rest of his life.

Jimmy was still in England when his father died in the spring of 1849, a belated victim of the cholera epidemic that had swept through Russia. With George Whistler gone, he withdrew even further from his mother, throwing himself totally into his passion for art. During the prep school years back home in America he became more intractable than ever; when he was admitted to West Point, he and his mother both felt a sense of relief . . . along with the now-familiar nagging counterpoint of mutual rejection.

On the train ride back home from West Point, Jimmy's feelings toward his mother had been a tangle of hostility and longing, anger and tenderness and shame. But when he came through the door of the little cottage in Stonington and saw her bent anxiously over the stove, hair graying and shoulders shrunken, with tiny new lines in the pink cheeks, everything else was swept away in a surge of compassion. Just a few months earlier Willie too, her good Willie, had inexplicably failed at Columbia University; now she had been betrayed by her eldest, her closest tie with her beloved George Washington Whistler.

Jimmy could not long endure the prayer-laden silence at Stonington; to redeem himself even momentarily, he was ready to grasp at any straw. His half brother, George William, had married into the Winans Locomotive family and was superintendent of their plant in Baltimore. George had already installed Willie there as an apprentice machinist. When he proposed to find a place in his drafting department for the banished cadet, Jimmy took the next train for Baltimore.

He spent an experimental two weeks among the plant draftsmen, spreading a dozen sketches not only over their work sheets but along the smooth wooden back-surfaces of their drawing boards. Included in this output were some river scenes and a much-admired study of a cavalier imprisoned in a lonely dungeon cell (an unconscious autobiographical protest?) . . . but nothing of the remotest use to the Winans Company. It was clear that Jimmy had no affinity for locomotive blueprints.

He continued across the D.C. line into Washington, and paid a call on Jefferson Davis. The Secretary of War, later to be President of the Confederacy, had known and liked George Washington Whistler. As George's boy sat before him, whimsically recounting certain "technical misunderstandings" at the Military Academy, Davis found himself tempted to intercede as requested. But if he made an exception for one "Southern gentleman," he would have a dozen other expelled cadets clamoring at his door. He postponed a decision.

Jimmy charged along to the Secretary of the Navy, James C. Dobbin of North Carolina, with the ingenious suggestion that he be admitted to Annapolis as a first classman, on the strength of his three years at West Point. Dobbin too was personally impressed, but hesitated to act.

Then a message came from Jefferson Davis: he had arranged for Jimmy to be appointed as a draftsman in the War Department's Coast and Geodetic Survey.

This suggestion went down very well with Anna Whistler. It struck Jimmy, too, as a big improvement over locomotives. For one thing, he would be surrounded by officers rather than artisans; for another, Washington was the center of a considerable social whirl.

He was rapidly disillusioned, at least about the job. The officer in charge, a Captain Benham, was crisp enough and eager to help any son of "Pipes" Whistler. But for their $1.50 a day, draftsmen were expected to report promptly at 9:00 A.M. at the Coast Survey complex a few squares south of the Capitol, and to labor till midafternoon superimposing topographical signs on highly technical military maps. It was a tedious mechanical operation for which Jimmy lacked either interest or patience. Soon he was trailing in late, and disappearing early.

The social scene was a brighter story. The Whistlers and McNeills had excellent connections in the capital, and Jimmy had inherited a full share of the familial gift for conviviality (a direct seventeenth-century ancestor, Dr. Daniel Whistler, was described by diarist Samuel Pepys as "a quaint gentlemen of rare humor"; another contemporary called him "the most facetious man in nature"). Jimmy became a familiar figure at embassy receptions, a Scottish tam-o'-shanter or broad-brimmed Rembrandt hat on his head, a blue and green plaid cape thrown over his shoulders. Lacking a dress coat for evening parties, he pinned back the skirt of a frock coat and counted on charm to see him through. He danced at the British Legation, entertained the Russian *chargé d'affaires* with oysters and cheese, and played billiards with nearsighted abandon at a parlor near his rooming house on 13th Street near Pennsylvania Avenue.

All this activity cut still further into his working schedule. When Porterfield, the fussy little attendance sergeant, remonstrated about his late arrivals, Jimmy replied: "I am never late. You open too early."

Captain Benham, fearful for Jimmy's future, decided on a stratagem. He summoned to his office Adolph Lindenkohl, the most methodical and reliable of his junior draftsmen.

The next morning at 8:30 A.M., Jimmy was aroused from slumber in his $10-a-month furnished room by a sharp rapping. He shuffled to the door in his nightgown to find Lindenkohl in the hall, round face beaming.

"Good morning, Whistler! I was just, ah, passing by. Thought we could go down to the office together."

Jimmy nodded drowsily; there had been champagne the evening before. "Oh yes, of course. Do come in." He swung open the door. "I'm afraid I'm not quite ready."

Lindenkohl pulled out a heavy railroad watch. "But it's getting on toward nine. We don't have much time."

"You mean, *you* don't," Jimmy murmured to himself. He was beginning to come awake. "Look here, Lindenkohl," he said aloud. "Perhaps you'd better go on ahead. I wouldn't want to hold you up."

"Oh, that's all right." Lindenkohl dropped his bulky frame into a chair. "I'll just rest here while you dress. That is, if you don't mind . . . ?"

"Oh no, not at all . . ." Jimmy fumbled in his shirt drawer. "Will you join me in a cup of coffee?"

"No, thanks, I've had breakfast. Been up since seven, you know. It's the only way to organize the day."

"Is it?" Jimmy seemed unconvinced. "Personally, I find it's coffee that's basic. I have this amazing little machine." He struck a match, and approached a French coffee-maker perched on an alcohol burner. Within minutes the aroma of strong Colombian coffee filled the room. Jimmy, drifting about leisurely in underwear and trousers with one shoe on, turned to Lindenkohl: "You *will* try some, won't you?"

Lindenkohl ostentatiously consulted his watch. "Well," he relented, "since you're making it anyway . . ."

Over the coffee, Jimmy told his guest about Igor, the Whistlers' pantryman in Russia, who hated Western food but always carted some off anyway. Igor could not resist helping himself to other people's property. "You might say stealing was a question of principle with him, of personal dishonor." Lindenkohl was much intrigued. Had Jimmy actually seen the Czar, and skated on the frozen Neva?

From Russia, the talk turned to Paris. Jimmy had been reading Henri Murger's *Scènes de la Vie de Bohème*, later immortalized in the Puccini melodies of *La Bohème*, and was full of enchanting anecdotes about student life on the Left Bank.

Ultimately, just as Captain Benham had planned, the two young draftsmen arrived at the office together. But the time was closer to lunch than to early morning. The stratagem was not repeated.

Once in the office, Jimmy generally kept himself busy—with sketches of passing pedestrians, water colors based on Dickens's *Pickwick Papers*—anything but map-making. His major opus was an informal mural project, covering with heads and figures the stairway wall leading down from his third-floor workroom to Captain Benham's office.

One chilly afternoon in February, the Survey artists were huddled at work around a smoky coal stove. Jimmy was struggling to chart the tidal currents around the Bay of Fundy in Nova Scotia, grumbling that anyone should have chosen to settle there. "If they weren't Scots, I should never forgive them."

A few minutes later he flung down his pencil in exasperation. "When I enrolled at West Point, I accepted the possibility of dying in battle. But I am *not* reconciled to dying of boredom!"

Little John Ross Key, a colleague whose grandfather wrote "The Star-Spangled Banner," stood up. "I have an idea, Jimmy." The etching department, he explained, handled assignments more congenial to a true artist: little views of harbor entrances, for reproduction on coastal maps.

Key brought Jimmy to the desk of Dan McCoy, a massive middle-aged Irishman with black brows and an enormous alehouse belly. "Dan, this is Jimmy Whistler that I was telling you about. He can draw anything."

"And is he interested in etching?"

Key looked inquiringly at his friend.

"I'd be starting from scratch, sir—if you'll forgive the pun. But it sounds a lot more interesting than logarithms."

"It is." McCoy reached out a brawny forearm. "See this chunk of metal? Copperplate. It's your drawing surface. And instead of a pencil or brush, you work with this . . ." He held up a steel needle. "Now, these may look to you like crude tools . . . but the technique is as delicate as . . . as the mists of Londonderry."

The phrase brought Jimmy to attention. He squinted hard at the copper.

"The first thing you do," McCoy went on, "is prepare the plate with a rosin ground, smoked good and dark. That's so you'll be able to see the lines made by the steel point. Then, when you have your drawing, you give your plate an acid bath. The acid follows your lines; goes through the ground and bites into the copperplate. That's your actual etching process. It's very tricky—has to be firm and even, not too shallow."

"Or too deep," said Jimmy.

"That's right. Because you still have the printing process ahead. And you want a neat, clean line. Of course, the printer affects the result, too. A lot depends on the amount of ink used, and the pressure."

"Can you make changes on the plate?" Jimmy wanted to know. "If it doesn't come out right?"

"Most etchers do. But you're getting into advanced problems. And you haven't even learned to lay the ground!"

By the next afternoon, with Captain Benham's permission, Jimmy had not only mastered the preparation of an experimental plate but had sprinkled it with deftly needled vignettes: Mrs. Partington and Ike from the pages of B. P. Shillaber, Breton peasant girls, himself in the haughty ruffles of a Spanish hidalgo. John Key watched with fascination as Jimmy proceeded to bite the plate, seeming to operate with the assurance of instinct. Before pouring the nitric acid, he packed the edges of the plate with wax to form a reservoir. Then, as the corrosive mixture bit and bubbled around the lines, he wiped them with a brush to prevent refuse from piling up and causing an uneven bite. Finally, he heated and washed the bitten plate to remove the ground, and brought it to the printer.

For the next few days, Jimmy turned up with astonishing punctuality and lingered till late afternoon studying the methods of the printers. He quickly concluded that a responsible etcher could not in good conscience turn over his bitten plate to a printer and forget about it, but had to supervise the inking and printing of every proof.

Captain Benham, delighted with this display of zeal, gave Jimmy an official etching assignment—and thereby precipitated the chronic Whistler dilemma: Jimmy might sit down to a drawing board with the soberest of intentions, but once an instrument of expression was in his hands, his private needs took over. For the government's purposes, a tree was simply an object, a general shape occupying a particular space along the shore; for Jimmy, any tree that he etched had to be beautiful and distinctive, or it had better not be there at all. Furthermore, if compositional balance demanded additional visual elements they would have to be introduced, whether or not actually present on the scene.

His first two subjects were harbor scenes from Southern California: a coastal town near Santa Barbara, and the Anacapa Islands some 25 miles offshore. Both were rendered with felicity, the first plate showing a deep bay curving in from a rocky coastline, and the second limning a barren rock-strewn inlet. Unfortunately, the Anacapa sketch was enlivened by two non-military flights of birds tracing a picturesque path across the plate, and the topographical features of the other etching were all but swamped by extra attractions: cottages with gaily smoking chimneys, and figures of peasant women, tattered soldiers, a bearded monk in a cowl.

Captain Benham was not charmed. He sent for the artist. "Mr. Whistler, you have not been engaged to spoil government coppers!"

"I was only trying out my point with those sketches, sir. I intended to stop them out in the biting. But I was, ah, delayed getting to the office yesterday morning, and someone put the plates into an acid bath without my authorization."

"You forget, Mr. Whistler, you *have* no authority here."

"I submit, sir, every artist has the authority to control his own work."

Benham was vexed; people were listening. "This is a military installation, Mr. Whistler. Perhaps you would be happier at the Beaux Arts in Paris!"

"That is very possible, sir."

Jimmy saluted—a gratuitous gesture for a civilian—turned smartly on his heel, and walked away without waiting for dismissal. The next morning, picking up his magnifying glass, Captain Benham was startled to find himself staring head-on at a nasty little demon. He knew who had painted it on the glass.

The Coast Survey adventure was over. Even without demons and insubordination, Jimmy's attendance record had become quite impossible. In November, he had been docked the equivalent of two days' pay for repeated latenesses; by February, he was averaging less than seven days of accredited work per month.

Jimmy lay half-awake in his room. Every meaningful landmark in his life—enrollment in the Russian Imperial Academy of Fine Arts, the volume of Hogarth drawings that made endurable his siege of rheumatic fever two years later—pointed in the same direction. Just once, at fifteen, he had tried to spread his wings toward a professional career in painting. He had been promptly and doubly shot down: by his father with the sorrowful suggestion that while art might be a splendid diversion for a gentleman, engineering or architecture were more suitable as professions; by his mother, with harsh finality. Anna Whistler did not hide her satisfaction that the adolescent notions of living by the brush once entertained by her husband had been soon abandoned —or her annoyance that her son had taken up the dream.

Again and again his yearning for art had been driven underground —but never buried. How long was he to go on marking time—and wasting it? He leaped to his feet and headed for the coffee machine. Enough of penances and sacrifices! He would put away the false-face of obedience, and follow his own instinct.

That could mean only one thing: the city of *La Vie de Bohème,* painters and palettes, lights and love and the Louvre . . . Paris.

His family reacted with surprising calm. Anna Whistler, confronted for once with an intensity of conviction equal to her own, voiced no protest. Nor did she raise her glance in mute appeal to heaven. Perhaps time and experience would accomplish what she had not. She went out and bought her son a half-dozen shirts . . . white and loose-fitting, art-student style.

George William arranged to send Jimmy a sizable slice of the $1500 annual income left by their father; the fledgling artist would receive an allowance of $350 a year, in quarterly installments.

On a bright June morning in 1855, Jimmy waved farewell to his family and skipped up the gangplank of a steamer bound for Southampton. He would pay a brief obeisance to his half sister and infant niece in London. A few hours beyond, lay Paris.

# Chapter Four

The angels guarding the gates of Paris were not kind. Jimmy had planned a splendidly theatrical arrival, something in the manner of the original Napoleon riding at the head of a triumphant column. He would be lolling back regally on the cushions of a sumptuous landau (a one-time extravagance to be justified by the special occasion), resplendent in freshly pressed white ducks, the black ribbon fluttering gaily behind his broad-brimmed, low-crowned straw hat. As his noble steeds capered past, the natives would crane their necks in awed tribute to this amazing foreign dignitary; he would nod benignly in acceptance of their homage.

Unfortunately, the nighttime crossing of the English Channel, followed by the crowded boat train from Calais, had left his stomach uneasy and his trousers rumpled; and there were no landaus or victorias in early morning attendance at the Saint-Lazare station. He was lucky to commandeer a mere one-horse fiacre.

In any case, Jimmy soon discovered, Paris itself made his lordly plan impossible. As the rickety four-wheeler clattered southward toward the Champs Élysées, he found himself hanging halfway out, overwhelmed by the sights and sounds of the French capital. He had rehearsed the fantasy a hundred times in his mind; he was still unprepared for the reality . . . the wide clean boulevards lined with lindens and chestnuts, the merrily striped café awnings, bawling street vendors, blue-shirted workmen, and occasional parasol glimpsed through a garden gate, bobbing above a feathered hat. He wanted to swallow up the city in great gobs: trees, bakery shops, flower markets, bookstalls; to embrace it like a man rediscovering a long-lost mistress. His hands itched for a paint brush.

The day was balmy, the sky a teacup-blue, without the hint of rain that constantly hung over the British Isles. And the architecture of

Paris, after the massive drabness of London, was intoxicating in its variety.

This was the Paris of the Second Empire, consecrated to the eternal glory of that most remarkable of nephews, Louis Napoleon. After decades of patient maneuvering in exile, the son of Bonaparte's younger brother had succeeded in exploiting bourgeois fears of the laboring masses; in 1852 he proclaimed a dictatorship in the name of order, prosperity, and national unity. Backed by merchants, clergy, and an army that was making a reputation in the Crimea, Louis soon felt secure.

He promptly set out to make himself historic. If he could not make France forget the first Napoleon, he could make sure they remembered the third one. To the impoverished workers he offered subsidies; to shopkeepers, credits; and to all Frenchmen a program of public works without precedent, starting with the virtual rebuilding of Paris.

By 1855 the great plazas and sweeping elegant boulevards were sprouting everywhere, wheel spokes grouped around the hub of the Place de l'Étoile. Throngs of frock-coated boulevardiers and their billowy-skirted ladies curtsied and bowed and flirted through the night under the soft romantic gas lamps of the City of Light. The new mood was captured by Offenbach in sprightly, impudent melodies that set the town on its ear and, along with a general outburst of artistic activity, attracted the creative talents of the world: Heine from Germany, Turgenev from Russia . . . twenty-one-year-old Jimmy Whistler from the United States.

The fiacre was rattling around the enormous Place de la Concorde at the foot of the Champs Élysées. Jimmy leaned forward and tapped the driver. "That must be the Place de l'Étoile farther up the Champs," he said in French. "So Montmartre would be behind us, to the right?"

The driver turned, revealing a mournful moonface with a long incongruous scar across the right cheek. "Your geography is not bad, monsieur. But your accent—formidable. Monsieur is English?"

"Never," snapped Jimmy. "American."

Cautious disbelief. "One speaks French in America?"

"I studied at college. The U. S. Military Academy."

"Ah, Monsieur is an officer!" The driver straightened his potato-sack figure. "I too have been a soldier. In the Crimea." He turned again and showed his scar, proudly.

"Very gallant," agreed Jimmy. "How far are we from the Bois de Boulogne? And the market district—Les Halles?"

"The Bois is at this end"—the man pointed straight ahead—"Les Halles is at that." He jerked his thumb back over his shoulder. "And half the Right Bank in between. Paris, monsieur, like Rome, was not built in a day."

"How much to rent your horse and carriage till evening?"

"Till evening?" the driver rubbed his nose. "Life is very dear . . . twenty francs."

"Twenty . . . that's four American dollars! I want to *rent* your horse—not buy him! I'll give you ten."

"Impossible . . . But for a young officer—very well, twelve."

Jimmy shrugged, already half-Gallicized. He was flush, flusher than he would be at any time till the next installment of his allowance arrived in three months. He had deliberately traveled first-class from England, to wipe out the ignominy of a second-class journey he had been obliged to make there at the age of fifteen. One had to know when to spend.

The fiacre continued its journey. By late afternoon Jimmy had climbed the winding streets of Montmartre, lunched in the Bois, gaped at the Royal Place (and, with fine impartiality, at the column commemorating the Bastille), and spun along the edge of the Right Bank past the vast Tuileries Gardens and the mighty eminence of the Cathedral of Notre-Dame on the Île de Cité. His head was a blur; he was quite exhausted.

"Monsieur has reservations at a hotel?"

"No."

"I can recommend a place near the Opéra—very respectable."

"No!"

The mournful face turned, the lumpy shoulders shrugged. "Very well then, if Monsieur prefers, *not* so respectable . . ."

"Just take me to the Left Bank," said Jimmy.

"The Left Bank is quite large, monsieur."

Jimmy ransacked his mind for memories of *La Vie de Bohème*. Ah, yes. "Place de l'Odéon," he said crisply. The driver cracked his whip.

Murger's admiration had not been misplaced. The Place de l'Odéon, centered on the handsome old theater of the same name near the Luxembourg Palace, was a modest jewel of architectural planning. Opposite the tawny-stoned Grecian colonnade of the theater entrance ran a fan-shaped arrangement of street diagonals and buildings, with each building-front cunningly curved to preserve the semicircular symmetry of the whole.

Skirting the eastern wall of the theater, with its lamp-hung archways, was the tiny Rue Corneille. No wider than a cart's breadth, the street held three buildings—the second of which proclaimed itself to be the Hôtel Corneille. Jimmy picked up his suitcase and trudged over for a better look.

The hotel had four and a half stories under a sloping roof. Grill-work balconies peered out from its middle floors. In the high, vaulted entranceway, two massive wooden doors stood ajar.

Jimmy walked through, and found himself in a cool dim arcade. Beyond was a cobblestoned courtyard, some forty feet long. A sign at its far end asserted the presence of a dining room.

Beneath the sign was huddled something presumably alive; under the twin handicaps of the twilight and his myopia, Jimmy could not be sure whether it was a small personage or large animal. He came closer: "Bonjour, monsieur." Or was it madame?

Ancient sleepy eyes looked up from a face like a dried apple. "Eh? Eh? What's that you say?"

"Do you have a room free here?"

"A room?" The concierge was male, Jimmy now saw, and rather deaf. "Yes, there's a room. But it's very small. No space to turn around. Even the mice complain." The concierge grinned. He had just enough teeth to make the grin visible.

"What floor is it on?"

"High, very high." A bony wrist flapped in the air. "One lives in the sky, like a bird." The concierge gestured toward the attic eaves directly overhead, facing northwest.

"How much is it?"

"Ah, monsieur, too much. Twenty-five francs a month."

"I'll take it."

The concierge shook his head and mumbled something, then produced a key. Jimmy took it, picked up his suitcase, and headed for the nearby doorway. A wide stone staircase, flanked by an iron balustrade, circled upward for as far as the eye could see. The journey from Connecticut was over. He was home, a student-citizen of Paris.

"Remember, gentlemen, the words of our master Ingres: 'Make lines.' Drawing comes first, the perfection of form. Then we may add color, to complete our effect."

The speaker was Charles Gabriel Gleyre, a Swiss painter of rigidly classical convictions who had inherited the teaching studio of his French colleague, Delaroche. High-domed, dignified, and precise, Gleyre laid out his words in neatly spaced intervals, as if assembling the elements of a design. "In drawing the figure, our primary concern is with proportion. We must be faithful to nature in reproducing the balance among the various parts. For example, you will be surprised to note that the human hand, spread open, covers as large an area as the face. Try it yourselves. Go ahead, everyone . . ."

Reluctantly, Jimmy brought his palm up to his nose. He was one of a score of students gathered around Gleyre in a clutter of stools and easels that, apart from an unoccupied model stand, was the only furniture in the bare-walled classroom. This was ridiculous. He hadn't come to Paris for a rehash of St. Petersburg academicism.

Gleyre was droning on. "We will now draw from the model." He beckoned toward the corridor, and a dark-haired plump young woman, draped in a brown robe, strolled in. She dropped the robe on a chair, turned a bored eye on the students and mounted the stand.

"The model will pose for twelve minutes, then rest for three," announced Gleyre.

Jimmy tightened his Ingres sketching paper, divided into four sections, on the easel and reached for a stick of charcoal. He squinted toward the nude model once, twice, and then began work, setting down his lines lightly but firmly in a sweeping, loose-wristed motion.

Soon the plump young lady began to emerge on the paper, somewhat more streamlined and dainty of limb than the original, but unmistakable. Jimmy became aware of a starchy presence behind him. "No, no, Monsieur Ouislair, you have violated the law of the vertical, observe with your plumb line. And the figure must stand well on her feet, not float in the air. You would do better to start with the lower body, and work up toward the head."

"But at St. Petersburg they said—"

"I do not care what you learned, or think you learned, in St. Petersburg. Or"—raising his voice for the other students—"in London or 'Lodelf.'" (Jimmy deduced after a moment that this must be a reference to Philadelphia.) "One question only, you must ask yourself: 'What would Raphael have done?'"

Gleyre had spent five years studying in Italy, and had come away with a fanatical devotion to Raphael—forefather, as he saw it, to the classicist Ingres. As the teacher moved along, Jimmy murmured to his neighbor, "Between Heaven and Hell, there is only Ra-pha-el." He himself was not that enamored of the Florentine. The few things he had seen struck him as slick: conventionally composed, floridly drawn, and dry in coloring.

But he wiped out his sketch with a chamois cloth, and extended his charcoal at full length in his right hand to measure the proportions of the figure with his thumb.

The model chose that moment to step down—rest period—and Gleyre resumed his discourse. "It is a rule of portraiture that the human eye is located about halfway up between the chin and the top of the head."

The man was developing a distressing resemblance to Dr. Parkington, the stuffy headmaster Jimmy had often caricatured in his Connecticut prep school days. His fingers twitched: Did he dare? He reached stealthily for the charcoal, then stopped in midair. Gleyre was saying something interesting:

"When we come to the matter of color, you will find that nothing can compare in importance with ivory black. Black is the basis of tone, the universal harmonizer that will pull all your values together. For that reason, the canvas should always be prepared with a black or dark ground; working from dark to light, rather than the reverse, one can better control the gradations of tone."

Jimmy's jaw dropped; the pedant was actually making sense. Could there be more nuggets concealed in these bleak Swiss hills?

There were, but not at that session. Three days later, Gleyre drew a comparison between "the foolish painter" who splashed his colors on the canvas helter-skelter, and the "prudent painter": "The foolish painter improvises a color scheme as he goes along, and often discovers errors when it is too late. The prudent painter arranges his palette carefully before he starts, assembling all the values he will use on the finished canvas. That way, he is free to concentrate on the essentials of his art: accurate drawing, and fine modeling to create the full roundness of the third dimension."

Now there, thought Jimmy, was a truly valuable idea—although not necessarily for the reason advanced by Gleyre. By experimenting with small quantities on the palette, one could develop varied possibilities in color relationships. And once a particular one had been arrived at, it could be repeated accurately elsewhere on the canvas.

These two concepts of Gleyre—the base of "universal black" or gray, and the pre-arranged palette—were to remain with Jimmy for a lifetime. Otherwise there was little to hold his interest at the *Académie*, where "the sun rose and fell with Raphael."

More to Jimmy's taste was the Louvre. Majestic in scale as it was exquisite in detail, the Louvre Palace rose in seventeenth-century splendor just across the Seine, its colossal arms beckoning across the rickety girders of the old Pont des Arts to the Left Bank world of artists and students. The Louvre collection was born of the French Revolution, when the great château galleries of the aristocracy were confiscated and nationalized; by 1850 the palace had gathered within its spacious halls an unrivaled array of Western painting and sculpture. Jimmy had seen other important accumulations of art: the 2000-painting Hermitage in St. Petersburg, founded by Catherine the Great; the National Gallery in London. But these were simply museums, institutions attached to capital cities; the Louvre was a universe unto itself. Every school and tradition was represented within its walls: Italians and Flemings and Spaniards, long-dead Greeks and living Frenchmen. As Jimmy often said, "What is not worthy of the Louvre is not art."

At first he merely rambled through the stately halls and gilded rotundas, nibbling at the hors d'oeuvres of the feast. Gradually he narrowed his focus, starting with the early Italian masters. He marveled at the powerful effects that the Venetians, especially Titian and his pupil Tintoretto, had achieved with simple pigments and straightforward brushwork. Years later he was to capture in his painting of the philosopher Thomas Carlyle some of the gray, haunting weariness of Tintoretto's self-portrait.

He paid his homage to the incomparable Rembrandt, virtuoso of light-and-shade; but it was another seventeenth-century Dutchman, Frans Hals, whose work spoke to him more personally. Hals had buoyancy and wit, a splashing immediacy of style; with a single swift, dashing stroke he penetrated to the heart of the moment, or the core of character. Like the more popular Rubens, he painted in the big, bold manner; but where Rubens seemed to Jimmy overblown, Hals wasted nothing.

French classical painting, apart from Corot's delicate seascapes, held little appeal for Jimmy. He dismissed the antiquity-minded Ingres as a "bourgeois Greek," and felt the Delacroix romantics had broken loose from mythology only to run afoul of historical anecdote.

One other master ranked near the very top of Jimmy's private pantheon: Velázquez, seventeenth-century court painter to Spain's Philip IV. Somber and dignified in his approach, Velázquez had achieved immortality with a relative handful of armored equestrian figures and tender Infantas. His canvases were rich in characterization and muted color harmonies. By contrast with the flamboyant Goya, Velázquez was a "painter's painter." For Jimmy, he was something else besides: a gentleman-painter.

Jimmy's contemporaries, he was well aware, were not contenting themselves with rhapsodizing over the masters; they were taking full advantage of the Louvre's facilities for making instructive copies. He would have to start doing the same. Any time now.

Meanwhile, Paris was at hand, more intriguing than Gleyre, less overpowering than the Louvre. He could sit at a street café, sketchbook resting on the cool marble table, and watch the life of the city unfold before him: milliners and ballet girls, farmers bumping along on fruit-laden two-wheel carts, a brawny half-naked forge worker with a hammer slung over his shoulder. A few blocks away, he could sketch portly bankers, rapt children gathered around a street acrobat.

And in between, gloriously walkable, the panoply of Paris, lush and inviting in the warm transparent summer light. One could wander freely for hours, observing, sketching, reflecting. Nobody paid attention, because half the population was doing the same.

Every shop window was a still life: wheels of golden cheese, fresh dark grape leaves set off against a pail of cream. Lovely detail bloomed in obscure corners—a lion's head on a courtyard pump, a helmeted charioteer in bas-relief over a butcher's door.

For all the grandeur of the new Right Bank thoroughfares, Jimmy far preferred the other, older side of the river opposite Notre-Dame, where the narrow tangled streets and disreputable cafés of Bohemia stretched southwest in a flattened half-moon arc. Heart of the Latin Quarter—so named because only the original Roman tongue was used there by the scholar-priests of the Middle Ages—was the Sixth Arrondissement, tucked inside the right angle formed by the intersection of Boulevard du Montparnasse and Boulevard Saint-Michel. A diagonal line running due north from the intersection directly toward the Louvre across the Seine, passed first through the pearl of the Arrondissement: the Luxembourg Gardens.

Standing between the old university buildings to the north and the painters' world of Montparnasse on the south, the Gardens were a seductive mélange of thick lime groves, chestnut-bordered walks and flame-colored rosebeds, interspersed with noble statuary. At the top of broad steps leading up from the central fountain, Jimmy stopped to admire a group of voluptuously sculptured female figures. One, he discovered, with long plaited tresses falling over opulent hips, was Sainte-Geneviève, patron of Paris. For the French, he reflected, even a saint had to be all woman.

Which reminded him—in this city of chic and sophistication, where even the mousiest midinette had a certain sexual elan, his own social life had thus far been nil. Very much like his progress in art studies. For three weeks he had been drifting and dawdling; had *accomplished*, as his mother liked to say, nothing.

A sudden panic seized him. Would his story be any different after three months—or three years? Painting was the path he himself had chosen. Was it possible he was going to fail again?

They would be wondering at home, as he was wondering here. Especially since he had not written beyond announcing his arrival. Well, he would take care of that tomorrow, make a full report—not too literal, of course, but something to allay their anxieties.

And his own.

At noon the next day he sat in a glass-enclosed corner of the Café Guerbois, composing for his mother an impressive if largely fictional account of his Paris regime, when he became aware of a well-bred English voice: "I say, Whistler!"

He looked up and recognized Edward Poynter, a fellow student at Gleyre's. "Good morning."

"Haven't seen you at the studio all week."

"And you won't, as long as the ghost of Raphael hovers. One can have too much . . . of a bad thing."

Poynter smiled thinly. He lived with several other Englishmen. Perhaps, he suggested, Jimmy would like to come for dinner that eve-

ning with "the chaps"—that is, if he didn't have anything more pressing
on hand?

Jimmy allowed that he just might be able to rearrange his schedule
. . . yes, on reflection he definitely could.

"Splendid. Eight o'clock, fourth floor, at 53 Notre-Dame-des-
Champs."

"The chaps" turned out to include George du Maurier, later famous
as a *Punch* cartoonist and the author of *Peter Ibbetson* and *Trilby*;
a brawny Highlander named Thomas Lamont, generally known as the
Laird; and a couple of other art-student refugees from Oxford and
Cambridge. Du Maurier was a slim, carefully tailored young man,
highly conscious of his delicate nose and upcurled mustache. The son
of a middle-class Frenchman and an English mother, he had a variety
of talents—among them, an excellent tenor voice—and limitless ambition. Lamont was a tower of bulging muscle and innocent good nature, immensely likable by contrast with the rather joyless Poynter.

Dinner *chez les anglais* Jimmy found tolerable, thanks largely to
an unexpected bucket of oysters. More disappointing was the discovery
that his new friends were passionate physical culturists. By day, their
habitat looked less like a studio than a gymnasium. Hanging down
from the central ceiling beam was a giant trapeze, flanked by a set of
rope-suspended rings for the somersault-minded. On the walls, Indian
clubs competed for space with boxing gloves and dueling masks.

The Englishmen lost little time in pouncing on Jimmy as a recruit.
"Do you box?" Lamont asked eagerly.

"Not him," surmised du Maurier. "He's a fencer, I'll wager. Eh,
Whistler?"

"He's a Military Academy man," put in Poynter gloomily. "So it's
undoubtedly all horses."

Jimmy's full nostrils twitched at this unpleasant suggestion.

"Well, which is it?" from Lamont. "What's your pleasure, Whistler?"

"Billiards," announced Jimmy decisively. "With a spot of dancing,
kept within limits . . . a cigarette . . . and a little whisky." Where-
upon, ignoring the general dismay, he stretched out on a couch and
lit up.

Jimmy could not see why grown men—and close friends, at that—
would want to pummel each other: "Why not hire your concierges to
fight?"

It was his special pleasure, while the body-building Englishmen
hammered or slashed away at each other, to lounge back in a comfortably stuffed armchair, ringlets over his eyes, feet propped up on a
table, puffing on a conspicuously unhealthful cigarette, pouring himself
occasional refills from a mug of cheap beer. Rebuked for this exhibition

of sloth, he would reply: "An artist should exercise only two things: his arms and his imagination!"

The Laird was frankly baffled: "You don't enjoy strenuous sports at all!"

"On the contrary"—with the loud, high-pitched, un-English but not quite rude laugh—"I enjoy *your* huffing and puffing enormously."

Jimmy had no idea that his cocksure insouciance was rankling du Maurier to the point of storing up bitter little notes that forty years later would explode into the character of Joe Sibley, the idle apprentice of *Trilby*. For the moment, du Maurier contented himself with a strip of cartoons on the wall in which a jaunty figure representing Jimmy, dangling a wand-like cane, grew gradually fainter until in the final panel it disappeared altogether, giving way to a large question mark.

Jimmy sensed no malice in his fellow artist, perhaps because he saw less of du Maurier than of the affable Laird. Lamont was in a perpetual death struggle with the French language—his attempts at "Kwell Cochong!" and "Bong Deoo!" were pathetic—and Jimmy willingly undertook to instruct him.

He was giving a verb-drill one day to the Laird, who was abed with a cold, when a bosomy French girl knocked on the door to explain that the Englishmen's laundry would be delayed.

"What does she say?" demanded Lamont.

Jimmy knew that the Laird was wearing only a thin nightshirt borrowed from du Maurier, which reached scarcely to his hips. "She says you must pay five francs at once, or all your linen will be sold at auction."

"At auction? What nonsense!"

"It's the local custom." The girl was talking again.

"I'm afraid," said Jimmy, "there may be an unpleasant incident."

The Laird thought that over. "Do you have a fiver, Jimmy?"

"Not a sou."

"There are some coins in my jacket—"

"I never touch another man's clothes. I'm afraid you'll have to get out of bed, Tommy."

The Laird looked over at the girl, who was finding this foreign colloquy a source of interest if not enlightenment. Tugging his nightshirt down toward his knees, he emerged slowly from the bed, like some ancient monster surfacing from Loch Ness. As the girl watched, bewildered, he skittered across the room, dug a few coins from his pocket, and gave them to her before retreating, face ablaze, to the covers.

Jimmy explained in French that his friend was making an advance payment on the laundry—"an old English custom." The girl moved away, bowing her thanks.

The Laird, too, was grateful. When Jimmy soon afterward wangled an invitation to dine at the residence of the U. S. Minister, Lamont not only offered his dress suit but prowled the post-midnight corridors of the Hôtel Corneille with his friend in search of formal patent leathers. Jimmy finally found—and unofficially borrowed—a pair of the right size, although he grumbled about the styling.

His evening-out on the Right Bank was diverting. Jimmy enjoyed the role of devil-may-care artist spying on the ultra-proper diplomats; it was a pleasant switch from his usual self-image of a prince incognito disporting himself among the Bohemians.

The trouble was, he had hardly penetrated the real life of the Left Bank. His doughty English comrades, with their earnest calisthenics and their Saturday night chops at a tavern in the Rue Royale, were about as Latin as Hyde Park Corner. Still, their aimless chatter was easier to live with than the dark self-questioning that too often gnawed at his solitude. So, he kept in touch.

It was just as well that he did. Through "the chaps," he met Fumette.

It was the Laird who, on an idle Thursday, proposed a short stroll to the Bal Bullier. The famous dance hall, scene of weekly revels and the annual Students' Ball, was at the far end of the Boulevard Saint-Michel on the southern tip of the Quarter, across the wide Place de l'Observatoire from the sweet-scented arbors of the Closerie des Lilas.

Jimmy, Lamont and du Maurier joined the long line before the Bullier façade, where colored lanterns lighted up bas-relief figures of students and grisettes. Somewhere inside, a band was thumping. From the sunken garden a flight below, treetops peeped out enticingly over the wall. Not only students were in the crowd; there were young workingmen, a sprinkling of Apache types, and well-heeled tourists eager for a glimpse of authentic cancan.

Jimmy paid his two francs at the box-office cubbyhole, handed his slim cane to a white-capped matron at the cloakroom, and presented his green ticket to an elderly silk-hatted gentleman who stood with two armed soldiers at the door (brawls were a standard feature of frolics in the Latin Quarter).

Jimmy found himself at the top of a broad wooden stairway, looking down on a whirling sea of color: blond heads and blue naval uniforms, yellow gowns, black sweaters and pink flesh, all mingling, blending, then breaking into new kaleidoscopic patterns as the dancers raced and tumbled about the floor. The ball was in full swing: fiery orchestra challenging the dancers to keep pace with the rising tempo of a *galop*.

"Mong Deeoo!" The Laird brought down a ham-sized palm on the back of each of his friends. "There's Fumette!" He pointed to a small, rapidly spinning girl in a low-cut, wide-skirted green gown. She was half-concealed by a lanky partner.

"Who?" asked Jimmy.

"Fumette. She did a little modeling for us a couple of months ago. Fantastic creature—recites de Musset, sings like a bird."

Jimmy reached into his waistcoat pocket for the monocle he had picked up on a whim the day before. Screwing it carefully into his right eye, he saw full petulant lips in a round, childish face, framed by an untidy torrent of blond silky hair. The whole effect was wistful, dissatisfied—and vaguely appealing.

"Does she have any other attractions?" Jimmy inquired drily.

"Ask George. He tried to, ah, press his attentions one afternoon."

"Not really," protested du Maurier. "I was simply adjusting her dress."

"She just about carved her initials into his cheek," said Lamont. "He passed it off as a dueling cut. Later we found out they call her La Tigresse."

Du Maurier started down the steps. "I dare say," he tossed back over his shoulder, "a man could have his way with her, if he wanted to take the trouble. Shall we get a table?"

Surrounding and overlooking the dance floor was the Bal Bullier garden, a charming affair of round ironwork tables and white gravel walks scattered among thickly leaved maples. Tiny summerhouses-for-two ran along one side, opening onto the *pièce de résistance* of the area: a bubbling, lantern-hung fountain of Venus featuring the goddess herself in an attitude of cheerful surrender.

As the three visitors took seats near the outside railing, shrieks and applause from below signaled the end of the *galop*. The mass of dancers, flushed and exhilarated, stampeded up toward the garden for a cool breeze and lemon ices. When the scramble for tables was over, Jimmy saw sitting a few feet away a boneless lizard of a man in maroon turtleneck. Although tall as the Laird, the fellow had a custard-pie pastiness that suggested he would be no match for the Englishman in a fair fight. However, a fair fight was the last situation in which one would have expected to find him. With the man was Fumette.

At just that moment, Fumette turned and saw Jimmy. Troubled gray eyes collided with dazzling blue.

The next few events overlapped. Fumette leaned out of her chair and spoke quickly to Lamont, who presented Jimmy. Fumette's escort bent over and hissed at her. Du Maurier mumbled something about being careful of the *maquereaux*—"they kick people in the nose!"

Fumette slapped the lizard-man across the cheek. He grabbed at her hair, and she dug long nails into his face. The man kicked back his chair and ran off howling. As he reached the bottom of the wooden stairs, Fumette's hard-flung shoe caught him in the back of the neck.

Fumette stood swaying on her remaining shoe at the table. Instantly Jimmy leaped up to retrieve the improvised weapon.

"May I?" Like Prince Charming attending Cinderella, he placed it gently on the girl's foot.

"*Merci,* monsieur. You are very kind."

"It is easy to be kind—when the lady is lovely."

"And also gallant."

Jimmy bowed. "A gentleman can be no less." He took the seat vacated by his predecessor.

"You are an artist?"

"One hopes. And you?"

"I sing, I portray poems, and for *la nécessité,* I work as a milliner. Sometimes I model." She flashed a dimpled smile. "Will you make me immortal?"

"I am afraid," said Jimmy softly, "the Lord has anticipated me in that."

They sat for a moment in heart-pounding silence, quite alone in the crowded garden.

"Once, as a small boy," said Jimmy, "I thought of being a lion-tamer . . ."

"Tigresses are better. And more appreciative."

"Jimmy, look out!" There was alarm in Lamont's voice.

Jimmy raised his head. The lizard-man was coming down the stairs.

The man came closer, glaring venomously. Jimmy kept to his seat without flinching. A few feet from the table, the *maquereau* suddenly spat, missing Jimmy's shoe by inches.

Immediately Jimmy started after him. Fumette seized his arm.

"Let me go," Jimmy protested. "I must teach him a lesson."

"He is too stupid to learn."

"It is a matter of honor!"

"Maurice has no honor. What he does have is a knife. He wouldn't have come back without it."

Jimmy shot her a glance from under his dark brows. "In that case, I shall call the police."

"No. You will be quiet and leave everything to me." She squeezed his arm intimately. "Everything, *mon petit amour.*" Her large gray eyes ranged over his face caressingly.

Jimmy shrugged. "*À bientôt,*" he said.

"*Very* soon," echoed Fumette. She walked quickly over to Maurice. The two exchanged a few sharp words, and then left together.

Late the next afternoon, browsing through *Le Figaro* in his hotel room, Jimmy heard light footsteps on the stairs. Instinct sent him rushing out to the corridor. On the edge of the landing was Fumette, a suitcase in one hand and several packages cradled in the other. In her simple yellow poplin and blue-ribboned straw bonnet, she looked even more the little girl than on the evening before.

"*Zut alors!*" she gasped. "Could you find nothing higher?"

Jimmy hastened to take over her burdens. "How did you find me?"

"Through Monsieur Lamont. But the concierge downstairs, he said he never heard of you."

"He will one day—if he lives long enough." Jimmy pushed open the door. "What about Maurice?"

"Which Maurice?"

Jimmy blinked. "The man last night—"

"Questions, questions. What are you, an artist or a police agent? I am here." She bent forward and kissed him lightly on the cheek. "You are happy to see me, or no?"

"Just let me put these things down, I'll show you."

His arms free, Jimmy came back to her. She melted toward him, all softness and warmth and faint perfume. He had a blurred memory of freshly squeezed milk in a musky Connecticut barn. Swaying slightly, he pressed himself against her.

Fumette broke away. "I have brought food," she announced. "You are too thin—even for a student. Where is your stove?"

Jimmy indicated an ancient woodburner in the corner.

"We have veal cutlets, rice, and cheese. You have some wine?"

"A half-bottle of passable red."

"Very good." Fumette started to open the packages, singing half to herself in a light, flute-like contralto:

> "Would you like to know
> How artists love?
> They love artistically
> Being artistic people"

The next line she spoke, matter-of-factly: "They go out the door saying, 'Come to my place, and I shall do your portrait.'"

She fumbled a moment with the lid of the stove. "Strange stoves," she murmured, "are worse than strange beds."

"Here, let me help you." Jimmy released the lid.

"Hand me the rice, please. It takes a while to boil properly."

Fumette busied herself at the stove. Jimmy came up behind her, placing his hands around her waist. "*My* boiling point," he whispered, "is lower."

How pliant her flesh, how willing! He moved his hands higher, his long fingers curling into her breasts.

Suddenly Fumette turned and threw herself against him, burying her hands in his thick curls, covering his mouth, eyes, and nose with kisses. Her tongue darted over his face, leaving a trail of moist and mounting excitement.

Jimmy was unprepared for such passion—on her part or his own. His previous sexual experience had been confined to some indecisive groping with Colette, the boardinghouse maid at West Point, and two bordello visits as an upper classman, both of them perfunctory and disappointing; the ladies had not been as young as Fumette, or as volcanic.

Now she was tugging at his blouse, and with her other hand loosening the buttons of her dress. Jimmy followed her lead; clothes fell to the floor in a haphazard tangle.

Staggering around the tiny room together, the two fell across the bed, limbs entangled, threshing wildly. Jimmy had never felt such desire, never known such an intense sensation of being alive. Fumette's nails were digging into his back, her breath came hot and sharp, she was panting "*Je t'aime . . . mon amour . . .*"

And then it happened. He felt a sudden loss of power and control, an oozing away of life . . . He struggled to hold it back, but he was helpless. He looked down, and was humiliated.

Fumette, too, had stopped writhing. She was gazing at him in astonishment. "But you have fired your cannon too soon, my little soldier." She saw Jimmy's acute misery, and patted him on the cheek. "But it is nothing. *Je m'en fou.* Lamont told me you used to be a cadet: later, we call up the reserves, *n'est-ce pas?* Meanwhile, we can eat."

She sprang up, and wrapped herself in Jimmy's blouse. "*Regardez,* the rice is exactly ready! I can give a new formula to the Gourmet Society: 'Cook rice, while stirring up Jimmy. When Jimmy comes to a full boil—the rice is ready!'"

Jimmy had to smile.

Dinner was excellent, and enlivened by Fumette's recitation of passages from Alfred de Musset, the bittersweet poet-playwright who had been an early lover of George Sand. "Poet, take your lute," she declaimed.

> "The wine of youth
> Bubbles this night within the godhead's veins."

Singing and chattering, she unpacked her suitcase and tidied up the room.

Afterward, they made love again. It was better, much better. Confident that he was wanted, guided by Fumette's sure fingers and knowing tongue, Jimmy leapt vigorously but unhurriedly to the attack. New sensations surged through his body, literally to the tips of his toes; he performed with a valor and adroitness that surpassed his own expectations if not those of Fumette. As he rolled over her, gyrating wildly, she squealed her delight. *"Mon Dieu, tu es formidable, mon petit américain! Je te décore de la Medaille Militaire."*

Jimmy crushed the tousled blond head to his chest. "Tomorrow," he panted, "tomorrow I go after the Légion d'Honneur."

# Chapter Five

Fumette opened the door to the Paris Jimmy had dreamed about. The grisettes of the Right Bank were linked to the art students of the Left by the Pont Neuf, a nightly passageway to Cinderella romance. Like the youthful poets, sculptors, and composers, the shopgirls crossing from the Rue de la Paix were outcasts from the world of privilege, but still rich in hopes and fancies; life had not yet closed in on them. The boys needed encouragement; the girls were thrilled at the prospect of intimate contact, however fleeting, with genius.

Painters and sculptors were especially esteemed as lovers, for their reputed tactile sensitivity. If a painter's mistress was, like Fumette, attractive enough to do some modeling, that was a bonus all around. A girl could make five francs in a single morning's sitting—better than a day's pay as a seamstress—and when otherwise unoccupied, she was a handy subject for her lover. The grisettes demanded little in return for their dedication. It was enough to dwell in the ambience of creativity, and thumb their pretty little noses at the barbarous bourgeois across the river.

Fumette's first move was to get Jimmy out of the Hôtel Corneille; he was paying far too much, she said, for too little. Together they trudged with their baggage past the bookstores of the Rue de l'Odéon, later famous as the haunts of Hemingway and Fitzgerald; threaded their way through the tall buildings of the Rue Saint-Sulpice; and after a bewildering jog or two in the road, landed before the ponderous wooden doors of 1, Rue Bourbon-le-Château. Three floors up from the usual paved courtyard, Jimmy and Fumette established residence.

For the moment at least, Jimmy's days of solo rambling were over. Latin Quarter couples traveled in large, overlapping groups, a roisterous sub-society as exclusive—and pleasure-loving—as any royal court.

The staple of merry-making was the studio party. However deplorable the condition of communal finances, everybody usually had some leftover he could contribute: onions shipped from a cousin in the country, a liter of wine, an empty loft with a rented piano. One perennial "student" of forty-five had a talented monkey who, lowered from a rope, could be counted on to pilfer some delicacy from neighbors: rare spices, or a jar of grape jelly. Pockets were scraped for the rest: five francs could produce a crusty bread, a fillet of beef, and a sizable chunk of pungent brie. Easels were pushed aside, feather boas and ostrich plumes tossed in a corner, and the piano rolled out to the middle of the room. Left Bank instruments were expected to survive everything, including wax dripping down from candle-holders and cheap punch flooding the strings.

Spacious quarters being at a premium, Jimmy once persuaded his English chums to convert their exercise-room-studio to a cabaret for the night. Du Maurier, merciless in the possession of a captive audience, performed nearly half the score of a popular new opera by Verdi, *Il Trovatore*. Finally, with some reluctance, he yielded the floor to Fumette and a gloomy Greek accompanist . . . and thereby acquired his models for the characters of Trilby and Svengali.

Less respectable evenings were passed in the dim lusty cafés of the Quarter—the Rat Mort, the Café d'Harcourt—drinking endless rounds of wine and bellowing rude student songs from the Middle Ages, in a stifling aroma of tobacco smoke, stale bouquets, alcohol, and perfume. When the revelers had exhausted the oil lamps, the credit possibilities and the patience of one establishment, they poured out onto the Boulevard Saint-Michel and headed for another. It was considered a point of honor never to retire until the brasserie shutters were being put up, market carts came clattering in from the country, and the first cock crowed.

Sundays were special. Lovers could picnic on the banks of the Seine (lunch provided by the girl, cigarettes and wine by the man); or, by a prodigious effort of thrift, spend the day in the woods at Saint-Cloud, making the outward journey by horse-omnibus and returning by moonlight aboard one of the new little *bateaux mouches* darting like fireflies along the Seine.

It was a splendid time and place to be young. With a good French meal in one's stomach, the soft amiable air of Paris to breathe, and a lively girl on one's arm . . . a room to work in, a canvas to cover with paint—who could be worried about tomorrow's incubating problems, or today's empty purse?

Fumette was, Jimmy discovered, undisputed queen of the local entertainment circuit. She recited de Musset with fiery conviction, and was equally effective pouting her way through the lighthearted songs of the tavern:

> "A young modiste am I
> And never sad or shy;
> To hearts that lack employment
> I offer sweet enjoyment.*
> But I'm not one who hankers
> For generals or bankers;
> The way a flower loves water,
> I love my Latin Quarter."

Dainty and adorable as she was in performance, Fumette became belligerently possessive where Jimmy was concerned. She permitted no approaches. If another woman offered to share an apéritif with him, Fumette La Tigresse would not hesitate to knock over the drink —or the drinker.

Jimmy pretended annoyance at such displays, but was secretly delighted. Fumette, the enchanting *enfant terrible* of the Left Bank, had eyes for him alone. He was her *homme*. The word had a nice ring to it. Returning from their first outing at Saint-Cloud, with the boat purring along under an orange-slice moon and Fumette's tousled head on his shoulder, he felt positively expansive.

Soon Jimmy too became part of the impromptu shows. He had been fascinated by private theatricals since his visit at fifteen to London; here, there was no mother or older sister to squelch him. He improvised an act based on the minstrel-show "plantation songs" he had heard from his numerous Southern cousins. Strumming an imaginary banjo (he used his cane first, until he found that an umbrella drew more laughs), he chanted in a high cracked voice:

> "Takey off your coat, boys
> Rolley up your sleeve
> For Jordan am a hard road to travel,
> I believe . . .
> De world was made in six days
> And finished on de seventh,
> According to de contract,
> It should have been de eleventh."

His voice was wobbly, his accent absurd; but the effect was hypnotic. Jimmy had the timing, the expressive hands and the motorized eyebrows of a born actor.

Word about *le petit américain* spread rapidly. The French liked the

* *Je suis jeune et modiste*
*Jamais je ne m'attriste*
*Et je tiens sous my loi*
*Tous les coeurs sans emploi.*

Whistler blend of personal chic, Southern chivalry and Bohemian arrogance. He was one of them, yet different enough to be that most prized of creatures, an "original."

And Jimmy liked being liked. Since childhood he had known that he was "bad" but charming; pirouetting in the limelight, he could forget his alleged sins. He expanded his party repertoire to include the tale of Poe's lugubrious "lost Lenore" from *The Raven,* and added monologues caricaturing gendarmes, tourists, and art lecturers.

The extent of his local reputation was demonstrated a decade later on the Civil War battlefield in South Carolina. A haggard officer one afternoon stumbled into the headquarters of Francis Vinton, a Union brigadier, and claimed to have known Vinton when both were engineering students in Paris.

The general reflected a moment. "Hm . . . who was the funniest man we knew?"

"Why . . . Whistler."

"Take that cot; you're no spy."

Yes, Jimmy was a success; he knew the actor's glory of "Encore!" Yet he had an uneasy sense of playing a game. Was it to massage his self-esteem that he had come to Paris? What was more important: To be noticed or to be productive?

It was a dilemma that took a lifetime to resolve. Meanwhile, to reassure his anxious family—and himself—Jimmy again wrote home at some length, describing the non-existent schedule of a non-existent Whistler-the-exemplary-student, who rose at dawn for a nourishing breakfast, attended drawing class from 8:00 A.M. till two in the afternoon, moved on to a modeling session for a couple of hours, and then, after a visit to the Louvre and a salutary walk along the Seine, spent dinner in discussion of lofty aesthetic problems with other earnest *etudiants* before blowing out his candle at ten.

Actually, he had given up totally on Gleyre; the morning class was generally over by the time he stumbled to the water basin for his pre-breakfast scrub. He was scarcely more active at the Louvre. Only his on-the-scene sketches, dashed off in billiard halls and cafés, on rainy street corners and in sun-dappled woods, were never abandoned. Here he struggled over and over, straining the capacity of his short-ranged eyes, to express in terse outline the forms and individual features of laborers and *grandes dames,* theater fronts and bridges.

But his misgivings were many. How could he master a difficult art, when he could not master himself? He remembered Colonel Lee's warnings about discipline, and was assailed by waves of self-doubt. Often he was caught up in alternating currents of euphoria and despair. He had a ready sunniness; but the opposite mood was never far away, a pervasive melancholy that in the presence of congenial company was likely to go underground like a cavern spring, then suddenly pop up again. His spirits were as unpredictable as the skies of the Mc-Neills' native Hebrides: sullen clouds giving way to bursts of sunshine, followed by gathering mists.

Bad days usually took him to the Luxembourg Gardens. The band music, the fluttering parasols under the rows of chestnuts gave him a lift. On one of his anisette-and-blank-verse evenings with Fumette, he had made a good friend. Nodding over a sketch in a noisy restaurant, he became aware of a shambling bear of a man peering over his shoulder. "Quick, chum—put a fifth leg under that piano, before it falls on the baby!" The criticism had been justified. Jimmy laughed and thanked the critic, who turned out to be a fellow painter named Ernest Delaunay.

Now, in the Gardens, Jimmy made another friend—of sorts. La Mère Gérard was the guardian of a makeshift flower stand under the huge spear-tipped gates at the southern entrance. Old beyond counting, unable to see at more than a few paces, Mother Gérard nonetheless held her bony frame erect and flailed at the world with a peppery wit. Gossip said she had been a respected poetess decades before. Further details, such as an alleged long-ago liaison with a cabinet minister, varied with the imagination of the speaker.

Certainly the spare, wrinkled old lady had kept a waspish tongue. Customers who attempted to bargain with her found themselves suddenly swamped with violets: "Here, take them for nothing. If you are so close to starvation you will need them for your grave!" When she saw Jimmy on a bench, jotting down studies of children's heads, she accused him of using his charcoals as a ruse for meeting pretty nursemaids: "It is not the Louvre that you seek, but the bedroom!"

Sensing a kindred spirit, Jimmy winked and begged her not to betray him to the police. He took to addressing her as "Madame la Duchesse." In turn she called him "Monsieur La Canaille," or "Mr. Scoundrel."

He never left the Gardens without buying a five-sou armful of violets or roses. This was not entirely out of solicitude for La Mère Gérard; it was also a form of insurance against the unpredictable humors of Fumette.

Living with any woman had built-in hazards for Jimmy. Years of conditioning by Anna Whistler had left him sensitive to criticism; and Fumette had a bold tongue locked onto a short temper. He was dependent on the attentions of women, deeply in need of their emotional support—yet suspicious of their reliability. Fearful of being maneuvered, he himself became the maneuverer . . . probing to see what he could get away with, testing the degree of Fumette's affection. He neglected obligations, was careless of promises . . . and then lavish with his attentions.

Fumette was willing, if not overjoyed, to take over the petty responsibilities of the household. What she found unendurable were Jimmy's capricious rebellions against his own dependency, when he would lash out against her for doing what he had obliged her to do. She was a cuddlesome French poodle, accustomed to being petted or dominated; a man who shifted from passivity to belligerence, from indifference to ardent courtship, baffled her.

And La Tigresse was a jealous girl of stormy impulses. She reacted badly to teasing. Thus, the elements of an explosion were always at hand. Quarrels could flare up over almost anything: the cost of coffee, a shirt that somehow had not been ironed. Inevitably the crescendo would be climaxed by Fumette's tearful charge that Jimmy did not really love her.

"But of course I do, *chérie!* How can you doubt it?"

"What do you love about me?"

A sly smile, the blue eyes gleaming. "Why—not much. Just your face —your body—your personal charm—your intelligence—and your character."

Fumette would purr, and slip inside the circle of his arms. Then she would lift her round, pale little face up to him wickedly: "As for me, all I like about you is . . . your love-making."

And it would be Jimmy's turn to arch his aristocratic profile and preen.

They were like wrangling children; such was their sense of play that they could be quickly diverted. Curiously, the strongest bond between them was their chronic poverty—and the pervasive air of comedy with which Jimmy surrounded it.

By Left Bank standards, Jimmy was theoretically quite rich. Many a student staggered through the year on a scanty $125 allowance, and Jimmy had three times that much. But he also had certain attitudes that precluded prudent budgeting.

Still under the impress of the Czarist years, he remained in his own eyes a kind of prince in disguise. Although his father had plumped hard and often for republicanism, Jimmy had never, as it were, renounced his claim to the throne.

With archaic courtliness he intervened with two gendarmes who were, as he thought, showing insufficient respect to a gentlewoman. Haled into court for his pains, he coolly referred the magistrate to "my banker, M. Rothschild."

And he spent money as if the airy invention were true. His allowance came in quarterly installments; the arrival of a check was the signal for a celebration that promptly reduced its value by at least ten percent. For a week or two, the vintage wine flowed; within a month it was at a trickle.

Jimmy did not spend selfishly: his purse was open to all comers. Even apart from his sense of *noblesse oblige,* he was a generous young man, instinctively sympathetic except where he felt threatened; and he dwelt among needy, deserving artists. Just as at West Point he had shared his homemade cookies and his linguistic skills, he would not in Paris deny his less fortunate friends anything of what he had.

He made occasional visits to London, where he was now "Uncle Jimmy" to a baby nephew as well as to six-year-old Annie Haden. One Christmas, when he was in England and Fumette was staying with her parents at Charenton-le-Pont, he left his studio in the hands of some "no-shirt" colleagues. They mixed grog in his new tin bathtub, shined their shoes with his towels, and when the dinner dishes were dirty simply turned them over and used the other side. Jimmy was stunned, but uncondemning.

Still, Fumette protested that their periodic plunge from the damask tablecloths of the Restaurant Magny to damp yellow cornets of fried potatoes was unnecessary. Jimmy readily agreed—and came up with a brilliant strategem. They would set up thirty pillboxes, covering such items of expenditure as rent, breakfast, tobacco, wine, art materials, stamps and laundry, and place in each box a carefully allocated sum that would have to last until the next check.

It was a brilliant stratagem, but not quite as brilliant as Jimmy's elaborate "borrowings" and mysterious exchanges among the boxes. Within two weeks there wasn't a sou left in any of them.

Eating on the Left Bank was not expensive. Breakfast at a *crémerie* —*café au lait* with a couple of crescent rolls and three pats of butter —could be managed for nine sous, or less than an American dime. For larger repasts, most of their group patronized Lalouette's, one of the many family institutions that shared the tribulations of the students and took pride in their successes. Managerial economies were forthright: the tablecloth was juggled to keep the worst of the accumulated gravy stains out of sight; the lamplight was skimpy, creating hazards for a nearsighted man like Jimmy. More than once, reaching for a plate of anchovies, he speared a neighbor. But for twenty sous, under the coat racks slung like hammocks along the wall, one could dine on soup, omelet, lentils, beans, sauced mutton, lettuce, cheese, and even a dubious blue wine.

Yet, often twenty sous seemed monumental. Jimmy then would enter the lists against Madame Lalouette, notoriously skeptical in extending credit. First he brought in an actor friend, in borrowed finery, to pose as Count Dubert, a wealthy intimate of the Whistler family. This was going well, until Madame Lalouette pulled back the "Count's" sleeve to expose a tattered shirt cuff. Another time, unable to pay up his past balance, Jimmy organized a pool among students on the no-credit list and raised enough to restore to good standing a Romanian youth, who thereupon promptly invited his indigent colleagues to his table.

When everything else failed, Jimmy would do a sketch of Lalouette's adored daughter, Bibi; the *patron* invariably wilted. Before leaving Paris, Jimmy had run up a debt of $600 at Lalouette's, all of which he later paid off from London.

In extremis, there was also the pawnbroker. One hot afternoon in August, yearning for an iced drink, Jimmy left his jacket for security and walked around for a week in shirtsleeves. To a friend who remarked on the sparseness of his furnishings, he confessed cheerfully, "We've eaten the washstand and we're halfway through my wardrobe."

Rent—or the evasion of same—had its own techniques. When the impoverished Ernest Delaunay faced a lockout by his inartistic landlord, Jimmy helped him to swing bed, chairs, and easel out of the window and into a lower-floor cubbyhole in the adjoining house. Pressed for their own rent, Jimmy and Fumette moved higher and higher to an ever smaller, cheaper room . . . up to the sixth, topmost floor of their building and then to a taller one, where by the end of the quarter they occupied a cramped attic that Jimmy insisted had been built for midgets. The floor level at which Jimmy was living was an unfailing gauge not only of the state of his finances, but of the corresponding time of the year; people in his intimate circle didn't need a calendar.

For sundries, Jimmy bartered sketches: of Garibaldi to appease an unpaid cobbler, of wealthy medical students to wipe out loans. It was Ernest Delaunay who pointed out that Jimmy was overlooking a broader, ready-made source of cash. Thus, poverty finally did what student tradition could not: drove Jimmy to making copies at the Louvre.

Ernest briefed him carefully. The sure-fire but low-fee market was in painting Stations of the Cross; dealers would even provide canvases with the outlines already traced in. Another steady sale was in saints. On a more ambitious plane, people never seemed to tire of excerpts from Veronese's magnificent panorama, the *Marriage Feast at Cana* . . .

"That sounds rather better," said Jimmy. "But what do I do for a big canvas? And paints?"

"You come with me to the Louvre tomorrow—and observe."

Ernest, with a drowsy Whistler in tow, was waiting at the door of the students' gallery when it opened at 8:00 A.M. Chatting with the guard, he moved briskly to the storage area where materials were left overnight, and with great self-assurance picked out a high easel, a

barely started canvas, a palette, turpentine, and a few brushes. As an
afterthought, he took up a stump of charcoal and in great sweeping
letters printed his name on the back of the canvas.

From his pocket, Ernest extracted the squashed dregs of a burnt-
sienna tube, and somehow coaxed enough paint out of it to obliterate
the original outline on the canvas. Then, as other students started to
drift in, he climbed a ladder and began his own sketch of a Bible subject.

A howl went up from the floor. A stout German lady was protesting
someone had stolen her canvas. "And other materials, too!"

From his lofty perch, Ernest turned in displeasure. "Please, madame,
you are disturbing the serious students!"

"You'd make a row, too, if an expensive canvas disappeared. With
two days of beautiful work on it!"

Ernest peered down fraternally. "How big was it?"

"About—about the same size as yours. Perhaps a little smaller."

"Surely it couldn't have walked off. Perhaps you took it home?"

"No. Some swine has pinched it."

Ernest clucked his tongue sympathetically. "In the very halls of the
Louvre! What is the world coming to?"

His sketch completed, Ernest was ready for his crowning coup: the
acquisition of expensive colors. Stepping down from his ladder,
palette over his thumb, he paused before the canvas of a blond youth
in maroon velvet. Such bold handling, he murmured. Such luxuriant
color! But if an older man—with full admiration—might venture a suggestion . . . ?

Eagerly, "Please do, sir!"

"Well, then . . . just a touch of cobalt blue, here . . ." Ernest
reached out to the profusely spread palette of his victim for a thick
"worm" of the blue that he himself needed, applying a tiny dab to the
canvas before him and leaving the rest on his own palette. "And a spot
of vermilion, here . . ." Ernest's hands flew between palettes and canvas, keeping pace with his comments, until he had a sizable roster of
colors.

"You will do great things, monsieur," he told the bewildered novice.
"Great things." He bowed and moved on.

Jimmy, now thoroughly awake, was enchanted. Within a few days
he was inventing his own audacities. He got along well, except for his
habit of rushing back abruptly from the canvas to survey his work. On
his first full day of copying, he backed into a scaffold, bringing irate
painter and ruined canvas down around his ears.

Before the week was up, however, he had stumbled into—or been
stumbled into by—the first paid commission of his career. He was standing before the 33-foot *Marriage Feast,* marveling at its sumptuous de-

tail and deploring the stiffness of his own purloined brushes, when a ruddy face interposed itself between Jimmy and the Veronese. "Blow me down if it ain't Jimmy Whistler! How are you, lad? Been looking for you ever since we got into port."

He recognized "Stonington Bill" Williams, a retired sea captain and friend of the Whistler family. "Good morning, sir."

"Say, that's a mighty snappy get-up, Jimmy. I see you're working— but would you have time to show an old sea dog around?"

"What would you like to see, sir?"

"Oh—everything."

So Jimmy showed him "everything." After miles of trudging through galleries and rotundas, Williams turned to him: "Could you copy some of these things?"

"Why yes, I think so."

"I mean to pay you, of course. What would the damages be?"

Jimmy quoted the first figure that popped into his mind. "Shall we say one hundred francs apiece?"

His patron pursed his lips. "How about twenty-five Yankee dollars, instead?"

"But—that's *more*, sir . . ."

"Is it?" Williams smiled innocently. "My bad luck." He chose three anecdotal subjects: a violent rainstorm, a pair of military couriers plunging through heavy snow, and a woman holding up a child toward a man locked behind prison bars. Pleased with the results of this first "collection," he then ordered copies of a haloed St. Luke, and, for a neoclassical touch, the *Deliverance of Angelica*, by Ingres.

This celebrated painting, an 1819 *Perils of Pauline*, showed a forlorn maiden chained to a rock, while a knight in burnished-gold armor tilted a lance through the jaws of a hissing dragon at her feet. It was not exactly Jimmy's idea of a contemporary subject, but he did what he could with it; and Ernest asserted that his silver-grays and warm flesh tints were an improvement on the original colors. Delaunay wondered, though, why his friend's paint was so thin.

"At these prices, I can barely afford linseed oil!"

"Stonington Bill" showed off his purchases to other American visitors, and soon Jimmy had commissions for a group in the *Decadent Romans* by Couture, and for François Boucher's *Diana at the Bath*. Boucher, like Ingres, was a consummate technician, but Jimmy found his work suffocatingly sweet.

He therefore welcomed the news of a forthcoming Velázquez summer exhibition at Manchester. He would have to go, of course. Unhappily, his recent wave of earnings had not at all altered his basic financial picture; he and Fumette had simply lived better for several weeks.

How to finance the Manchester visit—and ring in good old Ernest, who had put him onto the Louvre? There was a railroad engineer named Bergeron who had been extremely openhanded with art students. But, Fumette pointed out, Jimmy already owed him 80 francs.

"Ought that to make any difference?" Jimmy couldn't see why. Finally: "I'll ask him if he thinks I ought to ask him."

Bergeron, amused, financed what turned out to be a most stimulating trip. There were some fourteen Velázquez masterpieces lent from private collections, including *Don Balthazar in the Tennis Court, Duke Olivárez on Horseback, Admiral Pulido Pareja,* and a *Venus.* Each figure, Jimmy noted, had a flavor peculiarly its own; the very air breathed of individuality. And always there was the melancholy dignity, an execution that was careful without being pedantic.

They were supposed to be back on a Saturday morning, in ample time for an artists' outing at Saint-Cloud the next day under the sponsorship of Lalouette, the restaurateur. But they stayed overlong at the exhibition, missed their train, and finally stumbled into the Gare Saint-Lazare at sunrise on Sunday. Jimmy was weary but restless. Leaving Ernest at the Carré Odéon, he walked south to the Luxembourg Gardens.

There, dozing on a bench, sat the irascible Mère Gérard. Huddled under her shawls, gray and crumpled, she seemed suddenly pathetic. Yet a lingering defiance shaped her jaw, and around the corners of her mouth a tender half-smile reached back to the poetess of long ago.

The old lady stirred and blinked her eyes, gradually bringing Jimmy into focus. "So—it's you! Have you nothing better to do than run around spying on your betters?"

"I'm not spying. I've just had a prodigious idea. I want to paint you."

"Paint me!" She looked at him mockingly. "In the nude, I suppose!"

"In your Sunday best. Lalouette is running a carriage out to Saint-Cloud this morning. You'll come, as my partner. We'll work in the country."

"And my flowers?"

"We'll sell them to the students—except what we need for the portrait."

La Mère Gérard jeered, then protested; but at ten o'clock, amid general applause, she was hoisted up beside Jimmy in the hired carriage. On the way to Saint-Cloud, she told stories and even recited a few verses. But she would not touch wine, explaining that she suffered from a tapeworm.

"What can I give you, then?" asked the solicitous Jimmy.

"Some milk. He likes that."

In the woods, Jimmy hauled out a canvas rustled up by Ernest. With the grave cavaliers of Velázquez in his mind's eye, he already had the picture composed: four whitish masses of round bonnet, broad dangling strings, folded hands and tiny bouquet; for the rest, earth colors and black. The old lady sat straight in a chair, conceding nothing, against a gate. By the end of the day she was quite happy.

Not so Fumette. She had been left behind on the outing; tossed over, as she complained, for "a nasty old woman," humiliated before her friends. In vain Jimmy explained that it had been a matter of artistic necessity; one had to seize the opportunity of the moment.

"And what of me? Do I count for nothing?"

"You are everything, *chérie*. But this was such a perfect subject—"

"Fumette is not a good subject, *hein?* Fumette who shares your bed and your sorrows! Fumette is good enough for sketches. But when it comes to a real painting, your very first oil—then you go to someone else!"

"I will do an oil of you. Tomorrow—I promise."

"No. I do not want an oil."

"What do you want, then?"

Fumette sank down on the bed, glowering, making no reply. Such an earnest, appealing little face, thought Jimmy. The loose-hanging hair, the limp cigarette. It really called for a charcoal drawing, or—or—why not? He had been thinking of trying again with the medium he had picked up at the Coast Survey; had even acquired a few battered copperplates from the printer Delâtre. One of them already had a wax ground. There was a needle in his cupboard.

"I shall give you an etching," he announced.

Fumette, a trifle intimidated, watched quietly as he tracked the wooden-shafted needle over the surface of the copper. Once she got up to look, and complained, "You have lost my mouth!"

"Never that!" exclaimed Jimmy, and kissed her firmly.

For the moment the etching was forgotten; and in the amorous entwinings of the next two hours, all was forgiven.

The next morning, Fumette was pouting again. Jimmy had not brought back from Manchester, as promised, a souvenir beer mug for her: "Or did you give it to that old witch?"

Jimmy was indignant at the suggestion. To prove his ardor, right now, he would go downstairs and get her a suitable present.

On Saint-Germain-des-Prés, Jimmy ran into Ernest Delaunay. Ernest's news was depressing: he had been booted out by both landlord and girl friend, and was reduced in worldly goods to a huge copy of the *Marriage Feast at Cana*, languishing at a nearby studio.

Jimmy assured him the copy would bring a fortune, and offered to help find a suitable dealer. Balancing the canvas between them, they set out for one of the more prestigious galleries on the other side of the Seine. They asked 500 francs. The dealer laughed at them.

Well, what could you expect from the vulgarians of the Right Bank? They shouldered their cargo again and recrossed the Pont Neuf, heading toward a prosperous firm in the Latin Quarter. Here they tried for 250 francs. Again the answer was no.

Back again to the Right, Left, Right, with the price plunging steadily downward through the day, until at last they were rejected by the 10-franc pushcart merchants. Halfway across the iron-arched Pont des Arts, Jimmy looked over at Ernest. Ernest shrugged back. Together they approached the low webbed railing, and, with an "Un-deux-trois", heaved the painting into the Seine. For a few happy moments there was a tremendous hubbub as boats and hansom drivers raced to the scene, police whistles shrieked, and passers-by shouted "Man overboard!"

The row, and with it the exhilaration, subsided. Ernest was now not only homeless but emptyhanded. It was obvious to Jimmy that only one thing could save his friend's morale: a Lucullan evening. There was still some money left over from the Manchester trip.

They started with pernod on the terrace of the Closerie des Lilas. Eight hours, many drinks, and 96 francs later they sat at a sawdust-sprinkled all-night restaurant in the wholesale marketing district of Les Halles, surrounded by dangling carcasses, butcher-boy customers in stained uniforms . . . and an outraged manager. They had just consumed a mountain of mussels and a tureen of onion soup without having a sou between them.

The manager denounced Jimmy as a bare-faced thief. Jimmy challenged him to a duel. The manager, backing away, said he would give them two hours to round up the necessary 40 francs, before calling the police. It was decided that Jimmy would make the foray for funds, leaving Ernest as hostage.

Jimmy staggered off, trailing fierce military oaths. Ernest dropped his shaggy head onto the table and fell asleep.

Just before dawn Jimmy sauntered into view. He had quite forgotten his dueling impulses and was brimming over with good will toward the manager; coins jangled in his pocket. To Ernest he explained that an American fellow artist had come through with one hundred francs, although the fellow had had "the bad manners to abuse the situation; he insisted on my looking at his pictures."

"Les Vierges de Montparnasse . . ."
Jimmy's high, uncertain voice cracked on the top note, but it didn't matter; a little music helped a man get up the stairs.

He pushed open the door, holding a bouquet behind his back. "Fumette, my love—"

She wasn't there. The studio was deserted in the early morning light. Deserted, but not serene. His clothes were scattered over bed, chairs, dining table. And staring up at him from the floor were torn chunks of drawing paper. He bent over to confirm what he knew without looking: the fragments had been his most cherished sketches.

There was no message: only the empty drawers where Fumette's clothes had been, and the ruins of months of work. They were message enough.

Jimmy tossed his flowers aside and sank slowly to the floor. Perhaps if the pieces were not too small . . .

No, it was no use. Cruel, cruel . . .

What had he done to Fumette to deserve this? An impatient word, a harmless escapade or two. And oh yes—the present. It had slipped his mind at Manchester, and again when he encountered poor woebegone Ernest. But Fumette was a Frenchwoman, a Bohemian supposedly sensitive to art and artists.

Why had he been such a fool as to trust her? And how could he ever put his faith in any woman?

Weeping, he fell across the bed.

He was still there when Ernest came around in midafternoon. Delaunay's painter's eye took in the situation quickly: the disheveled room, the torn sketches, the tear stains on Jimmy's cheeks.

"Forget about it, Jimmy," he advised. "It is what one must expect between men and women. Sooner or later, they do it to us—or we do it to them." He strolled over to the cupboard, where Jimmy's copperplate of Fumette stood propped against the wall, unharmed. "What is this?"

"Nothing, nothing."

Ernest took up the plate by the edges, careful not to touch the wax ground, and held it up to the light. "But it is far from nothing! It will make an excellent etching. Which fits in perfectly with the plan I have to discuss with you. I propose we should get away for a while. Forget Paris, its women, its troubles. Not for just a couple of days, like Manchester, but a real trip. We must go to Alsace."

"What," Jimmy asked in a dull voice, "is in Alsace?"

"Old churches. Village streets. Unspoiled country people. Fresh subjects, Jimmy—not only for your pencil, but for your etching needle!"

Ernest waited. Jimmy sat on the edge of the bed, as if in a stupor. Suddenly he shot up, blue eyes dancing with excitement, black curls jiggling madly. "Stupendous idea!" He pummeled his friend enthusiastically. "Why didn't you think of it before?"

It was a theatrical transformation worthy of Henry Irving—except that in Jimmy's case it came from the inside, one of those shifts of mood that were both his plague and his salvation. "I shall get more coppers from Delâtre on credit," he crowed, bouncing around the room. "He likes me."

Jimmy stopped. "There is only one serious question."

Ernest returned his solemn gaze. "Yes?"

"Which hat to wear: The straw or the felt?"

They set out by train for Nancy the next morning: Jimmy's first venture, apart from brief trips to England, outside the circumscribed world of the Left Bank. Europe was in a state of relative quiescence; even the Italian *risorgimento* was a year away. It was Britain that dominated the international scene, building ships and expanding trade furiously while keeping a wary eye on Louis Napoleon's prancing cavalry. The only explosive news came from his own country, where anti-slavery abolitionists were squaring off against States'-rights secessionists. If war came, he would have uncles and cousins on both sides.

It was better to keep one's mind on painting. The two young artists, settling into their second-class carriage, were appropriately picturesque in bright yellow gaiters and broad-brimmed straws ("Why deprive the peasants?" Jimmy generously decided). Ernest had somehow got his hands on a pair of heavy walking shoes, but Jimmy wore his usual thin pumps. In a knapsack on his back were a dozen grounded copperplates, courtesy of the eminent etching-printer, August Delâtre. Jimmy had a fairly clear idea of what he wanted to do with them.

For the past month he had been dropping in at Delâtre's workshop in the nearby Rue Saint-Jacques, chatting with the quiet proprietor and studying the prints on the walls. Two etchers in particular had impressed him: Charles Méryon, who had lately restored a glimmer of prestige to the art after a lapse of 150 years, and the earlier Charles Jacque. Méryon brought great power to architectural subjects; his *La Morgue*, done in 1854, combined black rooftops, curling smoke and dark-robed angular figures. Jacque, more delicate, spun luminous landscapes à la Rembrandt.

The two travelers stayed overnight at Nancy, then continued 80 miles farther east to Strasbourg on the German border. From here they took a branch line northwest to Saverne, where Ernest had a painter friend . . . and Jimmy produced a masterpiece.

Saverne was a Vosges Mountain town on the edge of nowhere: weary, poor, bypassed by industrial progress. Crossing the main square at twilight, Jimmy was impressed by the brooding stillness of a narrow side street. Bony, hulking stone houses pressed together, forging deep gloomy shadows around a single street lamp. A gray-black sky looked down on a solitary foot traveler.

Jimmy unslung his knapsack and took out a copper. As Ernest

watched, he settled himself on an abandoned cart and went to work. Open-air etching, directly onto the plate without any previous sketch, was generally unheard-of; for Jimmy it posed no problems. Lightly and swiftly his hand moved over the wax ground, as sure with the clumsy needle as if it were handling a pencil. So close was the wedding of man and medium that his draftsmanship, sometimes erratic in large oils, was flawless. First to appear was the cobbled road in thick cross-hatching, then the battered façades of the old buildings, each with its own set of grimy wrinkles and sinister shadows. The endless hours of observing and sketching in the Paris streets had not been wasted.

In forty minutes Jimmy stood up, jubilant. He had brought the thing off, caught the eerie moment in mid-passage; he knew it. And he was right. What was to emerge from Delâtre's presses some weeks later would be simple, true, and stark as a gallows. It would have a faint echo of Méryon's *La Morgue*, a hint of the Gothic terror in a passage from Poe, and something more that was uniquely Jimmy's, foreshadowing the nameless mystery of the Nocturnes.

Ernest next proposed a boat trip northward down the Rhine. This turned out to be a capital idea except for one detail: Germany, and its coinage, had not yet been unified. The two artists found themselves entangled at each stop in a maze of Prussian thalers, imperial florins, and assorted groschen. After a cosmic miscalculation of the exchange rate by Jimmy, they debarked at Cologne in their familiar state of total insolvency.

What to do, worried Ernest.

"Order breakfast," said Jimmy.

They did, then sent off SOS letters to various points in Europe. Jimmy made an etching of the landlord's daughter—*Little Gretchen*. And every morning the two foreigners went to the post office, to be greeted by a chorus of small boys echoing the clerk's "*Nichts, nichts.*"

Finally Jimmy wearied of the game. He turned over his copperplates as security to the landlord, to be redeemed by payment of their bill from Paris—misgivings were about equal on both sides—and, armed with a gift of two groschen from Lina the chambermaid ("I too am a stranger here, from Coblenz"), they set out on foot for Paris.

It was a forced march on the most elemental basis. As their feet propelled them westward, their hands earned food and shelter. They sketched for their supper—and for breakfast and lunch, too. Their currency was pencil portraits; their patrons not merchant princes, but plain country folk.

Jimmy's first "commission," a drawing of a fat little boy, earned him a glass of milk, supplemented the next morning—when the lad's mother posed—by black bread and a fresh egg. In between, the two artists were separated from their modicum of German silver as the price of a bed of lumpy straw.

Their third morning on the road, the autumn rains descended. Ernest's brown Holland linens shriveled; Jimmy's patent-leather shoes shed their uppers and were reduced to flapping gypsy slippers. But autumn also brought county fairs. They teamed up with a pair of soggy troubadours, one of them a lady harpist. Ernest pounded the drums to announce the fortuitous presence of "two great artists from Montparnasse," who would do drawings at the ridiculous price of 5 francs for a full portrait, 3 for a head.

Business was not impressive. It picked up when the fee dropped to sous.

After five days, they reached Aix-la-Chapelle and salvation. Jimmy, still presentable by virtue of nightly washing and ironing of his shirt, persuaded the U. S. consul to advance 50 francs. At Liège, Ernest rustled up twenty more from the French. The worst was over.

A week later they turned up triumphantly at the Café Molière, where the usual hyperboles of Parisian gossip had reported their demise. The return of *le petit américain* in particular was loudly celebrated in song:

> "For he is not dead, not dead I think
> He simply is asleep
> To wake him up, let our glasses clink . . ."

Actually, Jimmy's mind was on other things. He had lost no time in retrieving his copperplates from Cologne, and biting the best half-dozen of them in a nitric-acid bath. Then for a long, anxious afternoon he had stood beside Delâtre as the veteran inked the bitten plates and then, with infinite care, wiped each one before running it through his roller press. At Jimmy's insistence, he had mixed the dark pigments for his ink with unburnt linseed oil, after the manner of Méryon. Although unburnt oil was thinner, and therefore had less of a grip on the powder, it could be dragged up from the etched lines to produce a subdued, subtle film of surface tone.

As he picked up each proof from the pressed plate, Delâtre's judgment was unequivocal. The rendering of Fumette, crouching like a wary cat, vast skirt spread tent-like before her, was superb; *Street at Saverne* was even better. Jimmy should do more at once, he asserted; perhaps issue a whole series of his etchings.

That was all the encouragement Jimmy needed. The bust portrait of La Mère Gérard was turning out well; now he went back to the Gardens and set her down full-length in copper, a thin, hostile old lady in layers of loose raglike shirts. He did shopkeepers at work, and on a London visit caught his niece Annie in a delicate plate reminiscent of *My Little Daughter* by Charles Jacque.

Etchings printed better, he had learned from Delâtre, on soft un-sized paper that soaked up the inked lines; so he spent hours prowling the bookstalls on the *quais* of the Seine, tearing the flyleaves out of old volumes.

In the late fall of 1858, he had Delâtre issue the limited-proof French Set, twelve plates plus a whimsical frontispiece showing Jimmy at work in Alsace, surrounded by inquisitive sailors and urchins. The set, published and sold by Jimmy himself, was priced at 50 francs: £2 for an Englishman, $10 to an American.

The entire edition of one hundred sets was sold out, as George du Maurier reported in an envious letter to his mother. "And he has just sold the 12 plates for another 100 pounds, that makes each etching 25 guineas, and I for a drawing on wood, more elaborate, only get 3. And he doing anything he likes, while my subjects are cut out for me. If I had barely an existence I should etch, as I feel sure my etchings would be wonders like Jimmy's."

Wonders or not, the French Set brought Jimmy a total of £300, four times as much as his annual allowance in Paris. He was on his way.

# Chapter Six

"This weather," said Degas, "is unspeakable."

"That, at least, you cannot blame on Louis Napoleon."

"Why not, Legros? It is probably God's punishment. The man is a disgrace to the name of sovereignty."

Fantin-Latour looked over at Édouard Manet, frowning. "We shall not be able to work at the Louvre today. It is too dark."

"Be thankful," interposed Jimmy. "Copying can become a vicious habit. Worse than cigarettes." He sat back and drew a long contented puff under the huge black Rubens felt, wide as a sombrero, that had replaced his straw. His mustache was fuller; an elegant polka-dot kerchief matched his blue velvet jacket.

The five young artists were gathered around a battered table in the Canard Fou, an alleyway café off the Rue Vavin, so small and questionable-looking that only habitués of the *Quartier* knew about it. Its virtues included good coffee, superior croissants, excellent cheeses from some obscure family source, and—most importantly—modest prices. Workingmen patrons and artists were separated by a bulky stove in the middle of the room, indispensable safeguard against the damp Paris winter. Outside, a dismal drizzle fell from a low-hanging February sky. It was the time of year when the gas jets on the walls burned constantly.

Hilaire Germain Edgar Degas, ten days younger than Jimmy, was a formidable figure on several counts: a draftsman already comparable to Ingres, whom he revered; a caustic wit; and the practitioner of an austere integrity that rejected all airs in matters of art. He had even simplified the aristocratic familial spelling of his name, "De Gas," much as a monk might shave his head or don a haircloth shirt. The pampered son of a cultivated Catholic banker, Degas had all the prejudices of his monarchist class. He despised Protestants, Jews, pacifists, socialists, and the "anarchy" of the Left Bank. But he dropped his xenophobic baggage outside the studio door; Camille Pissarro, a Jew, was his honored friend, and he collected the paintings of Gustave Courbet, Villonesque apostle of realism-and-rebellion.

In appearance, too, Degas was a paradox. Slender and dark, of funereal mien, he combined the remote air of a bishop with the calculating eye of a faro banker. And below the black mustache, in startling contradiction to the bland mask of his upper face, heavy sensual lips proclaimed his part-Italian origins.

Beside him sat Manet, at twenty-six the oldest of the group. Tall with wavy blond hair, relaxed in his checkered waistcoat, Manet was middle-class in background and in his frank ambition to be hailed as a latter-day Velázquez. He and Degas consistently harassed each other in public—and were as consistent in praise behind each other's backs.

The two youngest artists were Fantin-Latour and Legros, fellow students of the memory expert Lecoq de Boisbaudran. Fantin was stocky and serious, with a prow-shaped nose and a non-combative air in all matters save his avant-garde realism. Legros, a grave Burgundian of fine ascetic features, had lately—like Jimmy—created a reputation as an etcher.

Jimmy relished these daily encounters, which were less exchanges of ideas than ceremonial duels. Every man had his own established role and weapons. There were no surprises, no blood drawn, no opinions altered; yet the lunchtime ritual seemed a necessity to the group, a kind of orchestral tune-up before returning to the day's labors.

Degas, with his decisive manner, led the conversation. "I too have a copy to finish at the Louvre," he observed. He addressed Jimmy. "Raibolini. Do you know him?"

"Not intimately," Jimmy drawled. "I was a very small boy in the fifteenth century."

"You are careless of our treasures!"

"Or, unlike you, Degas, simply not burdened by the weight of tradition," teased Manet.

Legros ventured a comment. "Perhaps Whistler, instead of borrowing from the Louvre, intends to improve it."

"No." Degas curled his heavy lips. "With his sacks of American gold, our friend is going to buy the whole museum and ship it back to . . . to Brooklyn."

"Never," said Jimmy calmly. "That's in Yankee territory. To Baltimore, perhaps."

"My apologies. I thought they were the same place."

"My views on copying are very simple," Jimmy went on. "I think that if overdone, it can become a burial ground. A tombstone of classics is a tombstone nonetheless. I am not trying to become Rembrandt. My problem is to become Whistler."

He felt the weight of Degas's heavy lidded eyes. "Mr. Whistler is very clever. But—like me—he is harmless. He makes a lot of noise because he is afraid he may not be able to live up to his talent."

Jimmy flushed and laughed uncomfortably. "Thank you for the compliment—if not the forecast." Degas alone could penetrate his guard, make him feel naked and unmanned. Perhaps it was because they were so similar in their aggressive façades.

They were different enough in other ways, as were all five young artists. Quite separate in their aesthetic approaches, half-serious in their rivalries, they were linked by their common distaste for the standards of the official Salon, which waved over French art the bloodless banner of Classicism. Some fifteen years later, they would be lumped loosely together, along with Pissarro, Renoir, and Claude Monet, as the progenitors of a new outdoor art emphasizing light values and juxtaposed patches of color: Impressionism.

A plump brunette passed outside, picking her way through the puddles, and Manet indicated the curve of her rump. "Now, that's the kind of bottom I approve of."

"As an artist?"

"As a man!" Manet had a theory about a woman's sexual experience being reflected in her walk, which he proceeded to expound with many a sly glance at "our expert here, Degas." Degas was notoriously shy in female company.

"Ah, women!" shrugged Legros. "They are all alike."

"On the contrary." Jimmy had recovered his poise. "What makes women endurable is that they are all different. The plainest of them has something special: a firmer bosom, a softer smile."

Degas was back with one of his epigrams: "Women are like the Salon; they crave courting, but they are unable to love."

"The poor things do their best," returned Jimmy. "They are limited by nature—from which, after all, one learns not to expect too much."

With seeming artlessness, he had raised the red flag. The bulls lost no time in charging.

"Nature is our great teacher!" objected Legros.

"The source of all truth!" agreed Fantin.

Jimmy looked expectantly toward Degas, who did not fail him. "Nature is . . . insipid!"

Jimmy nodded vigorously, dislodging the monocle he had just screwed into his right eye. It would be some time before he would master the technique of keeping it in its place, much less the nuances of using it for emphasis. "Nature is without taste or selectivity," he said. "In a word, without art. And shamelessly spoiled by those who worship her naïvely."

Degas expanded the theme: "These landscapers fouling up the

countryside need a dose of bird shot. Painting is a convention to be practiced in the studio. It requires patient observation, a trained memory, as much wiliness in planning as a crime!"

"But you have to agree," pursued Fantin-Latour, "one must start from reality, the here and now. That, after all, is our revolution."

"Revolution!" Degas grimaced. "An odious word. I reject your God, Courbet—the unwashed Socialist who paints with dirty hands to prove he is sincere!"

"A better God than Ingres, whose hands are lily-white and lifeless!"

Now, this was more like it! Jimmy followed the duel avidly, in his peculiar fashion of a West Pointer on parade: head erect and immobile, but bright blue eyes shifting back and forth between the combatants.

"One must get out of the studio, Degas," said Manet. "You can't paint just for yourself."

"And why not? Who is a better judge?"

"He has a point," agreed Legros. "Art is a reflection of one's individual soul."

"Pretentious!" boomed Degas. "Of one's *eyesight!*"

Jimmy had to admire the man. Degas's impartial saber slashes at all shortcomings, not excepting his own; his refusal to take refuge in comforting clichés ("I am sorry, there are no accidents in art!") appealed to the Puritan strain in Jimmy's own background. In Fantin and Manet, Jimmy recognized distinctive talent embellished by marvelous technical skill; in Degas, the disagreeable and seemingly ruthless perfectionist, he sensed the singleminded power of genius.

He also envied the Frenchman. Degas was part of this setting; he had been born into the right time and place. No one had ever questioned the rightness of his course; his father had provided not only ample financial backing, but steady advice and encouragement. Jimmy would have welcomed a greater intimacy with Degas, but he knew the Frenchman could function only behind his own barrier of aloofness.

Degas pushed back his chair. "Well, we have done what we could for French art today at the café table. Now, to our easels."

Accompanied by Fantin, Jimmy went back to his new studio at 3 Campagne Première. This was well south of the river and the university quarter, in an area saturated with working artists. The Rue des Peintres was just down the street; a few blocks away, at the intersection of the Boulevards Montparnasse and Raspail, was a cluster of popular sidewalk hangouts: the Dome, Coupole, Select, and Rondpoint.

Jimmy's building had the inevitable inner courtyard, dotted with acacias and limes and surrounded by a ground-floor tier of spacious sculptors' studios. Upstairs—he was on the third floor—were the painters' quarters, with high studio windows and 22-foot ceilings. Jimmy had moved there soon after the departure of Fumette. In line with his new keep-it-casual philosophy of women, the sad-faced little Tigresse had had a series of successors.

Models and grisettes were a fixture of Montparnasse life, constantly drifting in and out of the studios, as eager as the artists for new liaisons. And Jimmy's sexual appetites, once released by contact with the tempestuous Fumette, were strong. He liked the creamy roundness of breasts and thighs, the touch of soft young skin under his fingers, the soaring ecstasy and sense of personal power that came with climax. When he wanted a woman, it became a matter of pressing urgency. More than once, confronted at his drawing board with a voluptuous morsel, he took her to bed simply to "get the delightful pagan business out of the way" so he could settle down to work.

His current inamorata was Finette, a dancer at the Bal Bullier, where she was usually partnered with Alice la Provençale or Rigolbache in a celebrated quadrille. Of uncertain North African origins, Finette had tawny skin and extraordinary legs; gossip said her sexual habits too were extraordinary. One afternoon she turned up uninvited at Jimmy's studio: "I have come to pose for you." She pulled up her dress to expose a long supple limb. "Are my legs not beautiful?"

"I can only see one of them."

With a quick gesture she slipped out of her dress. "Better?"

"Much better." Jimmy ran a hand along the smooth curve of her shoulders. "And not just for your legs."

"I have never had an American lover—male or female."

"A pity." His hands were exploring. "I shall write to the consulate on your behalf."

"But I want *this* American . . ."

As a Southern gentleman, Jimmy was happy to oblige. He found the dancer a spectacular bed partner, fierce and tender, deliciously knowing. Jimmy had respect for an artist, in any field.

Finette was around a good deal after that, between out-of-town engagements. At the moment she was in London, astonishing staid Britishers with the cancan.

Fantin too was an element in Jimmy's new arrangements. The two had met in the Louvre, where the Frenchman was finishing one of his innumerable brilliant copies of *The Marriage Feast*. Fantin, reserved almost to the point of monasticism, was a trifle alarmed at being approached by the eccentric foreigner in the outlandish straw, until Jimmy spoke: "Such fresh, beautiful colors!" It was not a bad start for a friendship.

They quickly discovered a common enthusiasm for the Dutch: Hals and Rembrandt, of course; less obviously, the work of two so-called minor masters of the seventeenth century, Gerard Terborch and Jan Vermeer. Terborch they admired for his semi-abstract compositional patterns, Vermeer for his silky evocation of space. Fantin, like Jimmy, sought overtones, emanations, atmosphere; he was a confirmed mystic, bent on translating the music of Wagner into paint.

But he was also a student of Lecoq de Boisbaudran, whose training in the techniques of observation and memorization provided strong underpinning for the "new realism" of Courbet. Standing in the Louvre before Hans Holbein's *Erasmus,* which portrayed the sixteenth-century scholar in profile at a writing desk, Fantin demonstrated how every detail of a painting—as of a landscape—could be stamped into the memory.

Although two years younger than Jimmy, Fantin had been painting most of his life, and studying formally since 1851—the year Jimmy entered West Point. He was exceedingly knowledgeable about the interaction of muscles in human anatomy, the properties of paints and varnishes, and the thousand tricks of the studio: how to model an expressive eyebrow with a single brush stroke; the knack of building up a smile through a chain of widening shadows spreading away from the mouth, like ripples from a stone thrown into water.

Fantin was astonished to find how much of this lore Jimmy already possessed by instinct. The way a composer could hear and shape a melody without conscious reflection, guided by an inner ear, Jimmy could grasp the sweep of a line. He did a striking pencil sketch of Fantin working in bed, bundled literally to the teeth against the near-zero rigors of a December night. As the Frenchman huddled over his drawing board by candlelight, ludicrously top-hatted and scarf-wrapped, sharp nose burrowing into his coat collar, Jimmy captured in a few vigorous lines not only the comic details of the scene but the furiously concentrated attitude of his subject.

Ernest Delaunay, intimidated by the prestige of Jimmy's new friends, had more or less retreated from the American's studio. But often Fantin and Jimmy were joined by Alfonse Legros. And always they were surrounded by the ambience of Courbet, the incomparable Master of Ornans. Fantin glowed when he talked of his prophet, and even the somber Legros showed a spark of fervor. From their accounts, Jimmy pieced together an intriguing picture.

Gustave Courbet had come to Paris in 1840 at the age of twenty-one, a big brawling mountaineer from the Franche-Comté vine-growing district near the Swiss border. Sent by his prosperous father to enroll in law school, he soon dropped out of college, started prowling the Louvre, and began to paint. By 1844 his work was accepted at the Salon; within a few years he had earned a Second Class medal there.

Then he met the Socialist Deputy, Pierre Joseph Proudhon, and his career took a sharp turn to the left. He seized enthusiastically on Proudhon's anti-Establishment doctrines ("Property is theft!"), and drew sweeping aesthetic parallels: classicism à la David and Ingres was decadent irrelevance; the heroic battle scenes of Delacroix, sentimental fakery ("The next time you run into an angel, let me know!"). In place of allegory and idealization, he offered *la vraie verité* (genuine truth) rooted in the simple experiences of ordinary people.

And he carried his thesis into his paintings: everyday subjects treated in a frank, everyday manner. In the huge, desolate *Burial at Ornans*, he dared to devote yards of canvas not to saints or duchesses but to common peasants.

Predictably, the Old Guard resisted. He was no longer so welcome at the Salon. In 1853 he showed *Les Baigneuses* (*The Bathers*), portraying two overblown ladies of pleasure disporting themselves on a river bank, one with her ample buttocks facing the viewer. Napoleon III was so irritated that he personally flayed the picture with his riding crop. Two years later, when the Salon judges turned down several of Courbet's most ambitious paintings, he launched his own private showing. For half a franc, visitors could examine forty specimens of the new realism.

Courbet was praised by Baudelaire, caricatured in the press, talked about everywhere. A satirical revue had him singing:

> "To paint the truth is not enough to make a realist;
> One must pain ugliness!
> I tear out all beauty as one pulls up weeds.
> Give me muddy colors, bunions, plenty of warts!"

Courbet fought back cheerfully; the public rough-and-tumble suited his swashbuckling style. A lover of taverns and practical jokes, a free-wheeling sensualist who never bothered to "carry a woman" because there was "always one around," he was the antithesis of the shy Degas, the trailblazer-in-spite-of-himself. Soon he was to ridicule the venality of the clergy in *Return from the Conference;* and when the bourgeois screamed in protest he would hurl at them *The Sleepers*, a pair of nude heavy-hipped lesbians, legs entwined after an obviously exhausting night of unsanctioned passion.

His women were as juicy as the overripe pears of his native Jura Mountains: robust, almost meaty, with flesh that demanded to be touched and embraced. For Courbet was not a mere pamphleteer. He understood paint, and flung it onto the canvas with characteristic boldness, from a brush, thumb, or palette knife loaded with rich impasto. No Ingres-like reticence disguised his brush strokes; like the man, they were there for all to see. His palette was restricted, and his treatment of space likewise simplified by the creation of three or four separate planes with little modeling, almost in the flat manner of a Japanese woodcut.

Courbet was a one-man revolution. True, his theorizing sometimes led him into a narrow photographic exactness; but it was largely his frontal assault against the sterilities of the Salon that opened up a path for the Impressionists.

Jimmy was eager to meet this pioneer of truth and independence. But Courbet was traveling in Germany. At long last he returned, and Fantin set up an appointment for him to come and see *La Mère Gérard.*

Jimmy found the physical reality of Courbet no less impressive than the legend. A ruddy stalwart, arrogant with animal vitality, Courbet always looked fresh from a deer-stalking tramp through the hills. At forty, his fine features were coarsening, but the expression under his thoughtful brow was friendly. He laughed easily, in a deep voice that was like the rumble of cartwheels over cobblestones, sometimes in spurts and wheezes that ended up as a gurgle into his fanlike black beard.

He stood before *La Mère* for a moment, the crow's feet crinkling above his high cheekbones, and turned quizzically to Fantin: "But what do you want me to tell you? There it *is*, eh?" To Jimmy he said, "You are a painter, my friend. Welcome!"

Jimmy was delighted. Over a bottle of vintage Bordeaux, he listened as Courbet thundered out pronouncements: "It is impossible to stick to one woman if one wishes to understand women . . . The Salon slams its doors against me, but I rise constantly to defy society and assert my own nature."

Courbet's politics, although stirring faint echoes of George Washington Whistler, were essentially alien to Jimmy; the man's courage was not. Here was no dry ideologue, but a crusading knight. Courbet's ardent realism, Jimmy felt, was mainly a protest against academic artifice; not so much an uncritical worship of nature as something akin to his own search for essence. Years later, he would have second thoughts about this.

Courbet declared that he took no pupils—"every artist must be his own master, applying his abilities to the age he lives in"—but if Jimmy wished to work at the studio of his friend Bonvin, well, he would be happy to look in now and then.

That, from *le grand Courbet*, was quite enough for Jimmy. Bonvin was a contemporary of Courbet who painted in the minor-Dutch style and had a modest following among connoisseurs. His Atelier Flamand in the Rue Saint-Jacques provided a base where a handful of young artists could work from the model under the unofficial guidance of Courbet.

Jimmy had barely plunged into his new routine when, hanging out of his bedroom window one morning, he saw a small bow-legged figure carrying a chamber pot across the courtyard. In answer to his "hallo!" a battered seamy visage was raised skyward, a pipe wedged into one corner of its mouth. Reality, indeed! This was the spiritual brother of La Mère Gérard.

"Come on up here!" Jimmy bawled.

"What for?"

"I want to paint your picture."

"I do not wish to be painted."

"I'll pay you."

"How much?"

"Five francs, complete," said Jimmy recklessly.

The squat figure hesitated. "I have just become a model. As soon as I get my carriage."

The "carriage" turned out to be a cartful of clattering chamber pots. Leaving them in the courtyard, the old man ascended to his new career.

He was an ex-sailor who quickly tired of posing, but professed a fancy for music. Jimmy obliged with some racy café songs. The old man responded with sea chanteys, and they had a working arrangement. Fifteen years earlier, at exactly Jimmy's present age, Courbet had broken into the Salon with a portrait entitled *Man with Pipe*. Now Jimmy followed in the master's footsteps.

He kept to the same full-faced Rembrandtish attack, with thick browns and blacks against a gray-green background. For the white shirt front, he laid on his color freely with a long palette knife, in the manner of Courbet.

The portrait refused to come to life. Jimmy painted and repainted; got the broad hat the way he wanted it, and the grim weary lines of the mouth. But something—was it the expression of the eyes?—eluded him. He rubbed out the left eye with a rag soaked in turpentine, and tried again. The effect was worse than ever. And—particular anathema to him—it reeked of visible effort. Aiming for grandeur, he had achieved only heaviness.

Well, one could learn from disasters. Clearly, he would not become Whistler by submerging himself in Courbet.

He had been crossing the Channel more often lately on visits to his half sister, of whom he was very fond. It was the after-lunch custom in the Haden household for Debo—the daughter of "Pipes" Whistler—to spend an hour or so improvising at the piano while her surgeon-husband relaxed over the paper. Their young daughter, Annie, already the subject of a Whistler etching, liked to stand in the curve of the parlor grand, folded arms resting on the open top, listening raptly.

It was on just such a mother-daughter scene that Jimmy chanced one sunny April afternoon. He made a quick pencil sketch.

The next day, he decided to risk it on canvas. His composition would be a clean rectilinear affair, spare and simple as the patterns of Terborch: horizontal lines of the rug, piano, wall dado and—a notion borrowed from Fantin—the bottoms of two picture frames, balanced against the vertical figures of mother and daughter facing each other in profile, left to right. Modeling of the two faces would be minimal: far from the elaborate chiaroscuro of Rembrandt, less even than the flattish forms of Courbet.

He planned his colors carefully. Painting "from dark to light," based on a ground of black or gray, made possible more subtle modulation of color effects; the under-color would "bleed through" to dilute harshness and unify the whole. But the scheme worked poorly with blatant primaries, and required dulling of even the secondary orange-green-violet shades; it flourished on cool grays, warm browns and delicate flat tints like pink and russet.

For *At the Piano*, black was Jimmy's keynote: established in Debo's black dress and the long gleaming instrument, then repeated in Annie's shoes and hair, and the violin cases stacked under the piano. For the contrasting white, he had the little girl's dress and stockings. From the rug came a muted note of smooth deep rose, echoed in the drapery over a table at the extreme left. On the table was a Chinese bowl of blue and gold; more gold shone discreetly from the picture frames and dado.

On the wall in the background, pinks mingled with soft streaks of green and gray; for Jimmy was seeking not merely a record of the event but its dreamy essence. In pursuit of atmosphere, he put aside the heavy impasto of Courbet and picked up what his own instinct recommended: thinner paint, applied with the light supple brush strokes of Fantin-Latour.

This time, he succeeded. So pervasive was the mood of the canvas that, standing before it, one could almost hear the melancholy chords drifting up from the strings.

He submitted *At the Piano* to the 1859 Salon, along with a couple of etchings. The etchings squeaked by; but the graybeards of the Salon had no taste for young "slice of life" painters, especially for protégés of the infamous Courbet. Fantin had entered portraits of his sisters and himself, while Legros submitted a portrait of his father; all were turned down. The *Piano* painting fared no better.

Bonvin, indignant, gathered together the rejected canvases of the realist insurgents at his Atelier Flamand. Critics rallied around, people talked. Jimmy, Fantin, and Legros—they were beginning to call themselves "The Society of Three"—had a *succès de scandale*.

Courbet had been away on a hunting trip. He returned to see what the fuss was all about. Arriving before *At the Piano*, he paused and stared. He leaned into the picture and felt the paint. Then he stepped back and opened his arms wide in a gesture of admiration: "Magnificent!"

There was more to come. The Royal Academy in London accepted the picture for its 1860 exhibition, hanging it at eye level in the coveted "on-the-line" position. Critical comment was generally favorable, although the *Telegraph* sounded a note that was to become depressingly familiar over the years: "eccentric, uncouth, smudgy." The *Atheneum* reviewer, while deploring Jimmy's "recklessly bold manner," found praise for his "splendid power of composition and design" as well as his "genuine feeling for color, atmosphere, and judicious gradations of light." The august *Times* was reminded "irresistibly of Velázquez . . . the most vigorous piece of coloring in the exhibition."

Even more satisfying were the accolades of Jimmy's British colleagues. The hearty John Everett Millais, then at the height of his brilliance, told the American newcomer: "I never flatter, but I will say that your picture is the finest piece of color that has been seen on the walls of the Royal Academy for years." And the Academician John Philip, just returned from a pilgrimage to El Prado in Madrid, tracked down the "unknown youth" to ask how much he wanted for *At the Piano*. Jimmy, pleased and confused, left the price up to the purchaser. Philip paid him £30, the equivalent of $150.

Jimmy paused for reflection. His career had reached a major milestone. In America, Lincoln had been nominated for the presidency by the Republicans; within months the guns would be barking at Fort Sumter. Jimmy would scarcely hear them. He was totally wrapped up in the problem of deciding his next move, now that he had found his own path at last.

Paris had been good to him, had provided masters to emulate, subjects to draw, a congenial climate for working. Now he wanted more: recognition.

In France, he might have to wait a long time. Even the most towering talents—men like Courbet, Degas, and Manet—were having a struggle; and they all had deep roots in the native soil. The small group of French purchasers were not likely to bypass accomplished fellow nationals in favor of an unknown American.

London, conversely, had fewer great painters . . . and a large rising class of merchant-collectors, accessible to him through his in-laws. Once he had a foothold among them, he could pave the way for his deserving friends, Fantin and Legros, staggering under heavy familial obligations. His own sense of family would be strengthened in the ancestral

British Isles; Debo alone, gracious and loving, was reason enough to be in London.

Finally, there was the Thames, to which he felt curiously drawn. The Seine had rarely touched his imagination: it was too neatly arranged, already shaped by the beauty-conscious Parisians. But the disorderly Thames—crude, disheveled, muddy, powerful—lay ready for his remaking, with its cranes and ships and docks that no Englishman had ever seen as he did. He had done some experimental etchings, and was eager to do more.

Perhaps it was time to cut loose from the sheltering arms of the Louvre and the frowning shadow of Degas, to end Bohemian disguises and take on the challenges of the real world.

For most of 1860 he shuttled back and forth across the Channel, lingering longer in England each time; by the following spring he was ready to move to the foggy capital that would be his main base for the rest of his life.

The day before pulling up stakes in Paris, Jimmy went with Courbet and Fantin for a farewell drink at the Closerie des Lilas. Passing the gate of the Luxembourg Gardens, Courbet saw La Mère Gérard. The old lady was poking in a basket of flowers, barely able to sort out violets from red roses. Jimmy, who had incurred La Mère's wrath by giving her merely a copy of his painting, hung back a few feet, out of range of her vision.

"Good morning, madame," said Courbet. "I hope business is good?"

"It stinks like old gardenias."

"I am very sorry. What do you hear from your good friend, the little American artist?"

"Ah, that one. I hear he went to England, caught the chill, and died."

"You must be very sad."

"Sad?" La Mère spat. "One no-good rascal the less!"

Jimmy, unable to contain himself, let loose the shrill diabolical cackle that was his trademark, and La Mère knew she had been celebrating too soon.

Paris was to hear that wild laughter only intermittently in future, but in the galleries and drawing rooms of London it would be a harbinger of amusement—and sometimes despair—for the next forty years.

# Chapter Seven

"You're being stubborn, Jimmy. Why blame hydrochloric acid for false bites?"

"Because that's my experience."

"A very limited experience, my boy. Do as I tell you."

Seymour Haden peered down at Jimmy through slitted eyes. A big, rangy man with thin lips in a full sensual face, the surgeon wore his habitual expression of half-amused contempt, a sneer waiting to be lowered. The two were in the lamplit workroom on the top floor of Haden's Sloane Street mansion adjoining the Royal Cricket Grounds.

Haden had resumed an interest in etching, after early dabblings in Italy, with the arrival in Europe of his young brother-in-law. He had won a small reputation, and helped find subscribers to Jimmy's French Set.

However, he had a condescending manner that a decade earlier infuriated George Washington Whistler. Born to wealth, with a physical presence that was commanding if not precisely handsome, Deborah's husband had been raised on the assumption of an innate Haden superiority. As he gradually acquired an attractive family and such patients as the Archbishop of Canterbury, he saw no reason to change that view. Seymour Haden was the sort of man who could proclaim a "lifetime devotion to the true and beautiful"—and run his household like a medieval jail.

Haden regarded Jimmy, sixteen years his junior, as a promising but wayward protégé. After a visit to Paris in the late 1850s, he wrote to Anna Whistler expressing his concern for Jimmy's health (to Deborah, he said "morals"). He urged Jimmy to spend more time in London, and in a burst of magnanimity (not unmixed with shrewdness) broadened the invitation to include the younger man's talented, struggling friends. Fantin-Latour, Legros, and even the apprehensive Ernest Delaunay briefly crossed the Channel to be overwhelmed by the squadrons of servants at Sloane Street and the upstairs shower bath— *cette espèce de Niagara!* From each grateful guest, Haden picked up a few drawings and oils, thus attaining at minimal cost the status of a generous and far-seeing art patron.

Jimmy remained his chief vexation. The boy had persisted in submitting *At the Piano* to the Royal Academy despite Haden's dissatisfaction with the color scheme, and in the face of the surgeon's dire forecasts of certain rejection. Worse, the boy's immature judgment had been upheld.

So it was more important than ever that he bring Jimmy to heel. Haden lowered a copper carefully toward its acid bath. "I've warned you before, Jimmy, about that all-steel needle. It's really a dental instrument, you know."

"Redesigned for me."

"Quite unsuitable for etching. Now, *my* needle—"

"Your needle is too damned thick, Seymour. Frankly, I find it clumsy."

The copper slipped with an angry splash into the porcelain tray. "It's *you* who are clumsy!"

Jimmy's head snapped up; blue-gray murder flashed from his eyes. With an effort, he controlled himself. Haden was Debo's husband and his own host. Sooner or later the fellow would have to be put in his place, but for his part Jimmy would defer the unpleasant moment as long as possible.

The surgeon flourished an enormous gold watch. "I have an urgent consultation at the hospital tonight, so I won't be able to keep an eye on your biting."

*Thank Heaven.*

"Give that plate of mine a minute or so. And forget about nitric acid. Use my Dutch Bath yourself, four to one strength." Haden paused on the landing for a final admonition. "And watch the way you handle the coppers. Sunday, you left finger marks."

"Yassuh, massa," murmured Jimmy. The stately tread receded down the stairs.

Jimmy fished out Haden's copper, washed it with ammonia, and reached for one of his own drawn plates. An interesting notion had occurred to him: why not start biting with the slow, sensitive hydrochloric acid, to pick up the most delicate lines, and then switch over to the broad, shallow bite of nitric for the heavier passages? He bent over bottles and varnishes, forgetting Haden, retribution, everything but the task at hand.

The next morning, Jimmy found a surprise waiting: Haden had rented a private ketch, complete with crew, for a joint etching expedition along the Thames . . . presumably to give Jimmy the benefit of his immediate supervision. Already the brothers-in-law had collaborated, with dubious results, on a woodland landscape of Haden's choosing. This time they would do separate treatments of an identical subject.

Their prize model turned out to be a white-haired, piratically mustached pensioner caught drowsing in the mild spring sunshine at Greenwich. But it was bosky dells, not portraiture, that had provided Haden with his burgeoning reputation as an etcher. As Jimmy's plate took sharp, intriguing form, the surgeon, fussing with his metal scraper to correct a false start, grew restive. Finally he threw down his needle. "It's that damned Traer!"

His medical assistant, Haden explained, had been poking about in his supplies of mastic and asphaltum. That, no doubt, was why the ground on his plate was so hopelessly brittle.

"No doubt," Jimmy agreed, his slender needle flying over the copper.

Thereafter Haden retreated from head-on competition. By tacit agreement he made his river journeys westward toward Richmond and Henley, the conventional stamping-grounds for British etchers, where the green fields and lofty maples were more congenial to his ladylike curlicues. That gave Jimmy a clear field for the part of the Thames he really wanted: the gaudily dirty, gorgeously atmospheric East End with its cranes and docks, its baggy-trousered pipe-smoking sailors, and the faded ancient masonry of its workshops and forges.

Jimmy plunged into the life of the river, a small spruce figure in white ducks among the grimy sweatered bargemen and stevedores. No seagull swooping over the Thames explored more avidly its great landmarks and secret places: towering bridges, dingy taverns, the marshy retreats of stiff lordly cranes. Working usually from a rowboat, copperplates tucked into a knapsack, Jimmy would circle and maneuver like a fencer seeking an opening till he found the precise arrangement he wanted, the sudden angle at which spars and tackle and crumbling piles could be shaped into enduring beauty.

More than once, venturing out onto the mud-flats, he was trapped by the 24-foot tides that swept in twice a day. On a Rotherhithe wharf, as he was sketching two fur-capped Norwegian seamen, a brick crashed down from an overhead scaffold. It missed Jimmy's head by inches, but left a record of its passage in the inadvertent sharp line creasing the middle of the plate. The next morning, a bandage over his bruised right arm, Jimmy was back perched on a loading crate to finish up the job.

By rowboat, oil lighter, and penny steamer he cruised up and down the river, searching out details that few had noticed and no one had dreamed of trying to record on a tiny plate: the curve of a sail before the wind, waterlogged timbers under a sagging pier, the queer slash of light from a broken factory window, masts piled up in the Pool of London like a forest of slim leafless birches. Brick by brick—or so it appeared—he charted the lineaments of tumble-down alehouse, four-square police station, cluttered warehouse. Courbet had sung the virtues of the simple contemporary subject, directly expressed; Jimmy brought the theory gloriously to life. One could smell the tar and brine imprisoned within his plates, feel underfoot the squooshy mud of the riverbanks, almost touch the hard wood of the pier planks.

When he had finished a score of plates, the Thames was no longer a dreary-brown commercial waterway but a fresh pattern-world of subtle line, sudden sunshine, and haunting shadows. And etching was no longer a mere illustrator's tool, but once again—as with Rembrandt—an expressive art form.

The first few prints elicited the usual quota of critical head-shaking. The eminent P. G. Hamerton, second in prestige only to Oxford's John Ruskin, complained that Jimmy's version of the Thames was not sufficiently "tranquil."

Others looked beyond what was not in the plates, to what manifestly was. Serjeant Thomas, a wealthy retired barrister and sometime art dealer, offered Jimmy a roller press at his house on Old Bond Street, where the etcher could sip vintage port and turn out his proofs without benefit of the meddlesome Haden.

Jimmy handled every detail of the printing himself. Spreading his ink across the plate with a horsehair dabber, he wiped it with a muslin pad that picked up most of the surface liquid without disturbing the ink in the lines. For the next step—the creation of delicate surface tone —Jimmy wiped the plate by hand, using the base of his palm.

For printing paper, he used only Old Dutch, free of the discoloring bleaches introduced after 1820, with a warm golden surface brought about by the decay of its gelatinous size. He damped the paper himself before placing it atop the copper on the blanket-buffered traveling bed of the press. A vigorous turn of the handle produced a proof—the "first state" of the etching. It was never the last.

Only at this stage could Jimmy judge how close he had come to his objective. Often the examination sent him back to the acid bath for rebiting of weak lines, or even back to redrawing. Sometimes new lines were ploughed directly into the metal with a stout, ax-sharp dry-point needle, a process requiring considerable physical strength. Integration of drawing, biting, inking, and printing presented a formidable challenge; rarely was Jimmy satisfied before the tenth state.

But when he emerged from the lawyer's attic with the dozen subjects of the Thames Series, resistance to his etchings largely collapsed. Even Hamerton conceded the "linear virtuosity" of the young American. Others noted admiringly the space and depth achieved on a few inches of copper, the technical precision that produced a man's pipe so tiny it could be seen only with a magnifying glass . . . and something more: a poignancy of feeling that pierced to the heart.

Comparisons were freely made with the immortal Dutchman. And Jimmy's prices rose accordingly. Where the French Set had netted him two guineas for a whole series of twelve, he was now able to get that much for a single proof.

Since early boyhood, two currents had raced through Jimmy's life, sometimes in rip-tide collision: the need to create beauty, and the longing to be noticed. Although this second yearning was for a time overshadowed by the lure of the Thames, it was not long in reasserting itself, especially under the bleak auspices of the Haden household.

The climate of tyranny at Sloane Street was unbearable. Deborah's children, like their mother, were reduced to whispering shadows. Jimmy, no longer an engaging pet but a formidable rival, got short shrift. Nonetheless he made fitful efforts to strike up a brotherly rapport.

"I say, Seymour, listen to this from the *Atheneum:* 'With all its faults, *Lear Recovering His Reason at Sight of Cordelia,* by Mr. Herbert, is a picture full of the earnestness of this great painter's later style. The drawing is in part faulty and the face of Cordelia is not only weak but ugly. Lear's short legs can hardly be accounted for on any but telescopic principles, and the physician to the right certainly does not put the best face upon things. The head of Lear, however, is a massive form of saintliness that *atones for much,* and the bit of sea seen through the tent opening is calming and thoughtful.'"

Jimmy put the paper down. "Now, there's a perceptive critic! Wouldn't you like to have him under your knife on the operating table?"

"Really, Jimmy, that suggestion is quite unjustified."

"You're right. It's the *painter* who should be disemboweled."

Haden frowned. "I must say, I find your jokes in very poor taste."

Jimmy shook his black curls impatiently, turning in mute appeal to Debo. But that veteran sufferer was long past rebellion. "You should listen to Seymour, Jimmy. He has your best interests at heart."

It was too much, coming as it did on top of a growing sense of spiritual isolation. In France, where anyone could become a painter, artists enjoyed the privileges of their poverty: cheap meals, agreeable mistresses, sanctioned eccentricity. Here, painters were all gentlemen or, like other middle-class citizens of the prospering Empire, aspired to be. They hobnobbed with their patrons and dreamed of being invited for grouse-shooting weekends at country estates . . . then, of owning the estates. Typical was the career of John Everett Millais, boy-wonder-turned-capitalist, who had exchanged an early individual-ism for the pleasures of the hunting season in Scotland.

Temperamentally, Jimmy felt doubly estranged: from America, and now from France. He loved London, but he was chilled by Londoners.

In desperation, he cast about for more congenial company. He found it in the person of George du Maurier, lately returned from the Continent. The two bachelors took a 10-shilling-a-week flat together in Bloomsbury, a drafty high-ceilinged affair with a towel dangling from a string to mark off the "bedroom" area.

To the well-timed rescue of both came another crony from the past, Luke Ionides: in Paris student days a black-bearded hanger-on among the boisterous art students, always available for a loan, a bit of posing, an amorous errand; but here in London, like the fairy-tale frog who turns into a prince, revealed as the scion of a powerful, picture-collecting family.

The Ionides clan, headed by Luke's father Constantine, claimed descendance from the early Byzantine emperors; a dashing uncle gave his name to the Russian seaport of Sevastopol. There were Ionides manors in three countries, and banking millions from which a tiny but much-appreciated trickle reached down to astutely selected artists. By happy coincidence, the family was as rich in beautiful women as in pounds sterling, providing an additional magnet, if any were needed, to feisty young painters.

The white Ionides villa at Tulse Hill in Surrey, porticoed and Levan-tine with cool marble floors, silken curtains and quiet fountains, was headquarters for the Anglo-Greek colony in London. Here the gallants of the town were invited of a Sunday afternoon to feast their bellies on stuffed grape leaves, and their eyes on equally well-stuffed Mediterra-nean bosoms; and here Luke Ionides brought his chums Whistler and du Maurier.

The two had become virtually inseparable. The birdlike du Maurier, troubled by failing eyesight, had been trying without success to break into the magazine field as an illustrator. Now his letters glowed with enthusiasm for his selfless friend "Jemmy," who had introduced him to Charles Keene of *Punch* and was bringing him to meet Seymour Haden. The day would come when du Maurier's fragile tenor would be raised in quite a different tune, but for the moment he could not find superlatives enough for his brother artist, "the enchanting vaga-bond." Jemmy was "the grandest genius I ever met . . . a wonder, a darling."

At irregular intervals, Tulse Hill sprouted dinner parties, masquer-ade balls, and private theatricals. By du Maurier's account, the new-comers were an instant success: "Jemmy talks the women over to him, I sing them back to me." They performed together in a Drury Lane farce of 1843, *The Thumping Legacy*, giggling their way through the parts of the Brigadier (du Maurier) and Jimmy Ominous (Whistler). Du Maurier, losing track of his dialogue on the line "I would arrest you," ad-libbed "I would eat you!"

"Are you quite sure you wouldn't throw me up?" Jimmy shot back.

When du Maurier sold his first two cartoons to *Punch*, his roommate was prominently featured in them: ribboned straw, jutting jaw, monocle, and all. "I am beginning to be a little lion," du Maurier exulted to his mother, "and the big lion Jemmy and I pull together capitally *dans le monde*." Only occasionally did a wistful note of rivalry creep in. Du Maurier surmised that although Jimmy was making the more dazzling impression, "I am more *liked* than he"; and he noted privately that one of his own paintings had qualities of "drawing and prettiness" that were beyond Jimmy.

Jimmy for his part felt like an escaped prisoner. The Ionides warmth spread through his Haden-chilled vitals. He loved being recognized and hailed at gatherings—he was hard to miss with his tumbling black curls, gleaming eyeglass, and trim, alert parade-ground air—and made no protest when he was hoisted onto a high stool to run through his repertoire of Negro spirituals, French cabaret songs, and imitations ("fat man snoring" always brought down the house).

To cap his triumph, there were two commissions from the senior Ionides: for an oil of Old Battersea Bridge, and a portrait of Luke. Jimmy promptly dashed off the first of many letters to Fantin-Latour, urging him to come back and share in the British Klondike: "No idea, theory, or other nonsense must prevent your coming here immediately. It is England, my dear fellow, that advances with both hands outstretched to young artists."

Less satisfactory was Jimmy's progress in the romantic arena. It was not for lack of attractive targets; Tulse Hill fairly overflowed with them. Marie Spartali, daughter of the Greek Consul-General and an Ionides cousin, was the very prototype of the tragic Rossetti "stunner," tall and slender, yet with an aching voluptuousness; her younger sister Christine, who would figure importantly in Jimmy's painting career, had huge dark eyes, black hair, lips the color of Salonika cherries. Seeing the two at a garden party, the poet Swinburne put his hand to his brow: "They are so beautiful I feel I could sit down and cry." And yet the Spartalis did not surpass the Ionides girls: Helen, Chariclea, and gray-eyed, sparkling Aglaia—already, to Jimmy's despair, out of bounds as Mrs. Coronio.

Actually, the issue went beyond marital status. London ladies of good family were not about to entrust their hearts—or any favors more transient—to the notorious caprices of artist chaps. Jimmy's real misfortune was his era, misnamed Victorian but actually rooted in the

Germanic middle-class prejudices of the Queen's Biedermeier husband, Prince Albert. It was Albert, of the massive thighs and bulky watch chain, who gave Englishmen their knee-length frock coats to curb the frivolity of their checked pants, and it was he who imposed the "Victorian" moral code of ostentatious respectability.

Under Albert's *Weltanschauung,* man's animal nature was a regrettable oversight of the divinity, to be excised from public view and even verbal allusion. Legs being inflammatory, the undersupports of tables were soon being referred to as "limbs"; discreet restaurateurs served "bosom"—not breast—of chicken.

Matrimony alone became the acceptable female condition. Divorcées—even the titled wives of foreign diplomats—were unwelcome at the Court of St. James's. As if all this were not enough to discourage healthy grappling between the sexes, on top of it arrived the mid-century wave of aesthetic romanticism . . . the etherealization of women in neomedieval painting and Chopin's languorous nocturnes.

From this background emerged the astonishing phenomenon of the crinoline, a light-metal underskirt guaranteed to screen off the lower female regions from lascivious masculinity by several yards of steel-wire framework. The crinoline, worn over tight corset pants and a reserve petticoat or two, satisfied every Albertian requirement. Topped by a copious full-length dress with a sweeping train in its wake, the crinoline assured its wearer, bulging fore and aft, of undisputed sway over at least six feet of floor space.

Thus bottled up and packaged, the Victorian female was transformed from a vivaparous two-legged animal into an exquisitely unreal supernatural being with a lily-stalk waist, who moved without visible means of locomotion in a perpetual sighing rustle of trailing silks. The sight of a handsome brunette gliding across the floor like a fourmaster under full canvas, proud and unassailable, was enough to shake the stoutest masculine heart; who could bed a Cape Horn frigate?

And Jimmy was not that sure of himself in the first place, with these heavily festooned creatures of his own class. What if he were to make an approach and be cut down like a presumptuous child? The prospect was terrifying.

Because he was so uncertain, he tried doubly hard. He joked and flirted, titillated and shocked. But always he had the uneasy sense that his triumphs of badinage were hollow, that Aglaia Coronio in particular saw through his façade of boldness.

One evening as he arrived at the Ionideses' for a dinner party, du Maurier was regaling a group of ladies with a tale of a model he had known in the Latin Quarter. "Most curious ways she had," said the cartoonist with a fetching twirl of his brown mustache. "If a man was kind and generous to her, she would become totally cold, turn her back

on him. But let him be vicious—abusive—insulting—and she'd be crawl-
ing at his feet."

"Love at first slight, eh?" drawled Jimmy, and moved along. He had
spotted Aglaia Coronio coming down the stairs, incandescent in a
damask-pink evening dress that displayed tenderly rounded white
shoulders above her long black gloves . . . and seemed on the verge of
displaying a good deal more. Whatever kept the clinging silk from
dropping the inch or two that would expose her breasts? And what
would he do if it did?

Aglaia watched him watching her. "You seem terribly preoccupied,
Jimmy Whistler." Her voice was cool and mocking. "Does your artistic
eye detect a flaw? Do you have some complaint to make about my
dress?"

Jimmy waited until she was very close, the polished-ivory skin all but
brushing against his upraised monocle. "Only one, madame. That it
covers *you*."

Effie Ionides, Luke's little blond wife, fluttered by. "Isn't Jimmy the
wicked one!"

"Only conversationally, I'm afraid," Aglaia responded. Her light
laugh cut through Jimmy like a descending sword. "I suspect his de-
pravity is all in his tongue." Her gaze fixed on him steadily; the
monocle dropped from his eye. "And I do believe even that is para-
lyzed for once!"

Jimmy flushed, furious. He wanted to kiss her and to kick her, to
dispel all doubts of his manhood. Instead he merely bowed and
showed his teeth—much, he realized to his dismay, as Seymour Haden
might have done.

He was in a foul humor the rest of the evening. At dinner, he was
far too free with the muscatel; descending the stairs to the garden, he
tripped and nearly took a header. "Who the devil was your architect?"
he growled to Luke Ionides. "Some damned teetotaler, no doubt!"

The autumn night became dewier, and so did Jimmy. He volunteered a capsule critique of English social organization. "Too blasted
many husbands and brothers! What I'd like to find is a beautiful, affectionate orphan!"

Pantomime time came, and Jimmy borrowed a hat from one of the
reigning local beauties, Rosa Moscheles. Discovering that it was a pork
pie, he decreed that pork pie was impossible without mustard. So he
emptied a half-pot of England's best into the hat.

Rosa, angry, told him that since he'd ruined the hat, he might as well
keep it.

"By Jove, Miss Moscheles! If I'd known that was the way things are
to be obtained in your family, I'd have poured the mustard into your
*hand!*"

The sally temporarily redeemed his public standing, but did little for the gathering loneliness in Jimmy's heart. He needed a close relationship with a woman, some replacement for the evanescent mother, in his struggle against a frequently uncomprehending world.

To this problem, too, it was the bountiful Thames that provided an answer.

Ever since *At the Piano,* Jimmy had been uncertain about what his next step should be in painting. He had a number of options. He could try to climb on the shoulders of the Anglo-Greeks into the ranks of the society painters, turning out sleek portraits of fan-twirling countesses. But he resisted the handmade-snapshot style of the Royal Academicians, with its standard dead-white flesh coloring; if the faces in the Academy portraits were right, then those of the living spectators admiring them were all wrong. And he was bothered by the attitude which argued that, since the portrait was fundamentally a showpiece to be stared at, like a new hat from Paris, it should leap vigorously out of the frame and do everything but knock down the beholder.

A surer path to acceptance lay in joining the British parade of anecdotal painters. Yet he could not stoop to the infantile moralizing that ran through their sermons-on-canvas, the artful catalogue descriptions that had nothing to do with line or form. And their blatant colors literally hurt his eyes; the wild reds and piercing blues were like an idiot conversation conducted at an incessant shout. House painters, God bless them, had the right idea: flat tints.

Jimmy felt a certain sympathy for the school of Pre-Raphaelites, who reached back for the medieval simplicity prevalent in painting before the birth of Raphael in 1483. Millais had been a bellwether of this group until he succumbed to the lure of popularity, leaving the movement in the hands of its two other founders, Dante Gabriel Rossetti and William Holman Hunt. The Pre-Raphaelite motive was sound; essentially they were in rebellion against the empty conventions of the Academy. Unfortunately, their sincerity was not matched by their grasp of paint. Except for Millais, who was descending to banality as he rose to prominence, they created dry, hard pictures devoid of transparence or velvetiness. Their forms, painted on a still-wet white ground, had a glittering angularity that tended to kill any suggestion of mystery or atmosphere. And they had their own literary-moralistic fixation, a flight from sordid commercialism to a knightly fantasy-land. In Jimmy's view, the Pre-Raphaelites were essentially dilettantes; their hearts were in the right place, but their brushes belonged in inkwells.

Jimmy's dilemma was resolved by happenstance. On Christmas Day, 1860, bored by the unctuous sentimentality at the Hadens', he strolled southward to Sloane Square in Chelsea. There the Thames was a short walk away, through the byways off King's Road. The day was sharp and frosty, unusually chill for London, where a softening misty curtain normally hung even in the winter air. Striding the pavement with his brisk, clipped steps, Jimmy was reminded of February mornings at West Point.

Arrived at the water, he knew at once what had drawn him there. The sluggish brown stream was sheathed in ice: slim motionless patches of it and bobbing granite-like slabs . . . stretching upstream for miles, hammering here against the protesting timbers of the Chelsea Bridge.

Jimmy reached into the pocket of his overcoat . . . his trousers. Nothing. Damn!

In the watch pocket of his waistcoat he found a stub of charcoal—and his passport.

Well, why not? On a blank page opposite his stamped British visa—one had to have a sense of nicety about these things—he began his sketch: on the left, dominating the scene, a bulky round-hulled sailing vessel with several sailors perched in the rigging; beyond and to the right, smaller skiffs and fishing boats; in the dim distance, smoke curling up from a factory chimney; in the foreground a lanky police officer, perhaps guiding an oarsman ashore. And everywhere else, hemming in schooners and barges, charging down upon piers, spreading its whiteness against murky water and scowling leaden sky: ice.

*The Thames in Ice.* He had the title before he had smudged in the dark mass of the ship's hull; and, rushing his prize to the easel at Newman Street in Bloomsbury to fill in his tones of black, gray, and white, he had a splendid full-blown oil in three days, done in crisp, almost reckless slashes that had more than a touch of Manet.

Only one sour note marred the project: the crafty Haden, sniffing a good investment, took possession of the picture for a 10-pound note: "Three pounds for every day of work you put in, and an extra one besides. A very fair price, Jimmy, I assure you."

Jimmy was not at all assured, but for Debo's sake he kept his peace. What mattered, after all, was that he had found his métier. In painting as in etching, there was nothing for him—as yet—to compare with the river.

But his Bloomsbury flat was in the middle of town, a long haul from the composition-rich docks of the East End. Jimmy abandoned Newman Street to du Maurier, and took rooms at a seventeenth-century inn adjoining the Wapping pier. From here, he could prowl the barges and shipyards of the waterfront.

Evenings, he amused himself at the noisiest of the local pubs, the Angel at the Cherry Gardens pier across the river. It wasn't Tulse Hill,

but the company was hearty and gratifyingly unpredictable. Irish seamen and stevedores, some from families in England five hundred years,
others in recent flight from political turmoil and the potato famine,
lived in thick clusters along both sides of the river, in Limehouse,
Rotherhithe, and Whitechapel as well as Wapping. Poor ( 10 shillings,
or $2.50 weekly was an aristocratic income ), something less than slaves
to ambition (they preferred free-lance floating to the monotony of regular employment), the Irish had their own formulas for fending off
depression, revolving mostly around strong ale and loud music.

Bound together by common hardship—a tumble into a hold could
break a man's neck—they were fiercely clannish. Any misfortune in the
community, Jimmy discovered, was followed at once by a "Friendly
Lead" concert in the pub. Each new arrival would toss a florin onto a
benefit collection on the bar, stand the house a pot of porter (the dark-
brown heavy beer preferred by the Irish to stout), and launch the
company into some lugubrious air. There was a macabre impressive-
ness in the sound of an ancient dirge wailed by several dozen Irishmen
with five or six pints apiece in them. Gradually, as whistles grew moist
and the immediate occasion receded, the wretched howling gave way
to jollier sentiments like *The Jug of Punch:*

> "What more diversion can a man desire
> Then to sit him down at an alehouse fire
> Upon his knee, a pretty wench
> And on the table, a Jug of Punch!"

This was usually followed by an ode to the healing powers of porter,
each stanza of which ended with the earnest supplication: "Give the
child a porter!" After a piano-accompanied chorus or two of "Nancy
Whisky" (a sort of beguiling Irish cousin to John Barleycorn), the
customers were well warmed, inside and out. Shouts went up for local
favorites. A clog dancer would stumble out of the shadows, followed
by a sailor doing a rubber-face act, and perhaps the tavernkeeper on a
jew's-harp.

And that was where Jimmy first saw Jo. She came out of a side room
one stormy February night, a tall, pale girl in blue calico with a plaid
shawl flung over her head. As she crossed to the derby-hatted Dubliner
at the piano, she passed for a moment beneath the gaslight flickering
on the wall. Jimmy saw green eyes, fresh glowing skin, a wide sensuous mouth. From her proud carriage, the lift of her shoulders, he had
an impression of individuality and strength. He put her age at twenty-
odd.

She was not, by classical standards, a beautiful girl. Her nose was a
trifle sharp—if noses could be judged independently of the faces they
sat on. Her jaw, too, had more north-south dimension than was strictly

desirable. And the brow was wrong: too short for the graceful neck, too high for the small ears. Yet the whole had an agreeable asymmetry, as if some capricious designer had decided to experiment with a new combination. And there was a haunting, elusive quality about the girl, a wild melancholy that both disturbed and elated him.

She began to sing, and Jimmy stopped his mental note-taking. Her voice was low, and cool as a mountain stream; then suddenly alive with yearning, and passionate with regret. Jimmy knew the tune—James Molloy's *O the Days of the Kerry Dancing*—but he felt as if he had never really heard it before:

"O, the days of the Kerry dancing, O, the ring of the piper's tune;
O, for one of those hours of gladness, gone, alas, like youth too soon . . .
O, to think of it, O, to dream of it, fills my heart with tears."

The song was the soul of Ireland, pensive yet sprightly, remembered laughter in a minor key. Jimmy was deeply moved.

He was to be more so. The girl finished. Instead of applause, there was a prolonged hush. Were they waiting for something?

With a swift gesture she flung off her shawl, loosened her hair, and began stamping her feet: a wild clattering of left toe beating behind right heel. Yet there was discipline within the wildness, the grave precision of a flamenco gypsy, as she exploded into a whirling hornpipe, feet tapping and kicking in intricate rhythm, upper body under perfect control. She was heartily proportioned, Jimmy was pleased to observe: breasts frank and full. And—Heaven be praised—the line running upward to them from her hips was no mere lumpy padding but long, smooth, unbroken.

The legs clacking along the floor, now lost in shadow, now spinning into a soft pool of light, were well carved and satisfactorily firm. But Jimmy had ceased looking at them. His eyes were on the girl's hair, a tumbling cataract of long shiny strands . . . leaping, swinging, gyrating on a mad dance of its own. And the *color!* A deep, rich, coppery-golden red, more vivid than Titian, more lustrous than Arabian silk. Even in the muted world of candlelight, its splendor was unmistakable; what radiance would it shed by day? For once, Nature had vindicated itself, had created a masterpiece any artist might envy. He had to paint that hair. He had to know that girl.

But she had vanished as mysteriously as she had appeared.

At the bartender's brisk "Last round, gentlemen," Jimmy sidled up to the bar. "Who was that girl, Dennis? The one who danced?"

"Jo? She's not after being anything special. Captain Heffernan's colleen."

"*Colleen?*" Jimmy's heart turned over.

"His daughter."

"Does she work here?"

The bartender spun a suspicious glance at the outsider from the West End. "You might say yes—and then again you might say no. It's mostly at a tackle shop she works, near Bermondsey." The bartender turned away and started polishing a glass.

Jimmy dropped a half-crown on the counter. "Her father—did you say he has his own ship?"

"An old scow, more like."

"Is he a regular here?"

"Ah, that he is. Stiddy as the tide." The bartender pocketed Jimmy's coin and pointed toward the window. "It's a sildom afternoon you won't find him in that corner. He generally docks about five. He's in here three minutes after."

And so he was the next day, a sturdy deep-chested man in battered military cap and oil-stained horsehair jacket. Blue eyes, and blue stubble along the squarish well-cut jaw. Only in the thin nose and flaring nostrils was there any suggestion of his daughter.

Jimmy approached his table. They were alone except for a sailor dozing at the bar. "Care to throw a few darts, Captain?"

The bargeman shook his head. "It's bewitched the little creatures are. They niver do go where I send them." His speech had a musical lilt, an arching of phrase that bespoke birth in Ireland.

"A drink, then?"

"It's an eloquent appeal ye make. A man would be a scoundrel to refuse."

"Ale or whisky?"

"Ale, says me pocket. Irish whisky, says me heart." He tapped his muscular neck. "But me parched throat clamors for gin."

Jimmy ordered two gins and water, and sat down. His companion raised his glass. "Heffernan's the name."

"Jimmy Whistler."

"Captain of the *Limerick Queen*."

"Is that your native county—Limerick?"

"Aye. Filt the famine a-comin' twenty years ago. Sorrow's the taste of work I could get on the Shannon, so I packed me woman and two baby colleens and whisked them off to London."

"I'm American, myself. But there's a touch of Irish in the family," offered Jimmy, discreetly omitting the detail that the Irish Whistlers were Ulstermen.

"Is there, now?" The captain brightened. "Then perhaps you've heard of Owneybeg near the Tipperary border. We were chiefs there for hundreds of years. Here, I'll show ye our coat of arms." He took a stub of pencil from his jacket and bit the point clear, then fished out a bill of lading and started drawing on the back. "Blue lion on a gold field, and for the crest, as the book says, 'a cubit arm erect in armor, hand gauntleted and holding a broken sword proper.' There. Well—I don't seem to have quite got it."

"Perhaps," said Jimmy politely, "you mean something more like this." He took the pencil and did a rapid sketch.

Heffernan stared, disbelieving. "Whoosh! But that's grand, man! Better than in the book!"

Jimmy explained that he practiced art for a living, and that in fact he was interested in his companion as a subject. Would Captain Heffernan be willing to pose for a couple of hours every afternoon? "All the gin you can drink, and five bob a week besides."

"I'll have you bankrupt, man!" cried Heffernan delightedly.

Jimmy's gambit worked out better than he had dared to hope. On his third afternoon with Heffernan at the Angel, the tall girl strode in, green eyes blazing, red hair trailing in a long knot down her back. Ignoring Jimmy, who sat with charcoal poised a few feet away, she went directly up to her father and swept his glass from the table. "So, Patrick Heffernan! This is how you've been financing those elegant sprees! And how do you expect to pilot a boat with gin spilling out of your ears?"

"Now, now, Joanna," the captain remonstrated. "What harm can a thimbleful of gin do, strayin' around in a mighty wilderness of a man like me?"

"Enough harm to knock you off the shipping list and into the poorhouse," she snapped. She wheeled around to face Jimmy. "And you— the great gentleman-artist from Mayfair . . . or so I'm told!" She lacked her father's heavy brogue, but there was a dainty emphasis in her neatly sliced t's and clear liquid l's.

She glared at Jimmy scornfully. In no specific feature did she resemble Anna Whistler, yet there was a certain spare angularity, a crispness of movement . . . and the same hint of resolution in the firm proud line of her mouth.

Captain Heffernan got to his feet with precarious dignity. "Mr. Whistler, may I have the honor to present my second daughter, Miss Joanna Heffernan?"

Jimmy bowed, his very best West Point bow. "It is a most distinct pleasure to make your acquaintance, Miss Heffernan."

Did the angry green eyes soften just a little? "I cannot honestly say the same, Mr. Whistler. You must understand, my father is a poor working man."

"So are we all, each in his way."

"Indeed?" Her voice rose. Her hands, gripping the table, were very beautiful, with long slender fingers and delicate articulations; not red and coarse, he noticed, like those of English girls.

She was lashing out at him again. "And is it nothing better you have to do than sit in a tavern, drawing cartoons of my father like a silly schoolboy?"

"I've just thought of something better. Much better." Jimmy paused. "I will happily release Captain Heffernan from our little business arrangement—"

"Ah, very good," said Jo.

"—if *you* will sit for me instead."

"Me?" Her astonishment was obviously genuine.

"Yes."

"But why me?"

"Oh—your hair, your hands . . . reasons that only a painter would understand." Did he detect a faint flicker of disappointment? "I would pay you, of course. In cash, not gin."

"What would I have to do?"

"Just stand—or sit—naturally. Confront the world, exactly as you're doing now. Oh, perhaps a trifle less ferociously . . ."

Jimmy smiled, and Jo's features relaxed into an answering grin. "Suppose," she asked, "I am not pleased with what you put down?"

"Then you can eat the painting alive. Or the painter."

Both were laughing now. Something had changed, and the captain too was aware of it. He banged on the table cheerfully. "Hear, hear! Let's not be after forgetting the noble entrepreneur. I demand me commission!"

He settled for another, by common agreement final, double gin.

It was several days before Jimmy hit on the setting he wanted for Jo. He thought of posing her aboard the *Limerick Queen*, but that was too theatrical. The tackle shop where she was a sometime salesgirl? Drab. Then he saw her one morning sitting on the balcony of the Angel, sharing a plate of herring and potatoes with Dennis the bartender. Directly behind them, the crew of a sailing vessel were lowering a giant boom. Farther out, toward Wapping, the Thames was a tangle of barges, spars and ropes; a corner window framed an intriguing glimpse of rowboats and fishing smacks.

This was it! A thick-textured, multi-layered composition, soaked in rich color, dripping with atmosphere . . . a sort of super-paean to Realism. He had never attempted anything so ambitious.

He would need at least one experienced model. Alphonse Legros, his partner with Fantin-Latour in the informal "Society of Three," had heeded Jimmy's summons and come to England to make his fortune. Legros was drafted, to take his place on the balcony with Jo and another local recruit, a young sailor. Jimmy set up his easel in the door-way and began work on a charcoal draft.

Jo baffled him. She seemed quite uninterested in what he was doing. Casually, an arm draped along the railing, she made small talk with the young sailor who—in Jimmy's initial design—sat alongside her. Yet, every now and then Jimmy felt her eyes upon him: silent, speculative. Later, he was to learn that she had already marked him for her own—"men dream and dawdle about these things, women know at once"; had decided with her Irish mysticism that Jimmy Whistler was to be her destiny.

But for the moment she seemed quite detached. She flirted mildly with Legros, pretending to be awed by his black beard and his gruff Burgundian manner. She donned long earrings and an imitation-pearl necklace as requested. She posed without complaint—and without apparent involvement.

Then, on the third day of work, he found her hanging over his easel, frowning in concentration.

"I haven't finished the faces," he said hastily.

"I know." She pointed. "That coal barge: that will be a heavy black shape, to balance against the pillars of the balcony on the right?"

Jimmy was surprised. "Yes." How did she know?

"I read about it in a book once," she said as if hearing his unspoken question. "You'll have to be careful with the sky, won't you . . . cool tones, to keep it far away."

Jimmy blinked. "Quite. It's a damned complicated color scheme."

"You'll manage," Jo said serenely, and walked away.

Actually, Jimmy was having his troubles; and they multiplied when he shifted from charcoal to oils. The demands on his palette were ex-hausting: black, vermilion, pink, purple, green; subtle sea tones of sun-tinted blue and gray. He moved his canvas from the makeshift studio at Wapping out onto the balcony—and found that half his boats had changed position. The faces of his models—obscured by the weather-blackened beams of the balcony, yet picking up scattered rays of water-reflected light—would not come alive.

He poured out his worries to Fantin-Latour, the one painter-friend who had his total confidence, in a letter sprawled over the margins and corners of four pages (the strain of Scottish frugality in Jimmy took odd forms, mostly in fare disputes with cab drivers and an adamant refusal ever to use an extra sheet of stationery). In his small, neatly slanted hand, Jimmy outlined his hopes for what he was sure would be a masterpiece, if he could overcome the technical hazards. Not a word of his project must be mentioned to Courbet!

He drew a sketch of his canvas for Fantin, a pen-and-ink miniature occupying less than half of his opening page, and then went on to describe it: the vivid expanse of the Thames in the background, "done like an etching and unbelievably difficult," the row of low-slung coal barges unloading in the center; and close in, practically overwhelming the balcony, the bowsprit and towering mast of a large sailing vessel, its rigging spread across the canvas like harp strings.

Finally, in the foreground, the seated figures on the balcony that were the heart of the picture, two men and a girl. And such a girl! "The most beautiful hair you have ever seen, of a red that is not so much golden as *copper*, like all the things Venetian one ever dreamed of. And a skin of lemony-white, or gilded, if you prefer." The head of the girl, Jimmy explained, was the glory—and the challenge—of the painting, for she wore an expression he was determined to capture, a secret smile as maddening as that of the *Mona Lisa*. Twice he had rubbed out his work in disgust, and on his third try the look had emerged: the jeering, knowing half-curl of the lip that said, "What can you tell me, friend? Whatever it is, I have been there before" . . . the world-weary wisdom of the demimondaine.

He was still not sure, he wrote, that he had done everything possible with the girl's face, but one had to call a limit. He did not want to wear himself out; and there were other sections that needed further work. At best, he was afraid there would be cries of "Not finished!" because his boats were painted on the move, under full sail, so that they could not be rendered honestly other than by deliberately indistinct splashes of tone. To those conditioned by "battle fleets" painted in scrupulous detail from toy models in the studio, his real ships would seem "unfinished." Ah, how he wished Fantin were here to help him unravel these matters . . .

But in any case, not a word to Courbet!

Jimmy dismissed his sitters. There was nothing more he could do at the Angel; he wanted to concentrate now on refining the spatial aspects of his composition, to distribute the large and small ships along the central corridor of his canvas in a deep-thrusting series of receding planes. That was a task for the studio.

He was aware that Jo attracted him enormously—sometimes, at night, obsessed him—but he had decided to make no move until the *Wapping* undertaking was disposed of. Now, as he was packing up his paints, once again she startled him: "Do you always work alone in your studio? Is no one else welcome there?"

"My friends. And models."

"And is it that I qualify as neither, Mr. Whistler?"

"You qualify as both. Please come tomorrow." He looked at her gravely. "Would three in the afternoon be convenient?"

"No," she said suddenly, turning away. "It wasn't really your idea."

He took a step after her. "It *would* have been," he assured her. All at once it was terribly important that she come to see him, that the confrontation not be permitted to slip away. "I was going to ask you."

"For a social visit?"

"If you like."

"Don't painters use models in their studios for studies and sketches?"

"If they're lucky enough to get good ones. Who don't mind the hours, and the possibility of boredom."

Their eyes were conducting a different, more intimate conversation, to which the words were a mere obbligato. "I don't believe," said Jo slowly, "that anything you do could be boring."

Jimmy's pulse quickened. "Tomorrow at three, then." He watched her leave the balcony. She descended the steps with a curious big-girl awkwardness that dissolved into grace as, reaching the ground, she broke into a long-legged loping stride.

Her knock sounded promptly on the hour. Jimmy came to the door of the little third-floor room, scarcely larger than one of his Paris garrets, palette in hand. He wore a white painter's smock and a lush blue-foulard bow tie. His curly black locks danced in a multitude of discreetly pomaded ringlets.

Jo, too, had taken special pains. The simple gray-wool frock was freshly washed and ironed; her hair was piled into a coppery-gold crown on her head.

Jimmy motioned her to his only chair. In a way, he felt very sure of himself. This situation was home terrain: devilish painter, model of humble origins. Here was no self-confident society matron prying through his surface nonchalance to the uncertainties beneath. With the Jo Heffernans of the world, as with its lighthearted French cocottes, he could cope.

And yet he sensed a tremendous inner tension, partly because of a subtle change he had detected in the girl. What met the eye was still the careless, full-breasted hoyden of the Angel balcony, but now he was sharply aware of something else, something he had first glimpsed under the gas jet as Jo prepared to face the tavern crowd: a remote, dreamy, unreachable quality, an aura of lost bewilderment. This impression of Jo was to grow in Jimmy's mind until ultimately her physical traits would recede into a background of mere trappings, as transient as clothing, and the mysterious melancholy became the only reality.

"You're working on the river scene," she said softly. "I've come too early."

"You could never come too early!" He was surprised at his own earnestness. It was the sort of gallantry he had uttered a hundred times, yet this time the usual hollowness was not there. The realization both thrilled and chilled him.

"May I take your shawl, Jo?"

She smiled enigmatically. "At the very least."

Fingers trembling, Jimmy lifted the shawl from her shoulders. A faint tangy aroma came to his nostrils: Her skin? Hair?

"Perhaps you would like me to sit for some sketches, Mr. Whistler?"

She had always addressed him by his last name, when she used any name at all. But under the circumstances—in the face of what was about to happen—the "Mr. Whistler" seemed ridiculous.

"I should like that very much," he said. "But not this way. We must get the full benefit of your hair."

He started to remove the fretwork of pins. Jo sat very still, her gaze calm and unflinching, as Jimmy carefully unwound each coil, then shaped the golden mass into a cascade that fell below her shoulders. "You mustn't hide your light beneath, under . . ." he began, and could not go on.

"Jo . . ."

The green eyes were opened to him, opened wide.

"Would you very much mind if"—he heard his own voice, hoarse and unfamiliar—"if we put off the sketching till later?"

For answer, Jo stood up. He took her hand and led her toward the bed.

"Just a minute, Jimmy Whistler."

He turned, apprehensive.

"I've always wanted to do this." She reached out and pulled loose the knot of his bow tie.

Jimmy paused: "If there are any other yearnings you would like to satisfy, please feel free."

"Ah, but I do, Jimmy. Free as a sea bird."

They both undressed quickly, eyes fixed on each other. Jo sank to the bed.

Jimmy fell upon her, onto the statuesque breasts and the warm round thighs, the supple throat and the miraculously long waistline. His lips traveled over her body—curves, hillocks, hollows—until they fastened at last on the lips.

Jo's kiss was like nothing he had ever tasted: yielding yet possessive; passion filtered through a cotton-cloud of serenity.

The kiss was only the beginning. He did not know what he had expected—physical release, the delirium of omnipotence, perhaps the ardor of Fumette blended with the technical virtuosity of Finette?— but certainly not this, because he simply had not had any idea that such depth of feeling existed, that such rapture could be distilled from the marriage of two naked pleasure-bent bodies. Perhaps something more than pleasure was involved; later, he could think about that. For the moment he was busy, busier than he had ever been in his life . . .

Jimmy fell back, exhausted. For several minutes he lay still. Then he became aware of Jo stirring beside him, unmistakably ready to resume combat. For an instant he felt desire wakening in response—then incipient panic. How could he keep pace with this magnificent Amazon?

The thought pierced him that he might fail Jo, and in failing lose her. The physical consequence was immediate, a chain reaction between mind and body that left him helpless and ashamed.

He felt something silky brushing across his face, like light rain or tassels of Indian corn: Jo's hair. She was on her elbows above him, beginning with mouth and tongue a wordless journey from his neck down . . . gliding over bare chest, belly . . .

Jimmy writhed with pleasure and anticipation, content to be clay under the hands of a master sculptor, harp strings plucked by an infinitely sensitive musician . . .

Dimly, he became conscious that she was moving away. "No," he gasped. "Don't stop . . ." Then he realized that he needed her aid no longer.

He reached out an arm and drew her to him, confident in his restored manhood, elated at her enclosing grasp. The two pressed together . . .

"Harder, Jimmy, harder . . ."

He was a knife-blade, thrusting deeper and deeper, an elemental force locked into its opposite. Jimmy Whistler no longer existed, nor Jo Heffernan; only blind driving need, and wild roaring release.

A wave of exultation swept over his body, an exquisite sense of aliveness, heightened by the momentary-death from the explosion in his loins.

Afterward there was peace, ineffable peace; and somewhere far away, a gentle rhythmic clasping and unclasping, as of coils reluctantly working loose. His breathing deepened; he fell asleep.

The room was dark. Outside a boat whistle sounded. Jimmy yawned, scratched his head. He tried to turn over, and his elbow sank into a soft surface. With a surge of delight, he remembered: Jo!

He opened his eyes. She lay in the crook of his arm, breathing softly, trustful as a child; in a sliver of reflected light from the pier lamp below, he saw long delicate burnished-copper lashes.

He couldn't be—?

But he was. He wanted her again, had a consuming need to lose himself—or was it find himself?—in that abundant forest of mutual passion.

She made no resistance; only, eyes still closed, raised her lips to his and entwined herself around him until there was no certainty where one flesh ended and the other began. Jimmy pressed urgently.

"Not yet," Jo murmured. "Stay there a while."

But he could not. In Jo's arms, surrounded by her warmth, he felt tireless, prodigal of his strength, a giant among lovers.

Jo lay back, unprotesting. She was rolling on a bottomless sea, rocked by gentle waves. In a fishing boat—or perhaps she *was* the fishing boat—on the North Sea.

The wind picked up, pushing the boat along . . . shivering and trembling under increasingly insistent gusts.

Now the storm was breaking: enormous waves, crashing seas, a mast plunging up and down against the darkened sky in a furious arc. A blazing streak of lightning; and then calm.

"Jimmy, Jimmy . . . I love you, Jimmy."

"My angel, my darling, my dearest love!" The words gushed forth beyond conscious control . . . feelings long hidden in some subterranean cave, prisoners bursting free into sunlight.

# Chapter Eight

Jimmy was charged with energy. He had a mistress-model whose very presence made him want to create, and whose emotional support was constant and unstinting. Jo seemed able to ride lightly on the surface of his gay moods, yet shift effortlessly to accommodate deeper needs, as if she knew without being told what was happening inside him. That gave him a wonderful feeling of freedom.

There were adjustments to be made. The very fact of a powerful sexual connection altered their relationship profoundly. It was like exploding a structure into midair: the falling bricks realigned themselves in a new pattern. Jo gave up the remaining shreds of her tackle-shop job at Bermondsey, along with her room there; Jimmy took larger quarters at the inn, and Jo moved in with him. He presented her proudly to his friends of the milieu: du Maurier, the painter Tom Armstrong, Luke Ionides.

But it was understood that Tulse Hill itself, the source of his immediate income from Ionides commissions, was off-limits; there he had to appear as the gentleman-artist, available for decorous flirtations, with his monocle alert to the cycle of well-heeled patrons, Royal Academy showings and prestigious notices that spelled a London success.

The *Wapping* picture was ninety percent right. The other ten percent, the final grouping of the figures on the balcony, might come in a half-hour's tinkering, or might elude him for years. He decided not to show the painting until he had what he wanted. Meanwhile, he made endless studies of Jo—standing, walking, reading, sleeping—in search of the unique attitude that would express her, or his vision of her. For once, he felt no great anxiety; the idea would come; it was hovering just beyond the horizon.

Jo wanted to see Paris—and Jimmy wanted Paris to see her. So off they tripped in April to the capital of Louis Napoleon and Eugénie, then as ever the fashion center of the Continent. Jo Heffernan of Bermondsey, who had never owned a formal dress or even, as she said, a "proper bonnet"—Irish girls covered their heads with shawls—was turned loose among the milliners and couturiers of the Rue de la Paix. She formed an instant and fanatical attachment to Paris hats: perky straws, lacy bonnets, basket-like assemblages of pagodas and cherry trees that were large enough to house a family of birds. Jimmy winced. Why hide the glorious copper strands under these gargoyles?

But he wanted Jo to be happy. She did, after all, cut a striking figure among the little midinettes of Paris. His heart sang as, along the Champs Élysées, jaded boulevardiers turned to stare after La Belle Anglaise.

He could deny her nothing—not even his own treasures. Poking through an old trunk, Jo found his broad-brimmed Rubens felt of the Paris student days, wine-stained from some forgotten prank of Ernest Delaunay, with the smoke from a hundred café nights clinging to its crown. How perfect for her! All it needed was a bit of ribbon and a few feathers. There was this clever Russian woman on the Rue de Rivoli . . .

The hats were of course useless without complementary dresses. Any woman knew that the ensemble was the thing; and no artist, least of all Jimmy, could deny the importance of harmonious color schemes. So Jo went shopping again, and for three days messengers were bringing perfumed packages to their hotel room off the Rue Bonaparte.

"What do you think, Jimmy? The yellow muslin or the blue crepe? Then there's this pale green—" She held it before her. "Wouldn't it make a lovely tea gown, now? The style isn't as new as the muslin, though. But you said you liked me in tarlatan . . ."

Jimmy put down his newspaper. "I would like you in a potato sack."

"Not being worn this year," Jo told him cheerfully. "I'll leave it to you, Jimmy. Which shall I be after taking?"

The blue-gray eyes blinked in dismay. Jimmy put up his monocle, and put it down again. "For Heaven's sake, Jo! I can't possibly choose. Take them all!"

Jo took the dresses—and the cue. Obviously, Jimmy did not like to make decisions; in fact, on almost every issue but his art, he preferred to have them made for him. And even in his work, she had noticed, he vacillated painfully under other people's opinions. He had ruined a charming drawing of his niece Annie Haden because a fellow artist objected to the arch of the eyebrows. Jimmy showed distinct relief whenever Jo took charge of petty everyday matters—stamps, laundry, bath reservations—and seemed to welcome, even while mildly protesting, personal admonitions: against smoking too much, or riding a steamy omnibus in damp weather. It was as if he found reassurance in the evidence that somebody cared enough to scold him.

When Jimmy proposed a trip to "Courbet country"—the seashore of Brittany—it was Jo who bought the train tickets and packed the bags. Jimmy made a brief show of superintending the preparation of his painting materials. But when he saw that Jo knew exactly what she was doing, had anticipated his needs in canvases and had even put in extra stocks of the Venetian red and yellow ochre that were always running low, he retreated happily.

They headed for the fishing village of Concarneau, about three hundred miles west of Paris, where the rugged coast bent inward from the Brest promontory to the north. Jimmy had decided to give a serious trial to the open-air methods of his Impressionist friends, although fully aware of important differences from them. He disliked the raw, unglazed colors of the new French school, their determination to proclaim rather than hide their effects. He mistrusted their direct, never-mind-the-sketch attack on the canvas. Most importantly, he did not share their central aim. They wanted to capture the precise light values of a given instant; he sought rather to absorb and then project the essence of a passing mood, in pursuit of which he was quite ready to alter actual details.

Still, he was intrigued by the notion of seizing nature on-the-fly. He and Jo found rooms with the retired mayor of the village, and Jimmy hauled his easel out to the fishing beach, a rocky cove commanding a fine northward view of the Atlantic. The June morning was brisk and clear, breakfast had been excellent, and Jimmy had high hopes.

These vanished with the first solid gust of wind from the east. Cloud patterns shifted, the sun disappeared, and he was confronted with a totally new set of light problems. Doggedly, he made a fresh start, and this time succeeded in getting the background down—only to find that the foreground was no longer what he had been looking at a few moments earlier. Whitecaps were scattered through the blue.

For a week he labored patiently—and achieved nothing but scarred canvases. There was always something—glaring sun, sudden cloud, drenching downpour—to deflect him from the firm grip he needed on his subject. The conclusion had to be faced: open-air bravura might be feasible for a Manet, whose hand was faster and whose vision stayed closer to the surface. It was wrong for Jimmy Whistler, for reasons of temperament as well as limitations of technique. Nature for him was merely a point of departure for a personal statement. He wanted to record an impression, to be sure; but in his case it was an impression of emotional content, not of laboratory-certified fact. And once the elements were fixed in his head he needed, like Degas, to cart them off to the studio for developing and refining. Only there, he felt, could an artist practice art.

So he took instead to long walks and picnic lunches along the beach with Jo. Jimmy told her about West Point and his family's early years in America—"The first Whistler, Francis, was listed on the ship's manifest as 'gentleman'"; Jo told him about growing up in the galley of a derelict barge, surrounded by hard-drinking stevedores, sheltered at odd moments by a curiously gentle father who taught her to read under a swaying oil lamp.

Usually, on these jaunts, Jimmy carried along sketching materials, just in case. Late one afternoon, as they were trudging along the shore hand in hand—Jo in summer organdie and sandals, Jimmy wearing whites and his usual dancing pumps—she stopped and pointed.

Jimmy squinted. He saw a far-off dot on the rocks near the water's edge. "What is it, Jo?"

"Put up your monocle."

Jimmy obeyed. Now he could make out the figure of a sleeping peasant girl, stretched out among great slabs of brown and russet stone. Simple bonnet and collar made a splash of white above her loose black dress. Behind the girl, a sea of intense blue; above the horizon, a streaky sky of paler blue, with a few puffy clouds hanging down almost to the whitecaps. Strong, somber Courbet colors.

Jo was fumbling with the knapsack on his back. "Hurry, Jimmy. It's perfect."

"Not on your life." The black curls waggled emphatically. "It's no good working with amateurs on a big spread like this. The moment I get started, she'll be bothered by the breeze, or remember that she didn't feed the chickens, or want to stare at the sunset. Worse yet, she'll have some wretched uncle who is sure I am trying to seduce her, and will demand one hundred thousand francs payment in advance."

"But it's such a grand picture, Jimmy. So much atmosphere!"

"Yes, it is," he agreed. He studied the scene a moment, walked a few yards inland to check it from another angle.

"What are we going to do, Jimmy?"

"*You* are going to be the peasant girl."

"In these clothes?"

"No. In those."

The negotiations were brief but picturesque, Jimmy taming his Paris street argot to the formalities of the countryside, the girl glancing from one to the other of the strangers in brown-eyed, chubby-cheeked confusion:

"Remove my skirt? But that is impossible, monsieur!"

"Why? Is it riveted on?"

"I am a decent girl! Ask any fisherman in the village!"

"As if the rascals would tell the truth! Especially the married ones. But we are getting away from the point. I do not wish to strip the

clothes from your back. I simply want you to exchange them temporarily for those of madame, these exquisite garments of Paris."

The brown eyes widened. "Of Paris?"

"But of course. A Paris dress of sheerest organdie. You may wear it
for a day or two"—now it was Jo's turn to look startled—"not in the cow
barn, of course, while we are using your costume for my picture. And
you will be paid, besides. Not in halibut or sole, but in gold. At least,
in francs."

"How many?"

"How many do you want?"

Now the girl was on more solid ground. She rolled her tongue along
the edge of her fine white teeth. "For how long do you wish to engage
my dress?"

"Aha! She speaks like a broker. Very well. I want exclusive rights
to your outer garments for a period not exceeding one week . . . at
three francs a day. Shall I have my attorney prepare a contract?"

The girl drew up her chunky figure. "That is not necessary, monsieur. The word of a Breton is enough."

A smoking shed used by the local herring fleet served as an impromptu dressing room for the exchange. Jo emerged looking suit-
ably bucolic; the Breton maid, somewhat smothered in organdie three
sizes too large, preened her way homeward across the fields.

The whole operation had taken less than three-quarters of an hour;
and for once, Nature had held still. Even the waves were just as Jimmy
left them: the tide, still at late-afternoon ebb, was just beginning to
creep back up the tawny sand. He had ample time to pose Jo carefully
in the left foreground of the canvas, her head just below a broken line
of small rocks that swelled gradually to a mass of jagged boulders on
the right. The sketch went quickly, but they worked outdoors with charcoal for three days more before Jimmy was satisfied that he knew what
to do with every inch of the canvas.

Now he couldn't wait to get to a studio. They returned to London,
and took the first place Jo could find: the lower half of a brick cottage on Queen's Road near the Thames in Chelsea. Here Jimmy translated into oils his non-Impressionist impression of the Brittany coast.
He produced a powerful canvas, severe in coloring and extraordinarily
palpable in its textures of rock and sand. In vigor it rivaled Courbet;
in atmosphere it went beyond the father of Realism, expressing the
desolate serenity of an empty beach under an endlessly stretching
summer sky. He called the painting *Alone with the Tide*.

A gust of salty October air swept in from the Thames. Jimmy looked
over at Jo in bed beside him, incredibly formed and tinted, her skin
the muted gold of ancient Chinese ivory. He knew every detail of her

body: the waist curving down from the custard-smooth breasts, the eyes whose color could be conveyed only through the chemistry of the palette. He knew what she was like beneath the splendid exterior, too; and what he knew rejoiced him. Jo was totally honest, totally dedicated to him and his well-being. Her one lapse—the splurge on clothes in Paris—had been the subject of endless self-recrimination ever since she discovered the actual state of his finances. She was constantly plotting little economies, usually at the expense of her own comfort.

It was eight months since he met her, and in those eight months his world had changed. He who had never felt that he had a home, had one at last: in her arms. Because Jo loved him, everything had become sharper, more meaningful. He could not imagine going back to a life without her.

The painting he planned of her had not yet crystallized, but he felt it ripening steadily in his mind, awaiting only the final stimulus that would pull all the components together. Meanwhile, he had minor commissions to occupy his easel, mostly portraits of children from families in the Ionides social circle. Little boys and girls being something less than ardent models, the work went slowly. Likewise the payments. Although he continued to write airily to Fantin of the fortunes waiting to be picked up in London, actually he had been obliged to borrow a shilling from du Maurier the day before to buy cigarettes. But things would improve; if only—irrationally—because he now had Jo.

She murmured something, and turned over on her side to confront him with an eloquent patch of naked back. A handful of freckles were scattered discreetly, like poppies in a field. Jimmy reached over, and with his long fingers started tracing letters on the ivory skin: "J-W a-d-o—"

Jo stirred sleepily. "What are you doing?"

"Writing you a letter."

"Can't you send it by post?"

"Too slow. And I don't trust Her Majesty's mail with confidences."

"Is it such a secret, now?"

"Not really. Du Maurier's been blabbing it all over London: 'Whistler is quite loony about his Irish Amazon.'"

Pause. "How do you spell 'Amazon'?"

"L-o-v-e-l-y."

Jimmy could sense her smiling into the pillow.

Suddenly the smooth shoulders quivered. "You opened the window last night!" She turned accusingly.

"But of course. That's what the pulleys are for."

"I've told you, it's dangerous."

"Oh yes," he teased. "The damp river air creeps in."

"And the Little People."

"Flying all the way down from Limerick. How is it that *I* never see them?"

"You're not Irish enough. Anglo-Irish doesn't count." Jo coughed; a sharp, hacking cough that brought a look of alarm to Jimmy's face.

Instantly he was out of bed, scrambling across the floor in bare feet to close the window. "Are you all right, Jo?"

"Perfectly. It's just a bad habit."

"In that case, as Colonel Lee would say, you should discipline yourself."

"Ah," sighed Jo. "Colonel Lee. Eternal Lee. Infernal Lee."

"Two demerits, for a ghastly pun."

Jo shrugged. "I'm not clever with words, like you. You should be happy when I make any kind of joke."

"Happy, no. Tolerant, yes."

Jo slipped out of bed and wrapped herself in a robe. "I've a good mind to cancel my surprise."

Jimmy, busy in the small dressing room, declined the bait.

"It's lessons I'm taking," she went on. "In English cooking."

The curly head, comical in dismay, popped into sight again. "No, not that! Take up musketry, sabers. Skewer me with arrows. But spare me mutton and treacle!"

Jo sat on the edge of the bed, crushed. "I was only trying to save restaurant money." Jimmy came over and put his arms around her. "You just concentrate on saving *me*," he said. "My wizardry in matters financial is the talk of two continents. Tonight, for example, we are dining utterly without cost, courtesy of a friend of du Maurier's just down from Oxford. Poet fellow by the name of Swinburne."

Algernon Charles Swinburne was a creature beyond invention, a fugitive from never-never land. His head loomed, red-maned and imposing, above a fragile, almost girlish body that sloped downward from narrow shoulders to flaring hips.

Within this inadequate shell was locked a tremendous reckless energy which, like a genie squeezed into a bottle, was constantly exploding through the lid. Swinburne jumped, jiggled, twisted, and jerked; his fingers twitched, his feet were never at rest.

His features sprawled inconclusively. Above and below the well-cut nose, a repertory company mustache and scraggly red beard made feeble gestures toward conventional virility. But the real man was in the eyes: tiny, green, and glazed, they floated free of the face, of time and place, into some remembered fairyland.

Swinburne, then twenty-four, had made a small splash in a very limited puddle with two plays written in blank verse. He was of good family—his father was an admiral, his maternal grandfather the third

Earl of Ashburnham—and had charming old-fashioned manners. But he took pains to establish for Jimmy early in the evening that he was exceedingly wicked. "If I am a great poet," he crowed, "it is only because I was properly flogged at Eton." His excesses, he made plain, were not confined to flagellation: "I shall construct a castle of seven great towers, and enact one deadly sin in each." Chided by du Maurier for gulping down a glass of yellow chartreuse, he replied, "I have the perfect antidote: two glasses of the green."

The little-boy naughtiness behind this "decadence" was so transparent that Jimmy could react only with amused sympathy, especially since Swinburne had greeted him with a guileless, "You too are a poet for the ages . . . in paint." Although barely three years older than Swinburne, Jimmy felt a fatherly protectiveness; beside the unworldliness of the poet, his own inadequacies seemed nothing. Clearly Swinburne shared this view; within months he was addressing Jimmy in letters as "Cher Père."

After dinner at the Café Royal, the party repaired to Swinburne's flat in Bloomsbury, where the poet recited from Walt Whitman's *Leaves of Grass* and his own *Rosamond*. The metamorphosis in personality was astonishing. Head flung back, eyes aflame, voice suddenly deepened in timbre, the little man rolled forth stanza upon stanza of perfectly articulated verse whose pounding meter was more important than the sense of the words. He was Pindar making high incantation to the gods, a cathedral organ with all the stops pulled out.

But his lyrics themselves were not negligible. Sometimes immature, often undisciplined, they nonetheless had a torrential flow, a gushing-forth as if from some volcanic inner core of molten earth. Jimmy was impressed, and said so.

In that case, Swinburne had something more to show him. Leaving du Maurier with the ladies, he led Jimmy to the library. From a locked cupboard, he drew out a slim folio: early sketches and water colors, he explained, by his poet-painter friend Dante Gabriel Rossetti.

The dean of the Pre-Raphaelites, never too sure of his painting skills, had an aversion to Academy showings or other public exhibitions. For that reason, Jimmy's acquaintance with his work was limited to the Rossettis he had seen in private collections, mostly medieval-anecdote oils of the quick-order genre that Rossetti himself described as pot-boilers. Regarding the poet's relationship with Liz Siddall, the tragic little cockney whom Rossetti lived with, married, and who soon after died and was buried along with his unpublished verses, Jimmy knew only the bare outlines. Here in Swinburne's library was the product of that period, a dozen sketches of the original "stunner," a record of the doomed love between consumptive shopgirl and spiritually tormented genius.

In these forgotten sketches—slight, evocative, with a loose, instinctive draftsmanship not yet overlaid with Pre-Raphaelite rigidities—the poet in Rossetti shone through. The thin sheets were crowded with hints of things unspoken. Jimmy particularly admired the luxuriant sensuousness of a pencil drawing showing Liz seated quietly against a wall, hands folded, eyes closed, rich sheaves of hair enclosing a delicate face. Her neck-high dress was simple and flowing, uncluttered by crinoline. Here perhaps was a clue for his portrait of Jo.

The next morning, Jo had a visit at Queen's Road from her sister Kate, who was to be married on the following Sunday. With the girls bustling about the flat, exchanging gossip and articles of clothing, painting was difficult. Jimmy picked up a book and took refuge in the bedroom.

By some lingering association with Rossetti, he chose a volume of Edgar Allan Poe. He was deep in the adventures of the unfortunate Ligeia, when—as it seemed to his startled eyes—the lady herself floated through the door. It was Jo, dressed in the old-fashioned gown that would adorn her as bridesmaid, a loose, trailing all-white affair last worn by a long-departed aunt.

Jimmy leaped up from the bed. This was the image he wanted: Jo in the lost paradise of the Rossetti angel-women, Jo in ethereal, virginal white.

He had no illusions abut the actual state of Jo's virginity. But there were other, more consequential forms of purity; and these Jo had in abundance.

Everything snapped into place. He would create a symphony in white: white dress, curtains, walls . . . His mind raced. For the background, colors; yes, a lavish palette. But the heart of the painting would be masses of white, with form delineated by a bold grouping of subtly graduated tones.

For this picture, no improvised corner in a London cottage would do. He needed a real studio, the kind that Paris offered in abundance. Within ten days he and Jo were installed in a bright, bare third-floor walk-up on the Boulevard des Batignolles, in Montparnasse.

"Damn!"

The sable-hair brush, flung from Jimmy's hand in exasperation, left a trail of alizarin crimson along the floor. He could not get the flesh tones right for Jo's face. Yellow ochre, white, Venetian red—and what? Perhaps the answer was burnt sienna after all, but very diluted.

He retrieved the brush and picked up another. "Could you hold your head a little higher, Jo? And turn just a fraction to the right? You're getting too much light."

Jo shifted, and stumbled slightly. "Jimmy—do you suppose we could take a few minutes' rest?"

"Of course, my dear. I'm sorry." And he was. As ever, he had quite forgotten that the model before him was human, had muscles that ached, joints that grew stiff in the damp air of a Paris winter. It was after ten in the morning; Jo had been on her feet without complaint since eight. That was his way, and he would never get over it.

His plan for *The White Girl* was dramatically simple: Jo standing in belted cambric, under strong light from a window on her right filtered through a white muslin curtain; behind her, a set of heavy-textured drapes; at her feet, a wolfskin-covered rug. Dress of brilliant lead-white; draperies shaded toward off-white by a delicate film of yellow ochre mixed with green; rug of Prussian blue broken up by patches of olive; wolfskin staring head-on, teeth bared, from the bottom of the canvas, in varying tones of umber with a delineating edge of alizarin crimson. And for the crowning note of color, of course, the magnificent red hair (burnt sienna, brightened with Indian red), tumbling in loose mass around the shoulders. Simple, but not sentimental. The painting would be daring in its high-key palette, almost stark in the purity of its design: no racy earrings of *Wapping* memory, only a sprig of green starflower hanging from Jo's left hand.

Jimmy sank into a chair, the only one in the room; he could never unwind enough to lie down while painting. Jo was already stretched out on the sofa, her eyes closed.

God, what a terrible grind—for both of them. Six weeks now, three complete scrapings-out and rebeginnings, and he was no more certain of success than on the day he started . . .

He must put aside such thoughts; no general ever backed his way into victory. Panic was the enemy, panic and doubt . . . the fear of waking each morning to find that yesterday's labor was wasted, and with it the sickening conviction that today's also was doomed . . . the paralysis of confidence that reached out to suspend the brush in mid-air. Half the problem was to conquer the difficulties of concept, of materials, of technique; the other, perhaps more devastating half, the quaverings of self.

Above all, he must not worry about Royal Academy deadlines, the onrush of time. That was the sure way of never finishing at all. One had to hammer away stubbornly, blind to all distraction, putting the best one had into every day. Then one woke on a certain unexpected day to find that the job was done.

Jimmy brushed at his eyes, felt a brief clutching pain in his stomach. Lead fumes, from his copious use of white paint. The air was saturated with the stuff. Only yesterday Fantin-Latour had warned him that it was a dangerous poison, the source of "painter's colic" affecting the blood and bone marrow. Well, that was a chance he had to take, a hazard of his profession. But was it fair to expose Jo, with her tendency to coughs?

She was sitting up now, smiling over at him. "I'm all right now, Jimmy."

Dear Jo. She would stand on her head if he asked her to. And not simply out of obedience. She was developing a considerable grasp of a painter's technical problems; her questions were few, but always intelligent.

He nodded to her, and picked up his palette. Perhaps he should forget about the flesh tone for the moment. Perhaps if he focused on the wolfskin at the tricky area where it merged with the folds of the dress, working on the canvas from the bottom up as Degas used to recommend, he could generate enough momentum to carry him forward into the complexities of face and hand. He freshened up his thin "soup" on the palette . . .

Ah, that was better! In fact, it was perfect, that sweeping brush stroke back from the head. One could positively feel the fur under one's fingers. Now, just a dab more of raw umber for the crucial section in the corner . . .

Splendid! Things were definitely picking up. Jimmy began to sing in a cracked falsetto his favorite air from Offenbach:

> *"Pour seduire la belle Alcmène*
> *Il prit les traits de son mari*
> *Je connais beaucoup de femmes*
> *Auxquelles ça n'eut pas réussi."*

Jo responded happily to his new mood. "What *is* that silly thing you're always singing?"

"It isn't silly. It's a profound piece of operetta philosophy. Tomorrow you shall have a full, custom-designed translation."

The next morning, on the tea tray that Jimmy brought to her in bed, there it was:

> To seduce the fair Alcmène
> He took on the traits of her legal lord-and-master
> I know multitudes of women
> With whom that tactic would have brought disaster

"You mean," said Jo slowly, "women are not always that enchanted with their husbands. It's true. I was thinking last night about poor Kate. Here it is less than two months since she and Willie were married, and from her letters . . . well, they just don't have anything to say to each other."

"Perhaps they never really did," suggested Jimmy. He stood before the mirror, admiring his new Oriental dressing gown; expensive, but he had not been able to resist it.

"It's very possible. You know, most couples just stumble through the day together, improvising here and there, pretending a good deal. People are like . . . like fish bowls pressed together, touching at only one point, missing all the rest."

"You a fish bowl? I deny it," protested Jimmy.

"You know what I mean. But we're different. We have contact in so many ways . . ."

Jimmy looked at her. "Yes," he said, suddenly serious. "Painting you is another way of touching you."

"We have our little jokes, and our impossible restaurants . . ."

"And our bodies."

They lay together, legs intertwined, in the special jumble of fingers and limbs that had become their own. Jo listened to Jimmy's even breathing against her chest. He had become a wonderful lover—tender, surprising, inventive—but impossible to hold beyond the moment of climax. Within seconds he was off and away, drifting down some deep and private river where none could follow. This was Jimmy's way, a selfishness that was perhaps inseparable from creativity. And she was content to be part of that creativity, connected in her own way with its godlike mystery.

*The White Girl* gathered force rapidly. So, unfortunately, did the inroads of the lead fumes. Both painter and model suffered continuous headaches; once Jimmy, mixing his "soup" for the white dress, was momentarily overcome, and only a quick lunge by Jo saved him from a nasty fall. But he was eager, in spite of medical counselings to a vacation and his own earlier self-admonitions about not hurrying, to be ready for the Royal Academy showings in May of 1862. Jo was scarcely less so; the painting had become their life.

And not without reason. Standing back from the gleaming canvas one morning in late April, Jimmy felt that it marked a major breakthrough. With its dazzling but controlled seas of white, *The White Girl* asserted the right of the artist to go beyond Nature in choosing his effects and techniques. It also had something to say about the importance of placing the subject well back within the frame, where it could be bathed in an appropriate reinforcing atmosphere (Courbet was to find the setting hypnotic, the girl "an apparition"). For Jimmy, *The White Girl* was the beginning of a detour from Realism that ultimately would take his portraits to the dim far side of psychic frontiers.

# Chapter Nine

Jury time. Along with *The White Girl*, Jimmy had submitted *Alone with the Tide, The Thames in Ice,* and a waterfront etching, *Rotherhithe*. All three water scenes were accepted. *The White Girl* was not.

For the first time, Jimmy was confronted by the reality of the British art scene. Under the domination of the stylist-social reformer John Ruskin, sentiment and literary pretension were as firmly enthroned in London as Queen Victoria.

From the viewpoint of the Academy jurors, *The White Girl* lacked a "subject." There was no uplifting message to soothe uneasy mercantile consciences; only, as a newspaper reviewer would later complain, "a powerful female standing on a rug." To the judges of Prince Albert's era, the subtle scaling of tonal values was simply baffling. With their anecdote-conditioned eyes, they could scarcely see what Jimmy had put on the canvas; and what they saw, they didn't like.

Jimmy was crushed, then angry. He took little comfort in the praises of the Thames painting as "broad and vigorous," the Brittany scene as "perfectly expressed." To his mind these earlier oils, which occupied him for days rather than weeks, were scarcely more than preparatory exercises for *The White Girl*. Here he had poured out the best of himself; and here he had failed. He felt vaguely humiliated before Jo, as if their love itself had been found wanting.

When a new gallery on Berners Street offered to feature the picture along with a catalogue note about its rejection, he quickly assented. He made no objection to a parade of sandwich men along Piccadilly with their boards ballyhooing WHISTLER'S EXTRAORDINARY PICTURE, *THE WOMAN IN WHITE*—until an *Atheneum* critic foolishly connected the painting with a popular novel of the period, observing that although the face was well done, "it is not that of Mr. Wilkie Collins's *Woman in White*."

This irrelevancy drew from Jimmy his first letter to the press, advising that he had not even read the Collins novel, much less attempted to illustrate it.

Disappointed and upset, worn out by the accumulated tensions and noxious vapors of the past winter and spring, Jimmy and Jo were ready for the long-prescribed holiday. They set out by rail for Biarritz at the western tip of the Pyrénées, in the sheltered corner of the Bay of Biscay just above the Spanish border. Two factors guided the choice. A few kilometers down the coast was the celebrated health resort of Guéthary. Farther south was Madrid.

Since the early Paris days, Jimmy and Fantin-Latour had day-dreamed of a joint pilgrimage to El Prado, there to stand in reverence before the Velázquez collection. It was a frequent theme of their cross-Channel correspondence, which at that time consisted mainly on Jimmy's side of exhortations for his friend to come to London and get rich, and on Fantin's of reminders that there were perils in worshiping success. More than once Jimmy thanked him for restoring perspective —"your letter was the cold shower I needed"; on the other hand Fantin *had* come briefly in 1861 and, entirely thanks to Jimmy, obtained a number of life-saving commissions.

Now the plan was for Fantin to join the holidaying couple in Biarritz, from which the trio would make the march on Madrid. If Fantin was held up, Jimmy might go anyway, and bring back photos of the master's work. "As for making sketches, I scarcely dare to risk the idea. If I acquire courage . . . we shall see. You know, this must be the kind of glorious painting which is beyond copying. Ah, how he must have worked!"

Meanwhile, there was a vacation to be enjoyed. At first, still restless, Jimmy didn't know what to do with it. Automatically, he had brought painting materials. Almost without thinking, and in spite of his qualms about open-air painting, he did *The Blue Wave:* giant breakers coiling across the canvas in huge whitecapped masses, under a glowering Michelangelo sky. Powerfully organized in space, the new seascape represented a striking advance compositionally over *Alone with the Tide.*

Gradually, Jimmy untensed. He and Jo lay around the sands, did a little reading (*Martin Chuzzlewit* by Dickens, short stories by Théophile Gautier), and sipped Pernod on the hotel veranda looking out over the sea: toward America to the West, the British Isles to the north. One evening after sunset, Jo claimed to sense ancient galleons hovering offshore, and to hear the murmur of voices.

"Delicious Lorelei?" inquired Jimmy. "Shipwrecked sailors?"

"I cannot tell," she answered gravely. "But they are very sad."

"Because they're dead?"

"Whoosh, no! It's living on and on that's hard. Some are terribly old."

Did she believe in immortality, then? And reincarnation?

"We never called it that. But the return of spirits from the past, yes. My grandmother used to have conversations with them."

Jimmy shivered slightly; the breeze from the sea? He looked over at Jo: tall and serene, with that evanescent air that suggested unreachability, some part of her always withheld, unfathomable. "Do you think it is possible," he asked, "that you may be inhabited by some lost spirit from the past?"

"I am sure of it," she replied softly.

Jimmy felt uneasy. "I know who it is," he declared. "A barefoot Irish princess of the fields. And I—my body is the modern dwelling place of some medieval McNeill of Barra, come with kilt and dagger across the wild seas to court you."

His tone was light, almost mocking; but he found his own words strangely persuasive. They fell silent, lost in a fantasy—or was it a remembrance?—of some misty Celtic past.

At first they swam a good deal; Jo with the assurance of a girl brought up on the river, Jimmy with more enthusiasm than skill. But Jo soon discovered that some element in the salty waters aggravated her cough. Unsympathetic spirits, she decided, were operating off-shore; Jimmy must be extremely careful. He agreed.

Two mornings later, the mystic in him was overcome by the venturesome little boy. The day was windy and overcast, with a chill in the air that sent Jo scurrying back between covers. On the veranda a group of late breakfasters dawdled, but the beach was deserted except for some children and a local fisherman who doubled as occasional painter's model.

Jimmy stood at the edge of the surf. Waves were soaring up from the sea like huge black stones, crashing down in fierce breakers that splintered into a myriad currents. Magnificent! He must taste that sea.

He waded out, ducked under a breaker and started swimming, cresting with the waves. Ha! Nothing to it. He swam on.

Looking back, he was startled to see how far he had gone from shore. Time to head for home . . .

Easier decided than accomplished. As he swung around, a great roller caught him behind the ear, knocking him under. Gulping for air, he came up only to encounter a 20-footer that spun him around like a leaf in a whirlpool. He swallowed what seemed like gallons of water.

What followed, he described in a letter to Fantin: "I swam and I swam, and the more I swam the less near I came to the shore. Ah, to feel my struggles useless and to know people were looking on saying, 'See how the foreign gentleman amuses himself, he must be strong!' I cry out, I scream in despair, I disappear three, four times. At last they understand. A brave railroad man rushes toward me, and is rolled over twice on the sands. My fisherman-model hears the call, arrives at a gallop, jumps in the sea like a Newfoundland, manages to catch me by the foot, and the two pull me out."

Back in the hotel room, huddled under a mass of blankets, Jimmy whispered to Jo through purple lips: "We must get to Madrid before I succeed in drowning myself. You know—see Velázquez and die!"

They had already made one tourist-excursion across the Spanish border to Fuenterrabia, where the balcony-covered houses, bold red blouses and swaggering berets of the natives left Jimmy enchanted. "Comic-opera Spaniards in the streets," he rhapsodized to Fantin. "Green balconies filled with beautiful brunette maidens, stuffing themselves with chocolate all day, as in a bad painting. Wild children like little Turks!" And all this only twenty minutes from France.

The projected journey to Madrid would be another matter: a long, bumpy railroad trip of some 250 miles; then the same distance back to Irun, and five hundred miles more of return to Paris or London. Jo's cough, a source of mild annoyance in the foggy British capital, had become actively worrisome in the supposedly tonic air of Guéthary. Jimmy hesitated.

He was almost relieved when word came from Paris that family problems would oblige Fantin to stay at home for the moment. That settled it; once again, the plan to visit El Prado would have to be postponed. Gradually, it was abandoned.

Jimmy was fed up with rambling. A little money was at hand, the proceeds from the sale of Wabash Railroad bonds left by his father. He spoke of finding a cottage in Surrey, made vague inquiry about acquiring some moldering palazzo in Venice—and settled in Chelsea.

Instinct had always drawn him, despite sojourns in Belgravia and Bloomsbury, back to this London equivalent of the Parisian Left Bank. The Borough of Chelsea, in the southwest corner of the city, stood like a short boot planted firmly on the northern bank of the Thames, with its rear uppers reaching northward through Sloane Street past posh Belgravia to Knightsbridge. A long diagonal marking its borders ran from the toe of the boot at Walham Green up Fulham and Brompton Roads to the same intersection at Knightsbridge; a second, more southerly diagonal—the legendary King's Road—sliced northeast through the heart of the borough to Sloane Square.

Chelsea was clubby, quaint, informal: a tangle of sleepy squares, neat rows of red-bricked Georgian houses, and sleazy side streets. Under the brooding skies of London, it presented a charming, huddled silhouette of slanted rooftops and fluted chimneys.

The borough boasted a long, gaudy, and sometimes bawdy history.

As a tiny Thames settlement grouped around a fourteenth-century church it was chosen for the site of his retreat by Sir Thomas More, the scholarly Lord Chancellor and author of *Utopia*. Sir Thomas dwelt in isolated splendor among the meadows and river fowl until he was beheaded by Henry VIII for refusing to swear to the Act of Succession.

More was succeeded on the Chelsea stage by a somewhat earthier character, the ribald Restoration monarch Charles II. Charles bathed and romped along the Thames for years; the pristine King's Private Road was a path hacked through the woods to facilitate his visits to the delectable Nell Gwyn. Following the royal example, a number of courtiers built manors along the river for their mistresses and, in a few rare instances, even their families.

Two hundred years and much roistering later, Chelsea was once more an oasis of tranquillity, relatively untouched by industrial ferment. The poet Leigh Hunt, settling there in 1830, rejoiced over its quiet "no thoroughfare" alleys "so full of repose that I felt I could sit forever, embalmed in silence."

At the time of Jimmy's arrival, the population of Chelsea was a mixed bag: of 15,000 persons, some eight hundred men and two hundred women were in the arts or professions, with painters predominating. The bulk of Chelsea's men were building-trade workers. Most of the women were listed as domestic servants. Whores did not appear in the official census, but there was no scarcity of them elsewhere. They generally conducted their business in solemn-fronted brothels tucked away on the lampless side streets near the river, in accordance with the Victorian dictum that high-spirited gentlemen could indulge their inclinations at will, so long as they did not do so publicly.

West of the Battersea Bridge at Beaufort Street, where the river sprawled untidily among ramshackle boatbuilders' huts, were the remodeled remnants of several imposing seventeenth-century residences. Jimmy found his home in Lindsey Houses, originally a baroque white palace spreading along 250 feet of waterfront. Redesigned for the Earl of Lindsey by Sir Christopher Wren, it housed the first performance in England of Italian opera. A century later the palace was partitioned into five separate buildings, and plastered over.

Jimmy rented the westernmost and smallest house, 7 Lindsey Row, separated from the river only by a winding footpath lined with weather-beaten trees. Although narrow and less than three full stories high, it had front and rear gardens, two bedrooms, and an oak-paneled drawing room with a 14-foot ceiling and a magnificent view of the Thames. At the rear of the same floor was Jimmy's studio, a squarish room with good north light overlooking lime trees, black mulberries and vines.

Because the place was in rundown condition, Jimmy was able to get it for the modest annual rental of £60 ($300). By the beginning of 1863, he and Jo had the house ready.

Alphonse Legros, meanwhile, having been launched among the merchant-collectors by Jimmy, was earning respectable commissions but had no fixed abode; he bounced among rooming houses, quarreling with landladies who objected to his careless ways, and with fellow lodgers unsympathetic to his nocturnal working habits.

In years to come, after many trials, Jimmy would write with ironic relish abut *The Gentle Art of Making Enemies*. But in the early 1860s he was still a man who made almost a cult of friendship. He invited Legros to move into the extra bedroom. There was a vague understanding that the Frenchman would contribute to household expenses.

The vagueness turned out to be a mistake. So, it developed, was the whole arrangement. Jo and Legros had diametrically opposite views on nearly everything, including the prompt payment of debts and the desirability of frequent bathing. Jo complained that although Legros left coal fires burning all over the house and counseled Jimmy to do the same, he was never around when the bills were presented: "I'd like to see some pounds shillings from him, instead of advice!" Legros was unhappy because Jo insisted he clean up the March mud dragged through the halls by his boots. "Who does the woman think she is?" he stormed to Jimmy. "She issues orders like Marie Antoinette, parades your name around London—and she can't even cook a decent omelet!"

The atmosphere grew thick. Jimmy suggested that Legros join him in a visit to Amsterdam, far more accessible than Madrid, where they could luxuriate in a leisurely study of Rembrandt and perhaps make etchings of some major oils. The two were in the Dutch capital, marveling over *The Night Watch,* when word arrived of a bombshell that had struck the Paris art world.

The official French Salon, administered by the Academy of Fine Arts, was if anything stuffier than the Royal Academy exhibition. Its jury, controlled by a cabal of older members, had become a private club for the protection of faded painters and outmoded ideas.

With the biennial Salon coming up in the spring of 1863, Jimmy had made a routine submission of *The White Girl*. As he anticipated, it was turned down; at Fantin's suggestion, he authorized a Paris dealer named Martinet to display the painting in his window.

However, this time the judging committee overreached itself. Not only Jimmy was shut out, but Édouard Manet, Claude Monet, Fantin, Legros, Bracquemond—virtually all the young Frenchmen of talent. Clearly the jurors were concerned less with the canvases of the candidates than with their birth certificates. Several newspapers were stirred to protest.

On April 24, the Emperor intervened. In a gesture half-enlightened, half-calculated (the Salon graybeards had no political following), Louis Napoleon decreed that a special exhibition of rejected works—a Salon des Refusés—should be held in the same building that housed the official showing, the Palais de l'Industrie.

The controversial display was caricatured in the press, satirized in the theater—and drew larger crowds than the Salon itself. Two paintings left all the others standing at the post: Manet's *Le Bain* (later called *Déjeuner sur l'herbe*), which displayed a group of fully dressed young men seated on a lawn with a naked young lady recently emerged from a dip in the river . . . and *The White Girl*. The Manet was shocking enough to arouse the ire of the belatedly circumspect Empress Eugénie; the Whistler was debated even more.

First reactions were not encouraging. The ubiquitous P. G. Hamerton, who earlier had excoriated Corot as an "amateur," had sneered at Courbet, and found Jimmy's etchings of the Thames insufficiently "moving," reported with visible enjoyment in the *Fine Arts Quarterly*: "Mr. Whistler's famous *Woman in White* is amongst the rejected pictures. The hangers must have thought her particularly ugly, for they have given her a sort of place of honor, before an opening through which all must pass, so that nobody misses her.

"I watched several parties, to see the impression it made. They all stopped instantly, struck with amazement. This for two or three seconds; then they always looked at each other and laughed.

"Here, for once, I have the happiness to be quite of the popular way of thinking."

French reviewers, however, disagreed. Paul Mantz of the *Gazette des Beaux Arts* pronounced Jimmy's work the "most important" in the exhibition, a veritable "symphony in white" exerting a strange charm. Fernand Desnoyers found it the "most original" on display, "of so individual a beauty that the public does not know whether to find the girl ugly or pretty." Burger-Thoré said it was "conceived and painted like a vision." The poet Baudelaire praised the painting, and the novelist Émile Zola scolded those who found it grotesque.

Monstrosity or marvel, the painting was at least recognized as a breakthrough into new terrain. Degas, speaking in the fifties of the common debt to the Dutch masters that he shared with Jimmy and Fantin-Latour, had observed that "any of us could have done the early work of the other two." With *The White Girl*, this was no longer true.

Jimmy, still at work in Holland, reveled in the clippings forwarded by Fantin. What, he demanded, were the boys saying in Manet's crowd at the Café de Bade? The imperial intercession delighted him; it was exactly the sort of aristocratic salute that he considered the due of James McNeill Whistler.

He soon had further cause for rejoicing. A set of his etchings, mysteriously entered in a May exhibition at The Hague, was awarded a gold medal; while a dozen more were bought in London for the Print Room of the British Museum. Jimmy was in the news, and the repercussions were not long in coming.

Two days after his return to London, a note was delivered to 7 Lindsey Row under the letterhead of Sir Francis Grant, president of the Royal Academy, inviting Jimmy around for "a little chat." Jo was elated, but Jimmy hopped aboard a hansom on King's Road with mixed feelings.

The grimy bulk of Burlington House stood at the far end of an enormous courtyard flanked by the Society of Antiquarians and the scientific Royal Society. Jimmy paused before the statue of Sir Joshua Reynolds, a swashbuckling figure in tight doublet; crossed to the seven-arched portico, and started slowly up the wide, richly carpeted staircase. Most of his associations with the Academy were unpleasant. Not only was it a haven for incompetent painters and a barrier to artistic progress; it was the quintessence of starched pomposity. This was the organization that had denied membership to a fine sculptor, Alfred Stevens, on the grounds that he was "living with a lady to whom he was not legally married."

On the other hand, these august halls were unquestionably the royal route to fame and handsome commissions, perhaps even one day to . . .?

"Sir James Whistler" had such a nice, natural ring to it. At the Arts Club, for instance: "Your newspaper, Sir James?" Knighthood would be a lovely gilding to one who could never forget the luster of the Czar's court.

But was he willing to meet the R.A.'s terms? Could he accept their empty idols and their mutual back-scratching? How could you scratch a man's back when what you wanted to do was kick him in the pants?

Sir Francis Grant came out from behind his desk to greet the American. He was a lanky middle-aged Scot with thin sandy hair offset by bushy whiskers. After a few mumbled civilities, he came to the point: "There's been a wee bit of talk in London"—he rubbed his ear—"well, perhaps more than a wee bit . . . about this str-range exhibition in Paris, and your gr-reat success in it."

His r's smelled of heather; Jimmy was beginning to like him. Grant frowned and waggled a finger: "Now, ye see, here in London we have this nonsense of Pre-Raphaelitism coming up, and we want some young men who can paint in the Academy. And ye can paint. And if ye behave yerself, we'll just make ye an Academeecian."

That was really all he had to say. Jimmy expressed his appreciation of the honor implied, and of the president's courtesy in conveying the message personally; then he bowed and started for the door.

Grant called him back. "Mind ye, there'll be no more prancing about like a peacock at private showings, or running down perfectly good chaps because they aren't Rembrandt. Ye'll have to curb your tongue. Ye can learn that, can't ye?"

The Scottish burr was no longer engaging. Jimmy felt more insulted than flattered: Did they think he could be patronized like a delinquent schoolboy? He flashed an angry look under the thick, dark brows; murmured a barely audible "Good day, sir" and stalked through the door, quickening his pace in the hall. He left the Academy much more rapidly than he had entered it.

At the next R.A. private viewing, Jimmy was conspicuously in attendance. He joined an admiring throng gathered around *Britain's Realm*, a seascape by the Academician John Brett, hung prominently "on the line." An elderly gentleman with a towel-length white beard stood before the painting, shaking his head in awe. "It's a *tour de force*," he declared solemnly.

"An *amat*eur de force," snapped Jimmy. "Or, if you like, a tour de *farce*." He walked up to the canvas and pretended to rap it with his knuckles. "Pure tin! If you threw a stone into this it would make a rumbling noise. Ha!"

A stoutish matron drenched in diamonds raised a lorgnette. "The trouble with modern English pictures is, they fade."

"No, madame," Jimmy corrected her. "The trouble is, they don't."

A minor critic thrust himself waggishly into the conversation: "Tell me, Mr. Whistler, is there anything you approve of here?"

"My *Last of Old Westminster* is acceptable—if you can ferret it out among the rubbish in that side room. And oh yes—there are some really handsome picture frames, quite worth the bus fare to look at." He turned and walked off.

Wherever he went in the next few months, Jimmy gibed at the Academy. When a waiter at the Café Royale, puzzled by his request for "flapjacks," protested "I can't make out what you mean," Jimmy whipped out his monocle and stared: "Gad, sir—are you an R.A.?"

During a reception at the Garrick Club, he referred to the forthcoming Winter Exhibition of Old Masters at Burlington House as the Academy's "annual atonement." Later in the evening, as he was having a whisky-and-soda in the bar, John Everett Millais pulled up a chair.

Millais was almost alone among Academicians in holding Jimmy's respect. Five years older than the American, the one-time child prodigy had shown in his first Pre-Raphaelite canvases a healthy disregard for anecdotal convention, and a considerable sensitivity to both line and color. His subsequent *Vale of Rest*, depicting a gravedigging at a nunnery, had emanated a brooding power; and his *Eve of St. Agnes* prompted Jimmy to advise Fantin: "A real picture, in every respect artistic, you will like it very much." *St. Agnes*, based on a poem by Keats and modeled by the painter's wife Effie, portrayed a handsome woman about to retire in the cavernous bedroom of an old castle, bars of moonlight bathing her half-clad, reverie-lost figure through a casement window. Although Millais's most recent canvases were showing signs of a creeping commercialism, he was still individualistic enough to be regarded with suspicion by the ruling elders at the Royal Academy.

Millais raised his striking profile toward the ceiling, apparently uncertain how to begin. The man was as physically impressive as Frederick Leighton, the "Greek God" of the London painting scene, but in a more rumpled, outdoors-tweedy way. Visionary blue eyes blazed out of an open, cleanly chiseled face. Millais had the kind of looks that enabled people to use the term "manly" without wincing.

Finally: "I, ah, heard your little joke about the Academy, and I quite understand how you feel. They've given me a pretty terrible time, you know, because I won't play their game with dealers and galleries. I sell direct to collectors, and get better prices than they do. Frank Grant and his bunch, they can't forgive that. They'll stop at nothing to shoot me down."

"Even at soliciting *me*."

"Really?" Millais stared.

"Yes. I was informed by Sir Francis that if I would mend my wicked ways, he could find a place for me in the holy war against the Pre-Raphaelites."

"That's the reason they built up Leighton." Millais bit at his lower lip. "They're very powerful, you know. And completely in league with the press. There's more than ignorance behind some of those funny notices."

"I was beginning to suspect that. Anyone who bucks the Academy must be ready to take on the critics, too."

"Quite. And it can be done." Millais pulled his chair closer. "It can be done, if you don't overlook one factor: the public. They are the only true, disinterested critics. You can go your own way, as long as you have them behind you."

"But they hardly know I exist."

"Not true. You've been noticed. This is the time to strike."

"Strike?"

"Turn out more canvases. And along the proper lines."

"I intend to. The proper lines—as I see them."

Millais shook his fine blond head. "Don't overdo the boyish fervor. Look what happened to me on *Christ in the Home of His Parents*."

"One of your noblest pictures."

"Denounced by Charles Dickens as 'odious and repulsive.' I was twenty. I know better now." He knocked the ashes from his pipe. "How many canvases have you turned out so far this year?"

"I'm not sure. Perhaps five or six."

"I've done twenty-two. You should paint more, my dear Whistler. Gets your name around."

Jimmy lifted an ironic eyebrow. "Boost the product, eh?"

"Why not?"

Jimmy adjusted his monocle. "Any other suggestions, Millais?"

"Yes. Don't be afraid of homely sentiment: you know, children, domestic bliss—the kind of subject you treated in that *Piano* picture."

"My intention there was atmosphere and design—not sentiment."

"True—for your taste and mine. But you were sensible enough to put it in a pleasant package. There's nothing wrong with having a catchy title, like . . . like my *Black Brunswicker.*"

"Or in going along with popular opinion?" suggested Jimmy. *Brunswicker,* idealizing a German grenadier at Waterloo, was shown at a time of strong anti-French feeling in England.

"Certainly. You can give them good painting; but like a thoughtful doctor, you have to sugar the pill. That's what the masses want."

Jimmy turned to face him, small sparks glittering in the blue-gray eyes. "What on earth have the masses got to do with art?"

"Everything," said Millais. "They pay for it." He fingered his sherry glass. "Be realistic, man. Basically, you're a sound fellow—not one of these queer birds like Rossetti. You like a good wine, don't you? And a juicy leg of mutton?"

Jimmy wrinkled his nose. "Could we make that a chateaubriand?"

"You can make it fresh pheasant—and bring the bird down yourself. Which would do you a world of good, by the way. Chap ought to get out of the stuffy studio every few months: trout streams, fresh air, exercise. But you've got to face facts, man. Traveling, houses, wives—these things cost money!"

"I wouldn't want more than one wife."

"One will cost you quite enough."

Jimmy smiled his sympathy. Millais had acquired the wife of John Ruskin and the critic's predilection for the country-gentleman life, without Ruskin's enormous income.

Millais stood up and waved his pipe earnestly. "Believe me, if you paint only to please yourself, you'll pay a terrible price. And for what? A hundred years from now, nobody will know the difference."

"Ah, but I will."

"You'll be long in your grave."

"Yes, but lying among the worms in sweet serenity, not twitching or twisting."

Millais looked shocked.

"My dear Millais, by your logic I ought to cover a series of 8-by-12 canvases with romping puppies. If the English public gapes lovingly at a single three-month-old beagle, they should swoon in ecstasy over a field full of them."

Again the worried waggle of the beautiful head. The fellow's sincerity was really touching. "It won't do to be *too* clever, Jimmy. A man can't live on the praises of his friends."

"But he can make a meal or two from the abuse of his enemies. Anyway, thanks for the advice."

"Well—I must be off. We're dining with the Lord Chancellor. Cheerio."

Jimmy looked after the tall athletic figure. He didn't really feel all that isolated. To begin with, there was Jo, warmer and closer than ever now that the tension with Legros had subsided. Happily, the Frenchman had been taken up by the young ladies of some genteel country families. He had become much more fastidious in his habits, and—even better—was away a good deal.

Jo had moved comfortably into the role of "Mrs. Abbott": aide and agent, intelligence operative, household manager, mistress-model-companion. The name was an inspiration of Jimmy's. "Mrs. Whistler" would have been awkward, "Miss Heffernan" seemed inadequate; so he retrieved for Jo the familial middle name discarded soon after he began embellishing his own signature with "McNeill."

Jo bought his paints and canvases for him, took his work around to dealers, kept more careful records than he did, and drove a harder bargain. She managed to modify in his favor the 50-50 split on his etching sales worked out by the wily lawyer Serjeant Thomas, who had tied up profitably the work of the fledgling Millais and clearly intended a similar fate for the young American. She attended exhibitions for him and, her perceptions sharpened under Jimmy's patient tutelage, soon developed a highly discriminating eye. The next logical step was to risk drawing a sketch or two herself, and Jo was more than up to it. She had a distinct gift for the light, graceful line, and absorbed instruction rapidly.

The inevitable happened. One day, departing hastily for Bond Street, she accidentally mixed in several specimens of her own work with a batch of Jimmy's drawings. The dealer accepted the lot without batting an eyelash, paid liberally on the spot—and Jo did not disabuse him. "It seemed a pity to give back those nice pound notes," she explained apologetically.

Jimmy was annoyed; then—as usual—amused. "We'll have you hanging in the Royal Academy yet!"

Everything, even struggle and exhaustion, was grist to their mill. When Jo sank back into a huge armchair after a day of stretching canvases and haggling with dealers, Jimmy made a chalk sketch. Later he converted it to the etching *Weary,* using drypoint to create soft masses of flowing hair.

Their greatest pleasure was simply in being together: long evenings of talking, of reading by the fire while the soft rain dripped against the leaves outside. Jimmy introduced Jo to Poe and Bret Harte; she picked up secondhand anthologies of poetry, and read to him aloud in her cool, clear voice. Sometimes she sang the new ballad by the young Irish rebel John K. Casey, who would be dead before he reached twenty-five:

> "Over the dim blue hills
> Strays a wild river
> Over the dim blue hills
> Strays my heart ever . . .
> Were I Tyrconnell's chief
> Or Desmond's earl
> Life would be dark,
> Wanting Maire my girl . . ."

She had another tune, softly trilled in Gaelic, but for a long time she wouldn't translate it.

"What does it mean?" Jimmy would persist.

"Och, it's a lot of nonsense," she finally told him. "About this girl who sleeps at the foot of her lover's bed, ravaged by his sweet talk—and he hardly knows she's alive."

"What's it called, the title?"

*"Buachaill an Chúil Dualaigh—Youth of the Ringlets."*

# Chapter Ten

Jo was the fulcrum; but with important reinforcement.

George du Maurier had ceased to be fun. As his difficulties in gaining a foothold on *Punch* continued, his essential craving for status was rising to the surface. So was his envy. His little sarcasms about "the fiery Jo" and the "Duchess of Dublin" did not escape Jimmy; du Maurier was having a bad time with a slow and exceedingly circumspect courtship of his own. Unwilling to take a mistress until solvent as urged by his French mother, yet guilt-plagued by his occasional "wastrel" flings at Brighton, he was on the point of nervous collapse.

This Jimmy could view sympathetically, and even attempt to alleviate through Haden. What he found intolerable was du Maurier's transparent willingness to make any accommodation necessary to get onto the staff of *Punch*. The man had abandoned all pretense of dignity. True, he had reason to be seriously concerned about his eyesight; but did that justify an eagerness to black the meanest boots? Beneath du Maurier's strained geniality, Jimmy descried the snobbisms of Seymour Haden.

On both sides, relations were crumbling. Du Maurier's letters no longer boasted of his intimacy with the incomparable Whistler. Jimmy was out of town, he reported tersely, "and good riddance. Nothing is more fatiguing than an egotistical wit."

The worn cord snapped with the appearance in Jimmy's neighborhood of a more than satisfactory replacement. Dante Gabriel Rossetti, poet and painter, outsider and uncompromising individualist, had much in common with the young American. He was foreign, mystery-loving, whimsical and gifted. He had even, like Jimmy, rearranged his name to suit his privately held image; the "Dante," like "McNeill," was inserted as an afterthought.

Jimmy's new friend was the dazzling sun of an erratically spinning planetary system, the Rossetti Circle, a heady crew of artistic dissidents

who in talent, depth, and personality simply left du Maurier miles behind. Within weeks, du Maurier was noting gloomily in his diary that
Jimmy had joined this dissolute band who indulged "the strangest and
most childishly irresponsible affectations," all the while breathing "a
noble contempt for everybody but themselves."

This was the judgment, of course, of a man excluded, who would
have to wait thirty years before taking his vengeance. Actually, Rossetti and his friends were deeply concerned with art, literature, philosophy, human relations—everything, in fact, except the Victorian
clichés that preoccupied their critic.

Dante Gabriel was a plump, dark-eyed man of volcanic intensity,
a seething Vesuvius transplanted to the mild damp shores of the British Isles. The son of a Neapolitan poet exiled for Republican activity,
Gabriel was technically one-quarter English, on his mother's side; in
temperament he was 110 percent Italian. His studio dress consisted of
a mud-spattered shapeless overcoat knotted at the neck, with notes
spilling out of its bulging pockets; and beltless trousers sagging in limp
waves to scuff the floor. He shuffled about in oversize Moroccan slippers like a sailor crossing a slippery deck, muttering obscenities, reaching up for the tankard of beer on the mantelpiece, dropping to all fours
to hunt among his floor-scattered sketches. Sometimes, with his drooping mustache and fat little goatee, he suggested a prosperous Hong-
kong merchant—except that his clothes would never have passed
muster in a respectable Chinese home.

And yet, at thirty-four this apparent travesty of a Bohemian had an
unmistakable grandeur. Authority flowed from his dark smoldering
eye. His lofty brow was Shakespearean (he had modeled for a portrait
of Chaucer). And in the massive carved smoothness of his face, the
thick arched brows flanking the still-sensitive if coarsening nose, there
were traces of a princely beauty.

He ate with royal gusto, a miniature Henry VIII. And there was
splendor in his voice, whether rendering imperious judgment on Dante,
Shakespeare, Blake, Browning . . . or fragments from his own pen:

> "From the fixed place of Heaven she saw
> Time like a pulse shake fierce
> Through all the worlds . . ."

Decades later, Jimmy would refer affectionately to the southern magnanimity, forgiving of lapses, with which Rossetti ruled over his "bar-
baric court"; the gates of his palace and the strings of his purse were
always open. And he *did* live in a palace. Tudor House at 16 Cheyne
Walk, a short stroll east along the riverfront from Jimmy's, had been
the official residence of Catherine of Braganza, the neglected Portuguese bride of Charles II, as attested by the elaborately initialed scroll-

work atop the 15-foot entrance gate. Some said the four-story mansion had been lived in earlier by Catherine Parr, sixth wife of Henry VIII, and then by Queen Elizabeth.

It was a rambling affair of some fifteen rooms, notably a 40-foot parlor spread across the first floor front overlooking the river. Stout oak doors and serpentine corridors made it the sort of place where a brooding literary man might hole up for days undisturbed; besides Rossetti's first-floor-rear studio and his bedroom above, there were three suites of bed-sitting rooms for tenants and guests.

Behind the house, a pleasant stone terrace led down to an acre of garden. The serenity of this retreat was not long maintained; for Rossetti had much to forget, and his major antidote to sorrow was the cultivation of a private menagerie ranging from armadillos to geniuses.

He started modestly enough, with an assortment of birds: parrots and parakeets, Chinese horned owls, a raven, and a peacock. He was momentarily put off when a green parrot screeched one Sunday morning, "You ought to be in church!"; a believer in the supernatural, Rossetti feared the spirit of some angry ancestor was rebuking him. But he went ahead with his collection. Shopping in Ratcliffe Highway, an area of sailors' hangouts and opium dens, he came back with salamanders and chameleons, woodchucks, a wombat and a wallaby, and a variety of other small animals. He graduated to a deer, a jackass, and a full-scale kangaroo, and bought a Brahman bull at Cremorne "because it had eyes like Janey Morris," one of his favorite "stunners." He was dissuaded from buying a lion because of the heating difficulties, but kept looking for a bargain in elephants. "I could teach it to clean the windows," he explained to the poet Browning. "People would ask who lived there, come in and buy pictures."

Never since Noah was there such a tangle of brays, squawks, hoofs, and feathers. Naturally, crises abounded. The armadillo dug up neighboring gardens and had to be banished to a zoo. The raccoon and wombat, of more varied appetites, feasted respectively on the letters of the Pre-Raphaelite Holman Hunt, and the hunting-hat of a patron-sitter ("Poor wombat," murmured Rossetti. "It will ruin his digestion"). There were terrible duels: a battle to the death between mother and son kangaroos, and an epic between peacock and gazelle which left the once-gorgeous bird bare as a plucked chicken. Servants, unnerved by the sight of monkeys bolting out of fireplaces, fled.

The squire himself was a near-casualty. It was his custom to engage in a daily chat with the Bull of Bashan, tied up at a stake in the garden. One morning after a turf-loosening rain the bull broke loose, leading to a confrontation not conducted according to the rules of the arena at Seville. Around and around a giant elm the two galloped, purposeful beast on the heels of reluctant, tubby toreador. Rossetti, who loathed exercise, made an exception in this case. Finally he risked a dash for the terrace steps, and succeeded in slamming the oak door of the pantry against the lethal horns.

The human denizens of the Rossetti circus—Jimmy met them gradually and in random succession—were no less picturesque, except for Dante Gabriel's staid and thoughtful brother William, who provided the necessary note of contrast. One permanent tenant already known to Jimmy was little Swinburne, who with his flaming crest and hopping, chirping manner might well have been classified with the tropical birds. Swinburne was there because, in addition to his literary promise, he had been a close friend of Rossetti's late wife. The older poet kept a tolerant eye on him, sometimes pinning the Tudor House address on his lapel before an evening of on-the-town revelry to ensure his safe return.

Other intimates of Rossetti included the novelist George Meredith; William "Topsy" Morris, social reformer, poet, designer of the morris chair and energetic husband of the languid Janey; the artist Frederick Sandys; and Charles Lutwidge Dodgson (Lewis Carroll), whose Mad Tea Party in *Alice in Wonderland* was modeled after the antics at Rossetti's dinner table.

The Circle sometimes shrank but rarely expanded. Jimmy gained entry by a curious route. In Paris, he had been among a handful of artists—notably the bird etcher Bracquemond and the poet Baudelaire—who in 1860 stumbled across the treasures of Oriental art. Japan had been opened to the West only since 1854, after Commodore Matthew C. Perry's visit with the United States Fleet; France had been quick to sign a cultural agreement. Soon La Jonque Chinoise, a shop on the Rue de Rivoli, was giving away superb jars of blue-and-white porcelain with sales of China tea, and packing its curio boxes with colorful woodblock prints by the Japanese landscape masters, Hiroshige and Hokusai.

The discoverers of the Rivoli shop trumpeted their finds to colleagues and patrons, and overnight a cult was born. Jimmy, abetted by Luke Ionides, brought the fad to London, where they enlisted the aid of the art connoisseur Murray Marks, a scholarly Dutch Jew with strong contacts among the Far East traders of Amsterdam.

Reports of Jimmy's collection reached the ears of the ever-inquisitive Rossetti, who asked Swinburne to bring him to the American. Jimmy had an instant convert. Legs planted far apart, dark eyes shining with excitement, Rossetti stood before the ginger jars and prunus-blossom vases and lacquered boxes. "What is this one, Whistler?"

"Ah, you have a discerning eye. That is my finest piece, Old Nanking of the K'ang Hsi period, 1662 to 1722. Notice how the cobalt blue is refined here to a pure sapphire, without purple or gray."

"Magnificent. And these—they are newer?"

"But not precisely new. Yung Cheng, and Ch'ien Lung of the late eighteenth century."

"Quick, let us go to this fellow Marks. I must have some pots before nightfall."

For Rossetti, ever in search of escape from his melancholy, the new vogue was custom-made: it gratified both his love of beauty and his child-like delight in games. He would "beat Whistler" in digging out hidden treasures from the Orient. For months his dinner invitations carried the salutation "Pots, Pots!"; visiting a surgeon friend, he became so intrigued by a pink salmon drawn on a blue plate that he turned the dish upside down, quite forgetting that it was filled with vegetable soup at the time.

One of the bed-sitters in Tudor House was occupied by George Meredith—but not for long. Elegantly slender, vivacious, short of cash but long on opinions, the author was too conscientiously English in upbringing for his Mediterranean host. One noon-day Jimmy was sitting at the breakfast table in Tudor House, skimming through the London *Times* for Rossetti. A patriotic letter-writer was worried about the leanings of Louis Napoleon's new advisers; an editorial questioned whether the United States would "absorb the British provinces."

"Ah," sighed Rossetti, "the momentary momentousness and eternal futility of so many political questions."

Jimmy had shifted to the virtues of Dorman's Prize Medal Dog Soap —"removes doggy smell, leaves Rover refreshed"—when Meredith breezed in, pink cheeks aglow.

He stared aghast at the scene. The gloomy ground-floor dining room was a clutter of recent Rossetti purchases: mirrors, chairs, fireplace tiles. Dante Gabriel, rumpled and unshaven after an all-night bout with insomnia, wore a tattered robe on which he had just splattered yolk from one of five poached eggs swimming in his plate. Undeterred, he jabbed at a chunk of bacon as if it were a mortal foe.

Meredith recoiled. "This is really ridiculous, Rossetti! You're stuffing yourself like a starved carnivore. What you need is a salubrious walk in the sunshine!"

Rossetti stopped chewing for a moment, egg yolk dribbling down his brown beard. "What I don't need," he growled, "is a young fop who can hardly pee for himself, lecturing me on everything from manners to Canaletto!"

"There's no occasion to be vulgar!"

"A little vulgarity is healthier than sanctimonious gossip." Swinburne

had accused Meredith of discussing the affairs of Tudor House with
cabbies.

The novelist twitched his red-brown mustache. "I won't stay here to
be insulted!"

"Please don't."

As Meredith retreated, Rossetti mockingly tossed the remains of a
teacup after him. A few days later, the friendship between the two was
resumed—but not the tenancy.

Cut more to Jimmy's style was the effervescent Frederick Sandys,
a painter of considerable gifts and more considerable borrowings; Rossetti called him "The Tomb of Loans." Tall, blond, and handsome,
Sandys sported a gaudy white waistcoat that never left his chest except
for visits to the laundry or, alas, the pawnshop. Sandys—pronounced
"Sands"—was a superior draftsman whose drawings on wood showed
appreciative study of Dürer. He had ample commissions for portraits
and magazine illustrations, but as a consequence of his expensive
amours was too busy dodging creditors to execute them. Rossetti, a
limerick fan, scribbled wryly:

> There is an old painter named Sandys
> Who suffers from one of his glandys . . .

The real victims were Sandys's indulgent friends, and especially the
archcapitalist among them, Dante Gabriel. Rossetti had learned to survive outside the art Establishment by shrewd cultivation of a half-
dozen extremely wealthy patrons. Robin Hood-like, he shared this
booty from the Philistines with his friends. He even shared the patrons,
with important consequences for Jimmy.

Sandys, for whom the nearest thing to a permanent address was the
pawnshop, was a frequent guest and visitor at Tudor House. At the
first dinner party Jimmy attended there, Sandys turned up with a Royal
Academician by the name of Wilkinson Ames. Ames was a mobile
soporific, the kind of man for whom people staged farewell parties the
moment he arrived in town. It was Sandys's not illogical premise that
after an hour or two of Ames, the other guests would be glad to pool
their resources to get the pair out of the house.

Rossetti writhed and groaned as, over the soup, Ames expatiated
on the names and interrelationships of England's "county families."
After exhausting the theme—and his listeners—he turned to his host.
"And what about your name?" he demanded. "Is it a symbol, or some
sort of flower? Just what is 'Rossetti'?"

Jimmy could almost hear the grinding of Italian molars. "Rossetti,"
he interposed, "is a state of suffering."

Talent, even when backed by a sympathetic mistress, was not a total bulwark against loneliness; in Rossetti, Jimmy found the on-the-scene male confidant he needed. Blue china was merely a convenient handle for developing a rapport that on both sides was deep and instinctive. Rossetti was another southerner-in-exile on the British scene, a fellow-romantic who preferred the nighttime bewitchment of the Thames to the purchased plaudits of the Academy. Like Jimmy, he idealized women as the mysterious wellspring of life and creativity, dreaming of the perfect soulmate he would eternally serve; meanwhile he too lived in irregular semi-matrimony with a mistress-model, the blowzy, busty Fanny Cornforth.

Jimmy dropped in frequently at Rossetti's, for evening walks or marathon discussions of life, death, life-beyond-death. In the first glow of new acquaintance, there had been some talk of arranging a four-man painting exhibition: Rossetti, Whistler, Fantin-Latour, and Legros. This was quickly abandoned in recognition of its stylistic incongruities. By tacit agreement, Jimmy and Dante Gabriel thereafter met as gentlemen rather than fellow painters.

Only once was the silent understanding breached. On a gusty March afternoon, returning from a shopping expedition in King's Road, Jimmy stopped in at Tudor House for a spot of tea. He found the place a trifle more chaotic than usual. Swinburne was capering around the entrance hall, quite nude; en route, he proclaimed, to a "gloriously indecent" encounter in St. John's Wood with fellow admirers of the Marquis de Sade. Fred Sandys was in the reception alcove playing some lunatic form of soccer football against a nearsighted marmoset. From the dining room came queer sounds as of an animal gnawing. Jimmy went to investigate.

Stretched out under the table, chewing on a two-inch timber, was Dante Gabriel. "It's that idiot Morris," he explained. "He's not coming to dinner. Or Janey, either."

Jimmy decided that he too might better return another day. He was intercepted in the hallway by Sandys. "I say, Jimmy, have you seen the news? A valuable Frith stolen from the Academy."

"Impossible."

"But it was in the World."

"No doubt something was taken. But if it was a Frith, it couldn't be valuable."

"They're scouring the gang hideouts in Soho."

"They would do better to check on escaped morons." Sandys raised a blond eyebrow.

"Put yourself in the place of such a thief. You have years of experience, can walk softly as an Indian scout, pry open a lock with the deftness of a surgeon. You have standards, a sense of pride in your work.

Now, do you waste all that preparation on stealing what is, after all, scarcely better than garbage? No, the man is a second-rater."

Rossetti was in the doorway, listening. "Jimmy—would you look at something for me?"

"China?"

"No . . . a sketch for a painting."

"Of course."

Jimmy followed him upstairs, very aware of the Rossettian self-consciousness that kept the Italian, a confident poet but a relatively untrained painter, from showing in exhibitions.

Dante Gabriel stopped before an easel drawing of a young woman in flowing robes, standing at the top of a curving flight of stairs. Tentative colors were indicated in the margin.

The sketch had possibilities. For once the trademarks associated with Rossetti—elongated neck, extravagantly curved lips, intense eye—were missing.

"What do you think, Jimmy? It's Sibylla Palmifera, Beauty the Palm-Giver, who draws to her altar all men of fine sensibilities."

"An excellent start. Very promising."

"Any suggestions?"

"No. Well . . ." Jimmy stroked his imperial. "Have you thought of possibly placing her farther down the staircase—for balance?"

"You mean, like this?"

"Not quite. May I?"

Rossetti handed him the charcoal. Jimmy drew a few swift lines.

"Marvelous, Jimmy. That's much better! Now let's have some beer."

Over the next few weeks, Rossetti periodically reported on his progress. He was modifying his color plan for *Beauty;* had acquired a stunning gold frame for the canvas; was keeping it hidden from the two assistants who usually touched up his pot boilers.

Then, a long silence. Finally Jimmy could not contain his curiosity. Had Rossetti finished the painting?

"Well, not exactly. It's over here in the corner . . . But I've written a little sonnet on the theme. Would you like to hear it?"

"By all means."

Rossetti threw back his shoulders.

> "This is that Lady Beauty, in whose praise
> Thy voice and hand shake still—long known to thee
> By flying hair and fluttering hem—the beat
> Following her daily of thy heart and feet,
> How passionately and irretrievably,
> In what fond flight, how many ways and days!"

The rich quivering voice faded to silence. Jimmy looked over for a moment at the painting, stiff of line, barely developed in composition from the charcoal sketch, its original purity muddied by strident purples.

"Frame the sonnet, Dante."

# Chapter Eleven

Seymour Haden was not pleased. The young brother-in-law he had introduced to London society and virtually worn on his watch fob was no longer at his disposal. To compound the injury, Jimmy had become a personage in the art world. And—final insult—in preference to the respectable solidity of Sloane Street, Jimmy had chosen the questionable pleasures of Chelsea. Jo was the prime symbol of Haden's defeat.

The surgeon fumed, but out of family considerations he and Jimmy continued to exchange visits. The uneasy truce was exploded by an affair of Haden's own making.

He had bought from Legros a quiet oil called *The Angelus*, a soft blur of gray stones merging into blue sky, depicting a country church at the end of day. Staring at the painting across the breakfast table one morning, he decided the Frenchman's perspective was wrong.

Nothing that his own agile hand couldn't repair, of course. He got out his oils . . .

What finally emerged was a morass of reds and yellows, no longer a Legros canvas but a parody of Turner: in Jimmy's eyes, as to the outraged Legros, an act of murder.

The two painters conspired to make the criminal pay. They whisked the picture back to Lindsey Row, rubbed out Haden's "improvements," and invited the surgeon to dinner, where the smudged canvas faced him in silent reproof all evening. For several weeks, at every encounter with Haden, Jimmy dexterously steered the conversation around to unnamed "amateur busybodies" and "vulgar retouchers" who were the abomination of the art world.

When the riposte from Haden came, it was aimed not at Jimmy's relatively unassailable position on the art front, but at a far more vulnerable target: Jo. After accepting a routine invitation to dinner, Haden dispatched a haughty letter announcing that of course he could not come if Jimmy's mistress were to be among the company. Propriety, he asserted, made it impossible for him to countenance by his presence the irregular domestic arrangements at Lindsey Row, the implicitly scandalous household *à trois*, etc. etc.

Since Haden had dined several times with the full ménage and had even joined once in painting Jo, it was not hard to trace a connection between his acute attack of virtue and his humiliation over the *Angelus* incident. Things were getting down to bare knuckles.

Jimmy went over the next morning to Sloane Street, where he found Haden sorting etchings in the top floor workroom.

"Ah, good morning, Jimmy. So you've come for a chat."

"An apology, rather."

"Indeed? Excellent. Here, let me have your hat . . . So you've come to your senses at last?"

"As usual, Seymour, you don't understand. I've come to *receive* an apology—not make one."

"Ah, Jimmy, Jimmy . . ." Haden wagged his ponderous head. "Sit down. It's time we had this out, man to man." He reached for his pipe. "Because, like it or not, you're no longer a boy-about-Paris. You're a grown man, accountable for your actions—and their effect on other people. Your loving sister. Your widowed, helpless mother.

"You are, after all, fairly presentable. You have access to people who count. Anyone in such circumstances who keeps his nose to the grindstone can rise swiftly to the top."

"Presenting a ridiculous picture along the way."

Haden ignored the interjection. "With a push or two from the right quarter, you could have prestige, money, even a title within your grasp." He paused weightily. "Now, what does society demand of you in return? Only that you do not publicly lower the standards built up over centuries of progress. Here in England, it's the unspoken rules that hold everything together . . . the things one *doesn't* do . . ."

"Such as?"

"Illicit liaisons . . . romances. Call them what you will, they've destroyed more careers than drink."

"You mean, it's wedded bliss or nothing?"

Haden nodded. "And wedlock only when one can afford to raise children decently."

"Suppose one cannot so afford, or finds marriage otherwise inconvenient? Do you, as a scientist, deny the existence of, ah, pagan impulses? What do you suggest a bachelor do about them?"

"Continence," replied Haden promptly. "It conserves the energy for more constructive purposes, and develops the will power essential to success."

"Continence, indeed?" Jimmy smiled broadly. "I'm told you didn't follow your own prescription during your holiday in Paris. Or was that in the interests of medical research?"

The small eyes of the surgeon narrowed; his lips clamped together. "I'm sure I don't know what you're talking about!"

"Then you have a remarkably poor memory. I don't see how you ever passed your exams at medical college. Think hard, Seymour. Georgette? On the Boulevard Raspaille?"

Haden's fist crashed down on the etching table, scattering his prints. "I see I've been wasting words. You're the same impudent, vicious little guttersnipe I've had on my hands for fifteen years!"

"And you are the same pompous, pretentious hypocrite!"

"I've warned your mother again and again—"

"And I wish I had warned my sister—as my father surely wanted to! That was why you wouldn't wait for his approval, because you knew he would see through you at once! You crept into my family by guile, like a thief in the night!"

"Out! Out! Get out!" In his rage, Haden was on his toes, finger pointed toward the open landing.

"I shall be happy to." Jimmy stood up.

"Go back to your Indian wilderness. You don't belong in a civilized English home!"

Jimmy paused at the top of the stairs. "If you are a specimen of English civilization—God save the Queen!"

By Haden's edict, visits between members of his household and Jimmy's were thereafter barred; his wife could not set foot on any soil where the wicked Jo held sway.

But if Jo was insufficiently pure for Sloane Street, she satisfied perfectly the requirements of Tudor House. Fanny Cornforth, Rossetti's blond mistress, welcomed Jo with cockney heartiness. She had herself been raised in Wapping, and was delighted to have reinforcement from the East End. The sober William Rossetti likewise confessed to being "prepossessed by the person and conversation" of Jimmy's lady. And Dante Gabriel himself was strangely tender with her. From Swinburne, Jimmy learned why: Jo reminded the poet achingly of his lost Liz, who had likewise been tall and pale, sensitive and remote, with striking red-gold hair.

On Jo's first dinner visit, Gabriel took up his customary post-prandial throne in the drawing room, propped up on an open-ended divan with a pillow behind his back. Without warning he raised his voice in passionate declamation:

"I have been here before, but when or how I cannot tell:
I know the grass beyond the door, the sweet keen smell, the
sighing sound, the lines around the shore.

You have been mine before,—
How long ago I may not know:
But just when at swallow's soar
Your neck turned so,
Some veil did fall—I knew it all of yore."

Then he fell silent, and did not speak again all evening. William told Jo the lines were from a poem written to Lizzie at Hastings in the summer of 1854, and never before mentioned since her death.

In the months that followed, Jimmy caught other glimpses of the poet's haunted inner world; beneath the *bizarrerie* was an undertone of wild despair. From Swinburne and William Rossetti, Jimmy gradually pieced together the story of the beautiful wife who had died at twenty-eight under circumstances that placed at least a strong burden of moral guilt on Rossetti.

He had married Liz Siddall, a fragile ex-milliner, in 1860 after a long and tormented relationship that had already passed its peak. Their first child was still-born. That, and the knowledge that he was secretly seeing Fanny Cornforth, threw Liz into a deep depression. One evening after a quarrel early in 1862, Rossetti came home to find her dead. Beside her was an empty phial of laudanum, and thirty-two lines of verse written in a faltering hand:

> Life and night are falling from me,
> Death and day are opening on me.
> Lord, may I come to Thee? . . .
> How is it in the unknown land
> Do the dead wander hand in hand?

Nearly mad with grief, Rossetti placed in the coffin with Liz the gray calfbound volume containing the only manuscript copy of his collected verses, as yet unpublished.

Then he took refuge in Tudor House and the ample charms of Fanny, as coarse and slovenly as Liz had been ethereal. He lay munching strawberries with her in the garden, as if trampling his past idealism along with the grass. He worked long hours by day; took drugs to fight off the ghosts that came by night; and tried to fill the gaps between with a sideshow atmosphere.

For this task, Jimmy indirectly supplied a spectacular recruit. For it was the Whistlerian blue-china wave that washed ashore at Rossetti's one of the most curious, scandalous, and engaging characters of the nineteenth century, Charles Augustus Howell.

Howell's appearance, like everything else about him, was controversial. Some people—usually male—found his good looks extravagant, theatrical, vaguely transcending the bounds of good taste. The large languorous gray eyes, they asserted, in combination with the wavy chestnut locks, smacked of the professional boudoir hound; the long heavy jaw and powerful 6-foot frame belonged in the prize ring. Other observers—mostly female—thought he was "quite the handsomest chimney in London," a reference to the cigarette smoke that poured out of him night and day. One non-admirer insisted he had "the face of a whipped cab-horse"; another objected to the "insinuating purr" of his accent.

For Howell was not a full-blooded Englishman. His mother was Portuguese, which in many quarters made him more suspect than an outright foreigner ("half-caste, you know; never can trust them"). His maternal ancestry was reflected in his full lips and swarthy complexion, and also in a certain air of reckless confidence. Howell claimed direct descendance from Boabdil El Chico, last Moorish King of Granada; and more than one painter transferred his casual arrogance to the canvas in the garb of a lance-tilting knight.

Jimmy first encountered Howell one sunny morning on the sidewalk outside Rossetti's. A hansom cab had just pulled up as Jimmy came out of the house, and the driver was engaged in heated discussion with his passenger. The latter, catching sight of Jimmy, gave a cry of relief.

"I say, old chap, could you give me a hand? Deuced awkward situation. I've come out without any change."

Jimmy looked the man over. He saw clear, intelligent eyes in a youthful arresting face. Was there some note slightly overdone, some tinge of rascality in the square cut of the red velvet jacket, the slimness of the tightly trousered leg? No matter. Jimmy was not fond of cab drivers.

He reached for his wallet. "How much is the fare?"

The cabbie answered. "Six bob."

Jimmy picked out some coins. Before he could turn them over, the passenger reached into Jimmy's wallet and plucked out a pound note. "You don't mind, old chap? Can't send the blighter off without a tip." To the cabbie he said, "I'll take twelve shillings, please."

Mildly stunned, Jimmy waited for his change. But the stranger pocketed the money himself, flashed a debonair smile and disappeared through the gate. "Forgive me for now, old chap," he flung back over his shoulder. "Rossetti is waiting."

That was Jimmy's initiation into the financial world of Charles Augustus Howell.

Three days later, he met his man formally. Howell was in the garden displaying a green China vase to Rossetti, who presented him as London's "foremost authority on Oriental art."

"I would scarcely have recognized you, Mr. Marks," said Jimmy gravely.

"Marks?" Howell smiled indulgently. "For an amateur, he gets his hands on quite good things. Of course, his personal contacts in the cultural sphere have been limited."

"That's true," Jimmy agreed. "Nonentities like Schopenhauer." Rossetti chuckled.

"And who was Schopenhauer?" inquired Howell blandly. "An eccentric German foolish enough to hate women. Need one say more? As my tribesmen in the desert used to put it, 'Maalesh.' "

It developed that Howell, now all of twenty-four, had served as the sheik of a Bedouin tribe in Morocco. He had also, by his own account, been a treasure-diver in his native Portugal, a railroad engineer, a diplomat in Rome, a guerrilla fighter near the Spanish border, an art student, and the proprietor of a curio shop. The astonishing fact was that he seemed exceedingly knowledgeable in all these areas.

Lately he had been employed as secretary, translator, and intellectual handyman to John Ruskin, also distributing largess for the wealthy critic. Now, on the strength of his expertise in rare china, he had extended his operations to the Rossetti camp as a dealer-collector.

Once inside the door, however, it was his resources as a raconteur and inventor of outrageous tales that commanded attention. To Rossetti, hounded by sleeplessness, the insouciant young man with the expressive actor's face and the five-language vocabulary was a modern Scheherezade to be cherished carefully and honored in a limerick:

> "There was a young fellow named Howell
> Who laid on his lies with a trowel.
> When he gives over lying
> It will be when he's dying;
> For living is lying with Howell."

Jimmy and Jo were at Tudor House on the evening Howell turned up late for dinner, breathless and disheveled. His hansom cab, he declared, had been in a collision. The passenger in the other vehicle was a tall, distinguished-looking gentleman with a vaguely familiar air who, upon parting, presented his card. "It read, 'Charles Augustus Howell.' "

Rossetti, a devotee of the occult, was spellbound.

Jimmy provided the newcomer, who had somehow left his tobacco behind, with a cigarette. "Do tell the ladies, Charlie, about the time you were medical adviser to the Empress Eugénie."

"It was not Eugénie," Howell corrected him gently, "it was her cousin, the Marquise de la Chambonette. Her husband, the Marquis, was a fanatical horseman, in the saddle day and night. He even took his meals while mounted on one of his favorite hunters; sometimes, to show off, he would finish his coffee while taking a jump.

"Well, you know, a terrible thing happened. Very subtly, the Marquis began to develop the notion that he himself was a horse. He started kicking at people in the evening. Of course, as long as they were only servants, nobody noticed. Then he wanted hay and oats at dinner. Finally he started to whinny at the most, ah intimate and inappropriate times.

"The Marquise was quite distraught, but I told her we had no choice. I put him quietly out to pasture, with a barn full of hay to sleep in."

"Cool", said Fanny Cornforth. "And what 'appened finally?"

"He broke a leg and we shot him."

One evening Howell invited Jimmy, Rossetti, Luke Ionides, and a few other collectors to dinner to see a choice piece of Nanking imperial ware he had picked up at Hammersmith.

As the party was breaking up, the prankish Rossetti tucked the prize under his cape and carried it home, hiding it in his cavernous hall closet. Then he invited all the guests and a dozen more to a return party for three nights later, intending to show off the elegant temple jar as "the equal of Howell's."

The "wily Portugee," as Jimmy called him, was one step ahead of Rossetti. Correctly deducing what had happened, he stopped by at Tudor House on a fictitious errand, ferreted out his imperial ware, and left another piece in its place. When Rossetti came to the climax of his dinner and unveiled his "surprise," he found himself staring at a wretched, cracked specimen of Delft.

"Look what the spirits have done!" he croaked.

But Oriental art was not only blue pottery from China. It was also, among other things, the woodcuts of the Tokyo masters. Woodblock prints from Japan shattered the conventions of Western art—and transformed Jimmy's universe.

European painting was three-dimensional, concerned with creating an illusion of volume through Rembrandtian modeling of light and shade. A picture was considered successful to the degree that it reproduced nature.

In the Orient, by contrast, painting was an acknowledged artifice, an instrument for the projection of beauty. Nature was mere raw material, to be distilled down to its essence and then reshaped for the most powerful possible statement. The flat surface of the canvas was accepted as a limitation to be utilized, not camouflaged. Oriental art, with its emphasis on pictorial values and interior illumination, exemplified what Jimmy and his caustic friend Edgar Degas had been arguing for in the Paris cafés.

The woodblock prints that reached Paris were of the popular ukiyoye school (literally, pictures of "the floating world" or everyday life), mostly early nineteenth-century landscapes series by Hokusai and

Hiroshige. They specialized in scenes of highway travel, depicting merchants, wrestlers, officials, fishermen, and geisha with superb natural backgrounds in the distance.

The Japanese used bold linear effects, with little concession to "laws" of perspective. Their colors were subtly tinted, enabling combinations —such as blue and green—that in Western hands would clash. And they organized space according to the principle of the Zen Temple rock garden: to achieve tranquillity by the suppression of clutter.

Not all of this was immediately evident to Jimmy. His first reaction to Oriental art, like that of his Impressionist friends, was emotional. The avant-gardists were like a party of children who have inadvertently stumbled on an attic full of exotic delights; for a time they wallowed in the sheer novelty of their discoveries. Manet, Claude Monet, even Degas (who hated fashions) filled their studios with pottery and fans. Jimmy surpassed them all in his collection of kimonos and combs, painted screens, lacquered boxes and cabinets, Oriental willows and bamboo matting. If he ran across something that came from the Far East, he bought it.

And he put his acquisitions into his paintings. Decking out Jo in a floral-patterned pink-and-rose kimono, her hair done up in a top-knot, he posed her amid a forest of plates and vases as an Oriental curio dealer. Lesser models—the Alices and Pamelas of Chelsea—were draped in flowing scarves and perched strumming the koto on softly tinted rugs to become instant Hisaes and Michis.

The little second-story studio bulged with delivery men, costumed girls and curious visitors. From next door, the Greaves brothers were drafted to stretch canvases and improvise Anglo-Japanese bamboo railings.

Out of this whirl of activity there emerged several completed paintings in 1863, notably the *Lange Leizen of the Six Marks*. Named for the long-limbed maidens decorating a particular rare piece of porcelain, this was the portrait of Jo as the lady merchant. Despite its remarkable high-key colors, it suffered from an awkwardness common to all these canvases: the English girls in them were not neutral sticks of wood but living creatures, creating associations of their own that jarred with their Oriental surroundings. Jimmy would have come closer to his revolutionary purpose if he had done something he often dreamed of but never dared attempt: simply set down abstract slabs of related color.

Nonetheless, if only for their oddity, the paintings had buyers: the French dealer Gambard paid £100 for one. Two others were sold to a steel magnate after a successful exercise in Whistlerian ingenuity. Inviting his prospective patron to dinner, Jimmy borrowed the last twelve shillings in Swinburne's purse to buy four bottles of cheap claret. He then took four sticks of sealing wax—blue, green, yellow, and red—and sealed one onto the cork of each bottle.

As the soup course was finished, he beckoned to the maid. "Bring up a bottle, please—the one with the yellow seal." After each course the little ritual was repeated until the fourth bottle—presumably masquerading as a ruby port—was consumed. Whether awed by this epicurean display or otherwise impressed, the guest reached for his checkbook.

Toward the end of 1863, Jimmy had a new sitter. Christine Spartali, daughter of the Greek consul in London, was one of the brunette beauties of the Ionides set. Jimmy painted her as the *Princesse du Pays de la Porcelaine:* a Japanese figure in rose robe and silver-gray kimono, with a white fan in her hand, a blue-and-cream rug at her feet, a painted screen in the background—and a strong Greek face crowned by loose-flowing Mediterranean hair. For all of its tonal splendor, it was a disconcerting mixture of Tokyo's Utamaro with Rossetti.

Christine came for long sittings twice a week. Confident that he was onto a major project, Jimmy served her and her sister the kind of lunches appropriate to the studio of a rising master: pheasant, cold tomato salad (unheard-of among the Greeks), canned apricots (unfamiliar to London)—and champagne.

Such flourishes, along with his costume costs, were expensive; as he remarked to Rossetti, he often found "a long face and a short account" at the bank. But Jimmy wasn't worried. He was immersing himself totally in Oriental art. Where the Impressionist school systematically absorbed Eastern influences, a cobra swallowing a goat, he was content to risk becoming the goat, convinced that out of his experiments would come something valuable.

He was struggling with the outlines of Christine's head, seeking to soften the edges, when the news came from America. It had the suddenness and force of a hurricane at sea, and was scarcely more welcome: his mother was en route to England. For years Debo had been urging Anna Whistler to come to stay in Sloane Street, and Jimmy had politely echoed the suggestion. Now, with the United States wracked by civil war and the tide turning against her beloved South, Anna had decided to take sanctuary. She would, of course, stay where she felt "most needed": with her oldest and closest child.

Jimmy had little time to react. As he explained in a hurried note to Fantin, he had barely a week to find comfortable quarters for Jo, help Legros get settled elsewhere, and cleanse the erstwhile love nest from top to bottom for its new Puritan tenant.

What he did not mention to Fantin, and in fact only dimly admitted to himself, was his sense of foreboding about his mother's arrival. How would his life in London look to Anna Whistler? By her relentless standards, what had he after all achieved at thirty? And what would be the effect on his relationship with Jo?

*Book Two*
# Challenge and Disaster

# Chapter Twelve

The rain dripped steadily through a heavy fog, blurring the steamship dock at Portsmouth. Under the pier shed, Jimmy stood among the soaked, steamy crowd, straining for a glimpse of the passengers coming down the gangplank.

There she was! Smaller and thinner than he remembered her, and just a trifle faltering of step. Now she had a firmer grip on the handrail, and the neat proud head snapped back. She was quite erect as she stepped from the gangplank into his arms.

There were tears and exclamations, and a fumbling of damp embraces. Then Anna Whistler took a pace back and surveyed the son she had not seen in nearly ten years. "You still have your curls, Jemie!"

"Flourishing like the green bay tree."

"Thank the Lord!"

"And the British climate."

Anna took in the silk top hat, the gray frock coat and the gleaming monocle. "You've become quite the man about town, haven't you?" Was there a hint of reproof in her voice?

"I should hope so," Jimmy replied lightly. "But tell me about Willie. Is he still at the front?"

"Where's Debo?" his mother was asking simultaneously. "Does the new baby look like a Whistler?"

They both laughed. "It's going to take a little time to go into all that," said Jimmy. "We'd best look after your luggage, first."

He extended his arm, and they started toward the baggage depot. Suddenly Anna Whistler stopped, frowning.

"Is there something wrong, Mother? What's the matter?"

"About your curls, Jemie. Don't you think you're wearing them a wee bit long?"

For better or worse, his mother was back in his life.

The new regime at Lindsey Row was installed quite smoothly. For several days Jimmy and his mother were busy catching up. Anna described her visit to Willie at Richmond, Virginia, where he was a medical captain with the Army of the Confederacy. Despite his father's long government service, and a maternal grandfather who had moved north to get away from slavery, Anna Whistler's younger son had unhesitatingly opted for the South.

Anna had been troubled by bronchitis, as well as her eyes. Jimmy in turn catalogued *his* recent ailments ("You should walk more in the fresh air, Jemie"), and told of his falling-out with Haden, putting it on the basis of his brother-in-law's busybody tendencies, but not mentioning Jo. Assured that she could see her grandchildren at Sloane Street, Anna took the news calmly enough.

Soon she was preparing fluffy biscuits ("Such a nice, roomy kitchen, Jemie!") and getting the measure of the greengrocers in King's Road. On her first Sunday in London, Jimmy took her to the snug graystone Old Christ Church of Chelsea two blocks away, where Anna sampled the Presbyterian pastor's sermon and pronounced him highly satisfactory: "Small churches have a more evangelical spirit."

Unlike her late husband, Anna did not distrust the British. She would have preferred to make a home for her boys in the United States. But she sent her cronies there glowing accounts of Chelsea's royalty-tinged past. On the whole, she was content.

Not so Jo. From the moment Jimmy spoke of the imminent change in his situation, referring delicately to his mother's "rather strict Puritan notions" and "old-fashioned ways," Jo began retreating into those private depths where pursuit was impossible. For her, no matter how Jimmy couched it, the message was clear: models and mistresses were one breed of mortal; gentlewomen, another. A girl from Wapping might be sported with at Cremorne, cheerfully displayed before semi-pariahs like Rossetti and Swinburne, even defended against the slurs of a Seymour Haden; but she could never be admitted to equality with a mother or sister. Basically, Jo felt, she had little more status than the upstairs maid.

But she kept these sentiments to herself, sensing that Jimmy was uncomfortable enough already. With a minimum of fuss she nodded her understanding and gathered up her things. He had rerented for her the flat they occupied earlier on Queen's Road, a few blocks from Rossetti's.

Three days after his mother's arrival, Jimmy came to her door there. His top hat glistened under the lamplight in the falling snow; masses of rosebuds peeped from the bouquet in his arms. "I've come a-courtin'," he announced.

Jo welcomed him gravely, taking his overcoat. Jimmy looked around.

"Bookcases, fireplace, flowers for the mantelpiece. Everything is exactly as it was."

"Is it?"

Something in her voice made him uneasy, made him rush to declare himself precipitously. "Ah, Jo, it's been an eternity! The house is so empty without you!"

"Should I be sorry for that—or glad?"

"Don't tease me, my darling." He reached out for the warmth of her lips. "I've had a trying few days."

"And do you think I haven't?"

She let herself be kissed, and be pulled toward the bedroom. But when they lay together across the familiar blue woolen spread, the response that had so often quickened his loins was not there. Her embrace was mechanical, reluctant; and the more fiercely Jimmy pressed his protest, the farther Jo withdrew.

"What's wrong, Jo? What's happened?"

"I don't know."

"Have you—don't you—love me any more?"

"Of course."

"Then why—?"

"Maybe that's the reason, Jimmy. I'm afraid I can't go back to being a whore."

"Jo!" The blue eyes filled with tears. "How can you say such a thing?"

"It's easy, when it's true."

Jimmy got up and dressed in silence.

Jo's withdrawal did not extend to her modeling role. As Jimmy resumed his working schedule, she turned up faithfully each morning at Lindsey Row. Jimmy was painting *The Golden Screen*, the most extravagant of his essays in flat silhouette and striking color, a sprawling composition of silk screen, kimono, dappled rug, and assorted Oriental knickknacks. Jo sat very still, sometimes reading, while Jimmy spread his ravishing purples and luscious vermilions across the canvas. They lunched together quietly, on soups and salads brought up by a maid. But there were no after-hours liaisons; Jo left his private life entirely in the hands of Anna Whistler.

They were hands as competent—and as uncompromising—as ever. Anna's avowed purpose was to re-create the orderly household she had enjoyed—and Major Whistler had endured—in St. Petersburg. Prayers, meals, and duties were regulated by the clock. Hospitality "in a rational way" was not discouraged, although it was really much better for Jimmy, she confided in a letter to friends in America, "for him to spend his evenings tête-à-tête with me." His artistic friends, if fascinating, were "visionary and unreal."

The "unreal" friends took the cue. They dropped in to pay their respects, spoke in polite praise of Jimmy's "improved health"—then stayed away. Rossetti made two visits; Howell could not survive Anna's benign disapproval for all of one. The sole exception was Swinburne, whose spectacular helplessness and craving for discipline were perfectly matched to Anna's grim efficiency. He attached himself instantly to Jimmy's mother. He read aloud to her by candlelight, sharp longish nose spun out like a bridge over his retracting chin, from the Bible (her choice) and Walt Whitman (his). Soon he was reciting his own verses, taking care, however, to expurgate the franker passages.

It was a wretched time for Jimmy. He did not enjoy being the exclusive target of a relentlessly pursued missionary campaign. He was annoyed when Anna proudly assured visitors that her son "found God through his paintings"—and then was annoyed with his own intolerance.

Far more acutely, he missed Jo's warm presence in his bed. Anna Whistler's theories notwithstanding, evenings tête-à-tête with a fifty-six-year-old Puritan were no substitute for nights in the embrace of a red-haired young Irish mistress. Seeing Jo every day in the studio did not make things easier.

The first break in the dreary regime came one evening in early spring. Jimmy had descended to dinner in silence, his *Princesse* portrait behind schedule, the day's work ruined by an intermittent fog. Afterward he read aloud to his mother as usual from the *London Times*. There was no comfort in the war news from America: Sherman was carving a fiery path across Georgia.

"That's enough, Jemie." Anna Whistler shook her head. "Ah, if people would only understand. My poor Southland is not fighting for slavery, but only in defense of its homes. Even Algernon has been taken in by this *Uncle Tom's Cabin* nonsense." She raised her eyes heavenward. "Let us pray together, Jemie, that God will bring both North and South to repentance. No true prayer goes unanswered."

The doorbell rang: remarkable speed, Jimmy thought to himself, even for divine intervention. Peering through the curtains, Anna saw a man in uniform.

Ulysses Grant, bearing a peace proposal? Not quite, but a welcome messenger nonetheless. It was the postman bringing a small, carefully wrapped package for Jimmy: the gold medal awarded to him in Holland for etching a year before.

With the medal came a letter from the president of the Academy of Fine Arts, offering "earnest congratulations" to the "newest master of an ancient art."

Jimmy jumped up and down in his thin dancing shoes. "'Master!' Do you hear, Mother?"

It was the tonic he needed, more bracing than his mother's rhubarb-and-iron formula from America.

Two days later came another welcome interruption. Jimmy had remained steadily in touch with Fantin-Latour, confiding the discouragement of his bad days—"everything is so slow, painful, uncertain . . . I rub out so much . . . when will I know more?"—as well as his admiration for the "magnificent" still lifes forwarded by Fantin. He continued to find patrons for his friend's work, at prices that made the Frenchman gasp.

Now Fantin proposed to do a large group portrait in tribute to Delacroix, the great romantic and colorist who had died the year before. Featured would be the painters and poets of the new Realist-Impressionist school who, even though hoping to supplant Delacroix's lush historical narratives, owed him so much for breaking the impersonal mold of classicism. Manet and Baudelaire had agreed to take part; Fantin wanted a few sittings from Jimmy and Legros.

Jimmy rushed his acceptance by return post. He wanted to bring along Swinburne, whom he had introduced to the French poets, and also Rossetti, who had "a superb head." But Swinburne was out of the city and Rossetti protested that he was too busy. Actually, Dante Gabriel had a low opinion of Frenchmen—"a million of them, cast up, will make one Englishman . . . perhaps"—and of Impressionist painting: "beastly slop." So Jimmy simply collared Legros and hastened across the Channel.

He had no cause to regret it. Fantin gave him center-stage on the large canvas, the standard-bearer for the troupe, holding up a bouquet before a bust portrait of Delacroix. Jaunty and erect in a black frock coat, gleaming curls falling to his shoulders, Jimmy made an appealingly boyish contrast with the austere head of the French master. He was flanked by his partners in "The Three," Fantin at an easel behind him and Legros standing above. Manet was on the far right, his reddish-gold hair and blue tie carrying out Fantin's reticent color scheme; Baudelaire sat on the other side, a trace of weary skepticism on his high-domed face. Rounding out the group were Bracquemond, Champfleury, and de Balleroy.

*Hommage à Delacroix,* with its quiet grandeur, was a smashing success at the 1864 Paris Salon. But Jimmy could rejoice in his friend's triumph only from afar. Personal and financial anxieties kept him in London.

Although *Wapping* had at last been submitted to the Royal Academy, prominently hung, and compared in the *Times* with Velázquez, Jimmy had run into a dead end with the *Princesse* portrait. After numerous delays caused as much by his hesitancies as by the illness of the sitter, and heavy costs to Jimmy for costumes, her father had rejected the portrait outright. The Greek consul did not recognize his daughter in this pseudo-Oriental aristocrat, and he did not want the painting—on which he had paid no advance—in his home.

Rossetti was indignant. He would show the picture in his own studio, he declared; he was sure it would find a buyer. Meanwhile: "What the devil has happened to Jo? I haven't seen her in weeks!"

Jimmy eyed him narrowly. He decided Rossetti's ignorance was feigned. "Jo has been, ah, confining herself to quarters."

"From what I've seen of the quarters, that cannot be an unmitigated delight."

"It's what she prefers."

"Well, un-prefer her. I'm having a table-rapping Sunday night, and we need her."

Spiritualism, which held that the material body was merely a temporary dwelling place for a "cosmic reservoir of life-mind," was at its zenith in London. According to the reigning theory, upon physical death the immortal spirit was liberated to one of some forty-nine spheres, there to gambol or suffer its way upward toward perfection. Under proper persuasion a spirit might be induced to return for a chat to earth where, because of its broader outlook, its guidance was invaluable. An astral visitor would signal its presence by rapping on or tilting a table—although some puckish spirits had been known to befuddle believers with false answers.

For Rossetti, steeped in medieval demonology, spiritualism was an ideal distraction. Had not his beloved Liz urged him in her farewell poem to "seek me in the throng of spirits floating past"—and lately spoken to him from beyond the grave in the voice of a chaffinch? Jimmy and Jo too had dabbled in séances. He, devoted to Poe's tales of the supernatural, was far more the pagan mystic than his mother dared imagine; she, raised on Irish folklore, was held by mediums to be a "natural transmitter."

There was no difficulty, therefore, in getting Jo's acquiescence to what was after all a social visit on neutral grounds. She and Jimmy turned up a little after nine o'clock at the summer tent in Rossetti's garden, where Howell, Fanny Cornforth, and a few others were gathered by candlelight around a bare round table. The medium, an enormous black-haired woman hung with dubious pearls, instructed them to spread their hands flat on the table, little fingers touching thumbs to form an unbroken circle.

Then she commanded silence: "We must make a mighty mental effort to breach the unknown." The ladies and gentlemen strained to oblige.

"Spirits of the other world," the medium began in a low throbbing voice. "Merciful spirits. Is there one among you who wishes to communicate?"

Eerie silence, the sound of breathing. Then, slowly, the table began to rock.

"Lizzie!" Rossetti hissed. "Are you out there?"

"Sh!" admonished the medium. "You'll frighten it off!" She turned to Jo. "Miss Heffernan, you have very good emanations. Will you address the spirit?"

"Is it you, Mother?" Jo asked softly. "Do you have a message for me?"

One sharp impatient knock—the signal for negative.

"If it is not for Miss Heffernan, it is for someone extremely close to her," said the medium. She looked at Jimmy. Before he could speak, three rapid knocks sounded: affirmative.

"Gentle spirit," whispered Jimmy cautiously, "are you my father?"

The spirit indicated not. Nor did other queries yield any result, until he mentioned a young cousin from North Carolina. Abruptly the medium's head slumped to the right. Eyes staring, she began to talk rapidly in a boyish treble: "Ah, Jimmy, you were the wicked one, teaching us all to smoke in the woodshed. Uncle Ben is with me here in the Sixth Circle, and don't you think I haven't told him about it. He says—"

The message from Uncle Ben went unrecorded, because the medium suddenly sat upright again. "A spirit has passed close by," she said in her normal voice.

"Right through yer mouth, 'e did," giggled Fanny Cornforth. "And gave poor old Jimmy what for."

Jo reached out a hand to Jimmy, who was trembling slightly. "Donald always was a nasty little tale-bearer," he said, "and immortality seems to have done nothing for his character."

The candles went out. Jo gave a little cry, and Jimmy put a protective arm around her shoulder.

"It's nothing," said the medium. "Pure spite. But he won't be back tonight."

The party trooped back across the lawn to the house, where Howell delivered a lugubrious tale about a country curate and his cat. "The curate's wife was long dead, and his children departed. The only companion of his old age was Roscoe, the cat. They dined together every night; Roscoe had his own plate and bib and chair. He ate whatever the curate did: fish, cheese, a salad if he was in the mood.

"One day the curate received word that the bishop would be passing through town, and would like to sup with him. On the urgent recommendation of his housekeeper, he decided not to set the usual place for Roscoe that evening. So, while the two clergymen discussed philosophy over their Madeira, Roscoe dined alone in the storeroom.

"The next morning, as the housekeeper arrived to light the fire, she was surprised to see a black object streaking out of the curate's room. She went inside and found him lying in his nightclothes, his throat ripped open."

"Coo!", breathed Fanny Cornforth. Her ample chin dropped to her still more ample bosom. "I'll never trust me tabby again!"

That fervent resolve broke the tension. Howell went down to the cellar for some champagne, and with the uncorking of the first bottle the party took an earthier tack. Soon Rossetti and his lady were rolling around the floor in their famous amorous-bear act. Jimmy and Jo were pressed to perform their satiric apache dance, in the course of which Jimmy as the willing but underweight bravo gradually disintegrated until the two, helpless with laughter, collapsed onto Rossetti's couch.

Their host brandished a beer bottle above them. "Look here, Jimmy, it's started to rain. There's an empty suite upstairs—we've sent Sandys out of the country to give him and his creditors a rest. Why don't you and Jo stay the night?"

Jimmy eyed the beer bottle. "Is that an invitation or a threat?"

"Howell," added Rossetti, "swears it is going to storm."

Jimmy looked over at Jo, her ivory cheeks flushed, her breasts heaving. He felt as if his life depended on her answer.

"I would never think," Jo said gravely, "of challenging Mr. Howell's veracity."

Jimmy led her upstairs, where they fell on each other with silent ravenousness. Afterward, they lay staring at the inlaid sixteenth-century ceiling.

"I need you, Jo."

"I need you, too."

"I'm only half-alive without you. You mustn't leave me."

"I never did. I was dismissed."

He drew her to him again, the pliant lips and golden shoulders and radiant hair. "We'll talk about it tomorrow."

It *did* storm that night. But Jimmy and Jo never noticed.


Thereafter the barriers were dropped at Queen's Road, but Jimmy still longed for the old, full intimacy. The opportunity came in autumn. A few months earlier his mother had been away to visit an oculist in Coblenz. Now, as the fogs came tumbling in, she spoke of finding sunshine at the seashore. Jimmy quickly suggested Torquay, a sheltered resort on the Devonshire coast two hundred miles to the southwest. She could stay through the winter untouched by the raw wind from the Thames, and there would even be a few scraggly palms within view from her hotel window.

Anna packed her bags, and on a quiet Sunday afternoon Jimmy took her to Waterloo Station. An hour later Jo was reinstalled as mistress of 7 Lindsey Row.

The moment she crossed the threshold, she slid shut the front door panel that told visitors to come another day. Then she tossed her Paris bonnet on the hat rack, shook loose her long red hair, and ran through the house singing, flinging open windows . . .

With Jo by his side night and day, Jimmy returned to an easier rhythm of living and working. The inhibitions and obligations of life with Anna Whistler fell away. He awoke refreshed at dawn, and was able to stay at his easel until long after shadows engulfed the lime tree beneath his studio window.

Returning one evening from a walk along the river with Rossetti, Jimmy found Jo standing before the burned-out fire in the drawing room, gazing dreamily into the mirror above the mantelpiece. She wore a white nightdress, and held a book in her hand.

Within minutes—it seemed to Jo seconds—he had his composition. Girl in three-quarter profile, red hair flowing, facing her mirror image to the viewer's right, just above her left arm stretched out along the mantelpiece. In her right hand the book—no, not a book but a Japanese fan. In the upper right, at the tip of the outstretched fingers, a slender Oriental vase . . . balanced in the lower right corner by a few sprigs of azaleas. The whole effect pleasantly asymmetrical, with intersecting verticals and horizontals formed by segments of the mantelpiece, fireplace, and mirror frame.

The colors took more planning. White again would be his keynote, contrasted with the flaming-copper hair and lightly flushed skin tones that were Jo's particular glory. But for the rest, parsimony. He would not repeat the restless clutter of shape and hue that overran the *Golden Screen;* at long last he would dominate his Japanisms, not be swamped by them. A few muted tones were all he needed, supporting the basic color scheme: blue and white for the porcelain, an echoing red in the mirror frame, splashes of pink and purple in the flowers for an unobtrusive decorative touch.

Jo responded enthusiastically to the new approach, throwing in a helpful suggestion for integrating the fan. She showed her usual patience while Jimmy fretted over the drawing of the hands, impossible to sidestep in this instance because of their prominence in the composition. And she rejoiced with him over the perfect rendering of the mirrored flesh tones—a technical problem, Jimmy asserted, that would have "given Degas a nightmare."

As with the first *White Girl,* they were more partners than artist and model; the closeness in the studio carried over to the bedroom, and then back. Jimmy became unwilling to let her out of his sight. One Sunday at breakfast when she proposed a visit to her sister, he demurred: "You're my good luck."

"That's interesting," said Jo. "According to the Irish, red-haired girls are supposed to be *bad* luck. If a fisherman sees one on his way to the beach, he'll turn back and go to bed."

"A very ingenious arrangement for a lazy man," said Jimmy, "but what if he's already got a redhead *in* bed?"

"In that case," Jo laughed happily, "I've run out of Irish sayings."

Later that morning he heard her singing in the kitchen, a mournful-lilting folk tune he hadn't heard before:

> "As young Rory and Moreen were talking
> How Shrove Tuesday was just drawing near
> For the tenth time he asked her to marry,
> But says she, 'Time enough till next year.'
> 'Then ochone I'm going to Skellig:
> O Moreen what will I do?
> 'Tis the woeful road to travel;
> And how lonesome I'll be without you.'"

Jimmy came into the kitchen. "What on earth is Skellig?"

Jo seemed embarrassed. "Oh—just some more Irish nonsense."

"But what does it mean?"

Reluctantly, Jo explained. It was the custom in the Irish country-side, since weddings were banned during the forty days of Lent, to march to the altar en masse in the few days preceding Ash Wednesday. Those unfortunates who were passed over in the choosing made an annual pilgrimage to the monastery ruins at Great Skellig Rock off the Kerry Coast.

Jimmy, always hazy about the calendar, realized they were well into February. He asked no more questions.

Except of himself. Marriage? To a queenly redhead who saw the world through the same multicolored lenses, with whom there was no necessity to explain every sigh, justify every frown . . . whose very presence melted away his sense of isolation?

Marriage to the daughter of a drunken tugboat captain, an untutored Irish Romanist from the docks? What would people say in the Carolina mansions of the McNeills—and the Mayfair salons where artistic destinies were decided?

Did he dare inflict still another disappointment on his widowed mother—and invite another reproof?

He thrust the idea aside.

*The Little White Girl* was settling into shape, under a brush made freer by Jimmy's Japanese experiments. His paint was thinner than ever before, mere streaks as against the massive layers of Courbet.

Others had made good use of the Japanese example: Manet in cutting down the degree of third-dimensional illusion, Degas in spatial composition and the poses of Utamaro's women. But it remained for Jimmy to penetrate Oriental color harmony, blending it in *The Little White Girl* with a Rossetti-like poignancy. He had captured the inner poetry of his subject, imprisoned forever the transient dream.

It was this last quality that seized Swinburne when Jimmy invited him to the studio late in March. Poet and painter had been spending a good deal of time together, partly because their mutual friend Rossetti rarely stirred beyond his own doorstep. There had been theater evenings, a trip to Epsom Downs for the Derby races, and a memorable January afternoon when Jimmy displayed some of his early work.

Surrounded by drawings, etchings, and oils, Swinburne had breathed his admiration. "I don't see how you can bear parting with any of these things."

"I can't, really."

"I know when I finish a poem, I tremble at the thought of sending it out into the harsh world. It's like a child, and something more."

"Exactly," Jimmy agreed. "You're afraid it may not be loved."

"How much more terrible it must be in the case of a painting—the only one of its kind—when you see it pass into alien hands, perhaps to be stupidly hung, or left neglected in a corner." The bright green eyes shone with compassion.

"You understand perfectly," said Jimmy.

The next morning, *La Mère Gérard* was delivered to Swinburne at Tudor House with a graceful little note. Thenceforth Jimmy became the "Cher Père" of Swinburne's confidences.

Now the poet stood before the new painting of Jo, wagging his large head in silence. Jimmy looked on in dismay. "You don't like it."

Swinburne did not answer at once. "On the contrary," he said finally. "I—I cannot tell you what I feel. But perhaps I can write it."

Two days later Jimmy found a poem in his mailbox:

> Come snow, come wind or thunder
> High up in air,
> I watch my face, and wonder
> At my bright hair . . .
> I cannot see what pleasures
> Or what pains were;
> What pale new loves and treasures
> New years will bear;
> What beam will fall, what shower,
> What grief or joy for dower;
> But one thing knows the flower; the flower is fair.

There were four more stanzas of seven lines each, accompanied by an apologetic note from Swinburne saying he would try again if Jimmy found the words unsuitable for catalogue printing.

The verses led to a curious argument. Jimmy promptly pronounced them superior to his painting. Swinburne indignantly dissented; his poem, he wrote to John Ruskin, was not "so complete in beauty, in tenderness and significance, in exquisite execution and delicate strength as Whistler's picture. I stood up against him for himself, and will, of course, against all others."

Jimmy appealed to Rossetti: "What do you think, Gabriel?"

"I think you had best leave such judgments to the imbecile-geniuses of journalism, and both go back to work!"

The painting was accepted for the 1865 Royal Academy, with two of Swinburne's stanzas reproduced in the catalogue. The verses, printed on gold paper, were also pasted to the picture frame.

But just before the opening, the idyll with Jo came to an abrupt end. Anna Whistler had had enough of Torquay.

The timing of her return to Lindsey Row did not make things easier. Jimmy was tense over the upcoming exhibition; it was all very well to rail at the Academy and expose its tinsel gods, but there was really no other artistic showplace in London.

He supposed his mother's return would mean Queen's Road again for Jo. "Yes, it is a nuisance—but, well, after all, my dearest, what else can we do?"

She stared at him for a long moment, her face suddenly grown older. "If you don't know, Jimmy—then I can't tell you."

Once again, critical reaction gave Jimmy a jolt. The world was not standing on tiptoe, looking eagerly for the new idea, listening with excitement for the fresh voice. The only applause came from the direction of Tudor House, where William Rossetti reported for the *Saturday Review* that Jimmy's "exquisite" portrait successfully met the challenge of *Esther* by Millais in the same exhibition, "retorting delicious harmony for daring force."

The Rossetti smile floated alone in a sea of scowls. The *Atheneum* scolded Jimmy for transforming his helpless model into "the most bizarre of bipeds." Another weekly, complaining of unorthodox chiaroscuro and dim flesh tones, dismissed the American as "half a great artist." Even French opinion, so ecstatic in discovering him two years before at the Salon des Refusés, was summed up in the guillotine slash of the *Gazette des Beaux Arts:* "A weak, tiresome repetition. The Academy judges might have rejected Mr. Whistler. It was clever of them to show his work instead and deliver it to judgment."

That was the start of a bad cycle. The elder Rossetti had persuaded

James Leathart, who had the best Pre-Raphaelite collection in England, that he ought to own Jimmy's *Princesse* portrait; now Dante Gabriel advised that after the spate of hostile notices, Leathart was balking at the bold lettering of the painter's name in the upper left corner. Jimmy declined to become anonymous.

To compound his irritation, the once-sturdy Legros was becoming obligingly commercial, depicting a fat Anglo-Greek merchant in the flattering guise of an Athenian patriarch. Jimmy turned in disgust to Albert Moore, who thumbed his nose impartially at princes of the marketplace, the cloth, or the blood. What did Jo think of the idea of his doing an intimate studio scene, showing her, Moore, and himself?

Jo was non-committal. No longer his eager partner, she did what she was asked to do, and no more. Jimmy dropped the plan. And after one visit to Queen's Road—tense, quarrelsome, and abortive—he stayed away.

Now a new worry assailed him: What if Jo were to take up with someone else? The Irish were notorious extremists, fanatically faithful or uncontrollably wild. And Jo was a strong-willed, impulsive girl who had never been at a loss for admirers.

This fear gained impetus in the summer when Anna Whistler scheduled another medical visit to Germany. Jimmy pointed out to Jo that there would be ample room again in Lindsey House.

"I'm a woman, Jimmy—not a stick of furniture!"

It was Jimmy's turn to sulk. Surely Jo should realize his predicament. He had obligations on both sides. An artist fighting for recognition could afford only one total commitment: to his work.

And yet he needed her desperately. He had become overattached, he told himself, allowed her to slip inside his armor, confused a sporadic physical and emotional need with romantic idealization. That was a mistake: look at poor Dante Gabriel and his unhappy Liz. How had he ever let himself fall into such a trap?

Frustrated sexually and artistically, pursued by guilt and even more by his sense of helplessness, Jimmy was ripe for a fall from grace. The opportunity came in an evening at Albert Moore's studio. Moore's Cardiff-born mistress had brought along a Welsh friend who danced in a Soho cabaret. Gwen was pert, pleasantly rounded—and instantly smitten with the debonair American. Jimmy accepted the invitation to see her home, and spent the night with her.

The adventure was briefly soothing to his bruised ego, but it resolved nothing.

Once again it was Rossetti who made at least temporary repairs. Shrewd and intuitive, he saw how things were going with his friend. Such details as he could not surmise were filled in for him by Fanny Cornforth, who had become Jo's confidante. With Fanny's connivance, he arranged for Jo to stop by at Tudor House on an evening when he knew Jimmy would be there.

Over strawberries and cream in the garden, he confronted the discordant lovers. "You two look like a couple of specters out of Poe," he growled. "And you're behaving more childishly than Swinburne. What you need is a holiday."

"In a sense we're having a holiday," said Jimmy mildly. "That's the problem."

"I don't mean *from* each other. Together. Don't you know some Yankees with a pile of tin and a villa in Nice? Or a grandee with a cosy castle in Spain?"

Jimmy shook his head. "There's Trouville, of course. But that wouldn't be a holiday. Courbet and Manet want me to join them doing seascapes."

"Trouville! But that's perfect! Sunshine, sea air, a casino!"

Fanny leaned her blond head into Jo's face. "Rizzetti knows best, dearie. 'Ow soon can you leave?"

"Jimmy hasn't said he's going yet. Or that he wants me."

"Wants you!", exploded Rossetti. "Good God, woman—just look at his face!"

Dante Gabriel stood up and started toward the terrace steps, reciting softly. His words floated back into the garden:

> "A little while a little love
> May yet be ours who have not said
> The word it makes our eyes afraid
> To know that each is thinking of.
> Not yet the end: be our lips dumb
> In smiles a little season yet:
> I'll tell thee, when the end is come,
> How we may best forget."

"Faster, Jimmy, faster! Half the afternoon is gone, and you're still on the same canvas!"

Jimmy, fussing to adjust the legs of his easel in the sand, glanced over at Gustave Courbet, a bit fuller in the paunch and cheek but merry-eyed as ever. Before Courbet's campstool a gray and green seascape had sprung startlingly to life, thickly textured, charged with rugged authority. It was at least his tenth canvas since their arrival a week before at Trouville. How did the man do it? Jimmy shook his head, scowling. "You're not a painter, Courbet. You're an acrobat."

"Not 'crobat—*Courbet!*" The Master of Ornans roared his laughter, delighted with his appalling pun. He winked at Jimmy. "If I had your model, I would do twenty canvases a day!"

Jimmy twitched his mustache skeptically. If you had my model, he thought, you would paint zero canvases. You would spend all your time trying to get her into bed with you.

Courbet, who made no secret of his taste for heartily proportioned girls, had soon after their arrival done two oils of Jo. Strong, earthy, with the juicy-pear flesh of his peasant women, they were a far cry from Jimmy's ethereal *White Girl* studies.

Jo did no other modeling at Trouville. For most of the day she and Jimmy reveled in the crisp, tingling air and the mild surf that drew thousands to the resort below Le Havre on the Normandie coast. For 50 francs a month—the equivalent of ten American dollars—they had a large room in a villa on Rue Carnot behind the casino. A short walk through an alleyway flanked by tent-shops led to the beach.

They swam together every morning, Jo scorning the horse-drawn "bathing machines" available for lady-like immersion. Usually Courbet joined them in the water, playful as a porpoise. Then the trio breakfasted on fresh-caught shrimp and country butter under the striped awnings of the casino terrace.

Afterward, Jimmy and Jo strolled along the shore. Trouville, with its broad quiet beach and streaky gray skies, had been a fishing village when it was discovered by painters in 1825. A decade later Alexandre Dumas came there to work, followed by Alphonse Daudet, Flaubert, and then a sprinkling of minor aristocracy who promptly lined the waterfront with an eruption of outlandish summer homes. Norman spires popped up into the sky, surrounded by a farrago of Turkish domes, Chinese pagodas, and Roman arches.

As Jimmy remarked to Jo, "If there's anything left out of the house you're looking at, you're sure to find it in the one next door."

"But the effect is rather charming," Jo protested. "Like *Grimm's Fairy Tales.*"

"So long as you don't confuse it with architecture."

The walk was followed by a cutlet-and-fruit lunch at the casino, pronounced by Courbet "much too good for the leisure classes." Then Jo went back for a nap, and the two painters got out their canvases.

Jimmy was at an impasse aesthetically, his confidence shaken by the failure of *The Little White Girl.* He was glad enough to have the sea, with the relative freedom of its large masses and broken lines, as a subject.

He found Courbet's ebullience a little unsettling. The Frenchman, who in explanation of the black ground used in his landscapes once remarked "Like God, I draw light out of darkness," plunged directly into color after the briefest of sketches, gurgling, whistling, keeping up a running fire of chatter: "Nature is before you, Jimmy, asking only to be captured, taken—like a woman! The rest is technique—for example, so!" He smoothed a lump of paint with his thumb, and it became the prow of a boat.

Courbet still regarded "the Englishman Whistler" as "my pupil," an illusion not shared by Jimmy. No longer a wide-eyed student in his twenties, Jimmy continued to admire the courage and elan of the older man, and the painterly eloquence of Courbet's palette knife, which could reproduce the very shape of an onrushing wave. But he was increasingly mistrustful of rapid-fire realism as an approach for himself. And he was aware that the exercise of influence had become reciprocal: the crashing breakers now appearing in Courbet's seascapes had not been there before Jimmy's *Blue Wave* of Biarritz was put on display at the Boulevard des Batignolles.

Courbet was openly contentious about Jimmy's treatment of the horizon. Both men were preoccupied with creating a sense of space. But where Courbet kept his picture plane far back, creating his light through cloud formations spread across a low horizon, Jimmy brought the picture plane forward in the Japanese manner. Figures and boats in the foreground were given more importance, and the horizon raised to become no more than an embellishing background.

One afternoon as Courbet was gazing out to sea, Jimmy persuaded him to hold the pose. Three days later he showed his colleague the *Harmony in Blue and Silver:* the imposing bulk of Courbet suggested in three short, firm strokes at the lower left, and the eye then being led diagonally upward past a floating log, a fishing boat and finally to a lonely sail in the upper right corner. The colors—whitish sand shading into blue-gray water and silver-black sky—were as delicate as anything Jimmy had done; the receding planes had infinite depth, a hint of mystery. The horizon was indisputably low—and indisputably perfect. There were no more genial lectures.

After sundown, Trouville was pleasure unalloyed. The evenings were given over to Jo, and she filled them with a music and laughter neither man would ever forget. She had Irish hanging dirges to stir Courbet's revolutionary ardor; broad rustic comedy like *Paddy Heggarty's Breeches,* in which an innkeeper broiled a pair of leather pants to appease a hungry mob; and rollicking Rabelaisian airs:

> "Oh there was a young lady from Grosvenor Square
> Who said that her clock was in need of repair;
> In walks a young German and to her delight
> In less than five minutes he had her put right."

Reserved for the late-night hours alone with Jimmy were the sentimental ballads she cherished most, and had sung only sparingly before. New treasures tumbled forth, as if answering a last-call-before-curtain-time.

As the days passed, a gravity settled over the two, a tender savoring of each passing moment. Nothing was said of Anna Whistler, but her presence in London hung over them like a cloud, urging them back to the city—and by the very urging, impelling them to stay. The future was closing in. Neither knew what waited at the end of the holiday, but it would not be as good as this.

Through more than one long, moon-soaked night, Jimmy lay sleepless at Jo's side, listening to the wash of the tide and brooding on the two women who shared—and refused to share—his life: Jo queenly, spirited, not yet thirty; Anna tiny, indomitable, twice his sweetheart's age. In their strength and faithfulness, the major's lady and the barge captain's daughter were a good deal alike; by the whim of fortune, they were implacably opposed. He could not satisfy his mother except by hurting Jo; he could not please Jo without offending, if not repudiating, his mother.

Late in October, Jimmy spoke vaguely of getting back to the city. Two weeks later he mentioned the matter again. With November disappearing from the calendar, they reluctantly packed their bags and met Courbet at the casino for a farewell dinner. All three laughed a good deal, and drank far more than was necessary, and finally—each for his or her own reasons—wept.

# Chapter Thirteen

Jimmy returned to a London suddenly quivering with the aftermath of the American Civil War. The previous spring of 1865 had seen the surrender of Robert E. Lee at Appomattox. In the months that followed, uprooted officers of the Confederacy flocked to England, where their cause had generally been viewed with sympathy, to hunt up old friends, seek new careers, or simply take refuge over a friendly pot of ale.

Among the exiles was Dr. Willie Whistler, grown taller, plumper—and, astonishingly, acknowledged as a hero of heroes. The once-timid younger brother who in Russia begged Jimmy to fight his schoolboy battles had cut a very different figure on the Virginia front. Going into the field with the famous Orr's Rifles, a South Carolina regiment, Willie manned a surgical tent alone for weeks, then gave up his horse to a wounded infantryman and took the man's place in the line. Later he made a spectacular courier run through the Union lines to New York, dodging sentries, shifting disguises, hiding in river shacks and burned-out barns.

The soldierly family name had lost no luster in the War between the States. But it was the younger son of Major George Washington Whistler, not the West Pointer, who won distinction under Robert E. Lee. What had been expected of Jimmy had been delivered by Willie, the mild McNeill.

That fact was lost on no one, least of all Jimmy. Mingled with his pride in introducing Willie around London was a certain disquiet. He was particularly uncomfortable among the keen-eyed young Southern veterans, with their noisy chatter of raising an expeditionary force "to oppose tyranny everywhere." Nobody ever asked, of course, but why had James Whistler been sitting out the war in England while his brother faced shellfire?

Jimmy was still wrestling with that issue when his mother presented him with another one. For what reason, she inquired suddenly one evening after dinner, had he lingered so long in Trouville, nearly till Christmas?

Jimmy looked up, puzzled. "But surely you know, Mother. I had work to do."

Anna Whistler carefully marked her place, and closed her Bible. "What sort of work, Jimmy? Yours—or the devil's?" She fixed her eyes on him with a solemnity that was unmistakable.

A stabbing pain shot through his abdomen. Undoubtedly his mother had long been aware of his liaison with Jo. But the subject had never been mentioned between them; by tacit agreement, a moat stretched between Jimmy's private life and their household world. Now Anna Whistler was dropping the drawbridge to send her troops across.

Again he felt his stomach tighten. He would have to be careful of his words. "I gather"—his attempted lightness was marred by a slight tremor—"you've been talking to our friend Seymour Haden."

"He *is* your friend, Jemie. Far more than many who pretend to be. But I've been taking counsel with others as well. Your sister. The widow Whitcomb next door. Parson Fuller at the church."

"A truly learned crew," murmured Jimmy. "Except for Debo."

This conversation was going to end in a terrible explosion. He could sense it, like the distant rumble of an approaching train; but, as with the train, he felt powerless to head it off.

"Believe me, my dearest Jemie, I speak with the greatest reluctance. I have no wish to arouse your anger—and still less to cause you pain. Until this moment I have stayed scrupulously aloof from your private affairs. But as a conscientious mother, I now have no choice. Silence gives consent; and I cannot consent to what I see."

"And what is it exactly that you see?"

Anna Whistler rose to her feet, tiny but regal in her wrath: "My eldest son wilfully destroying his reputation as a gentleman and his future as an artist, to indulge a weakness of the flesh!"    .

"Rubbish!" Jimmy cried.

"Is it? Let me read you something from last month's issue of *Mayfair*. I dare say it may have escaped your attention in Trouville." She picked up a clipping from the curved table beside her armchair and bent over to get the lamplight.

"Here, don't go straining your eyes!" He got up impatiently to take the paper from her. "I'll read it."

"No," his mother insisted. "This time it's I who must read to you." She continued from the clipping in halting but emphatic tones: " 'Unlike the Continent or America, the distinguishing mark of good society here is a respect for moral' "—she squinted hard—" 'moral character. No degree of rank, wealth *or celebrity*' "—she looked up at Jimmy significantly—" 'will induce a well-bred English lady to admit a man or woman of *questionable character* to her drawing room . . .' "

"What pious hypocrisy!" snorted Jimmy, resuming his seat.

"Wait, there is more. 'Society is pitiless. Once fallen, no matter how sincere and complete the repentance, the sinner finds the door shut on him or her forever.' "

She put down the clipping and faced her son again. "There it is, Jemie. The code the British live by."

"Not quite. The code they ask others to live by."

"However you put it, you are a guest here. Your behavior reflects on all Americans abroad. You have among other things an obligation to your countrymen."

"My first obligation is to myself!" He heard his voice rising. "I am not going to conduct my personal life to suit every prig in London! You would prefer that I give no offense to anyone. The only way I can do that is to roll over and die. That, no doubt, is what many of my so-called 'well-wishers' may well wish; but I do not intend to accommodate them!"

"And will you do nothing to accommodate your mother? 'A tree is known by its fruit,' Jemie. For months I have endured the humiliation of an illicit attachment going on under my eyes, of sudden whispers and averted glances. Night after night I have prayed that the Lord should come to you, and bring you the light. 'Blessed is the man that endureth temptation; for when he is tried, he shall receive the crown of life.' What, after all, does a widowed mother have to look forward to, but the successes of her sons?"

Oh Christ, thought Jimmy, don't let her raise that old refrain about good-boy-Willie.

It was a hopeless supplication. Anna Whistler charged on relentlessly. "My younger boy, with the help of God, has found an honorable profession. He has carried forward his father's memory as a defender of the right. But of you, Jemie, what can I say? Talent thrown to the winds. Fits of hard work, mingled with idleness and dissipation. The butterfly has a short life, Jemie—and an unproductive one."

Out of long habit, Jimmy found himself apologizing. "I *am* working, Mother, really. You don't understand how difficult it is to develop one's own style, to fight against prejudice and ignorance—"

"I understand very well where you have been turning for solace. The convenient evenings overnight at Mr. Rossetti's. The extended stay in France. And the open scandal last year when I was away in Germany, and you actually had a strange woman living with you in this house of ours, within these very walls! 'Honor Thy Father and Mother,' indeed!"

Something turned over violently in Jimmy's mind. "What about some honor and respect for the rights of children?" He was on his feet now, blue eyes blazing, a Whistler in counterattack.

His mother fell back a pace. "You're shouting at me, Jemie."

"Forgive me. I mean no disrespect. But I am no longer a little boy, Mother. I have put away my childish things. I'll take you to church and respect your ways where I can, but I won't be told where to go and how to stand and whom to see. At thirty-one I will not submit again to the nightmare of my childhood!"

"Nightmare!" The thin lips pressed tight. "You had every benefit of a good Christian home."

"And every torment."

"Were you denied good food, loving care, guidance?"

"I was denied nothing—except what I wanted most: the right to grow in my own way, make my own mistakes. Always it was your standards, your ideas . . ."

"Were they imposed selfishly? For my gain?"

"No, no." Jimmy shook his head impatiently. "You did what you thought was right—because it was right for you. It never occurred to you that it might not be right for me."

"It is a mother's duty to show the way. I placed you on the path of the Lord."

"You offered theology, a throne in the next world, to a child who needed affection in this one! Every time I obeyed an impulse, I lived in terror of your disapproval. I felt condemned, useless . . ."

Anna's face was going gray. "Why didn't you speak up, then?"

"How could I? I was afraid I'd be thrown out completely!"

"Oh, Jemie, Jemie!" Anna came forward slowly, extending her arms. "And I thought you were my *strong* boy. I would never willingly give you pain."

Jimmy returned her embrace. "Nor I you, Mother."

"You were my first-born, the center of my hopes. I wanted only to make you the man your father was, build your character, protect you from tendencies in yourself. I acted in your interest, just as I do today."

Jimmy drew back slightly. His mother clung to his arm. "We are not always able to see what is best for us. People can be blinded by emotion, by despair—especially if they have strayed from the true church. And you have the artistic temperament, Jemie. Sensitive, impulsive. You must admit you can be easily influenced. Especially by the opposite sex."

"If that is so, you've had a hand in it."

"I?" Anna Whistler was astonished. "I pointed out the true path, the straight and narrow!"

"Children can't be driven down a path like oxen," her son said impatiently. "A child is a creature of nature, like—like a flower. It needs air and sunshine and warmth, not doctrine!"

"You speak like a pagan!"

Jimmy shrugged. "The Greeks produced magnificent works. So did the Japanese. Life has too much mystery to be encased in a single dogma."

"So we should make room for Papists as well?"

Jimmy did not respond to the thrust. Mother and son stared at each other in silence.

Anna Whistler took a new tack. "If I have been such a complete failure as a mother—"

"I never said that."

"—how do you explain Willie's fine record?"

"What works for one person can be hell for another."

"Jemie!"

"Forgive my language." He bowed coldly.

"It is the sentiment that gives offense. You hate me. My own son." Anna turned away, lowering her head.

Jimmy came after her and took her hand. "I don't hate you," he said urgently. "I can't, I never will. The problem is loving you. Why else do you suppose all this anguish?"

"You hate me," she repeated dully. "I can no longer stay under this roof."

Jimmy forced back the tears. "I'm sorry, Mother. I didn't invite this. But now that it's happened, it's I who will go."

He left abruptly, clattering down the stairs. A moment later the door slammed, and Jimmy was out on the street.

It was a damp, murky night, warm for midwinter; puddles awaited the unwary pedestrian except along the patches of paved sidewalk. Jimmy's quick, clipped stride took him to the corner, and then northward toward King's Road. A plan was forming in his mind, a plan that he felt would have had the blessings of George Washington Whistler. He would be no man's lackey—and no woman's, either.

At King's Road, he hailed a hansom. He headed for the Stag and Horn, a Soho pub adopted as an informal headquarters by the footloose Southerners. There he sought out Captain Roger Hall, an elegant, erect young Atlantan who had attended the Virginia Military Institute and had shown marked respect for Jimmy's West Point background.

"I say, Hall . . ."

The Georgian turned from the bar. "Mr. Whistler! How nice to see you. So you've come to hoist a glass with us?"

"Or perhaps a sail."

"Indeed?" The captain's yellow-green eyes sparkled. "Let me stand you a brandy and soda."

"Thank you . . ." Jimmy sipped at his drink. "There was some talk last week of forming up an expeditionary force and departing for parts unknown."

"Not unknown. Just unstated."

"Have those plans become any more definite?"

"As definite as a bullet through a man's chest."

"You express yourself vividly, Captain."

Hall smiled. "We are in the process of organizing a reinforced company for service in . . ." He dropped his voice. "Chile."

The Spanish government, he explained, had two years earlier seized the Chincha Islands of Peru in support of indemnity claims filed by absentee landlords living in Madrid. The Chileans, acting in the spirit of the great Latin American liberator Simon Bolivar, had gallantly gone to the aid of their northern neighbors. As a result, the Spaniards had turned their wrath against Chile, threatening the key seaport of Valparaiso.

"And the Chileans have appealed to you for aid?"

"Nothing as primitive as that, my dear Mr. Whistler. There are in Europe certain interests with, shall we say, a limited affection for the Spanish royal family and crowned heads generally. Dissidents; or, to honor them with a better word, *rebels*. Negotiations are in progress regarding ship's passage, equipment, command structure—and, of course, reimbursement. We are fond of underdogs—but gentlemen do not live by platitudes alone."

"Can you use another officer?"

"That depends. Do you know him well?"

"Exceedingly."

"And do you vouch for him?"

"On the whole, yes. I am speaking of myself."

The young officer pulled back. "I did not think you were serious, sir!"

Jimmy raised his monocle. "I am rarely 'serious.' But I mean what I say!"

The Southern group would be glad to take aboard a West Pointer, and one from a Carolina plantation family at that, Hall assured him. It would probably be some weeks before the actual sailing—"but I dare say you'll need the time to put your affairs in order."

"You mean, arrange to store my paintings and all that?"

Hall looked at him soberly. "I should prepare for *all* contingencies, Mr. Whistler. They tell me the Spaniards are better shots than our Northern cousins."

He could be killed; that was one of the disagreeable things about war. As ever, he was fascinated by its trappings but abhorred its substance. In the late '50s, when Britons were growing nervous about

Louis Napoleon's intentions, Jimmy had made a brief show of joining the volunteer "Artists' Corps," turning up at the end of drills just in time to shriek his mockery of Rossetti (who always marched left on "Squads right!") and the nobly proportioned Leighton, whose idea of combat gear was twenty pounds of braids, epaulets and buckles.

Well, if he stopped a Spanish bullet his family would have just what they wanted, glory enough to trail the Whistler name through the clouds of eternity. A soldier's death on exotic shores would be the very peak of respectability, more than compensation for all his scapegrace sins. Ah, what a lovely thing his mother's preacher, Parson Fuller, could make of it!

Meanwhile, there were more mundane matters to set straight: paintings unfinished, commissions hanging in midair, bills to be collected and paid. He went to Rossetti's for the night, arranged in the morning for his personal belongings to be sent there, and spent the next two weeks with Anderson Rose, a lawyer friend of Dante Gabriel's, going over his affairs.

His basic decision was already taken: everything he had would go to Jo. A one-page will on pale blue paper, naming Dante Gabriel and Rose as his executors, affirmed Jo's absolute status as sole heir to his estate. Meanwhile, except for some etchings whose sale was entrusted to Rose, she would exercise total control of his property in his absence. A separate power of attorney authorized her to invest Jimmy's money or dispose of his works as she saw fit; a letter to the manager of the Bank of England specified she could sign checks, borrow against Jimmy's account, and represent him in any business dealings.

When Andy Rose raised the question of a provision for Anna Whistler, Jimmy sat in silence for a moment. Then, after a deep breath: "Mrs. Whistler has a small income, as well as an exceedingly wealthy son-in-law with a large house and a pious tongue. She will be more comfortable there than I could possibly make her—and also more at home."

He did not see his mother again before sailing, and had time only for brief visits with Jo; the Southerners had drafted him for their planning staff. Early in February of 1866 he embarked from Southampton with an advance party of officers, aboard a slow steamer bound for Panama. There—barring piracy, accidents, or bad weather—they would cross overland to the Pacific and pick up a South American coastal vessel down to Valparaiso.

The outward voyage was bleak. Later, Jimmy would transmute it into a golden tale of adventure; but the reality was a blur of heavy seas, leaden skies, dull table fare, and duller company. Jimmy's companions displayed little interest in anything but bourbon whisky or poker. He began to wonder what he, an artist, was doing on this strange journey.

Daybreak at sea, gray and mysterious, reminded him of Trouville and Biarritz and Jo; after a while, so did nearly everything. The trip itself gradually took on a trance-like, unreal quality, as of a dream where he was only half-present.

The dream exploded into unpleasant reality on arrival at the Isthmus. The neck of land stretching between Atlantic and Pacific was narrow, but every inch was impassable jungle or rugged mountain. Roads were few, and the March rains plentiful. Earthquakes periodically rumbled across the forbidding landscape.

The warriors were much relieved to transfer from muleback to ship's deck again at Panama City. As the southward trip toward the long sliver of Chile began, Jimmy stirred to life. Santiago, one of the "little Paris" capitals of the world, beckoned. Jimmy practiced his Spanish with the ship's crew and even did a few marine sketches from the bridge.

They docked at Valparaiso late in March, and were taken inland by coach to Santiago to pay their respects to government leaders. While they were being entertained at the capital, word arrived that the Spanish fleet had been sighted at sea.

Back to the coast sped the dignitaries, local and imported. At sunset they reached Valparaiso harbor, a beautiful curving bay with the town on one side and a line of hills on the other. Ranged before the entrance to the port were not only a formidable Spanish armada, but "observer" warships flying the flags of England, France, Russia, and the United States, on hand to see that the Spaniards stuck to the rules of the game. It was the era of gunboat diplomacy, when colonial regimes were expected to enforce their wishes through a discreet if unmistakable demonstration of superior firepower.

The assembled cannonry made a spectacular array; but more impressive to the gray-clad *capitán americano* on the roof of the customs building was the translucent shimmer of the Pacific twilight. Now, that would be something worth capturing . . .

Early the next morning, Jimmy and his friends gathered in the town plaza, mounted on the finest stallions of the Chilean army. Remembering the capricious Quaker of his cavalry drills, Jimmy had an uneasy moment or two; but it was too late for regrets.

A shout went up; the French force at the mouth of the harbor was pulling away. It was followed by the other neutral fleets, moving out to sea in great sweeps and flourishes, until only the Spaniards were left.

Semaphores flashed, and the enemy force churned forward into the harbor, half a dozen strong. They drew up in formation before the town, and boomed an opening shell.

The population disappeared no faster than the generals. Jimmy found himself riding behind the deputy chief of staff, toward the hills on the other side of the bay. Since there could be no serious thought of defense, one might as well watch from a good vantage point.

As he told the story later, the bombardment was conducted in "most gentlemanly fashion." The attackers waited several minutes for the local citizens to get out of the way, then pumped in a few more ceremonial shells, setting fire to some waterfront houses.

Once, sportively, the gunners shifted their cannon and sent a shell whizzing in the direction of Jimmy's group in the hills—causing the only panic of the morning. Cabinet ministers, admirals, and foreign advisers wheeled their mounts around, dug in their spurs, and galloped off furiously, anywhere. The riding was, according to Jimmy, nothing less than splendid; "and I, as a West Point man, was head of the procession."

By noon the show was over. The Spaniards sailed out, the English and Americans sailed in and helped put out the fires. The *Henriquetta,* the vessel manned by Confederate veterans, was marooned somewhere down the coast and put in no appearance whatever.

Jimmy was stranded in still another foreign land, thousands of miles from home, his Great Adventure reduced to a semi-comic footnote in the history books—and with no immediate prospect of getting back. Repeating the Panama route was out of the question; he would rather walk. Direct service from Valparaiso to London was theoretically available through the new Pacific Steamship Navigation Company; but the line had only two ships whose infrequent runs were subject to the vagaries of wind and tide.

The Chileans did their best to help. They billeted him in the home of a leading banker, and introduced him to the handful of European artists working in Santiago. It was through a non-painter, however, that Jimmy drew the only artistic dividends of his Chilean journey. Alistair McQueen, a member of the thriving British commercial colony in Valparaiso, put Jimmy up for membership in his club. The club windows commanded a sweeping view of the harbor whose soft twilight had so fascinated Jimmy; and there was no objection to his setting up an easel in the library.

Jimmy decided to work out his tonal combination on the palette in advance, as he had begun to do in Trouville. That way, with any luck, he could execute the whole canvas at a single sitting. For his setting, he chose a sundown when the harbor was crowded with sailing vessels riding lightly at anchor. Pale motionless water, dim half-furled sails, scowling black-streaked sky were to be coalesced into an atmosphere of breathless mystery, of time suspended. A study of light, yes; but not light analyzed into spectrum components, as with the Impressionists. Light synthesized, rather, with other elements, to effect a personal statement of mood.

Hovering over his easel in the clubhouse study, Jimmy felt a tingle of excitement. It was coming to pass. The sky, covering the top half of the canvas, howled soundlessly. The ships whispered of ghosts. The water, beneath its faintly rippled surface, hinted of bottomless depths.

This was the effect he wanted, more a remembrance, a hazy summoning-up of past impressions, than reality à la Courbet. A phrase of Coleridge's came to mind:

> As silent as a painted ship
> Upon a painted ocean.

In *Crepuscule in Flesh Color and Green,* he was free of Courbet, free even of Velázquez. Nor was he submerged in the mechanics of Orientalism. The painting was pure Whistler, an evocation of feeling through space-mass abstraction and delicate tonal relationships, and a harbinger of the Thames Nocturnes to come.

At long last, Jimmy was in his cabin aboard the paddle-wheeler *Chile.* The steamer had come down from Ecuador and Peru, picking up passengers at Valparaiso before continuing southward. Soon it would pass through the Strait of Magellan at the tip of the continent and, after final stops in Argentina and Brazil, would nose its way across the Atlantic to Southampton.

Jimmy was in wretched humor. He had wasted months of time, resolved nothing either for the downtrodden Chileans or for himself, and had just been involved in an absurd quarrel over a deck chair with one of the other passengers, a black Haitian known as the "Marquis de Marmalade." The "Marquis" had been smirking for days at the defeated Southerners, finally arousing Jimmy to a martial ardor not evidenced against the cohorts of Spain. Since the incident, Jimmy had been, if not confined to irons, encouraged by the captain to remain in his quarters.

What was he going to do with himself? Would Jo be waiting with open arms, after his quixotic flight? And if she was, was he ready to plunge into them? Would Willie be lost to him, along with Debo, if he did not patch things up with his mother?

His eye fell on an edge of canvas sticking out under the berth. The *Flesh-Color and Green* of Valparaiso harbor. It was good. Yes, better than good; it would endure, whether he himself did or not.

Of course! That was the answer: his work. To concentrate on his painting to the exclusion of everything else, cutting through at last to the essence of a personal style. He was close; he knew that.

To hell, then, with all this nonsense of families and mistresses, of country cottages and peaceful firesides! No man could have everything; least of all, the artist.

He sighed and stretched out on the berth. Giving up what he had found with Jo would not be easy. Every man was a twofold prisoner: first, of his own mortality, living under a sentence of death that would be executed without reference to his wishes; second, of his particular past, unique and unshakable, condemning him at some innermost core to walk alone. To break through this double isolation and link up with another human being was a major coup.

It wasn't just sex. That occurred in a hundred times and places. Its techniques were learnable; whores performed them best. Sex was only a channel for the communication of deeper needs.

And yet—marriage? From his observations among family and friends, it was an arguable business at best: restrictive, monotonous, hypocrisy-breeding. If a conventional institution served so indifferently the needs of conventional people, how could it be expected to suit those of more original stripe?

The artist was a man apart, paying for his gift in the frailty of his human relationships. By his nature, his insatiable drive to reshape "reality," he needed to be born anew each day. This meant consuming people as well as ideas; it was as essential to his growth as the discarding of old petals by a flower to make way for the appearance of new buds. To survive, one had to destroy: intimacies as well as canvases.

Disappointment in personal life was virtually a condition of being an artist; one had only to look at poor haunted Rossetti, the flailed and flailing Swinburne, the embittered Degas . . . How could a man find fulfillment in a life that belonged less to him than to his creative passion?

There was no solace in the knowledge that others, too, were trapped behind bars; one could see them plainly there, but rarely could an arm reach through. It was as if each man were surrounded by an anti-magnetic field that assured the separation necessary for artistic individuality . . . and at the same time blocked true contact with others.

Well, so be it. The artist had god-like privileges and pleasures; it would be strange if his punishments were on a lesser scale. The only real failure was to suffer the deprivations of the creative life without achieving any comparable compensation in one's work; that truly would be disaster.

Work: that was the anodyne and the justification, Nature's balm for personal loss and spiritual crippledom. He had to become a master of his craft.

# Chapter Fourteen

The *Chile* tied up at Southampton in mid-November. Arriving in London, Jimmy went straight from Waterloo Station to Jo. She had a right to be first to hear about his new program.

Besides, he was dying to see her.

The little red-brick cottage on Queen's Road looked dingier than he remembered, and smaller. He paid the cabbie and started toward the steps. A lamp fluttered into light in the parlor, and beyond the white curtains he made out a familiar silhouette.

Jimmy broke into a run. In seconds he was across the threshold, Jo was in his arms, and his monastic resolution disappeared. "Jo! Jo!" He sought out her lips, buried his face in the copper-red hair, flung aside her dressing gown to caress the warm dear flesh of neck and shoulders.

"Jimmy, dearest Jimmy!" She clung to him with a consuming intensity, limb against limb, mouth against mouth. He was surrounded by Jo: her scent, her husky murmuring voice, the subtle pressure of her moving fingers.

Breathless, they finally fell back from each other. "How long it has been, Jimmy!"

"And how terrible!"

"But you show no sorrowful effects." She ran her fingers up his cheek and into the tangle of black hair. "You have such bright rosy color."

"Six weeks of salt air and sea breezes—and I hated every minute of it." He stared at his girl; memories flooded over him.

"One letter I had from you, and that not saying very much. What happened with the Spaniards? Did you do any painting?"

"Later," he commanded.

The bedroom was unchanged. He had no recollection of tearing off his clothes, turning down the lamp, disappearing under the covers: only of the furious embrace that followed. Everything—nine thousand miles of distance, eight months of mutual loneliness, two lifetimes of alternating elation and despair—was poured into a few moments of bruising, surging contact.

Jo was crying. Softly, so that he didn't notice it until he brushed his lips over her long, closed lashes. "Turn off the waterfall," he whispered. "That was yesterday."

She opened her eyes and looked up at him. "It's tomorrow I'm weeping for."

Jimmy shivered. Had she, with her Irish mysticism, divined the renunciation that was in his mind an hour ago? Had Jo somehow been hovering in the corridor on the night he lay in his cabin off the Brazilian coast, grappling with the dilemma of his future?

No matter. That was all empty theorizing, meaningless alongside the physical reality of Jo. "We're going to stay together, Jo," he said firmly. "I'll get a little house in the country—Surrey or Kent. We don't have to be in London."

"You can't do it, Jimmy."

"I can and I will. A man has to run his own life."

"You're not just a man, Jimmy—you're an artist. You can make plans, but it's a demon inside you that makes the decisions." Jo drew up her knees and swung out of bed. "And when he does, you're not much more than a helpless bystander."

"But I need you, Jo!"

"No, you don't. Not the way ordinary people need each other. Men like you and Dante Gabriel and Swinburne live in another country. You ride across the sky in a golden chariot, traveling with the gods. There's only one thing you need, Jimmy: faith in yourself."

"You can give it to me, Jo."

"No, I can't. It has to come from inside, where the demon lives. Where it should have been planted by your mother."

Jimmy stiffened. "We're not talking about my mother."

"Whether we do or not, she's *there,* Jimmy . . . hanging over you, eating into your manhood."

Jimmy sprang up and followed her across the room. "Not any more, Jo. That's all done with!"

"Some day—but not yet. They're burned deep, those early years. Like —like an etching."

He threw up his hands. "All right, I'll prove it to you. We'll get married!"

Jo, slipping into her robe, stopped and looked at him tenderly. "Ah, Jimmy, Jimmy. How lovely that sounds. And what a foolishment it would be."

"Why?"

"You're not ready. You could never stand the confinement, the re-sponsibility, not on top of your other troubles. You'd begin to hate me. Or else you'd start leaning on me, make me a mother instead of a wife —and soon you'd hate me for that, too. There'd be more running away to show your independence, more little adventures like Gwen Richards."

"Gwen Richards?"

"The girl you met at Albert Moore's."

"Ah. You know about that."

"More than you do, I'm afraid. She's had a child, Jimmy."

"A child?" The black brows shot up in alarm.

"A little boy. Yours."

"How do you know it's mine?"

"I've seen it. She went to Moore and then Dante Gabriel and—well, I know the whole story."

Jimmy regarded her in silence a moment, stunned. Mechanically he got into his shirt and trousers. Jo had gone into the parlor. He sat down beside her on the sofa. "It was an escapade, Jo, a reckless moment. I was miserable and—and she was available. The woman means nothing to me. I hardly remember her name."

"She has reason to remember yours," said Jo softly.

Jimmy dropped his head. "Very well. I transgressed. I committed an infidelity, and deserve to be punished. But not this much. Are you say-ing that, because of a single slip, you would refuse to marry me?"

"No," said Jo slowly. "Whatever you did, I could endure. It's what others would do to you."

"Damn the others!"

"It's you who would be damned." She looked at him soberly. "I'm from the wrong end of London, Jimmy. With the wrong accent and the wrong religion. Seymour Haden and his opinions would not lack for company."

"To hell with Haden! You're worth a hundred of him!"

"Not at the dinner tables of your patrons. Or in the reception rooms of the Royal Academy. There would be insults, quarrels, challenges. And after all the shouting, what would be left of your career?"

Jimmy stared at the floor. She was right, of course. He had known it all in the back of his mind, that night in the cabin. "Is there no sal-vation for me, then?"

"Only in succeeding as a painter. Nothing less will make you feel complete. For that, I'd just be in the way. And be blamed in the bar-gain—by your family, your friends, and finally by you."

"Never! You are what makes my work possible."

"If that were true, it would only prove what I've been saying. You have to be able to stand by yourself as an artist, without leaning on anyone."

"And so, to speed the process, you would cut me adrift." His full lips curled into an ironic smile. "To save me, you're prepared to desert me."

"I would never desert you, Jimmy. For as long as I'm in London, you're welcome to my modeling services, my bed—anything I've got."

Jimmy leaped up. " 'As long as'— What are you talking about?"

"You know the sorrow I've had with my lungs, how I've been wanting to get away from the soot of London. Well— I've been offered a job at Chalfont St. Peter in Buckinghamshire."

"What sort of job?"

"Governess to a little boy. His mother is a permanent invalid."

There was a long pause. "And his father?"

"A hardware merchant. A decent, plain man. My sister was taking care of his wife in the hospital. That's how I met him."

"I see." Jimmy paced for a moment, then turned. His voice trembled. "You've made . . . an arrangement."

"No. My only duties are to the child."

"Unless"—the blue eyes gleamed angrily—"you choose to expand them."

Jo made no answer.

Jimmy sighed. "That doesn't leave much to discuss, does it . . ."

"Only your little boy."

"What about him?"

"He's in a foundling home at the moment—courtesy of Howell."

"The ubiquitous owl—who sees all, manages everything."

"Jimmy . . . that's no place for the son of James Whistler to grow up."

"Are you suggesting I convert my studio to a nursery?"

"No. I'd like to take him with me to the country."

Jimmy blinked; it was all too much to absorb. "You want to raise my . . . the product of a liaison with another woman?"

"He's a part of you, Jimmy, a part I can help without hurting. I'll be a good mother, I promise you."

He looked at her mutely, and felt the tears rising. "I'm sure of that."

"I've told Mr. Gordon I have a baby nephew whose parents are separated. He doesn't mind, so long as expenses are paid."

Jimmy tugged at his imperial. "You would go to all that trouble for a child who means less than nothing to you, the child of another woman?"

"Your child."

"Why, Jo?"

"Because I love you."

He slammed his hand down on the coffee table. "If you love me, stay with me!"

Jo stood up and went to the window. "The tides on the Thames rise and fall, Jimmy, and there's no man can push them forward or hold them back. We've had our moment, and more than a patch of glory in it, too. One day the world will bow to you, and you'll find your peace. But it will be with another woman."

The affair was over. From that moment the happy-go-lucky Jimmy of Montparnasse and Cremorne began to recede from view, and the first dim outlines emerged of the public Whistler, the legendary battler with fists and tongue who would keep London alternately terrified and amused for the next two decades.

Jimmy needed a truce with his mother if he was to reorganize his life. He enlisted the aid of his brother Willie, Willie the magician who always had the right medicines, and so often had the right words as well.

Willie arranged a quiet dinner à trois at his home. Anna Whistler was already at the table when Jimmy arrived. He kissed his mother formally, and the two picked up the conversation as if he had been away on a short holiday.

Afterward, Willie discreetly remembered an appointment at the Chelsea Hospital clinic. Anna and her first-born were alone.

Jimmy took the plunge. "I owe you an apology, Mother. I'm afraid that, in the heat of the moment last winter, I said some harsh things, some thoughtless things, that I very much regret. I now ask your forgiveness."

For an instant his mother's pink, roundish face was unresponsive. Then the firm thin mouth softened. "It is granted without the asking, Jemie."

"I suggest we regard the incident as closed."

Anna nodded. She raised her head heavenward. "'A word spoken in due season, how good is it.'"

To underline the fresh start, Jimmy moved into a larger house at 2 Lindsey Row, five doors to the east and, as he pointed out to his mother, one hundred feet closer to her beloved church. He seized the occasion to execute his own strong notions of interior décor, a sphere where Victorian convention yielded nothing in stuffiness to the galleries of the Royal Academy.

London homes were a suffocating clutter of massive carved furniture, noisy wallpaper, dreary statuary, and aimless knickknacks from which no corner was spared. Red damask hangings, dribbling down onto green velvet carpets to "set each other off," merely set Jimmy off in howls of denunciation.

To the William Morris formula of "harmonious"—and unlimited—detail, he opposed the Japanese concept of refined simplicity, an elegant spaciousness relieved by selected ornamental motifs. His main departure was to create restful expanses of flat unbroken wall, painted in cheerful pastel tints that would "bring the sun inside." Against the fogbound gloom of London he pitted walls of pale pink and turquoise, of off-white, flesh-color, and, most abundantly, of a hue he came to claim as his own: lemon yellow. Charles Augustus Howell, stepping across the threshold for the first time, observed that it was "like standing inside an egg."

But Howell was quick to voice his appreciation of the gold-flecked dado in the entrance hall, showered with rose and white flower petals; the blue-on-blue dining room, with its purple Japanese fans sprinkled along walls and ceilings in a deft arabesque; and the daintily appointed drawing room, where a black-and-white porcelain bath filled with goldfish and lilies sat with a few pieces of light furniture on a floor covering of straw-yellow matting.

Jimmy's studio, painted gray with black doors, was again one flight up in the back, overlooking a thickly planted garden. His bedroom, alongside that of his mother on the floor above, boasted a huge Chinese bed, a collecting coup engineered by Howell's rival dealer, Murray Marks.

At the turn of the year, Jimmy and his mother moved into the new establishment, and she resumed housekeeping for him. But the pre-Chilean episode hung like a veil of disquiet between them. Although Anna continued to scold her son for smoking, and to prescribe walks for his health, the old closeness was gone.

Sharp little incidents broke out, mostly involving observance of the Sabbath. Jimmy was willing enough to escort his mother to church; but, scornful of the twenty-four-hour piety flaunted by habitual weekday sinners, he reserved to himself the option of painting on Sunday.

To Anna Whistler this was an offense against God. She was determined to end it. Jimmy was equally resolved to establish that his retreat at Willie's house was not a total surrender.

The showdown came on a Sunday morning a few weeks after they moved in. Anna, returning from church services, found Jimmy sprawled before a wood panel in the front hall, putting the last strokes on a trim white schooner skimming over the sea with billowing sails. Beside him, the Greaves brothers were busily mixing colors.

Jimmy heard her come in. "Look, Mother," he called over his shoulder. "Isn't she magnificent?"

"Magnificent?" echoed Anna Whistler. "Or blasphemous?"

"We're having guests this evening," Jimmy protested. "One doesn't entertain in an unfinished hall."

"This is God's day," Anna retorted sharply. "What was wrong in the young boy with his toys cannot become right in the grown man with his paints!"

Jimmy scrambled to his feet. "I intend to finish, Mother. In accordance with the wisdom of St. Mark: 'The Sabbath was made for man, and not man for the Sabbath.'"

"I need no instruction from you in the Gospel!" Anna Whistler tilted her head and marched up the stairs.

But thereafter she kept her criticisms to herself. She was silent even when, venturing into Jimmy's studio late one afternoon, she found him sketching the parlormaid *sans* apron—or anything else.

Jimmy had turned to experimentation with nudes, at the suggestion of Albert Moore, in an attempt to strengthen his handling of formal composition. His first showing since the Chilean trip, at the French Universal Exhibition early in 1867, had not been successful; a reviewer lumped the lovely Valparaiso twilight with a pair of Trouville marines as "blurred foggy imperfections." Now he was concentrating on a studio piece, the *Symphony in White No. 3*. This featured Jo, temporarily back on the model stand as promised, half-reclining on a long sofa with another girl kneeling on the floor alongside.

The arrangement of the figures, Moore noted approvingly, was unusual: an ingenious distribution of lines and curves that avoided clumsy parallels. Jimmy, as quick to enthusiasm as to despair, forwarded a sketch to Fantin-Latour, asserting that he was making "truly enormous progress."

Back came further encouraging word. Degas—the scowling, cynical Degas—had glimpsed the drawing on Fantin's studio table and asked permission to copy it into his notebook as a model of composition.

Could there be a more auspicious accolade? Jimmy hurried to finish up the painting for the 1867 Royal Academy exhibition. This time, surely, the critics would not be able to hold back their praises.

But they did, and emphatically. The *Gazette des Beaux Arts* curtly reiterated its disappointment: Whistler had "failed to fulfill his earlier promise." And the owlish P. G. Hamerton grumbled in the *Saturday Review* that the painting wasn't even a proper symphony in white; Jo's hair was red, he pointed out. There were also flesh colors, yellow in the other model's dress, and a scattering of blue and green in the accessories.

Coming on top of the unfriendly comment at the French Universal Exhibition a month earlier, this was too much. Jimmy sat down at his writing desk and dashed off a note to Hamerton's editor:

*"Bon Dieu! Did this wise person expect white hair and chalked faces? And does he then, in his astounding consequence, believe that a symphony in F contains no other note, but shall be a continued repetition of F,F,F . . . Fool!"*

That made him feel better, but did not entirely vent his spleen. The world seemed to be sharply divided: Jimmy Whistler on one side, the rest of mankind on the other. After the shipboard skirmish with the Marquis de Marmalade, he had taken a few boxing lessons from a London professional. It was just as well. Within three weeks, he was involved in as many brawls.

The most spectacular was a return bout with his old nemesis, Seymour Haden. The surgeon had for some years employed a medical assistant, one Edward Traer, a gentle soul very popular among the artistic fraternity.

In the summer of 1867, Traer died unexpectedly in Paris. Haden, taking charge of the funeral arrangements, ordered that expenses be kept to some 23 francs or a little under five dollars . . . enough to provide a small plot of ground, but not a marker.

Traer's indigent mother and sister appealed to Jimmy, and succeeded instantly in raising not only his blood pressure but £31 in art-circle subscriptions. Jimmy and his brother Willie were joined by Rossetti, du Maurier and Alec Ionides in putting up five guineas each; the rest was pledged by Howell, Swinburne, Frederick Sandys, and Charles Keene. The two Whistlers went to Paris to confront the unspeakable Haden.

The three-way meeting at a café table was short and fierce.

"The man died penniless," declared Haden, "as incompetent in terminating his life as he had been in managing it."

"Even if that were true," protested Willie, "you don't bury a friend like a stray dog."

"Traer was an employee. He had no claim on my friendship."

"Or your conscience, either," interjected Jimmy. "You hound a man for a lifetime, slander him before the Medical Board of Commissioners, and then would deny his family even the solace of a religious service!"

"Have a care, Jimmy. I've thrown you out of my house once—"

"You *crawled* after me down the stairs."

"Impudent puppy!"

Jimmy reached across the table and backhanded Haden's imposing jaw. The bigger man, inarticulate with rage, jumped up and grabbed Jimmy's head under his left arm, uppercutting with his right. Careening drunkenly, the adversaries skidded toward the plate-glass window fronting on the street. With a nimble movement—Jimmy's teacher had stressed footwork—Jimmy broke free, and Haden's momentum sent him crashing through the window.

The pair landed in a Right Bank court, where the magistrate gave an unpleasant bark of recognition. Jimmy had been in the same tribunal some ten days before, as the result of an altercation on the Rue Colisée.

Passing through the narrow thoroughfare, he had been showered with plaster from a workman on an overhead scaffold, and reacted with loud cries of indignation.

The burly laborer above was amused at the sight of the fuming little foreigner. "Why don't you look where you're going?" he shouted back.

"Clumsy bastard!"

"What was that?"

Jimmy repeated the epithet, then obligingly spelled it out.

The man swung onto a ladder and clambered down, fists clenched for action. Five seconds later he was sprawled on the sidewalk, victim of a rapid-fire left-right combination.

On his first appearance before the magistrate, Jimmy had been able to invoke the protection of the American consul. His encore in the Haden case did not, predictably, sit well with either the consul or the magistrate. He was fined 100 francs, but considered the satisfaction well worth it.

There was one more account to settle, and he lost little time in settling it. Back in London the following week, he ran into Alphonse Legros at an Ionides reception. Relations between the two had been cool for some time. Suddenly, during a discussion of copy-making from old masters, they became very hot indeed.

Legros was remarking to Luke Ionides that he had enjoyed some lucrative commissions in this field, and—with a glance at Jimmy—had been "elbowed out of" a number of others.

"I presume," said Jimmy slowly, "you are referring to Lady Ashburton?"

The Burgundian nodded his long proud head.

"I shall tell you precisely what happened. She approached Rossetti, he referred her to me, and I told her that either you or Fantin-Latour could provide her with excellent copies."

"That is not true!" exclaimed Legros excitedly. "I heard from—"

What he heard, and from whom, was lost to posterity; for at that instant Jimmy struck him a mighty whack across the cheek. He had given Jimmy the lie direct . . . a dangerous act for a man of sturdier moral fiber and more prepossessing physique than Legros.

Like all of Jimmy's physical encounters, the battle was brief. Legros tore out a tuft of Jimmy's hair before he was downed by a blow over the eye and retired from the field. In later years, Legros would be remembered for the witticism that in taking out English citizenship, he had managed to "win the battle of Waterloo." He did not win the battle of Tulse Hill, and it marked the end of his friendship with Fantin-Latour as well as with Jimmy.

Jimmy's adventures in pugilism had immediate repercussions, public as well as private. Seymour Haden, a prominent member of the Burlington Fine Arts Society, threatened to resign unless Jimmy were forced out. The Rossettis came to Jimmy's defense, courageously but ineptly. William introduced a motion for reinstatement; Dante Gabriel, unwise in the ways of parliamentary procedure, missed his cue, and the motion was defeated, 19 to 8. The Rossettis thereupon departed from the club in protest.

Within Jimmy's family, there was a bewildering round-robin of hurt, angry correspondence. Dr. Willie wrote to Debo that her husband got exactly what he deserved; Jimmy assured his half sister that he had been provoked, among other things, by a long history of un-answered insults to herself and his mother; even Anna Whistler informed her stepdaughter of past chicanery on Haden's part. It was sadly and mutually agreed that all intercourse between Hadens and Whistlers must be terminated; and even though the women later found ways to circumvent the rule, Jimmy was now effectively cut off from Debo.

It was a serious loss to him. There had been a special intimacy between the two most lighthearted Whistlers since childhood days, when both had chafed under the censorious eye of the major's second wife. Jimmy had looked on sympathetically as "Dashka," the nickname given by the American colony in Russia to its piano-playing belle, was obliged to choose between invitations to dinner and the opera, since to enjoy both in the same evening would have constituted what Anna Whistler regarded as ungodly frivolity. And Debo, nearly a decade Jimmy's senior, had looked after him in London during the year before his father died, superintending his health, education, and recreation with a solicitude equaling that of his mother, but with far more humor and a sweet tolerance for his shortcomings; Debo could scold without lacerating.

Cut off from mistress and sister, fretful under the shadow of his mother, with his paintings—as he wrote to an American friend in Paris —"more or less damned by all," Jimmy was at a dangerous impasse.

# Chapter Fifteen

What had happened to his recent clarity of vision?

That moment of insight in the cabin of the *Chile,* that recognition of work as the only answer, was still valid; he must cling to it or perish.

An image from his Washington days returned: the lonely knight sketched in a castle dungeon, friendless but fighting on. He was that knight. He would find his solitary retreat, pull up the drawbridge behind him, and stay until he had slain his personal dragons of ignorance and uncertainty.

Castles were not abundantly at hand. But a friend, Frederick Jameson, had a flat at 62 Great Russell Street in Bloomsbury, near the British Museum, with a large studio that had once been used by Burne-Jones. Jimmy eagerly accepted his invitation to move in, and settled down to the most unsparing self-examination of his life.

*He was a faulty draftsman.* That was the first, and perhaps most terrifying, realization that had to be faced. He ought to have studied harder at Gleyre, worked to perfect his line. There was so much he didn't know and couldn't do—things that Fantin and Degas had absorbed in their endless copying and analyzing, while he was sliding by on mere native glibness. He knew, vaguely, why he had rebelled against systematic study; life under Anna Whistler had left him permanently allergic to discipline. Now he was paying for that exaggerated reaction. He was in the worst of hells: to have beautiful visions and be unable to execute them.

*His excursion into Courbet-land had been a mistake.* Courbet was a master, yes, but a master with a totally different view and purpose. To the young Whistler emerging from student days, gifted and impatient, realism had been an enormous temptation. One had simply to put down what was there, and *voilà*—an end to all anxieties and uncertainties, fame would be waiting. Only now could he perceive that this apparent shortcut was actually a detour; in the pursuit of accurate detail, poetic

essence could be lost. Realism, unlike his still inconclusive experiments
with Oriental and neo-Greek forms, would have offered him a comfortable niche. But security was a deadly trap; he was determined to
grow, to unlock the full potential within him.

Jimmy felt painfully ill-equipped for the decisive struggle ahead.
Nonetheless he worked with monastic singlemindedness from dawn
to dark, seeing no one but his roommate Jameson, and confiding only
to the faithful Fantin-Latour the depth of his crisis:

"Ah, my dear Fantin, what an education I have been giving myself!
Or rather, what a fearful lack of education I feel! With my fine natural
gifts, what a painter I should be now if I had not, in my vain contentment with those gifts, turned up my nose at everything else!"

He passed merciless judgment on the youthful achievements that a
short while before had seemed to him so striking: "The *Piano*, the
*White Girl*, the *Thames* and the seascapes were turned out by a clever
rascal puffed up with vanity at being able to show other painters his
splendid qualities, qualities which required only a rigorous education
to make their possessor a master."

No longer, wrote Jimmy, was he the amiable and careless fellow
who "tossed everything pell-mell on the canvas, knowing that instinct and beautiful color would see me through." After a bitter reflection on the "pernicious influence"—for him—of Courbet, Jimmy
turned to the classicist Ingres, long overshadowed in the eyes of the
younger men by his romanticist rival, Delacroix:

"Ah, why was I not a pupil of Ingres? His work I like only fairly well
—I feel there are far finer things to be done—but what a master he
would have been, how soundly he would have guided us!

"Drawing, by God! Color of itself is vice. Color well guided, however, by her master, drawing; color firmly grasped with a strong
hand, becomes a splendid bride with a husband worthy of her.

"But coupled with indecision, with drawing that is weak, timid, and
easily satisfied, color becomes a swaggering jade who makes sport of
her mate, treating him like a clod who bores her—which he does. And
one sees the result: a chaos of drunken swirls, of tricks, regrets, work
that is never finished."

"Well, enough. That explains the prodigious task I have set for myself. I shall make up for time thrown away. But what labor, what a
battle!"

His battlefield was the studio; his weapons, paint and canvas; and
his enemy the slapdash, loosely improvised working methods that had
brought him to this impasse. It was annoying enough to be compared
unfavorably with the purveyors of gilt-framed gingerbread; far worse
was the knowledge that he was not meeting his own standards, was

expressing with no more than random success the visions of color and design in his head.

It was the loneliest, most consuming kind of mortal combat, full of bold charges and exhausting stratagems, of invisible victories and humiliating retreats. He experimented endlessly: with medieval design, fine sable brushes, canvas as porous as blotting paper, thinned-out pigments that trickled in rivulets down to the floor. He fought the elusiveness of the liquid colors and the resistance of the tough-grained, closely woven cloth, groping toward a goal he could not articulate, but that instinct told him was just around the corner.

For days he would feel as if he were trying to carve through a stone wall with a penknife; and then a small breakthrough would come, the rightness of a sweeping curve or a delicate flesh tone. And he would experience the peculiar ecstasy of the artist, at once humbler than his fellows in the realization that he can never execute totally the dream in his mind, and more arrogant in that he dares to try, to presume that his tiny vision, lonely as it hangs in the vast void of the universe, is unique and of value. In those moments Jimmy felt nothing was beyond his doing, and no other creature on earth could quite duplicate his achievement. This sense of towering above the mass of mankind would linger until some fresh failure reminded him how far he was from his dream; then, like Satan, he plunged from heaven to hell.

Unexpectedly, in the midst of his strivings came a commission for a group of paintings. The patron was a long-time supporter of Rossetti's, the shipping magnate Frederick Leyland. Leyland left the choice of subject to Jimmy.

With his renewed interest in the power of pure line, Jimmy opted for a decorative series to be called the Six Projects, featuring, in the Albert Moore fashion, supple long-waisted young ladies bending in graceful arabesques to arrange flowers, or floating like water lilies on a seaborne wind. If he could no longer hope to draw an anatomically perfect line, at least he could create a beautiful and expressive one. Joined by Moore, he spent long hours at the National Gallery analyzing the design elements in Titian and Tintoretto.

These investigations slowed his work more than ever. Entry time came for the 1868 Academy, and he had nothing ready.

Tense, unhappy, his whole being on the alert for the revelation that would not come, he had little appetite for social life. Twice a week he visited his mother for a late dinner, but conversation was sparse. To Anna Whistler's credit, she did not press him. He felt badly about his protracted silences. But he was the vat where the brew was fermenting, the crucible heating over the fire; how could people expect him to behave "normally"?

In this trying period, moral support arrived from an unlikely source. During Jimmy's absence in South America, Algernon Swinburne had published his *Poems and Ballads,* and metamorphosed from the bad boy of Chelsea to a national celebrity. Fame, however, had only made him more obstreperous; at the Arts Club, where he circulated ribald satires on Queen Victoria's sex life and improvised erotic sculpture from the tableware, Jimmy was constantly defending him against expulsion proceedings. In another gesture of loyalty, Jimmy had etched his erratic friend, capturing the reverie-lost dreamer's face with its wasteland of forehead, forest of red beard and mustache, and brilliant far-seeing eyes.

Now, in the spring of 1868, Swinburne came to Jimmy's studio, where the walls were covered with chalk and pastel sketches for the Six Projects, only one of which was ever finished in oil. Swinburne was fascinated by the seductive Greco-Japanese figures under their flimsy veils. In a pamphlet on the 1868 Royal Academy, he wrote glowingly of these minor gems "not submitted to the loose and slippery judgment of an Academy," which conveyed a "freshness and fullness of the loveliest life of things, with a high, clear power upon them which seems to educe a picture as the sun does a blossom or a fruit."

Jimmy was momentarily heartened. As long as at least one pair of eyes responded sympathetically, there was point in carrying on.

It was a dampish midnight in June when the idea burst upon him. He was alone in his candlelit bedroom, leafing through a folio of rare Hokusai woodcuts that had somehow come into the possession of the redoubtable Charles Augustus Howell. Suddenly he was struck by the precision and consistency of the color combinations. It was as if the Japanese master, like an Oriental Beethoven, wrought his intricate variations from a single scale of tones.

Beethoven? Well, why not?

Jimmy's intuitive response to music was limited—he laughed openly at operas performed by bathtub-shaped prima donnas—but, thanks to Anna Whistler's four-handed piano drills, his grasp of musical principles was something else. What was painting, after all, but a kind of visual music, an arbitrary arrangement on two-dimensional canvas where line, form, and hue replaced melody, harmony, and orchestral color, and the palette was substituted for the keyboard?

Corollaries tumbled rapidly into place. The painter should be as free as the composer to express himself in abstract patterns, without benefit of literary contraptions. And thus liberated, he would work most effectively within a particular tonal setting, creating harmony by the subtle association of closely related tones.

Jimmy was amazed to discover that Fantin was embarking gingerly along the same path. He noted in a letter that the Frenchman's most recent bouquets could boast not only dazzling brushwork but "stunning color composition, which for me is what really constitutes color." Fantin's pigments, he declared, were "so to speak embroidered" onto the canvas, with individual hues reappearing from time to time "in accordance with their significance."

For his new approach, Jimmy did not need a rainbowful of colors. But those he did use had to be precise. He had always ground his own pigments, and slimmed down his brushes to ensure better control of his thin paints. Now he devised a system of "prepared tones," basic formulas for such recurring effects as "daylight pavement," "evening sky," and "interior floor." His prescription for flesh-tone—subject of course to individual variations—was a blend of yellow ochre, white, Indian red, and Venetian red.

To accommodate these combinations, he designed a large table palette, essentially an oblong tray fitted onto a sloping desk. The "prepared tones" were ranged down the center, with galipots of individual colors to the left and bowls of oil and turpentine on the right.

Cautiously, he advanced from theory to test. For *The Artist's Studio*, he first did a fragmentary oil sketch: himself at the easel in gray, Jo and another model at the sofa in pale tones of blue and gold. The full canvas was to include also the figures of Fantin-Latour and Albert Moore in black.

But, "prepared tones" notwithstanding, he could not bring off the whole group to his satisfaction. He lacked the Hals-like command of anatomy and drawing that would enable him to handle all the elements at one swoop; and he was unwilling to execute the canvas piecemeal, in individual portraits done at different times, because that would sacrifice unity of tone.

Whatever the merits of his color-harmony theory, they would not be evidenced in *The Artist's Studio*.

The blow was scarcely softened by word from Jo that she could not delay any longer her departure for the country. Her new employer wanted her—and Jimmy's infant son—to come now, if they were coming at all.

Jimmy packed his suitcase, folded up his easels and asked his mother to prepare his bedroom at Cheyne Row. The experimental sojourn in Bloomsbury was over.

He had come out with one concrete souvenir: the Whistler butterfly signature, modeled after the identifying tablets used by the Japanese woodblock masters and always worked into their pictorial compositions. He chose the gaily blazoned butterfly for its grace, its suggestions of evanescence and rebirth, and for the wry pleasure of remembering that it had always been Anna Whistler's horrible example of the idle saunterer, dilettante dissipator of precious Time.

He had also acquired in his hibernation a knowledge of his limitations, and a concept that would overshadow them. Color harmony would ultimately be the hallmark of his greatest portraits; but before that, it would lead him down a more personal and in some ways more rewarding path.

# Chapter Sixteen

Once again the Thames was at Jimmy's doorstep. But now he saw it with eyes sharpened by his Japanese studies. In the Bloomsbury studio he had become aware of tonal arrangements; contemplating the river, he began to grasp the greater purpose which they served.

The heart of Oriental painting was its mystery. As a Chinese landscapist put it in the sixteenth century, "The shadow of a tree reflected on the earth at dusk contains a deeper sense of art and beauty than the tree itself." Gazing out over the twilight-hushed Thames three hundred years later, Jimmy could only breathe, "Amen." These ghostly skiffs and motionless sails, the great reaches of mist-covered water dotted with tiny lights, were the stuff of poetry.

By instinct he had touched this chord in the dream-like *Valparaiso Twilight*. Now, in a series of Thames scenes, he set out to crystallize all he had learned into a conscious technique: to fuse the broad color masses and simplified planes of Hiroshige with the refinements of space, atmosphere, and water painting that he had absorbed in Europe. His unifying agent would be tonal harmony.

What emerged was neither Eastern nor Western but Whistlerian. With a handful of fugitive tints that glided meltingly together—dim shadowy blues or grays transformed by a faint flush of something gold or beige—he created a twilight universe of impalpable air and light, of haunting mystery and aching beauty. He painted the soul of the riverside.

It was his mother who responded first to the mood paintings of the Thames; her appreciation was a significant step in drawing the two together again. But Jimmy had little hope that the pictures would enhance his standing at the bank or in the art columns; they were too open to the familiar charge of sketchiness. He kept painting them anyway—at nearby Battersea Bridge, Westminster, the Pool of London in the East End—and called them Moonlights until an important new patron suggested they be called Nocturnes. Promptly and gratefully he accepted the amendment: "It does so poetically say all I want to say, and no more."

The big new fish that had swum into Jimmy's waters was the multi-millionaire proprietor of the Leyland Steamship Lines.

Frederick Leyland was an odd blend of sober businessman and secret aesthete, a self-made tycoon with a Medici flair for the arts. An avid amateur pianist, he read Balzac and Dante in the original and was an assiduous collector of painting and sculpture. If he lacked the technique to perform Chopin in public—a dream reluctantly relinquished—he was determined at least to win immortality as a patron. That he succeeded was one of the triumphs and tragedies of Jimmy's life.

The two first met through Rossetti, whose work was the backbone of Leyland's English collection. At the urging of Dante Gabriel, Leyland had taken over from James Leathart the Oriental-style portrait by Jimmy of Christine Spartali, *The Princess from the Land of Porcelain.*

One morning Jimmy had a note asking him to come at once to Tudor House. Below his friend's signature was a playful sketch of a fat checkbook.

He found Rossetti in his studio, reviewing paintings with a grave, slender man dressed entirely in funereal black. The lower half of the man's long, ascetic face was masked by a beard and mustache, equally black. Above, anxious brown eyes fixed Jimmy with a steady judicial gaze.

"I am Leyland," the man announced without waiting for a formal introduction. "I recently acquired your *Princess* painting."

"To my great pleasure."

"I find your work extremely interesting, Mr. Whistler."

"I take a certain modest interest in it myself."

Leyland did not return his smile. "At your convenience, I should like to see what else you have available for sale."

"Are you staying in London, sir?"

"No. But I shall be back on the sixteenth." He produced a card. "You can communicate with me at this address." Leyland started toward the door, then turned back abruptly to Jimmy. "Are you free to accept binders on future work?"

"Perfectly."

"I have a rather flexible arrangement in mind—something along the lines of my understanding with Mr. Rossetti."

Jimmy bowed. "Anything that has been agreeable to Dante Gabriel will be quite satisfactory to me."

"Good. You will have my check for a hundred guineas in the morning." Leyland inclined his head stiffly and was gone.

Jimmy looked after him quizzically. "So that's the fairy godfather! The clothes are all wrong, Dante, and the manner is somewhat less than enchanting."

"Ah, but the signature is splendid! At any bank between here and Alexandria."

A few days later Jimmy received a note saying Leyland had been called abroad, and suggesting the pick-your-own-subject that became the Six Projects. Meantime, Rossetti filled Jimmy in. Not since the celebrated Plint of Leeds, the eccentric cotton merchant who insisted on paying for canvases long in advance, had British art known such a generous patron. Leyland's collection was hand-picked, in most cases directly from the painters themselves. He had started with Bibby, Sons & Co., a Mediterranean shipping line, as an office boy; within fifteen years, thanks to his intense application, his genius for detail, and his imaginative grasp of steamship design, he was running the company. Ultimately it became the Leyland Line, famous for the unorthodox methods of its owner: Leyland kept a constantly updated card file on his desk recording the exact position and cargo load of every one of his vessels.

Reticent and imperious, fanatically precise, Leyland worked hard at extending his commercial empire. He displayed little interest in conventional social activity or even in his own family. He allowed himself only two diversions: accumulating masterpieces, and playing the piano. It was his frequent habit to arrive late in the evening at Speke Hall, his mansion on the outskirts of Liverpool, and stomp straight upstairs to a secluded music room, ignoring his wife and whatever guests happened to be present.

Frances Leyland was not, according to Rossetti, a wife many men would have chosen to ignore: "an absolute smasher, Jimmy!" Auburn-haired and dainty, with a mocking, provocative air, she had been a widely courted North Country belle and was at thirty-three by no means reconciled to social retirement.

But the magnate's mind was on other things, mainly a project that would establish him as a caliph among merchant princes. He intended to acquire a palace in the heart of London, and stock it with the greatest art collection that money and taste could assemble.

Toward that end, he laid about lavishly with commissions. For a man who in business made a fetish of neatness and punctuality, he was remarkably indulgent with his artists. It was as if he felt they belonged to another world where he was only a privileged visitor. He would willingly overlook, if not positively enjoy, the slovenly disarray of a Rossetti, the improvidence of Frederick Sandys, the effronteries of Howell. Never quite comfortable in the small talk of dinner parties, more at ease with figures than with people, Leyland could relax among artists who were as devoted to hard work, in their way, as he was in his. Toward one or two, he even extended the warmth that he denied his wife.

The intriguing possibilities of the Leyland ménage were soon enough made evident to Jimmy. Like Rossetti and others before him, he was invited up to Speke Hall for a couple of weeks to ramble in the woods, fortify himself with the clean air, and work if he wished at the nearby beaches. Unlike the morose Rossetti, however, he was a charming bachelor of thirty-five.

Jimmy's curls were as appealing as ever; enhanced, in fact, by a jaunty white lock that had materialized mysteriously after his Chilean adventure. His profile was as sharp, his bearing as courtly. And he was no longer the awkward outlander of the Ionides drawing rooms; he could cope better with women of his own class. Frances Leyland, like many a bored housewife before and after her, was gratified by the attentions of an attractive stranger. Jimmy was unfailingly deferential, with that Southern gallantry whose essentially condescending character is always deftly concealed. Unlike Frederick Leyland, he was not given to fits of temper, and was flatteringly aware of small things: a new scarf, a vagrant feminine mood. With the master of the house frequently bottled up with his executives or his beloved Chopin, it fell upon Jimmy to brighten the Leyland teas.

All too soon the holiday ended. But when Mrs. Leyland came down to London a month later to supervise the renovation of the mansion her husband had found at Queen's Gate, she invited Jimmy to dinner. She remarked carelessly that, with Leyland in Italy, she and her sister had an extra ticket for the opera tomorrow. Was Jimmy fond of Verdi?

"Curious you should ask," Jimmy replied, blue eyes gleaming. "I've just developed an irresistible passion for him."

Frances Leyland flicked him an appreciative glance. She pushed forward her full lower lip in the most imperceptible of gestures. "Then perhaps we could impose on you—?"

"I should be most delighted to serve you—in *any* capacity."

Ten minutes of watching Jimmy squirm through a tenor aria were enough to establish the fragility of his passion for Verdi. But there were more invitations, and more small parties at the theater and concert halls. The situation was circumspect if titillating; Mrs. Leyland's sister Cynthia was always present. To discourage gossip, and head off possible husbandly objections from "the baron," Frances Leyland dropped word among her friends that Jimmy was much interested in Cynthia.

Upon his return from the Continent late in 1869, Leyland broadened his Speke Hall hospitality to include Jimmy's mother. The spacious many-gabled country house, with its handsome grounds and incredible kitchen (hothouse grapes and tomatoes in midwinter), was a welcome retreat for Anna Whistler—who promptly earned her keep by nursing eight-year-old Fanny Leyland through a siege of the grippe. Socially, things were going swimmingly.

Less spectacular was Jimmy's progress at the easel. After tinkering inconclusively with the Six Projects, he had begun moving outdoors for his Thames mood pictures. However, apart from a few etchings, almost nothing ordered by Leyland had been completed.

Jimmy was therefore surprised when the shipowner proposed a massive new commission: a series of portraits recording for posterity the entire Leyland family. The artist would be bound to no deadlines, could come and go as he pleased with full access to the phaeton, the wine cellar and all the other amenities of Speke Hall. There would be a substantial down payment, and further advances as required.

It was really too good to turn down. Money was a perennial problem at Lindsey Row. With a gentlewoman on the premises, certain minimal living standards—a cook, a butler—had to be met. Although servants were paid meagerly in Victorian times, they had to be paid something, regularly. And the major financial responsibility was Jimmy's; Willie Whistler was still struggling to gain a foothold as a doctor in a foreign land.

At Leyland's, Jimmy could enjoy virtually the court-painter status of his revered Velázquez—right down to the English "Infantas" represented by the magnate's three young daughters. And it was in portraits that reputations—and fortunes—were made.

On the other hand, as he was painfully aware, portraits also held pitfalls—and for no artist more than Jimmy Whistler. He talked over his reservations with Albert Moore. "To begin with, there is the dreary business of anatomical accuracy. A Nocturne is imprecise almost by definition; who can challenge the fuzzy outline of a bridge at twilight? But do the same thing with a nose or leg—especially if it happens to have been on public display because it belonged to a Disraeli or a Henry Irving—and a thousand self-anointed 'experts' will jump on you!"

"That's ridiculous, Jimmy. You're a superb draftsman."

"On a small scale, yes. In etchings. But with the large and often ungainly human figure . . ." He shook his head. "Then there is the matter of intent. A serious painter is interested only in his own response to a subject."

"True," nodded Moore. "His communication is one-directional: with himself."

"That does not necessarily produce flattering results. Now, a bouquet of flowers is in no position to complain that it has been maligned or distorted. A sitter can—and often does. You waste time and energy coping with some dullard's exalted image of what he looks like."

Moore puffed solemnly on his cigar. "Tell me, Jimmy, what other delights do you find in painting your fellow creatures?"

"They're too damned *available*. A Thames twilight won't sit for you fifty times; you have to commit yourself then and there. With a model, you're always tempted to have one last shot at the brass ring."

"A sad, sad tale," Moore sympathized. "Just remember, as they're voting you into the Louvre, that your old friend Moore told you to stop grappling with phantoms and get on with the job."

Jimmy had one more worry, not mentioned to Moore: How to preserve in portraiture the other-worldly dimension of the Nocturnes?

He went back to Velázquez, never in any case far from his consciousness. The princelings and clowns of the Spanish court, stately on horseback or broodingly pensive, had long seemed figures almost of his own imagination. Now, as he bent over old photographs with a new intentness, he realized why.

Velázquez was beyond all else a painter of atmosphere. His farmers, musicians, and biblical personages, no less than his proud, sad kings, each breathed a special aroma. It was much what Jimmy had been groping toward in his *White Girl* pictures: somewhere between the viewer and the physical body of the subject hung the mystery of human personality.

Part of the Spaniard's effect came from the shrewd choice of costume, setting, and accessories. The rest, Jimmy decided, grew out of an adroit manipulation of chiaroscuro: all objects, and space itself, were treated as softly graduated interruptions of light.

It was a technique he had neither the capacity nor the desire to emulate. Yet he was determined to arrive at an atmosphere equally expressive.

A daring alternative began taking shape in his mind: Could harmony of tone by itself be the key to poetic unity? To give the plan a chance, he would have to first strip down all other considerations to a minimum, confining himself to a single model, one-source frontal lighting, and a correspondingly simple pose in full face or silhouette. Then he could concentrate all his resources on the handling of color.

With layer upon layer of thin coatings, he would build up his entire canvas at a single pace. Kept uniformly wet, the picture would advance steadily in tone and definition, growing like a photo negative under the action of chemicals, from the first faint hints of values to its full range of lights and shadows. There would be no random treatment of a single section, no spotty patchwork to replace a faulty brush stroke. Like a tender shoot that is not yet a plant but is in its own way complete, the portrait would at any given stage be "finished" . . . and in its final form, perfect.

Jimmy had his campaign plan. Now armed with a theory as well as his talent, he advanced on the Speke Hall bastion.

Ten weeks later, he walked somberly into the drawing room at 2 Lindsey Row. "I'm back, Mother. I've run into trouble."

Anna Whistler, seated by the late-afternoon fire, fluttered to her feet. "Jemie! It's not your chest again?"

"No, no. Nothing like that."

"Anything else, with the Lord's help, we can overcome."

Jimmy bent and kissed her. "I hope this long winter hasn't been too hard on you."

"An ache or two that Willie looked after. But with you home again, I shall be better."

"I didn't intend to stay so long. There was so much to do . . ."

The brown eyes searched his face anxiously. "Did your efforts bear fruit, Jemie? You wrote that you were starting with the children."

"Yes. They had the most free time. Unfortunately, they did not wish to spend it standing still in a chilly studio."

"But they're so fond of you!"

"As a parcheesi partner, quite. And they adore Uncle Jimmy's tales of West Point. But when it comes to posing—" He shook his head. "Restless, hungry—and inventive. As models, they have all the adult vices, compounded."

He did not tell his mother, but he had thought back often to the uncomplaining Jo, and for a change the accompanying twinge of regret had no sexual overtones.

"So you accomplished nothing?"

"Oh, a few things. The little boy quit after a couple of pastels. And the older girls weren't much better. But Florence, the baby, sat for quite a nice dry point. And a promising oil, blue on blue."

"Like Gainsborough?"

He smiled faintly. "I fancy Gainsborough had less trouble with the mouth of his little boy."

"It seems to me you've done quite well. Everyone knows children are difficult subjects."

It was astonishing how much she had picked up of studio shop talk and attitudes. She had always demonstrated a keen sense of color, rhapsodizing in her letters over gardens and sunsets that were "the glory of creation." But since coming to London and being exposed to the hard realities of the painting life, she no longer scorned art as idle frippery; in fact, curiosity had expanded to fascination and concern.

"Children aren't the problem, Mother. Please sit down."

Anna returned to her chair. Jimmy paced a moment. "You see, Leyland himself decided to stay home for a week and stand for me. I devised a most effective composition: black on black, with the figure melting into the background; delicately carved, as it were, into the canvas. Just a few touches of silver, brown and white: on the shoe buckle, the hair, the shirt front."

Anna nodded.

"Leyland is posed very straight, with a light coat flung over his left arm and his right hand resting on his hip." Jimmy demonstrated. "The fellow has a certain dignity, you know."

Jimmy explained that he had dispensed with any preliminary drawing, and gone directly into oil. Then, as he began stripping away the surface resemblance and penetrated more deeply, he realized the legs weren't going right. They had a thin, insubstantial look; the portrait wasn't standing up firmly.

"I scraped and fussed at them a bit—and, well, I've told you my feeling about portraits. You can't do them in segments, not if you want a unity of tone and atmosphere. If some part doesn't work, you've got to do the whole thing over. Keep the canvas wet.

"I wasn't worried, at first. I had my prepared tones, and I knew where I was going. So I picked up my nice, flat house-painter brushes and started all over, this time working up from the bottom. One of Degas's tricks, for better control."

Jimmy stared past his mother into the fire on the grate. "It didn't help a bit. The legs still wouldn't come out. I must say, Leyland was very sporting about it. He stayed until after dark one afternoon, slapped me quite cheerfully on the back, and told me he hadn't the slightest doubt about the outcome."

"He's a Christian gentleman, Jemie."

"That's the worst of it. He's never once pushed or complained."

"Why should he? He's picked his man. He doesn't mind waiting a bit."

"A bit? You don't understand, Mother. After he left that day, I lighted a lamp and took a good look at the canvas. And you know, I simply cried. The more I had painted, the worse things seemed to get. Streaks and patches were showing up, where I had just laid down a smooth lovely veil. And then it dawned on me: my whole technique, the 'one-skin' approach, was at odds with the *medium*."

"The medium?" Anna Whistler strained to understand.

"Oil paints dry at different tempos, so it's extremely hard to keep an entire canvas wet. And the thin glazes I use tend either to sink into the underpainting, or run down leaving nasty streaks. A novelist or composer can erase his mistakes; a painter builds them into his canvas."

"Surely you can modify your method?"

"I don't want to! Its potentialities are wonderful—if the hazards can be kept under control. This time, they weren't." Jimmy removed his monocle and passed a long, bony hand across his forehead. "There's really no sense in stumbling on. Later, perhaps, I can do some leg studies from a nude model, and make a fresh start. But at this point, I'm at the bottom of a ditch." The hidalgic jaw quivered. "That's the plain truth, Mother. But I just can't face Leyland to tell him."

Anna Whistler waited a moment. Never had she seen her son—usually so debonair, or at worst stoic—so near defeat. The corners of his black mustache drooped wearily. Jimmy was getting older, she realized: small lines around the corner of his mouth, wrinkles above the fine brow, that brow so reminiscent of George Washington Whistler. Finally, "Would it be wiser to write him a note?" she asked gently.

"I can't." He raised his eyes. "But you can. Leyland has great respect for you. Tell him I've worked hard, but have run into difficulties . . . that the picture won't be ready for the Academy this year. Tell him I'll need more time, but am too embarrassed to ask him for it."

"He's a sensitive man, Jemie. I'm sure he'll understand."

Jimmy walked to the window. "If he wishes, he has a right to have his four hundred pounds back. Oh, I know there are bills to be paid, fuel and taxes. But I'll get the money somewhere—perhaps from brother George. I will not play the dishonorable man with Leyland."

"You could not with anyone. You are Major Whistler's son."

He came to her chair. "And yours as well."

She reached up and stroked his arm. "Ah, Jemie, Jemie. When will you have your reward for all the patience and struggle?"

"In the next world, no doubt. But it would be so gratifying to have at least a foretaste in this one."

Anna Whistler frowned. "I cannot help thinking, Jemie: Is this not perhaps a manifestation of the Lord's displeasure over work done on the Sabbath?" She felt him grow tense under her hand. "No, my son— you are right. This is no time for sermons. I shall attend to the letter at once." She looked up brightly. "Will you be dining at home? I have an excellent leg of veal."

"Tomorrow, Mother dear. Anderson Rose is waiting for me at the Arundel."

Walking down the path to his front gate, Jimmy turned to wave a farewell. His mother stood silhouetted at the drawing room window. A fading sunbeam gleamed momentarily across the pane, lighting up black dress, gray shawl, old-fashioned white lace bonnet . . . and beneath, the stubbornly youthful patch of color in her cheeks.

# Chapter Seventeen

He really would have to paint her one day. The thought had crossed his mind often in the past couple of years. Several times, toying with a self-portrait before bedtime, he had tried sketches of his mother, but the composition had never fallen quite into place.

He dropped off from his hansom at Trafalgar Square, to walk the last few blocks to the club in the April twilight. The setting for Anna Whistler would have to be simple, even stark: a blank wall broken by one or two picture frames, a dark adjoining drapery with perhaps a faint floral motif. The tonal effects, very subdued . . . a study in silver gray? Harmony in brown and silver?

Turning into Adelphi Terrace for the Arundel, he paused to make way for the lamplighter, a dim ancient little man shuffling along the Strand in a black ulster.

Black. Gray and *black*. Yes, that was it: an *Arrangement in Grey and Black*.

The chance came sooner than he had anticipated. Frustrated over Leyland, Jimmy had turned back to a commission started earlier at Dieppe for William Graham, a wealthy M.P. The subject was the legislator's fifteen-year-old daughter: *Maggie, Girl in Blue on Seashore*. Things were going very nicely—at least from Jimmy's point of view— when a footman brought word that Miss Graham had "sprained her ankle" and would be unavailable for an indefinite period.

Jimmy spent the afternoon in despair. He had no doubt that Maggie's indisposition was diplomatic; the girl had been showing signs of growing impatience with his slow, meticulous methods.

That evening, he reached a decision. If he was going to be plagued by contretemps anyway, he might as well be working on something of his own choice. After dinner, his mother noticed him preparing the other side of the *Girl in Blue* picture, which was painted on a large canvas of very fine white batiste. He volunteered no explanation. Anna Whistler, aware of his keen disappointment over the Graham setback, respected his moody silence.

The next morning, he asked her to come into his studio. "Would you mind standing over there, Mother?" He pointed toward the wall.

Mystified, Anna complied. Jimmy went to the single north-lighted window and lowered the shade carefully, about a third of the way. "A bit farther back, please, so that the light falls on you directly . . ."

"If I am going to stand for one of your patrons, I shall charge you regular model rates. Is it little Maggie I am posing for?"

Jimmy stepped back absently, making a slight adjustment to the shade. "No."

"Who then, if I may ask?"

"Yourself."

"Jemie!"

"I have wanted to take your portrait for some time. Would you mind?" He was suddenly anxious. "Could you manage the strain?"

"I should be most flattered, Jemie dearest."

"Good! We'll take another look at the pose this afternoon, eh?"

"What about my dress?"

"Oh, that's fine. Black is what I want. But perhaps you could wear that other bonnet, the white lace with the longish streamers down the side?"

Anna nodded. She was beginning to find the prospect quite exciting.

When she returned after lunch, she found her place marked with chalk. Jimmy had set up his easel near the window, with the table palette on its left and the model about four feet away on the right, so that the light fell over his left shoulder, slanting onto the right of portrait and sitter. Replacing his monocle with a pair of steel-rimmed spectacles, he studied his mother's features in silence. As he had circled the docks of the Thames a dozen years before, he moved lightly around the room, noting the juncture of neck and shoulder, the shadowed depth of an eye socket. Finally he picked up a pad and sketched a few tentative notes.

Three times in the next two days the ritual was repeated, with Jimmy quite forgetting his initial solicitude, and the standing periods stretching to nearly half an hour. Anna Whistler was Spartan and conscientious and determined to aid her eldest boy; but she was also sixty-five, in a damp climate unfriendly to aging joints. At last a sigh escaped her, and she asked if she might perhaps pose leaning against the wall?

As ever, Jimmy was instantly overwhelmed with remorse. "How stupid and cruel of me!" But of course, she would do no such thing.

He would put away his sketch pad at once, and when they resumed in the morning she could pose sitting down at her ease.

Anna protested; it would be foolish to stop now, with the spring light so clear and steady. Tomorrow might bring showers.

So they compromised. Anna went upstairs to her "Japanese bedroom" to rest, while Jimmy fetched a graceful straight-backed ebony chair from the dining room, and his mother's fireside footstool.

Now she sat, facing her son. Yes, she agreed, she was quite comfortable . . .

But Jimmy wasn't. The pose was too obvious, conventional. And it lacked the long, sweeping line that he cherished. Now, if he could only get a flat, clean profile effect à la Utamaro, a kind of modified silhouette . . . Why not?

"I'm sorry to trouble you, Mother, but—"

He swung the chair and stool around so that she would be at a right angle to him, the left side of her face exposed to the light. Anna took her seat again, automatically folding her hands in her lap in an attitude of calm dignity.

Jimmy rushed forward, whipping a white silk handkerchief from his breast pocket and placing it in her hands. Then he stepped back.

This was it! The design and color harmony were assembling in his mind faster than he could jot them down.

Spatial arrangement had periodically fascinated him. Like his engineer father, Jimmy was intrigued by abstract linear patterns, the interplay of vertical and horizontal to create distance and atmosphere. *At the Piano* had been a successful excursion into this domain. The portrait of his mother, with its crisscrossing lines of drapery and dado, picture frames and bare floor, would be another.

His colors would be absurdly simple in the telling, infinitely subtle in execution: gray on the wall and floor, whitish-gray for the bonnet and handkerchief, black in the dress and the drapery; with relief notes of gold dotting the drapes, pink flesh for the face, and chestnut in the headband and the *Black Lion Wharf* etching on the wall. The trick would be in the variations of tone within that narrow range, the discreet repetitions, the all-enveloping harmony of shadows and reflections.

The pose at which painter and model had arrived would be the subject of speculation for generations to come. Critics would trace it to the sculptured likeness of Nero's mother, Agrippina, in Rome, and to Canova's statue depicting the mother of Napoleon. Actually, it was simply the way Anna Whistler liked to sit.

Anna held herself quite still, wondering when the painting would begin. At the very edge of her faltering vision, she was aware of Jimmy on her left, evidently fussing with some tubes of color. But he had not yet approached the canvas.

As if divining her thoughts, he spoke from the table palette. "Please be patient, Mother. This process is very important, but I can't do it until the sitter is before me. I am mixing my prepared tones, the basic colors I will use in this canvas: the gray of the floor, for instance, with its variations as it appears in half-tone and deep shadow."

Since the development of his color-harmony approach, his pictures were increasingly "pre-painted" on the palette. He spread over the middle of the table a mixture for the flesh tone, and into the local color dragged his favorite shadowing elements, raw sienna and ivory black. His blacks were greenish for the drape, tinted variously for the dado and dress. Gradually the palette was covered with a network of related tones, a schematic miniature or forecast of what would appear on the canvas.

After fifteen minutes, Jimmy was ready. Picking up two small round hog's-hair brushes with 3-foot handles, he loaded them with a brownish-black mixture and walked back to the far end of the room. For several seconds he stood still as a pointer, scrutinizing the scene; then he darted forward and started sketching his main outlines—figure, drapery and wall—using the broomlike handles to maintain a distance from the canvas that enabled him to shift his glance occasionally to the subject. The lines were traced quickly with long, firm strokes.

To fill in the surfaces, Jimmy changed to his short-tapered house-painter brushes, building up a broad map of light and dark areas until figure and background emerged in foggy grayish-brown shades.

Now the stage was set for the first, tentative application of his pre-pared tones. Again Jimmy retreated to his corner, several loaded brushes in hand, this time to study a localized area of the subject. His visual impression obtained, he translated it mentally into the requisite pictorial equivalents, then slid forward to fix it in line and color while the original image lasted in his mind's eye.

For the better part of an hour, totally oblivious to the sitter as a human being, Jimmy repeated the process: the full charging of brushes with paint; the fierce, almost scalding gaze across the length of the room; the clean saber strokes that climaxed his dash to the canvas.

Then he let his mother see what he had done.

Hobbling stiffly to her feet, Anna Whistler peered over his shoulder. "But that's wonderful, Jimmy! Such a likeness—it's practically done!"

Jimmy laughed lightly, placing a hand on the bent frail back. "My dear Mother—it has just begun."

Now came the real test, the business of evolving the tonal refinements through which personality would be revealed. Jimmy worked intensively with his mother for the next two weeks, rising at seven for a row on the river with the Greaves boys, breakfasting *à deux* at eight, and proceeding directly to the studio.

Slowly he built up the depth and intensity of his colors, first in the figure and then in the background, covering the canvas again and again with a thin film of paint. Each coat, he explained to his mother, had to be light and transparent, "like breath on the surface of a pane of glass." He gave special attention to the crucial area where model sank into background, since the distance between the two could be created only by exact color values. Pressing his brush firmly into the canvas, he achieved an effect that was crisp, yet without hard edges because the tones were so closely related.

It was a long, tiring procedure, at first endurable for Anna only out of maternal loyalty. Jimmy might look twenty times, with that searching scrutiny that seemed to drain away the very life of his subject, before finding the exact place to put in a touch of prepared tone. Then, as he brought the brush to the canvas, he would like as not change his mind at the last minute and discard it for another. In a day's sitting he might piece together fifty such touches—or be totally absorbed in isolating the precise half tone of a neck shadow.

Yet he seemed relaxed and confident. Watching him carefully lift residual pigments into overnight saucers one evening, Anna asked if he thought the picture would be favorably received.

"My dear Mother, I am doing this picture to please myself—not for payment in any other coin. If I succeed—as I believe I shall—the critics also should rejoice. But if they do not . . . it will still be a fine picture."

The weather, Jimmy told himself, had something to do with it. There was a freak May storm, and then a succession of drizzles: damp, gloomy days when the rain never came down hard but never stopped either, and the muddy light trickling into the studio was almost worse than no light at all.

But it wasn't only the weather: he was having trouble with the expression around Anna Whistler's mouth. Publicly, in his vehement reaction against narrative sentimentality, he would one day snap angry denial of any personal associations connected with the picture. It was an *Arrangement in Grey and Black:* "To me it is interesting as the picture of my mother; but what can or ought the public to care about the identity of the portrait?"

In practice, he could not detach the withered features before him from what he knew and felt about their owner: the plain "best friend" of Mary Swift who stepped into the satined slippers of the former campus queen; the much-tried mother who lost three of her five boys in their infant years; the prayerful widow whose pious harangues pursued him from dawn to midnight, but whose fresh baked bread was as indispensable to his youthful years as her comforting good-night kiss. He had seen the firm flesh of her cheeks grow flaccid, while resignation overtook anxiety and hope.

Jimmy was as fervent as Degas in rejecting story-telling on canvas. But where Degas, like a frightened anemone closing up its petals, cut himself off totally from emotional contact with his subject, Jimmy kept his sensitivity intact under the barbed armor of his wit. The difference emerged in his best portraits; they had a warmth that was absent from the Degas ballerinas of the rehearsal hall.

The struggle for that extra dimension was all too evident to Anna Whistler. Although Jimmy was silent, his tension filled the room. She sat quietly, hands peeking out from plaited white cuffs, eyes fixed in an unseeing stare, her vision turned inward. And she prayed.

"Blast it!"

Anna intensified her appeal to the Lord. She was growing tired, but she would not add to Jimmy's difficulties, not now.

"No, no, I can't get it right!" She heard a brush clatter to the floor, and her heart wept for him. "It is impossible to do it as it ought to be done, perfectly!"

Ten minutes more. Footsteps, an occasional sigh. Anna felt a trifle dizzy. Probably he would call a break any moment. An interruption by her now might negate the cumulative effect of his endeavors.

Another passage of time, and she could not catch her breath. She managed a faint gasp: "Jemie!"

Jimmy looked up like a man coming out of a trance. For an instant he blinked in bewilderment, then rushed to her side. "Oh, this time I have really been neglectful! I am so sorry, Mother." He looked out over the garden, where the clouds were giving way at last to bright afternoon sunshine. "The weather is clearing. Let us go down to the river for some air."

At Cadogan's Pier, near the Battersea Bridge, they boarded a tuppence sidewheeler for a breezy cruise to Westminster half an hour away. Anna had changed to walking shoes, and thrown a maroon shawl over her perennial black dress. Jimmy was resplendent in fawn trousers under a dark gray frock coat, his broad-brimmed topper tilted back above his monocle to expose the white lock. He carried one of the slim canes that were the latest addition to his wardrobe.

Just beyond the Houses of Parliament, he helped his mother disembark and led her toward the sprawling greenery of St. James's Park. For a leisurely hour, they sauntered along the tree-shaded walks, admiring the grave-faced children trotting beside their white-capped nannies, pausing frequently at benches where Anna could rest.

Then Jimmy snapped his fingers for a hansom cab, and treated his mother to a final flutter of soft fresh air through the streets of Pimlico and Chelsea. As they arrived at Cheyne Walk, the sun was retreating toward the railroad bridge to the west, spreading a purplish fan of light over the Thames; the water glowed with a rare transparency.

Jimmy's eyes grew bright. "I must catch that, before it disappears into twilight." He ran ahead into the house, galloped up the stairs, and by the time Anna reached him had set up an easel at the huge drawing-room window. Responding to his excitement, Anna hastened to fetch his eyeglasses and the tubes of paint he needed: ivory black and lead white, Prussian blue, vermilion . . .

And, of course, the diluting turpentine. She hung over his shoulder as, with the deftness of a water-colorist, he washed his "soups" across the canvas in great loose-wristed sweeps. "Like magic," she thought to herself as the enchanting scene emerged; and she was reminded of Jimmy's insistence that for him, God was made manifest by the mysterious beauty of the cosmos.

Twilight crept over the water; the picture was virtually done. Then a new silvery glow appeared over the Battersea Marsh to the south. "Look, Jemie dear!" Anna pointed up at a brilliant rising moon. "There is light enough for you to do another painting if you wish, a Nocturne!"

Jimmy wished; and he did, most satisfactorily. By the time they sat down to a dinner of cold lamb and potato salad, the clock in the old church tower across the river was chiming ten.

It was never quite clear to Jimmy exactly what had made the difference—whether it was the break in the weather, the relaxed afternoon of sightseeing, or a reborn confidence growing out of his virtuoso handling of the Thames scenes—but when he resumed work on the portrait of his mother the next morning, the confusions were gone. Within ten minutes after starting, he saw the transition from lip to creased cheek that had been evading him; five minutes more, and he had translated it into paint.

Anna Whistler was quite startled to hear him cry out, in tones that would have been unthinkable a day before: "Oh, Mother, it is mastered! It is mastered and it is beautiful!" With the words, he bounced across the room and planted a kiss on her brow.

"How happy I am for you, Jemie!" And to herself, "Thank you, dear Lord."

"The rest will go quickly," Jimmy exulted. "I promise you. A few touches of gold on the drape, then a fine new skin over the whole. We shall be finished before the day is done."

And he was. Jimmy's "grand manner" was upon him; he worked with uncommon speed, humming his off-key airs from Offenbach, sometimes pursing his lips to blow out the air between his teeth . . .

a sure sign of euphoria. Only a half-dozen times in his life was there to be such a confluence of buoyant mood, splendid light conditions and sympathetic subject.

He stepped back at last. "Come and see, my dear mother."

Anna Whistler's gasp of admiration was pleasant to hear, but told him nothing he did not already know. It was a great painting: taken as linear composition, as color harmony, as atmospheric portrait; and, most remarkably, in the subtle fusion of all three. Purpose and means were so smoothly interwoven as to be inseparable.

No less than in the Nocturnes, he had achieved a universal statement, so poetic and diverse in its implications that for a century afterward, men and women of sensitivity would be stirred in a myriad of different ways. Some would see "modesty charged with loving tenderness"; others, only a stark Puritan austerity. The suggested motifs were to roam the compass: "humble fortitude," satisfied contemplation of a life well spent, the transcendental mysticism that sent the Pilgrims in flight to a New World. A French critic in 1910 would liken the painting to a classical tomb-carving, a somber forecast of the death that would soon separate mother and son; a famous American playwright of the 1960s, from Anna's own cherished Southland, would complain of her "irritatingly sweet, passive image." People would respond to the picture according to their private histories and associations; but they would all respond.

That, however, was still to come. A dozen years of adventures, rejections, and hairbreadth survivals lay between Whistler's *Mother* and reluctant critical approval; and nearly a decade more would pass before it was officially raised to immortality.

# Chapter Eighteen

The *Mother* portrait had barely been finished when it came within inches of being destroyed.

For several days the canvas stood on its easel at 2 Lindsey Row to receive the homage of Jimmy's intimates. The insomniac Rossetti, increasingly dependent on chloral, stirred from his melancholy long enough to pronounce it such a picture as "must make you happy for life"; Swinburne was moved by its "tender depth of expression." Anna Whistler, relaying the general flattery to her correspondents in America, hoped they would not think the "human weakness" had overtaken her.

On his return to Speke Hall for the Christmas holidays, Jimmy carted the portrait along, as much to reinforce his own morale as to impress his patrons. It was carefully packed and, along with two other crates containing uncompleted canvases, stored in the baggage car.

As the train was pulling into Liverpool Station, word swept through the passenger section that there had been a fire aboard. Jimmy collared a conductor. "The fire—where was it?"

"I'm not certain, sir. I believe the baggage car."

"Badly damaged?"

"So they say."

Jimmy dived through the compartment door and sprinted madly along the platform. Patches of blue smoke trailed up from the direction of the baggage car; he smelled charred wood and burning leather.

Drawing nearer, he saw trunks, suitcases, and cartons, some still spurting flames, strewn on the ground. A burly policeman guarded the open entrance to the baggage car. "No entry 'ere, sir," he told Jimmy.

"But I must!" Jimmy panted. "You don't understand." He flapped his arms excitedly. "My mother . . ."

"Yer mother?" The policeman raised a skeptical eyebrow. "Now, sir, if you'll just get a grip on yerself . . . The boys are bringing everything out. Everything wot's left, that is."

"*Left?*" Jimmy tiptoed, trying to peer over the big man's shoulder.

Then he saw his crates coming—one, two, three. There—that was the *Mother,* he knew it from the shape. And his heart stopped. A thick black smudge creased the lid.

Seconds later, he had snatched the packing case from its bearer's back and was tearing at the thin wooden stripping. It was still hot beneath his fingers; he dreaded what he would see.

Miraculously, the canvas was untouched. The flames had licked to the very edge, scorching the right side of the frame—and gone no farther.

It was like the Red Sea parting for Moses. There was something to be said for Anna Whistler's God.

Jimmy was still shaky on arrival at the mansion. His tension was quickly dissolved by the reception accorded the *Mother.* The ladies were enraptured; the head of the house insisted on moving the canvas from Jimmy's bedroom to the main salon, where it shared the place of honor with a Velázquez . . . and by general agreement (in which Jimmy concurred) lost nothing in the comparison.

On Easter Tuesday of 1872, the picture was dispatched to the Royal Academy. Despite the applause of his friends, Jimmy had no illusions about its prospects there. Most of the elders who made up the Exhibition jury resented his style, his tongue, or both. The title of the new Whistler—*Arrangement in Grey and Black #1: the Artist's Mother*—was not calculated to diminish the charges of pretentiousness.

Jury procedure was to sift through the hundreds of entries in two days, at a pace that allowed about a minute per painting. Most, marked with an ugly black cross on the back, never got beyond the ground-floor meeting room. A handful were favored with a white-chalked "A" for "approved," and taken to the huge lift running up to the gallery floors. A final group were marked "D" for "doubtful" and held for reconsideration, to be checked for size against the remaining space available.

This was the category to which the *Mother* was first assigned. Upon review by the full jury, it drew the praises of several prominent members, including Ford Madox Brown—but harsh attacks from the dominant Old Guard faction.

"We cannot leave out a work of such obvious distinction," protested Brown. "It would invite a public scandal."

But the conservatives had the votes. With visible relish a grizzled nonentity by the name of Dobson applied the damning black "X."

At this point Sir William Boxall, a member of the R. A. Council who two decades earlier had done a portrait of the adolescent Jimmy, arrived and asked where the Whistler picture was going to be hung. Informed that it had just been rejected, Boxall picked up his top hat: "It shall never be told of me that I served on a jury which refused a work like that. You have my resignation, gentlemen."

Such gestures had been made by members before, and ignored. But Boxall was the director of the National Gallery, a favorite of Queen Victoria.

Resentfully, the anti-Whistler clique agreed to compromise: the *Arrangement* would be hung as part of the "black-and-white" exhibit, among the drawings and engravings, but in a fairly conspicuous position. A last-minute move by Dobson to "sky" it higher, ostensibly to cram some smaller canvases below, was firmly turned down. "Touch it again," reiterated Boxall, "and you have seen the last of Sir William Boxall."

The portrait had breached the ramparts of the Academy—but only after overcoming an opposition whose bitterness Jimmy never forgot.

The day after the opening, Jimmy had a note from G. F. Watts, the most distinguished traditional portraitist in England, congratulating him on "a work of such merit," despite the "little weight you will probably attach to my praise."

That praise was not echoed in the press. The *Examiner* dismissed the *Mother* as "another of Mr. Whistler's experiments . . . it is not a picture." To the critic of the *Hour,* it was "stiff and ugly enough to repel many." *Punch* sniffed in disbelief. Was it a practical joke? Or a reflection of severe optical delusions? The painter violated "all accepted canons of good drawing, good color, good painting." And the *Times,* shuddering at the "dim, cold light" of the "solemn chamber," reported that the portrait had "found few admirers among the thousands who seek to while away the hours at Burlington House."

The Establishment seemed as determined as ever to throw Jimmy overboard.

But they could not stop him from painting. Already he was occupied with important sequels.

One of his neighbors at 24 Cheyne Row a few blocks away was Thomas Carlyle, Scottish author of *The French Revolution* and *Sartor Resartus,* a giant among the intellectual figures of the century. Gaunt and fierce at seventy-seven, Carlyle felt cast aside by a country that preferred to take its guidance from "mediocrities" like William Gladstone. From his shabby citadel in Chelsea, he stormed at the hypocrisies of an age whose gift to slum children was "the liberty to starve."

On a mild spring afternoon, Carlyle was lured into Jimmy's house under pretext of a domestic errand by a mutual friend, Madame Emilie

Venturi. Madame Venturi, a disciple of the Italian revolutionary
Giuseppe Mazzini, maneuvered the old man upstairs to the studio and
left him alone with the *Mother*.

The dissenter from Glasgow planted himself before the portrait of
Anna McNeill, great-granddaughter of the clan chief Black Daniel
McNeill from the Isle of Barra. He tapped the floor meditatively with
a gnarled cane.

Carlyle had come down to London as a divinity student, the son of
a Puritan stonemason; the hardness of the older man's materials, along
with his moral fanaticism, had rubbed off on the boy. In 1866, after
forty poverty-plagued years of marriage, Carlyle's wife Jane had died.
Although their domestic life was something less than blissful—rumor
said Carlyle never made love to her—her tuneful piano and lively
tongue had been a comfort to the dour "Sage of Chelsea." Since her
passing, he had grown more cantankerous than ever, railing against
church bells, crowing cocks, and "yellow demon" organ-grinders, as
well as parliamentary policy. He scorned the pleasures of society and
the senses: poetry was "jingles," nonsense that would be "retired to
the nursery" in the coming age of science. Art was (shades of the
young Anna Whistler!) trivial; Michelangelo intrigued him, but only
as an engineer. Foppish display was, of course, inexcusable; Carlyle
had snubbed Robert Browning because the poet came to see him
wearing a purple frock coat.

To such a man, who considered Voltaire "insufficiently earnest," the
becurled little American painter on Lindsey Row was naturally anathema; in fact, Carlyle publicly referred to Jimmy as "the creature."

That was before the philosopher confronted the painting of the
*Mother*. He had stopped tapping now, and was staring with undis-
guised interest. There was something very like a glint of approval in
his sharp blue eyes.

Emilie Venturi drifted to his side. "Is it not very simple and real,
Mr. Carlyle?"

"Humph . . . Aye, 'tis real."

"You would make an equally fine subject. Mr. Whistler is most eager
to have the opportunity."

Carlyle turned to Jimmy, discreetly busy with his paints in a corner.
"Ye ken, Mr. Whistler, I'm a mon of little patience. How many days
would ye take?"

"As few as possible, sir, I assure you."

The ambiguity of the assurance was not lost on Carlyle. Scot faced
Scot (Jimmy had become all McNeill), the beginning of a stubborn
confrontation. "Well, let's gie it a try. Just two or three sittings, mind
ye."

And so the famous author consented to sit to the most unpopular painter in England.

At ten the next morning, Carlyle clumped up the stairs and threw himself heavily into the same chair that had held Anna Whistler. "All right, mon, fire away!" At Jimmy's startled expression, he explained: "Whether ye're fighting a battle or painting a picture, it's the only thing to do: fire away!"

"You remind me of my West Point days, sir. But the command was a little different there." He eyed his adversary. "Fire *when ready*." He turned back to his palette.

This was to be an *Arrangement in Grey and Black No. 2*, a deliberate reprise of the *Mother* composition but with significant differences in detail and mood. He studied the restless old man planted gloomily in the chair, right hand clutching a stout walking stick. He saw the face of an Old Testament prophet: craggy, austere, with straight nose and stony jaw under shaggy gray thatch. The eyes were deep and gleaming, and sunk in a sadness near despair.

Jimmy stepped forward. "If I could trouble you, sir, to turn your head a little to the right . . . and place your hat on your knee. There, so . . . and let us loosen the front of your greatcoat, so we get a curving line . . ."

Drily, "Would ye like me to do a little dance?"

"That won't be necessary, Mr. Carlyle—unless you cannot control your exuberance."

It was a good silhouette line, quite different from that of his mother, broken in sinuous descent from brow to shoetops by the bulge of the greatcoat, the projecting top of the cane, and the broad hat angled across the old man's knees. Hiroshige would have approved.

He wasn't so sure that Carlyle did, but that couldn't be helped. He picked up one of his long sketching brushes, dipped it in a brownish mix, and approached the canvas. His sitter suddenly perked up. "I see ye don't use those wee brushes."

"No. I find these more suitable."

"Why don't all painters use good, straightforward tools?"

"I cannot speak for others. A man must pursue his own way."

Carlyle liked that. He looked over at the carefully arranged table palette. "Ye have the methods of a workman," he said approvingly.

"I'd better have. Painting is hard work."

Carlyle fell silent.

At their second session, the old man suddenly expressed curiosity about contemporary Paris. Jimmy told him of the boulevards and museums, the bright crowded cafés like the Foyot and the Anglais. The historian leaned forward slyly: "Ah, but can a mon get a good chop there?"

Before leaving, Carlyle took a "wee peek" at what Jimmy explained was the painting equivalent of a very rough first draft. The old man was pleased to note that his shirt collar was indicated in white: "I sat once to Watts, and he painted my collar green. I told him, 'Mon, I have always been in the habit of wearing clean linen!'" Carlyle smiled in triumph. Jimmy smiled back. There was no further talk of "two or three sittings."

On his next visit, Carlyle was unexpectedly expansive, touched off by an ingenious American-made umbrella in Jimmy's hallway. Canny wights, the Americans. But their politics? The massive unkempt head waggled. "Democracy is anarchy dressed up with a street constable. Against the nature of the human beastie." Abruptly, "Ye're from the South, I believe, Mr. Whistler?"

Brush in hand, studying the tones of the brown cape thrown across Carlyle's lap, Jimmy nodded.

"They've turned out some leaders at least, aye, men of strong principle like Robert E. Lee."

"My superintendent at the Point."

"Indeed?" Carlyle brightened. He was off on his favorite subject, the interpretation of history as the creation of a few super-heroes.

Jimmy made no interruption to these élitist sentiments. His own politics were vague and fluctuating: a grab bag of St. Petersburg snobbery, Swinburne republicanism, Old South prejudices and even the fire-eating socialism of Courbet. Although his emotional sympathies were with the oppressed, he had never tried to fuse these discordant elements into a coherent political philosophy. Now he listened solemnly, occasionally nodding. His one concern was to capture Carlyle afizz, in this moment of revelation. He would cheerfully have signed the Communist Manifesto to prolong the necessary mood.

The flush of excitement passed; and still Jimmy toiled on. After two weeks, Carlyle's habitual impatience returned. What the devil was taking so long? And what was the point of continuing into late afternoon, when the light was reduced to a flicker and all sensible people were settling down to a good cup of steaming tea?

"My dear Mr. Carlyle, I must tell you there *is* a point. As the light fades and the shadows deepen, all petty and exacting details vanish. Everything trivial disappears, and I see things as they are, in strong masses. The buttons are lost, but the garment remains; the garment is lost, but the sitter remains; the sitter is lost, but the shadow remains; the shadow is lost, but the picture remains. And that, night cannot efface from the painter's imagination."

"Humph!" Carlyle stumped out.

The next morning, he returned to the attack. Why was Jimmy fussing so much over the painting of his coat? "Ye give that more attention than my phiz!"

"Naturally. The coat did not have God for its tailor."

"Ye're toying with blasphemy. But I still dinna ken why—"

"Mr. Carlyle, I do not pretend to advise you on how to analyze the Fall of the Bastille."

"Aye, and a good thing you don't!" Carlyle pounded his cane angrily on the floor.

"For God's sake," Jimmy screamed, *"don't move!"*

Nobody had shouted at the King Lear of Chelsea and gotten away with it since Jane Carlyle died. This, the old man recognized, was a duel to the finish. Jimmy might cozen a bit and cajole, but the present message of flashing eyes and jutting jaw were unmistakable. Thomas Carlyle was confronted with a will as stubborn, a temper as irascible as his own.

Up to this point he had conceded to Jimmy only a certain "lunatic talent." Now he had to admit evidence of something he valued much more: character. He clamped his lean jaw shut and sat still.

The decisive assault came almost by accident. Dropping in one night at the Duke Street tobacconist, Jimmy found Carlyle at the counter. They emerged together, the painter dexterously rolling a French cigarette, the author puffing contentedly on his pipe. "Och, mon, 'tis a bonnie evening for a walk," observed Carlyle.

"And there's no lovelier path than the Embankment."

That was the beginning of a twice-a-week arrangement. Carlyle had prowled the Thames shore with Emerson, Dickens, Tennyson, and John Stuart Mill; now it was the turn of the little American. They were the original odd couple: tall, spare ascetic striding powerfully in his sacklike black cloak, small jaunty bon vivant in dancing shoes stepping along briskly beside him.

Carlyle talked of his most intimate beliefs. Even Jesus now disappointed him; the Son of God lacked humor. "I would not for all the disciples gie up the ragged company of Falstaff." And Jimmy, for once, listened, sucking up the spiritual bone marrow of England's Angry Old Man.

By day, he recorded his impressions in paint. For a last rendering of the coat, he put in two sessions with a professional model. Then he called in Carlyle to look.

The old man stared for several seconds. He cleared his throat, and the heavy mouth relaxed into something like a smile. "'Tis very like, Mr. Whistler. Very like indeed."

It was far more than that. The painting had the monumental simplicity of a great Velázquez, recalling the Spanish master's portrait

of the sculptor Ivan Martinez. In composition, it was if anything superior to the *Mother*, with the butterfly cartouche at the extreme right
balanced exquisitely against the two framed prints on the left. Its
mysterious grays and subtle browns created an atmosphere palpably
weighty: "In painting a thinker," Jimmy had said, "one must fill the air
with thoughts."

But beyond all that was the man himself, a ruined Rome of a man.
Jimmy had set down the disillusion and sorrow, the emotional con-
tradictions that for Carlyle made personal relationships all but impossible. The world would be years in recognizing Jimmy's achievement;
but in the furrowed granite countenance, the averted melancholy eye
contemplating a dream gone down the drain, were the tragedy of defeated genius.

Meanwhile, Jimmy had launched into another project, at the opposite extreme of the atmospheric spectrum. Pert, blond Cicely Alexander was nine years old, the daughter of a long-time Whistler patron.
The day her mother brought Cicely in by carriage for her first sitting,
Carlyle was just departing through the garden gate. He turned to the
coachman: "And who might that be?"

"Why, that, sir, is Miss Alexander, come to 'ave 'er portrait taken by
Mr. Whistler."

"Puir lassie," muttered Carlyle, and strode on.

For his young sitter, Jimmy did a turnabout in tactics, summoning
up his resources of fey charm. He recited nonsense poetry, fashioned
her a puppy from leftover gold leaf, even promised to paint her doll.
He also enlisted his mother to select a white gown of sheer muslin, all
ruffles and dancing lightness.

He posed Cicely standing in the center of a striped carpet, plumed
hat in hand, left leg slightly advanced, with the careless haughtiness of
a modern Infanta. His color arrangement—*Harmony in Grey and
Green*—was the sunniest since *The Gold Screen* done with Jo a decade
before, and far more intricate. The grays ranged from iron-dark in the
dado through the still-rich tones of her hat, down to the near-white
of the floor covering. Pale green accents appeared in waist sash, hem-
line and trailing hat feather. Splashes of gold glittered in hairpin and
shoe buckles, and in the matching grace notes of daisies at the child's
side and butterflies fluttering over her head.

But beyond decoration lay the mystery of atmosphere—and that
proved maddeningly hard to pin down. Time and again the inspirations of twilight proved deceptive, and had to be scraped off with the
palette knife in the morning.

As session followed session, and weeks melted into months, with
Jimmy as usual oblivious to the reactions of his model, Cicely's initial

self-importance gave way to ennui and then irritation. It was not comfortable to stand in a fixed position for long, slow hours, being stared at as if one were a mannequin. Jimmy showed no concern whatever for his empty stomach—or, what was worse, hers. Notified that lunch was ready, he would mutter an absent "Be along in a moment," then work right on into an un-English teatime of biscuits and tinned peaches.

Soon it was open warfare, more strident than the contest of wills with Carlyle: "You're a horrid, wicked man!" from the weary child, "Stand still and be quiet!" from the exasperated painter. Cicely wept a good deal, and Jimmy shed a few tears himself.

If the little girl was outgunned, she was not ready to surrender. Now each time she resumed her pose, her lips were shaped into a proud, defiant pout.

It was that sullen stance that gave Jimmy his clue. He had been chasing the wrong quarry! What Cicely emanated was not so much guileless innocence as the impatience of youth, the eagerness to throw aside the restraints of childhood and step across the threshold into grown-up life. That was quite a different story . . .

Cicely saw the painting-hand slacken . . . a worrisome sign. "You're not going to start all over again, Mr. Whistler?"

"Let us have tea, and I shall tell you all about the gay court life of St. Petersburg." Jimmy didn't tell her "all," but he made the account diverting enough to lighten the little girl's mood.

After she left, he started scraping away at the dress. As he studied it for repainting, it occurred to him that it didn't need any; the palette knife had created exactly the spare effect he wanted. Such happy accidents were rare; he embraced it as a good omen.

Which it was. On the next sitting—Cicely's sixty-eighth over a period of ten months—the new concept emerged smoothly. It seemed that even the early experimentation was not wasted; previous layers of delicate pigment peered through, imparting an exquisite luminosity of tone. The canvas was a unified surface of subtle color embroidery, the perfectly woven tapestry-in-paint that he had held out as a remote ideal in his anguished letters to Fantin-Latour. It was also an affirmation of his insistent musical analogies: the line of black that wound down from velvet hair ribbon to waist cockade, hatband, and shoes was as precisely ordered in its intervals as a rich chord on the piano.

Never again, in his large oils at least, would Jimmy spin such a web of joyous color . . . or know such a streak of unbroken productivity.

Jimmy was thoroughly worn out. In the intensity of his concentration, he had quite lost touch with events outside his studio. The past few years had brought major changes to Europe: Germany's Bismarck, having overthrown Louis Napoleon at Sedan, was now a figure to be reckoned with. The United States had been altered even more drastically: with the plantation aristocracy destroyed, and the South in the agonies of Reconstruction, Northern enterprise was sweeping westward on the rails of the New York Central and the transcontinental Union Pacific. Only Britain held to a familiar course, carving new outposts of empire in India and Africa.

Jimmy needed time to collect himself, and a breath of fresh air. Both were suddenly put at his disposal, in an invitation to an extended stay at Speke Hall. He could rest and walk in the country; and when he felt up to it, engage in leisurely final bouts with the adult Leyland portraits.

There was another, more interesting reason prompting his eager acceptance: he wanted to press his suit with the delicious Frances Leyland.

His friend Degas might turn an ascetic back on women, muttering "There is love and work, and a man has only one heart." For Jimmy, work alone could never be enough. The rustle of a skirt, the caress of a gentle voice, the enigma of a smile were as necessary to him as air. Like many another artist, he carried his own romantic nimbus around with him, seeking a target in every female figure that swished mysteriously past.

Not that he wished to repeat the bittersweet experience with Jo, where he had committed and submerged himself utterly. That was a lingering ache, a door in his heart he preferred not to open. In future, his sexual life would be modeled on the butterfly of his painting signature: swooping down gracefully to admire, taste, and enjoy . . . then darting off unpinioned. That way lay freedom—and safety.

During the past year, between occasional working visits to Speke Hall, he had maintained a discreet but obliquely feverish correspondence with Mrs. Leyland, never quite proposing an affair but hinting that he was available for one: London without her, he wrote, was desperately lonely, bereft of all sunshine; he felt like an orphan tossed out in the cold; the mere thought of Speke Hall (and its implied forbidden delights) inspired delicious reveries.

Now he had a legitimate excuse to continue his courting in person. The portrait of Frederick Leyland had at long last been virtually completed, after a male model was drafted in desperation to sit for the legs. The studies of the children were at an impasse, except for one of the girls with whom half-hearted efforts would continue until she quite outgrew the canvas. Only the sleek and slender Mrs. Leyland remained to be painted.

She stood, aristocratic of profile, glancing over her shoulder at Jimmy in the top-floor playroom that had been converted into a studio.

Her husband was on a trip to Glasgow, her children all at school. Her red-flecked brown hair was piled into a demure bun, oddly provocative against the ultra-romantic accessories of pink dress, rose-flushed walls and sprays of whitish almond-blossom. This *Symphony in Flesh Color and Pink* would be one of Jimmy's last essays in light-toned portraiture.

"I hope," said Frances Leyland, "we will not be working too hard. I should hate to be associated in your mind with drudgery."

"My dear Mrs. Leyland, no one would dream of associating you with anything but pleasure."

The long lashes fluttered. "You are too *galant*. I wish that were true."

He looked at her meaningly. "It would be, if you let it."

Frances colored. "Pray tell me, Mr. Whistler, is this pose, ah, satisfactory?" She dropped her arms to her sides.

"Whatever is comfortable." Jimmy put down his large brush and went over to her. "You must try to relax." He brought her hands gently together. "How does that feel?"

"Quite natural."

Something in her voice signaled him forward. He slipped a wiry arm around her waist. "And this—does this too not seem natural?"

When in doubt, attack! That was the West Point credo. His hand, unopposed, moved boldly to the collar of her loose silk frock, then crept beneath to probe at the lacing of her stays.

"Jimmy! What are you doing?"

"What I have longed to do these many months!" His search was rewarded; his fingers sank into soft cool flesh.

"No, no!" Frances protested, and at the same time squirmed toward him. Grappling under her dress, Jimmy was conscious of lilac perfume mingled with hot quick breath. One hill taken, one to go . . .

"We are well-matched in desire," he whispered.

"But not in situation."

"Please, my darling. Just the other breast."

"And then what?" Frances wrenched herself away. Jimmy pursued her across the room: "You are meant to be loved, not displayed like a trophy! Do you pretend to be happy with Leyland?"

"I pretend nothing. But if we go one step further, there will be no turning back. I can't afford that, Jimmy. I am not one of your Paris models—although sometimes I wish I were."

"You are more beautiful than any of them!"

"I have children to think about—and a husband who would not hesitate to bring down scandal on the heads of all of us."

"Leyland need never know."

"He would find out. Already he has made remarks, about my unusual good humor on the days when there is a letter from you."

"The bully!"

"Your patron. And in the eyes of God and Queen, the lawful liege of my household."

Angry, frustrated, Jimmy plunged ahead recklessly. "If it's marriage you want—"

"Come now, Jimmy, you're not serious. You don't want to be burdened with a wife."

"You could never be a burden."

"And *I* don't want to be at the mercy of the artistic temperament. The moods of a dilettante are bad enough."

"Please don't compare me with that monster!"

"I'm not. But the sad fact is, you're a lover, Jimmy—and I'm not free to be loved."

"Only to be painted, eh?" He was annoyed that his voice had become so shrill. He flung himself out of the room.

Ultimately, the sitting was resumed; but it was a perfunctory performance on both sides. Several times Jimmy pronounced the portrait done, only to wipe it out the next morning and start again. Because Frances grew bored, Jimmy brought in a chic new professional model from London, Maud Franklin, to sit for the dress. Finally, dissatisfied with the hands, he thrust the canvas into a corner.

The rebuff by Frances Leyland made things just about unanimous. The critics had not yet passed judgment on the *Carlyle* or *Miss Alexander* portraits, but he had no reason to think they would fare any better than their predecessors. With his fortieth birthday around the corner, he was a crashing failure in practically every department of human endeavor.

Although presumably at the peak of his creative powers, he was being widely dismissed as a mountebank or a bungler. The highest price he could command (or rather, muster from his little clique of supporters by something unpleasantly close to wheedling) was 150 guineas per picture, against the 11,000 raked in by the solemn Pre-Raphaelite Holman Hunt. John Everett Millais, that practical earthbound grouse-shooter, was earning £40,000 a year; Jimmy had made scarcely £3000 since coming to England.

A particular source of anathema were his abstract titles. But when critics condemned him for showing a story-less *Nocturne in Blue and Gold*, he itemized publicly their technical blunders—some could not tell a Delacroix from a dishrag—and came back with more nomenclature deliberately borrowed from the concert hall: Symphonies, Harmonies, Arrangements. He refused to temper his emphasis on what Gauguin would one day call "the total liberty of the act of painting." And dealers, with a respectful eye toward press opinion, were not interested in putting such heresies on display.

Gloomily he consoled himself: If he had remained in America, he would by now have become a New York or Philadelphia portrait hack, respectable, married—and miserable. Early success would surely have been a disaster. Well, fate had spared him that—more emphatically, he reflected, than might have been absolutely necessary.

To assuage the sting of daily rejections in Bond Street and Pall Mall, Jimmy took to staging mock exhibitions in his studio. With the Greaves brothers as an audience making up in enthusiasm what they lacked in numbers, Jimmy played all the parts: dealer, ticket collector, fashionable viewer, and critic. His oily entrepreneurial smile of greeting was faultless: "Come one, come all, to see the strange wild American with his even stranger titles. Be prepared to smile, but under no circumstances to comprehend . . ."

Then, hand limply extended, he became a languid Mayfair beauty pausing before a canvas: "Is that an oil, Lord Rumplebottom?"

A hideous squint, a stumbling forward on an imaginary cane, and the answer in a faint octagenarian squeak: "Oh no, my dear. Oils are always in red or yellow."

His most cherished caricature was, naturally, the critic: bulging with stomach and importance, advancing across the floor portentously with lorgnette raised. "Ah, what have we here? A *Nocturne in Dried Noodles*, perhaps? Ha-ha."

The dealer, hastily sidling up to him: "You're looking at Lord Rumplebottom, sir. The paintings are on this side."

Walter Greaves, weeping with laughter after one of these improvisations, ventured that the world was really missing something. Wouldn't it be marvelous to have a *real* one-man Whistler show, with the artist himself presiding?

Why not? mused Jimmy.

He knew very well why not. Bloodied as he might emerge from an exhibition where he shared space with many others, how much worse would it be to stand naked and alone in the arena, facing a phalanx of starved critical lions? He understood the terror that public showings held for Rossetti and Degas.

Early in 1874 he was struck by a severe attack of bronchitis. Weak and dispirited, he could not execute the simplest commissions. In this moment of travail, encouragement again came from surprising sources: the two most distinguished misanthropes working on either side of the Channel.

First it was the bilious Degas who turned up, blue and shivering in his greatcoat. "These fogs are a national disgrace. And with my eyes" —he had incurred a puzzling ailment while on sentry duty in the Franco-Prussian War—"I had a devil of a time finding your house."

"Please sit down. You're just in time for tea and biscuits. Now tell me—what news of the fellows on the Impressionist front?"

Degas stared at him gloomily, his thick lower lip drooping: "When we were youngsters, battling the Philistines of the Salon together, we clung to each other like lovers. Now that we have all 'arrived,' we quarrel: Manet with Pissarro and me, Fantin with Legros . . . If we had fought the Germans as we do each other, Bismarck would be in his grave."

"You are still doing your studies of movement—those wonderful horses, and the ballet girls? You strike a very special note, my dear Degas."

"As do you," the Frenchman said with unexpected emphasis. "I wrote it to Tissot last year, and I repeat it to you here: you have really found a personal way of expression, especially in those river pieces. It is something unique, the mysterious mingling of land and water."

"The London critics don't—"

"Please!" Degas raised a slim imperious hand. "Nothing of critics. I am eating."

The following morning, it was Carlyle who stood in the bedroom doorway. "I've just heard ye were ailing. My cook has brought some fresh barley soup and Spanish oranges to your kitchen."

"That's very kind of you, Mr. Carlyle."

" 'Tis the least a neighbor can do. They say you were very bad last week. But when they told me you'd made up your mind not to die, I knew it would be all right." He nodded curtly, and let through the ghost of a smile. "When a mon decides not to die, half the battle is won."

Good fighting words, from one Celt to another. They were all Jimmy needed to hear. A month later, when the Royal Academy made an across-the-board rejection of his entries, he decided, like Courbet and Manet before him, to take the solo plunge. He ferreted out Henry Graves, a dealer at 48 Pall Mall who was rash enough to hazard a Whistler show, and assembled a dozen of his most recent oils along with fifty etchings.

Several major critics, including those from *Atheneum* and the *Saturday Review*, didn't even bother to come. Those who did stayed briefly, before repairing to their writing desks to deliver what many obviously hoped would be the *coup de grâce*. Under the mastheads of *Life, Truth, Knowledge,* and lesser journals, in elegant opera pumps or middle-class brogans or hobnailed boots, they stomped on the audacious American. The Whistler canvases were "blue and black smudges," mere "riddles" or "rub-ins of color" done in a "mad new style." "Painting to Mr. Whistler," snorted the *Times*, "is the exact correlative of music, as purely emotional, as released from all functions of representation." Nobody quite suggested that it was the artist, rather than his canvases, that should be hanging, but the note of violent dismissal was clear.

Sir George Scharf, curator of the National Portrait Gallery, was coaxed through the door to consider the *Carlyle*—already publicly condemned by the prestigious Frederick Wedmore as "doleful." Scharf stared incredulously for a moment, then burst into a loud cackle. "Well, and has English painting come to this?"

The artist popped up at his side. "No, Sir George," Jimmy hissed into his ear. "Unfortunately, it hasn't."

The *Carlyle* did not reach the walls of the Portrait Gallery.

No warmer was the reception accorded the "puir lassie" who had followed the ancient Scot into Jimmy's studio. The shimmering *Miss Cicely Alexander*, Jimmy's marvel of tonal delicacy, was "devoid of color" according to the *Western Daily Mercury*, a "rather unpleasant yellow" in the opinion of *Echo*, and a mass of "murky tints left wet in a room where chimney sweeps were at work" to the eyes of the *Era* reviewer, who protested this slur on the "roses and lilies that adorn the cheeks of our blooming English girls." *Punch*, although omitting the Union Jack, was equally scathing: "A gruesomeness in gray. Farewell, J. Whistler!"

Jimmy, grinding his teeth, carefully clipped out and saved every last stinging paragraph. These were his war wounds, for grim contemplation and proud display. One day, when the battle was won—as it surely would be—he would hurl back the insults in the bastards' faces.

# Chapter Nineteen

The fact was inescapable. He was still under siege: if no longer by his own inadequacies, by an outside enemy even more implacable. He had to bolster his standard for the long haul with a retinue of loyal supporters.

The first problem was a matter of basic housekeeping, the day-to-day requirements of his table and his studio. Anna Whistler was clearly failing, diminishing in energy if not in will. She who over the years had nursed so many of her family and friends, now needed nursing herself; Willie was increasingly at the house to prescribe strong bark for her heart, and soothing solutions for her eyes.

The situation demanded a woman. If domestic competence could be supplemented by sexual attractiveness, so much the better.

Maud Franklin unmistakably filled the bill. Small, trim, with well-spaced features in a smooth oval face, she had been engaged as a model originally because of her similarity in type to Frances Leyland. She was not as patrician as Mrs. Leyland, or as witty as other society beauties such as Louise Jopling. Although her hair was, consistent with Jimmy's romantic history, red, it was not the flamboyant voluptuous mass of Jo Heffernan, but something darker-tinted and more discreet. Nor could she measure up to Jo in fey charm or artistic sensibility.

Yet she was in her dainty, small-boned way an agreeable creature: thrifty and efficient, with a knowledge of bookkeeping and a façade of elegance that more or less camouflaged her lowly origins. The daughter of a widowed brewery worker, Maud had been hired as an apprentice by a seamstress aunt, and had taken the opportunity to study the manners of her aunt's fashionable clients. Delivering a gown in Mayfair one afternoon, she was spotted in the anteroom by the libidinous Frederick Sandys, and was soon launched on a career of modeling.

Her passage into Jimmy's bed was accomplished with ladylike urbanity: in fact, with a detachment that he found irritating. If he had a complaint about Maud, it concerned her British matter-of-factness in the sexual sphere; there was more fire in her jealousy than in her performance. He could scarcely have anticipated the storm that the appearance of a prepossessing rival to Maud would create a decade later. But it wouldn't have made any difference; his immediate need for companionship was too great.

Equally acute was the need for an artistic representative who could expand Jimmy's narrow band of patrons. The Rossetti Circle, spinning on its merry-lugubrious way, had flung into Jimmy's orbit first the great man himself, then the effervescent Swinburne. Now it was the turn of Charles Augustus Howell, foremost of agent-middlemen.

Over the years Howell had broadened his operations, handling everything from avant-garde poetry to thoroughbred race horses for the European nobility. But his specialty remained art objects. Recently he had been active (some thought overactive) on behalf of Rossetti. The dashing Portuguese had brought a good deal of income into Tudor House—and undoubtedly carted away quite a lot, too. Portable items of value—a drawing here, a water color there—tended to be missing after one of Howell's friendly visits. The DGR monogram was likely to turn up on a sketch of the agent's own authorship, and be passed off on some unsuspecting baronet as an original. But what really exasperated Rossetti was the Howell's labyrinthine bookkeeping. The Owl, as Jimmy sometimes dubbed him, could not simply enter a charge for his services; he was constitutionally unable to follow a straight line. Rossetti made several futile protests, then broke off business (but not social) relations.

Swinburne had already done the same, after Howell tied him up to a nearly disastrous publishing contract. Howell's managerial talents were therefore at the disposal of Jimmy, who was pleased enough to inherit them. To Jimmy, these contretemps of personality were less important than Howell's money-earning skills; and both considerations paled before the exploits of the "wily Portugee" in hoodwinking the duffers of the Establishment.

Howell was a living mockery of Victorian society, skimming over its surface like a sea bird, footless and inconsequent as the hero of a Fielding novel. The range of his rascality was staggering, running the gamut from boy tenor to basso profundo of crookedness; he could devise a royalist plot of noble proportions, and the next moment devote the same meticulous attention to separating an innocent clubman from a few shillings. Never did he lose his sure sense of style; he was, as Jimmy insisted, "criminally speaking, an artist."

There was the time he was charged with swindling a collector out of forty pieces of blue china pottery. Howell hired forty cabs, each carrying one item, to trundle up to the courthouse in stately procession—a theatrical gesture that quite overwhelmed the jury.

Even more spectacular was the Kien Lung coup, in which Howell pitted wits against a cabinet minister reputed for his shrewdness. Visiting Howell's home at Fulham, the minister had noticed a small group of pieces done in black china: a teapot, a pair of cups and one saucer. "What are those, Mr. Howell?"

"Oh, nothing of importance. Part of a batch I picked up last week at auction in Hammersmith."

"But what are they?"

"Really, not suitable for your collection. As you can see, quite lacking in beauty. Apart from their rarity, they're not worth looking at."

The ministerial eyes narrowed. One hand reached out to pick up the teapot.

Howell sighed. "Just a bit of Oriental eccentricity. You probably know that when the Emperor Kien Lung lost his favorite wife, he ordered the entire court into total mourning. Black was ordered everywhere: in clothing, hanging, carpets . . . even the garden paths were covered with cinders. Well, as you know, by that period there was no black china being produced; so a special service had to be made, exclusively for royal use. Naturally, most of it has disappeared. These few odd pieces are probably all that is left."

The official concealed his excitement. In his best offhand manner, he inquired what Howell was asking for the black china.

"Oh, I'd rather hold onto them. Historical interest, you know. They couldn't possibly mean as much to anyone else as they do to me."

"But if you *were* to consider selling—as a personal favor?"

"Well—on a personal basis—let's say a nominal two hundred pounds."

Flushed with triumph, his precious acquisition carefully tucked under his arm, the minister departed soon afterward.

A year later, strolling along Wardour Street, he spied another black teapot in a store window. He dropped in casually, bought an Indian drum and a silver snuffbox to throw the dealer off guard, and then pounced on his prize.

"Oh, that, sir? Why you can have that for two shillings."

"You're joking, of course?"

"Oh no, sir. If you're interested in black china, I have hundreds of pieces in the storeroom. Mallinson's brought them out several years ago, and I stocked up heavily. But the confounded stuff never caught on!"

Howell himself always *did* catch on, sometimes in the most unexpected circles. Visiting Fulham in early 1873, Jimmy was startled to find the Owl entertaining a small, rotund gentleman wearing a clerical collar. With a flourish, Howell presented "the Reverend Canon Cromwell, my colleague on the School Board." It developed that Howell, without lifting a finger (and indeed despite apparent protestations of inexperience) had been elected a Governor of the Board.

"By an overwhelming majority, sir," Canon Cromwell squeaked proudly to Jimmy. "And I may say we are most fortunate in obtaining the services of so distinguished and public-spirited a gentleman."

Jimmy nodded in grave agreement. "Mr. Howell is not the man to deny his country in its hour of need."

"And so unselfishly! Although himself a Catholic, Mr. Howell has volunteered without discrimination on grounds of race or religion personally to meet the costs of educating every illegitimate child in the borough!"

Illegitimate children! It was a pricelessly wry gesture, not without its moving aspects—and altogether typical of Howell. Whatever his depredations, he was equally careless of his own worldly goods, especially where friendship or art was involved. Any time an appeal went out—to relieve Sandys's crushing debts, to aid Walt Whitman stricken by paralysis in 1873 across the sea—it was the agent's name that headed the subscription list.

In Howell, Jimmy saw a gallant rogue who planted a foot in the backside of dull respectability. Nothing could have been better matched to his own new mood.

For years, critics had been tossing at his feet the grinning mask and multicolored cloak of the clown: "Mr. Whistler is jesting again . . . another harvest of American bad jokes." Suddenly he saw an opportunity to capitalize on their ridicule by embracing it. He would accept the gaudy costume, even round it out with jangling bells. What better way to lull the enemy into overconfidence?

New Whistlerisms, calculated to amuse, were soon titillating the salons of Mayfair: God was "a careless workman"; Turner canvases impossible to authenticate "because the difference between real and imitation is infinitesimal."

One riposte in particular created a stir. At an Ionides dinner party, Jimmy was all but run over by a bejeweled matron who had seen the *Miss Cicely Alexander* at his one-man show, and could not wait to discuss her impressions. "Ah, Mr. Whistler—such an *impasto,* such a *je ne sais quoi* of rare *chiaroscuro!* I have studied art myself, you know, and attended the lectures of Mr. Ruskin. 'Art is long,' *n'est-ce pas,* 'and life is short.'"

Jimmy drew back instinctively before this Niagara of platitudes. Beaming, the lady pursued him: "To me, there are only two painters in the world: you and Velázquez."

Jimmy flipped up his monocle and peered at the creature: jowly, vacuous, hideously dressed in a green gown and purple silk boa. "Why," he purred sweetly, "drag in Velázquez?"

The remark was repeated all over London, and cited as proof of his "insufferable vanity." It was, of course, nothing of the sort; to anyone with the slightest knowledge of Jimmy's reverence for the great Spaniard, the notion was unthinkable. He was "taking down" the aesthetic pretender with straight-faced irony, crowning her absurd proposition with a still more absurd one of his own. And audible to all but the deaf was the note of calculated self-mockery.

The role of the Puckish eccentric could be misunderstood; but it had clear advantages. Jimmy would not be forgotten so long as his sallies were quoted around town. Nor could he be hurt so long as his cloud of persiflage, flung out like the self-protective blue ink of a squid, surrounded him with a foggy impenetrable screen.

Meantime, he kept peering from his watchtower. And now he saw something: the gaunt, scowling figure of Henry Irving.

Jimmy had been fascinated by the stage all his life, even before his mother whetted his pre-adolescent appetite by banning attendance at anything but puppet shows in St. Petersburg. In his youth, he had been warmed by the applause of drawing room audiences. He had sung his doggerel verses in Paris cafés, shared the spotlight in amateur theatricals with George du Maurier, and afterward appeared with Frances Leyland in the sketch *Twenty Minutes Under an Umbrella*.

Under the influence of the peripatetic Howell, he became in the mid-'70s a regular theatergoer. Much of what he saw—ponderous melodrama, stilted Shakespeare in outlandish costume—was simply fodder for his cynical wit. But Henry Irving was something else.

Irving had emerged from obscurity with his tour de force in *The Bells*, where he played Mathias, a hypnotist who slowly and relentlessly wrung out the confession of a murder long hidden. Unlike most of his contemporaries, the new star of the Lyceum had the intelligence to probe into the subsurface complexities of character. And with his tall, angular frame, his brooding eye, thick wavy locks and long tapering jaw, he had the power to project them.

Irving's *Hamlet* in 1874, restrained and psychologically penetrating, ran for an unprecedented two hundred performances and catapulted him to instant immortality. Soon after, he shifted to the Spanish court as the crafty Philip II in Tennyson's *Queen Mary*.

Jimmy attended the opening and was entranced. Here, in Irving as the organizer of the ill-fated Spanish Armada, was a superb and unusual portrait subject that might give him just the public recognition he needed. He had known Irving casually since the actor's admission to the Garrick Club—and therefore the Bohemian inner circle—a couple of years before; he penned a hasty note and sent it backstage.

For answer, Irving turned up at his studio the next afternoon, traveling bag in hand. "Here I am, me boy," he said in his heavy North Country voice. "With King Philip in the suitcase. What do ye use for a dressing room?"

"Curiously enough," replied Jimmy, "the dressing room." He pointed. "But now I'll have to put a star on it."

Nearly two hours later—Irving's make-up was an elaborate ritual—the collaboration began, in an atmosphere of considerable mutual tension. For Jimmy, the picture was a possible spring-board to national prominence. All London, and especially the people who counted, knew Henry Irving. If the theater idol liked the painting, talked about it, and displayed it in his home, Jimmy might at one bound leapfrog over the heads of his critics into the limelight.

For Irving's ambitions, the engagement held equal promise. British actors, thanks largely to the disapproval of the Church of England, still were condemned to distinctly inferior social status, closer to that of circus acrobats than of opera divas. Their intellectual capacities, like their morals, were traditionally suspect. Irving was determined to change all that—and in fact did in 1895 become the first British actor to win knighthood. By posing for the man who had painted Thomas Carlyle, he would promote the claims of the profession to dignity.

But he had never faced the searching close-up scrutiny of a painter, and he was nervous about it. Irving had grappled his way slowly up the theatrical ladder, overcoming a native stammer and an initial awkwardness (one of his earliest roles was as the Ugly Sister in the Christmas pantomime). He had endured a painful nine-year apprenticeship in the provinces, in the course of which he had suffered at the hands of newspaper critics almost as much as Jimmy. "Spindleshanks," he had been derisively dubbed when the padding around his skinny legs was detected; and "the Crab," in mockery of his once-ungainly gait.

Jimmy's concept for the painting was in his mind's eye before he picked up a brush: he would do a defiant kingly figure with head slightly averted and legs planted well apart, somewhat in the manner of the *El Bufon de Vallodolid* of Velázquez. His first shock came when he studied his model, and looked in vain for the noble lineaments of the Bourbon monarchy. Instead, he saw a nearsighted, blinking countryman of nearly forty who said "gaw" for "go" and hid behind a fixed, mechanical smile. Without the romantic glow of the footlights, the red plush draperies of the Lyceum, and the majestic verse of England's Poet Laureate, Henry Irving was once again reduced to John Henry Brodribb of Somersetshire. Somewhere between the bustling Strand and quiet Chelsea, the magic had been lost.

Jimmy would have to work from memory, a memory that came into jarring conflict with the uneasy figure before him. There was another complication: his best portraits were based on his own distillation of the essence of a subject. But here the subject was already an actor's impression of someone else; in effect he had to do a portrait-within-a-portrait.

For Irving, shivering in short Elizabethan doublet and light black cape, his long thin legs covered only by sheer white stockings, there were different problems. The studio had no heat to counter the raw winds of early April; Jimmy, obliged to cut expenses, was more willing to give up coal than pheasant.

He couldn't pay for the pheasant, either, however, and that meant frequent interruptions by angry tradesmen. Usually Jimmy vanished before he could be cornered, leaving his sitter to face the mercantile music. Once Irving was denounced as a double-dealing scoundrel by a baker who assumed he was Whistler; another time, unable to find his glasses, he stumbled into an easel and barked his unprotected shins.

But the worst offense, to the actor's methodical mind, was the painter's erratic pace. After a dozen sittings—and half as many scrapings-down—nothing was left on the canvas but the model's upper body and the flung-around cloak. Outraged, Irving demanded to know why.

"Ah, but such a cloak," Jimmy told him. "Observe the brush strokes. Who save the Master could have painted it?"

They sparred constantly, neither willing to back down before the other.

"Your hand is too stiff, Irving!"

"That is my characterization."

"But this is *my* painting!"

Irving had his revenge. A few mornings later, when Jimmy was visibly at breakfast in the dining room, the servants were startled to hear his rasping "Ha-ha!" echo from the studio. Irving, having assiduously practiced the painter's mocking laugh, had slipped up the stairs unnoticed to confound the household.

"You're moving your head, Irving!"

"And my feet as well. It's after four."

"Damn it, man, artists don't work by the clock!"

"Mere theater people do. When that curtain goes up, we have to be ready." Irving lowered his famous stare from *The Bells*. "Even the *geniuses*."

Jimmy hurled his brush at the closing door. "Blasted ham!"

In such a competitive atmosphere, he could not flourish. At best, Irving posed technical problems, especially with his legs. Of a woman-ish thinness, scarcely picking up girth at the thighs, the actor's underpinnings had given him a good deal of trouble. They gave Jimmy even more. He painted and repainted, and ran into his familiar bugaboo of thin surface oil that either trickled down the canvas, or in being wiped out took some earlier work with it.

Still he persisted, never mentioning his difficulties with the legs aloud in view of Irving's notorious touchiness on the subject. At long last Jimmy was satisfied. He invited Irving's inspection.

The actor surveyed the canvas meticulously, from white-plumed black hat down past gold-bordered cloak to the silver-buckled shoes. The figure, with its blond pointed Spanish beard and sweeping lines, had an unmistakable majesty. Finally Irving spoke: "The cape is gud, very gud. And the face not bad. But I can't say I admire those . . . *fins* at the bottom."

In capturing the legs, Jimmy had lost the sitter.

With sinking heart, he suggested that Irving might like to show the picture to his friends. "I would be honored to have it hanging in your flat. The price is really of no consequence."

"Hm . . . I dunno. I'll think about it."

But thoughts of Macbeth intruded, and Irving for the moment did not acquire the painting.

It was a crushing disappointment. Putting a further strain on Jimmy's resources, both nervous and fiscal, was the condition of his mother, who after a severe illness in 1875 had been transferred to the more salubrious climate of Hastings.

Nothing was going right. Jimmy caught himself staring at the brown, torpid waters of the Thames, wondering what it would be like at the river bottom . . .

Ridiculous, impossible, and obscene! He would not be beaten into submission by the London conspiracy of fools. If collapse was what they expected, he would show them how a Whistler responded to bad news.

He threw open the doors of 2 Lindsey Row to a mad round of parties and entertainments. Anyone who could play a tune or mix a drink was welcome; one thirsty pianist came for an evening and stayed a month. The empty bottles piled up beside the unpaid bills. When Maud reported that their regular vintner had discontinued credit, and she would have to get a less palatable port elsewhere, he cried gaily, "Any port in a storm!"

The revelry was not as haphazard as it appeared. Every campaign had its slow phases, when one had to conserve fire and hold on. And for maintaining battle morale, there was nothing like sparkling at one's own table, making fullest use of soaring eyebrows, mesmeric fingers and flying monocle.

In all this, Maud's role was indispensable. Between stints of modeling for Jimmy—as a Walter Scott heroine, or a nonchalant "Young American" from the pages of Henry James—she shopped, cooked, intervened discreetly when a nearsighted countess mistook the Japanese bath for a divan and tried to sit on the goldfish.

Yet bed remained for her a cyclical duty, as it was for the well-bred Victorian ladies she was always striving to emulate. Pushing himself to prodigious efforts, Jimmy had the brief satisfaction of arousing his diffident mistress to unfamiliar transports ("Oh, Jimmy, you *are* an artist!")—and the recurrent vexation of hearing her whimpers subside, brought under firm British control. Sexually, he was left restless.

Jimmy was restless—and Rosa Corder was an exciting woman. That combination in itself would not have been enough to set off a conflagration, because Rosa was part of Charlie Howell's entourage, and the Southern-cavalier tradition discouraged poaching. But Rosa was also bold and self-possessed, an avant-garde Liberated Career Woman who made her own choices.

Still in her early twenties, the daughter of a prosperous City merchant, Rosa was that rarest of Victorian anomalies, a female painter. Respectable ladies were expected to commission portraits, not commit them; their delicate fingers might be permitted to dabble with needlework, but never with messy oils. Rosa went further; she specialized in painting horses, and had a studio at Newmarket as well as one in London.

She had studied with Rossetti, and fallen briefly under his spell before switching her affections to the more ebullient Howell. So frank and engaging was her personality that Howell's wife, Kate, actually welcomed her visits to the Bohemian manor in Fulham.

As befitted a follower of George Sand, Rosa was handsome rather than pretty. Her major attraction was her figure, rounded and ripe-to-bursting as a black Homburg grape. Her face was small, overwhelmed by a mass of ash-blond hair. By painterly standards, the eyes were too close, the mouth and nose too broad. Yet there was a strong, calm dignity that set her off from the crowd; as the actress Ellen Terry put it, Rosa was "one of those plain-beautiful women who are so far more attractive than some of the pretty ones."

Howell brought her often to Jimmy, who was impressed by her work and agreed to instruct her in the rudiments of etching. Arriving for a lesson one summer afternoon, Rosa found Jimmy alone in the garden, apparently lost in thought. She waited by the potting shed; and it was there that, looking up after several minutes, he saw her.

"Rosa! How long have you been there?"

"Long enough to see you are not in a teaching mood."

"You are quite right." He fixed a speculative eye on his pupil, an elegant figure in severely cut brown jacket, framed against the black door of the shed. "Today," he said unexpectedly, "you must sit for me."

Gathering in his mind was a solution to the perennial problem of background. English portrait painters favored synthetic landscapes, easy to fill in after the sitter departed. Even among the Impressionists, plain black was in disgrace. But it was precisely the black of the shed door that had set off Rosa's outlines so subtly, creating an effect like that of a Pompeian fresco.

He posed Rosa against a black velvet drape, her body turned more than halfway to the left, a plumed hat dangling from her right hand. With a series of exquisitely differentiated browns—in jacket, hat, furs, feathers, and floor—he brought the figure forward out of the darkness.

It was Rosa, finally, after a month of sittings, who refused to let him experiment further. "You've already done what no one else would even attempt. Why risk ruining it?"

"Just a few hours more, my dear. It is Sunday, Maud is visiting her aunt, and there is no one to interrupt our work."

"Yes, there is. *Moi.*" She picked up her skirts and headed for the dressing room. Reluctantly, Jimmy started to wash his brushes.

"Jimmy! Would you come here, please?"

She was calling from the little dressing room. Puzzled, Jimmy went out into the corridor.

"The door is open. Come in!"

Jimmy obeyed. The sumptuous Rosa stood before him in long black stockings and boots—and nothing else. Her breasts rose like twin pink-tipped melons.

Jimmy sucked in his breath. Normally he would have leaped joyously to the attack. But this, dammit, was Charlie Howell's girl; and under the West Point code one did not help one's self to a friend's whisky, his horses or his women. "Ah—excuse me!" he said finally.

"For what? You haven't done anything."

"I'm afraid I don't understand—"

"Do you require a drawing, Sir Artist?" She stepped closer and kissed him lightly on the lips.

"I must confess, I am at a loss. Charlie, after all, is my friend. And you are . . ."

"Charlie's friend. So, since we are all friends, why shouldn't we be friendly?"

"I thought your relationship with Charlie was somewhat more intimate. Of the sort that would preclude a third party from, ah—"

"Injecting himself?"

Jimmy bowed. "I wouldn't have put it quite so graphically."

"Let me assure you, Jimmy, I am a modern woman. My arrangement with Charlie leaves us each quite free to pursue our fancies elsewhere. I am no more restrained than he by the—accident of my sex."

An appreciative gleam lighted the blue eyes. "A very happy accident."

"I might add that your notions of propriety—as well as of property—are quite wasted on Charles Augustus Howell. He has no concern for either."

"You mean, if the situations were reversed—?"

"He would not be standing there playing an uncertain Hamlet."

Thus encouraged, Jimmy obliged with Mercutio.

There were no complaints about his performance. But it was never repeated. Both parties understood that what had been delicious as a Sunday interlude, might be disastrous as a sustained liaison.

The Rosa Corder portrait was a landmark in two respects. It established the black background, later regularized as a large square of black velvet nailed onto an easel, as the preferred base to which Jimmy repeatedly returned after adventures in lighter tonal schemes. And it brought forth from Howell an actual purchase in hard cash. Jimmy offered him the portrait as a gift, but the nimble agent insisted on tendering one hundred guineas. It was only months later that Jimmy realized Howell had paid him with his own money, adroitly borrowed the week before.

The intramural episode left Jimmy's basic situation unimproved. With each passing week it grew more perilous. Like the seemingly doomed hero of a Greek tragedy, Jimmy could avert his fate only through the intervention of a *deus ex machina,* a rescuing god floated down obligingly from the wings.

# Chapter Twenty

The god arrived on cue—once again in the frowning person of Frederick Leyland. The salvation he bore was the Peacock Room.

The shipping magnate had been systematically assembling treasures for the Hyde Park mansion at 49 Prince's Gate that would establish him on the London social scene. Like the original Medicis, who were wary of arousing popular envy, he kept the outside of his new house quite simple, and concentrated on creating a breath-taking interior.

To stun the arriving visitor, he brought into the entrance hall the famous stone staircase of the Percys, lately removed from their demolished mansion in Trafalgar Square. At the top of the gilded bronze balustrade were a trio of first-floor drawing rooms, linked with movable screens to embrace an area 94 feet long. Within this not-so-miniature museum, Leyland scattered his collection of Oriental rugs, Venetian statuary, inlaid cabinets from India and Germany, Beauvais tapestries, Botticelli portraits, mosaic floors, Renaissance bronzes and Ming vases. Balancing the period pieces were a score of contemporary paintings, mostly by Rossetti and Burne-Jones.

Through Murray Marks, the Dutch-Jewish art connoisseur, Leyland had accumulated a considerable array of blue and white china. Since he also owned Jimmy's portrait of Christine Spartali, *The Princess from the Land of Porcelain*, it was agreed that these cousinly elements should be brought together in the ground-floor dining room. The task of decorating the room was assigned to the architect Thomas Jeckyll, known as "Jeckyll of the Gates" in tribute to a set of wrought-iron gates that had figured as a wedding gift to the Prince of Wales. A tense, pale little man with a dark beard and a bald pate, Jeckyll numbered among his eccentricities a penchant for Puritan knee breeches and buckle shoes. Jimmy had known him for years as a minor member of the Rossetti Circle, equally ready to design a Japanese billiard room for Alec

Ionides or to guide the stumbling Swinburne into a hansom, and had recommended his engagement by Leyland.

Jimmy himself had been commissioned in midsummer of 1876 to decorate the dado of the great staircase. He contributed a chain of pink and white Oriental floral patterns on a background of cocoa flecked with gold. Now, as an authority on color harmonies, he was invited to survey Jeckyll's reconstruction of the dining area.

He found himself in a large oblong room, some 33 by 20 feet, with a lofty ceiling. The pine-paneled walls were lined to a height of 7 or 8 feet with open shelves of carved and gilt walnut, subdivided vertically to show off Leyland's plates, pots, beakers, and vases.

Above the still-empty shelves rose a covering of rare Cordova leather, brought to England three hundred years earlier by Catherine of Aragon, and hanging since then in a Tudor mansion in Norfolk. Of a dull yellowish-brown, the leather was embellished by "German gilding," a mixture of silver leaf and amber shellac. In the center of each panel were red-painted pomegranates (Catherine's heraldic symbol) and flowers.

From Jeckyll's ceiling, broken up into solid hexagonal panels, dangled eight heavy pendant lamps. A red-bordered Oriental rug covered the floor.

Looking out over this somewhat jumbled grouping, from a dominant position above the turquoise fireplace, was Jimmy's *Princess*.

Leyland turned to the artist. "What do you think, Jimmy?"

"I am still thinking."

"Murray Marks is very pleased. He says this will make Jeckyll's reputation."

"Tommy has already got a reputation; he's an exceedingly clever designer. The question is, Does he have a *room?*"

"You have doubts about the color scheme?"

Jimmy put up his monocle and looked down carefully at the floor. Then he walked over to the leather panel alongside his picture and examined the floral decorations. "Fewer and fewer, unfortunately."

Leyland held his ground. "Marks feels it will set off perfectly the blue and white china."

"At the expense of murdering the *Princess*."

"What?"

"Let us be clear about the keynote of the room, Leyland. What is the first thing the eye encounters, coming through the door? It is the *Princess* on the left, looking down from the mantel. Is that not correct?"

"Well, yes. But the porcelain is also important."

"As a setting, a framework for the lady. What we require here is a total atmosphere that blends with and reinforces her. What we presently have, I regret to inform you, is a series of discordant effects among which her pale tones of rose and silver cannot possibly breathe. The border of your rug, for example: a purplish red that swears horribly against the delicate streaks of vermilion in the canvas."

"Well—I suppose we could have the border removed."

"But what really sins is the leather. Just look at it."

Leyland obeyed. "You mean the subdued red of the flowers?"

"Not subdued—muddy. But it's more than that. The basic tone of the leather is too low. It needs to be brought up, perhaps with discreet patches of gold."

"What? Paint over that beautiful Spanish leather?"

"Most assuredly—if this is to be a boudoir worthy of the *Princess*."

Leyland shook his head. "I paid a thousand pounds for that wall covering."

"It's not worth a thousand pennies if it defeats our grand purpose." Jimmy looked up proudly at his painting. "The *Princess* is no ordinary lady, Leyland. Her surroundings must be finished off by the Master, who knows her best."

Leyland stroked his black beard. "You wish to alter the leather, eh?"

"A few exquisite touches will make a world of difference."

"I really hadn't planned on any further outlay for this room."

"My dear Leyland!" Jimmy regarded him reproachfully. "I am not talking about installing a ship's engine, or a new quarterdeck. It's a matter of judicious changes here and there, to restore the color harmony."

"I see . . . something in the neighborhood of five hundred guineas for the job?"

"In the neighborhood," said Jimmy carelessly. He glanced up sidewise and put a finger to his lips. "Please, the princess is listening. Let us not have her overhear this bickering."

"Very well, Jimmy. I leave it to you."

The rug was a simple matter. A long-handled razor swiftly disposed of the offending border.

No such solutions were possible with the leather. Jimmy's first try—modifying the surface flowers with a primrose tint—merely underlined the incompatibility of the somber brown background.

A Draconian move was required. Jimmy ordered a pail of deep Prussian blue. For several days he tinkered with it on a corner of the leather panel adjoining the *Princess*. While he was working, Leyland stuck his head in.

"What on earth are you doing, Jimmy?"

"Experimenting, my dear Baron. This tone is of course quite wrong, but it provides a starting point."

"Will you be able to get your 'experiment' off my leather?"

"Of course. Have no fear."

Leyland looked skeptical, but there were other things on his mind; he was launching his shipping line into the Atlantic trade. "I'm counting on you. I shall be away for the rest of the summer."

"You will return, I assure you, to an enchanting harmony."

Jimmy cleared off the leather. What the room needed most, he decided abruptly, was gold, already introduced by Jeckyll in the form of a few speckles over the woodwork.

Jimmy brought in masses of gold leaf, artfully tarnished in the old Japanese fashion to temper the raw crudity of the color. He spread the foil liberally along the dado. Then to round out his harmonic balance, he lightened his blue paint with yellow and white to a shade matching the turquoise of the fireplace, and spread it over a few open spaces in the woodwork. The result was gratifying, ready for inspection.

In the September issue of the *Academy* a friendly description of the room appeared, followed up by a letter from Jimmy expressing lavish appreciation for the inspirational example of "the distinguished architect, Thomas Jeckyll." Relaying the notice to Leyland, Jimmy remarked that what his patron had seen in August gave no more idea of the splendidly revamped ensemble "than you could have of a complete opera judging from a three-finger exercise." Jimmy concluded that, content with his labors, he was preparing to depart for Venice on an etching trip.

He never finished packing. Something kept pulling him back to 49 Prince's Gate.

Still lacking in Leyland's dining room was an organizing force, a unifying motif. It should be something Oriental in flavor, yet no mere imitation; the execution ought to be Western. A variation on pine cones? An abstract design based on a flock of swooping plovers? With only broken spaces left to work in, it would have to be fluid, flexible, untrammeled . . .

He picked up a broad studio brush, dipped it into a pail of his greenish-blue paint, and started almost aimlessly tracing a pattern along the gold-encrusted dado. What gradually emerged was a series of wavy overlapping lines, imbrications . . .

The graceful tumbling tiles, perhaps, of a pagoda roof? No. Jimmy looked again. After a moment, he recognized the stylized form that his hand had improvised: it was the breast-feather pattern of the peacock.

Three years earlier, consulted by the father of little Cicely Alexander regarding the décor of the family's Campden Hill mansion, Jimmy had proposed a drawing room scheme based on the peacocks frequently adorning Japanese screens. Later he had dropped the plan in favor of a more modest arrangement in white; but evidently the plan had never loosened its grip on him.

He returned to the dado. With each stroke his brush gathered momentum, and his excitement grew. The design was flowing so smoothly, effortlessly, growing as he painted; every touch had an exhilarating sense of freedom. And there were all these splendid sections of space to be covered! For once he would not be confined to a few narrow feet of canvas; he could work on a generous scale, like the fresco-painting Old Masters. He reached a corner, joined the angles with a bold curving line, and swept recklessly on.

Halfway around the room, his spectacles blurred with paint, he paused and stepped back. He had his peacock-feather theme; it was time to plan elaborations. The first one was obvious: to repeat the same motif in reverse, i.e. as a semi-disc of gold leaf laid over a solid blue background. But the low dado would not provide enough painting area. Where could he find the necessary space?

He looked around the room. At scattered intervals, panels of virginal Cordova leather stared innocently down. Jimmy stared back, not so innocently. A malicious little smile crinkling his cheeks, he loaded his brush and advanced on the nearest panel. With serene confidence, he buried its quiet brown presence under a glittering coat of blue.

All through the day Jimmy painted with furious energy. Conscious effort was left behind; Jo Heffernan's "little demon inside" had taken over completely. He forgot lunch, Leyland, Tom Jeckyll, Venice. A major work was opening up before him; he trembled at its implications, for art and for himself. More quickly than his hands could keep pace with, his mind darted ahead to new combinations: a dot-within-circle pattern based on the "eye" of the peacock's iridescent tail fan, a parade of full-size prancing birds to adorn the window shutters. Jimmy locked the doors, hummed his mangled Offenbach, and breathed in paint fumes happily.

This would be his riposte to the enemy, wiping out the hostile reviews, the vicious attacks, the endless disappointments. With one powerful blow, he would redeem years of frustration. Other men had painted canvases attuned to the rooms they would hang in; Whistler alone could remake an entire room to harmonize with his picture.

He felt in total control of the project; all the help he needed was extra muscles. Early the next morning, after scarcely closing his eyes, he roused Walter and Harry Greaves to assist him with mixing paint, cleaning brushes, laying down gold leaf and rigging ladders. Overnight he plunged into the most demanding schedule of his life.

He rose daily at six. By seven a hansom was disgorging painter, assistants, and cartons of materials at Prince's Gate. Paints and lacquers flew furiously until lunch, at first taken in Chelsea but soon, to save time, prepared under Jimmy's meticulous direction in Leyland's unfinished kitchen.

Work then resumed, up to a theoretical quitting time of eight. More often the church clocks were striking nine before the brushes were washed and the gold leaf put away. The night work was important; since the room would be viewed mostly by gas lamps, during the dining hours, Jimmy wanted to be sure his color harmonies would hold up under artificial light.

Only Jimmy was allowed to wield brushes. The brothers devoted themselves first to developing contraptions that would enable "the Master" to reach high surfaces: ladders, scaffolds, finally a beam-slung hammock from which the reclining painter dabbed at the ceiling with brushes attached to broom handles.

Later the assistants were allowed to gild and lacquer flat areas. By evening the trio were half-gilded themselves, gold flakes sparkling in their hair, on their cheeks, on their clothes. Within a few weeks, Jimmy's costs in materials, labor, and laundry bills were enormous.

But so was his progress. The walls and dado were covered with alternating patterns of breast and "eye" feathers, and the "eye" motif was being repeated in blue over the gilded surface of the ceiling, imparting to the staid Tudor panels an exotic Oriental flavor. On the wooden window shutters, a row of magnificent peacocks advanced in perspective, tail fans outflung like billowing clouds.

Jimmy could not contain his agitation; his peers must see what he was doing. Brief scribbled notes summoned moguls of the art Establishment: Millais, Edward Poynter, the neoclassicist Lawrence Alma-Tadema. They stopped in, stayed, blinked their admiration. Sir Henry Cole, director of the South Kensington Museum, came; so did Manet, who was more impressed with the Peacock Room than he had been earlier on meeting its owner.

The circle of visitors was extended to family and intimates: Debo, slipping away from Sloane Street and Seymour Haden; Jo Heffernan, bringing Jimmy's little son Charlie in from the country for a dazzling treat; and two new cronies who would figure profoundly in Jimmy's future, the avant-garde architect Edward Godwin and his piquant bride, Trixie.

In the late fall Jimmy wrote to his mother in Hastings: "It is a noble work enough, Mother, and one we may be proud of—it is so entirely new and original as you may well fancy it would be—for at least *that* quality is recognized in your son."

Wistfully, Anna regretted that her boy's talents should remain hidden from the world: "But a gentleman's private residence is not on exhibition."

She was very shortly proved wrong. Just as Jimmy had put the gentleman himself on exhibition in August to Manet (who sniffed and inquired "What does he sell?"), he now threw open Leyland's doors to the fashionable public. He made sure to give them a show.

Strollers to Prince's Gate were likely to find the Yankee artist stretched out on a mattress in the middle of the floor, surrounded by paints, palette, and a half-dozen bamboo fishing poles with brushes fixed to their tips. With these he made occasional long-distance strokes at the ceiling, pausing now and then to remove his monocle and confirm his results through a pair of enormous binoculars. "Now, wouldn't I be a fool," he demanded of a visiting journalist, "to risk myself on a scaffolding and nearly twist my head off my shoulders trying to look upward, when I can so easily annihilate space this way?"

To sustain the circus atmosphere, he wore a picturesque flowing smock or a black outfit featuring velvet knickers and eight-inch ties with diamond buckles. When Louise Jopling, the society matron and sometime painter, dropped in for lunch, he gaily assigned her a tiny corner to decorate. Lady Ritchie, a friend from the old Paris days, found herself whirled around the bucket-cluttered room in an impromptu waltz. Princess Louise turned up with the Marquess of Westminster to marvel at the peacocks and request that Jimmy make her a copy of the *Mother* portrait. He casually snubbed her by sending a photo; mere royalty could not be permitted to dictate to artists.

In his enthusiasm for the Peacock Room, Jimmy spread himself like the peacocks. All perspective was washed away. The *Harmony in Blue and Gold* became his life, solo substitute for the Royal Academy to which he had not been elected, the handsome sales unachieved, the flattering notices never written.

Lord Redesdale, a Chelsea neighbor, found Jimmy perched like a gnome atop a high ladder. "What are you doing up there?"

"The loveliest thing you ever saw."

"But have you consulted Leyland?"

"Why on earth should I? I am creating the most beautiful room that has ever been done."

"I hear he's upset about all the publicity."

"Well, what can you expect from a *parvenu?*"

Others, too, had heard that the globe-trotting Leyland was annoyed, particularly when the *Morning Post* couldn't even get his name right. Charles Howell bearded his client directly. "You're looking for trouble, Jimmy. Leyland is already touchy about your relationship with Frances—which I dare say has been closer than his own lately. If he feels you're humiliating him further by using his house as a private court—"

"To hell with Leyland! This room is more important to me than any grumpy moneybags!"

"He could be a dangerous enemy."

"The world is full of Whistler enemies. But this will overturn the whole conspiracy. A room is something they can't just bury in a corner; it's a complete environment. Anybody who steps in here must become aware of Whistler, whether the critics want him to or not!"

"You don't have to chop up Leyland in order to broil the critics, Jimmy."

"Perhaps not." Wicked smile. "But it would be such fun."

Before the Leyland issue could come to a head, there was the distressing episode of Tommy Jeckyll. Jimmy had long been fond of the odd little architect, once even paying his back dues at the Arundel Club—a considerable gesture for a man in Jimmy's economic circumstances. He had supplied advice freely for Jeckyll's two-story ornamental pavilion at the American Centennial Exposition in Philadelphia earlier in the year, and had taken pains to give the architect public credit for the early arrangement of the Peacock Room.

He was therefore quite unprepared for the news sweeping the Arundel, according to which Jeckyll had visited the Peacock Room, gone home and spread gold leaf over his own walls—and taken leave of his senses. Apparently things had been going badly for him lately, and he had counted on the room to rescue a career already often clouded by collaborations.

Jimmy realized that several members were staring at him, evidently intrigued by the tears springing to his eyes. The room had become silent.

They were all waiting for his reaction, damn them, hoping to spot some chink in the glittering Whistler armor. He gave them instead a cold, brilliant smile: "To be sure, that is the effect I have on people."

Like his famous refusal to be paired with Velázquez, the remark was widely repeated . . . this time as evidence of Whistler's heartlessness.

Leyland arrived without notice soon after, early in the new year of 1877. Jimmy, working alone on the dado, his face and body spotted with gold leaf, became aware of a silent black-clad presence in the doorway. He turned, and the two exchanged long, silent stares.

"Welcome, Baron."

"Thank you. I wasn't sure I was."

"You've been misinformed."

"I know only what I hear from my friends."

"A notoriously inaccurate source."

Leyland advanced slowly into the room, wheeling around to take in the shining expanse of golden-blue design. His lips twitched a little in his tightly held face. "What," he asked finally, "have you done with my leather?"

"It's all there," Jimmy assured him. "Beneath my peacock patterns. And a very good ground it made, too."

"And my porcelain? It would be drowned in this avalanche of color."

"But the bare shelves have a nice linear quality."

"You were not authorized, Mr. Whistler, to redo my room."

Jimmy put down his brush. "I find your attitude extraordinary, Leyland. If you were a *blind* man—"

"What did you expect?"

"Gratitude. I have made you famous. Shipowners, like their ships, come and go in the night. You alone may survive, in the dim ages to come, as the proprietor of the Peacock Room."

Leyland managed a bitter smile. "I am eternally indebted to you."

"That is very true. I am glad to see it is sinking in."

The magnate put a finger up to one of the blue-covered leather panels. "What do I owe you for ruining my dining room?"

"More than you can possibly pay. My costs alone have been in the hundreds of pounds. As for my time and talent—there is no saying. However, in consideration of past kindnesses, I shall charge you only two thousand guineas."

Leyland fell back. "Two thousand—that's ridiculous!"

"I know. A work of genius is entitled to far more. But I am an artist, not a businessman."

"It's out of the question, Jimmy. We never spoke of more than five hundred guineas. And you already have had more than a thousand in advances from me for paintings never delivered!"

"I am not disposed to haggle, Leyland. You will pay my fee—or accept the entire Peacock Room as a gift. Now, if you will excuse me, I have one last wall to finish." He turned back to his brushes, tossing a final word over his shoulder: "The art world has begged for a formal critical showing next month. I suggest you may prefer to stay at Speke, as they are coming to see the work of the Master, and naturally you may feel a little out in the cold."

Leyland retreated, sorely wounded. He had been a free-handed patron and solicitous host; had invented the Nocturne designation and backed the artist during years when most of London turned away. Now he was being elbowed out of his own home and, to crown the indignity, in effect being held up on the street outside!

The room might indeed be—probably was—a landmark in Western art; and the sum Jimmy asked was not beyond that commanded by other artists of highly perishable reputation. Yet the American had behaved with outrageous arrogance, the same arrogance he displayed in his easy familiarity with Frances Leyland. Jimmy Whistler had to be taken down a peg.

Leyland dispatched a check, marked "payment in full," for one thousand *pounds*—not guineas . . . twice the sum originally mentioned, half of what Jimmy wanted. The downgrading to pounds, although amounting to only a shilling less per unit, was symbolically important. Professional men, including artists, were paid in guineas; tradespeople, in pounds.

Jimmy ignored the check. He traced his response in gold leaf on the final wall of the Peacock Room, opposite the *Princess*. Originally this panel had been intended to house another Whistler canvas, the *Three Figures*. Instead, Jimmy painted over the blue leather two radiant golden peacocks in angry confrontation. The larger one, smothered in a shower of gleaming guineas, clutched underfoot a pile of silver shillings. Capering disdainfully away to its left was a smaller peacock, head arched in defiance under a cloud of fluttering feathers, trailing an interminable elegant fan. Thus Jimmy recorded for the ages the conflict between proud artist and ducat-drenched patron.

Before he finished, word arrived via Rossetti and Howell that Leyland would raise his price to 1500 pounds if Jimmy would only clear out.

"Absolutely not, Charlie! He will have his room complete. There he will sit at dinner, his back to the *Princess* and always before him the apotheosis of *l'art et l'argent*."

In February the press came, not a little prodded by a publicly circulated pamphlet in which Jimmy expatiated on the glories of his room. For once, the critics were constrained to agree. "Singularly captivating," reported the *Academy*, adding with unusual prescience —transfer of the room to Washington, D.C., for permanent display was still thirty years away—"it will long remain to eye and mind a type of what artistic enterprise and conception *sui generis* can effect in combination with opulence." *London* found "a solitary spectacle, all the beauty that *bizarrerie* can give, and something more." The *Pall Mall Gazette, Standard,* and *Examiner* used adjectives usually reserved for Royal Academy favorites; even the *Times* carried a lengthy and respectful account.

Leyland, referred to in the *Harper's Bazaar* review as "T. J. Leyburn," was not gratified. Letters snapped and snarled back and forth between patron and artist. Leyland asserted that Jimmy had "degenerated into nothing but an artistic Barnum," blinded by vanity "to all the usages of civilized life." He was forbidden to communicate in future with the Leyland ladies.

Jimmy retorted that he would continue to honor his duty as a gentleman, "little as you know about it." He sneered at Leyland as a frill-shirted "Chevalier de Commerce," compounded by his doctors from Sir Walter Raleigh, Don Quixote, and William Pitt, "with the aid of a chest cold."

The shipowner mailed back some glowing notices on the Peacock Room: "An advertisement of this kind is of such importance in the absence of (or incapacity to produce) any serious work that I feel it would be an unkindness to deprive you of it." He also forwarded a bill contracted by Jimmy for lamp fixtures. Commented Jimmy in a letter to a mutual friend: "He promised me a horsewhipping and sends me his gas bill!"

Meanwhile, he finally cashed Leyland's check.

The Peacock Room affair was one of the most complex and damaging of Jimmy's life. Called upon to give a casual opinion, he had wound up imposing a total private vision; like a volatile gas turned loose in a vacuum, he had been unable to stop expanding until he permeated every crevice. He might, had he been more secure as an artist and a human being, have created the room without provoking the crisis.

But the *Harmony in Blue and Gold* could not be separated from the trials that preceded it: the quarrel with Anna Whistler over Jo, the difficulties with Henry Irving's legs and Frances Leyland's stubborn virtue. Quite innocently, Frederick Leyland had come to represent in Jimmy's eyes all that was oppressive in the Victorian world, where the artist was the hireling of merchant princes instead of being a prince among hirelings. The fact that Leyland himself pursued artistic interests merely compounded his sins; by Jimmy's self-serving logic, the man was a dilettante, a piano-thumping pretender.

A sharp dichotomy was crystallizing in his mind: on one side, the Philistine persecutors of the virginal Muse; on the other, Jimmy Whistler as the lady's visored defender, obliged under the stress of mortal combat to forego his chivalrous ways. It was a self-image that within months would plunge him into a battle beside which the Leyland affair was a mere preliminary skirmish: the head-on collision between James McNeill Whistler and the mighty John Ruskin.

# Chapter Twenty-one

For some years, a small coterie of London art lovers had been grumbling about the absence of an alternative showplace to the Royal Academy. At long last, one of them decided to do something about it.

In May of 1877, the bustle of activity outside a handsome gray mansion in Bond Street—scurrying messengers, workmen delivering crates, carriages ranged along the curb—portended an event of great consequence. And indeed it was: the opening of the Grosvenor Gallery, London's first major exhibition hall for dissident painters.

Sponsor of the project was Sir Coutts Lindsay, a banker and sometime artist. Eager to demonstrate that financial solvency was not synonymous with cultural poverty, Sir Coutts had invested heavily in architecture and décor. His main hall was decked out like the interior of a Florentine palace, with red damask wall hangings and a blue firmament overhead dotted with powdery stars.

More importantly, every painting on display would be set off from its neighbor by six to twelve feet of breathing space. The artists themselves would be consulted on lighting and placement. Although disclaiming any hostility toward the Royal Academy, Sir Coutts made it plain that there would be no lost-in-the-rooftops "skying" of unorthodox work, no burial in remote corners, no careless catch-alls of scale, style, or color.

To publicize his challenge to the Art Establishment, the banker had drawn on prestigious family connections. Heading his guest list for the sumptuous opening banquet was none other than His Royal Highness, the Prince of Wales. And heading the list of critics invited to the afternoon preview was no less a personage than John Ruskin, Professor of Fine Arts at Oxford and archarbiter of the London aesthetic scene.

Chief beneficiary of all this solicitude was to have been the dean of the Pre-Raphaelites, Dante Gabriel Rossetti. But Dante Gabriel, increasingly ill and chronically mistrustful of public exposure, had at long last declined. The ensuing vacuum had been filled largely with the work of one of his colleagues in the "Brotherhood," Edward Burne-Jones . . . and of James McNeill Whistler.

As the afternoon wore on, the little knot of men gathered around Sir Coutts near a first-floor window grew larger—and gloomier. The *Times* man had arrived, and reviewers from other major journals like the *Pall Mall Gazette* and *Atheneum*. There was the usual fop or two from the frivolous weeklies; but no Ruskin. For the third time, the gallery manager assured Sir Coutts that the great critic and social reformer was definitely coming down from Oxford for an evening lecture at the Society for the Prevention of Cruelty to Animals. Ruskin had been advised of the preview; surely he would stop by, if only out of courtesy to Burne-Jones, his former pupil at Oxford and long-time bosom confidant.

A buzz of excitement at the window ended the speculation. At the curb below, two passengers were descending from a carriage with a kind of choreographed deliberation. From their surface resemblances —both were slender, fair, dignified, and conservatively dressed—they gave an initial impression of perhaps being brothers. But as the younger man, first to reach the pavement, extended an arm in deferential assistance, and the other stepped down with something akin to royal daintiness, it was clear that their relationship was one of pupil and mentor. Edward Burne-Jones had personally fetched John Ruskin to the exhibition.

At fifty-eight, Ruskin cut an imperious figure. He was tall enough— just under six feet—to make permissible and even interesting his slight stoop, relic of countless hours spent poring over essay drafts and illuminated manuscripts. As he raised his eyes to scan the new gallery building, his long thin face caught the last rays of the waning sun. It was a face stained with melancholy, pleasant-featured but singularly lifeless. Light brown hair, ample at the crown, flowed down his cheeks in thick rust-colored sideburns unsupported by beard or mustache. The blue-gray eyes, surrounded by tiny freckles and violet wrinkles, were still attractive; but their lingering luster was diminished by the prim, severe mouth and especially the loose, petulant lower lip. A noble serenity in his expression struggled against a haunting despair.

Ruskin's was a curious story. Like Jimmy, he too had been brought up as something of a princeling: a princeling in chains. The only child of Puritan first cousins who married late in life, he had been marked from infancy for a career of intellectual distinction: "a bishop at least," as his father, an exceedingly prosperous wine merchant, averred. His childhood was a chronicle of lopsidedness: too much attention, theological dogma, instruction—and solitude. His only "toy" was a box of bricks.

When after extensive travel in Europe he entered Oxford as a wealthy "gentleman-commoner," his mother tagged along to keep an eye on him, more proud than if she had been "the mother of kings."

In 1843, he burst into print with *Modern Painters*, and at twenty-four was instantly famous. His subtitle, which asserted that British landscapists and especially J. M. W. Turner were superior to "all the Ancient Masters," pleased merchants and fox-hunters alike. The book advanced a quasi-theology of art: the artist was a carrier of divine messages, whose role was to promote morality by recording the universal truths of nature. Since painting was "nothing but a noble and expressive vehicle of thought," all talk of art for art's sake was an absurdity.

Ruskin expanded rapidly into sociology and economics. He attacked the laissez-faire bracketing of profits and poverty, proposing instead rigidly organized communities of farmers and artisans who would be protected from corrupting influences by the burning of "impure" books. From his pastoral retreat in Brantwood near Oxford, a widening torrent of words—on architecture, botany, drawing, mythology, the education of women—cascaded over the clubrooms and dining salons of the land . . . a hodgepodge of brilliant wit and simpering banality, of lofty inspiration and petty malice.

The sheer force of the stream, especially in matters of art, swept dissenters aside. Canaletto, the Eighteenth-century Venetian master, was dismissed as a "little and bad painter"; Dante Gabriel Rossetti, daring to disregard a piece of unsolicited advice, was told: "You are a conceited monkey."

Unchallenged, with a powerful command of language, the Oxford Professor became a kind of schoolmaster-general to the nation. To the actor-manager Henry Irving he wrote tartly: "It greatly surprises me that you have not taught Miss Ellen Terry a grander reading of Portia." To Elizabeth Barrett Browning he complained of "sharp blemishes" in *Aurora Leigh*. He would undoubtedly not have balked at reordering the sequence of Genesis if that had entered his head; and such was his prestige that much of England would have hastened to conform.

For the Grosvenor Gallery preview, Ruskin had dressed with antique formality. His Ascot-style gray frock coat, with its rich velvet collar and outsize sleeves, bespoke wealth as well as indifference. His fawn waistcoat was double-breasted and tightly buttoned. Around his neck was his sole concession to modernity (if not to outright bohemianism): a bright-blue cravat.

Burne-Jones, trailing a half-step behind, was even paler and thinner than the critic, a long blond stick of a man with bony cheeks and a reddish pointed beard. He had created on canvas a world half-celestial, half-medieval, a romantic never-never land of soaring castles and enchanted forests, peopled by dreaming knights and grave-faced maidens; and he himself looked as ethereal as the bloodless, sexless creatures of his imagination. His small ascetic mouth seemed to be framing an unspoken "Repent, ye sinners!"

By now the pair had reached the ground-floor lobby. A scurrying of relieved officialdom hastened to greet them, take their hats and canes, and express appreciation for the great man's visit. Would Professor Ruskin care for a cup of tea, an illustrated catalogue, a boutonniere? Sir Coutts Lindsay would be happy to escort him personally around the gallery . . .

Gracefully, in his low musical platform voice, Ruskin brushed aside the offers. It was clear that he relished the attention; and equally clear that he intended to see the gallery in his own way. "Ned here will show me around," he murmured.

Executives and flunkies retreated, still mumbling their eager good wishes. From a respectful distance—as Ruskin was delightfully aware —they continued to peer out at him from behind doorways and pillars, overwhelmed by a reputation that not only preceded the critic but surrounded him.

As the two men mounted the stairs, Burne-Jones turned diffidently. "Where shall we start, John?"

"Not with *your* work, my dear Ned. One doesn't begin a meal with dessert."

The painter smiled. "Shall we follow the alphabet, then?" He pointed in the catalogue to the name of Alma-Tadema.

"Why not?" Ruskin started toward a side gallery with stately stride, as if conscious that his legs were entrusted with delivery of a priceless cargo, i.e. himself. Lesser critics, and other privileged visitors, fell back, staring.

They had good reason. Ruskin had single-handedly raised Turner to international eminence, won acceptance for the much-censured young Millais, and boosted the fortunes of a dozen lesser lights; conversely, he had shattered the ambitions of countless anonymities. As high priest of British art, he hurled from his mountaintop Jovian thunderbolts against which there was no defense, and from which no man recovered. To be crushed by Ruskin was never to rise again.

*Punch* had summed up the plight of his victims in the dolorous verse:

> I takes and paints,
> And no complaints,
> And sells afore I'm dry;

When savage Ruskin
Sticks his tusk in,
And nobody'll buy . . .

Flanked by Burne-Jones, the critic floated through the halls with
the serenity of a deity . . . an attitude understandable in a man who
years earlier had not hesitated to chastise Michelangelo, and had never
been taken to task for it.

There were no surprises in the mock-Athenian household scenes of
Alma-Tadema, whose claim to unorthodoxy was at best dubious. *Love
and Death,* a gloomy allegory by the academician G. F. Watts, likewise
earned the briefest of Ruskinian glances. He paused before works by
Tissot and Millais, to jot a note or two in his catalogue.

At last Ruskin came to rest back in the main gallery, before the
Burne-Jones section. The critic's friend had sent two water colors, *Hope*
and *Faith;* a pair of large canvases, *The Mirror of Venus* and *The Beguiling of Merlin;* and an elaborate six-paneled version of *The Days of
Creation.* It was an ensemble typical of the painter: drenched in piety,
striking in color, and hopelessly wooden in anatomical construction.

Whatever the aesthetic qualities of Burne-Jones's work, its impact
on the female public was unmistakable. Two leading society beauties,
Louise Jopling and Trixie Godwin, were not only gazing raptly at the
*Mirror of Venus;* their trailing red gowns, high-piled virginal coiffures
and languid attitudes mirrored those of the female figures jostling for
space among the Cupids, halos, and floral wreaths on the canvas.

Ruskin breathed deeply. "Splendid, Ned. The very embodiment of
truth and goodness." Burne-Jones opened his little goldfish-mouth in
gratitude, but could find no words. "Is there anything more I should
see?"

"Well, there's, ah, Whistler."

"Whistler?" The critic's voice shot up an octave; his thick eyebrows
tightened. "Very well; I suppose I must." He followed Burne-Jones
across the parquet floor.

Jimmy had entered seven paintings, including the portraits of
Carlyle and Henry Irving, and several Thames Nocturnes borrowed
from their owners. One other Nocturne was on display: the Cremorne
fireworks scene originally sketched on the night of his expedition with
Albert Moore and the Greaves brothers. This alone, entitled *The Falling
Rocket, Nocturne in Black and Gold,* was offered for sale, at a price of
£200.

Ruskin paused briefly before the *Carlyle;* the venerable historian
had been one of his few preceptors. He sniffed at the Irving, wrinkling
his sharp thin nose. But it was the Nocturnes that engaged his attention. He advanced on the canvases and backed away; cupped a hand

over his right eye to screen off the light; came forward again to examine the paint of *The Falling Rocket* under a magnifying glass. Then he turned toward Burne-Jones and emitted a short unpleasant laugh.

"Rather Impressionist, eh?" ventured the painter.

"That," pronounced the august critic, "is the least of its sins."

Jimmy's favorite rendezvous, in a city organized for the convenience of its bons vivants, was the Arts Club in Hanover Square. It offered a congenial mixture of creature comforts and literacy, with just the necessary spicing of Bohemianism. On the evening of July 6, 1877, Jimmy was in the smoking room with George Boughton, a plump, convivial fellow Yankee who was a member of the Royal Academy. Boughton was sunk in one of the squat, ugly black-leather library chairs, a cigar in his hand and a magazine propped up on a reading rack before him; Jimmy was lighting a cigarette from the gas jet on the wall.

"I see they're still quoting you, Jimmy." Boughton read aloud: "'The painter James Whistler was once approached by a female admirer who reported she had just come down that evening from Putney, and the Thames was a "perfect Whistler." 'Ah,' murmured the painter, 'nature is creeping up.'"

Jimmy inhaled slowly. "Old jokes, like old horses, should be retired after a decent interval."

"You know, it might be fun to do an article about the females who gush over paintings."

"Yes. I have a title for you: 'Shall We Enjoin the Ladies?'"

Boughton snorted his appreciation. He picked up another magazine from the nearby table and started leafing through its pages. "Old Ruskin is back in form," he observed. "In five pages he has managed to call Goldwin Smith a goose, accused Sir Henry Cole of setting back British art instruction by twenty years, and demolished Manchester University . . . I say, what's this?"

"What's what?"

"A notice by Ruskin on the Grosvenor opening."

Jimmy's eyes narrowed. He took a step toward Boughton, then dropped instead into one of the trim, uncushioned Queen Anne armchairs. "Read it like a good fellow, eh, George?"

Boughton adjusted his glasses. "'I must not close this letter without . . .' Ah, never mind that. Here we are: 'Sir Coutts Lindsay is at present an amateur in both art and shopkeeping. He must take up either one or the other business, if he would prosper in either . . . The upholstery of the gallery is very grievously injurious to the best pictures it contains, while its glitter as unjustly veils the vulgarity of the worst.' And so forth."

Boughton ran his eye down the page. "Ah, yes. 'The work of Mr. Burne-Jones is, first, simply the only art work at present produced in England which will be received by the future as "classic" in its kind—the best that has been or could be. The action of imagination of the highest power in Burne-Jones, under the conditions of scholarship, of social beauty, and of social distress in the nineteenth century are alone in art—unrivaled in their kind; and I know that these will be immortal.'"

"A very detached and balanced judgment."

"Uh—I think you'd better read this next part yourself, Jimmy."

Boughton extended the paper, an odd look in his eye. Jimmy hesitated, swept by a chill of impending disaster. Then he screwed his monocle into place, took up the sheet, and sat down again. He looked at the title of the publication. *"Fors Clavigera.* What the devil does that mean?"

*"Fate,* ah, *Fate Bearing a Hammer,* you might say. His monthly prescription for improving the soul of the British workingman. Your part is at the top of the second column, where he talks about 'eccentricities of the modern schools.'"

"Oh yes." Jimmy read to himself for a moment, a pallor spreading over his ruddy cheeks. He continued aloud, in a high strained voice: "'For Mr. Whistler's own sake, no less than for the protection of the purchaser, Sir Coutts Lindsay ought not to have admitted works into the gallery in which the ill-educated conceit of the artist so nearly approached the aspect of . . . of . . .'" The light voice broke slightly, the full sensitive lips twitched. "'. . . of wilful imposture. I have seen and heard much of Cockney impudence before now; but never expected to hear a *coxcomb* . . .'" Jimmy came down heavily on the word, paused and went on. "'. . . a coxcomb ask two hundred guineas for flinging a pot of paint in the public's face.'"

"Pretty strong stuff, Jimmy."

"It is the most debased *style* of criticism I have had thrown at me yet."

"Rather a stab in the back, I should say."

"And with a kitchen knife!"

"Is there any more?"

Jimmy picked up the sheet and read to the end of the column. His name was not mentioned again. It appeared that Ruskin having thus, as he fancied, decapitated the upstart painter, he felt free to turn to more edifying matters, concluding his homilies for the month with an inspiring tale of the tender relationship between a race horse and its stable kitten.

Boughton was watching him expectantly. "No, there's no more. But what there is, is quite enough." Jimmy stood up and crossed to an alcove off the fireplace, where an enormous dictionary was mounted on a rostrum. He shuffled the bulky pages a moment. "'Coxcomb: a cap once worn by professional fools, resembling the comb of a cock. By extension, a fop—dude—popinjay—jackanapes!'" The underslung Whistler jaw tightened. "Jackanapes, I believe, is a kind of monkey!"

"Sounds rather like libel," suggested Boughton.

"That," replied Jimmy, "we shall try to find out."

A misty summer rain tapped against the sides of the carriage, muffling the clip-clop of hoofs along gaslit Piccadilly. Inside, Jimmy was wrapped in mists of his own. The material damage to him was hardly the point, though he supposed it might be the basis for legal action. It was his sense of justice that was outraged—and his pride. He was the son of Major George Washington Whistler, a man who in seven years of royal service never bent the knee to the Czar; and on his mother's side, descended via plantation-owning North Carolinians from a clan chief in the Hebrides. He did not take insults lightly from any quarter; certainly not from a, a . . . actually, who *was* Ruskin?

He had only the dimmest personal knowledge of the critic. A decade earlier, Swinburne as a mutual friend had tried unsuccessfully to bring young painter and middle-aged critic together. Afterward, vague reports had come to Jimmy's ears of a professorial broadside at Oxford against "impudent daubs," presumably Whistlerian. And Jimmy recollected being outraged by one of Ruskin's grandiose social projects: "It's a scheme for badgering the unfortunate. God knows the poor suffer enough without being patronized!"

Like everyone else in London, Jimmy had heard of the sensational love triangle of the '50s involving Ruskin, his vivacious wife Effie Gray, and the painter Millais. Ruskin had invited Millais to join the couple on a holiday trip to the Scottish Highlands. There, by accident or design, bored wife was thrown repeatedly into the company of handsome, vigorous young artist. The flirtation led to annulment of Ruskin's marriage, after which Effie became Mrs. Millais.

Spicy details were supplied by the omniscient Howell. Ruskin had been unwilling to consummate his marriage, Howell asserted, because he was repelled by the reality of the nude female form in contrast to the hairless perfection of Greek statuary. According to Howell, the professor's repeated emotional frustrations, added to his confessed inability to "compose a picture" himself on canvas, had now brought Ruskin to the brink of nervous collapse.

This portrayal, Jimmy felt, might be questionable; Ruskin's position of entrenched power was not. The man had inherited more than £200,-000 on his father's death in 1864. He had the prestige of an appointment to a chair at Oxford five years later. And he had the best of con-

nections in the invisible, impenetrable web of landowners, clergy, public officials, and press barons who governed England; when he wept
aloud in his rich, rolling prose for the neglected soul of the British
worker, not only schoolgirls but cabinet ministers wept with him.

Could such a colossus be toppled? Jimmy needed a legal opinion.

"Forget about it, Jimmy."

They were sitting in the rear garden at Lindsey Row, Jimmy and
his small, agile-minded solicitor, Anderson Rose. The air was heavy
with the late-afternoon scent of honeysuckle and lime.

"But why?"

"Ruskin is practically invulnerable. A British jury would only need
to be reminded that he has passed most of his life among the world's
great paintings."

"By that yardstick," snapped Jimmy, "every washroom attendant
in the Louvre would qualify as an art expert."

"The people of this island regard him as an oracle."

"Which gives him the right to trample on my work?"

"Not the right—but the power."

"What about the famous British concern for protecting a man's good
name?"

The solicitor pursed his lips. "It's true that we go beyond American
law in our zeal for defending personal reputation. But in this case—
that factor would have to be balanced against British concern for free
speech, for the right of a critic to express an opinion. Libel is a very
slippery business: not only a matter of language, but of intent. Was
Ruskin being honest, or malicious? And again, is your reputation in
England such that it *could* be damaged? Ruskin would trot out the
trained seals of the Academy to testify that, aesthetically speaking, you
are all but a naked barbarian."

"But there must be some honest painters—"

"Honest but scared. Nobody is eager to join the whipping boy in the
stocks. You would be astonished at how many of our boon companions have suddenly become hard of hearing, or developed important
engagements that will take them out of London." He ticked off names
on his fingers. "Alma-Tadema, for one, would find it inconvenient to
take the stand. Charles Keene, whom you have praised as the successor to Hogarth, is sure the trial will be 'the greatest of larks'—but
begs you to get along without him if you can. Poynter objects even to
his letters in appreciation of the Nocturnes being quoted."

"What about the Rossettis?"

"William might be persuaded to speak for you, as a critic. Dante has
already been approached by the other side, and turned them down.
But as for turning up on your behalf"—the lawyer shook his head—

"Ruskin was his patron, even put up money for his wife's poems. So, no matter what Dante thinks of his manners or his qualifications as a judge of art . . . besides, Dante would rather face a firing squad than a court. You know how he hates publicity."

"Howell is clamoring to be unleashed. Says he has devastating information on Ruskin's business methods."

"Suppose the defense chooses to go into *Howell's* methods? The peculiar way that so much of Ruskin's capital stuck to his hands or wound up with his relatives? If you ever expose Howell to cross-examination, he'll probably be indicted for larceny. Or seduction, or perjury. He has the kind of character it's impossible to assassinate."

"I could count on Albert Moore," Jimmy persisted. "And Freddie Leighton. We go back to Paris days together. And he's going to be the next president of the Academy."

"Maybe, maybe, Jimmy. But you're outgunned."

Jimmy fell silent. It was hardly worth raising the question of the critics. In the public prints and private encounters, he had made many a meal of the reveiwers from the *Times* and *Truth;* could yesterday's poached filets be expected to defend the man who had gobbled them up? Besides, what critic, given their generally middle-class origins, would dare to enter the lists against Ruskin and run the risk of being wiped out forever by the Preacher and his formidable friends?

There were his French partisans—some major talents who might cross the channel if he called. Degas, Manet, Fantin-Latour. But the applause of unorthodox outlanders would merely underline his alienation from British respectability.

Jimmy's long, nervous fingers wandered disconsolately over his imperial. Those willing to help his case would be useless, or worse. And those whose support would be valuable were not willing to help. He became aware of a shadow in the pantry doorway. "Yes, Joseph?"

"Mrs. Whistler"—Maud had lately commandeered the title—"will be here a little after eight."

"Very good. Will you join us for dinner, Andy?"

"Thank you, no. I'm expected in the country." Rose heaved himself to his feet, motioning Jimmy to stay seated. "I'll find my way out." And he was gone.

The butler came forward. "Mr. Albert Moore sent this by messenger." He handed Jimmy a pamphlet.

"Thank you, Joseph."

"Will there be anything more, sir?"

"Another mint julep, please."

A boat whistle sounded from the river on the other side of the house, mingling with the far-off cries of children at play. From the garden wall, a brown and white cat dropped noiselessly to the ground and curled up in the shade of the lime tree. Peace spread over the garden: was it the peace of utter defeat?

He felt a surge of helplessness. Why wasn't there someone to tell him what to do—not a detached legal adviser, but someone close? Maud was willing, but she didn't quite fill the bill. His mother was away. His brother Willie was preoccupied with a recent marriage and a growing medical practice.

Alone. Damnably alone, as ever.

The blue-gray eyes blinked rapidly. A sensation of dampness crept across his face.

He was crying, crying even as Joseph with ostentatious discretion deposited a fresh drink and slipped away. With a breast-pocket handkerchief, Jimmy dabbed at his cheeks. He reached for the julep, and his eye fell on the pamphlet sent by Albert Moore.

NOTES
on some of
THE PRINCIPAL PICTURES
exhibited in the rooms of the
ROYAL ACADEMY
1875
By John Ruskin

A segment of the Holy Scripture. Mechanically, Jimmy picked up the leaflet and glanced at the titles on the index page. *The Babylonian Marriage Market*, by Edwin Long. Now, there was a sure-fire combination of exotic prurience and tongue-clucking virtue. And an execrably vulgar painting, to boot. Even the Great Man must have noticed . . .

Curious, Jimmy popped his monocle into place and turned to Ruskin's review. "A remarkable picture," he read, "even as a mere piece of painting" (than which, presumably, nothing could be lower). Ruskin had praise for the work's "anthropological merits;" he regretted only its inadequate concern for "moral beauty."

Jimmy read on. Ah, here was a learned reproof to Rembrandt! One J. Pettie, in creating a facial wrinkle, had dared to use a boldly projecting ridge of paint instead of the "proper dark line." Ruskin was stern: "Rembrandt's bad bricklayer's work, with all the mortar sticking out at the edges, may be pardonable in a Dutchman sure of his colours; but it is always licentious."

The light was dimming and the air growing chill. Jimmy crossed the stone flagging to the rear of the house and went upstairs to the drawing room, where an armchair and gas lamp beckoned near the fireplace.

The critic was equally put out, he discovered, with the "clumsy hand" of Constable. But Ruskin's rancor faded before a "pretty little scene" called *Domestic Troubles*, in which a wicked little boy has taken apart a fireplace bellows; and a sympathetic portrait of a kitten was, to the Oxford Professor of Fine Art, "unsurpassable."

Except, perhaps, by a thumping cavalry charge at Waterloo: "Of all in the Academy, the picture which an Englishman of right feeling would least wish to overlook."

Jimmy put the catalogue down. It simply wouldn't do. Ruskin might be a giant of literature, but in the groves of the painting Muse he was a destructive monster. If no one in England had the courage to lop off the dragon's head, who better than an American-born child of revolution?

There was something else that made it necessary to resist, a vague indefinable bone-in-the-throat sensation. The smothering of dissent was intolerable from any source—whether it be a self-appointed guardian of aesthetic standards, a pontificating brother-in-law . . . or yes, one's own mother. Ruskin, the professional zealot, stirred painful echoes of Jimmy's boyhood.

He had to fight back, although it would not be easy. The British press, from whose attacks the memory of the 1776 insult was never entirely absent, would make a carnival of the case. He would himself be placed on trial . . . ridiculed, maligned.

But the Great Preacher would not escape unscathed, either. If he could smash Ruskin's power, the game would be worth the candle—although the candle might burn James Whistler very badly indeed.

# Chapter Twenty-two

On July 21, 1877, the bombshell burst on London: Whistler was suing Ruskin for libel, claiming damages of £1000. The story ricocheted through the small inner world that held the reins of nation and empire.

To begin with, painters didn't bring lawsuits. They were too erratic, improvident a breed. True, they might be involved with the law occasionally—but always on the other side, as alleged violator and incipient victim. Rarely had one invoked the aid of justice.

Not that they didn't have occasion to. Most of them were periodically cheated—by unscrupulous dealers, patrons who exploited their fragile economic condition, sitters who became bored and vanished with an unpaid-for portrait half done. But they generally complained to their friends, had a drink, or wove the incident into an amusing anecdote. Painters didn't go to court.

And if they did, no painter in his right mind would sue a critic. For an artist to pick as his target the high priest himself of British aesthetics was inconceivable. Does the criminal in the dock dare to challenge the Chief Justice?

No less titillating were the personalities of the principals, two of the arch-individualists of the age. After declining to contest his wife's charges of "incurable impotency," Ruskin had stunned London by continuing to champion the work of his successor, Millais.

As for Whistler, he had long been an unwelcome guest. In a society publicly preoccupied with its laundering and laces, privately uneasy over its monstrous inequalities, the American was too quick to slash at façades. Since the Whistler heresies could not be acknowledged as dangerous without undermining the Victorian pose of insouciance, the safe response had been to laugh.

Now the venom behind the laughter came into the open. The weekly *London* editorialized on August 18:

We fear the Oracle of English Art has simply said in fit words what many silent persons thought . . .

In the birth of the Whistleristic principle we are struck, as in all great discoveries, with the simplicity of the germinating idea. For ages this idea lay dormant, as it were, under the very thumb of everyone who cleaned his palette and spread the refuse on a bit of wood or paper. Year after year dullard men were appealed to in vain by oily coagulations . . . What glory to Mr. Whistler! He it was who first saw the use of such accidental mixtures.

We sometimes picture the scene. A piece of newspaper is set to receive the refuse paint; a prophetic glow overspreads the young American features; and on a contemptible patch of the New York *Herald,* glitters the first genuine Whistler.

Mr. Whistler's brave attempt to enlighten the Britishers is lost to us should that cold douche of Ruskinese freeze, rather than invigorate. But we can't despair, remembering as we do that the Whistlerian idea arose in the land of progress and Presidents, the land where Barnum blows and Whitman catalogues. Before taking our leave of Mr. Whistler (perhaps never to meet him again!) it is our solemn duty to warn him against giving way to discouragement.

Jimmy had more to be discouraged about than heavy-handed satire. He had hoped for an early court judgment, and Ruskin too was eager for the contest to be joined, writing to Burne-Jones when the pleadings were closed on December 11: "It's mere nuts and nectar to me . . . the whole thing will enable me to assert some principles of art economy which I've never got into the public's head by writing, but may get sent all over the world vividly in a newspaper report or two."

But the confrontation so ardently desired by both sides was suddenly sideswiped. At fifty-nine, Ruskin was fifteen years Jimmy's senior. He had lived for decades under extreme tension and in abnormal isolation. There had already been signs of either arterial degeneration in the brain, emotional disturbance, or both; now the long-gathering mental crisis erupted. Delirium swept over him for days, alternating with periods of quiet and of violent rage. His physician, diagnosing "brain fever," requested postponement of the trial.

Courtesy as well as self-interest obliged Jimmy to go along. The delays were repeated several times. By fall of 1878, it became clear that no permanent improvement in Ruskin's condition could be anticipated; at best he would be too weak to take the stand. It was agreed to go ahead in November without him. The spectacular personal duel would be eliminated; but Ruskin's political power had already been marshaled. His chief counsel would be the Attorney General himself, John Holker.

Meanwhile, another Whistler showing at the Grosvenor Gallery resulted in negligible sales. This might strengthen Jimmy's court case, but it did nothing for his battered pocketbook. At the same time he had acquired an unanticipated set of expenses in connection with a new mortgage-financed house in Chelsea.

Even the one flicker of cheer on the horizon was quickly dimmed. Frederick Leighton, the newly elected president of the Royal Academy, had consented to appear as a witness for Jimmy. But on the weekend before the trial date, Leighton was summoned to Windsor Castle. On the morning of November 25, when Jimmy went out like a Christian gladiator to face the British Lion, his old comrade would be kneeling for knighthood before Queen Victoria.

The Court of Exchequer in London reverberated to the drum rolls of British history. Jutting out from the northwest corner of the parliamentary complex, it stood a few feet from Westminster Hall, oldest surviving segment of the medieval royal palace. Under the Gothic flying buttresses of Westminster, English kings beginning with Edward the Confessor in the eleventh century had been crowned; Thomas More, Guy Fawkes, and King Charles I had faced their accusers in state trials.

The courtroom itself was majestically scaled, with arched beams sweeping upward to a paneled-oak ceiling thirty feet above the floor. Enormous casement windows looked out across the New Palace Yard toward Big Ben in the Clock Tower. The judge's bench stood on a dais at the far end, flanked by the witness stand and jury box; rows of benches for spectators provided some 150 seats.

On the morning of November 25, 1878, they were not nearly enough. By 10:00 A.M., when the doors opened, a crowd was waiting in the halls. An hour later, with court scheduled to convene, they were spilling over into the aisles.

At the plaintiff's counsel table, little Anderson Rose was in earnest colloquy with Messrs. Parry and Petheram, the two barristers he had engaged to conduct Jimmy's case. No, he assured them, the erratic painter had not taken off for parts unknown. Jimmy was chronically late for appointments: a matter of temperament, and perhaps perverse principle, long ago congealed into habit. Whistler rejected even the "slavery" of carrying a watch. But he was probably somewhere in the environs right now.

And indeed he was. In a cloakroom just off Westminster Hall, Jimmy was adjusting the snowy forelock that floated among his curls like a lone whitecap on a dark sea. It had to thrust forward crisply under his silk topper, the first sight to meet the gaze of the enemy. There! That was a fine battle standard. He stepped back into the corridor.

The guard at the courtroom door shook his head. "No more room, sir. You're too late."

Jimmy flipped the monocle up to his eye and stared.

"You wouldn't be—? Oh, beg pardon, sir. Right this way, Mr. Whistler."

Standees fell back as Jimmy made his way down to the front row. He had not been in court since the Paris street brawl with Seymour Haden; this promised to be more interesting. For one thing, the room was superb, a suitable setting for an important artistic dispute. For another, there was the audience, distinctly top-hat and Paris-bonnet. Without unseemly craning of his neck, Jimmy could see that it was of a caliber more familiar to Ascot or an opening night at the Lyceum than to the somber halls of justice. In fact, there was Henry Irving himself in the fifth row: Checking up on the competition? And clustered together farther back were a group of the Whistlerite faithful: Howell and Rosa Corder (Howell had actually roused himself before noon!); Luke Ionides; Ned and Trixie Godwin; the dealer Murray Marks, the young critic Malcolm Salaman. Some painters were scattered about—rather discreetly, Jimmy thought: Sandys, Keene, Boughton . . .

The day was gray; not dark enough to require the gas lamps mounted along the walls, but reinforcing the air of theatrical anticipation.

Now the jury filed in, a special panel. From what Andy Rose had told him, they were mainly merchants and retired civil servants. Jimmy looked his peers over with mild curiosity. The foreman, he decided, was a chemist. That was a bad sign. Chemists meant ugly mustard plaster, painful and stubborn bouts with the grippe . . .

"Silence in the court . . . the court will rise."

A gangling man, half-lost in trailing robes, shambled out of a side door in the back and, as he took his place at the bench, was promptly surrounded by lawyers and court functionaries. This was Baron Huddleston, the presiding justice. Jimmy diverted himself by comparing the several wigs on display. Although the judge's frizzy white headpiece would never have passed West Point inspection, those of opposing counsel were quite well fitted.

An amiable fancy struck him. Why not formal court costume for all participants in the case? The plaintiff in garb of outraged innocence, spiky hair standing angrily on end? The defendant with a halo mounted over his head? And every witness, according to the nature of his testimony . . .

The judge was nodding solemnly to some procedural suggestion. Baron Huddleston was long-limbed and cadaverous; a typical upstanding—or in this instance upsitting—representative of the minor

British aristocracy. He wore the expression of a nervous basset hound, his small brown eyes shifting rapidly in his head as if he were fearful of having missed something. And the chances were, Jimmy reflected, that he had. When Huddleston leaned back, fumbling with a pen-holder, there was a hint of a draught or two sitting comfortably in his tummy. The baron was clearly no molder of empire; this was some-body's elder son, pitched onto judicial shores by the winds of political fortune. There was little prospect of sympathy from that quarter.

The clerk was droning an "Oyez, oyez . . ."; the trial was under way. Jimmy was faintly depressed to note that the very phrasing of the action served to reverse the position of plaintiff and defendant, and place him in the dock; the case was announced as that of James Whis-tler, "an artist," against John Ruskin, "the well-known author and art critic."

Serjeant Parry, Barrister, now came forward to lay out the essence of the plaintiff's case: a sincere and hard-working artist had had his living seriously impaired by vituperative criticism far beyond the bounds of legitimate comment. As his first witness, Parry called on the painter himself.

Conscious of the buzz of voices behind him, Jimmy rose and care-fully peeled off his long sealskin coat, lately acquired from Howell in part payment for the portrait of Henry Irving. He crossed to take the oath from the clerk, then mounted the three narrow steps to the wit-ness box. For just an instant he turned toward the spectators, parade-ground trim in his black frock coat and gray trousers, left hand resting on his hip in the jaunty carelessness of a cavalryman at the trot. The blue, knife-blade eyes flashed defiance. Under the drooping-willow mustache, the sardonic mouth twisted into a sneer.

Then Jimmy sat down in the box, placed his hat alongside him, and slowly drew off his yellow gloves. Serjeant Parry lumbered for-ward and asked the artist where he was born.

"In St. Petersburg, Russia," came the serene reply.

Jimmy was perfectly aware that he had entered the world in the humdrum surroundings of Lowell, Massachusetts. But how could a few years in a New England mill town compete in memory with a land of pageantry and princes? He had no patience with inconvenient de-tail; in life as in art, if "accidental" fact interfered with an agreeable "arrangement," the fact would have to go.

Besides, the "St. Petersburg" conceit would stun the stodgy Brit-isher. What better credentials to fling before the caste-conscious is-landers than the glittering decadence of the Czarist court?

Parry waited for the hum to subside. "Where were you educated, Mr. Whistler?"

"At the United States Military Academy."

This time, Baron Huddleston stirred. "You are a professional soldier, Mr. Whistler? A graduate of West Point?"

"Not quite, milord. I attended the Academy for three years . . ." Jimmy paused, drawing in his audience adroitly. "If silicon had been a gas, I would be a major general."

The line went down well; it always had. Huddleston rapped for order.

Now counsel for the plaintiff got down to business. Briskly, Parry established his client's professional status: eight paintings shown at the Royal Academy, representation at the Paris Salon, a gold medal at the Hague, etchings in the British Museum and Windsor Castle collections. Jimmy testified that in the group reviewed by Ruskin at the Grosvenor Gallery, only the painting condemned by the critic was for sale. Most of the others were on loan from purchasers who had paid from 150 to 200 guineas . . . the amount being asked for *The Falling Rocket*.

"Since that criticism, Mr. Whistler, have you sold any more Nocturnes?"

"Not by any means at the same prices as before."

Parry then asked Jimmy to explain his definition of a Nocturne.

"I have perhaps meant to indicate an artistic interest alone in the work, divesting the picture from any outside anecdotal sort of interest which might have been otherwise attached to it. It is an arrangement of line, form and color first; and I make use of any incident of it which shall bring about a symmetrical result. Among my works are some night pieces, and I have chosen the word Nocturne because it generalizes and simplifies the whole set of them."

Parry turned the witness over for cross-examination to the Attorney General. John Holker was a large, fleshy man who affected a light jocular manner—rather like, Jimmy thought, a hippopotamus attempting the ballet.

"Ah, Mr. Whistler . . . two hundred guineas is what we ordinary folk who are not artists would call a stiffish price, is it not?"

"Very likely it would be."

"Artists do not seek high prices irrespective of actual value?"

"That is true, and I am glad to see the principle so well established."

Holker nodded. He fingered his ear delicately. "When you exhibit, you do expect your work to be criticized?"

"Of course; but on a technical level, and by a man whose life is passed in the practice of the science which he criticizes. For the opinion of a man whose life is not so passed, I would have as little regard as you would if he expressed an opinion on law."

Holker beckoned one of his assistants to bring forward a canvas. "Do you recognize this painting, Mr. Whistler?"

"With some difficulty. You're holding it upside down."

The Attorney General was all contrition. "There . . . would that be better? Now, would you tell us what this is?"

"The *Nocturne in Black and Gold* is a night piece representing the fireworks at Cremorne."

"Not a view of Cremorne?"

"As a view of Cremorne, it would certainly bring about nothing but disappointment on the part of beholders" (appreciative laughter). "It is an artistic arrangement."

"Like your, ah, rendition of Mr. Henry Irving. Why do you call Mr. Irving an *Arrangement in Black?*"

More ripples of amusement. Baron Huddleston waggled a finger at the Attorney General, smiling. It was the picture, he pointed out, not Mr. Irving, that was the arrangement.

"Each of these pictures," said Jimmy, "is an impression of my own, a problem worked out . . . the result of much study."

"You've been told that your pictures exhibit some eccentricities?"

"Yes—very often."

"But you send them to the gallery to invite the admiration of the public?"

"That would be an absurdity beyond contemplation."

Some minor verbal scuffling followed. No, the painter did not expect his work to be universally accepted; yes, he considered *The Falling Rocket* to be a finished picture, in the sense that nothing more could be done to improve it. The painting was mainly "dependent on the instantaneous work of my hand."

Holker eyed the canvas thoughtfully. "Can you tell me how long it took you to knock off that Nocturne?"

The eloquent eyebrows flew up. "I beg your pardon?"

"Ah, forgive me . . . I'm afraid I'm using a term that applies rather to my own work . . ."

"Oh no, permit me!" The long nervous fingers traced a delicate arabesque, the eyes flamed with malicious delight. "I am too greatly flattered to think that you apply, to work of mine, any term you are in the habit of using with reference to your own. Let us say then how long did I take to—'knock off,' I think that is it—to knock off that Nocturne; well, as well as I remember, about a day. I may have put a few more touches to it the next day if the painting were not dry. I'd better say I was two days at work on it."

Holker, suddenly not so flabby, darted in for the kill. "It is for the labor of two days, then, that you ask two hundred guineas?"

"No. I ask it for the knowledge of a lifetime."

A burst of warm applause spread from the center of the courtroom. Baron Huddleston rapped sharply. "Silence, please! If there are further manifestations from the spectators, the court will be cleared!"

Holker motioned to his counsel table for another painting to be brought into evidence. This time, the canvas was handed first to the jurors, and made a bumpy passage through the court. Jimmy watched with increasing distress as, banged against a solid bald crown, it was jarred part way out of its frame.

Finally the canvas reached the witness box. "Is that your work, Mr. Whistler?" demanded Holker.

Jimmy raised the monocle to his eye. "Well, it *was*," he said tentatively, screwing the eyeglass tighter. "But if it goes on much longer this way, it won't be!"

He identified the painting as the *Nocturne in Blue and Silver,* a representation of Old Battersea Bridge by moonlight.

Baron Huddleston squinted down from the bench and motioned for the picture to be brought closer. "Which part of the picture is Battersea Bridge?"

The sally drew loud laughter from the courtroom—a "manifestation" which, curiously enough, the judge made no effort to squelch.

"Your lordship is too close to the picture at present," Jimmy explained, "to perceive the effect which I intended to produce at a distance. The spectator is supposed to be looking down the river toward London."

The judge paused; expectant giggles from the front row awaited his next thrust. "Do you say this is a correct representation of the bridge?"

"I did not intend it as a 'correct portrait' of the bridge."

"Those figures at the top: Are they meant to be people?"

"They are just what you like," replied Jimmy. Of what use to discuss the subtleties of Japanese painting, the geometric intricacies of a Hiroshige or the graceful sweep of an Utamoro line with men to whom these names would only conjure up dishes in a Limehouse restaurant?

The judge continued his low-comedy inquisition. "Is that a barge beneath?"

"Yes. I am very much encouraged at your perceiving that. My whole scheme was only to bring about a certain harmony of color."

After a brief adjournment, Holker had a last fling at *The Falling Rocket.* "Do you think, Mr. Whistler, you could possibly make *me* understand the beauty of that painting?"

Jimmy studied the Attorney General gravely. Then he looked over at the painting. Back and forth his gaze went, several times, while the court fidgeted in suspense. "No," he said at last. "I fear it would be as hopeless as for a musician to pour his notes into the ear of a deaf man."

Jimmy was followed to the stand by William Rossetti. Bald and solemn, with a long monkish face, William sat like a bearded Buddha, hands folded calmly in his lap. If Dante Gabriel looked the genius, William looked the sage.

A former civil servant, he had given sanctuary in his home to leftist political refugees from all over Europe. He was the author of an excellent biography of Shelley, and one of the few literary and art critics with no cliquish affiliations. As an old friend to both parties, he had been "rather dismayed" to receive a subpoena; but he had written sympathetically in *The Academy* of Jimmy's Nocturnes at the Grosvenor ("the *Blue and Gold* is a masterpiece of tone, tinting, solidity, and sentiment too"), and was of no disposition to recant.

Holker, having won from the witness the concession that *The Falling Rocket* was not his favorite Whistler, drove relentlessly for more. Was it a "gem?" An exquisite painting? Very beautiful?

No, no and no. But was it a work of art?

Firmly, "yes." And definitely worth 200 guineas, although "I am too poor to give it."

Albert Moore, slight and smoldering with indignation, testified next. Jimmy felt a wave of affection for the little fellow. It was Moore who had asserted "there is not a single R.A. who could design a button" and who, hearing of an Old Guard painter at work retouching in a private room at the Arts Club, had hissed: "Don't miss the chance. Lock him up till he promises to take the picture home."

Moore was more emphatic than Rossetti about *The Falling Rocket*. It was "marvelous, a consummate work of art." Far from retreating under cross-examination, he asserted that the word for Whistler should not be "eccentric," but "original." "He succeeds as no other living painter could; I wish I could paint as well."

A short appearance by William Gorman Wills, Irish playwright and portrait painter, concluded the plaintiff's case. Wills testified that Whistler was a "man of genius."

The Attorney General now moved for dismissal, on the grounds that no libel had been established. The judge declined. Whistler had clearly been ridiculed; it was for the defense to prove that Ruskin's criticism was fair and honest.

Holker chose, in his opening statement the next morning, to pursue the line of still greater ridicule. He conjured up a bevy of beautiful but fatuous ladies gaping at the Whistler display at the Grosvenor, with one murmuring: "How delightful that Mr. Whistler should have discovered a connection between music and art. Just fancy a moonlight in three flats!"

Holker paused for the obligatory laugh. Having received it, he pictured his imaginary ladies standing in wonderment before the *Nocturne in Blue and Silver, Old Battersea Bridge*. "What is that part in the middle?" they would ask. "A telescope, or a fire escape? Or is it the great tubular bridge over the Menai Straits which has escaped to Chelsea?" Loud merriment in the courtroom. "And those figures at the top: Are they men and women, or horses and cattle? How did they get on the bridge, and how, in the name of fortune, are they going to get off?"

Holker derided the painter for "seeing things others cannot see, and hearing artistic voices we cannot hear"; if such a man wished to risk his livelihood by exhibiting a silly daub, he ought not to complain when it was so identified. In sum, Mr. Whistler was indeed demonstrably a coxcomb or jester, since never had "so much amusement been afforded to the British public" as by his pictures; and Mr. Ruskin was the protector of the unwary buyer, the defender of all that was truly beautiful: "Do not paralyze his hands."

The defense too led off its witnesses with the main gun: Burne-Jones, in effect standing in for Ruskin himself. Jimmy shook his head, dismay mingling with a sense of outrage, as the slender, ascetic-featured Pre-Raphaelite mounted the steps to the box. Jimmy found it simply incredible that a fellow painter, especially one who himself had long been castigated for clinging to a private vision, could line up in the enemy camp. Granted, Burne-Jones was Ruskin's disciple and friend; true, his fervent preoccupation with legend and moral uplift placed him at the opposite pole aesthetically; still, he was a man of the brush . . .

Burne-Jones himself was visibly uncomfortable; for years afterward, he was to refer to the trial as a "hateful affair." He squirmed, smoothed his long yellow beard, and wiped the perspiration from his face repeatedly as Holker led him through a series of increasingly severe judgments:

"Perfect finish" was indispensable to a work of art. Whistler's first *Nocturne in Blue and Silver* was "masterly" in color, but incomplete: "Neither in composition, detail, nor form has the picture any quality whatever." The Nocturne of *Old Battersea Bridge,* employing a similar palette, was "even better" in color, but "bewildering as to form," and utterly without composition. He didn't think Mr. Whistler intended it to be regarded as a finished picture.

As for *The Falling Rocket,* it did not "have the merit of the other two," or qualify as art; it was merely "one of a thousand failures which artists have made in their efforts at painting night." It was not worth 200 guineas, "seeing how much careful work men do for so much less."

Defense counsel conferred briefly, then beckoned forward a clerk staggering under a large portrait canvas. As he set it down, juror number seven muttered irritably and quite distinctly: "Ah, we've had enough of these Whistlers!"

The painting turned out to be a Titian, introduced for the purpose of illustrating true classical finish.

On cross-examination, Burne-Jones agreed that Whistler had an "unrivaled" sense of atmosphere. He also volunteered once again, as if in response to nagging conscience, that Jimmy's color was "beautiful, especially in his moonlight pieces." But he stuck with his basic contention that Whistler never carried his work beyond the sketching stage, and had therefore betrayed his early "infinite promise." It was not the beginning that mattered, but the challenge of meeting steadily increasing difficulties. "If unfinished pictures become common we shall arrive at a stage of mere manufacture, and the art of the country will be degraded."

Flushed and trembling, Burne-Jones stepped down to make way for an unlikely bedfellow, William Powell Frith. Frith, a stocky, red-bearded man of sixty, specialized in "authentic" mob-scene canvases like *Derby Day* and *The Railway Station*. Much satisfied with a career that had brought him the patronage of Dickens and Prince Albert, he grinned at the court in a frequent display of bad teeth. Jimmy was vexed to note that several jurors, in a show of mercantile camaraderie, grinned right back.

Frith favored high finish and blinding colors. It was his boast that he had tossed a coin to decide between art and auctioneering; in Jimmy's view he had achieved neither. Jimmy remarked once of a Frith collection, "They may be finished, but they have certainly never been begun."

Frith ticked off his opinions crisply. Whistler had "very great power as an artist," but it was not displayed in any of the works under discussion. The picture of Old Battersea Bridge by moonlight had a "beautiful tone of color, but it does not represent any more than you could get from a bit of wallpaper or silk." Was *The Falling Rocket* a serious work of art?

"Not to me."

Tom Taylor took the stand. Editor of *Punch* and art critic of *The Times*, he was the author of some seventy plays including *Our American Cousin*, the comedy that Abraham Lincoln was watching on the night he was shot. Taylor did not look the illustrious part. He was small, bunchy of figure, and haphazardly dressed, with steel-rimmed glasses precariously held aboard by string. Nor were his critical credentials impeccable, despite his university honors at Glasgow and Cambridge. He had once written glowingly of a "Turner" that turned out not to be, and had described the Velázquez classic *Las Meninas* (Maids of Honor) as "slovenly in execution, poor in color, and ugly in its forms."

Jimmy had at first been infuriated by Taylor's pomposities; with time and closer acquaintance, he had become positively fond of the little bumbler. At a gallery showing, when Taylor commented crossly "It's not good, you know," Jimmy had corrected him gently: "Don't say it's not good; say you don't like it, and you're safe. Now come and have something you *do* like." And he led Taylor to the whisky bar.

As a trial witness, Taylor was in his element; his secret yearning was to be an actor. With very little prodding he produced copies of his *Times* reviews on Whistler, and declaimed them for the jury: Whistler was a sketcher, not a serious artist, whose work belonged "in the region of chaff." The Nocturnes, including the disputed *Falling Rocket,* were only "one step nearer pictures than delicately graduated tints on wallpaper."

Taylor squashed his clippings into his overcoat pocket and stepped down, smiling at his friend Frith. The defense rested.

In charging the jury, Baron Huddleston observed that some of Ruskin's language was indisputably libelous; the critic should not use his position as a "veil for personal censure or for showing his power." But—did Whistler's notions of art invite such language? "The further question is whether the insult offered—if insult there has been—is of such a gross character as to call for substantial damages?" The judge suggested the alternatives of damages "in some small sum," or "merely contemptuous damages to the extent of a farthing, or something of that sort, indicating that the case is one in which no pecuniary damage has been sustained, and which ought never to have been brought into court."

The jurors took the cue. After an hour's deliberation, they returned with a judgment for the plaintiff—awarding Jimmy damages of one farthing, or half of an American penny. Baron Huddleston, to underline his endorsement of the verdict, refused to assess Ruskin for costs; both sides had to pay.

The newspapers lost no time in pointing out the rebuff to the American. Gloated the *London Standard:* "The farthing, even if economically expended, will hardly go far to satisfy the claims of Mr. Whistler's legal advisers. But he has only to paint, or as we believe he expresses it, 'knock off' three or four 'symphonies,' and a week's labor will set all square." The *Entr'Acte Almanack* featured a cartoon of Jimmy captioned "Damages One Farthing—An Arrangement in Done-Brown." Even the sympathetic George Bernard Shaw, writing as a twenty-two-year-old in *The World,* observed that Jimmy should have talked less of his "Artistic Conscience" and more of the damage to his commercial reputation: "That sort of thing can be understood by lawyers, and he would have been awarded one thousand pounds."

Not surprisingly, Jimmy put a different front on the matter. When the jury foreman announced their findings, he had listened in puzzlement, then turned to Serjeant Parry. "That is a verdict for me, is it not?"

"Nominally, yes."

Jimmy reflected a moment, and his face cleared. "Well, I suppose a verdict is a verdict. After all, we were fighting for a principle—not money."

"That," said Parry slowly, "is one way of looking at it."

It was the way that Jimmy chose—at least publicly. He leaped with glee when, two days after the trial, Ruskin surrendered his chair at Oxford; he cited the gratification of the American author, Henry James, at seeing Ruskin "brought up as a disorderly character." To a friend who dissented from his cries of triumph, he condensed his scorn in a single sentence: "My dear fellow, you are just fit to serve on a British jury."

In his heart he knew better. The British papers were right. True, he had toppled the All-Powerful from his throne; the question was, could the "victor" survive his victory?

The financial blow to him was devastating. Legal fees for each litigant came to some four or five hundred pounds (between $2000–$2500). For Ruskin, the millionaire, a public subscription launched by his friends netted more than half the sum in ten days. In Jimmy's case, a more private appeal drew a single pathetic contribution of £25—accompanied by a request for an etching or two in exchange. When Jimmy offered the Arts Club a picture in lieu of back dues, the Secretary sent an acid reply: "It is not a Symphony in Blue and Gray we are after, but an Arrangement in Gold and Silver."

Even worse was his sense of isolation. Almost without exception, his colleagues had gone over to the critic-enemy or taken refuge in neutrality. More than ever, in his mind, the fate of knight-errant Whistler was inseparable from the fate of Art.

# Chapter Twenty-three

The knightly back was against the wall. Work and income had been brought to a standstill by Jimmy's long struggle against Ruskin, but not his sybaritic way of life. Throughout, the sparkling Moselle and Hochheim Berg had flowed freely at his table, washing down oysters and lobsters, fine cheese and hothouse pears. New shoes lined his closet. Ticket stubs scattered through his dinner jacket—for boxes at the Globe, the Princess, the Gaiety—attested to his support of the British theater.

None of these items, of course, was paid for. The stack of old bills on his desk—for painting frames, delivery vans, floor matting—was buried under new tabulations for back income taxes and such miscellanea as "Something Nice" toilet lotion from the pharmacy.

Now the disregarded invoices were being followed up by their outraged senders. Jimmy was reluctant host to a parade of visitors who kept him practically locked up in his house.

He met the onslaught with equanimity. Oddly, the farthing-verdict had refreshed him; he had defied the lightning and remained alive. Ultimately, he was convinced, the brave and deserving would get their reward; his merits would be recognized, and the sheep would flock to Whistler as they now did to Millais and Leighton. Every creditor would be paid. Meanwhile, was he to starve until the great British public awoke from its snoring to discover the master in its midst? Absurd. In a world managed by and for drones, the genuine artist had to bend a few rules to survive. No one would be cheated, of course; but *noblesse oblige* had to be tempered with "talent entitles."

Millais was visiting Jimmy one evening when there was a terrible thumping at the front door. Jimmy peered down through the curtains. "It's poor old Drimble the stationer. I really must do something for him. So sorry I'm not in."

"You can't go on this way, Jimmy. What are you going to do?"

"Do? Why, go to bed, of course. Let my creditors pace the floor."

One or two food merchants had to be placated, unless Jimmy was willing to give up eating. To a greengrocer who had unaccountably let him run up a debt of £600, Jimmy made what seemed to him a reasonable proposition: "Now, Mr. Nelson, you realize that at my table your tomatoes have gratified some of the most distinguished palates in London. But there have been, you know, lapses of quality in your vegetables, which would inevitably be called to general attention if these, ah, unseemly discussions should continue. Why don't we, instead, make you a present of these two excellent Nocturnes, forget about the past, and in future keep a weekly account? Wiser, you know."

Mr. Nelson was not interested in exchanging his grade-A produce for dubious Nocturnes. And although Jimmy offered to Mr. Perkins the fishmonger the salt-scented Valparaiso Harbor scene, and spoke eloquently of this "opportunity to demonstrate both your personal taste and your financial acumen," Mr. Perkins too was unimpressed. Word had filtered back from Glasgow that a Whistler Symphony originally purchased for 200 guineas had, since the Ruskin trial, been disposed of at auction for £13.

However, a few Whistler canvases still had some negotiating value. During the trial, when the winds from the Thames were growing chilly, Jimmy had looked enviously upon Charlie Howell's sleek sealskin coat. The coat, along with £10 in much-needed cash, had become his, in exchange for the portrait of Henry Irving. Now, in the hope of securing a substantial loan from a dealer, Jimmy entrusted to Howell's maneuvering skills his two most precious pictures, the *Carlyle* and the *Mother.*

The *Carlyle* had already been pawned once for £150, and redeemed. Even the *Mother,* which Jimmy usually hung in his bedroom and hated to let out of his sight, had seen brief service as security. For a few days it wound up with Mrs. Noseda, a books-and-prints seller on the Strand, who put it on sale for £100 until the infuriated artist threatened to dismember her.

Howell went to Henry Graves, Jimmy's sympathetic gallery owner in Pall Mall, who had already declined to advance £200 for the *Mother* on the grounds that it wouldn't bring in 20. Shifting to a package deal that combined the two major portraits with three Nocturnes, the ingenious agent managed to part Graves from £500.

Thus Jimmy skated by for a couple of months more, spinning out breezy letters to his mother in Hastings that made no mention of his difficulties. He had his little techniques for forestalling doomsday: the ostentatious delivery of a rented grand piano to impress his creditors, the casual engagement of a hansom that would cruise Bond Street and Piccadilly until he ran across someone who would put up the fare. He did rather resent being tapped for the Poor Tax—"I should be receiving, not paying it!"—but on the whole he might have carried off his improvisations indefinitely, had it not been for the disaster of the White House.

Edward Godwin, the dissident architect and stage designer who was Jimmy's newest crony, shattered the stereotype of the decorous Albertian male. Tall and patrician, with feverish brown eyes in a long blond-bearded face, he was fancied by susceptible females to resemble Pericles of Athens, the French King Henry of Navarre, or Cardinal Manning. Godwin was as celebrated a womanizer as his clubmate at the Arts, Charlie Howell, although operating at loftier echelons; not only had he been the paramour of the delectable Ellen Terry, but countesses and the wives of cabinet ministers were also the accomplices of his mysterious rendezvous. Twice he had been horsewhipped publicly by cuckolded actors. He kept a life-sized statue of Venus in his chambers.

It was as a renegade in his profession, however, that Ned Godwin made his appeal to Jimmy. The architect admired the Japanese aesthetic of simplicity and selectivity, seeking in his own work an abstract emotional statement that balanced mass, light and line. He also agreed with Jimmy on the fundamental unity of the arts, and helped the painter lay out the muted décor for his one-man show.

In 1876, having discarded Ellen Terry, Godwin married Beatrice Philip, the twenty-one-year-old daughter of a prominent sculptor. He brought his vivacious bride to meet Jimmy at the Peacock Room. "Trixie" had a flair for decorative painting. She also had an obvious weakness for gifted older men, and was soon, with or without Godwin, a regular visitor at Jimmy's studio. The trio were mutually enchanted, and—to Maud's great annoyance—for a time inseparable.

In the midst of the Ruskin proceedings, Jimmy's lease at 2 Lindsey Row had expired. It occurred to Jimmy that if he had a large house of his own, he might combine it with a painting school and bolster his sagging fortunes. Naturally he turned to the Godwins. Together they created the White House, a few blocks east of Lindsey Row on Tite Street, overlooking at the rear the grounds of the Royal Chelsea Hospital.

It was a three-story building of revolutionary simplicity, in the complaining view of one critic "plain as a pikestaff." Facings of white Portland stone were crowned by a roof of green slate; moldings were few and classical. Lending charm and character to the exterior, however, was Godwin's capricious, witty scheme of fenestration; windows of different sizes and shapes were scattered irregularly over the façade in accordance with function.

Inside, each room had its own color, broken up by simple lines and ample empty spaces. A "minstrel's gallery" of delicate ironwork surmounted the pale yellow reception hall. On the top floor was a 47-foot studio for Jimmy, with medium-high windows running along the north side. Furniture was minimal: a sprinkling of cane-seat chairs, bamboo sofas, and spindle-legged tables, rounded out by flower vases, goldfish bowls and some pictures. The accent was on visual beauty, not voluptuous luxury: "If you want comfort," Jimmy told a visitor, "go to bed."

The entire concept was not one to gladden the hearts of the die-hard medievalists on the Metropolitan Board of Works, who rated buildings according to how much they exhibited of parapets, cornices and similar architectural ribbonry. For purposes of pacification, Godwin threw into his blueprints a number of ornamental carvings (later conveniently forgotten), and the project moved on triumphantly into the construction stage.

Unfortunately, Jimmy and his architect shared not only a penchant for beauty, but a total disdain for bookkeeping. When they thought of an idea for lengthening the skylight or deepening the fireplace, they had it executed at once; extra costs would be absorbed by the mortgage loan.

They were, to the tune of nearly £1000 in new architectural fees, bringing Godwin's bill up to £2830. Piled on top of this, however, was an unexpected but fully itemized accounting from the contractor, Benjamin Ebenezer Nightingale, demanding £635 for chimney and landing alterations, "close copper nailing" in the pantry, and recoloring of the dining-room walls. "The Nightingale," quoth Jimmy, "hath soured his sweet song."

The contractor did more than that. When no money was forthcoming either from Jimmy or from his now-wary mortgagors, Nightingale was not content to join the long line of grocers, tax collectors, vintners, and frame-makers chasing the painter around London. He went directly to court. On the morning of December 25, 1878, Jimmy awoke to a disagreeable Christmas present: a judgment against him for £450.

An urgent call went out to the heroic Howell, who eased the immediate crisis by issuing a series of complicated personal notes that, if they perplexed Nightingale, also momentarily appeased him.

Howell had been a bottomless well of ingenuity, more than justifying Jimmy's faith. Immediately after the Peacock Room imbroglio, he had kept Jimmy afloat by promoting a new printing of long-neglected etching plates. He had not only obtained loans from Henry Graves, but had inveigled the dealer into issuing mezzotint engravings of the

*Mother*, the *Carlyle* and the *Rosa Corder* which had sold surprisingly well.

There were, of course, the peculiar penalties attached to any dealings with Howell. One morning, Jimmy could find on his etching press only five of the eleven proofs he and Howell had pulled the night before. "We must have a search," the Portuguese averred solemnly. "No one could have taken them but me, and that, you know, is impossible!"

What was truly impossible was to nail him, although Jimmy came close. He intercepted a letter from Howell to Graves, instructing the dealer to keep the mezzotint engravings out of Jimmy's hands: "Of course you will not give Mr. Whistler the proofs he desires."

The Owl's feathers were unruffled. The gallery, he "explained," had sought permission to scrawl identifying numbers—"large, horrid numbers"—across the prints. "I wrote them, 'Of course you will not. Give Mr. Whistler the proofs he desires.' Two separate sentences, you see. You know how wretched my punctuation is in English."

His arithmetic was even worse; through a network of indecipherable ledgers, he kept his clients constantly in his debt.

All these annoyances were washed away, however, by Howell's magnanimous behavior in "the railroad matter." The Metropolitan District Railway, in a moment of bad judgment, had chosen to build its new underground right of way through the Queen Anne mansion rented by the agent in Fulham—which instantly acquired the glowing outlines of an Aztec palace. By the time Howell finished reciting the details of his "tragedy" to a jury of sympathetic neighbors, they awarded him damages of £3650. Howell had massive obligations of his own. But before spending a shilling, he allocated enough to Jimmy to stave off again the impetuous Mr. Nightingale.

He also had a brilliant thought. Jimmy must paint Her Majesty's Prime Minister, Benjamin Disraeli. Disraeli had been among the first to purchase a *Carlyle* engraving; surely he would be receptive.

Jimmy was delighted at the idea. He had unbounded regard for the slight, dandified "Dizzy," who after a successful literary career (one novel sold 80,000 copies in the United States alone) had battled his way to the pinnacle of political life.

Henry Graves liked the notion, too; enough to promise £1000 for copyright to the portrait . . . and to put up £100 for Howell and Jimmy in advance.

But the statesman eluded the Butterfly's net. In later years Jimmy would spin an airy tale of a visit to Disraeli's country estate at Hughenden, where Disraeli expressed admiration for his pictures ("Which have you seen?" "None. That is why I can admire them."), but declined to sit ("My life is spent in sitting. Parliament does nothing else"). According to Jimmy, Lord Beaconsfield promised that if he ever sat to any artist, it would be to Whistler. "He kept his word. He sat to no artist, but posed for Millais."

Unfortunately, the encounter was fictional, as was the variation in which Jimmy paraded down Whitehall with Beaconsfield, crowing "If only my creditors could see me now!" He never caught up with Disraeli at all.

But the creditors, alas, were catching up with him. Inspired by Nightingale's example, one and all were hiring solicitors. Jimmy's fragile web of charm, bluff and postponement, effective in putting off notices of "final warning" from apothecaries, dissolved to shreds before the more determined assaults of lawyers.

From every corner of the compass—Brompton County Court, Middlesex; High Court of Justice, Common Pleas Division; Westminster County Court; Queens Bench Division, Highest Court—the neat sheafs of light blue legal paper poured in: Whistler vs. Duffield . . . vs. Winsett . . . vs. Le Clerc, Bernstein, Herrman.

Whistler, reflected Jimmy gloomily, vs. the whole bloody world. He stopped opening his mail; it would only be another lawsuit. Never had he realized there were so many varieties of court in London, and so many remedies at the disposal of aggrieved creditors; wherever he turned, he was set upon by summons-servers, constables, solicitors, and sheriffs. Vainly he tried to shuffle accounts à la Howell. It was too late. Trapped in the inexorable machinery of the British judicial system, he was tossed about like a gatepost in a hurricane.

Heavy-jawed bailiffs began turning up at the White House—Jimmy had finally moved in—bearing writs and processes that attached his breakfast table, his fireplace tongs, even his paints and brushes. A frantic appeal to Anderson Rose got rid of the first invader; others followed, like a procession of termites. No sooner had Mr. Nightingale's man-in-possession been sent packing by a down payment than Mr. Winsett's representative took his place, thumbs tucked in waistcoat, threatening to snatch Jimmy's bed out from under him unless thirty of Her Majesty's golden guineas were forthcoming at once.

Jimmy borrowed, promised, issued checks backed by little more than a prayer. His personal capital shrank to five pounds, then to three shillings ten pence. Forwarding an engraving ordered by the prosperous academician Watts, he apologized for the stampless envelope (a budgetary necessity) and implored speedy payment. If he could keep from going under, there was a glimmer of hope: the Grosvenor Gallery was talking of another Whistler show, and a few dealers were showing signs of interest.

Then came the last straw: the auctioneers. Brusque and fast-talking, flanked by gimlet-eyed appraisers, they bustled through the rooms, waving gaudy sales posters. It was impossible to work in the house, and increasingly difficult to survive. Jimmy plucked a half-crown from Howell's hand and took a hansom to Anderson Rose's office.

"It is time to run up the white flag, Andy. I am being badg-ered, bludgeoned, and bedeviled. I have already been sliced, salted, smoked, and left for dead."

"Not quite dead," Rose corrected him. "But bankrupt, yes."

His net worth, they calculated, was less than £2000; his outstanding bills, about £4600. By filing a petition in bankruptcy, he could obtain at least some relief from harassment until a receiver took over his af-fairs.

Jimmy was practically relieved at the prospect, except for one thing: his pictures. He had painful visions—all-too-accurate, Rose agreed—of superb Nocturnes being knocked down to bank clerks for the price of a box of cigars, and invaluable etching-coppers winding up as play-things for schoolboys. These products of a lifetime's effort had to be transported to friendlier climes. But how, with the house overrun by bailiffs?

Heading the force in residence at the moment was a huge blunder-buss of a man by the name of Davis. It was clear from a glance at his bulging midriff that Davis was a beer drinker.

A dozen years earlier, aboard the *Chile*, Jimmy had been fascinated by the steward's account of a snuff-and-beer combination guaranteed to induce slumber. What better time for a test?

He set up a large pitcher of beer in the garden and mixed in a packet of snuff. Then he approached Davis & Co.: "Do come outside, gentle-men. I have the ideal refreshment for a mild May afternoon." The bailiffs trooped out into the sunshine.

Within half an hour, heads were nodding like so many wilting lilies all over the garden. By nightfall, not a man was awake. Howell and Albert Moore, arriving on cue, helped Jimmy load a half-dozen of his most important paintings, as well as a stack of copperplates, out of the back door into a Grosvenor Gallery delivery van. Jimmy had no conscience qualms. Some butchers and hatters might be deprived of income; "but I am extending to them a privilege they would never have the wit to seize for themselves . . . that of becoming Whistler patrons, sponsors of the sacred cause of Art!"

The next month, a meeting of creditors set up a committee headed by Leyland, Howell, and the printer Thomas Way to liquidate Jimmy's affairs. The gathering was enlivened by a speech from Jimmy attack-ing Leyland as the "quintessence of plutocratic putrefaction." That evening Jimmy went home and, trailed by a few friends, swept through his studio with a palette knife. Two years before, irritated by the presence of men-in-possession, he had carved up the nearly completed portrait of Lady Redesdale rather than appeal to her husband for an advance that would have canceled out his debts. Now, armed with an authorization from the receivers for the destruction of "unfinished" Whistler works, he interpreted the term very broadly.

His slashing knife ripped through oils, drawings and studies. "*This* they shall not have—" The blade demolished a *White Girl* portrait. "*This* is not to be hawked about for the greater riches of some Bond Street speculator; but *this*, my dear Howell, you must somehow take title to at the sale, and hold for me by one of your slippery stratagems until I can buy it back. . ."

By the end of his rampage, two-score canvases lay in ruins, some chopped up beyond recognition, others hastily obliterated with glue or great swatches of ivory black. When the committee of creditors arrived to make their examination a few days later, they found the studio virtually empty.

But not entirely. Three hideous caricatures of Leyland, all ridiculing his penchant for frilled shirts, glared down from the walls. The largest, entitled *The Gold Scab—Eruption in* Frilthy *Lucre,* depicted a skinny creature covered with a rash of gold coins seated atop the White House pounding on a piano.

The sale of the White House and its effects was officially set for the end of summer. Meantime, Jimmy sat back to enjoy his catastrophe. The burly bailiffs who were his day and night companions were not a bad lot, apart from a professional predilection for wearing their derby hats indoors. A few sharp thrusts of the long Whistler cane remedied that, and also discouraged smoking strong cigars in Jimmy's bedroom.

One Belkins, an ex-sergeant in the Indian service, proved quite companionable. He suggested a small immediate payment would ease his personal situation: "If you don't give me nuffin, Guv'nor, then my people won't, and what am I to do?"

"Do? Why, get yourself a man-in-possession, like me!"

Alternatively, Jimmy thought he might do a portrait of Belkins—an *Arrangement in Smoke and Sympathy.* "I do appreciate your plight, Belkins; I am in a rare position to share your sorrows. What shall we do, then? Ha-ha. Here is what we shall do. You have a face, Belkins— not without interest, I assure you—and I still have brush and canvas. We shall pool our resources. I dare say we can make a sale to the National Gallery—or perhaps the police files?"

"Not them, Guv'nor. They've already got one!"

Without exception, the bailiffs were well set-up fellows. It struck Jimmy that they would fill butler's livery very nicely. They made no great protest, and at his next Saturday dinner party, three were pressed into service with great success. One of the guests, Lady de Grey, remarked on the cheerful mien of Jimmy's servants: "They seem so attentive, so eager to please!"

"I assure you, madame, they wouldn't think of leaving me!"

Another admiring guest, pleased to see him "grown so wealthy," was told: "See how smartly they wait on table! Next month, you can see them sell the chair you sit on, every bit as well. Amazing."

Buttressed by this enviable staff, and making the most of Maud's skill at still squeezing out credit, Jimmy stepped up his entertaining to Nero-esque heights; he would go down with colors flying. A haberdasher bearing an ancient invoice found him in the White House garden with friends one warm July evening.

"Ha!" Jimmy greeted him. "I suppose you think I haven't the money to pay your wretched bill? Well, I haven't." He took the man by the arm. "But do sit down and enjoy some champagne."

"Really, Mr. Whistler! I am astonished to see a man who cannot settle his legitimate accounts, indulging himself in expensive wines."

"Oh, don't let that worry you. I don't pay for that, either."

As the sale date approached, the auctioneers came back to plaster their announcements all over the building. Jimmy merely added a postscript to his dinner invitations: "You will know the house by the bills posted outside."

Coming home one evening, he noticed that some of the posters had come loose and were flapping in the wind. He promptly summoned the auctioneer. "Your bills of sale," he announced, "are flying about wildly, distorting the perfect lines of the White House. You will please have them properly pasted down."

Early in September, Jimmy gave a buckwheat breakfast party to introduce the American beauty, Lily Langtry; later in the day the furniture was tagged and numbered for sale. After dinner, Jimmy attended a costume ball at George Boughton's, dressed as Hamlet but in no visible respect melancholy. He buttonholed John Everett Millais who, having stuck faithfully to his please-the-public formula, was about to move into an imposing marble-halled mansion at Palace Gate: "I heartily recommend to you, Millais, that you acquire some men-in-possession. They assure you of police protection day and night, they are very clever at sweeping bottles out of the cellar, and some, you know, some really have an eye for modern art. Drunken bailiffs make better judges than sober critics."

The following Sunday, Jimmy gave a farewell reception of his own. By a most welcome stroke of luck, the Fine Arts Society of London, which had long been negotiating with Jimmy to do a set of twelve etchings in Venice, had never either withdrawn its proposal or actually put up any cash (which would have been gobbled up at once by his creditors). Now the Society was ready to pay his travel expenses and put up a hundred-pound advance besides; he would be leaving for Italy the next morning.

After his guests departed, he climbed a ladder and wrote in ink over the lintel of his front door: "Except the Lord build the house, they labor in vain that build it. E. W. Godwin, F.S.A., built this one."

Then he lighted a cigarette, picked up a copy of *Punch*, and sat down calmly among the rolled-up rugs and crayon-scrawled crates.

For a man who detested opera, he played a rare Pagliacci.

*Book Three*

# Comeback

# Chapter Twenty-four

Jimmy arrived in Venice in the autumn of 1879 with his finances shattered and his reputation scarcely healthier. Even the box of copperplates under his arm was a gift from one of the few faithful, the printer Thomas Way. He had one grim consolation: matters could hardly get worse.

He had reckoned without the Venetian winter. It came suddenly and early, all but obliterating the fall, and it was the most severe within native memory. The November rains slashed at the city with near-hurricane force. Sharp winds blowing down from the Adriatic numbed his fingers; ice forming along the canals chilled his heart. To hold a copperplate steady was a formidable challenge; to control an etching needle, impossible. Ten days after settling in at the huge, drafty Palazzo Rezzonico on the western loop of the Grand Canal he had a heavy cold, with Willie Whistler and his magic syrups hundreds of miles away.

Jimmy prowled aimlessly, mostly on duty tours, while waiting for more congenial skies. He took in the Tintorettos at the nearby Scuola di San Rocco, climbing a ladder for a better look, and the Titians at the Church of San Giorgio. Squinting up at the magnificent ceiling of St. Mark's Cathedral, he pronounced it not superior to that of the Peacock Room. All the while, as in his first weeks of apparent idling in Paris, he was storing up impressions, reconnoitering the terrain for the battle ahead.

But the rains continued, and the jeweled wonderland of the eastern Mediterranean, the fabled "floating city" of glittering domes and sparkling lagoons, remained largely a matter of hearsay. His lire were vanishing, with nothing to show for them. The Fine Arts Society, which had been promised twelve etchings within three months, grew querulous. They wanted plates; Jimmy wanted another advance. Angry letters were exchanged.

Christmas found Jimmy barricaded in his gloomy seventeenth-century room, peering down through rain-smeared windows at the swollen waters of the Grand Canal. It was all too easy to fill out the scenario: once again he was the lonely knight of Washington days, raised in rank to dukedom but still condemned to his cheerless dungeon. All his life, it seemed, his bags had been kept at the ready; even in the White House, as a visitor once observed, the only sign of permanent occupancy had been the dinner invitations ranged around his fireplace mantel. What other artist of stature was subjected to such uprooting?

What other? Well, Courbet, for one. At the height of his troubles with Ruskin, Jimmy had had a pathetic letter from his old friend and mentor, then exiled in Switzerland and near death after years of persecution for his association with the short-lived 1871 Commune. Courbet, as President of the Federation of Artists and an elected official of the revolutionary regime, had endorsed the dismantling of a Place Vendôme column bearing a statue of Louis Napoleon in the garb of a Roman emperor. When the Right returned to power, he was thrown into jail. Only Daumier, Corot and Daubigny came to his defense. He was hounded incessantly and finally saddled with a back-breaking fine of half a million francs.

Courbet's letter, written from the mountain-fringed Lake of Lenan, was crowded with poignant memories of the 1865 seaside idyll at Trouville: the carefree frolics on the beach, the fresh shrimp salads and endless discussions of how to paint space. With special affection he evoked the image of Jo . . . singing, dancing, bubbling with humor. He still had with him his portrait of Jimmy's incomparable mistress; penniless or no, he would never part with it.

Jimmy turned away from the window. Courbet's ramblings were of another world. Jo Heffernan had grown plump, almost matronly, the once-blazing red of her hair turning toward a nondescript brown. Her wit still flashed occasionally, like lightning crackling over a dry summer landscape; but a dozen small changes had given her the façade of a respectable countrywoman, vigilant "auntie" to his twelve-year-old son. The Jo of the Trouville days existed only on canvas . . . and in memory.

His loneliness was unbearable. Suddenly he felt a wave of nostalgia for Maud. She was a good sort, and she really cared for him; she'd have seen to it somehow that he never caught that damned cold. A continent away, Maud's virtues loomed large, her shortcomings seemed insignificant. Throwing a coat over his shoulders, he sat down and wrote Maud a letter asking her to join him. He knew she would not hesitate.

What saved him meanwhile was the discovery of "the boys." Crossing the bridge below the Academy of Fine Arts one blustery morning, he ran into an American named Grist, an aide to U. S. Consul John Harris. Grist was surrounded by a troupe of colorfully garbed young men whom he presented as "Duveneck's boys"; fledgling American painters, they had followed a Kentucky-born artist by the name of Frank Duveneck from his studio in Munich down to Florence, and then to Venice. Gravely, Jimmy greeted each in turn: "Whistler is charmed to meet you."

Two weeks later, at the first sign of a respite from the howling winds, Jimmy dropped in on the young Americans. He was immaculately turned out in white ducks and low-collared white shirt under a dark sack coat. Below his battered but fastidiously tilted soft brown hat, a relic of Left Bank days, the famous white lock curled imperiously upward.

Jimmy was surprised at the warmth of their reception. Otto Bacher, a chunky fair-haired boy who was a would-be-etcher, scrambled up from the one comfortable chair. "Please sit down, Mr. Whistler!" Another lad offered wine—"local red, but it's better than nothing"—while a third leaped up to light Jimmy's cigarette.

"Don't disturb yourselves, gentlemen."

"Disturb? We are tremendously honored."

These neophytes, it developed, were not only aware of his work, but had actually seen a few things—and, in a general way, even understood them. "You are the pioneer of new color harmonies," said a dark slim boy introduced as Robert Blum of New York. "The Richard Wagner of painting."

"Wagner?" Jimmy put up his monocle, pretending to be annoyed. "I had rather fancied myself as Beethoven."

Here there were no stupid echoes of the Velázquez episode. The allusion to the classical roots of Jimmy's art was taken as it was offered: comically. It was very gratifying.

He was as impressed by the location of the students' lodgings as by their friendliness. They occupied a set of rooms above an ancient watch-mender's shop on the Riva degli Schiavonii, commanding a majestic view of several intersecting waterways. Otto Bacher, leading Jimmy to a window, explained that Venice was laid out "like a long-handled Japanese fan. Over there in the west you have the head of the fan, with the Grand Canal threading through in the form of a huge figure two. We are situated in the southeast, just at the juncture of the head and the handle."

"You talk like a man from the Coast and Geodetic Survey," objected Jimmy. "What interests me is what I can see from here." He pointed. "That fine promontory, for instance, with the thin church spire rising."

"The Salute, where three major canals come together—the Grand,

St. Mark's, and the Giudecca. Directly ahead of us is St. George, and beyond that the Lagoon and Lido."

"You have the soul of a tourist guide," murmured Jimmy. "But perhaps the eye of an etcher." He smiled, and Bacher was emboldened to go on.

"Because of the way we jut out into the water, we even have a view of St. Mark's Plaza."

Jimmy nodded. His eye was on the scene directly below, the marble-edged flat stones of the Riva and the little fishing boats moored to the embankment. "Would it be possible," he asked Bacher, "to work for a few hours from one of these windows?"

"Of course. My room down the hall has an excellent view."

"It's not only the view. For purposes of etching, I find terra firma superior to wobbly gondola—and less exposed to public curiosity."

"You're welcome to come any time. And you needn't worry—I'll get out of your way."

"That won't be necessary. Perhaps we can even"—the blue eyes gleamed slyly—"pick up a pointer or two from each other."

Upon Maud's arrival, Jimmy had taken a small house near the Church of the Frari on the west side of the Grand Canal. Now he boarded a gondola every morning to work from the windows of the Casa Jankovitz. When a large room became available there, he and Maud promptly moved in.

The changeover, enthusiastically greeted by "the boys," gave him an enormous lift. The Duke-in-exile now had his court, a resident company of retainers who, in return for his guidance, would be expected to render due homage. Agreeably but unmistakably, Jimmy let them know how matters stood. The day after he moved in, Bacher took him by gondola to the picturesque Ponte del Pistor (in ancient Venetian dialect, Bridge of the Breadmaker), a sleepy corner of narrow waterways hugged by tall crumbling buildings.

"This is a very good subject, Bacher. When did you find it?"

"Why, a week or so ago. I've already done two plates."

Jimmy shook his head. "Bad show, my boy. When you find a subject as fine as this, you should not do it. You should come and tell Whistler."

The habit of referring to himself in the third person, if not quite the equivalent of the royal "we," was an engaging variant: "Whistler must definitely etch the Riva"; "This plate will be prepared with the swellest ground, as you know only Whistler can do"; and, on appearing for dinner in a formal jacket but without a tie, "Who but Whistler would so dare to defy convention?"

If later generations would see in such godlike pretensions a semi-departure from reality, a grandiose cover-up for inner hollowness, to "Duveneck's boys" they were merely charming eccentricity. Jimmy was, after all, at forty-six, in every sense the senior American painter in Venice; Frank Duveneck was barely thirty, John Singer Sargent a gawky twenty-four. The Master was entitled to his foibles.

He was also, at long last, primed for the serious business that had brought him to Italy. And so, happily, was Venice.

In mid-March the high winds gave way to light breezes; the city threw off its veil of winter mourning and unfolded like a tulip in the sunshine. Gracefully curved gondolas, with jerseyed oarsmen in their sterns, poled between jade-green islands. Tourists and pigeons crowded each other aside amid the columned splendor of St. Mark's Plaza, where lofty bell towers recalled the medieval reign of the Venetian Republic as the world's greatest sea power. In the stately halls of the Doges' Palace, the imaginative ear could still pick up the overtones of masked revels.

And in the backwaters winding away to the hidden interior of Venice, there were subtler charms: orange-slice bridges curving over quiet canals; faded gardens, broken balconies, abandoned doorways. Here the residue of centuries had painted the stones with mottlings of dark moss and patinas of purple or rusty-orange. This was the Venice that Jimmy chose to record.

It was a bold decision, consciously made. Etchings, he knew, were his last refuge, the lone life raft that had survived the flood. The safe course would be to apply his needle to the familiar Venice of the tourist guides and the learned Ruskin essays: monumental buildings, straw-hatted gondoliers plying lazy lagoons. No subjects were more beloved to London collectors.

But this was ground already covered, and expertly, by the great eighteenth-century colorist Antonio Canaletto and his brilliant pupil, Francesco Guardi; it would be an impertinence as well as a redundancy to repeat their labors. Besides, he had to respond to the city in his own way. Steeped in the space-and-mood mysteries of the Orient, he gravitated toward secret corners rather than chronicled cathedrals, people rather than palaces.

The choice would create problems, perhaps even the necessity for a new, more painterly technique of etching. The medium might not yield to his demands. Well, that was the risk an artist took every day if he would grow rather than stagnate. In any case, there could be no repeating—of others or of himself.

At least he would not be alone. When things went wrong, Maud was there to pick up the pieces. Once, working in their crowded room, he tipped over a tray of boiling acid; only her prompt intervention saved his shirts in the bureau drawer beneath.

"The boys" too came through handsomely: with a broad flat-bottomed *barca* steady enough to hold an easel; a heavy printing press brought from Munich by Bacher; and, not least, the odd *soldo* at the end of the day necessary to buy a cup of coffee, and all too often missing from the Whistler purse.

Jimmy did not try to hide his financial condition. His importuning of the Fine Arts Society was yielding the most meager of advances, and those at widespread intervals. His white ducks, though kept spotless, were worn threadbare. His soft brown felt, he conceded, was "over-bitten." But when Maud discreetly mended the large hole in its crown, he ripped out the stitches: "A tear is the accident of a moment, but a darn is premeditated poverty."

He returned as best he could the hospitality of his young friends, usually offering American-style pancakes-and-potatoes cooked over a spirit lamp. Inviting Robert Blum to a fried-fish dinner, he added: "Better bring some newspapers; we're out of serving linen." For a table-cloth they used the front page of the Boston *Transcript*, where Jimmy was delighted to run across a full column of "Whistler Impertinences." He read his misdemeanors aloud with great good humor.

Such accounts of Whistler bumptiousness hardly prepared the students for the interest he displayed in their work. Jimmy was a sympathetic counselor. Where he could not praise, or make a constructive suggestion, he merely twirled his mustache and murmured, "Pretty, yes, very pretty." He invited Harper Pennington to come study with him in London, and gave fatherly lectures on the Italian masters: "Canaletto could paint a white building against a white cloud; that was enough to make any man great." As with children, servants, and all others who did not threaten him, he was gentleness personified . . . evidence of a truth already grasped by a discerning few: the waspishness from which London recoiled was only the scar tissue of terror.

One afternoon he took Otto Bacher and Robert Blum on an etching expedition. "Would you like to know the secret of how Whistler works? What would it be worth to you—in dollars? Rubles? Pounds? Ha-ha!"

"More rubles," replied the whimsical Blum, "than are locked in the U. S. Treasury. And more dollars than the Czar can command."

"Quite right, quite right," chortled Jimmy. "Therefore—observe." He picked up a plate from the bottom of the gondola. They were in the lower reaches of the Grand Canal, at the northward turning where the Rialto Bridge came into view. "The first thing I do is seize upon the chief point of interest. It might be a doorway, a figure—or, as in this case, something in the extreme distance, like the shipping beneath the bridge. This I set down in elaborate detail, so that by itself it is already a picture. Then I expand from it to the objects next in importance—the little group of palaces to the right—and so on, until I come to the bridge itself, which I will draw in one broad sweep. If by chance I do not see the entire bridge, I do not put it in. The process continues, in a steady diminuendo, until I reach the foreground figure that is no more than a hint, an intimation. In this way, the picture must necessarily be a perfect thing from start to finish; even if one were arrested in the middle of it, it would still be fine and complete."

Blum nodded. "But do you set it down just as you see it, as in a pencil sketch? Won't everything come out reversed on the proof?"

"Of course. What of it? It is not the topography that matters, but the poetry that Whistler extracts from it. Have you not read my 'Propositions No. Two'? The masterpiece requires no reason to explain its presence, has no mission to fulfill."

Whatever the charms of Venice, it was London that held Jimmy's gaze. The only decoration in his quarters was a photo of the coin-clutching patron-peacock on the wall of Leyland's dining room. "Whistler must get back to the world again," he fretted to Otto Bacher. "Whistler has been away too long. But the return must be properly planned."

Anxiously he had followed the accounts from London of his affairs there. Although Howell was an erratic and baffling correspondent, a lucid report came from Jimmy's sister-in-law Helen Ionides Whistler, who had married Willie a few years before. The Whistler auctions were over, Nellie wrote, with the best remaining canvases in the solicitous hands of Thomas Way. But the White House had suffered an incredible fate, becoming the property of the sniffish anti-Whistler critic Harry Quilter!

This was a cruel postscript to his troubles. It was not enough that at forty-six he should be reduced to scrounging among art students for paper and paints; his home had to be taken over by a despised interloper! "Sometimes," he wrote to his mother in Hastings, "I get a little despondent." But he rallied quickly, on paper at least, assuring her that Venice was "a fairyland for the painter"; he was "at work the first thing at dawn and the last thing at night, and loving you all the while."

The White House wound was scarcely eased by a chance meeting in May along the canals. Returning one bright morning to a nook spied out by his gondolier the week before, Jimmy was dismayed to see a boat already tied up in the narrow passage. He looked again, and recognized the gangling figure sitting at the drawing board in the bow. The color scheme alone—beige blazer against the Trinity College scarf of dark blue with red and yellow stripes—was enough to identify Harry Quilter, youthful Ruskinian art critic for *The Spectator* and more recently the *Times*.

"I say, there," bawled Jimmy. "Out! Out!" He jerked a finger in the general direction of the Austrian Alps.

The young man turned. "What do you mean, 'Out'?" He blinked. "Why, it's Mr. Whistler!"

Jimmy did not acknowledge the point. "You'll have to leave," he repeated. "You've got my doorway."

"Your doorway? Confound your doorway! It's *my* doorway, I've been here for the last three days."

"No matter. I'm the one who found it. I got that grating put up."

"Much obliged to you, I'm sure. It does improve the design."

"It's kind of you to say so. Now, if you'll just get out of the way—"

"But I'm not *in* the way. My boat is comfortably moored to the side of the canal. You're the one who's blocking the passage."

"Dammit man, this is my subject!" Jimmy's voice rose with his temper. "There isn't room for two gondolas here."

"That's quite true. Why don't you come aboard and work from my stern?"

Jimmy hesitated, then broke into a smile. "Splendid idea," he said, picking up his materials and clambering into Quilter's boat. "You know, as an art student, you may be interested in a recent and rather fantastic adventure of mine. I built last year, in collaboration with the eminent architect Edward Godwin, a beautiful home in Chelsea, London. Owing to a series of reverses, I was obliged to dispose of this unique property, this gem of taste, imagination, and craftsmanship.

"Who do you suppose acquired it? Brace yourself, my dear fellow: none other than the notorious 'Arry the Quilter. Surely you've heard of him?"

Quilter, helpless, eyed his tormentor in silence.

"Could anything be more absurd? Caliban, let loose in the Taj Mahal! Naturally, he lost no time in tearing everything apart. He installed shower baths in the lovely studio, billiard tables in the drawing room, and w.c.'s!—w.c.'s everywhere. Ah, the 'ygienic 'Arry!" Jimmy pulled his slender etching needle from its bed of cork. "I say, old chap, do you have a cushion I could sit on?"

It was amusing to discomfit the critic; but an incident a few days later made clear that Jimmy was longing for deeper revenge. Surprising a scorpion as it crawled across his windowsill, he impaled it on his etching needle and brought his prize to Bacher. "Look at the beggar!" he cried as the insect thrashed about, lashing with its curved spur at the needle handle. "See him strike! Isn't he fine? See how hard he hits! And the way the poison comes out when he strikes! That's right, that's the way!"

So he would strike back at the panjandrums of art in London. He had a growing pile of etchings, far more than the dozen pledged to the Fine Arts Society. The few collectors who had seen them were offering

tidy sums. But not even his chronic shortage of cash would induce
Jimmy to put them on the market, although he finally parted with three
proofs out of concern for Maud, whose health was being affected by
their Spartan régime.

But that was as far as he would go. His prints were the shock troops
of his redemption.

He also had a reserve force up his sleeve, quite unknown to his critic-
adversaries: pastels.

Some seven or eight years back, he had begun using black chalk on
brown wrapping-paper to make notes for his Nocturnes. Soon he was
touching in an occasional pastel tint. Gradually a novel technique
emerged, combining colored paper, black chalk or charcoal to set down
the main outlines of the subject, and a handful of pastel tones, applied
sparingly in pure form.

Traditionally, pastels had always been used as a substitute for oil
paint, with pigments blended in a stumping-and-smearing process that
covered the whole surface of the paper. Jimmy's approach employed
the pastel sticks like crayon to impart dainty, incisive touches. It
worked best on unusual subjects: leaves blowing across a sunlit balcony, a red-sailed fishing fleet glimpsed along a canal at dawn . . . exactly the sort of thing in which Venice abounded. For months, he
roamed the back alleys on foot with sheets of brown, red, and gray-
tinted paper fixed to his drawing board.

By the summer of 1880, he had assembled a "perfect gallery" of pastels that, as he wrote his son Charlie, should fetch nearly a thousand
pounds: "People here are very much struck, they acknowledge I have
found something quite new and utterly different."

*Most* people, he should have said. In the restaurant of the Bauer
Grünwald Hotel near St. Mark's, a gathering-place for the international
painting fraternity, one Wolkoff, a plump Russian, professed mystifi-
cation at the fuss over Whistler's pastels: "Really, they are quite ordinary."

Jim Williams, an American at the far end of the table, entered a hot
protest. How dare Wolkoff malign the Master?

The Russian was unmoved. "Whistler's pastels are nothing," he insisted. "They could be done by anybody."

"*Anybody?*"

"Anybody!"

"You, for instance?"

"Why not?"

Williams leaned forward. "Would you care to make a little wager—
say, champagne dinner for the entire company?"

"With pleasure!"

Details were fixed quickly. Nothing was to be said to Jimmy. Wolkoff would prepare a set of pastels, which would then be mixed in with a group by Jimmy and submitted, without identification, to a committee of six judges: one each from Austria, Holland, Spain, and England, plus Frank Duveneck and Otto Bacher from America.

The Russian made one condition: that he be given a chance first to review Jimmy's work. On the following Sunday, describing Wolkoff as a "keen student of pastels," Bacher took the challenger to Jimmy's room.

In all innocence, and with considerable flourish, Jimmy trotted out his treasures, pinning each pastel onto a large cardboard and propping it up on a chair as easel. To each of Wolkoff's seemingly idle technical queries, he made careful answer.

Wolkoff then dropped out of sight for several weeks. Meanwhile, word of the contest spread through the artistic community. Inevitably, a local framer made a chaffing remark to Maud Franklin, who repeated it to Jimmy.

Confronted, Otto Bacher confessed the "plot." He had taken part, he explained, because all the Americans were fed up with Wolkoff's bragging. "We knew that in pitting himself against you, he had finally overreached himself." Bacher added hastily that if Jimmy found the whole notion distasteful, there was a graceful way out; Wolkoff was now complaining that the kind of pastels Whistler used were unavailable anywhere in Venice.

Jimmy reflected. He was confident that his work could not be duplicated, not by a finer hand than that of the reputationless Russian. Of course, there was always the element of chance: Wolkoff might come up with a happy accident, judges were fallible . . .

Still—back down before a challenge? "Tell Wolkoff to come to my room tomorrow morning. I shall be out. The pastel sticks will be on the table. He can take what he wishes."

Wolkoff, deprived of excuse or retreat, picked up the colors and went to work. A week later he announced that he was ready.

The "trial" took place in a schoolhouse overlooking the Lagoon. The six judges, surrounded by a throng of spectators, gathered around a table in the main classroom. Down a nearby corridor, in adjacent cubicles, the rival pastel collections were stacked. Jimmy presided over his own; another Russian filled in for Wolkoff, who was ill.

A neutral painter—from Switzerland, naturally—was designated to pick up a few specimens from either group, or mix them together according to his fancy, and place them before the judges for identification. He began by selecting three from the American's room.

Jimmy tiptoed into the corridor. Would they recognize the Master's touch?

Silence. Then a booming German voice. *"Das ist nach meiner Mei-*

*nung ein echter Whistler.*" An indistinct mumbling, in which he thought he could make out an impatient "*Si, sì*"; followed by the clear treble of Otto Bacher, blessed Otto: "These are all by Jimmy, every one!"

The Swiss returned, and this time picked up a single Whistler pastel, *Stormy Sunset.* Jimmy heard him go into the adjoining room and, after a long pause, head back down the corridor toward the judges. Obviously, he was now going to offer a mixed bag. Would they spot the work of the impostor?

His brow was dripping. Why the devil had he let himself in for this? Suppose Wolkoff turned out to be a superb copyist, a veritable Charles Howell who could fool curators? "Wolkoff exposes Whistler." The story would be all over Venice by midnight, and within a day or two reach a newspaper desk in London or New York, to be adorned with trimmings and joyfully circulated . . .

A shout went up from the classroom; then groans and laughter. They were laughing at him! He bit his lip in agony.

Above the hubbub, he recognized the cool, clinical tones of Woods, the R.A. from England: "In sum, we have here one work of art—the Whistler *Sunset*—and four exceedingly shabby imitations."

He could almost forgive the R.A. its long catalogue of sins.

There were further tests, with Whistlers and Wolkoffs jumbled together cheek-by-jowl, but no difference in the results. Not a single Wolkoff squeaked through. "Anybody" could *not* dash off a Whistler.

With this second, somewhat more cheering, trial verdict behind him, Jimmy settled into the happiest weeks of his stay in Venice. He concentrated on bringing his etchings to perfection.

They were, even more than the pastels, a radical departure. A couple of years before, in etching the Adam and Eve pub in Chelsea, he had begun moving away from the literal precision of his early Thames plates. In Venice, he brought this impulse to flowering. With swift, free strokes of broken line he depicted a beggar woman and her child scurrying through a dim tunnel; a group of figures huddled frieze-like in the doorway of a ruined garden; or the stunning panorama of the Rialto exchange. By deft suggestion—sometimes no more than a cunning arrangement of hatched tone—he conveyed the grandeur of a crumbling palace, the weary head of a bead-stringer.

His water subjects—tiny sailboats in a vast lagoon, far-off islets vanishing into the sea—had the poignancy of Hiroshige. They were in effect Nocturnes in Black and White, unlike anything that he—or anyone else—had ever done. By deliberately not setting out to etch the departed glory of Venice, he had captured its lingering aura.

As ever, he pulled his own proofs, meticulously and alone, returning again and again to the original copper to make changes. Officially, there were an average of ten separate "states" of each etching; actually, some were revised as much as a hundred times. "Work alone," he told Otto Bacher, "will efface the footsteps of work." In the case of the celebrated *Traghetto*, a study of gondoliers lounging at a Grand Canal ferry-crossing, he spent weeks on a complex reconstruction of the lines in a spoiled plate.

Such labors were balanced by convivial evenings around a table in St. Mark's Square. Once the circle of artists sipping absinthe at Florian's was joined by Robert Browning. The stout white-bearded poet declined to recite *Fra Lippo Lippi;* but he did extemporize a bristly "letter-from-Whistler" to the editor of the *World*, denouncing Ruskin, Pre-Raphaelitism, the Royal Academy . . . and British bathtubs. The American's appreciative cackle led the laughter.

By now he was "Jimmy" to everyone, quick to join in student pranks, and sometimes to lead them. One John Wharlton Bunney, a fanatic Ruskinite, was devoting his life to an elaborate canvas of St. Mark's Cathedral which would delineate every detail of the building. It was Jimmy who slipped up behind him and, pretending absorption in Bunney's minute brushwork, pinned a sign onto the painter's smock: I AM TOTALLY BLIND.

He was quite as ready to figure at the other end of a joke. Belatedly, he had discovered the new American mode of diving, and spent hours in the Lagoon trying to emulate "the boys" as they arched cleanly into the water. One morning, he was groping nearsightedly for position on the flat crossboard of his gondola when Otto Bacher came churning by. With a sharp kick, he sent Jimmy tumbling headlong over the side.

The Master came up spluttering but undismayed: "That was a good dive, wasn't it? I didn't splash with my knees, did I?"

Toward the end of summer, on the rumor that Jimmy was about to depart, he was the hero of a farewell party. An enormous coal barge, decked out with studio drapes, lanterns, chianti bottles, and garlands of ripe fruit, was floated down the Grand Canal with Jimmy perched on a throne in the bow. Passing gondolas joined the procession, rending the air with raucous song. The celebration was only slightly marred by the guest-of-honor's announcement at 3:00 A.M. that he wasn't quite ready to leave town.

A few weeks later, he was. Art students, consular officials and a few others were invited to the one-room apartment in the Casa Jankovitz, where Maud served a six o'clock snack of sardines, boiled eggs, fruit, and excellent coffee. Over cigarettes, Jimmy showed a sampling of his Venetian etchings and pastels, accompanied by wry commentary: "What are they going to make of these things in London? Befuddling enough, I am sure, for the critics. But that's not the half of it. What of the orderly, respectable City merchant who is always called at exactly eight-thirty, close-shaved at a quarter to nine, and tucked behind his desk at ten? What on earth is *he* to think? Serve him right, too. Ha-ha!"

A solemn flourish of the monocle. "Now—now, I am afraid, we approach a serious moment. All of you gathered here have been very kind to me. You have made endurable, and even pleasurable, what might have been an insufferable purgatory. And so, it is only fitting that you should be rewarded."

He reached into a folder and pulled out a proof of the *Rialto* etching, quite ruined by marks left by a hand-vise in the course of heating the plate. "How many are we here? Let me see . . . eighteen." He took up a pair of shears and cut the proof carefully into eighteen pieces. With great ceremony, he handed out one to each guest as he bowed them to the door: "Let it never be said that Whistler forgets."

# Chapter Twenty-five

The Venetian etchings were served up in early December at the Fine Arts Society, and the British press did not flinch from what was by now a ritual duty. "Eminently vulgar," roared the Glasgow *Herald*. "Criticism is powerless here," seconded the scientific weekly *Knowledge*.

Leading the wolf pack were three particularly prestigious "authorities": Frederick Wedmore of *Nineteenth Century*, P. G. Hamerton of *Saturday Review*, and the ineffable Quilter, who complained in the *Spectator* that Jimmy had failed to portray "the Venice of a maiden's fancies."

History would say that no such prints had been seen since Rembrandt; but history had not yet come to sit in judgment. What Jimmy had to live with were the critic of the *Observer* ("beyond the understanding of an ordinary mortal") and a visiting journalist from Moscow ("Subversion!").

One of the few visitors to express praise was Debo's husband, Seymour Haden. The surgeon-etcher hated his brother-in-law as fiercely as did any man alive, but he loved fine etching; the critics were unburdened by any such sensibilities.

The whole performance had all the charm of a public whipping. When the exhibition was shipped across the Atlantic to New York, and only eight sets of proofs were ordered there, the rout of the American "eccentric" was complete.

It was time, Jimmy knew, to throw in his reserves, the Venice collection of fifty-three carefully hoarded pastels. The operation could not be handled casually; beyond the pastels there was nothing. Still ringing in his ears was the scolding from Ned Godwin over the offhand way his etchings had been displayed: "Helter-skelter, and on a maroon background that deadened the tone!"

He would have to do better. For the pastel exhibition, he and Godwin redesigned completely the gallery of the Fine Arts Society in Bond

Street, bringing everything—down to the shoes of the attendants—within a coolly elegant color scheme of yellow and green gold. The pictures were hung "on the line" at eye level, mostly in scumbled "Anglo-Japanese" frames of rich yellow gold.

Talk of the unusual décor buzzed through London, and the private preview on Saturday, January 29, 1881, saw a crush of carriages in Bond Street. Nobody in society wanted to miss a possible reprise of the Peacock Room merriment or the Ruskin affair. They came to see Whistler and each other and—in a very few cases, as a remote after-thought—the pastels. Most didn't know a pastel from a parakeet.

Suddenly confronted by Jimmy's wispy canals and brooding sunsets, the visitors hung back. Were they expected to laugh, swoon, or merely nod sage recognition? They waited for the critics to provide a clue.

The critics duly arrived and pronounced judgment. The décor was offensive, Jimmy's brown paper inartistic; and although a certain "trans-atlantic impudence" marked his technique, the subjects were unworthy. So much for the Whistler pastels.

Strangely, however, people continued to look. And to be pleased. A grave little girl, not knowing any better, clapped her hands in excite-ment before the *Stormy Sunset* that Wolkoff had tried in vain to emu-late. She was quickly shushed, but the undercurrent of agreeable surprise persisted.

Then brawny, handsome John Everett Millais, bursting with health and confidence, bustled into the room and headed straight for Jimmy. "Magnificent!" he bawled. "Cheeky, but magnificent!" He laid a hand of benediction on the little American's shoulder.

That was all the crowd needed. If the dean of popular painters, the darling of the drawing rooms, approved the Whistler pastels, surely they could, too. New and gratifying adjectives—"fresh"—"spontaneous" —"happy"—came to Jimmy's ears. Although nothing would go on public sale until the following week, there were queries about prices.

"Sixty guineas?" a top-hatted baronet was protesting to his wife. "For a little drawing? That's enormous!"

Jimmy appeared at his elbow. "Not at all, sir. I assure you it took me quite half an hour to do it!"

By the end of the day, his spirits were rising rapidly. The test of sales was still ahead, but there was a distinct chance: his reserve-battalion of pastels might just do the trick.

On Monday morning, as he was dressing for the opening day of the public exhibition, all speculations on career were swept aside by a telegram from Hastings: Anna Whistler was near death. Numbed, un-thinking, Jimmy rushed hatless from the house and directed his wait-ing hansom to Charing Cross Station. Much as he hated traveling alone, he dared not wait to hunt down Debo or Willie. He caught the 11:25 train, found an empty compartment, and sat back to brood through the three-hour journey some 60 miles southward to the sea.

At least, he reflected, his mother had spent her declining years in gentle, hospitable surroundings, a picture-book England where ghostly knights clanked along the high cliffs, and the centuries fell away. Hastings was the site of a monumental milestone in British history, the successful invasion by William the Conqueror in 1066, still marked by the crumbling red battlements and archery-slitted towers of the Norman's eleventh-century castle overlooking the Channel. Sheltered in an eastward-curving fold of the Sussex coast, Hastings frequently sparkled while London was shivering in dense fog.

Wheeling out of the railway station, Jimmy's hansom crawled up the steep incline of Castle Hill Road, turning left on Plynlimmon, where the Angel Inn stood like a spearhead pointing toward the sea. Below it was a cosy little rival pub, the Beresford Arms; and beyond that his mother's street, St. Mary's Terrace.

This was a hidden sliver of road, actually no more than a cart path, winding down the edge of a hillside between rows of quaint gable-roofed little cottages and their flower-dotted gardens. It overlooked a magnificent panorama of rolling cedar forests and billowing sea; Anna Whistler could feast her eyes incessantly on the glorious works of the Lord.

A few yards short of No. 43, white among the neighboring greens and yellows, Jimmy saw two somber figures in the doorway—his mother's housekeeper and the local doctor—and he knew it was all over. He grasped the woman's hand and went swiftly up the stairs. Anna Whistler lay in her small white bed, her features quiet and composed. She was the Mother of his portrait; as he had once said, "grace wedded to dignity, strength enhancing sweetness." She even wore the bonnet in which he had painted her. He kissed the still figure. Then he knelt by the bed and wept.

Willie and his wife Nellie—slim, beautiful, gently understanding—arrived on the next train. But Jimmy's brother could not stay long. He was now Senior Physician to the London Throat Hospital, and at this peak of a harsh winter he had scores of the living to claim his attention. For once, Jimmy would have to assume burdensome details.

He made arrangements for a Friday funeral. In the intervening days he walked the cliffs, staring down unseeing at the jumbled rooftops of the medieval Old Town, the open-air fish stalls along the flat tawny beach. Gusts of wind whipped his hatless curls into disarray and flapped his long black coat around his ankles; pebbles along the cracked-clay paths dug unnoticed into his thin-soled pumps.

In his grief and self-reproach, he pushed out of mind all past resentments. Anna Whistler's autocratic ways, he told himself, had always been well-intended; even when she opposed him, it had been in what she considered his best interests. Nor did she spare herself from the demands she made on others. She had been faithful to the end, only months ago knitting woolen cuffs with her aging fingers to ease his Venetian winter. In everything she displayed a superb consistency; could he say as much for himself?

Sometimes his sister-in-law walked beside him, and he voiced his thoughts aloud: "Why didn't I come to see her more often—on her birthdays at least? Why did I always leave it to you or Willie?"

"You came when you could, Jimmy. You had problems."

"Everybody has problems!"

"And your visits gave her great happiness. It was in her face when she talked about you. Especially the time you brought a Nocturne to show her, all the way from London."

"I owed her more than a Nocturne."

"She didn't feel that way. She told everybody about the portrait you painted of her: the noblest gift, she said, that a son ever made to a mother."

"Ah, if she only knew of its wanderings!"

"But she didn't. That was one of your kindnesses. Your letters spoke only of the good things, your great prospects."

Jimmy shook his head. "Fictions, fictions . . . except for the love they conveyed."

"Jimmy, stop it! She never uttered a word of censure. Why should you?"

But he would not be comforted. "You know, Nellie, she always wanted me to be a parson. It would have been better for all of us if I had."

Anna was laid to rest in the Borough Cemetery due north of the town, among the oaks and pines of winter, under a simple white marble slab that carried the inscription:

> Blessed are they who have
> not seen
> And yet have believed.

On his return to London, Jimmy went straight to the Graves Gallery in Pall Mall. He had £50 in his pocket, advanced without any question by Willie; he offered it to redeem the *Mother* portrait. "You may keep the others as guarantee against the 450 pounds I still owe you; but the *Mother* must go with me." Graves, still convinced the painting was of little value, made no objection.

Coming out into the street, Jimmy saw a billboard screaming from the corner newsstand: *THOMAS CARLYLE DIES!* It was an evil omen, he felt, extending the series of disasters that had followed the Ruskin trial. He trembled to think what news might be waiting at his lodgings in Alderney Street.

He was therefore quite unprepared for the exuberant report from Maud: the pastel show at the Fine Arts was a smashing success! For whatever reason, the public had brushed aside the critical attacks (the only good notice had been written by Godwin), and, at prices of 20 to 60 guineas, had put down £400 on the very first day. By now the sum had been more than doubled, with every prospect that it would go up to nearly £2000, far surpassing his original hopes.

The cash was important; the implications far more so. If the critics could be outflanked by direct appeal to that public which he (but not Millais!) had always held so lightly, new possibilities opened up, perhaps a whole new style of campaign.

The next morning, a letter from Degas lifted his spirits still higher: his insurgent comrades on the French front, where the odds favoring the Establishment were not quite so one-sided, had scored a major coup: hereafter the Salon jury would no longer be made up of former prize-winners—whose gaze was inevitably fixed backward—but would be named by the exhibitors themselves, the membership of the Society of French Artists. The new art, stressing purely pictorial qualities of color and form, would no longer stand in the shadow of classicism and literary narrative. Already there was talk of a Salon medal for Manet. Jimmy had reason to hope for similar recognition; a forthcoming article in the *Gazette des Beaux Arts* by his admirer Theodore Duret would link the subtle coloring of the Nocturnes to the daring new harmonies of the composer Richard Wagner.

Meanwhile, life in London had to be reorganized, beginning with two pieces of unfinished business. The first, and more pleasant, concerned Maud Franklin. Maud had endured a good deal in Venice: physical privation, alien surroundings, Whistlerian crises, and, worst of all, tacit isolation: there were homes, mostly rich and American, to which it was understood she could not be invited. All this she had suffered without complaint. Jimmy could not bestow in return a deep romantic love that he did not feel. But now, with a few shillings in the till, he could make some expression of his appreciation. Maud was given carte blanche to ransack the Regent Street shops, and went on a glorious 100-pound spending spree.

That left the matter of Howell. Relations between the "wily Portuguee" and his clients were always, like his complex ledgers, in delicate balance, a question of weighing his services against his depredations. With Jimmy as with others, Howell had long steered an uneasy course between friend and exploiter. While generally loyal to Whistler, he had also taken care to be loyal to Howell; for every generous gesture such as the outlay of his railroad money, there had been a blatantly crooked one . . . the sort of thing that had led to his alienation from Ruskin, then Swinburne, then Rossetti, until Jimmy alone remained more amused than offended by his shenanigans.

The day of reckoning, however, had arrived, as it always did with Howell. It was the agent's misfortune that he had too much taste to practice all-out commercialism, but not enough discipline for the creative life. Constantly short of funds, he sooner or later fell back on his collection of scurrilous letters, and his undeniable talent for "copying": less politely, artistic forgery.

During Jimmy's absence in Venice, Howell had done a tolerable business turning out "originals" by Reynolds, Gainsborough, and Henry Fuseli, an eighteenth-century Swiss who specialized in nightmarish quasi-pornographic illustrations. One day the busy forger made the mistake of carefully signing a "Gainsborough" . . . something the portraitist himself almost never did. Howell's market for Old Masters disappeared.

Desperate, Howell began dropping word around London that Jimmy Whistler was enjoying voluptuous idleness among the American millionaires on the Grand Canal and would probably never return. The inference was that the Whistler canvases on hand—most of them, it so happened, held by one Charles Augustus Howell—would be the last ones available.

This story was not long in reaching the returned traveler's ears. Topping it off was an account of the outlandish adventures that had befallen a nine-foot Oriental pagoda-cabinet left by Jimmy with Howell for delivery to its buyer.

Jimmy was incensed. It was one thing for Howell to help himself to an occasional etching; it was quite another for him to embroil a friend and client in one of his colossal fleecings of the bourgeoisie. At best, Jimmy was not the most forgiving of men; under the press of adversity, he had come to demand all but total loyalty.

He found Howell in a borrowed Bond Street office with Rosa Corder, copying a drawing—was it an early Rossetti?—that was quickly spirited out of sight.

"Why, good morning, Jimmy. We were just wondering what had happened to you."

"A number of things, Charlie. A number of things."

Rosa caught the glitter in his eye, the edge in his voice. She stood up hastily. "Perhaps you gentlemen would prefer to be alone?"

Jimmy did not deny it. He bowed Rosa out, and drew off his yellow gloves. Did the muscular Howell pale?

"You're looking very fit, Jimmy," he offered. "I gather things got warmer in Venice after that first nasty winter."

"Not as warm as they're going to get for you, Charlie." He advanced a step. This time Howell definitely fell back. "When I left for Italy," Jimmy continued, "it was with the comforting conviction that I had left behind a loyal friend in London, the one man I could count on in a pack of traitorous jackals. Steadfast, unselfish, devoted through thick and thin."

Howell waved a deprecating hand. "Ah, you embarrass me."

"Impossible!" The monocle popped into Jimmy's right eye. "I have since discovered that, while I was freezing in Venice, working my fingers to the bone, you were circulating stories of my slothful indolence and hopeless unreliability!"

Howell opened wide his languorous gray eyes. "What an idea, Jimmy! Why in the world would I do that?"

"For the excellent reason that if Whistler was finished, played out, and there would be no further etchings from Venice, those remaining with C. A. Howell could command better prices!"

Howell shook his head sorrowfully. "Ah, Jimmy, I'm afraid you have a devious mind."

"Not devious enough to keep up with you!" He banged his fist on the table, upsetting a pot of ink. "What have you done with my cabinet?"

"Cabinet?" Howell looked blank.

"Oriental cabinet, nine feet high by four feet wide, Japanese copy of a Chinese original. Four vertical panels at the bottom, two middle shelves, and an elaborate pagoda roof with carved human figures on top. Does that refresh your memory?"

"Oh, *that* cabinet . . . well, there was, ah, a little trouble with that cabinet. Yes, quite a bit of trouble."

"You fascinate me. Go on."

"Not very good workmanship, you know—and little bits kept falling off. The fact is, it's been such a continual nuisance that I haven't been able to deliver it to this day."

"So I hear from the legal owner, Mr. Sydney Morse."

"Oh, you've been to him, have you?"

"No, he's been to me. Several times. And we have succeeded in piecing together, if not the cabinet, the full story."

Howell fumbled for a cigarette. "You mustn't believe these merchant types, Jimmy. You're too credulous."

"You will recall, Charlie, that when I left the cabinet with you I jestingly expressed the hope that you would not cut it up like a steer in a butcher shop and sell the various parts separately. I saw your eyebrow go up, and I thought, 'Oh God, I've given the rascal an idea.' But I never thought you would go through with it.

"Almost too simple, wasn't it? You delivered the bottom half to Morse, telling him the top had been damaged and was in repair. Then you took the top to a pawnbroker, telling him the rest was being fixed, and meanwhile securing a tidy advance. After that you persuaded Morse you needed the bottom back for matching-up purposes, and took that to another pawnshop. Soon you were shuffling the pieces around so that nobody knew who had what—except that Morse ended up with nothing but promises!"

Howell repressed a yawn. "Really, Jimmy, it was a tedious business. I'll get the whole thing over to Morse tomorrow—"

"Indeed you will, or explain yourself to a London judge! You have compromised my reputation, Charlie!"

"Why don't we open some old port at Fulham tonight, and forget it?"

"Because I don't intend to. Ever."

And Jimmy didn't. Thereafter each man joined the other's growing list of ex-intimates.

Jimmy was now representing himself. With Maud away on a trip to Paris, he took a studio-apartment in Tite Street a couple of doors from the White House—an ideal location from which to pepper the unhappy 'Arry Quilter. He noted in a letter to the *World* the absurdity of his "living in this fashion, next door to myself," while Quilter refused to make the civilized gesture of yielding the premises to their natural owner. He roared public protest about Quilter's alterations: "History is wiped from the face of Chelsea. Shall the birthplace of art become the tomb of its parasite in Tite Street?" And he pounced gleefully on the blunders of the critic, who obliged regularly, first by praising a water color done of John Ruskin as a "fine oil portrait," and later by confusing a photograph with an etching.

But critic-sticking, however soul-satisfying, paid no bills. For that he needed commissions, perhaps from the "fashionables" who had bought his pastels. He had visions of Sir Joshua Reynolds a hundred years earlier, briskly working his way through five sitters a day, like a doctor with a crowded waiting room.

He quickly discovered that for Londoners, alas, he remained a mountebank: a mountebank who had, to be sure, struck off the pretty Venetian scenes in a lucky moment, but not a painter to be taken seriously. Of the few sitters who came, most were offensively condescending. The first was a fussy little nobleman intent on impressing his heirs. He had very precise ideas on the image he wished to leave behind, and insisted on examining the portrait at every stage. "That eyebrow, Mr. Whistler: too high. And what about the left ear?"

Jimmy, to whom individual features were an irrelevant detail, looked up carelessly. "I haven't finished that yet. In fact, I haven't started it."

Two weeks later he announced that the painting was ready. His patron raised a pince-nez disapprovingly. "Do you mean to say that is my portrait?"

"Not until you have paid for it, Your Lordship."

"But the left ear! It is still—"

"Oh, you can put that in when you get home!"

To a giddy matron who brought in her "Pussums" to be painted in her lap, Jimmy demanded, "Would you like the cat in the foreground, or the backyard?" Lady and tabby fled together.

In two cases, his ventures as a Mayfair portraitist fared better. Lady Meux was the wife of a successful brewer lately knighted for services to beer and country. A full-blown young brunette, she was beautiful enough to yield a dramatic *Arrangement in Black and White,* notable for the inverted-U sweep of a white fur mantle that hung from her shoulders to the floor. When the Prince of Wales admired the portrait, she came to sit for more.

On Jimmy's third *Lady Meux,* a study in sable furs, he was unable to obtain the ultra-thin raw canvas he wanted. After several mutually irksome delays, the lady turned up late one afternoon with the news that she could only spare Jimmy an hour; she was expected elsewhere.

"The hairdresser, no doubt," Jimmy snapped. "Mustn't keep the really *important* people waiting!"

A gloved finger waggled in his face. "See here, Jimmy Whistler. You keep a civil tongue in that head of yours, or I shall have someone in to *finish* those portraits you've made of me!"

Outraged, Jimmy brandished his brush like an avenging mace. "How —how—dare you!" he finally spluttered.

Instead of keeping her next appointment, Lady Meux sent her maid, a poor thin creature swathed in the precious sables. By way of reprisal, Jimmy painted in the maid's face—and then never delivered the picture. The price that the canny brewer had maneuvered him into was ridiculous anyway.

From Lady Meux, Jimmy graduated to an even more demanding belle, Lady Archibald Campbell. Daughter-in-law of the Duke of Argyll, Lady Archie put her blond good looks on frequent display in amateur theatricals at her country estate, Coombe. She was tall and regal. She was also so rich that she could afford to go around London with two shillings in her purse. Jimmy, who always had to pay off her cab, remarked: "Those two shillings have been turned down by all of London."

Lady Archie was a slippery subject. Jimmy tried posing her in court dress, in theatrical costume; then, as she was leaving one afternoon after a social call, Lady Archie paused at the door to draw on her gloves—and he had what he wanted. So he painted her: a slim, haughty figure looking back over her shoulder, head cocked, small white face peering out enigmatically between the black furs of hat and mantle.

Lady Archie was delighted, then not so sure. She brought her husband, who was worried about Jimmy's ambiguous reputation, and the maidens of her Anglo-Greek dramatic chorus, who made suggestions. Jimmy, anxious to please an important patron who was also a good friend, vacillated. He added "one last beautiful skin"—then sent an assistant back before dinner to wipe it all out: "I shall only be nervous and begin to doubt again."

The sitter changed her mind a few times, too, until the inevitable explosion came, with Jimmy finally shouting, "What you really want is a different picture!" The lady stormed out, to be followed into the street by Theodore Duret, who leaped onto the step of her hansom: "Madame, you must come back. You cannot deprive the world of a painting that will make both of you immortal!"

It was an argument no famous beauty could resist. Lady Archie came back, and Jimmy finished "The Yellow Buskin."

But the rest of Burke's Peerage was beating no path to Tite Street. Clearly, the normal routes to lionization were closed; the moneyed gentry of the British Establishment were no more eager to promote the Whistler fortunes than were its artistic Solons.

Two possible sources of salvation remained. Recognition could come from a new unspoiled generation of local artists or, more likely, from abroad. Meanwhile, he would not starve. The pastels had brought some good notices, and put his work on display in prominent homes. He had a backlog of etchings and drawings, easy to supplement in the streets of Chelsea. Between old supporters who would snatch up the odd Nocturne, and an occasional new sitter tempted to dabble in the forbidden, he could survive materially, if not flourish.

More difficult was the persistent drain on morale. How to fight off the insidious tendrils of despair while waiting, how to preserve the squashed and trampled ego?

Gradually, without conscious planning, he slipped into a phase where every move was calculated, flamboyant, designed to force attention. He became Whistler the Poseur.

The new style served several purposes. It proclaimed, like an extension of his defiant white tuft, his nose-thumbing refusal to submit. It provided him with an audience, and the sheer fun of play-acting. And it might promote his career: if he could make people stop long enough to look at him, conceivably they would become curious and look beyond the man at his work.

He had taken on a deliberate role before, in the bitter clowning that followed critical rejection of his 1874 one-man show. For a time he had competed with Howell in mocking all things, including himself. But there were important differences from the earlier period. He was nearly a decade older now, and by that much more desperate. Where he had sought previously only not to be forgotten, now he craved overt acknowledgment.

To the superficial eye, however, Jimmy was merely discarding the tassels of the jester for the bows of the dandy. Nor did he stint on the bows. His clothes surpassed anything England had seen since the elegant idlers of the late eighteenth century. The skirt of his long fawn-colored frock coat was specially designed to match the flowing lines of his shoulder cape. His immaculate white ducks, below a Navy blue waistcoat, reached to exactly a quarter-inch from the pink ribbons on his shoes. As startling as the impossibly tall silk hat on his head was the slender bamboo cane that rarely left his hand ("I keep this for the critics"); sometimes, in threatening weather, he substituted a rolled-up American umbrella, but declined vigorously to open it: "It would get wet!" When a friend attempted to adjust a salmon-hued silk kerchief in his dinner ensemble, he recoiled in mock horror: "You've destroyed my precious note of color!"

A Whistler visit to his tailor in Bond Street had the pomp and ceremony of a papal benediction. It began with Jimmy checking before a mirror the sweep of vertical line from shoulder to heel. A tap of his cane on the tailor's wrist would signify approval: "It is your duty to see that the Master does not appear badly clothed."

Further scrutiny generally revealed some objectionable detail. Up popped the monocle. "What have you done with the lapels? They are far too broad!"

"But, sir—you distinctly specified the measurements—three inches in the—"

"How dare you quote me! I am a painter! This is not my craft; it is *you* who are supposed to be the expert!"

Such would be the urgency of Jimmy's complaint that the entire clientele of the store would be drawn into his private drama. Once, as he stood haranguing an elderly retired general—"What are we to do about these cuffs?"—another customer came in from the street. Taking Jimmy for the store manager, he objected that the hat he bought last week didn't fit. Jimmy looked him over impatiently. "Neither does your coat," he remarked, and turned away.

The ritual at the hairdresser in Regent Street was equally demanding: first, the light trim by a trembling barber with Jimmy serenely directing the snipping of every lock; then the shampoo, followed by the wrapping in a towel of the white lock to be pinched dry; finally the scream for "Comb, comb!" with slaveys rushing forward to oblige.

Jimmy combed the tuft into a feathery plume, then shaped the black ringlets around it for the proper effect of carelessness.

Now he was ready to promenade through Mayfair, a walking billboard for himself. Gallery owners who had business with him were instructed not to be casual in their payments: "It is a privilege to deal with the Master; all checks should be offered in a kingly way, on a rich old English salver." Other owners watched apprehensively as he strutted briskly through their rooms, uttering only a sharp and baffling "Ha ha! Amazing!"

Frequently bands of urchins, scenting a celebrity, trailed him through the streets. With the geniality that he always displayed to innocents, Jimmy chaffed them: "How old are you, lad? Seven, you say? I can't believe it. Nobody could get that dirty in only seven years."

He was like a man on a tightrope, thinking up tricks to keep his audience amused, averting his eyes from the awful drop below. His public extravagances were alternated with private performances certain to be circulated widely. A journalist arriving for an interview was greeted with cries of dismay: "*Parbleu!* What a nice get-up to come and see me in! Scarlet tie and brown jacket—*quelle dissonance!* I must request that you leave immediately!"

The interviewer, shedding the tie, observed humbly that he wished to "help the world share your revelations."

"Impossible! Why, I myself am compelled to stand on tiptoe to reach my own height, metaphorically speaking!"

To another reporter he confided that he was ordering a custom-made hansom: white body, yellow wheels, a lining of canary-colored satin, and the driver in matching costume. "I shall petition the city to let me carry one lamp on it, and on the lamp there will be a white plume. I shall then be the only one."

With public and dealers indifferent to his canvases, Jimmy concentrated his imaginative resources increasingly on himself, becoming his own major creation. Inevitably, the public character he invented— brusque, amusing, unpredictable—sometimes took over, not always serving his rational interests. Offered a good commission if he would undertake to produce "a serious work," he sent his regrets: "I cannot break with the traditions of a lifetime." He made a cult of the studied insult. To a wealthy American matron who asked his advice on the décor for her new mansion, he replied: "To begin with, burn all your furniture."

Just once the impaler was impaled. When his French poodle developed a wheeze, Jimmy calmly sent for the eminent throat specialist, Sir Morell Mackenzie. The next morning, Jimmy had an urgent summons to Sir Morell's place: "Ah, good morning, Mr. Whistler. I'd like to have my front door painted."

G. K. Chesterton and the Swiss Carl Jung, at that time both school-boys, later made shrewd assessments of the Whistler phenomenon. To Chesterton, a post-Victorian essayist, novelist and poet, Jimmy was a man of enormous gifts who lacked however the sublime confidence of genius, and therefore remained always anxious, uncertain, "taut with vanity." Jung, a co-founder with Sigmund Freud and Alfred Adler of psychoanalysis, writing more broadly in *Psychology and Literature* of the artistic temperament under prolonged stress, observed that an artist's work frequently "outgrows him as a child its mother," leaving the man himself far behind: "The creative force can drain the human impulses to such a degree that the personal ego must develop all sorts of bad qualities . . . in order to maintain the spark of life." The resultant ruthless selfishness, concluded Jung, was like that of "illegitimate or neglected children who . . . must protect themselves from the destructive influence of people who have no love to give them."

It was in full, if unspoken, recognition of this need that Jimmy launched his famous "Sunday breakfasts." These gatherings at Tite Street, without precedent in timing, menu, or guest list, brought together a baker's dozen of men and women from what later would be called "café society": free-wheeling aristocrats, poets and painters, city bankers, art dealers and connoisseurs; as Jimmy summed it up, "people with brains, and those with enough to appreciate them." Lady Archie Campbell was often there, as were the American painter Mary Cassatt and, in later years, the John Galsworthys. A sprinkling of theatrical types—Mrs. Langtry, Henry Irving, the French star Coquelin (who created the part of Cyrano de Bergerac)—assured that the stage would be properly dressed for Jimmy's bravura performances.

The breakfasts were beyond Jimmy's means, but not quite beyond Maud Franklin's ingenious resources. She had an occasional assist from Jimmy's son Charles, now raised by Jo to personable adolescence and attending a boys' school in London. Maud wheedled eggs on credit, juggled accounts, once induced an M.P. to bring a few loaves of bread —"we have buckets of butter from Lady Archie's country place!"

The guests, summoned by elegant hand-printed invitations that Jimmy carried to the post office himself to make sure that the stamps were affixed in exactly the right place, assembled as bidden at half-past noon sharp. Then they stood around waiting for their host.

All Jimmy's parties were, as an actor-wag observed, "standing-room only." The studio furniture consisted of a handful of cane chairs, already requisitioned for the dining room, and a bony bamboo sofa that nobody ever sat on twice. Maud ("Madame" to the servants, "Maud Whistler" in her correspondence) fluttered among the guests, making introductions.

At 1:30 a vigorous splashing from the direction of the bath heralded the ultimate, if not imminent, arrival of the Master. Half an hour later Jimmy emerged, white lock gleaming among the damp black curls like a jewel in the fez of some Mohammedan emir. Protests over his lateness—"We are so hungry, Mr. Whistler!"—dissolved in his smiling reassurance: "What a good sign!"

The breakfasts themselves were simple; Jimmy was chary of food faddists: "When you begin to talk about the juices of the stomach, it's time to leave the table!" His usual menu was onion soup, an omelet, salad, and a sweet—preferably American cake. Sometimes the whole breakfast consisted of Yankee buckwheat cakes and molasses, prepared by the host himself, in which case every guest was expected to express proper enthusiasm or be condemned to future ostracism.

Generally, the food played second fiddle to Jimmy's table décor. Pink-tinted rice, and butter stained an interesting apple-green, were typical Whistler whimsies to draw out the "amazing" qualities of his blue-and-white porcelain, Japanese goldfish bowl, and old English silver.

His wines were undistinguished. Jimmy had learned early that, with a suitable introductory flourish, he could palm off practically any white wine on the British. "Somehow they understand red—with a cheap vintage, they can recognize vinegar—but whites baffle them."

It was with his pouring of the two-shilling sauterne (from, of course, an exquisitely made straw cradle) that the party really got under way. At each setting, as he filled a glass, he paused to deliver some merry jingle (a favorite was Rossetti's "There is an old person named Scott, Who thinks he can paint and cannot . . .") or a bon mot: "You enjoy plaice only at dinner, Lady Furlong? Well, you know, on dit that in the well-run household there is a plaice for everything!"

All this was prelude to the full-scale Whistler stories, recounted with a panoply of eloquent gestures, gyrating eyebrows, pregnant pauses, and monocled stares that would have done credit to any of his actor listeners. His most versatile prop was the monocle: dangling from his right hand, inserted into his screwed-up face, blasted out like a cannonball by his explosive eyebrow.

Jimmy spun tales from Edgar Allan Poe or Bret Harte, or related anecdotes from his own well-traveled past, such as the celebrated Goldfish Story. Originally the prank of a fellow student in Paris, it had been appropriated by Jimmy and embellished beyond recognition:

"I was on the Left Bank and doubly poor: not only a painter, but a student, what? My money came from America, like this"—the long slim fingers crept snail-like across the table—"but went like this"—Jimmy's monocle shot out with the éclat of a champagne cork.

"Naturally, I was obliged to forego the Ritz in favor of a modest *pension*, eh what? Ha-ha! *'Pauvresse oblige,'* *n'est-ce pas?* Well, the landlady who ran the place had a very limited approach to cuisine. In fact, ha-ha, she served nothing but fish. Fish for breakfast, fish for lunch, dinner, and tea. Amazing, what? You might say"—a sly sidelong glance—"it was her *sole* specialty.

"One afternoon, returning home from a tiring day at the cafés, I became aware of a peculiar, intermittent flash of light at the window. Looking down, I saw on the landlady's ledge directly below a new goldfish bowl, with three residents taking their ease, don't you know, in the sun." Jimmy made slow, fin-like flapping motions, and pursed his lips as if gulping mouthfuls of water.

"I saw an opportunity to repay my landlady for her many, ah, fishy favors. Bending an ordinary pin into a hook, I attached it to a long piece of string, baited it with bread, and lowered it into the glass bowl. As an inexperienced angler, I had a little trouble at first. But, ah, practice makes perfect, what? Ha-ha. I soon had my little trio, and seconds later they were doing a merry dance in my frying pan!"

Invariably some shocked female interrupted. "You *cooked* them?"

"A delicious pale brown, my dear." Jimmy paused to enjoy the reaction to this imaginary execution.

"And then you ate them?"

"Perish the thought, along with the goldfish!" Jimmy began rolling a cigarette. "I lowered them back to the ledge with a charming note: 'Dear Madam—you have so often graced my table with fish that I thought it only proper to return the gesture.'"

Silence, as the company watched Jimmy push his cigarette into a long black holder. Finally: "Did she ever again give you fish?"

"Never. Not for lunch, breakfast, or tea. What she *did* give me"— an expectant pause as he lighted up—"was my notice!"

Entertaining so successfully, Jimmy was in turn entertained. It was his boast that he never dined alone, and his firm practice never to arrive on time. Urged by a sitter to leave off work so they could attend a dinner together, he became indignant: "What? Go and stuff myself with food when I am painting so beautifully? Never! Besides, they won't do anything until I get there. They never do."

Once they did. Making a grand entrance at 10:00 P.M., Jimmy found the company at dessert and all his untouched courses piled up before his empty chair. He tucked up his tails, calmly sat down, and worked his way backward from *marrons glacés* to soup.

There was usually some distraction stirring at Louise Jopling's; or George Augustus Sala, the portly journalist, might be at home for "Tea, Plum Cake, and Scandal," featuring the company of "Sir Benjamin

Backbite, Mrs. Candour, Lady Sneerwell, and Captain Masher (un-attached)."

When all else failed, there were the clubs. Somehow, on the eve of expulsion for delinquency in dues, he always managed to piece to-gether the necessary. He held a score of memberships, although the august Reform was not among them; his piercing laugh, demolishing the silence of the library one evening, had awakened the chairman of the Admissions Committee. He was a leading light, however, of the companionable Hogarth Club.

Caught up in this social whirl, he sometimes lost touch with old friends. He was vexed to find that, through an oversight, he had missed the dedication of a statue in Chelsea honoring Dante Gabriel Rossetti. The fiery Anglo-Italian had succumbed in 1882 to an assortment of ailments and torments.

Now, two decades since the heyday of Tudor House, a very dif-ferent kind of poet had entered Jimmy's life, an extrovert who sought the glare of notoriety as assiduously as Rossetti had dodged it.

Oscar Wilde was a large plump Irishman in his middle twenties, florid and bland of countenance, with wavy hair parted in the middle and a heavy, overripe mouth. His most attractive features were ex-pressive gray eyes and a pleasant tenor voice; even in later years when he acquired drooping jowls, discolored teeth and the jaded air of an aging Roman emperor, the combination of keen glance and musical speech gave him a certain appeal.

Wilde had made a brilliant career at Oxford where, during one of John Ruskin's forays into character-building manual labor, the young poet had been entrusted with personally filling the great man's wheel-barrow. Wilde was determined to expand upon this success in London, and began by searching for an equally distinguished pair of accessible coattails. He was happy to discover, a few doors away from his house on Tite Street, Ruskin's late adversary.

He plumped himself down at the Master's feet to absorb the new anti-Academic gospel, so nicely compatible with Walter Pater's art-for-art's-sake if not with Ruskin's art-for-the-masses, and coupled this obeisance with a lively wit. The British artist, he remarked, could be defined as a "curious mixture of bad painting and good intentions." And popularity was "the only insult that has not yet been offered to Mr. Whistler."

Jimmy was flattered and amused. He put down Wilde's name on his Sunday-breakfast list, and soon the two were lunching together regularly in the gilt-and-mirrored opulence of the Café Royal, where the poet's dapper knee breeches and languidly dangled sunflower (he was the original flower child) drew as much attention as Jimmy's sartorial arrangements-in-yellow.

It was a convenient pairing for both. Jimmy was assured of a worthy sparring partner for his verbal bouts in Mayfair; Oscar acquired public status, along with the chance to soak up not only Whistler on blue china and the unity of the arts, but Ned Godwin's intriguing notions about free-flowing neo-Greek clothing for women.

As a team, even more than separately, they commanded the attention that each sought for his work. All over London, at soirées, gallery openings, and the theater they joked and gibed together, the piranha and the whale: Jimmy short, fierce, and harsh of speech; Oscar huge and blubbery, floating paradoxes in his lazy drawl. The London press recorded their exchanges blow by blow, and clamored for more. *Punch* was filled with Whistler-Wilde caricatures; Edmund Yates, "Atlas" of the *World*, kept his column always open for their latest repartee.

Relations between Jimmy and Oscar were never really intimate. They wore each other like plumage; and each was at pains to ensure that the plumage did not overshadow the wearer. But in the public mind, which made no fine distinctions among Pre-Raphaelite medievalism, drooping sunflowers, and Whistler's Japanese fans, the two were inextricably linked, and would remain so for decades. The mere pairing of Jimmy's name with Oscar's conjured up a music hall billboard: "Whistler and Wilde—songs, impressions and pleasurable patter." Cementing the confusion was Gilbert and Sullivan's *Patience,* a lighthearted satire on the "deep" and soulful aesthetes:

> Though the Philistines may jostle, you will rank as an apostle
>     in the high aesthetic band
> If you walk down Piccadilly with a poppy or a lily in your
>     medieval hand.

Bunthorne, the crafty and pretentious "fleshly poet" of the operetta, had the languorous mannerisms of Wilde; but the monocle, white lock, and trim imperial worn by the actor George Grossmith were pure Whistler.

None of this was particularly irksome to Jimmy, however, until Oscar showed signs of actually presuming equality—and exploiting it to his own advantage. The poet-playwright, who up to this point had talked much but published little, saw an opportunity to break into the burgeoning lecture field. Gathering together a mélange of Sunday-breakfast notions advanced by Jimmy, Ned Godwin, and the reformer-decorator William Morris, he decked them out in glittering epigrams and began solo flights before fashionable female audiences. With his velvet beret, enormous green tie, plum-colored knee breeches and yellow silk stockings, all wrapped around a magisterial platform presence, he was an instant success. An American lecture manager invited him to tour in the United States, where self-conscious culture was on the march in the lyceum movement, and speakers like the theologian Henry Ward Beecher were collecting $1000 for a single appearance.

Jimmy was miffed. His own country, after ignoring his achievements for twenty-five years, was tossing bouquets to a callow, shallow "impostor." His public dialogues with Wilde grew more tart. When Oscar blithely asserted in a telegram: YOU AND I NEVER TALK ABOUT ANYTHING BUT OURSELVES, he rebuked the upstart sharply: NO, NO, OSCAR. YOU FORGET . . . WE NEVER TALK ABOUT ANYTHING BUT ME.

Nonetheless, upon Wilde's return from America, Jimmy agreed to brief him for a lecture on art to be given before students at the Royal Academy. Wilde emerged—having made no mention whatever of Jimmy's assistance—as a "well-known authority" on painting.

A week later, they were both guests of Henry Irving at the Beefsteak Club. Jimmy, discoursing on his most recent tangle with the Establishment, observed: "People will forgive anything but beauty and talent. So I am doubly unpardonable."

As roars swept the table, Oscar looked up, chagrined. "I wish I'd said that."

"You will, Oscar—you will!"

The association, always superficial, became increasingly fragile. Each man was using the other as a convenience: the painter, as he fought to stay in the limelight while waiting for the world to catch up; the writer, hoping to secure a welcome for a literary output still largely to come. They made the most unstable of compounds, bound to disintegrate—or detonate—at the shift of a single atom. In Jimmy's view, Oscar was a dabbler in the garden of the painting Muse, with little visual sense and even less fundamental purpose, who appropriated the Whistler masquerades without any of the high conviction that, in Jimmy's case, justified their use as protective armor. The poet, Jimmy grumbled to Ned Godwin, was cheapening the role of genius-mystifier into empty harlequinery.

The open struggle for pre-eminence, for settling who was the rising (or fading) star and who the satellite, was still a year or two away. But a clash had to come; for, as the London *Times* observed, "Whistler was a prophet who liked to play Pierrot; Wilde grew into Pierrot who liked to play the prophet."

The full seriousness of Jimmy's commitment was underlined when, with several of his long-time supporters out of the country, sales slackened and the financial noose tightened around his neck. He scraped together a show of water colors done in Venice; he repeatedly mortgaged the *Carlyle*, the *Mother*, and various etching plates; he let go the last of his remaining Thames Nocturnes of the '70s to Luke Ionides for a paltry £30. But he would not bend himself to cultivate the merchant families who furnished his fellow American and Tite Street neighbor, John Singer Sargent, such tidy commissions.

On this issue there were no poses: only an implacable, uncompromising determination. Never would he turn his "needy skill" to mere crowd-pleasing prettiness.

At best, most portraiture left him restive. He yearned for the day when painters would be free simply to cover a fresh canvas with shapes and colors, to toss their fantasies into the air and spread a feast for the eye as musicians did for the ear. For such freedom, he would gladly trade the material pleasures of this world and the promises of the next.

Jimmy rarely voiced his convictions. But one cool evening in early spring, riding to the Café Royal with a young admirer, he tapped with his wand for the driver to stop. Leaning forward in the hansom, he gazed out at the lush foliage of Green Park, fresh and sweet in the dusk after rain, and the long shimmering line of light reflected in the wet Piccadilly pavement: "As you know, my boy, I have not dined; so you need not think I say this in anything but a cold and careful spirit: it is better to live on bread and cheese and paint beautiful things than to live like Dives in the parable, and paint potboilers."

# Chapter Twenty-six

In 1883, the breakthrough came: as Jimmy had anticipated, in Paris. He had never lost contact with his French friends; his first move after the closing of his Venice pastel show had been to dash across the Channel for the new Impressionist exhibition. Before the "cruel beauty" of the Degas wax sculpture, *Little 14-Year-Old Dancer*, he had waved his bamboo cane wildly, shrieking his enthusiasm for a work that went far beyond surface realism to bite into the marrow of French life (almost nobody else approved of the thin tutu-clad figure, but nearly ninety years later in New York it fetched a world's record auction price for sculpture of $380,000).

Degas in turn had found the flesh-color and pink *Lady Meux*, Jimmy's first submission to the French Salon in fifteen years, a "stunning" canvas, full of character, worthy of comparison with Watteau. The affinity between American and Frenchman was amusingly confirmed when a Paris comedy satirizing Degas was adapted for London's West End, and the apostle of semi-abstract tonal masses became Whistler.

Deciding to show the *Mother* in France, Jimmy asked Degas to shepherd it through the newly liberalized Salon. He was breakfasting alone one morning when Maud burst in, hair in curlers, to thrust a rectangle of paper under his nose.

"Really, Maud," he protested. "My eggs!"

"There are other eggs. But there is only one official French Salon!"

He flipped the monocle up to his eye. The paper was a telegram from Degas, reporting that entry No. 2441, by "James Mac-Neil Whistler," had been awarded a third prize gold medal in the 100th Exposition of the Fine Arts—"founded 1693." Only a dozen canvases from the global assemblage were ranked higher by a jury which, although now made up of active artists rather than bemedaled ancients, was still weighted heavily in the direction of conservatism. An official notice from the Palais des Champs Élysées was on its way. And Jimmy was on his.

He pushed his chair back from the table, far too excited to eat. A gold medal from the Salon would make up for many things—including the indifference of his homeland to the *Mother*. Sent earlier to the Pennsylvania Academy of Fine Arts in Philadelphia, the painting had been relegated to a distant and little-visited corridor. It had an equally disappointing reception in New York, where there were no bidders at five hundred dollars.

But Paris was the acknowledged art center of the western world. No more than a handful of English painters, mostly the rajahs of the Royal Academy, had been honored there. Salon acceptance was beyond the mocking reach of the wags from *Punch*, or the sneers of their pontificating brethren. Jimmy's battle was far from over, but never again would his star sink completely from sight.

The first repercussions came quickly. A shipment of Whistlers was requested by the Dublin Sketching Club, where its showing touched off an aesthetic Donnybrook. Half the membership were ready to send the painter to Parliament; the other half, to jail.

A firm bid was made to purchase the *Mother*, prompting Jimmy to one of his frequent inconsistencies on the subject: "Please tell the Irish gentlemen the portrait was only *lent*. How can it ever be supposed that I offered the picture of my mother for sale? I would never dream of disposing of it!"

The commotion spilled over to the *Carlyle*. A public subscription to buy the picture for the Scottish National Gallery, at Jimmy's price of 400 guineas, was begun in Edinburgh in 1884.

Unfortunately, the subscription sheet carried a statement absolving contributors from any endorsement of Whistler's peculiar theories and practices. Learning of the disclaimer, Jimmy fired off an indignant telegram: THE PRICE OF THE CARLYLE HAS ADVANCED TO ONE THOUSAND GUINEAS. DINNA YE HEAR THE BAGPIPES?

The metaphor, apart from its relevance for the addressees, was calculated. Jimmy was growing more confident now, confident enough to take the knightly offensive. He could discard his dandy's paraphernalia and assume his natural trappings of Highland warrior on the march, kilts flaring and dirk tucked into his stocking. For too long Jimmy had held back his martial ardor, contenting himself with the rapier flicks of insult when he yearned for the clang of the broadsword. It was true, as some had already noted, that he took keen delight in the duel itself, the delicate footwork and nimble thrust; but it was also true that he sometimes wished to see the enemy squirm, as the pinioned scorpion had squirmed in Venice.

Jimmy's combativeness was more than a matter of Whistler soldier-

generations and McNeill blood feuds. It involved his small stature, his stifled childhood and the taunts of a hostile, uncomprehending world . . . all culminating in his counterfantasies of the artist-avenger on horseback. The result was a perennial crusading militance: frequently impish, always quixotic. His battles were against the arrogance and ignorance of the powerful, not the failings of the weak. Although born, as he said, "to collect scalps," he would never "tilt against a woman"; and except for cabbies, whom he regarded with Celtic suspicion, he was conspicuously considerate in his dealings with the lower economic orders.

Returning to combat in the mid-1880s, he was mildly surprised to discover that he was no longer alone. The movement among artists toward the Whistler banner was hardly a stampede, but it included some important recruits. Georges Seurat, youthful French leader of the neo-Impressionist *pointillistes*, was rhapsodizing over the Whistler innovations in night-painting and geometrical composition. One Vincent van Gogh of Holland singled out Jimmy among the few contemporaries whose work he cherished. And a whole band of young dissidents in Belgium, the "Society of XX," fell under the Whistler spell en masse, purchasing monocles, committing his artistic "Propositions" to memory, and begging the Master to honor them with a visit.

All this, and new British admirers too. The cult of Whistler followers in London had begun with a modest brace of disciples soon after his return from Venice. Even before that, there had been precedent: the Greaves brothers who in the '70s trailed after Jimmy to a drawing class in Chelsea, doffing their gloves in synchronization with the Master, breaking out cigarettes whenever he did, and faithfully recording their impressions—not of the nude model, but of the sketch emerging on Jimmy's pad.

The post-Venice team—the "Two Pupils"—were lads in their early twenties, Mortimer Menpes and Walter Sickert. Menpes, a cherubic little Australian with an obstinate cowlick and an eager, innocent air, first encountered Jimmy in the printing room of the Fine Arts Society. The older man invited him along to the National Gallery to study the Canalettos—and the National Art Training School at South Kensington lost a student.

Slight and boyish, Menpes tagged after Jimmy on Chelsea sketching expeditions like an adoring puppy, carrying a little pochade box of oils and water colors. In their wake floated a shoal of expectant children. Jimmy would pick out the grubbiest—"Not bad, Menpes, eh?" —obtain parental permission, and bring the child back to his studio for a work session that lasted until his subject grew fidgety: "Pshaw, Menpes, what's it all about? Can't you buy it a toy or something?"

In due course, the pupil-slave was permitted, after having observed

Jimmy's manipulation of inks and rags over the etching copper, actually to finish off some proofs himself. Jimmy would turn up at Menpes's house on his way to a garden party, resplendent in close-fitting frock coat and canary-yellow gloves, to issue final instructions: "We do not want the hard, mechanical wiping effect of a professional printer. Or the excessive dragging with muslin that produces what they call a 'full line'—and I call gummy. Remember, my boy: although yours is the palm that wipes the plate, you are merely the medium for translating the ideas of the Master."

Walter Sickert, although he deserted Alphonse Legros at the Slade School for Jimmy, was less meek in his devotion. Tall and clean-featured, with fair hair and sky-blue sailor's eyes that suggested his part-Danish origins, Walter was cut more to Jimmy's own mold of personality. He dressed exotically, spoke several languages—and courted ladies in all of them. For a time he had been a bit player with Henry Irving's company at the Lyceum, and retained an affection for theatrical pranks and disguises.

Among Walter's assignments was to carry a weighty stone by cab to dinners at the Café Royal, in case Jimmy should be overcome by the urge to try his hand at lithography. Walter was also entrusted with delivering the *Mother* to France for the Salon. Fully conscious of his role in the little drama, he thrilled to the narrow pinewood case "swinging from a crane against the starlit night, and the sleeping houses of Dieppe."

As a painter, Walter was Germanically precise. It was his confident plan to become a "living Master," recognized as a "literary painter illuminating the beauty of everyday life."

Between his vanity and his inventive high spirits, Walter took a good deal of trimming-down. Once he devised an elaborate pun in Latin, and passed it off as a Whistler witticism. Jimmy, at his next public outing, was greeted by his scholarly host in Ovidian verse—and could only look blank.

When Walter turned up for studio labors a couple of days later, he was soundly ticked off: "I appreciate your efforts as a Propagation Bureau for Whistler *mots*—but when they're in languages that I don't understand, better send along a translation!"

Flustered, the younger man dropped the etching plate he was heating.

"How like you, Walter!" Jimmy snapped.

A moment later it was Jimmy, bending to adjust the roller, who let a copper slip from his fingers. "And how unlike me!"

With Jimmy's recognition by the Salon, his following increased perceptibly. The reinforcements were all in their twenties, less than half the age of the fifty-year-old Master. Where Jimmy's contemporaries

were put off as much by his relentless classical standards as by his stinging tongue, the idealistic newcomers saw in those same standards an
alternative to the amorphous doctrines of Impressionism. Just as he
and Fantin-Latour had twenty-five years earlier rallied behind the embattled dissenter Courbet, so the new crop gathered around Whistler.

There were about a dozen of them, including Menpes and Sickert.
Most were English: slim, quiet Wilson Steer; Arthur Studd, who discarded a promising Gauguin-like style to develop a mediocre Whistlerian one; huge, gaunt William Stott, already honored at the Salon;
Sidney Starr, Antony Ludovici, Brandon Thomas, Francis James, and
Carrie Balestier, who later became Mrs. Rudyard Kipling. France provided Theodore Roussel: cheerful, mildly wicked, and so Whistler-
struck that he would not wear his hat even outdoors in the presence
of the Master. From America there was Harper Pennington, who had
been encouraged by Jimmy in Venice and turned up three years later
at Tite Street for closer guidance.

The entourage formed a public bodyguard around Jimmy. They ran
his errands, fought his battles and advertised his genius, competing
with each other to interpret every ambiguous rasp of Whistlerian
laughter. Was that a signal of benign merriment—or divine irritation?
Adoring, uncritical, insulating their idol from painful reality, they were
in a sense bad for Jimmy. They were also indispensable. He was still
fighting his way up against disheartening odds, and the Followers were
a welcome counterweight.

Sheer force of personality was all that bound them to him. The Followers received no formal instruction, but were allowed the run of the
studio, where—between chores of varnishing, cleaning, and making
deliveries—they had the privilege of watching him start work. Occasionally, with tongue-in-cheek asperity, he would issue devastating
judgments on departed Masters, mixing shrewd insights with shock-
effect hyperbole.

Raphael? Merely "the smart young man of his time." Rembrandt
"had his good days," although sometimes he let his pigment get too
fat. Velázquez "knew his trade and his tools"; while Hokusai was elevated to the lofty plane of Whistler himself. But Turner! "He alone
dared to do what no true artist would be fool enough to attempt—paint
the sun—the old amateur!"

Jimmy's awed audience, unaware of the Master's capacity for what
the youth of a century later would call "the put-on," hung breathlessly
on every word. With each dazzling thrust, their infatuation grew. A
room was rented in Baker Street where, unknown to Jimmy, they could
practice their rites of adoration uninhibitedly. Walls and ceiling were
painted in solid colors ("broad and simple" was a Whistler shibboleth).
A special stamp was put out, of an onrushing locomotive whose

Cyclopean red headlight blazed a warning to the Philistines: the reformers were on their track.

Then the members vied with one another to demonstrate the sanctity of their commitments. Did Whistler preach thin paint? The Followers used such watery mixtures that the floors of their studios looked like wading pools. Was sentiment not to be abjured? They rigorously divested their pictures of human values: a face was equal to a peach was equal to a soccer ball. To show their contempt for Nature in the raw, they squinted at their subjects through keyholes.

In portraiture, understatement was the goal. Menpes understated the flesh-and-sand tones of a child playing on the beach until his canvas looked like a blank page. A rival pioneer etched Carrie Balestier with a four-pronged fork, and was undismayed when his proof was mistaken for a rainy-day scene and hung sideways: "It only shows the unimportance of the representational element in art!"

For a time, after Walter Sickert was presented to and overwhelmed by Degas, everybody labored under the double burden of being both Whistler and "Digars." The ideal Follower canvas was a low-toned ballet girl.

Seeking to emulate, they caricatured. Like the Greaves brothers, they aped Jimmy's dress and mannerisms, creasing their innocent features with fierce scowls, periodically emitting the brittle "Ha-ha!". When Jimmy appeared at dinner in a white waistcoat denuded of buttons—the work of a careless laundress—Brandon Thomas, who would soon write a stage comedy called *Charley's Aunt,* rushed from the room to create the same effect. He didn't want to look like an outsider.

A French journalist diagnosed the ailment of the Followers as "Whistlerium Tremens." A London paper laughed them off as "penny-Whistlers."

Jimmy did a little laughing himself. One morning he came into his studio to find several youths swooning over a forgotten oil of a Chelsea butcher shop. He put up his monocle, while the gathering fell reverently silent. "God bless me," he murmured at last. "I wonder where that came from. It's not worth the canvas it's painted on."

On one subject there could be no joking. In his new phase of carrying the fight to the enemy, Jimmy was less tolerant than ever of what he considered disloyalty. Menpes submitted some etchings to a Belgian exhibition without consulting the Master. Jimmy flourished his cane: "How dare you! I found you in absolute degradation, studying under *Poynter;* and what did I do? Saved you, cleansed you, allowed you the intimacy of my studio. I made you a pupil, even gave my friendship. Now, don't you feel ashamed of yourself?"

Though his fury was misdirected, it was comprehensible. Followers notwithstanding, Jimmy was still an isolated figure in British art. The pendulum was slowly swinging his way, but only against bitter resistance. The great majority of critics, far from tempering their wrath, pilloried him in the middle '80s more savagely than ever.

Typical was the derisive judgment—"two large blotches of dark canvas"—passed on the *Rosa Corder* and *Henry Irving.* "When I have time," the reviewer added, "I am going again to find out which is Rose and which is Irving." The *Yellow Buskin* of Lady Archie Campbell was likened to a female "pursuing the last train through the smoke of the underground." Another society-woman portrait, *Scherzo in Blue,* was nothing more than "the sketch of a scarecrow." Objecting to its display at the Grosvenor Gallery, the *Pall Mall Gazette* snarled: "Mr. Whistler's counterpart in Paris, the eccentric Mr. Manet, at least has more sincerity than to exhibit his work in such an imperfect condition."

Jimmy struck back with McNeillian gusto. Declining the written support of an industrialist friend, he observed that most critics were not worth bothering with: "among sportsmen there is a certain sense of the ridiculous that prevents them firing at a skunk." Instead he concentrated his artillery on prominent spokesmen like Harry Quilter who, when the White House issue was worn threadbare, helpfully provided his tormentor with a new theme by getting himself nominated for the chair of Slade Professor of Art at Cambridge.

Jimmy, with the aid of his columnist clubmate Edmund Yates, promoted the quaint fancy that "'Arry" was no longer among the living, having been dispatched and scalped by Whistler; however, he added, no doubt the sleepy scholars of Cambridge, "ceasing to distinguish between the quick and the dead," would "prop up our late 'Arry as professor, long to remain undetected in the Chair!"

Even more satisfying was Jimmy's coup against another long-time nemesis, Frederick Wedmore. According to the most generous of Wedmore's published estimates, the American interloper ranked as "long ago an artist of high promise, now frequently agreeable" if "incomplete."

One evening Jimmy found himself at a Belgravia dinner party where the critic was the guest of honor. A fresh copy of the *Fortnightly Review,* featuring an article by Wedmore on the French etcher Méryon, was spread open on the drawing room table; the distinguished pundit himself, a portly figure of clerical solemnity, was on display before the fireplace.

At dinner, Wedmore was placed to the right, and Jimmy directly across the table to the left, of the hostess. To the consternation of that amiable lady, Jimmy, as if unaware of Wedmore's profession, launched into a loud discussion with his neighbor, a City banker, on the subject of art critics. "Dull dogs, my dear sir, I assure you. Dull dogs.

You, of course, being occupied all day with your business affairs, have not, I suppose, come across them . . ." He glanced over idly at Wedmore, who was reddening.

"They are quite easy to recognize: a certain gleam of anxiety, or perhaps it is avarice; an unhealthy pastiness of complexion; and a deplorable clumsiness in handling the English language . . ."

The hostess, her frantic head-shaking disregarded, was kicking Jimmy under the table. "Ah well—enough of this tedious subject. The poor wretches must eat, I suppose. And when one lacks any *genuine* talent . . . don't you agree, Mr. Wedmore?"

Wedmore, torn between apoplexy and dignity, remained silent. His hostess threw him a lifebelt: Would he care to tell the company of his experiences in France, researching Méryon?

Wedmore beamed and cleared his throat. "As you know," he began, "Méryon was not an orthodox practitioner. If we explore the influences governing his art, we find links with the medieval period; for example—"

Jimmy was not going to let him romp home *that* easily. "Speaking of French unorthodoxy," he interrupted with great *bonhomie,* "have you all heard the tale of the fabulous impostor the 'Count of Montezuma,' who dined all over Paris without paying a sou, and invoked his royal bastardy to avoid getting thrown off a boat?"

The guests hadn't heard—but they wanted to. It sounded like better fare than Wedmore's lecture; and, as related and enacted by Jimmy, it was.

Later, with a little help, Wedmore regained the floor. He started to pontificate about New York's Metropolitan Museum, opened fifteen years earlier: "nothing serious, of course, by our standards—"

Once again Jimmy derailed him. "Ah, the Americans, my compatriots! Frequently amazing, you know. For instance, that extraordinary cockfight in Liverpool, where they rigged up an American eagle as a rooster and tossed him into the pit, and— But perhaps you would rather hear more about the Metropolitan Museum?"

The eagle won at the table, as it had in the pit at Liverpool, and Wedmore wound up contemplating his truffles. Thereafter the evening was Jimmy's. Time and again, sparking the conversation and leading the laughter that followed, he left Wedmore at the post. He was indisputably the hero, and Wedmore the goat, of what was to have been a triumphal hour for criticism. Jimmy might be, as Wedmore claimed, "incomplete" as an artist; but there was nothing incomplete about his talents at demolition.

Slowly, inexorably, cracks were beginning to appear in the anti-Whistler front. Under the impact of English followers and French critics, backed by a handful of discerning collectors and an occasional independent spirit like the youthful George Bernard Shaw, the opposition showed signs of wavering.

Some friends counseled Jimmy to a more conciliatory posture. But, as any West Pointer knew, this was the time to hit harder, press the attack. The question was, How?

Oscar Wilde had shown the way: a public lecture. Ironically, Wilde and his *ersatz* aesthetics would be one of Jimmy's prime targets. With a single stroke he could advance his career, while rescuing his Muse from the unwelcome embrace of hucksters and pedagogues.

Content would be no problem. Unlike the egregious Wilde, he would not be obliged to piece together hand-me-down ideas. He had articulated his thoughts in a score of letters and after-theater discussions at the Hogarth Club; his theories of art were as clear in his head as they were manifest on his canvases.

He read a few sample passages aloud to a lecturer friend, who brought him to see the celebrated Gilbert and Sullivan impresario, Mrs. Richard D'Oyly Carte. After several animated discussions in her cubicle at the Savoy Theatre, where *The Mikado* was in rehearsal, there came a public announcement: Mr. Whistler would make an appearance, called simply *The Ten O'Clock,* on the platform of Prince's Hall in Piccadilly, the evening of February 20, 1885. The auditorium was situated at the northeast end of the famous thoroughfare under the new galleries of the Royal Institute of Painters in Water Colors, almost diagonally across from the Royal Academy's Burlington House.

The late hour, like all other details of the engagement, was Jimmy's idea. He had a horror of being interrupted by late-dining "fashionables" who had lingered too long over their port-and-scandal (once, squashed into his stall seat at the Lyceum by an overweight dowager who arrived after the curtain went up, he murmured venomously, "Madam, I trust I do not incommode you by keeping my seat").

The lecture itself would seek to define the true nature of art, as distinct from the fancies propounded by Ruskin and Wilde. Between them, the puritanical professor and his libertine ex-pupil had spread total confusion. Beauty was being confounded with pious intentions, and sensitivity with absurd affectation.

Actually, Jimmy would point out, art was a private, lonely affair, divorced from time, place, and fashion, concerned not with morals or stories but only with its own integrity as the creator of beauty. That integrity was being doubly threatened: by well-meaning pedants who would bury art alive in pigeonholes marked Nature-Worship, Anecdote, Morality, or Scholarship; and, from the other side, by cynics who would merchandise art for the masses in a tawdry Wildean package that blended boutonnieres with Botticelli.

He brought his draft over to Ned Godwin, who was ailing, and canvassed actor friends for technical tips. Then he rehearsed endlessly along the Thames Embankment with Mortimer Menpes, building up the sonorous cadences of his quasi-biblical passages. His one fear was that his voice would not carry.

As the lecture date approached, notes and reminders went out from Tite Street. Alan Cole, whose father headed the South Kensington Museum, was warned he would have to part with his guinea for a box seat—"even the D'Oyly Cartes are paying!" Walter Sickert, like brother Willie Whistler, could get by with a stall ticket at ten shillings and sixpence. Waldo Story was briskly instructed to "pawn something, but come!" Godwin, of course, would crawl from his sickbed without urging; but Jimmy even beat the drums to lure Sir Frederick Leighton, president of the Royal Academy.

Leighton, a meticulous draftsman from his studies of Greek statuary but a hopelessly arid colorist, regarded him sadly. "What is the use of my coming? You know I should not agree with what you said, my dear Whistler."

"Oh, come all the same; nobody takes me seriously, don't you know!"

At 9:30 P.M. on February 20, carriages began rolling up before the classically sculptured façade of 190–95 Piccadilly. Bewhiskered and bemedaled gentlemen handed their ladies carefully down to the curb, with instructions to the coachmen to return at eleven.

Expectations were for something "amusing." Nobody was sure whether Jimmy would turn up in red studio smock or acrobatic tights; to juggle oranges, etch the audience, or strum a banjo. There was some surprise, and even disappointment, when the painter parted the gray curtains and stepped onstage: in the words of a morning paper, "a jaunty, unabashed self-satisfied gentleman in faultless evening dress." Slight and erect, Jimmy stood his cane against the side wall, then removed opera hat and gloves and placed them on a table.

Turning to the podium, he set down his notes and raised his monocle. He lowered it quickly again. Ranged before him in the first two rows were a phalanx of impassive faces, the critics of London.

For a moment he was frozen. Then he swallowed, looked out over the audience and began: "It is with great hesitation and misgiving that I appear before you in the character of the Preacher . . ."

His voice sounded so thin and quavery! Where was the vigor of last night's dress rehearsal, when the Followers posted in the back of the hall had been able to repeat every word?

Angrily, he charged ahead. "Art is upon the Town!—to be coaxed into company as a proof of culture, chucked under the chin by the passing gallant . . ."

Ah, an appreciative ripple of laughter. Premature, but it gave him strength. "The people have been harassed with Art in every guise, their homes invaded, their very dress taken to task . . . until roused at last, they cast forth the false prophets who have brought the very name of the beautiful into disrepute."

A slender, tiara-crowned woman on his right was peering absorbedly through a lorgnette. Remembering Godwin's advice to focus on individual listeners, he stared boldly back. "Yet Art has naught in common with such practices. She is a goddess of dainty thought—having no desire to teach—seeking and finding the beautiful in all conditions and in all times, as did her high priest, Rembrandt, when he saw picturesque grandeur and noble dignity in the Jews' quarter of Amsterdam, and lamented not that its inhabitants were not Greeks."

He was conscious of nods and approving murmurs. More confident now, he put aside his notes and launched into a catalogue of sinners against the Muse, beginning with the Ruskin-hypnotized Nature-worshipers: "Seldom does Nature succeed in producing a picture. She contains the elements, in color and form, of all pictures, as the keyboard contains the notes of all music." It was the artist who was set apart by the gods "to pick and group these elements . . . into that wondrous thing called the masterpiece."

And it was this same artist, in his loving study of Nature, who was closest to her of all men. Jimmy's voice, suddenly rich in unexpected overtones, filled the auditorium:

"When the evening mist clothes the riverside with poetry, as with a veil, and the poor buildings lose themselves in the dim sky, and the tall chimneys become *campanili,* and the warehouses are palaces in the night, and the whole city hangs in the heavens, and fairyland is before us—then the wayfarer hastens home; the working man and the cultured one, the wise man and the one of pleasure, cease to understand, as they have ceased to see, and Nature, who for once has sung in tune, sings her exquisite song to the artist alone."

Not a cough broke the hush of the room; breathing itself seemed suspended.

With an adroit change of pace, Jimmy shifted his attack to the literary and moralistic "middlemen of art"—an accusing finger shot out toward the critical "enemy" in the second row—who looked "not *at* a picture, but *through* it" to the subject beyond. He pointed with scorn at the pedants, "sombre of mien, who frequent museums and burrow in crypts . . . classifying, contradicting, speculating in much writing upon the great worth of bad work;" and, unmistakably, at Ruskin himself, "Sage of the Universities, of much experience in all matters save his subject, bringing powers of persuasion and polish of language to prove—nothing."

That brought him to Wilde. He had previously noted the ascendancy of a new breed, the artistic "huckster who saw fortune in the facture of the sham." His voice regained its familiar rasp as he descended on Oscar, the apostle of knee breeches and shapeless dresses: "The Dilettante stalks abroad. The voice of the aesthete is heard in the land, and catastrophe is upon us . . . a weird cult in which all instinct for attractiveness is to give way to a strange vocation for the unlovely." Anna Whistler, who liked a touch of brimstone in her sermons, would have been delighted.

Jimmy concluded on a peaceful note. The true artist, beginning with the first caveman who shunned the pleasures of the hunt to trace "strange devices with a burnt stick upon a gourd," was forever "a monument of isolation," but forever joyous nonetheless; for his Muse was the most faithful of lovers, "turning never aside in moments of hope deferred—of insult—and of ribald misunderstanding."

The applause was long and generous. Edward Poynter, certainly one of those at whose "solemn silliness" Jimmy had scoffed, bounded backstage to congratulate the speaker on saying "a great many things that, er, ought to be said" . . . and rapidly vanished.

The newspapers, as ever, were patronizing. "Flimsy" was the general verdict; "smart but misleading," although the *Times* conceded that those "hoping for an hour's amusement" from the erratic American were not disappointed.

It was Oscar Wilde's notice in the *Pall Mall Gazette* that Jimmy looked forward to. If it had been rash to attack Ruskin in court, it was positively heroic to challenge Wilde on his own grounds. Their last encounter had not been amiable. Asked to judge a ballad thrust into his hands by Oscar, Jimmy had commented drily, "It is worth its weight in gold." The poem was written on thinnest tissue paper.

Wilde's review was alternately jeering and respectful, as if written with one eye on his laughter-seeking patrons in fashionable society, and the other on his credentials as an artistic confrere of the painter.

He started out with a purr: "Mr. Whistler spoke for an hour with really marvelous eloquence on the absolute uselessness" of all art lectures. "The scene was in every way delightful, a miniature Mephistopheles mocking the majority!" Wilde saluted fascinating wit, paradox, many passages "of pure and perfect beauty."

Having paid such tributes, he could not be accused of overtly bludgeoning a former sponsor. Once inside the door of the mansion, however, he achieved something far more damaging by introducing just the right, rib-tickling note of mocking condescension: "Mr. Whistler explained to the public that the only thing they should cultivate was ugliness, and that on their permanent stupidity rested all the hopes of art in the future. He was like a brilliant surgeon lecturing to a class destined ultimately for dissection, and solemnly assuring them how valuable to science their maladies were and how absolutely uninteresting the slightest symptoms of health on their part would be."

Oscar was cavorting before the gallery, delicately echoing the popular view that Whistler was a silver-plated Mayfair version of the Brighton tuppenny sidewalk mountebank. In one breath he scoffed at Whistlerian canvases that the common people were not to "attempt to understand, much less dare to enjoy"; in the next he gave as his judgment that Jimmy was "indeed one of the very greatest masters of painting," . . . only to set up a last, devastating reversal: "And I may add that in this opinion Mr. Whistler himself entirely concurs." It was a bravura display of feline ingenuity. "Nobody takes me seriously," Jimmy had remarked ironically to Fred Leighton; and Wilde seemed determined to reinforce that impression. His review marked the effective end of Whistler-Wilde relations.

However, their verbal salvos and counterrakings crackled on to the end of the decade. First came a mild scuffle over Wilde's bracketing of Jimmy with Benjamin West, an American who succeeded Sir Joshua Reynolds as president of the Royal Academy but who was never a very distinguished painter. ("To be great," protested Oscar in his reply, "is to be misunderstood")

The grappling grew harsher when Wilde was invited to assist in organizing the reformist National Art Exhibition. "What has Oscar in common with Art?" snapped Jimmy in an open letter to the Committee. "Except that he dines at our tables and picks from our platters the plums for the pudding he peddles in the provinces. Oscar—the amiable, irresponsible, esurient Oscar—with no more sense of a picture than the fit of a coat!"

Stung, Wilde struck back: "With our James vulgarity begins at home, and should be allowed to stay there." He followed this up with an article in *Nineteenth Century* sneering at Jimmy's foggy Thames twilights "where the cultured catch an effect, the uncultured catch cold . . . Whistler spells Art with a capital 'I.'"

In 1890, an article on plagiarists in *Truth* sent Jimmy to his inkwell: "How was it that you omitted that fattest of offenders—our own Oscar?" And once again he cited the evening in Waldo Story's home where, "in good fellowship," he crammed Oscar for the poet's appearance before Royal Academy students, so that "he might not add deplorable failure to foolish appearance."

Spluttered Wilde: "It is a trouble for any gentleman to have to notice the lucubrations of so ill-bred and ignorant a person." For once the fluent Irishman was reduced to impotent fuming. For what it was worth, Jimmy had another scalp.

# Chapter Twenty-seven

Late in 1884, when Paris recognition, Follower enthusiasm and D'Oyly Carte showmanship were beginning to build up a modest Whistler bandwagon, Jimmy caught a glimmer of a very different faction seemingly eager to lumber aboard.

The Society of British Artists had a long and notable history—all of it decidedly past. In recent years it had limped along, shabby and apologetic in its dingy quarters on Suffolk Street, as a kind of Cinderella sister to the Royal Academy. When the R.A. moved from neighboring Trafalgar Square to the Burlington House in Piccadilly, its overflow visitors no longer found the S.B.A. convenient. With the opening of the Grosvenor Galleries, its patronage was further depleted.

The eighty-year-old institution was moribund or worse; more than ready, many thought, for administration of the last rites. Its halls were chill and gloomy; its membership, mostly an Old Guard of commercial hacks, more so. Exhibitions by the Society were haphazard and perfunctory affairs, with anecdotal trivia and Ruskin-sanctioned pussycats jumbled together to cover every inch of available wall space. The S.B.A. could have been put out of its misery permanently by a concerted effort on the part of London critics; it was allowed to linger on as a catch-all for painters and paintings rejected by the Royal Academy.

Such was the ancient and wheezing maiden that, via a chain of discreet inquiries, was approaching Jimmy to ask his hand in marriage. Jimmy, sensing a broader platform for his gospel, sent back word through Walter Sickert that he was interested. Two days later a deputation from the S.B.A. arrived.

On the face of it, this would be an improbable union. But the Society desperately needed a new and livelier image; so desperately that its leaders were willing in courting Jimmy to risk the displeasure of R.A.

President Leighton, their Colonel in the "Artist's Rifles" (S.B.A. painters never quite abandoned hope of attaining the R.A. heaven).

And Jimmy had reason to accept. At fifty, he was still without official
status in England. In joining, he would move instantly to the forefront
of the Society, the magnet both for the public and for its restless
younger members. Instead of charming bastardy—no longer so appropriate as he matured in years—he would acquire a legitimate background. And from his new platform he could tweak the tail of the
Academy lion.

Jimmy charged into the partnership with his customary enthusiasm.
He kicked at the corpse, jabbed it, startled it awake . . . and within
months put it on the map.

His first move was to overhaul the exhibitions. S.B.A. practice was
to plaster the walls from floor to ceiling with a frame-to-frame bargain-
basement display. Unadorned wall was considered a scandalous waste
of selling space. If by chance a 9-by-6 inch nook was left uncovered,
members rushed back to their studios to find some potboiler that could
be squeezed in . . . or even painted a hurried sketch to meet the required dimensions. Décor consisted of cheap colored-paper hangings,
supplemented by scattered bric-a-brac.

Early in 1885, Jimmy took the floor at a Suffolk Street meeting:
"Gentlemen, such showings are a disgrace. They do no service to the
artist, and confuse the viewer. Each painting must be properly hung,
with sufficient room to set it off, and with proper soft lighting against
an unobtrusive background." Introducing the simplicities of plain-
colored walls, Japanese matting, battened muslin and minimal furniture, he changed the galleries from an ungainly barn to a dignified
exhibition hall.

Catalogues, which had declined to little more than dreary trade ad-
vertisements, were brightened up by sketches contributed by Follower
members, now listed as "pupils of Whistler." And there would be no
marking down from catalogue prices: "An insult to the artist!" cried
Jimmy.

He also, against much muttered protest, insisted on an end to grov-
eling before critics. The Society was £500 in debt; why not, Jimmy
demanded, cancel the annual Press Day debauch of whisky, caviar,
and cigars aimed at wheedling friendly notices from the newspapers
and weeklies? "Let us have standards, gentlemen! Dignity! Style!"

To show the way, he played host at the new exhibitions, guiding
society beauties through the rooms, tossing out playful—and quotable—
judgments. And he poked headline-making fun at the Royal Academy.

In 1885 one J. C. Horsley, a venerable Academician, appeared before a Church Congress to read a paper attacking the nude in art.
Horsley bewailed "the degradation enacted before the model is suf-

ficiently hardened to her shameful calling. Is not clothedness a distinct feature of our Christian faith?"

The S.B.A. was in the process of assembling its winter show. Jimmy borrowed from the printer-collector Thomas Way his own *The Purple Cap*, a delicate pastel study of a very thinly draped female figure. To the dismay of the Society's Executive Council, he hung it prominently with the attached label: *Horsley soit qui mal y pense*.

He spoofed the R.A. without mercy. When his atelier-boy proposed to enter some etchings in an Academy-sponsored show for novices, Jimmy outfitted him in a smart new top hat: "I do not wish you to be embarrassed among your colleagues."

And yet, perversely, he continued to hope himself for election to the Academy; his quiet enrollment on the candidates' list of several years before had never been withdrawn. Challenged at an 1885 banquet for Alma-Tadema to lead a toast to the R.A., he rose calmly: "Only those not acquainted with proper social usage could expect me to take umbrage at such a proposal. On the contrary, the pirate whose black flag skims the seas, floating at the whim of his fancy, never refuses, when the occasion presents itself, to salute the vessels of the State."

Meanwhile, he enhanced the Society exhibitions with some of his best work, including the brilliant new *Sarasate*, originally intended for the 1885 Academy. His successes at the French Salon—the *Mother* of 1883 had been followed by applause for the *Carlyle* and *Miss Cicely Alexander* in the following year—had spurred him to a burst of important portrait work. First came the journalist Theodore Duret. As a thrust against the Academy vogue for posing merchants in the robes of medieval barons, Jimmy painted Duret in evening dress: a simple, dignified canvas with an extraordinary gray background that picked up the pinks and flesh tones of the accessories.

With the *Sarasate*, he departed from convention a step farther. Pablo de Sarasate y Navascués was a Spanish virtuoso of the violin, perhaps the greatest since Paganini. Jimmy, reluctantly in attendance one evening at a Sarasate performance in St. James's Hall, was quite carried away—not by the moving strains of the Mendelssohn E Minor Concerto (his ear for melody was such that Sarasate might have been sawing a log), but by the violinist's mercurial personality, his lightning manipulation of the bow in *agitato* passages.

Sarasate was not inclined to be painted, until he dined with Jimmy and discovered they had much in common. The maitre d' actually took them for brothers, so close were the parallels in spare figure, tangled black curls, and vivid presence.

A physical mapping of his subject was, of course, the last thing on Jimmy's mind. He wanted to re-create the magic of the artist alone before the footlights, a phantom creature emerging briefly from the mists to wave his wand over the millions.

It was an Edgar Allan Poe concept . . . and he brought it off. His painting portrayed Sarasate on stage, lightly poised in evening clothes, violin held across his body: floating in space, yet with feet solidly planted; ethereal in feeling, yet masterful in composition. As he explained to Sidney Starr, "Everything is balanced by the bow."

The *Sarasate* was the main attraction at the S.B.A. Summer Exhibition in 1885. Thereafter Jimmy kept it dramatically on display at the end of a long corridor in Tite Street, haranguing visitors: "Isn't it beautiful, man? I mean, damn it, isn't it beautiful?"

Among the many who agreed was Henry Irving. The actor-manager, now grown to international stature, had at long last acquired the Philip II portrait done of him by Jimmy, after seeing the famous legs sticking out from a pile of canvases at the Graves gallery. In the interim, he had made two triumphant tours of America, become the first actor elected to the ultraconservative Atheneum Club, and been painted by Millais. The effects on his ego were predictable. Ellen Terry, left in the shadows by the Irving-centered spotlight in *A Winter's Tale*, complained: "How about having a few rays of the moon land on *me*, Henry? Nature, after all, is impartial . . ."

Irving now consented to give Jimmy a few more sittings. Jimmy trimmed down the hat plume, shifted the cloak, and added a gold chain around Irving's neck . . . all to the visible benefit of the portrait as hung in New York's Metropolitan Museum of Art nearly a century later. Before the painter could finish amendments to the legs and right hand, Irving took off again. But he displayed the picture prominently before the élite of England in his backstage Beefsteak Room, where he and Jimmy continued their eternal debate over whether the painter had immortalized the actor, or vice versa.

The merit of Jimmy's claim was curiously if negatively upheld a few months later when the estate of William Graham, M.P., was auctioned off at Christie's. Contemporary "classics"—by Burne-Jones, Millais, Rossetti—were bid up swiftly to hundreds and even thousands of pounds. Then a Whistler Nocturne—*Blue and Silver, Battersea Reach*—was propped up on the easel. Loud hisses and boos broke out, despite the gavel-pounding of the shocked auctioneer.

Jimmy was quick to note the incident in a letter to the *Observer*: "May I beg to acknowledge the distinguished, though I fear unconscious, compliment so publicly paid. It is rare that recognition so complete is made during the lifetime of the painter."

By 1886, the recognition was not entirely negative. An American critic, W. C. Brownell, was writing appreciations of Whistler in *Scribner's Monthly*. The French authority Marcel Roland declared flatly: "Whistler's work will leave his studio only to go directly to be bored forever on the walls of the Louvre's great halls. His place is reserved, between Paul Veronese and Velázquez." And more fellow artists, like the talented young Frenchman Toulouse-Lautrec, were speaking up on Jimmy's behalf. Mary Cassatt, the Paris-based American Impressionist and protégée of Degas, sent her sister-in-law to be painted by Jimmy: "It is a good thing to have a portrait by Whistler in the family." Another American artist and Whistler enthusiast, William Merritt Chase, tried to buy the pawned *Carlyle*, and wound up advancing to Jimmy the £250 needed to repossess it.

Even John Everett Millais came down off the fence. For twenty-five years, the most successful painter in England had been at war with himself on the subject of Whistler, unable to reconcile his British conservatism with his artistic sensibilities. He had alternately castigated Jimmy as a painter "ignorant of the grammar of his art, a great power for mischief amongst the younger men," and written warmly of Whistler's "gradations, tenderness, lovely tints"; had admonished the American to be more respectful of popular prejudices, and praised him as "really a painter's painter."

Meanwhile, Millais himself had become more than half a country squire. His grouse-shooting, deer-stalking holidays in the Scottish Highlands grew longer (once, interrupted at a canvas by a black cock flying overhead, he grabbed his rifle, fired, and returned to his palette); and his work grew spottier. Soon after the showing of Jimmy's *Mother*, he turned out the very similar *Mrs. Heugh*, mimicking successfully the stark accessories without, however, bringing a breath of life to the subject's face.

For years, Jimmy had seen Millais at receptions, meerschaum in hand, gold scarfpin glittering, surrounded by worshipful matrons. The two painters, each recognizing in the other what he himself might have become, were not comfortable together. As recently as 1884 they had barely averted an awkward clash at the Grosvenor Gallery, where Millais ground his teeth before the *Lady Meux:* "Clever, a damned sight *too* clever." A few yards away, Jimmy was groaning before a sentimental park scene by Millais—just sold, according to its tag, to a town in New South Wales. "And quite right," grated Jimmy. "Back to the bush with it!"

The following year, 1885, Millais reached twin peaks in his career. He was created a baronet by Queen Victoria—the first artist to be so honored—and his drippingly winsome portrait of his grandson, entitled *Bubbles*, was smeared by the Pears Soap company over every billboard in England. But a certain self-questioning had begun. Had he, like the "poor devil" magazine illustrators he publicly pitied, "gone wrong for the sake of a few sovereigns"? He tried to get some of his recent portraits back for reworking, but their owners liked them as they were.

In 1886, the Grosvenor spring exhibition included a retrospective of early Pre-Raphaelite work: Holman Hunt, Rossetti, Ford Madox Brown, and of course Millais, from the period that followed his emergence as boy wonder of the Academy. On the opening morning, Millais spent an hour before the collection, assembled mostly from museums. He lingered long before his own *Blind Girl* and *The Huguenot:* simple subjects, faithfully recorded.

When he emerged, his fine brow was wrinkled. Effusively greeted by the gallery manager as he went down the stairs, he nodded an absent acknowledgment.

In the lobby, Jimmy was handing his hat and cane to the attendant. "Ah ha, Millais. Up early, I see, to admire your own work. And who should do it better?"

"Good morning, Jimmy." He perked up slightly. "I say, Irving showed me what you've done with his portrait. Deuced fine piece of work. As good, in its way, as your *Sarasate.*"

"Thank you, Millais. From the man who did *The Eve of St. Agnes,* that is high praise."

"Ah, *St. Agnes.* Do you know when I painted that?" The sturdy jaw quivered. "Nearly twenty-five years ago . . . I must tell you, Jimmy. With the passage of time your work has gained something. While mine . . ."

He did not have to finish; the tears suddenly glistening in his eyes said the rest.

Jimmy gazed at him steadily, offering no consolation. For decades Millais had reaped the guineas and the honors, a man who had to belong at any price. Jimmy could understand, but he could not forgive.

"You are quite right," he told Millais, and turned away.

To the amazement—not to say consternation—of the London art world, Jimmy was elected president of the Society of British Artists in the summer of 1886. The vote was rammed through by the ebullient Whistlerites against disorganized opposition from more conservative members. It signaled a sharp split in Society ranks. "All the rising painters," predicted Malcolm Salaman in *Court and Society Review,* "to whom we must look for the future of British art, will flock to the standard of Mr.—why not Sir James?—Whistler."

Although Jimmy would not take office until December, the counterfire and sniping began at once; several leaders of the Old Guard resigned. Unimpressed, Jimmy more than filled the gap by enlisting Charles Keene, the scintillating draftsman from *Punch.* To relieve the Society's drooping finances, the president-elect sold several water colors, pawned his gold medal from the Salon, and extended a personal loan of £500.

And he organized the upcoming Winter Exhibition without compromise. He put Mortimer Menpes on the Hanging Committee and told him, "If there is any doubt in your mind—say 'Out!' We want clean spaces around our pictures. We are not providing advertising space for mediocrities, or pandering to the tastes of so-called patrons!"

The mediocrities in question, understandably, did not receive this news with joy. Sharp infighting broke out, intensified when Jimmy proposed Sunday afternoon tea receptions in the gallery. There were cries of sacrilege, and angry letters to the press. Jimmy, revelling in the battle, marshalled his troops about him with Antony Ludovici as trusty "aide-de-camp." While his enemies drew up protest petitions, he prepared a spectacular flank attack.

It was the year of the royal Golden Jubilee, half a century since Queen Victoria ascended the throne in 1837, and institutions throughout the Empire were declaring their fealty. Consulting no one, Jimmy took up a dozen old Dutch folio sheets, had them bound in soft yellow Morocco, and prepared an eloquent address to the Queen. He illustrated it himself with etchings and water colors celebrating Britannia's majesty, and concluded with an essay on the Society of British Artists: how lengthy and unswerving its service to country, and how pleased it would be to have this devotion recognized by the throne. Back from Windsor Castle came a decree awarding the S.B.A. a royal charter.

With the royal reply under his arm, Jimmy calmly took the chair at the next Society meeting. There were the usual screams of outrage against the president, and a querulous suggestion that something be done about the Queen. In the midst of the babble, Jimmy dropped his bomb: henceforth the gentlemen could claim membership in the *Royal* Society of British Artists.

The opposition collapsed, and Jimmy mounted their undefended ramparts. He had the doors and dadoes of the gallery painted yellow, and invited the Prince and Princess of Wales to the next exhibition. When the Prince inquired about the history of the Society, Jimmy replied: "Sir, its history dates from today."

While the Old Guard writhed, and computed in pounds, shillings and pence their losses from unused wall space, Jimmy introduced a new notion: photo reproductions of the catalogue entries.

The weekly Sunday reception was unabashedly a Whistler show. Seated on a circular yellow sofa under a butterfly decorated silk umbrella, Jimmy romped merrily over everyone in sight. The unwary critic who sidled in would be led by the painter up to one of the deft, charming little Whistler street scenes on the walls, and then publicly disemboweled: "Pretty, is it not? But of course, as your keen eye will perceive, not quite 'finished.' In fact—what is the critical phrase?—'little more than a sketch.' And the figures—so indistinct. Perhaps you would like a magnifying glass?"

A solicitous glance at the critic, then back to the picture: "Ah, it is small, very small indeed. You have a point there, a definite point. But come closer—not too close, because it might be a pastel, and then you would rub off the color with your nose! But just about here . . . *voilà!* You can smell the varnish, definitely establishing that we are dealing with an oil, not a water color. So you can't make *that* mistake again . . ."

The press retaliated: first with sardonic articles and caricatures (Jimmy was the "big frog" swallowing up the tadpoles of the Society), then, more devastatingly, with a virtual boycott of R.S.B.A. shows. Jimmy, noting the dwindling attendance at the galleries, read aloud to the membership a passage from Thackeray about an earlier gallery that was patronized only by spooners in search of privacy. "History, gentlemen, repeats itself."

Still he did not capitulate. He exerted himself to bring over from Paris a late canvas by Édouard Manet, who had recently died. He offered exhibition space and honorary membership to Claude Monet, whose mist-shrouded rendition of the Le Havre docks in 1874 had inspired the term "Impressionism." British critics, unable to tell the two Frenchmen apart, shrugged off both as "foreign nonentities."

Jimmy went further. He pushed for formal election of Alfred Stevens, a much-honored Belgian who was a holder of the Legion of Honor. When Stevens turned down membership in the Royal Academy in order to enter the Whistler fold, the gesture did not go unnoticed.

People were starting to talk about the R.S.B.A. in Paris, Brussels, Munich, Venice—even in New York. For the first time, the Royal Academy had a serious rival.

That suited Jimmy perfectly. He saw no reason why the Queen's own art fraternity—or its dynamic president—should play second fiddle to Burlington House. He had brought John Everett Millais to heel; now it was the turn of that other titan of the tea-tables, Sir Frederick Leighton, president of the R.A. For years, Jimmy had been vaguely resentful of Leighton's preening; once, when a covey of gallery ladies were gushing over "Freddie's" good looks, linguistic ability, fine voice and pianistic skill, the American had interrupted, "Paints a little, too, doesn't he?"

Already Jimmy had been accorded equal status with Sir Frederick at the Golden Jubilee ceremonies in Westminster Abbey, and the Naval Review at Spithead. Now he needled Leighton constantly for official brotherly recognition. Why had he not been invited to the Academy's annual *soirée?* Was this suitable treatment for a fellow president?

Finally he was placed on the guest list for an Academy reception. Sir Frederick, resplendent in white tie and gleaming shirt front, himself a far more agreeable visual experience than his muddy neoclassical canvases, advanced to greet Jimmy at the head of the stairs. "My dear Jimmy, this is the very first time I have seen you here."

"Quite true, Freddie. And I have such a rotten excuse to offer you. It is the first time I have been invited."

Even a knighthood, Jimmy began to feel, was within reach. It was the custom for the royal accolade to fall, sooner or later, on the shoulders of all art society presidents. Malcolm Salaman had been stirring up the breezes; George Bernard Shaw, writing as an art critic for the *World,* had just bracketed Jimmy with John Singer Sargent as virtually the only painters in England who could "swim on any tide;" brother Willie Whistler was sounding out several patients who had influence at Court.

"Sir James Whistler . . ." There was no denying it had a certain ring. "Your carriage, Sir James . . ." "Could you come to tea, Sir James?" Even, from a fishmonger bending low, "Your little account, Sir James . . ."

Unfortunately, while Jimmy's eyes were on fame and history, other eyes in the R.S.B.A. were on the cash register. Royalty was coming in to the galleries, but money was not. The suburban ladies who had been the financial bulwark of the Society were dismayed by the battened walls and yellow awnings, the storyless Monet canvases, and the spaced-out arrangement: "There's hardly a shilling's worth to look at, my dear!"

Veteran members, rallying their forces at a monthly meeting, increased their clamor for an end to "Mr. Whistler's eccentricities," and a return to good solid commercialism.

Jimmy put up his monocle and cast a slow, meditative stare over the room. "You know, you people are not well! You remind me of a shipload of passengers living on an antiquated boat anchored to a rock for many years. Suddenly this old tub is boarded by a pirate (I am the pirate). He makes her not only weathertight but a perfect vessel running down ships less ably captained. But her triumphant passage is stopped by the passengers themselves . . .

"You invited me into your midst as president because of these same so-called 'eccentricities' which you now condemn. You imagined I would bring notoriety to your gallery. Did you also imagine that when I entered your building I should leave my individuality on the doormat?"

The Old Guard risked everything on a last-ditch response. As Jimmy said later, "They brought up the maimed, the halt, the lame, the blind —literally, like in Hogarth's *Election*—everything but corpses"—and in May of 1888 nearly forced his expulsion. A few weeks later he was replaced as president by one Wyke Bayliss: Board School chairman and church warden in suburban Clapham, Fellow of the Society of Cyclists, lecturer and Shakespearean student, and "champion chess player of Surrey" . . . altogether, a suitable antidote to Whistler.

Jimmy complimented the victors: "You can no longer say you have the right man in the wrong place. Now I understand the feelings of all those who have tried to save their fellow men."

With Jimmy twenty-five members resigned from the Society, including Stevens, Keene, and such Follower stalwarts as Walter Sickert, Sidney Starr, Antony Ludovici, and Theodore Roussel. Dangling a toy that tinkled out "Yankee Doodle," Jimmy treated the faithful to champagne, and the press to a lively interview:

"The situation is not at all chaotic. Everything is in order—the survival of the fittest as regards the presidency, don't you see—and, well, Suffolk Street is itself again. No doubt their pristine sense of undisturbed somnolence will again settle upon them after the exasperated mental condition arising from the unnatural strain recently put upon the old ship! Eh what? Ha ha.

"You see, the S.B.A. had by degrees lapsed into a condition of incapacity, until it acknowledged itself a species of *crèche* for the Royal Academy. I wanted to make it an Art center; they wanted it to remain a shop.

"The Royal Society of British Artists tended to this final convulsion; they could not remain together, and so you see the 'Artists' have come out and the British remain."

Thus ended Jimmy's dream of becoming "Sir James." Ironically, Wyke Bayliss and also his successor as head of the R.S.B.A. were duly knighted. But the man who obtained the royal charter for the Society was ignored; the only knighthood Jimmy would know was the one he had long ago conferred upon himself, as defender of the Muse.

Bayliss made a long statement to the press accusing Jimmy of responsibility for the decline in Society sales, from £8000 in 1884 to less than £1000 in 1888. Replied Jimmy, noting that the big drop came in 1885: "The disastrous and simple painter Whistler only took in hands the reins of government at least a year after the former driver had been pitched from his box and half the moneybags lost. And when I last saw the mad machine it was still cycling down the hill."

One aftermath of the R.S.B.A. affair was the dispersal of the no-longer-neophyte Followers. In the case of the first disciple, Mortimer Menpes, Jimmy made it a dishonorable discharge.

Menpes, like Walter Sickert, had a long history of being "forgiven" by the Master. He had once slipped off on an unsanctioned painting trip to Japan. He had been first to quit the dissension-ridden R.S.B.A. —"the early rat," as Jimmy put it, "who leaves the sinking ship." A few months later, to cap his crimes, he opened a house in Fulham decorated with the soft lemon yellow that Jimmy had introduced twenty years earlier in Lindsey Row.

Furious, Jimmy denounced in the *World* "the Australian robber" who "like the kangaroo of his country is born with a pocket and puts everything into it." He then disposed of Menpes "permanently" in a private note: "You will blow your brains out, of course. Pigott has shown you what to do under the circumstances, and you know your way to Spain!" Richard Pigott was a notorious forger, author of a recent letter seeking to link the Irish Nationalist leader Charles Stewart Parnell with terrorist violence. Upon exposure of his machinations, Pigott had fled to Madrid and killed himself.

Far more serious for Jimmy than the theatrics over Menpes were the demises of two contemporaries: one literal, the other metaphorical. First came the death of Ned Godwin, architect and designer, ladies' man and lion of the theater.

Godwin's life, sadly unfulfilled, was a chronicle of beautiful women abandoned, great production schemes never carried through, and finally debilitating fevers. He did nonetheless break the Gothic-Queen Anne stranglehold on British architecture, and he pioneered liberating changes in women's clothes and stage costume. Ellen Terry, who treasured above stardom the two children of her liaison with Godwin, kept always among her papers an unsigned poem:

> Yet self-betrayed he fell in Fortune's spite
> His royal birthright sold for scanty wage . . .
> They tell me he had faults; I knew of one:
> Dying too soon, he left his best undone.

Jimmy, who was with the chill-racked architect to the end (they were planning a new and "more astounding" house), had the melancholy task of notifying mutual friends. He also, despite his childhood-rooted terror of death and funerals, gallantly accompanied Trixie Godwin and Ellen Terry to the burial. The trio fortified themselves first with several rounds of brandy at Jimmy's studio—"Ned would have insisted on it," Ellen maintained—and rode out to the cemetery swaying alongside the hearse, in mingled tears and laughter.

Different, but quite as poignant, was Jimmy's parting with Algernon Swinburne. The two were united by far more than youthful escapades. There had been years of sympathetic exchanges, including the poet's magnificent verses inspired by the *Little White Girl*, and his near-filial attentions to Anna Whistler, who had once nursed him through a distressing epileptic seizure.

When the *Ten O'Clock* was published in 1888 after repeat performances at Cambridge and Oxford, Jimmy decided nothing could give the printed version as good a send-off as a notice by the now-celebrated Swinburne. He remembered that his "devoted son" Algernon had come through handsomely many years before with a written appreciation of the Whistler painting style, and in 1870 had helped Rossetti with what Dante Gabriel called a "more than brotherly" review of newly published poems. Hence, "The Bard must write a dignified criticism of my lecture."

Swinburne, long ensconced in solitude at the Thames suburb of Putney, demurred; he was a greatly changed man from the *enfant terrible* of Tudor House. But Jimmy would not be put off. Finally the poet acquiesced. What he wrote did not make either man happy.

Swinburne had been whisked off to his retreat in 1879, his health failing after many bouts with epilepsy and whisky, by Theodore Watts, the tiny, walrus-mustached solicitor who had rescued him from the snares of Howell. In Watts's rambling, shabby-comfortable country house, overflowing with books and the smells of cooking, Swinburne was placed under a strict curative regimen. Watts took charge of his laundry and his allowance; his daily constitutional, his bedtime and his diet. Missing from the menu were the carousals and companions of Bohemia. No unscheduled visitors were permitted. From 6:00 to 7:45 every evening, Dickens was read aloud.

Gradually the poet was walled off from the world by his savior-captor. He led a hothouse existence—seeing, reading, and in his growing deafness hearing, only what "dear Theodore" approved. Jimmy Whistler's affairs did not come under that heading. To the fussy little solicitor, arch-conservative in all things, the American painter was a hangover from Swinburne's disreputable past, still engaged in dubious if not subversive artistic practices. Nor did Jimmy improve his standing when Watts, presumably to avoid being confused with the eminent portraitist G. F. Watts, hyphenated himself to Watts-Dunton; "Theodore What's Dunton?" chirped Jimmy in a telegram to Putney.

The Golden Jubilee celebrations arrived and, under the tutelage of his protector, Swinburne experienced a startling resurgence of British consciousness. The Republican firebrand who had idolized Victor Hugo and literally knelt at the feet of the revolutionary Mazzini, now became an ardent royalist; the poet who had written scandalous burlesques of Victoria's sex life composed a "Jubilee Ode" that was simply odious: as pompous, dreary, and cliché-ridden as Watts-Dunton's own sonnet to empire-builder Cecil Rhodes. Swinburne now eulogized all things British—authors, politicians, even the weather—and turned away impatiently from all things "alien." Such was the man, a once-great poet reduced to ventriloquist's dummy, to whom Jimmy was appealing in the name of old friendship.

Granted, Swinburne was reluctant and testy; granted, there was some misunderstanding about the deadline, so that his article in *Fortnightly Review* had to be written on an evening when he came in tired and chilly after being caught in a downpour on Putney Heath. Still, by any standard, it was an extraordinary document.

The tone, sarcastic throughout, was set in an early paragraph where Swinburne referred to himself as "one of those unfortunate 'outsiders' for whose judgment Mr. Whistler has such an Olympian contempt." He then went on to complain of Jimmy's vocabulary, his logic, and particularly the painter's suggestion that Japanese art could possibly be mentioned alongside that of Swinburne's beloved Greeks. The painting of the Orient, Swinburne asserted, was trivial, typefied by "the grin and glare, the smirk and leer" of Japanese womanhood. Emphasis on color harmonies meant the "immolation" of all nobler values; Phideas, after all, was concerned with "other things than 'arrangements' in marble."

As Henry James later pointed out, Swinburne's genius was "for style, not thought." Humorless as an essayist, he cut a stiff, awkward figure in the clothes of his friend Ruskin: "Mr. Whistler would do well to eschew a Greek term lying so far out of the common way as 'aesthete.' The only possible meaning of that word is an intelligent, appreciative person. Such abuse of language is possible only to the driveling desperation of venomous or fangless duncery."

Swinburne brought down his sledgehammer: "Mr. Whistler's theorem is that 'Art and Joy go together,' and that tragic art is not art at all"—something Jimmy had never said, or remotely intimated. Of course, the poet went on, intelligent judges would realize they were "not in a serious world, but in the fairyland of fans, the paradise of pipkins." Yet "a man of genius is scarcely at liberty to choose whether he shall be considered as a serious figure" or regarded as "a tumbler or a clown."

Reading the notice, Jimmy was stunned: to a long silence, then to tears. How could Algernon, himself so often misunderstood and abused, desert his fellow Christians in the arena to join the shouting mob in the stands? How could he deplete the never-too-robust ranks of the spiritual élite to swell the already-powerful hosts of the stranger?

Jimmy composed a brief letter to the *World*, taking care to dispatch a copy first to Putney:

"Bravo! Bard! and exquisitely written . . .

"The scientific irrelevancies and solemn popularities I seem to have met with before—in papers signed by more than one serious and un-qualified sage, whose mind also was not narrowed by knowledge.

"Thank you, my dear! I have lost a confrere; but then, I have gained an acquaintance—one Algernon Swinburne—'outsider'—Putney."

The letter was enough to enrage Swinburne, and prompt him to put *La Mère Gérard* up for sale; but it could not dislodge the poisoned arrow in Jimmy's heart. Some time later, he drafted a longer rebuke. After reading it aloud, with much bitterness and grief, to a few inti-mates, he published it. Entitled *Et Tu, Brute!*, it was a rare cry from the depths:

"Why, O brother! did you not consult with me before printing, in the face of a ribald world, *that you also misunderstand?*

"Cannot the man who wrote *Atalanta* and the *Ballads* beauti-ful, be content to spend his life with *his* work . . . that he should so stray about blindly in his brother's flower-beds and bruise himself?

"Shall I be brought to the bar by my own blood, and be borne false witness against before the plebeian people?

"Who are you, deserting your Muse, that you should insult my God-dess with familiarity? Do we not speak the same language? Are we strangers, then, or, in our Father's house are there so many mansions that you lose your way, my brother, and cannot recognize your kin?

"You have mistaken pale demeanor and joined hands for an inward spiritual earnestness. For you, these are the serious ones. Their joke is their work. For me—why should I refuse myself the grim joy of this grotesque tragedy—and, with them now, you all are my joke!"

# Chapter Twenty-eight

Marriage was an institution Jimmy had never found irresistible, although, as he said, "I tolerate it in my friends." His one real gesture in the direction of matrimony, made to Jo decades before in a moment of acute desperation, was at fifty-two scarcely remembered. He regarded himself as bound seriously only to the Muse. Flesh-and-blood females were for him, as for that earlier Chelsea bon vivant Charles II, essentially purveyors of flesh-and-blood delights.

This principle suffered only minor infringement during his long involvement with Maud, although her jealousy imposed the need for discretion. Off on an alleged business trip to Paris in 1883, he arranged for a male friend to post daily letters from the French capital to London, while he dallied with a lady in Dieppe. When a visitor to Tite Street left a coronet-embroidered nightgown behind, he hustled it to his indulgent sister-in-law for laundering.

Maud herself had no illusions about Jimmy's approach to domesticity. Soon after the return from Venice she found herself pregnant. She was promptly shipped off to Paris for the *accouchement;* medical attentions and personal comforts were carefully arranged, but that was all. Her infant daughter was treated by Jimmy as an accident of the chase, for which he accepted financial responsibility and nothing more. The child was placed with relatives of its mother.

Maud was on hand constantly during the Tite Street Sunday breakfasts, but did not resume living with Jimmy until 1884, when he acquired larger and less expensive working quarters in Fulham, north and west of the fashionable Embankment. They took a cottage in the Vale, a rural paradise tucked behind iron gates a few feet above the bustle of King's Road, where an informal colony of painters and sculptors lived in a cluster of old veranda-fringed houses and wild gardens.

The relationship between painter and mistress had altered substantially. Maud, first introduced to Fantin sheepishly as "the daughter of an old friend," was now known to half the tradesmen of Chelsea as "Mrs. Whistler." She dealt with the cook and the tax collector, pulled Jimmy's etchings and attended to much of his correspondence.

She continued to share his bed, with more zest than formerly. Englishwomen, Jimmy reflected, were like pinewood fires; they required a great deal of kindling, but once ignited they burned tenaciously. However, by now the libidinous cycle had reversed; it was Jimmy who had become the perfunctory partner. The frustrating battle against Maud's passivity had speeded up a process already set in motion by his advancing years: the channeling of sexual energies into his work.

Thus, by the middle '80s Maud had assumed almost the role of Anna Whistler: supervising, soothing, scolding. With expanded responsibilities came a change in her perspective. She dared to contemplate the day when, weary of butterfly rambling, Jimmy would want to settle down outside London and perhaps even formalize their union. Maud was gradually moving into "possession"—a term and a concept that Jimmy loathed.

He resented also her tendency to treat "the Master" like a wayward child, her knowing indulgence of his hesitancies—the more so because he was aware that he had largely created his own state of dependency. There were moments, too, when Maud missed the point of a drawing, or was unable to keep pace with some flight of Whistlerian fancy; and his mind went back to the old days on Lindsey Row with Jo. Then he was angry: at the world, fate, family. This was a wound, buried deep but never quite laid to rest, that would surface volcanically for years to come.

New tensions cropped up with Jimmy's ascendancy in the Society of British Artists. Maud, feeling her command threatened, instinctively harped back to the closely shared privations of Venice and the White House—periods that Jimmy preferred to forget. And she was increasingly touchy about being shunted aside; once content to take a back seat socially, she now had fits of uncontrollable weeping. Jo's outbursts had been brief, fierce and of a certain magnificence; Maud's were tearful and prolonged—as Jimmy complained to Albert Moore, "simply Maud-lin."

Typical was their clash at the Vale over the Royal Academy reception. Jimmy made plain that the invitation he had maneuvered did not include Maud.

"Why can't I go with you, Jimmy?"

"Self-preservation, my dear. You'd be bored to death. They are the dullest creatures on earth."

"But not too dull for you!"

"On the contrary. I go only to make a public demonstration of my superiority."

"I should like to be bored just this once. In a long, purple evening gown. There is an absolute stunner in Madame Cecile's window."

Jimmy turned from the writing desk where he was drafting an acceptance. "My dear Maud, why agitate yourself over trivia beyond our control? As we both know, the Royal Academy has its unwritten rules."

"Rules? You make a point of demolishing them where your art is concerned."

"Which is precisely why I must make some minimal concessions elsewhere."

"Such as me!" She took a few small, angry steps toward the door, then stopped. "Is Albert Moore taking Jossie?" Moore, too, had a mistress of long standing.

"Of course not. Look here—why don't you and Jossie go to the Gaiety on Saturday? They say the new burlesque is—"

"I have my own burlesque," declared Maud tragically. "Right here." She plucked a handkerchief from her sleeve and started sniffling.

"Looks more like an Ellen Terry matinee."

"That's right—make fun of me! Till you can't find your dress tie and the coal runs out and there's no one to print your etchings! Then it's 'Maud, my sweet' and 'What would I do without you, Maud!'" Adult sorrow sat grotesquely on the pleasant, child-like features.

"Oh, damnation!" Jimmy shouted. "Stop it, stop it!" He started up from his desk.

The whimpers blossomed into sobs. "Maud doesn't count. She's good enough for the nasty little jobs—but when the swells get together, we keep her below-stairs!"

Forcing back a grimace, Jimmy put his arms around her. "Really, my dear! All this over a silly reception. As if the R.A. didn't have enough crimes to atone for!"

He wiped away the tears gently. Maud permitted herself to be kissed: on the forehead, the cheek, the soft slim shoulder. Finally she looked up: "Will you be coming home early"—sniffle, sniffle—"or will you go tripping off afterward with your society friends?"

"I really can't say, my dear. I have been supplied neither with a guest list by the Royal Academy, nor with clairvoyance from Heaven. Therefore I don't know who will be there, or what social obligations I shall have to assume. But you can be sure I shall do no more than circumstances require—and no less, either."

So off Jimmy would go to his party, and Maud to her unwelcome distraction. Such was the situation late in 1885 when Trixie Godwin, Jimmy's sometime student, reappeared on the scene alone, her husband Ned no longer in attendance as insulation between his wife and his friend. Trixie and Ned had decided, after several years of quarrels and reconciliations, to make an amicable but definite separation; she found him impossibly philanderous, he regarded her as naïve. Jimmy's attachment to neither was impaired by the change.

In fact, he quickly showed signs of increasing intimacy with his pupil. Her painting sessions at the Fulham studio extended into amiable lunches and leisurely twilight walks. Maud, who had eyed with misgivings the earlier Godwin-Whistler trio, was scarcely comforted by the new duet.

On physical grounds alone, Trixie Godwin provided good reason for Maud's fears. At thirty-one, a few years younger than Jimmy's mistress, she was black-haired, full-bodied and sensuous, a ripe plum of a girl with dark reckless eyes set off by a tea-rose complexion. Jimmy, himself often described as "foreign-looking," took pleasure in the rumors that there was gypsy blood in her background.

Trixie's temperament supported the rumors. She was impulsive, pranksome, passionate in her enthusiasms. Perhaps most importantly for Jimmy, she was at home with the vagaries of the artistic personality. Her father, John Birnie Philip, had sculpted the podiums of Albert Hall and the Foreign Office. She herself had created charming panels to decorate Ned Godwin's "Anglo-Japanese" furniture, and, for a provincial church, a stained-glass Paradise that Jimmy proclaimed "well worth the mortal striving."

Maud was worried, but she held her fire. Jimmy had flirted before, and returned to the hearth.

When Ned Godwin died in 1886, Maud merely noted the fact primly in the postscript of a letter to a friend: "Mrs Godwin is now a widow. He died two weeks ago."

Doubtless the event and its implications did not impress her that lightly. But what shook her far more was the discovery of an unmentioned painting project. Rummaging through the studio loft one morning in search of a missing water color, she came upon a large canvas stacked among some long-abandoned projects in a corner. Freshly traced in burnt sienna were the lushly rounded outlines of Trixie Godwin.

"I see you've acquired a new model," she remarked to Jimmy when he came in. He looked startled. "The one you're hiding up in the loft."

"Oh, you mean Mrs. Godwin."

"Yes, Mrs. Godwin."

They stared at each other in silence. "I haven't, ah, got very far with that."

"Indeed?"

"I mean to say, it's an experiment. I'm trying to work without—"

"I'm sure," Maud interrupted, "your *experiment* will turn out brilliantly. In all respects." She left the studio, slamming the door so hard that an etching was knocked from the wall.

*Harmony in Red,* he would call it: *Lamplight.* He was painting Trixie in an atmosphere utterly subdued, the shades drawn down in the studio's high north-facing windows, a single gas jet on the wall amplified by a table-height oil lamp. Never had he retreated farther from the outdoor pyrotechnics of Impressionism. Severely classical, too, was Trixie's pose: full-length before rich crimson draperies, with a long cloak of warm-toned rose flung over her black dress.

Yet the feeling of the picture was intensely personal, atmospheric. Trixie peered out of the canvas wrapped in wistful yearning, as if seeking from behind a veil to penetrate the male-female mystery. Facial details, often slighted by Jimmy, were here rendered with ineffable tenderness; soft curving lips slightly parted, black eyes transfixed.

Standing before the completed 7-foot painting, Trixie became very quiet. The picture fairly glowed, suffused with an inner light. Finally she turned to the painter, eyes wide and moist: "But you love me, Jimmy!"

Jimmy reached slowly for his imperial. "Why—why, yes, I suppose I do."

Maud got her first look at the portrait when it was being varnished for the British Artists' Winter Exhibition. Her small rosebud mouth tightened, teeth sinking into her lower lip. Jimmy was watching her anxiously. "Well? What do you think, Maud?"

"It certainly is . . . different."

"Different? How do you mean?"

"I suppose the exact word is"—she groped for an adjective that would hurt—"*sentimental.*"

"Oh." His wince was almost audible.

"But then, every painter has his lapses. Which reminds me—William Stott of Oldham has been begging me to sit for him as Venus. It's a very important commission, and he says there is no one else in all London who is right for it. Would you mind?" She fixed her brown eyes on him intently, her heart in her glance.

Jimmy hesitated.

And then foolishly, because her only weapon was words, Maud hurried on: "After all, it's not as if you would be left without a model . . ."

She was challenging him, and Jimmy never failed to pick up a gauntlet.

"Of course, my dear. You go right ahead. And give Stott my best."

Maud had entered on an unequal contest. More than ever, Jimmy was thrown together with a younger, more beautiful woman who represented not carping domination but low-pressure companionship; a woman, furthermore, whose antecedents would make her welcome in any drawing room in London, or for that matter North Carolina. Trixie was fresh, frolicsome. She had the verve, if not the mysticism, of Jo, along with Maud's steady competence.

But she *managed* him so much better than Maud! She had a way of suggesting and cajoling, of laughing him into what she wanted.

Working against Maud most of all was the change in Jimmy's professional situation. Like many a self-centered artist before him, he had taken early sustenance where he could get it. With gradual acceptance, his need for enormous emotional support had diminished; what had been indispensable anchor was becoming predictable bore. The artist on the upswing, with his legacy of self-doubt, becomes uneasy about the woman of his floundering years; she has seen his weakness under fire, is associated with a dependent self-image he would like to put out of mind. That she may have sacrificed some of her own youthful appeal in the furtherance of his interests merely adds to his guilty discomfort. "Thanks for the ride," he says in effect. "You have helped set me free from my torments—and, free, I can leave you." Rationalizations come easy: "After all, nobody forced you to stay."

A man can emerge from such an experience wiser, firmer, more attractive; a woman only becomes older. Jimmy was joining a long line of gifted men whose talent was not matched by their gratitude, in dealing with an impasse not subject to facile solution. Trixie was simply a livelier consort than Maud, and a superior ornament to the knighthood-eying president of the Royal Society of British Artists.

It was Maud who remained "in possession," however, until the spring afternoon in 1887 when she returned home unexpectedly early—Stott had sprained his painting wrist—to find Jimmy tête-à-tête with Trixie in the drawing room.

"Mrs. Godwin has brought some etchings to show me," Jimmy explained hastily. "She is illustrating a children's book."

"How very fortunate for the children, I'm sure! But I am extremely fatigued." She turned pointedly to Trixie. "I must ask you to excuse us, Mrs. Godwin."

"Of course. We shall finish our business in just a moment."

"You can finish it tomorrow in the studio!" Trixie, startled at the stridency of her voice, frowned but did not move. Maud took a step forward. "This happens to be *my* home, Mrs. Godwin. I should think a lady—especially a lady of *breeding*—would not need to be reminded of that!"

Trixie colored. "How dare you!"

"How dare *you* invade my house in my absence—like a—a common woman of the streets!"

"Ladies, please!" Jimmy was too late. Trixie, dark eyes blazing, had slapped a gloved hand across Maud's cheek. Maud grabbed unsuccessfully for her rival's hair, and the two lurched around the room like a pair of featherweight catch-as-catch-can wrestlers.

"Slut!" Maud screamed. "Home-wrecker! Jezebel!" Her voice rose to a piercing shriek, then dissolved suddenly in a paroxysm of coughing. "Oh, my God!" She held up her handkerchief as Jimmy thrust himself between the pair. "I'm bleeding! Oh, Jimmy, I'm going to die!"

"What a happy thought," said her adversary.

Jimmy, lips twitching nervously, guided Maud to the bamboo sofa. "Just, ah, just sit here a moment, Maud. I'll, ah, go for a doctor." To Trixie he said, "You'd best come with me."

In King's Road, Jimmy interrupted a general practitioner sitting down to tea. While the doctor went for his kit, Jimmy hastily put Trixie into a hansom.

Back at the Vale, the doctor quieted Maud with a stiff gulp of brandy. He looked at her throat and reported there was no cause for worry: "It's a very superficial injury, just the rupture of a tiny blood vessel from some unusual strain or, er, excitement." He applied a long silver nitrate stick, and the bleeding stopped at once.

No such magic could salvage Maud's relationship with Jimmy. Two days later she moved out of the Vale, and Trixie Godwin moved in.

On their first night together in the cottage, Jimmy felt the stirring of old misgivings. Trixie was a vital thirty-one; he, approaching fifty-three . . .

Sliding into bed, he reached out his arms to her nakedness—and was astonished at the intensity of her response. Trixie, the captivating Trixie, was flooded with passion at his very touch. Their bodies had scarcely locked when she was heaving and gasping in climax: "Jimmy, Jimmy—I've waited so long. I love you so, my dearest!"

"Do you, do you?"

"I suspect I've loved you ever since the day Godwin brought me to the Peacock Room. I've never looked at anyone else—and I never shall."

She lay beneath him, flushed and golden. The years dropped away.

Henry du Pré Labouchère—"Labby" to Fleet Street and the City— was a feisty, garrulous little man with a large head and larger whiskers. Labby was a mover and pusher of assorted projects. He founded the *World* with Edmund Yates, and was a co-owner of the first Liberal

Party daily, the *News*. A drama buff, he cheerfully sank a fortune into making a star of Henrietta Hodson, then married her. In the 1880s, he thrust his way into Parliament, where he scandalized the Members by the outspokenness of his views on all subjects, and persuaded Gladstone to arrange a knighthood for Henry Irving.

The Whistler-Godwin romance offered an irresistible field for his talents. Labby had known the painter since both were sportive young men in Washington, Labby as an attaché at the British Legation. He owned a number of Whistler canvases, notably the portrait of the dancer Connie Gilchrist.

In the summer of 1888, the Labouchères were guests, along with Jimmy and Trixie, at a dinner party given by Louise Jopling-Rowe in Earl's Court. Brushing aside some vague talk of a Whistler-Godwin "engagement," the entrepreneur got right down to business: "Look here, Jimmy, will you marry Mrs. Godwin?"

"Certainly."

"Mrs. Godwin, will you marry Jimmy?"

"Certainly."

"Good; that's settled. Now, when?"

The principals answered simultaneously but imprecisely. "Oh, some day," said Jimmy; Trixie's contribution was "I don't really know."

Labby shook his head; that would never do.

"I wish," interposed Louise, "you two would get married before I go up to the country."

"When is that?" asked Jimmy.

"On Sunday."

"But this is Wednesday already. And the banns take three weeks."

"Oh, that's easy," volunteered George Rowe. "Mrs. Godwin has only to come up to my office in Lincoln's Inn Fields tomorrow, and we'll get a special license."

"While I," proclaimed Labby, "will get the Chaplain of the House, Reverend the Honorable Francis Byng, to perform the ceremony. In return for which I demand the privilege of giving the bride away."

"And what do I get to do?" inquired Jimmy.

"Oh, you simply turn up at the church on Saturday at eleven."

"Which church?"

"St. Mary Abbots in Kensington," Trixie offered promptly.

"There you are!" Labby beamed in triumph. "Now, shall we get on with dinner?"

Two days later, Labby ran into Trixie on King's Road: "Don't you forget about tomorrow!"

"Oh, no. I'm just on my way to buy my trousseau."

"Isn't it a bit late for that?"

"Not really. All I'm picking up is a new toothbrush and a new sponge, as one should really start with new ones when one marries."

St. Mary Abbots was among the most venerable and prestigious of London's churches, first recorded in the Doomsday Book survey of 1086. At 10:30 on Friday morning, Jimmy's hansom swung up the steep grade above Kensington's High Street. The painter alighted, white tuft gleaming smartly against broad-brimmed topper, his frock coat-cane-and-gloves ensemble a princely arrangement in blue and yellow. He was in excellent spirits. Only one doubt gnawed at the back of his mind: Had Labby been able to maintain secrecy? Jimmy had unpleasant visions of Maud, trailed by the gigantic William Stott, bursting in on the ceremony . . .

He was scarcely reassured when, stepping briskly into the vestry adjoining the church, he was greeted by a reporter from the *Evening Standard*. But further arrivals, including the Willie Whistlers, were all on the guest list.

The ceremony went smoothly, with Jimmy losing his voice only a little on the "I do." Afterward, Trixie kissed the ladies and started back down the aisle. Jimmy tapped her arm: "You haven't signed the register yet."

"Oh—must I?"

"Listen to the Master," Labby advised.

"My Lord *and* Master," Trixie corrected him. "Oh, very well. I just *did* promise to obey, didn't I . . ."

She went to the thick ancient volume in the vestry and completed official entry No. 303, dated August 11, 1888. Below Jimmy's scraggly signature—in his nervousness, he had written his name as "McNeile," and in his gravity, he had omitted any butterfly—she inscribed in a firm, strongly slanted hand the testimonial of Beatrice Godwin, widow, of "full" age.

The wedding party proceeded to the new flat that Jimmy had taken a few days before at the Tower House in Tite Street. The packing cases that served for chairs were in the Whistler tradition. So was the host's refusal to sit down with the three-tiered wedding cake ordered from Buszard's: "Yellow and purple! It is too monstrous!"

"If we eat it," suggested the bride, "the colors will go away."

"And if we don't," added Labby, "the guests will."

Jimmy indicated he would not be crushed by that prospect—so long as Trixie stayed.

# Chapter Twenty-nine

They honeymooned in France: lazily, amorously, in Jimmy's pet term, "artistically." For him, it was the first real holiday in years. He slept late, dawdled on the sands at Boulogne, ate melons in Touraine, sketched at Chartres.

And they explored each other with increasing delight. Although Jimmy could not bring to the bedchamber the physical powers of his youth, he did not require them. The slightest pressure of his fingers aroused Trixie instantly, and a few moments' mingling of bodies was enough to trigger a wild explosion . . . more satisfying, if possible, to her middle-aged husband than to Trixie herself.

They returned to London and wandered off again to Belgium, visiting friends, talking late into the night, painting and etching without pressure. Jimmy was happy to be alone with Trixie at dinner, flicking across the table the little gold-and-green metal frog that was her model for a set of children's-book illustrations; he was equally pleased to feel her eyes lovingly upon him in a room full of strangers.

His own serenity astonished him. It came in part from his confidence in Trixie and his respect for her aesthetic judgments; even before their marriage he had reconstructed an entire portrait because she objected to the color of the eyes. But the matter went deeper; she truly understood him. She knew, as Anna Whistler had known, when to chat and when to keep silent. Better than Anna Whistler, she could lighten a fogbound afternoon with a joke, or buck him up in the mornings when he was dubious about the labors of the previous day. Her grasp embraced his subtlest moods, went to his very marrow. If there was not the wild intensity of life with Jo—well, neither was he any longer a reckless young cavalier.

On the face of things, Trixie was repeating her close relationship with her sculptor father, playing the worshipful daughter to a gifted and doting older man. In practice, the emotional roles were frequently reversed; she was the imperturbable Mommy looking after the erratic little boy.

But Trixie's maternalism, unlike Maud's, was never condescending. She held Jimmy in loose check, allowing him to swagger publicly in full male glory, while watching out of the corner of her eye to rein him in quietly when he strayed too far off course. Instead of condemning his quarrelsome impulses, she chaffed about them: "Why waste your energies on the London critics, darling—those dreary, dessicated old men? Can you imagine Shakespeare turning away from his draft of *Hamlet* to draw a caricature of some stupid court scribbler?"

One morning she found him fuming over a society-column reference in the *Post* to a *Symphony in Succotash*. Scenting an imminent letter-to-the-editor that would consume several hours—and then might never be dispatched—Trixie retreated to the drawing room and calmly emptied the inkwell.

A few minutes later, Jimmy's anguished screams rang through the Tite Street flat. "My ink! Some scoundrel has made off with every drop!"

"What a pity, darling. Did you have something important to write?"

"Of course it's important. I must tweak the nose of that slanderer in the *Post*."

Trixie came over to the writing desk and examined the inkwell solicitously. "It must have been the cat."

"Cat?" Jimmy glared at her. "We have no cat."

"Well, you must admit, it's the sort of thing a cat would do, if we *did* have one. They're very curious, you know. And rather literary."

"Really, Trixie—"

"I'm afraid we can't send John—he's at the apothecary. I could pick up some ink myself on the way back from the dressmaker—but you know, by that time you might have forgotten what you were angry about. You might even be at work, touching up that dry point you promised Luke Ionides." She smiled, all merry dimples and teasing black eyes. "Can't you see his face if you actually had it ready on time? That startled-fawn-in-the-forest look?"

Jimmy found the corners of his own mouth curling up. "Hm . . . well. Where did I leave my needle?"

"Right here." Trixie produced it from her reticule. "Your press has been inked, and you'll find dampened printing paper on the window sill."

"You haven't overlooked anything, have you?"

"Only this." She came into his arms for a long, warm kiss. The *Post* fluttered unnoticed to the floor.

Thus reinforced at home, Jimmy made a daring etching expedition

to Holland, penetrating the very heart of Rembrandt territory. Shuttling between Dordrecht and Zaandam, he turned out seventeen plates
of the flat, endlessly stretching Dutch countryside with its winding
canals and distant ghostly windmills. Critical response surpassed his
expectations: the consensus was that what Whistler yielded to the
Dutch master in exactness, he made up in poetic atmosphere.

To the superstitious Jimmy, who stuck to his hearth on Friday the
13th and would walk a mile to circumvent a black cat, unearthly forces
were clearly at work: "Trixie has a mysterious way with the gods, don't
you know. Gypsy incantations or such." He began calling her his rabbit's foot—"rabbit" or "bunny" for short—and listened solemnly to her
forecast of great fortunes ahead: "Jimmy will be quite rich. People
with his kind of eyebrows always get rich."

Events soon gave weight to this thesis. The French Government,
after a showing at the Georges Petit Gallery in Paris where Jimmy
shared space with Rodin, Renoir, Monet, Pissarro, and Sisley, suddenly
elected him to the Legion of Honor, established by Napoleon I in 1802
to reward services "to France or the causes in which France believes."
A few weeks later a gold medal for the Dutch etchings arrived from
the Amsterdam International Exhibition. People were discovering Whistler in all sorts of places. Friendly notices appeared in Boston and
Florence. From Munich came word that he had won a second prize
for his portrait of Lady Archie Campbell. Never particularly fond of
Germans—"What can you say of a people who call a glove a 'hand-
shoe'?"—he communicated his "tempered and respectable joy" at the
"secondhand compliment."

The Awards Committee, conceivably missing the irony but in any
case not at all put off, promptly elected him an honorary member of
the Bavarian Royal Academy and followed that up by decorating him
with the handsome Cross of St. Michael. Jimmy began to have second
thoughts about "Dutchmen."

He was mellowing visibly. Friends and colleagues decided a celebration was in order—ostensibly in tribute to his accumulating honors,
but with a nod also to his newly found domestic tranquillity. In the
spring of 1889, a stag dinner was held at the Criterion, a massive granite complex of theaters, restaurants, and banquet halls at the top of
Regent Street in Piccadilly. Guests were hoisted via an egg-shaped,
leather-lined "lift"—one of the first in London—to Victoria Hall on the
top floor, a vast gilt-and-plush salon with four maneuverable chandeliers suspended from a Zodiac-covered ceiling 50 feet high. Gigantic
arched windows and a French-doored balcony looked down on the
lights of Piccadilly Circus below.

Some sixty-odd guests gathered to do Jimmy honor, most of them scattered in cabaret-style circular "sprigs" grouped around the long main table. Painters, most of them young, were everywhere: proud former Followers, delegations from the Belgian "Society of 20" and the Glasgow School, Americans, Germans, Italians, unaligned artists, and even a few bold Academicians. The Whistler influence, relished or not, was by now an accepted fact. Rounding out the place cards were some of the most prominent names in British arts, journalism, and politics: Henry Irving, W. E. Henley, Sir Henry Thompson, Thomas Hardy.

In the chair was the celebrated barrister-orator Thomas Underwood. He opened the after-dinner proceedings with a description of Jimmy as a gay and unique creature—the *papilio mordens* or sharp-toothed butterfly—"amply supplied with an acid that can penetrate the tough surface of a copperplate, or leave its mark on the thick wooden skull of a critic."

Sir Coutts Lindsay, on behalf of gallery owners and dealers, testified to Jimmy's courage. Archibald Wortley of the New English Art Club, a former pupil of Millais, drew cheers with the assertion: "Every young painter in this country owes a debt to Whistler. I will go further. There is not a man of the brush or etching needle among us, regardless of age, who if he is honest with himself will deny that Whistler has taught him something."

As the encomiums piled up, Jimmy's nervousness kept pace with them. He patted the thin sheaf of notes in his jacket pocket for reassurance. Curiously, he was more jumpy about his speech than he had been with the *Ten O'Clock*. There, it had simply been a question of getting past the initial stage fright; he had not really cared what the carriage-trade Philistines thought of him. Here, he did.

Wortley was followed by the bluff, sardonic Edmund Yates of the *World*. Yates confessed at once to a weakness for Whistler and a corresponding prejudice against Royal Academicians: "It is my good old pagan habit to love those who love you and hate those who hate you." Others, said Yates, were better qualified to dilate on Jimmy's excellences as an artist: "I only know that he has few equals as a man." In closing, the editor noted the "persistent and egregious failure of the Brittanic regal wand" to alight on Jimmy's still-unknighted shoulders. "Happily, the Court of Munich has been able to perceive at a great distance what myopic eyes could not descry at home. I propose a toast to our next and principal speaker: Sir *Michael* Whistler of Baltimore and Bavaria!"

Winches turned, and the great chandeliers slowly descended. There was a great clanging of silverware, mingled with roars of "Hoorah!" Jimmy pushed back his chair. He had not bargained on such an outpouring of affection. Reaching for his notes, he felt a stab of panic.

Ah—wrong pocket. He tugged hurriedly at the other side of his jacket, caught his hand on a button—and spilled his masterpiece in disarray over the red carpet.

There was nothing to do but improvise. "Friends," he began desperately. "Romans—will Mr. Pellegrini please rise? Countrymen . . . with a bow to Mr. John Singer Sargent."

There was generous laughter. He took heart. "I commend you for your fortitude in coming here—if not your good judgment. The wicked Whistler, you know . . ."

Total blank. What next? "The, ah, previous speakers, the speakers have been very kind." Mumbled afterthought: "They would have been even kinder to keep speaking, and spare me this display of ineptness."

That was wrong; he must not confess his plight. He groped frantically to recall some of his prepared gems, and a fragment came back. "Remedies, as we all know, insist on their diseases; similarly, rewards bring with them their own virtues."

More laughter, shouts of "Hear, hear!" deafening applause out of all proportion to the witticism. These people had not come to sit in stony judgment on him, or watch him turn handsprings. They loved him. He could say anything.

And so he could say nothing. "My dear colleagues," he began, and broke off, his voice catching. "The honor you do me . . . kindness . . . quite undeserved." Finally he stood before them mute, humble, and shy, no longer hiding his warmth behind a cold shower of darts, the Whistler of the Fantin-Latour letters.

At long last he heard his brother Willie at his side: "That part about the traveler, Jimmy!" He nodded; he could remember that.

"In surroundings of antagonism," he went on, "I may have wrapped myself, for protection, in a species of misunderstanding . . . just as that other traveler drew closer about him the folds of his cloak. But as with him, emerging into the sunlight of friendship and understanding, I throw from me all former disguise and disclose to you my deep emotion . . ."

It was more emotion than he could handle. His voice trembled; his eyes misted over, clouding his monocle. "Gentlemen, I have come to the end of my rope—if not of my prepared remarks." He sat down, head bowed, as Sir Quiller Orchardson, fierce-beaked and aristocratic, led in his rolling Scots burr a last toast to "that rarest of mortals, a *true* artist."

Enveloped in irresistible affection, Jimmy had dropped his guard and become like other men: open, vulnerable, capable of forgiving and forgiveness. The transformation was not quite complete. Even as the guests were leaving the banquet, he encountered among them in

Regent Street the journalist-historian Justin McCarthy. Hanging onto McCarthy's arm was the despised ex-disciple Mortimer Menpes. "Ha!" Jimmy cried. "No doubt, Justin, you took pity on this wretched outcast. But remember—Damien died!" (Father Damien was the Belgian priest who devoted his life to the lepers of Molokai and had just perished among them.)

Before long, Trixie had a pungent reminder that the new Whistler had not taken total leave of the old. In the library of the Hogarth Club, Jimmy came across an article in *The Hawk*, a ha'penny gossip sheet, sneering at Ned Godwin as "the late impresario of the boudoir." Knowing that Augustus Moore, editor of the tabloid, was an inveterate first-nighter, Jimmy bought a ticket to the Drury Lane opening of *A Million of Money* and at the first intermission descended on Moore in the lobby.

"Hawk!" he shouted, and brought down his slender walking-stick like a horse-whip across the offender's shoulders. The startled Moore, half a foot taller than Jimmy, fell back. Jimmy pursued him through the crowded lobby, crying "Hawk!" with every whack. In the ensuing scuffle—later described by witnesses as the liveliest entertainment of the evening—Jimmy lost his footing on the marble floor. Both parties later issued victory statements—Jimmy's the more persuasive because there was no camouflaging the purple welt around Moore's left eye.

Trixie was much disquieted. "You might have been badly hurt, Jimmy."

"By that bag of ill wind? Impossible."

"Suppose you had landed on your wrist when you fell? You do have obligations to your art, you know."

"My first obligation is to be a man. No one will defile Ned's memory while I am alive."

"My precious noble knight, my jousting James!" she mimicked his gesture of curling the downswept mustache. "Just make sure you do *stay* alive!"

"How can I fail, with my darling Rabbit to look after me?"

Trixie returned his smile and his kiss, but she remained unconvinced. Jimmy was on the threshold, she felt, of an international acceptance that would justify his decades of struggle. Yet, ravaged by unseen scars, he could be sparked by a word of provocation to a vendetta that was as self-destructive as it was self-perpetuating.

She had to keep him peacefully occupied. For a start, she found a house at 21 Cheyne Walk, a few doors from the old Rossetti mansion, with a large garden and a high-ceilinged drawing room that could be converted to a studio. Her program got an unexpected assist from Count Robert de Montesquiou, poet and decadent extraordinary, destined for immortality as the polished, vicious Baron de Charlus in Proust's *Remembrance of Things Past.*

Montesquiou's lineage, if not his private life, was impeccable. He claimed direct descent from several French kings and—with even greater élan—from the original D'Artagnan, Alexandre Dumas's famous musketeer. He commissioned a full-length portrait from Jimmy, and as down payment shipped over from Paris an Empire bedstead presented to an ancestress by Napoleon I.

Beds figured importantly in the Count's life. A slim, birdlike creature of a preciosity that made Oscar Wilde seem drab as a country deacon, Montesquiou slept in a black couch shaped like a dragon, on cushions of pure eiderdown. He inlaid the shell of his pet tortoise with priceless jewels (the ungrateful creature promptly died). Among his less endearing eccentricities was a habit of squeezing Jimmy's arm, accompanied by an intimate glance and a murmured *"Mon cher diable angelique!"*

He was a difficult man and a difficult subject. Yet Jimmy sensed, beneath the bizarre façade, a complex inner world. Probing for this essence, he drew forth from the canvas a serpentine figure with sallow unhealthy flesh tints, hovering wraithlike among gloomy shadows. The effect was weird—but so was Montesquiou. Between the twin perfectionisms of painter and subject—Jimmy had dim hopes that the nobleman would bequeath the canvas to the Louvre—the work dragged on, in London and then Paris, through twenty, thirty, fifty sittings. Jimmy was still engaged in it when an intriguing new project came along.

For several months, various newspaper syndicates had been nibbling at Jimmy to contribute an art column. Now Sheridan Ford, an American correspondent in London, came up with an alternative. Why not put together a vitriolic volume of vintage Whistler, drawing upon the Ruskin case testimony, the *Ten O'Clock* lecture, various truculent pamphlets and catalogues, and a juicy sampling of Jimmy's newspaper exchanges with his critics? Little new work would be required. The whole idea would add up to a kind of military history—the Whistler war, as it were, against the Victorian artistic Establishment.

It was an ingenious plan, calculated to make Ford rich and Jimmy happy.

Jimmy liked it. Most men wrote nostalgic memoirs of tender friendships; he would turn the tradition upside down and immortalize his adversaries. "It is they, after all, who helped me most. But we cannot wait. Tom Taylor is gone, Ruskin is fading. In a few years I shall scarcely have an enemy to call my own."

Trixie, solicited for the necessary "bunny blessing," approved: "I would rather see you record your old campaigns than embark on new ones."

Clippings, drafts, and memoranda, carefully preserved through the years, were delivered to Ford's hotel. It was understood that the breezy, youngish newsman would assemble them in attractive fashion and append a few illuminating footnotes. Everything went smoothly until Ford, in rainbow cravat and red spats, brought around his proposed layout.

His format and typography were dismayingly pedestrian. The interspersed headlines and editorial comments were often funny, but in a wise-cracking music-hall vein that jarred against the urbanity of the Whistler texts. And several items had been tossed in, notably of Oscar Wilde's composition, that had not been obtained from Jimmy.

Ford saw the heavy black eyebrows tighten. "You must trust me, Mr. Whistler. I know what the public likes."

"I, Mr. Ford, am concerned only with what *I* like."

"But you said I could have a free hand in arranging the material!"

"When I spoke of a free hand, I did not anticipate that it would be such a clumsy one."

Ford bridled. "That is not my reputation in the States. You must realize, Mr. Whistler, a project like this can have only one editor."

"In that case, Mr. Ford, since it is my life—perhaps it had better be me!"

Ford gathered up his papers and stormed out.

Jimmy took counsel with his "bunny" and their weekend guest, the graduate-Follower Theo Roussel. Trixie emphatically backed Roussel's advice that Jimmy go ahead on the project without Ford. "The fact is, darling, you've had this in the back of your own head for years. Why else did you save up every scrap of argument? I don't see what Mr. Ford has to contribute besides temperament; and with all due wifely respect, we have no visible shortage of *that.*"

Jimmy sent Ford a brief thank-you-and-farewell. He enclosed a £10 note in acknowledgment of a phrase he had plucked out of Ford's draft introduction and shaped into a title, *The Gentle Art of Making Enemies.* Then he tackled the editing job himself, puffing on a string of tiny hand-rolled cigarettes as he covered sheet after sheet with pungent annotations. Every page was laid out as carefully as a canvas— "my book must be beautiful to look at"—with wide margins and asymmetrical paragraphs. The *pièces de résistance* were the butterfly illustrations that punctuated each segment: graciously welcoming the reader in the preface, posing with calm dignity below the Artistic Propositions, clutching the British farthing with a kind of pathetic defiance at the bottom of the Ruskin judgment, and elsewhere capering, pirouetting, roaring with laughter or sulking in sorrow.

Jimmy took his book to William Heinemann, a twenty-seven-year-old publisher with no reputation but considerable taste and energy.

Heinemann had plans for bringing Tolstoy, Ibsen, and Maeterlinck in translation to the British public. The trio struck Jimmy as acceptable stablemates.

Sheridan Ford, meanwhile, was displaying some Yankee get-up-and-go of his own. Without a word to Jimmy, he bundled up the Ford version of the Whistler material and took it to the London publishing firm of Field and Tuer, capping his piracy with a prefatory note: "I commend this book to Mr. Whistler's enemies, with the soothing assurance that should each of them purchase a copy the edition will be exhausted in a week." The edition never reached the presses. As soon as the publishers heard of Jimmy's contract with Heinemann, they returned Ford's manuscript.

Undeterred, Ford shifted operations to Antwerp, where Jimmy met the move with a court order. At a brief trial, Ford's two thousand illegitimate copies were ordered confiscated, and the defendant (who remained discreetly in Paris well out of range of Jimmy's cane) was charged £150 in fines and damages.

Ford made another and last stab in Belgium. Pawning his clothes and furniture, he succeeded in printing four thousand copies at Ghent before the Procureur du Roi slammed down the law on him. A handful of books survived impounding, to turn up later in New York as collector's items. Ford had paid for them with his career.

Ironically, the "peaceful" editorial interlude had added still another scalp to the Whistler collection. "Ha!" chortled Jimmy. "The fellow is a rank amateur. After all, I cut my eyeteeth on Howell. Now, there is a *real* robber!"

Trixie looked up from the *Post*, a strangely thoughtful expression on her face. "There *was* a real robber."

"What's that? What's that? Are you trying to tell me Howell has reformed?"

"Not exactly." She passed him the paper. Squinting, Jimmy adjusted his monocle. There it was, on the front page. Charles Augustus Howell, "the well-known art connoisseur and bon vivant" (how the Owl would have loved that!) had died in the Home Hospital, Fitzroy Square, after being found unconscious in the early morning outside a Soho tavern. Unconfirmed accounts said his throat had been cut and a shilling thrust between his teeth.

"Poor devil," murmured Jimmy. "More likely he suffered an epileptic fit." Howell, never a heavy drinker, had been subject to occasional severe seizures.

This was not the first time he had been reported dead. In the 1870s, seeking to bolster his court case against the Metropolitan Railway (and also no doubt out of pure devilment), the Owl had circulated rumors of his sad demise. This time, as Ellen Terry wrote to a dilettante admirer, "Howell is *really* dead. Do trot around to Christie's and see what turns up."

Howell's uncertain reputation (only a year earlier, his famous locket-enclosed "tresses of Charles I" had been exposed as a snippet from the head of Rosa Corder) did nothing to discourage attendance at the Great Rooms of Christie's, and conceivably even swelled the crowd. Scores of sales ghouls were there, and others with a more personal interest: Theodore Watts-Dunton came from Putney to reclaim a batch of recklessly affectionate letters sent thirty years before to the handsome Howell by the young Swinburne.

Although enormous sums had passed through Howell's hands, his entire estate fetched less than £5000, all of it scooped up by waiting creditors. What finally wrecked the master of middlemen was the one factor he could not manipulate: the date of his birth. Had he lived half a century later, in the golden era of the silver screen, he would have been king of Hollywood agents.

Jimmy heard that Graham Robertson, Ellen Terry's delegate, had acquired two Whistlers—a *Valparaiso Nocturne* and the *Rosa Corder*— for £240 each. He braved a heavy fog to visit his paintings. Running a finger over the portrait lovingly—"Isn't she beautiful?"—he noticed an oval bed of black lacquer that Robertson had also picked up at the sale. "But that—that Chinese bed," he stammered. "It's mine! He never would let you remember where your things *were*."

Jimmy refused to believe Howell was really gone. "The painless Portuguee will turn up again somewhere," he told Trixie. "Spinning a fantastic tale of a trip to Mars."

"Or the nether regions."

"Yes. And bringing back an authentic set of the proprietor's horns to prove it—priced below cost."

No further trace appeared of Howell's corporeal being, but his exploits lingered on. The Oscar Wilde auction in 1900 included in the catalogue a "Whistler drawing of Sarah Bernhardt," duly if perplexingly signed by the great lady herself. The French star had never sat to Jimmy. But she had once been seen—and captured in a clever forgery—by Howell.

The last screech of the Owl echoed, appropriately enough, through a fashionable Bond Street gallery, where Jimmy saw a vaguely familiar sketch of a lofty church interior on display for £500. It was described as a "preliminary drawing by Michelangelo for St. Peter's Cathedral." Jimmy put up his monocle, and recognized the *Michelangelo* as a sketch of St. Paul's he had dashed off one afternoon while walking in the City . . . with Howell.

It was William Rossetti whose rueful judgment on Howell was seconded by virtually all who knew him: "I could have better spared a better man."

Trixie's diversionary tactics had, despite the detour with Sheridan Ford, kept Jimmy on fairly good behavior for nearly three years. Now, with the stirring of Whistler winds in the north, returns began coming in.

Ever since a second showing of the *Carlyle* at Glasgow in 1888, leading painters there had been urging their Lowland compatriots to buy the picture. "If the citizens of Glasgow," snapped Sir Quiller Orchardson, "assembled in their wisdom, have not the wit to welcome home a magnificent portrait of their greatest philosopher, painted by a true McNeill of Barra, they should abandon all claim to the title 'canny Scots!'"

The painting was indeed admired. But Jimmy's proud price of a thousand guineas? Scottish heads waggled: "Dinna know, mon . . ."

In 1891, a petition for the purchase was signed by nearly a hundred prominent persons, including Royal Academy President Frederick Leighton and president-to-be John Everett Millais. Millais had long ago resolved his Whistler dilemma in Jimmy's favor. He had painted a *Carlyle* of his own—sleek, photographically accurate, quite empty—and the contrast with Jimmy's poignant canvas was too striking to ignore.

The elders of the Corporation of Glasgow pondered. Despite some grumblings of "wasteful extravagance," it was decided to buy the *Carlyle*. But not, of course, at the price demanded by the artist. Although the exchequer could manage the sum, no true Scot could countenance such abject capitulation. A two-man delegation was appointed to negotiate suitable terms.

Officially in charge was Robert Crawford, a soft-spoken merchant who was chairman of the Galleries Committee. Because Crawford was suspected of surreptitious experiments with water color, he would be accompanied by Ian McLellan, a flinty six-foot farmer who had red hair as rough as an unplowed field, and a voice to match. McLellan had never been accused of painting anything more complicated than a barn door.

Jimmy greeted his visitors in the second-floor studio at Cheyne Row. He was dressed, as Crawford later described it, "very Boul 'Mich'": white blouse, flowing bow tie, brown velveteen jacket. He danced nervily about the room, served "Vienna tea" with lemon and rum, and talked of everything but the *Carlyle*. "Splendid afternoon, is it not, gentlemen? I have just been admiring the honeysuckle in the garden. I hope you have had a pleasant trip? The tea is rather special, but I could supply something stronger." He looked at McLellan, bulging out of a Harris tweed suit fresh from the rack. "A spot of Drambuie for our hearty friend?"

"Mr. Whistler," Crawford injected gently. "We have Drambuie in Scotland. But we do not have your painting of Carlyle. That is what we are here to talk about."

"Oh yes—the picture, of course. Well, gentlemen, the picture is yours. And I must say I am delighted. The great Corporation of Glasgow: enlightened, liberal, humane. I could not wish to see it in better hands."

"There is a certain problem about the price, Mr. Whistler."

"Yes," rumbled McLellan. "We cannot pay that much. But we might consider—"

"My dear, ruddy-cheeked Scots!" Jimmy teetered back like an astonished canary. "What is this we are doing? Surely one of the great cities in the Eastern Hemisphere is not going to haggle over guineas. If it were in my power to bestow this picture on the people of Glasgow as a gift I would gladly do so, to express my appreciation of their good judgment. But alas, I cannot make it a gift, and I wish you to have it. In any event, the picture will be back here from the framer's tomorrow, and we shall look at it together. Now, let us turn to other things. Would you care to see Mr. Irving tonight at the Lyceum?"

The Glasgow pair were back the next day, considerably more dour of mien. "Well, Mr. Whistler," Crawford began, "have you been doing any more thinking?"

"Indeed I have—but only on the anticipation of seeing you both again, and resuming our delightful chat."

"The price, Mr. Whistler." Crawford blinked his eyes hopefully. "Will you not change—?"

"Sir, I quoted you a figure. Whatever may be offered elsewhere, I am too much a man of honor to raise it by a single shilling."

Crawford looked to McLellan in despair. "Perhaps we had better view the painting."

"It is over here by the window."

The Scots stood before the canvas in silence for several moments: Crawford in open admiration, McLellan trying to look as though he reviewed masterpieces for the Louvre Council every day. Finally the farmer cleared his throat and spoke: "Do you call this life-size, Mr. Whistler?"

"No, I don't. If I put you up against that canvas and measured you, you would be a monster."

"What about the, ah, the tones, Mr. Whistler?"

"What about them?"

"Not very brilliant, are they?"

"Are you brilliant in tone? Am I? They are the tones of human flesh."

McLellan had run out of steam. He glanced helplessly at Crawford, who sighed and carried out his duty to the Corporation. "They say, Mr. Whistler, that modern pictures are inclined to fade."

"No, they do not—and therein lies their complete damnation! What I am entrusting to you, Mr. Crawford, is not a 'modern picture' but a Whistler, to be enjoyed for eternity, long after your thousand guineas have been spent and forgotten. I fear this discussion grows burdensome. Shall we light up some smokes, gentlemen, and relax?"

"Dammit, yes!" roared McLellan suddenly. "Tell me, Mr. Whistler—did you ever think of giving up painting for the healthy outdoor life of the farm? I could use a horse trader like you!"

With the Scottish outpost taken, the Whistlerite campaign in France moved into high gear. It was spearheaded by an important recruit. Stéphane Mallarmé was an avant-garde poet: the literary heir, along with Verlaine and Rimbaud, of Baudelaire. Mallarmé's art, which repudiated the conventional emotional associations of words in favor of the "organization of sound" along Poe-like principles of placement and repetition, had much in common with the Whistler doctrine of arranged harmonies.

Poet and painter were introduced by Claude Monet at the Café de la Paix. Mallarmé at once asked permission to translate the *Ten O'Clock*, and turned out a French text hailed by Jimmy for the "sympathy manifested in every line."

The two met again on Jimmy's next trip to Paris. Struck by the slight poet's simple dignity, his air of aching mournfulness, Jimmy offered to do a lithographic study for the frontispiece of Mallarmé's latest volume of verses. Posed before Jimmy's fireplace at the Hôtel du Bon Lafontaine, Mallarmé confessed that he was indeed miserable: crossing the Pont de l'Europe every morning to the Right Bank to give the English lessons that were the source of his livelihood, he was often tempted to hurl himself onto the tracks below.

"But that would be so inartistic!" cried Jimmy.

The fire scorched the poet's trousers twice before Jimmy got the effect he wanted. Conventional lithography, in which he had dabbled since the '70s, involved drawing with a greasy crayon directly onto a flat stone; by rolling ink and pressing paper over the stone, an image was reproduced. Jimmy, ever the experimenter, put down his drawing first on paper, and transferred these lines to the stone.

Mallarmé's patience was rewarded by a perfect miniature. The sad downcast eyes were there, with the extra note of melancholy formed by the inverted-V of mustache and beard surrounding the downturned

mouth; and, transcending all individual features, the expression of solitude, of remote, secret majesty. "It is a marvel," declared Mallarmé.

In turn, he set out to win Jimmy greater recognition in France. Although poor, Mallarmé knew everybody of consequence. His drum-
beating was reinforced by Theodore Duret and the sculptor Drouet,
and by the middle of 1891 Jimmy had been elevated from a mere
Chevalier in the Legion of Honor to the status of Officer. He was now
entitled to wear a rosette instead of a red ribbon on his street clothes,
and had a separate rosette to decorate the green-and-white medal prescribed for formal occasions. "Spread the word at the Royal Academy,"
he told his friends, "although it is essentially useless to talk of Whistler
to the British. What I say they do not understand; and what they understand, I have never said."

His real target in France, however, was something more: acquisition
of the *Mother* by the French Government. "It is a matter of destiny,"
he explained to Trixie. "The painting has survived so many trials and
near-disasters: fire, pawnbrokers, the covetous grasp of bargain hunters
. . . why, do you know, just a few years ago, when I was very hard-up,
a man in New York actually bought it from my Pall Mall dealer,
Graves, through my American friend Bill Chase."

"Then how were you able—"

"As I said, destiny. The gallery was closed and Bill's check needed
time to clear the bank. By the time it did, I had sense enough to change
my mind."

"When the gods speak," said Trixie solemnly, "it is wise to listen."

"Precisely, Rabbit. The French were the first to recognize the merits
of the *Mother*. She should belong to them forever."

Mallarmé firmly agreed. He brought his friend Claude Roger-Marx,
the Inspector of Fine Arts, to see the painting at the Boussod-Valadon
Gallery, and went to lunch with Claude's boss Bourgeois, the new Minister of Fine Arts. Self-effacing where his own interests were concerned,
Mallarmé was a tiger on behalf of Jimmy. He went after another tiger, the most famous in all France. Georges Clemenceau, who
would head the French Government from 1906–1909 and again during
World War I, was already leader of the Radical forces in the Chamber
of Deputies and publisher of *La Justice*. With his accession to the
Whistler cause, the bastions of conservatism fell.

On November 21, Jimmy received a letter from the Minister of Fine
Arts informing him that the French Government would like to purchase the *Mother* for the National Museum in Luxembourg Palace,
but were regrettably unable to offer what the picture was worth. In
fact, the Minister hesitated to mention the sum allocated to him: a
token figure of only 4000 francs, or about $600.

Although barely solvent—he was living on advances from Heinemann for *The Gentle Art of Making Enemies*—Jimmy was overjoyed; he would have parted with the picture for the single farthing of the Ruskin judgment. He had achieved, in his own lifetime, the dream of every artist; from the Luxembourg his painting would go in time to the hallowed halls of the Louvre.

He wrote to Paris that he was "deeply touched" by the honor: "The picture you have chosen is precisely the one I could most earnestly wish to see become the object of so solemn a consecration." Price was no obstacle; the government's "flattering evidence of sympathy," crowning earlier honors, was "too precious for me to wish to entertain any other consideration."

Privately, Jimmy was amused by the swarm of busybodies who came forward to hint with winks and nods that they had been instrumental in the government's decision. "It reminds me of the tidal waves of porters who grabbed my luggage at the quai in Venice, then waited for me at the hotel lobby. Each one recited what he had done: 'I took your trunk—your suitcase—your umbrella'—until it came to the turn of the last one. 'I didn't carry anything,' he admitted. 'But I was present.' All these braggarts were likewise 'present.'"

Jimmy also noted with irony the unblushing boast in the *Illustrated London News* that with the purchase of the *Mother*, "modern British art" would now be represented at the Luxembourg with "one of the finest paintings due to the brush of a British artist."

However, for the moment he was really too excited to mind. The picture was being displayed on an easel in the Salon d'Honneur of the Luxembourg for two weeks before going onto the walls: "So that, until, in the end of time, I go to the Louvre, the Louvre has meanwhile, so to say, come to me! Can anything be more royal?" He quoted to Trixie from the Songs of Solomon: "The stone that the builders rejected has become the cornerstone; this is marvelous to behold." And he stretched his purse to take a tiny flat near the Place de l'Odéon, so he could run across the street to the Museum to see the portrait whenever he was in Paris. The *pied-à-terre* was in the Rue Rotrou, a few paces from the old Hôtel Corneille where he had spent his first night in Paris as a raw novice from the States.

Jimmy had come a long way. He intended to go a good deal farther —and settle some scores en route. At a celebratory dinner in the Chelsea Arts Club, he announced he was burying the hatchet—"in the ribs of the enemy."

He started modestly at the Walker Art Gallery in Liverpool. As guest supervisor of hangings, he placed in the center of the main exhibition room *The Doctor*, Luke Fildes's famous (and mawkish) anecdote of a saintly faced physician ministering to a sick child. Jimmy grouped around it all the canvases of illness he could find: convalescents at the seashore, an elderly man in a wheelchair, a druggist filling a prescription, even a dying puppy . . . capped by a last-minute discovery that he delightedly dragged out of the storeroom, a large still life of medicine bottles. To inquiring reporters, he gravely explained: "I wished to emphasize this particular school of English painting."

Telling the story later, Jimmy sometimes insisted the motif of his arrangement had not been illness so much as "the Academy baby": canvases of British tots of every size, shape and condition. Each picture, he declared, was hung "on the line" without crowding, to the delight of the contributing artists—until each man turned around and saw all the others. "Babies in front of them, babies behind them; to the right, to the left. Amazing, what? They never asked me again."

It was for London, however, not Liverpool, that he reserved his thunderbolt: the Whistler retrospective at the Goupil Gallery in March of 1892. Jimmy's idea was magnificently simple. Gathering together from their owners his best oils of three decades, he hung them himself in Bond Street and printed beneath each what the critics had said at its first public showing ("vulgar . . . clownish . . . slovenly . . . nightmarish . . . madness"), the whole parade of foolish, cruel abuse offered as the sober judgments of London's professional sages. Trixie could not accuse him of belligerence; he was merely quoting verbatim, as ruthless in his accuracy as they had been originally in pillorying him. The ninety-three reviews, including fatuities by Ruskin, Wedmore, and other representatives of England's most illustrious journals, were assembled for posterity in a catalogue entitled *The Voice of a People*. Never had inept warriors been blown higher by their own misplaced petards.

As a parting blast, Jimmy cited the somewhat different opinion of the Parisian Chronique des Beaux Arts: "At the Luxembourg Museum there has just been installed Mr. Whistler's splendid portrait of his mother, a work destined to be admired for all eternity, upon which the consecration of the centuries seems to have put the patina of a Rembrandt, a Titian or a Velázquez."

The exhibit was mobbed. A whole new generation, not raised to prostrate themselves before Ruskin, paid their shillings and pushed through the turnstiles to gape at the sculptured splendor of *The Blue Wave* and sigh before the elusive tints of *Miss Cicely Alexander*. A special sixpence fee was set up for evening visitors, and a weekly half-crown day for those who wished to avoid the crowds. Artists and their families were admitted free.

Jimmy appeared briefly at the private view, speaking grimly of "sending Ruskin a season ticket," then retired with Trixie to the Chelsea Arts Club. He would not go back to the gallery: "They were always pearls I cast before them, and the people were always—well, the same people."

Still the throngs came, as intent on eulogizing Jimmy as they had once been on condemning him. The prices of Whistler canvases shot up, sparked by the sudden entry of American dollars into the market. Until now, American opinion of Jimmy had generally aped the British: Whistler was a monocled clown, perfect copy for the Sunday feature papers. This view was severely shaken by the French purchase of the *Mother*, and overturned completely by the Goupil triumph. Americans wakened to the fact that they had a great painter living abroad; they opened their checkbooks to claim him. Within a year, Croal Thompson of the Goupil was involved in negotiations for more than half the paintings from the show. Typical was the boost in price of the Ruskin-despised *Falling Rocket*. Railing at Jimmy's original price of £200, the critic had called the picture "a pot of paint" flung in the public's face. Now, Thompson had no trouble getting £800; as Jimmy said, "four pots of paint."

Society wanted Whistler portraits. One of the first to offer a commission was the Duke of Marlborough, who invited Jimmy and Trixie to Blenheim and collapsed before they could make the journey. "I accepted," drawled Jimmy, "and he died by return mail. Now I shall never know whether my letter killed him."

Other dignitaries were waiting in line. "Where were they ten years ago," Jimmy complained to Trixie, "when I wanted to paint them, and needed to paint them, and could have done them just as well?"

Trixie discouraged such backward glances. "This is what you've wanted all your life, Jimmy; it's those eyebrows of yours making good on their promise. You're going to have enough money to live where you please, do what you like, even make that trip to America you're always talking about."

America . . . Jimmy's "blessed America." He had been away from his homeland for thirty-seven years, and toying with a visit for the last seven of them. He yearned to go, and was fearful of being ridiculed by his countrymen.

For all of his fervor about the supra-national role of the artist, Jimmy's Americanism was deeply ingrained. His small library consisted mainly of Poe, Mark Twain, Bret Harte, and various histories of the United States. He had a habit of advancing his birth date from July 10 to July 4. And he took great pleasure in showing off the technical superiorities of such American imports as his slender cane-umbrella: "Look at that—and that! Perfection, what? Made in New York, New York. That's the way they do things over there!"

He had his suspicions about American culture, however, because of the prohibitive tariff placed on art works brought into the country. "Haven't you a law to keep out pictures and statues?" he demanded of Bill Chase in 1885. "Is it not written in black and white that the works of great masters are not wanted in America? A people that tolerate such laws have no love for art."

Nonetheless, he listened to Chase's reassurances of a marked change in climate. Major art museums were established along the eastern seaboard and as far west as Chicago; serious collectors like August Belmont were increasingly in view. When, after the stir caused by the *Ten O'Clock*, the celebrity-booker Major Pond in New York offered to sponsor an American lecture tour, Jimmy had agreed. With Mark Twain and Oscar Wilde in the field, lectures were more than ever the rage of the day. Jimmy entertained visions of tugboats rushing to greet him down the bay, and ship news reporters dissolving before his witticisms.

But he was elected head of the embattled British Artists, and it was the trip across the ocean that dissolved. In the next few years, attempts to revive the project ran into difficulties of scheduling.

Now, in 1892, circumstances had changed. Not only was Jimmy in a stronger position personally; he was being offered, through his prestigious American colleague John Singer Sargent, the perfect setting to frame a triumphal return.

The two American painters were on cordial terms, although very different types. Against Jimmy's diminutive ebullience, the younger Sargent was huge, bearded, and grave, with the stiff Bostonian correctness of his friend Henry James. However, he was an agreeable neighbor in Tite Street, and an appreciative listener to Jimmy's monologues at the Chelsea Arts.

Sargent, who rivaled Millais in popularity as a portraitist, was frankly admiring of Jimmy's work. Jimmy regretted that he could not return the compliment. Like Degas, he considered Sargent an excellent technician with a sharp eye for character, able to execute any assignment vigorously but lacking in mystery or inner radiance . . . a coloristically inferior Manet with a Yankee accent.

Jimmy made no secret of these views. Yet, some months before the Goupil breakthrough, Sargent had urged his name upon the skeptical Brahmins of Boston. The city was building a monumental new Public Library, modeled after an Italian Renaissance palace. Sculptured approaches had been entrusted to Augustus and Louis Saint-Gaudens; mural decorations to Sargent, the American book illustrator Edwin Abbey, and the aging French master Puvis de Chavannes, renowned for his contributions to the Panthéon.

The only man who could round out their scheme to perfection, Sar-

gent told the trustees, was Whistler. It was, as Jimmy quickly acknowledged, "an act of rare and noble camaraderie."

It was also an opportunity to let out his sails such as he had not had
since the Peacock Room. With freedom to create pure decoration, his
palette could roam beyond the bounds of naturalism. He could
conjure up a neo-Greek figure-harmony, an extravagant forest of impossibly beautiful flowers, even the monumental dreamed-of abstraction that had long haunted him, the *Symphony of Colors—Full Palette*.

"Think of it, my dear Bunny. To return to Baltimore and West Point
like a victorious Caesar, having vanquished foreign lands and planted
the Stars and Stripes in the Luxembourg; and then to contribute a
masterpiece that will elevate Beantown to a place among the world
centers of art."

"They will fall upon your neck in gratitude, my darling Knight of
the Brush. Especially the bold handsome American women. And I
shall be dying of jealousy."

"But you will be there beside me."

"For protection?"

"For proud display."

After Trixie retired, Jimmy went to the pile of clippings stored in his
studio cabinet. Would his countrymen really meet him with laurels?

From the time of his first showing there, when a circus-mood crowd
guffawed its way through a Baltimore gallery in 1875, until a few
months ago when a Philadelphia critic jeered at the Luxembourg for
"lowering its tone" to the degraded Whistler level, American reaction
had generally been hostile. Jimmy fingered a clipping from *McClure's
Magazine*, describing how "Whistler the Comedian" had allegedly
hurled his scissors through the studio window, exclaiming with glee
at the howl of rage below: "Ha, not yet nine o'clock and another enemy made!"

No, the land of the roistering pioneer and the land-grabbing railroad baron was not kind to artists. Perhaps some day; but Americans,
he had recently read, still hooted at poetry and looked with suspicion
upon wine-drinking. There probably wasn't a painting worth looking
at west of the Alleghenies, and very few east of them. Would he be
a fool to entrust his tender inspirations to Boston? He hoped to get the
answer at a Paris meeting set up by Sargent with the key trustee of
the museum, Samuel Abbott, and its chief architect, Charles Follen
McKim.

Abbott was gracious and knowledgeable. He spoke of a projected
$15,000 fee. McKim, the partner of Stanford White, was even more
persuasive. The most important room in the building, he explained,
climax to the vast marble entrance hall and noble stairway, would be
Bates Hall, the barrel-vaulted, mosaic-topped reading-room occupy-

ing the entire front of the second floor. Surrounded by huge arched windows, the 9,000 square foot area with its 50-foot ceiling would have the scale of a great Roman bath.

At its far end, commanding the attention of every eye in the room, McKim had reserved a giant panel. This was for Whistler. "My thought was, we might have a surge of color here, to contrast with the brownish-gray sandstone of the hall. But that, of course, would be entirely up to you."

At a second meeting, held over lunch at Foyot's, McKim described the main-staircase panels proposed by Puvis: allegories dedicated to Poetry, Philosophy, History, and Science. Sargent elaborated on his plans for a series of huge tableaux depicting the Divine Comedy, or perhaps the history of religion. Jimmy, fired by the Pouilly Fuissé, the company and the conversation, grabbed a stub of charcoal and started drawing on the tablecloth. He would decorate the Bates Hall panel with a 20-foot peacock in flaming gold, he announced. So rapidly that Sargent blinked in amazement, he outlined his design, and covered the cloth with arrow-pointed notes detailing the color combination.

It was agreed that he would complete a formal sketch of the mural within the coming weeks, and forward it to Boston. The four men parted, glowing with enthusiasm.

Negotiating the trip back to London—it was a bad Channel crossing, slow and rough—Jimmy's glow faded. By the time Trixie ran out to greet his early-morning hansom, he was ready to confess his fears: "One amiable official does not a nation make. I have no stomach for taking on another corps of Yankee Doodle Ruskins. It would be terrible to survive the rigors of the Atlantic, only to be wrecked by a reporter at the pier."

The golden peacock acquired no shimmering feathers at Cheyne Row. Two days later the tablecloth at Foyot's was delivered to an efficient Paris laundry, where Jimmy's sketch and its accompanying notes were scrubbed back to blank whiteness. Washed away with them was Jimmy's American journey.

# Chapter Thirty

Not Boston or New York, but Paris was the next Whistler port-of-call. For nearly a year, Jimmy and Trixie had been looking for something unusual in the way of a small house on the Left Bank, close to the excitement of the art world and yet secluded from it. In the middle of 1892 they found what they wanted: a seventeenth-century hideaway in the Latin Quarter set back 200 feet from the busy, colorful Rue du Bac. An imposing archway on the street led through a paved, covered passage, once used as a carriage road, to the elegant little building and a spacious rear garden. Across the garden wall was a Dominican monastery, where the nightly chanting of vespers provided a final note of Old World tranquillity. The location was ideal: quickly accessible to studios, shops and cafés, with the Louvre just a short stroll away on the other side of the Pont du Carrousel.

Jimmy was in a position now to experiment with his art according to his fancies. Thanks largely to Trixie's cool determination, he had achieved acceptance for his work and his ideas. The question was, would he enjoy his freedom, or fritter it away in devising schemes to trip up people of no consequence? Would he pursue new aesthetic challenges or, driven by his interior demons, keep flailing at phantom enemies in the manner of a punch-drunk fighter who cannot hear the final bell?

Trixie was not optimistic. She knew too well her husband's penchant for glowering over past grievances, searching out new injury, sometimes even going out of his way to manufacture it. The ensuing bouts were usually titillating, but they distracted the artist from his work. She had a suspicion that this was their hidden purpose.

She could sympathize; she knew herself the daily misgivings of creativity. And Jimmy had reason to shrink from the grinding demands of studio portraiture: the foibles of sitters, the "one last skin" that so often eluded him and resulted in a discarded canvas. Yet he needed

work for his psychic balance; without it, his restlessness sought release elsewhere.

Trixie nudged him gently toward lithography and water colors,
small-scale media that put less strain on the nerves and muscles.
"Lithos have hardly been tapped as a legitimate medium, Jimmy. But
your river twilights are like fine charcoal sketches; they really exploit
the broken granulated line." And she pulled him back from the ink-
stand. When he proposed sending a note to Edmund Yates "lest in my
absence too great a security should come over the enemies," she replied drily: "By all means, darling—if the World will pay you a guinea
per word. That is what I estimate the time lost from your studio will
cost us."

Mainly, in her campaign to "make Jimmy amiable," she concentrated on providing him with a warm home, the first permanent dwelling place of his vagabond life. Their long, blue-toned reception room
held a discreet blend of First Empire furniture and Oriental décor,
rounded out by two small Nocturnes, some etchings, and a pastel Venus
over the fireplace. In the back, a lattice-work trellis designed by Trixie
opened onto the winding gravelled walks of the garden.

"Enchanting serenity . . . aristocratic repose," murmured guests and
interviewers. There was no lack of either group at 110 Rue du Bac.
French journalists mingled with a new crop of Followers from England, and globe-trotting Americans for whom it had become de rigueur
to "see Whistler in Paris."

Never averse to adulation, Jimmy flourished at an endless round of
teas and receptions, drawing on his pantomimic accessories of elevator
eyebrows, dancing monocle, and eloquent hands. He clung to the
monocle even though both eyes needed help, and the strain of squinting was forcing unpleasant lines that had to be effaced each morning
with unguents. For some time he had been wearing spectacles when
he worked (with the recent addition of a patch of cloth beneath the
steel bridge to avoid leaving a mark on his nose), but he was indignant
when Bill Chase suggested he wear them regularly: "D'you expect
me to go around the world like a damned poky German student?"

No Heidelberg bookworm, he. Monocled and manicured, mustache now more tightly curled and flecked with iron-gray, he pranced
forth on the boulevards in short black coat and white ducks, the Legion rosette in his lapel. One evening he appeared at Maxim's, surrounded by an entourage of admiring young artists.

"Whistler!" a voice bawled out of the darkness. "You have forgotten
your muff! Along with your manners."

He recognized the harsh accents of Degas: friend and tormentor,
colleague and nemesis. The Frenchman was standing a few feet away

at the cloakroom counter. He had aged a good deal; his once-slim figure was bulky under a long black greatcoat.

Jimmy bowed. "Forgive me, Degas. I did not see you."

"But I saw *you*. Even with these bad eyes. That fine rosette lights you up like a street lamp on the Champs Élysées."

"It *is* fine, isn't it," Jimmy agreed. "You should wear one, Degas."

Degas snorted. "I? They offered me the Legion three years ago when they were honoring all the forgotten men. I threw it back in their faces. Let Monet and Renoir and Rodin be the dancing bears in the Salon circus. And Whistler, the once forward-looking Whistler!"

"Still forward-looking, my dear Degas. I wrote to you several times from London. I would like to see what you are doing, after those magnificent nudes. Can we have lunch together next week?"

"Bah, there is no keeping up with you. You are certain to be rushing off to the photographer, to pose in your new hat. It is a good hat—but it will never win us back Alsace-Lorraine!"

The maitre d' appeared meekly at Jimmy's side. "Sir, your private room is not quite ready. Could we put your guests—"

"What?" Jimmy shrilled. "Not ready?" He put up his glass, and impaled the man with a stare. "How dare you be not ready? Were you not advised that Whistler and his party were on their way? Lower your head, man, and do penance!"

Degas jammed his fedora onto his head in disgust. Loudly, so that the whole restaurant could hear his judgment, he roared: "Whistler, you behave as if you had no talent!" The buzzing of Jimmy's entourage gave way to shocked silence. The Frenchman's short, heavy steps carried him through the door.

Jimmy was stunned. How could Degas, himself such an outsider, inflict public discredit on one of the few men he had always respected? True, Degas had reason to be bitter. His eyesight was failing. He had never found the "happy little home" that, in spite of his railings against women, he admittedly yearned for. Though his work was praised now, and brought good prices, it had all taken so long that he had ceased to care; as he declared to *Le Figaro*, "I am like the old horse who is told he had won the Grand Prix, and all he wants is his bag of oats."

Jimmy knew all this, and that a Degas outburst was not to be taken seriously; the man had trampled with equal thoughtlessness on the sensibilities of his best friend, Manet. Still, it hurt; the attitude smacked altogether too much of Swinburne, insisting in his *Ten O'Clock* review on the obligation of the great artist always to be serious.

Well, Jimmy would not be. Where his behavior was concerned, he was willing to be peremptory, silly, undignified, to play the bully and the fool. As he once observed, he had no private life; what happened to him personally was not terribly relevant. It was a costly logic, but with it he purchased something: his art remained inviolate.

Talent, by Jimmy's reasoning, had a life of its own. To nurture that life, the man it inhabited sometimes had to twist himself into bizarre shapes. Good Lord! What more ludicrous spectacle than Swinburne in his cups, carted like a sack of coal under the arm of the huge explorer, Richard Burton? Or for that matter Degas himself, covering his naked shoulders like an elderly spinster when surprised in the act of dressing by his seventeen-year-old chambermaid?

Happily there were other, more sympathetic Frenchmen; and he had found one of them. His rapport with Stéphane Mallarmé had ripened into a close relationship, for Jimmy the last of the real intimacies between peers that had begun with Fantin-Latour and extended through George du Maurier, Rossetti, Swinburne, Howell, and Albert Moore.

The new friendship brought immediate entrée to the Tuesday evening salons in Mallarmé's small Rue de Rome apartment, where the poet played host to the cream of France's creative talent: Rodin, Claude Debussy, Paul Gaugin, the twenty-one-year-old Marcel Proust. Jimmy was a new and famous face to be fussed over. Young Proust respectfully submitted an engraving of the *Carlyle* for his autograph, and later formed the name of his painter in *Remembrance*, Elstir, by combining Helleu with Whistler. Debussy, whose *L'Après-midi d'un Faun* had been inspired by Mallarmé verses, expressed a feeling of similar kinship for the Whistler Nocturnes. With Jimmy the object of such attentions, Trixie had the first round of her battle well in hand.

In his new contentment, her husband entered the phase of James the Benevolent. One of the first to enjoy the blessings of the Rue du Bac Whistler, as edited and revised by Trixie in the early 1890s, was Aubrey Beardsley. Beardsley was an exotic apparition: bony, hollow-cheeked, a third-generation tubercular who moved like a spindly wraith in something between a glide and a shuffle. A frequent companion of Oscar Wilde, he spoke in high staccato tones, gobbled up concerts and lectures with the furious energy of the doomed, and was given to strange excitements.

His chief passion, however, was art; and his chief idol Whistler. Long before setting eyes on Jimmy, he had prowled through the Peacock Room filling a notebook with sketches. He was in raptures at obtaining "a gem of an etching" by the Master, and stood sobbing before the *Miss Cicely Alexander:* "Truly glorious, indescribable, mysterious."

At twenty-one, Beardsley already had a style: the long, sweeping neo-baroque line that would culminate in Art Nouveau. His pen-and-ink drawings in the *Studio* magazine exuded a faintly unhealthy air,

like some tropical plant grown to excrescence. Though thin and delicate, they were flamboyantly aphrodisiac. One of his most noted—and
hastily suppressed—efforts was a sketch of plump little Queen Victoria
as a Degas ballet dancer.

It was at a diplomatic dinner party in Paris that Jimmy and Trixie
met this most undiplomatic of artists. Jimmy was, of course, prepared
to dislike him; any friend of Wilde was a potential enemy of his. His
prejudices were affirmed by Beardsley's frenetic eye and the lank red
hair trailing down over his forehead. "The fellow is as overblown as
his work," he told Trixie.

"But Jimmy—he really has a Japanese sense of line."

"I am not arguing with you, my dear—I am telling you. His drawings
are no better than he is—all hair and peacock plumes."

In 1894, while Jimmy and Trixie were visiting with friends in Chelsea, a new edition of Sir Thomas Malory's *Le Morte d'Arthur* was published with illustrations by Beardsley. Trixie bought a copy and left it
on Jimmy's dressing table.

Thumbing through the drawings before the fireplace, Jimmy exclaimed in pleasure several times, then grew very silent. He took a
hansom directly to the house in nearby Pimlico where Beardsley lived
with his mother and sister. Ignoring the lurid décor of Beardsley's
room—orange walls, covered with Japanese pornography—he crossed
to the desk where the boy was working, and tapped his cane lightly
on Beardsley's shoulder: "Aubrey, I have made a terrible mistake. You
are"—he swallowed—"you are a great artist. I shall see that my publisher and my friends are properly placed on notice."

Beardsley shot up, cheeks flaming. "But I—why should you—oh, Mr.
Whistler!" Flapping long arms like a windblown scarecrow, he burst
into tears.

Willie Rothenstein was half-Jewish and all sweetness, the son of a
prosperous Yorkshire warehouse owner and a village lass. Born in 1872
—the year Jimmy was painting the *Mother*—Willie had made a small
ripple at Oxford with his neatly composed, penetrating character drawings; Jimmy was trying to spread the ripple farther.

His protégé was a moon-faced youth with thick scholarly glasses,
pouting mouth and the kind of slicked-down hair found in prep-school
yearbooks. Jimmy took pleasure in introducing this solemn-looking
innocent to prospective patrons as "an old bird who has knocked about
a good deal in Palestine and other places." Publicly, he always addressed Willie as "Parson" and pretended to censor racy smoking-room
talk in his presence. He teased the lad about Willie's voluptuous Italian
model: "Confess, Parson, have you outraged the poor girl?" And "How
are you going to explain this to the Pope?"

Privately, he and Trixie treated Willie like a son. They applauded his drawings (an early sitter was George Bernard Shaw), were among the first subscribers to his book of lithographs, and gave him a standing invitation to the Whistler dinners.


Scalpel-eyed as Rothenstein, startling in appearance as Beardsley, and more indebted to Jimmy than either was Henri, Count of Toulouse-Lautrec. Jimmy was on the Right Bank one April afternoon, sipping a Pernod with Mallarmé in the Cosmopolitan Bar, when Maurice Joyant, the Goupil Gallery manager who had arranged details of the *Mother* sale, came in. Trailing the heavy-set dealer was a dwarf-like creature of perhaps thirty who advanced with slow, halting steps, supported by a bamboo cane. Joyant introduced his boyhood friend, Toulouse-Lautrec. Jimmy saw a bulbous nose, thick red-rimmed lips framed by a wiry black beard, large dark eyes behind a velvet-ribboned pince-nez. The Count was not more than four and a half feet tall. Every detail of his dress was calculated to combat his deformity: close-cropped hair that minimized the disproportionate size of head to body, long jacket and baggy trousers to hide the shrunken waist, arrestingly handsome shirt and tie from one of the British shops on the Rue Saint-Honoré.

Scion of one of the most powerful houses in all Europe, Toulouse owed his tragedy to his noble lineage. His parents had been first cousins, brought together to keep the family fortunes intact; their son was a sickly child, with inbred deficiencies of the bone marrow. Twice in adolescence he had suffered bad falls, fracturing both legs which had thereafter ceased to grow.

Toulouse acknowledged Joyant's presentation in excellent English, speaking in a surprisingly resonant voice: "My pleasure, gentlemen. It is an honor to meet, at one stroke, two masters of tone in different arts."

"A valued tribute," returned Jimmy, "from one who can make claims to pre-eminence in a third field himself."

The Count would not be outgallantried. "If you refer to lithography, Mr. Whistler—I have seen your portrait of our friend Mr. Mallarmé here, and been properly struck dumb."

"Gentlemen, gentlemen!" cried Joyant. "Let us order drinks, before we suffocate each other!"

Toulouse twisted himself into a chair. The talk turned to his paintings in the 1892 Impressionist-Symbolist show, which Jimmy had been obliged to miss. "I would very much like Mr. Whistler to see my work." Jimmy felt the gaze of his fine, intelligent eyes. "But I am afraid my canvases have even shorter legs than I."

Jimmy picked up the cue. "Where is your studio?"

"At 19 bis Rue de Fontaine—directly across the court from Degas. A great convenience when I wish to steal."

"I shall be happy to come to you tomorrow."

Jimmy found Toulouse before an easel at 10:00 A.M., still wearing the dress clothes of the previous evening. The Count's stubby legs, not long enough to reach the floor, were hooked by the heels of his formal pumps onto the cross-bars of a stool. "I have not been to bed yet," Toulouse explained. "It bores me to go to bed alone. Besides, I have such delicious sketches to work from."

He held up several sheets alive with slashing pencil outlines: of a crowded ballroom floor, two brawling soldiers in a doorway, a bored dancer twirling a foot overhead in the successor to the cancan, the *quadrille naturaliste.*

"Where did you do these?"

Toulouse shrugged. "The Moulin Rouge. De Galette. I am the perennial tourist in Paris. The night life of the city exhilarates me." He did not have to add that, among the seamy denizens of after-dark Montmartre, his own aspect was less conspicuous.

Toulouse reached for his cane. "But I am being rude! I must offer you a morning eye-opener. Last night I learned two new American cocktails: the Prairie Oyster and the Love-Push. Ah, but I was a splendid pupil!" He hobbled over to a low makeshift bar littered with bottles.

Jimmy indicated it was too early for him to start drinking. However, to ease Toulouse's disappointment, he demonstrated the niceties of preparing a mint julep. The little Count was ecstatic: "Amazing, amazing!" (He sounded suspiciously like his visitor.) "Technique bartender, ha-ha!"

With remarkable energy for a cripple who had been up all night, Toulouse pulled out canvases from their hiding places. He stumped along beside Jimmy, keeping up a spirited line of chatter: "The painter of pure landscape is an ass. The figure alone exists." And he had painted the figure—in château gardens, dance halls, and circus rings—with unsentimental accuracy, and a power of dissection wittier than that of Degas if not quite so savage.

"I reject all schools," Toulouse volunteered. "I have traveled widely, and so been able to borrow from many sources. There are advantages to having a count's income. Technique annexation, ha-ha!"

Jimmy recognized a mélange of forces: the diagonals and strong rhythms of Japanese woodcuts, the light palette of the Impressionists, an oil-and-pastel medium probably derived from Degas, touches of crispness and decoration that might be attributed to Hals and Gauguin. And unmistakably superimposed on all these, an influence that could only be his own. Toulouse had taken much to heart the Whistler injunctions of "simplify, reduce, stylize, heighten"; his quietly ordered compositions were reinforced by careful color-harmony.

An early exterior, *Woman Sitting on Bench at Céleyran,* might have been signed with the Whistler butterfly. Still more allusive was a seated profile portrait, in restrained lines and muted tones, of the poet Georges-Henri Manuel. Jimmy examined it carefully, put down his monocle, and threw a Puckish glance at the other painter.

"I'm afraid I was young and impressionable," sighed Toulouse. "I had just seen your superb *Carlyle* at the Salon, after viewing the exquisite *Mother* the year before."

"I am flattered. You do not imitate; you strike your own note. The brushwork is quite distinctive."

"Ah, but that too is not entirely mine. The violent Vincent, you know. He and I used the same models in '86." But Toulouse glowed his pleasure. "You might say I am a thoroughbred pony, by Whistler and van Gogh out of Hokusai!"

A few months later, a new series of lithographed color posters by Toulouse were the sensation of Paris. He had changed his model from the voluptuous lesbian La Goulue (The Insatiable) of the Moulin Rouge to Jane Avril, featured dancer at the Jardin de Paris. Jane was a *fin de siècle* type: pale, pensive, angular, the out-of-wedlock daughter of an Italian nobleman and a French whore.

The new posters, cut clear of all superfluity, were fine specimens of Whistlerian "minimal art"—a genre that would later be vulgarized by people of minimal talent. Three autographed prints were delivered to the Rue du Bac with a gracious note from Toulouse.

The artist was invited to Trixie's next garden party. Afterward, Jimmy and Trixie sat under the trellis and talked. Jimmy conceded that the Count was not very pretty.

"And he drinks so much!"

"It's a miracle he doesn't run through the streets killing."

"The scandals they tell about him. From a family that was honored by Charlemagne."

"Little good that does the poor wretch today."

"Is it true that he lives in brothels—a Count?"

"Who has a better right? I dare say the conversation is livelier than at the family châteaux. Besides, he finds his subjects there. You don't suppose the Empress is going to rush to the poor man's studio? No, my dear: it isn't his drinking or his women that people really object to. It is his talent—and his courage! Most of them, with the same physical handicaps, would crawl off to a corner and die!" He gazed up at the vine-covered garden wall: "Imagine how lonely his childhood must have been—a puny little fellow growing up in a family of warriors."

Trixie wondered if he was talking only about Toulouse-Lautrec.

Jimmy's studio was at 86 Notre Dame des Champs ("Only the French," he often said, "have any taste in the naming of streets"), a huge skylight duplex at the top of six steep flights of highly polished, slippery stairs. Furnished in his usual scattering of old chairs, temperamental stove and battered sofa, it had a printing press, a balconied dressing room for models, and a planted terrace with a view that overlooked the Luxembourg Gardens and stretched northward to take in all of Paris. Trixie, who frequently worked there, heard a knock on the door one summer morning. She found Toulouse on the landing, bedraggled and perspired. "I—have—just climbed the Pyramids," he panted. "I hope the Pharaoh is here."

"Jimmy will be along directly. He had to stop at the printer's." She looked at the little man with something like maternal pity. "But you must be exhausted. Can I offer you some tea?"

Toulouse grimaced. "Too strong, keeps me awake. But if you had a cocktail—?"

Trixie checked the cabinet. "There's some brandy here. And a little absinthe."

"And of course some lemon? Good. I shall mix my own."

Jimmy arrived in a few minutes. He collapsed into a chair until he caught his breath. "Ah—good—morning, Toulouse. How do you like —my studio?"

"Splendid—if you don't get a heart attack walking up. Or pneumonia in winter. Why don't you move to the ground floor?"

"I will—when I die."

Toulouse, it developed, was planning to make some colored lithographic studies of Loie Fuller, an American dancer starring at the *Folies Bergères*. Loie's specialty was to stand in one spot on stage writhing sinuously as she manipulated a set of transparent veils; shifting hues from the footlights created intriguing patterns listed in the program as Fire, Butterfly, Serpent, and River.

The Frenchman was not concerned about capturing the colors; he had evolved his own methods of overlaying two or three primaries on the same stone. What he wanted was the Master's guidance in basic composition.

Jimmy, who had sketched the moving veils himself, bent over Toulouse's designs with him for several hours. The consultations were continued intermittently at Toulouse's studio, and finally at the apartment that the Count's mother had taken for him in the Rue Douai. Ultimately Toulouse published a series of sixteen prints, finished off in water color and gold powder. The first set, with an accompanying note of gratitude, went to his friend and mentor, James McNeill Whistler.

The mantle of Father Bountiful, alas, rested uneasily on Jimmy's shoulders. Trixie saw the signs of edginess creeping up. Her husband could not, she realized, be repainted with a once-over light glaze; like his own less successful portraits, he had absorbed too many haphazard and damaging early coats.

It was very possible that his success had come too late, that the legacy of private guilts and frustrations had congealed into a generalized anger that could only be sporadically appeased, never satisfied. Knowing his old fear-mingled starvation for love, she had given him more than she would have thought was in her; yet once again he seemed less concerned with love than with paying back his "enemies," avenging the years of helplessness.

The immediate cause of his grumbling was, ironically, the zooming prices of Whistler canvases. She had to admit he had reason for bitterness. Work long ago completed, and taken from his studio for paltry sums, was financing country homes and holiday sprees. Not only were handsome profits being raked in by "dull impertinent clods" who, as Jimmy saw it, "happen to own a Whistler"; even supposed friends, unable to resist the boom, were marketing canvases the artist had presented to them as gifts.

The *Princess from the Land of Porcelain,* which netted Jimmy 105 guineas, drew 420 at the sale of Frederick Leyland's effects in 1892. The *Lange Leizen,* bought for £80, was sold for 800; the *Battersea Bridge Nocturne* for which William Graham laid out £63 in 1886 had a post-Goupil value of £2000.

"Collectors, indeed," Jimmy stormed. "The main thing they are collecting is pounds sterling—for the product of *my* brain, *my* labors! Gerald Potter has just sold *The Blue Wave,* which cost him all of £50, for a cool thousand. Did he put any part of that sum on a cushion and bring it to me, kneeling and begging me to accept at last the value he would have given at the time had he been able to afford it? No!"

Jimmy had strong and personal views regarding the ownership of his creations. To him they were never commodities turned out for a market, but an intimate part of himself that he hated to part with. Often he would invent excuses—"the frame isn't right . . . let me print you a better proof"—to stall off delivery.

Yet, where he felt there was genuine appreciation, a love of beauty equal to his own, he might give away his work spontaneously. Money was never a consideration. Six shillings tendered with sympathy would shake him faster than cold guineas from a calculating dealer. Once, when a sitter had exhibited saintly patience through a long series of reworkings, he sent along with the commissioned portrait a valuable oil of a Chelsea child: "The man has been so nice, and he seemed so keen on that painting."

Most sales, made out of hard necessity and often through dealers, were to Jimmy an unavoidable evil. Since he felt no basic rapport with the buyers, a curious corollary followed: he did not in his heart regard such transactions as really binding. The unwary owner who "loaned" an old canvas to the artist for an exhibition, or "a week of freshening up," had a hard time getting it back. "These people!" Jimmy would fume at their complaints. "They think that just because they have paid some ridiculously small sum for the privilege of living with a masterpiece, they *own* it! Why, a Whistler would be out of place remaining on their walls; there is never anything else there to compare with it!"

The invasion of the art scene by American buyers complicated matters. Jimmy, rather than Sargent, was now *the* American painter; not to own a Whistler was to confess a gaucherie as embarrassing as the possession of one would have been a few years before. Jimmy's countrymen seemed determined to pour the gold of California into his lap; but their manner of going about it infuriated him. "They seem to think they are buying sides of beef, or chamber pots. 'Wrap it up,' they say, 'I'll take it!'"

A Croesus from Colorado came to the Notre Dame des Champs studio, glanced at the Nocturnes and Symphonies on the walls, and turned briskly to the painter. "How much for the lot?"

"Four million."

"*What?*"

"My posthumous prices," said Jimmy with equal briskness, and showed his visitor to the door.

On the one hand, he resented Yankee ignorance: "Heaven forbid that the Englishman's one undeniable superiority be challenged; but an Englishman is so honest in his stupidity that one loves him for the virtue, whereas the American is a smart aleck and therefore intolerable." On the other side, the surge of American buyers, imperfect though they might be, enabled him to indulge his far more longstanding Anglophobia.

In the 1890s, the British were still managing to irritate Jimmy regularly. They were looking the other way upon the death of Albert Moore—"the greatest artist," according to Jimmy, "that in the century England might have cared for and called her own." They had returned a letter addressed to Jimmy at the Royal Academy with the notation "Not Known Here," prompting him to boast sarcastically of "this final certificate of character." They had not even been able to handle a special French dinner he had ordered for Toulouse-Lautrec at the Café Royal.

To Major George Washington Whistler the subjects of the Crown had been merely untrustworthy, "the devious British." His son was far more categorical: "They beat their wives, neglect their poor, and boast about bathtubs they were obliged to bring in from the Orient. Their notion of art is a picture postcard of Westminster Abbey." The only thing in London that Jimmy admired, according to his Goupil Gallery agent Croal Thompson, was the way the Bobbies handled street traffic. Upon departing Cheyne Walk for Paris, Jimmy had asked Walter Sickert to find a suitable non-Briton to take over his house: "It would be deplorable to have built this gorgeous dining room for an English-man to sit and eat his beef in." Now he decided none of his pictures shoud go to English buyers or galleries. "Find a Scotsman," he told Thompson. "Or one of those filthy-rich culture hounds from New York."

He was angry at practically everybody. An etching dealer who after buying an enormous stack of prints asked Jimmy to sign a consular cer-tificate, was told: "My signature, sir, has value, and I refuse to put it on any such documents!" A duchess seeking his counsel on how to dispose of her expensive art collection got an abrupt answer: "Leave them to an asylum for the blind."

Jimmy was spoiling for a fight. Fate, usually obliging in such circum-stances, arranged two of them.

Sir William Eden was an exceedingly wealthy baronet from a family long active in the diplomatic service (his son Anthony was to succeed Winston Churchill as Prime Minister). Sir William bought paintings, and dabbled in water colors himself. But he never let his passion for the finer things run away with him; Walter Sickert, strapped for funds, had to part with three good oils to extract £20 from Eden.

Among the baronet's proudest possessions was a beautiful wife. Lady Eden had been painted by the leading Academicians; now her husband wanted a Whistler. But the thrifty baronet did not want to pay the 500 guineas that inquiry at the Goupil disclosed to be Jimmy's fee for an oil portrait.

Eden took his problem to the novelist George Moore, a mutual friend of his and the painter's. Approached by Moore, Jimmy agreed as a favor to do a small water color. The price was not fixed, but it was understood, in the loose manner of an arrangement among friends, that it would be between 100 and 150 guineas.

Lady Eden came to sit in January of 1894, and she was indeed a beauty; within an hour Jimmy knew he would not be content merely to sketch her in water color. He opted instead for a small but elegant oil.

The portrait went quickly; in a few weeks it was virtually done. On February 14—St. Valentine's Day—Sir William came to the studio to express his pleasure. With a great show of largesse, he handed an envelope to Jimmy: "For you, a pretty Valentine. Open it when I am gone."

Jimmy did—and found a check for 100 guineas, the rock-bottom minimum that had been mentioned for an expected little water color. He was incensed. He had taken great pains with the painting, had produced a work for which any gallery would have given 400 or 500 guineas—and had been paid off in what he considered shillings . . . with a fine show of fake generosity, no less!

He refused to turn over the portrait, all the more grimly when Eden offered to raise the fee to 150. The Baronet staggered up the six flights of stairs again to protest, and Jimmy slammed the studio door in his face. Eden retreated, howling threats of legal action all the way down. Jimmy poked out his head long enough to urge quiet upon the Briton, lest he "expose his nationality" by unseemly noise in a public place. Jimmy then calmly sent the picture to an exhibition in the Champ-de-Mars and deposited Eden's check, "as a Valentine."

This last gesture was clearly intended to provoke. Jimmy was inviting a trial of strength.

A trial was what he got, literally. Before a Civil Tribunal in Paris, Jimmy argued that a work of art, by its special nature, could not be treated like an ordinary commercial product; only the artist himself was qualified to judge when it was finished and should be delivered.

The court disagreed. Jimmy was ordered to give back Eden's money, pay 1000 francs damages and turn over the picture. He announced he would appeal.

At this point George Moore entered the argument—on Eden's side. In a letter to the *Chronicle,* he ridiculed Jimmy's claims and asserted that Lady Eden's face had been painted "about the size of a sixpence." Jimmy instantly and formally, through a pair of French seconds, challenged him to a duel.

There had been no serious combat-of-honor in England since 1852. Jimmy's qualifications as a marksman were dubious; on his one hunting expedition during a weekend at Speke Hall, his only hit had been on the tail of an understandably aggrieved pointer belonging to his host. Like the Russian generals of his Czarist boyhood, he liked parades but frowned on fighting because it "got everybody's uniform dirty." He was pleased to cite Sainte-Beuve, summoned to defend his honor on a rainy morning, who clung to an umbrella in his left hand: "I don't mind being shot—but I didn't come here to get wet." As for his own views, as he once told Mortimer Menpes: "I should hate to be standing opposite a man who was a better shot, far away out in the forest, in the bleak, cold, early morning. Fancy me, the Master, standing out in the open as a target to be shot at! Pshaw! It would be foolish and inartistic. I never mind calling a man out; but I always have the sense to know that he is not likely to come."

He had estimated his adversary accurately. Moore, languid and pale-mustached, a self-described terror on the amatory couch, was not anxious to extend his conquests to the dueling ground. He chivalrously declined to battle a man who was nearly twenty years his senior and nearsighted to boot. "I have praised Mr. Whistler's work for twenty-five years," he declared in mollifying tones. "I wish he would get back to it."

The odds were not good. Simultaneously with the Eden affair, Jimmy was embroiled with George du Maurier over *Trilby*. The erstwhile roommates had seen each other little through the years. Du Maurier had become a fixture at *Punch* as the caricaturist of leisure-class foibles; but his real ambition, abandoned only when he lost the sight of one eye in 1857, had been to make a name as a serious painter. His jealousy of the dashing Whistler had been encapsulated in a youthful letter to his mother: "People like me better. I am *plus sympathique*."

With the slow ascendance of Jimmy's star in the eighties, cartooned gibes at Harmonies and blue china began appearing in *Punch;* but the full extent of du Maurier's bitterness was not revealed until in 1894 he published *Trilby*, a novel about a Paris model who was mesmerized by the scabrous Svengali. Prominent among Trilby's art-student devotees was Joe Sibley, "the idle apprentice, king of bohemia." As depicted by du Maurier, Joe was of less than kingly character: "He had but one God, whose praises he was perpetually singing . . . Sibley. And he would hear no other genius in the world.

"Always in debt, like Svengali; vain, witty, and a most exquisite and original artist . . . genial, caressing, charming, the most irresistible friend in the world as long as his friendship lasted—but that was not forever.

"The moment his friendship left off, his enmity began at once. Sometimes this enmity would take the simple and straightforward form of trying to punch his ex-friend's head; and when the ex-friend was too big, he would get some new friend to help him. And much bad blood would be caused in this way—though very little was spilt. And this was not made better by the funny things he went on saying about the unlucky one who had managed to offend him—things that stuck forever! His bark was worse than his bite—he was better with his tongue than with his fists—a dangerous joker! But when he met another joker face to face, even an inferior joker—with a rougher wit, a coarser thrust, a louder laugh, a tougher hide—he would just collapse, like a pricked bladder!

"He is now perched on such a topping pinnacle (of fame and notoriety combined) that people can stare at him from two hemispheres at once."

The description of Jimmy-Joe (was there a hidden slap at Jo Heffernan here?) was rounded out by a pair of du Maurier drawings, one depicting the unmistakable Whistler curls, the other showing their owner fleeing in terror from a studio melee.

Du Maurier's not-so-playful satire appeared in the March 1894 issue of *Harper's Magazine*, which was serializing the book before publication. A copy was rushed to the Rue du Bac by a solicitous clubmate in London.

Once again Jimmy had solid initial grounds for distress. The problem lay, as with the Eden case, in the fanatical zeal of his reaction.

He fired off to the *Pall Mall Gazette* an answering blast against "that abomination, the friend," denouncing du Maurier's "pent-up envy and malice, the picric acid of thirty years' spite." But he didn't stop there. He demanded that everyone who knew both men should take sides: the Beefsteak Club must chose at once between victim and villain; mutual friends in the art world like Edward Poynter must henceforth cut du Maurier dead or forfeit all claims to Whistler's affection.

The club was spared a crisis when du Maurier, protesting that he had never been Jimmy's bosom companion, quit. The mutual friends were less obliging. "I like them both," averred Poynter.

Still steaming, Jimmy went to William Webb, a fussy little solicitor. He had visions of a colossal libel suit that would effectively kill the book if not its author. Webb, sniffing and peering over the top of his outsize spectacles, wasn't so sure.

Harper Brothers, who were also publishing the book, were willing only to make a public apology and to have the offending passages deleted or revised. Du Maurier spoke of a personal retraction, and went so far as to draft a letter to Jimmy, but never sent it. Jimmy had to settle for the conversion of the elegant silken-haired Joe Sibley to "bald Antony," colorless offspring of a respectable Swiss burgher. He rejoiced at the "humiliation" inflicted on the author in being forced to submit his copy for approval by Jimmy, but he kept pressing Webb for "my full pound of flesh" until advised there was no more to be had.

Later the magazine editor Comyns Carr, one of the crew who had been ordered to choose between the disputants, told Jimmy bluntly he had "made a mess" of the affair. Jimmy grew suddenly reflective: "Perhaps you are right."

There was no "perhaps" in Trixie's mind. And Jimmy seemed to be getting worse, turning his animus now against the French. Officialdom there, with the usual Gallic reserve toward foreigners, had acknowledged his presence and moved on to other things; no election to the sacrosanct French Academy was forthcoming. Nor were the young painters of the land salaaming before a man who, after all, stood aside from the mainstream of Impressionism. To crown Jimmy's vexation, he had been approached by friends of Willie Rothenstein for permission to have the celebrated poet Verlaine do some verses on his *White Girl*, now called the *Symphony in White, No. 1*; with much ceremony he had accepted "this apotheosis at the hands of a great poet"—and Verlaine had then decided to work from Rossetti's *Mona Rosa* instead. Soon afterward Jimmy had been inexplicably cold in a chance encounter with the unpretentious Fantin-Latour.

Trixie had nightmares of a Whistler war against the Third Republic. Her husband was a time bomb whose prime candidate for injury if he went off was himself.

She confronted him over dinner: "I don't know what to do with you, Jimmy. You're like a wicked little boy determined to get himself spanked. Just when you should be concentrating your energies on your art, you run about looking for trouble. Frankly, I'm discouraged. If you're going to give up on yourself—what's the use of my trying?"

Jimmy looked up from his *potage bonne femme*, blue-gray eyes troubled, teeth gnawing his lower lip. He said nothing, but he was clearly unhappy. After a long pause: "What do you want me to do, Bunny?"

"Be the great artist that God made you."

"I will, I will. Where shall I go?" He was like a penitent child.

"Well—you've always been happy at Dieppe."

"I'll go tomorrow morning."

History had imposed on Dieppe warriors and holiday-makers; nature had created it for painters. Even the slender harbor curving back from the English Channel was shaped in the form of a palette. Nestled between grassy bluffs topped by a fierce medieval château, the town lay in airy sunshine, softer and dreamier than Hastings across the water.

Behind the wide pebbled beach rose a wonderfully scenic jumble of fishing boats, church spires, and balconied storefronts; beyond a wooden footbridge sprawled the ancient Sailors' Quarter with its red-gabled rooftops and iron-arched, oddly elegant attic windows.

Dieppe was white sands, crowded with the parasols of the London-Paris society leaders who had been coming there since the Duchess of Berry launched pleasure-bathing in 1824. It was mineral baths, and a palatial Byzantine casino overlooking lawns laid out by the Empress Eugénie.

But above all Dieppe was sea and sky, an intoxicating mixture of filmy spray and iridescent light. Authors and composers—Dumas, Strindberg, Rossini, Debussy—were attracted to it; painters found it

irresistible. Constable and Turner had come, followed by Corot, Delacroix, and the Impressionists.

For Jimmy, the old port was as fresh to the eye in the spring of 1895
as it had been when he first saw it forty years earlier. He loved the
shifting moods of the sea: languorous in the soft morning light, saltily
bracing by night; and in between, especially after a late-afternoon
shower, afloat in a gray sky subtly penetrated by orange and violet
tints. If he had fumed in the past against "foolish sunsets," it was only
from annoyance with sentimentalists who, by swooning over every
show of gold on the horizon, debased the currency of beauty.

Unpacking his paints, he warmed up with water colors. From C. E.
Holloway, an English painter encountered at his printer's, he had absorbed the nuances of "bleeding" the fragile colors evenly across the
damped sheet. He breezed through several subjects: his *Flower Market* and *Sad Sea* were like silvery flute notes traced on paper.

Cautiously, he moved forward. Decades before, on the beach at
Trouville with Courbet, he had toyed with instant-seascapes in oil, but
found himself unable to keep pace with the scurrying winds. Now his
hand was as fast and sure as Courbet's. Why not combine the rich oil
medium with his etcher's drafting skills, arresting the moment in flight
on cigar-box-size wooden panels?

He had often and inaccurately been called an Impressionist; at
Dieppe he became one. But where Monet and Pissarro concerned
themselves with prismatic light, Jimmy remained in his own world of
geometric space effects and tonal harmonies.

His miniatures were miracles of compact expressiveness. Within an
8½ by 6 inch framework, he conveyed the grand reaches of atmospheric space. Brief dashes of paint produced a distant horizon, rolling
whitecaps, a sharp glimpse of character. Confining himself to a few
precisely graduated tones of gray or golden-brown, accented by a
bright note or two of positive color, he shaped "cabinet pictures" as
perfectly calculated and rhythmically organized as a Mozart chamber
quartet.

Jimmy returned to Paris with a stack of fine canvases, so keyed up
that he felt ready to resume portrait work. It would be nice to climax
his mature years with one crowning masterpiece, a flawless portrait
that would leave even the *Mother* and the *Carlyle* behind.

As if by Muse's command, his subject appeared in the garden of the
Rue du Bac: a meltingly wistful American girl named Louise Kinsella,
with ivory skin glowing against hair of midnight black. Nobody knew
who had brought her, but Jimmy didn't care. In his mind's eye he was
already recostuming her in a quiet ultramarine that would set off the
lustrous flesh tones.

And so he painted her in the studio at Notre Dame des Champs, seated on a sofa with a yellow iris in her hand. The serene, formal arrangement of line and the blending of muted colors recalled to Willie Rothenstein the altarpieces of the fifteenth-century painter-mathematician Piero della Francesca; the face and neck, according to an awed Toulouse-Lautrec, had "the golden tone of Titian."

Jimmy was in a state of euphoria. "It will be an exquisite ghost," he rhapsodized to Trixie. "Pathetic, but full of dignity. I have never painted better. And it is you, my darling Bunny, who are responsible. You have put me back on the right path."

"Now that you've found the path again, Jimmy, you must never lose it. Even if one day you have to travel it alone."

"What on earth are you talking about? Are you intimating that you have met some swaggering young lieutenant for whom you are throwing over your old Toiler?"

Trixie smiled her sunny southern smile and kissed him on the cheek. "There is no lieutenant as young or as brave as my Jimmy—when he wants to be."

Less than a week later, in the middle of the night, he found out what she had been talking about. Trixie was moaning, clutching her abdomen, in obvious pain. He filled a hot water bag, and the next morning took her to the doctor.

"Nervous exhaustion," was the brisk report. "Get her to the seashore."

The diagnosis was reassuring. After all, Trixie was only forty-one, a virtual stranger to illness. They went to Lyme Regis, a fishing village of thatch-roofed cottages in Dorsetshire on the rugged southwest coast. Here Trixie perked up in a few days, then decided she could rest more comfortably in the familiar surroundings of their Paris house. "But you must stay on and paint, darling. There'd be interruptions at home—and we can't have you lose your momentum."

Reluctantly, Jimmy agreed. Every morning at dawn found him trudging through the streets from the Red Lion Hotel; every evening he poured out his thoughts in long letters to Trixie. Perhaps from worry over her illness, he was in a new crisis of self-doubt. For a week he spoke of difficulties with the angle of the sun; but he was struggling on as she wished, he assured her, looking neither to right nor left.

His messages grew more fervent: he lived only for word that she was feeling better; he could never finish all the things he had to say to her. At last, he struck a cautiously cheerful note: despite the daily terror, and the fear of tomorrow that she knew all too well, he was making headway. He had done many lithos, and several excellent bust-size oils. He would match *Little Rose of Lyme Regis*, a portrait of a clear-eyed child in black pinafore and white collar, against anything out of Holland.

The letters that came back from Trixie—gallant but honest, in a hand now visibly faltering—were more than he could bear. He entrained for Paris, and took her to a professor of biology recommended by Duret. This time the report was not so reassuring: "All I can tell you, Mr. Whistler, is that it is an internal ailment, and it is serious." The professor recommended immediate hospitalization.

Jimmy refused to believe him. "These graybeards. Fattening on forecasts of doom. We shall go to London, darling. Brother Willie the magician will have you dancing again in a week."

But Willie did not. Nor could his colleagues at the hospital. Jimmy and Trixie took a suite high in the newly built Savoy Hotel on the Strand overlooking the Thames to await the arrival of a specialist commandeered from Berlin. Nobody said, but everybody heard, the terrible word: cancer.

Jimmy did not leave Trixie by day or night. Lines appeared in his face; graying curls straggled down his neck unattended. Medals were forwarded to the hotel: from Venice, Antwerp, Philadelphia; they sat in their boxes unopened. But Jimmy insisted everything would work out: "No ailment can resist a German doctor's 'Heraus!'—it wouldn't dare! You'll see: by spring we'll be on a holiday steamer bound for America."

"My darling Jimmy—you are Whistlering in the dark."

The German specialist was sidetracked to Versailles for a ducal emergency. "Well," joked Trixie, "he's getting closer." Meanwhile, she urged Jimmy to get back to his art: "The worst thing about this beastly illness is what it's doing to your work."

"Do you expect me to set up an easel in the pantry?"

"No—but you could do some lithographs, right from the window. The bridges, and the pigeons along the Embankment. There are pictures from every angle."

Jimmy faced her, his lips twitching miserably. "Pigeons? Is that what you want of me, Rabbit?"

"That is what I want of you."

He nodded. Once embarked on work, he lost himself in it as if welcoming the outlet. For six days and nights he sketched, rubbed in his shadows with a thick leather stump, tried a thin grainless paper suggested by Toulouse-Lautrec, and lithographic ink instead of the usual crayon.

Already, in his portrait of Mallarmé and his studies of the Thames, he had elevated lithography to much more than a means of mass reproduction. The slim new Savoy Series was his finest: filigree-light street scenes, a haunting impression of Waterloo Bridge, and the promised pigeons, fluttering along the eaves of the hotel.

But most moving by far was a portrait of Trixie in bed. Clearly exhausted, she sank backward among the sheets, head propped up by a pillow, left hand dangling limply toward the floor. An abandoned book lay open on the covers. In her eyes was a suggestion of patience . . . and resignation.

Jimmy ordered only twenty prints: "This is not for any publishers, but for ourselves." He called the lithograph *The Siesta*. The work itself eschewed any such euphemisms. It was the portrait of a beloved wife dying.

The German doctor arrived at last, but it was an anticlimax. He too had no formulas. In April of 1896, Jimmy rented St. Jude's Cottage in Hempstead Heath from a local clergyman. Walter Sickert had a brief note: *We are very, very bad.* Later in the month Jimmy was seen at the apothecary's distraught and unshaven, wearing one brown shoe and one black.

On May 10, the neighboring cotton merchant encountered Jimmy running wildly across the heath, hair flying, eyes bright with horror: "Don't speak, don't speak—it is too terrible!"

Trixie was gone; and with her, half of Jimmy.

# Chapter Thirty-one

Jimmy returned alone to the Rue du Bac, where every vase and rose-bush held memories of Trixie. He was rudderless, frightened; she had been the balm that healed his cracked-down-the-middle personal world and held the pieces together. "I am finally *toujours seul*," he wrote to Mallarmé, "alone as must have been Edgar Poe to whom you have found a certain resemblance on my part."

His circle of colleagues was narrowing. That same summer, Frederick Leighton had died, then John Everett Millais. George Boughton suggested that, under other circumstances, Jimmy might have succeeded either as President of the R.A. Jimmy was so subdued he could only murmur, "Who knows?"

His son Charles, "little Charlie" of the Venice letters, having been faithfully supported by Jimmy over the years and shepherded through college, was a grown man with an engineering degree and a wife of his own. Jo had vanished, a middle-aged housekeeper, into the mists of Buckinghamshire. How long could he himself fend off his old enemy, Time?

With a touch of the old defiance, he tried again. He pomaded his hair, brightened up when complimented on his erect carriage—"There's a West Point figure for you"—struggled with his face before the mirror like a fading matinee idol. To a tourist from Lowell, Massachusetts, who beamed, "We were born in the same month; that makes you sixty-three," he retorted: "I beg to differ. You be what you wish. I will not be sixty-three till I choose to."

He snorted his disgust at a portrait painted of him by Giovanni Boldini. The Italian virtuoso depicted him as a ravaged but superb old boulevardier in evening dress, a figure of diabolic intensity with marble-hard eyes, sharply cocked brows and a bitter subtle mouth. In a curious paraphrase of the detested Oscar's *Dorian Gray*, it was as if the torments and anguish of his past years had been transmuted not to inert canvas, but to his underlying nerve structure, and were at long last erupting to the surface. Standing before the canvas, Jimmy grimaced: "They tell me it is very like me, but, thank God, I am not like it!"

Yet it was with Boldini and the American couple Joseph and Elizabeth Pennell that he went to Dieppe. Pennell was an American graphic artist and critic, originally sent to London by *Harper's Magazine*, now anxious to write Jimmy's biography. At the beach, Jimmy momentarily recaptured the old Whistler spirit of fun, gravely intimating to the staff of the ultrafashionable Hôtel Royal that the bicycle-skirted Mrs. Pennell was a princess traveling incognito. In the dining room, he told an Englishman struggling with the menu, "I'm afraid, sir, you have just ordered a broiled staircase." But the light mood vanished abruptly with the news that Aubrey Beardsley lay in a nearby villa, dying.

Back in Paris, Jimmy spent most of his evenings reminiscing for the Pennells. Most of his tales were coated with a "one last skin" that concealed as much as it revealed. After a lifetime of covering up his heartbreaks, he had no intention of parading them before the world. He had even toyed with doing his own biography, before deciding the worshipful Pennells could be entrusted to record the Whistler gospel according to St. James.

Walking home along the Boulevard Raspail one evening, Jimmy found himself at the intersection with Boulevard Montparnasse. Without conscious purpose, he shifted direction southeast toward the *Observatoire*. He turned left at the sloping Rue Paul Sejourné, and made a sharp right at the first corner into Notre Dame des Champs. There, massive in the shadows opposite the Rue Joseph Bara, stood No. 86.

He climbed the dim stairs, resting at the third floor landing where an old sofa squatted under the flickering gas jet. On the top floor his studio was black, the moon above his skylight blotted out by dark clouds. He groped along the wall, found a candle, struck a match. Grotesque shadows leaped up toward the overhead balcony, danced among the neatly stacked canvases facing the walls.

Now he knew why he had come. For two hours he had been prattling confidently to the Pennells of his "scientific technique" in portraiture, as if it were an infallible approach that solved all problems. How sure, in fact, was his grasp? What had he really achieved?

Holding his candle aloft, he turned the nearest canvas around. It was a full-length study, in gold and gray, of a handsomely dressed young boy. He lowered his light, moving it slowly along the surface of the picture, peering so closely that his nose almost touched the paint.

Below the left knee, the picture stopped abruptly. The yellow straw hat, likewise, had no brim. He had abandoned the portrait a week after starting it.

Hands shaking, he lifted another from the stack, then two more. Abortive specters all: confidently begun, angrily scraped out; resumed, only to be cast aside in despair forever.

"Scientific technique," indeed! He was in a graveyard of failures, surrounded by cloth-and-pigment tombstones. How many times, especially on the big canvases, had he known frustration; how rarely the lightning-strike of success!

Ah, but when his methods did work . . . He looked over toward the darkened window, where the *Louise Kinsella* rested patiently on its easel, awaiting the day when he would take up a normal schedule again. This painting, properly finished, would redeem everything, define his status for all eternity. Should he permit himself just a peek, a restorative-from-dismay? No, there was not enough light. Patience; it would really be better to . . .

So he carried the candle, trailed by its restless, eerie shadows, across to the portrait and looked. Ah, she was exquisite indeed! The colors were alive, the modeling a challenge to the Renaissance.

Except—always the damnable "except"—the left hand. It was the portraitist Helleu who had first noticed it. The fellow might be a slick, empty technician but he was right. Somewhere, perhaps in the curve of the wrist, the values were awry. He could let the flaw go—it was really minuscule—yet, if he could overcome this last obstacle, it would settle permanently, for himself as well as others, the issue of his capacity to handle anatomical detail. Tomorrow, definitely, he would attack the problem.

But he could not walk away from the easel; the hand kept pulling him back. Oh, very well—he had nowhere to go, no one waiting for him; why not?

He lighted a second candle, took off his jacket, rolled up his sleeves. His glasses were in the cupboard drawer, his prepared tones on the table palette.

The difficulty, he decided, was in the blue shadows around the thumb. Perhaps if he warmed them up with a touch of neutralizing orange, slightly tinted . . .

He mixed his colors in the semi-dark, applied them carefully. No; he shook his head. That wasn't right.

Another, hastier slash. Worse still.

Staring in the gloom, weary, miserable, he was assailed by a wave of doubt. Maybe the trouble was somewhere else. How could he be sure the *neck* was really right? He could have been deceiving himself, and his friends applauding out of kindness . . .

With a quick, frantic gesture he picked up a rag, soaked it in turpentine, and started scrubbing. The neck disappeared. Should he wipe out the bust, too? Why not? It was his own maxim that if any segment was wrong, a picture should be repainted from top to bottom. He continued savagely until the canvas was reduced to a butcher's block of disconnected shapes: head, lower torso and limbs, sofa. Like a compulsive gambler who refuses to quit when he is ahead, he had returned for "one last killing"—and killed his finest canvas.

Trembling, Jimmy stumbled back and sank into a chair. What had he done? Why had he done it? He needed Trixie to tell him, and she wasn't there.

Jimmy's breezy air had always been a façade; only Whistler canvases hung in the Rue du Bac, because to open the doors on masterpieces of the past might sweep away his faith in himself. Now, with the full realization of his nakedness without Trixie, almost overnight he disintegrated. He was inconsolable widower one moment, sadistic schoolboy the next. There were flashes of his father's warm generosity, and Anna Whistler's stubborn strength. But mostly he was the bitter lonely knight, unhorsed and unforgiving, cleaving the air furiously with a poison-tipped lance.

His single consistency was fear. As after the debacle with Jo in 1866, he retired to his castle and pulled up the drawbridge behind him. Only a few allies and retainers were allowed to cross: Mallarmé, Duret, the Pennells, and the publisher William Heinemann, in whose Whitehall Court flat he often stayed during shuttlings to London. Steward of his household was his ward and heiress, Trixie's slim virginal younger sister, Rosalind Birnie Philip.

Without a sense of center or continuity, he brandished his spear and waited for the terror to strike. Twenty years before, at the Ruskin trial, Jimmy had been berated by the judge for being "thin-skinned." Now he had no skin left at all: only antennae aquiver to record injury. He saw goblins behind every tree; winced before an enemy blow landed, and felt some that were never thrown.

In this state of near-hysteria, his sole release from tension was in counteroutbursts of malice. He had the cruelty of the desperately hurt. Hearing of the death aboard ship of William Stott, the ex-Follower who had sided with Maud Franklin in 1887, he rasped: "Stott died at sea—where he always was!"

Trixie had once forecast half-seriously that if she preceded Jimmy to the grave, he would soon be without a friend. And few indeed could withstand the strains imposed by his obsession of beleaguerment. When Sidney Starr, a long-time admirer, urged him to accept the belated capitulation of the Royal Academy and send pictures to a Loan Exhibition at Burlington House, he exploded with rage. Starr had unpardonably "gone over to the enemy." A friendship of twenty years' standing was wiped out.

The Pennells poured fuel on the flames. Jealous of earlier Whistler disciples, Joseph Pennell haled Walter Sickert into court for publicly questioning the Whistler-Pennell technique of using transfer paper in lithography. Sickert enlisted Willie Rothenstein, and Pennell riposted with Jimmy in the ensuing wrangle, which subsided abruptly when Walter confessed his mischievous intent and paid a fine.

However, the quarrel picked up again with redoubled fury as the result of a new judgment in the Eden case. This time the highest appeals court in France reversed the original verdict, and upheld Jimmy's claim that an artist alone could determine when he was ready to part with a picture. Jimmy did not have to deliver the portrait of Lady Eden, the tribunal ruled, so long as he effaced her features and returned his fee—both of which he had already offered to do. Furthermore, Sir William was ordered to pay the considerable costs of the appeal.

It was a resounding defeat for the Baronet; but Jimmy wanted more. The world must be told of this Whistler amendment to the Napoleonic code. Why not, he demanded of Heinemann, flood France, Germany, and the United States with a reprint of the French Attorney General's admirable summation? "Take my word for it; the first duty of a good general when he has won his battle is to say so. The people, always dull—especially the Briton—fail otherwise to understand. Victory is not complete until the wounded are looked after, and the dead counted."

He intended to make sure that Sir William was very dead. Again he invoked the *Trilby* decree: no friend of Whistler should henceforth have any dealings with the Baronet.

This was a tactic manifestly doomed. The New English Art Club, to which Eden belonged, was loaded with ex-Followers; Sickert and Rothenstein were two of many. More importantly, the Baronet was a frequent patron of his non-millionaire clubmates. The first crisis arose when Willie Rothenstein served on a jury that accepted one of Eden's drawings.

Shortly afterward, Sir William decided to put part of his collection on the block at Christie's. Sickert, Rothenstein, Wilson Steer, and Charles Conder hastened to the auction house in King Street to discuss the question of putting small reserves on their paintings; and there Jimmy, strolling through with Heinemann, came upon the group of Whistlerites clustered around Eden. Jimmy put up his monocle and turned on his heel. "Sickert's mistake," he snapped, "is that he began life as an actor. On the stage there is always an exit; now Walter is going to find out there is no exit." A final blast against the other "deserters" was reserved for a Whistler pamphlet summarizing the Eden case, *The Baronet and the Butterfly*.

During the same period, Jimmy managed also to break with his lithographic printer of eighteen years, Thomas Way. Ostensibly he was dissatisfied with a catalogue; actually he thought the Ways had taken advantage of his 1879 bankruptcy to pick up valuable paintings.

His Anglophobia was quite out of control, part of a general negativism that threatened to engulf him. As he once said of the hapless R.S.B.A., Jimmy was plunging madly downhill and out of sight.

Yet it was an Englishman who restored him to reality. Charles Edward Holloway, a veteran water colorist, had been exceedingly kind a few years before in sharing his technical expertise with the far better-known American. Gentle and ample-bellied, a Papa Haydn of the art world, Holloway had been painted by Jimmy early in 1896 as *The Philosopher: Rose and Brown.* The 8¾ by 5½ inch wooden panel, richer in feeling and detail than many a monumental canvas, was snapped up by the Countess of Bearn.

Now Holloway was in trouble. In his quiet, unhurried way the big man had for years been soaking up more brandy than was good for either his painting or his liver. He had at long last, through Jimmy's good offices, been offered prominent space at the Goupil Gallery, but he was too weak to finish his work for the exhibition—or, indeed, to move from his bed.

It was Jimmy—the irascible, impossible Whistler—who came to his rescue. Even in his most rattlesnake humors, Jimmy could not turn his back on a vulnerability akin to his own; during the blackest days of poverty in Lindsey Row, he had sheltered a helpless drug-addicted designer. Now, in Holloway's moment of need, the external Whistler who moved like an overwound clock through a series of dreary alarms gave way to the faithful friend. Every afternoon he brought specially prepared food to the shabby little studio in Fitzroy Square. He paid the coal bills and hired a nurse to aid the invalid's distraught sister.

The doctor said it was a corroded liver, and almost certainly terminal. Jimmy had Holloway removed to a private hospital. Late that afternoon the sick man, who could barely speak, beckoned Jimmy closer. "Oh, for one long day's painting," he whispered. "An artist should only paint, Jimmy. Not drink, not quarrel . . . There is enough work for any man's lifetime." He turned his head weakly toward the bureau, where *The Philosopher,* borrowed from its purchaser, rested against a flowerpot. "You—you are a painter for the ages, Jimmy."

"Ha-ha. At the Academy, they think life-size means six-foot-three. But an artist can render life on a postage stamp."

"Not all artists. A Whistler. You must not stop for anything or anyone, Jimmy—not even yourself."

Later that week, the Goupil show opened, and Holloway's Venetian water colors went on display. The Princess Louise was impressed; so was the new critic of the London *Times*. Yes, he would definitely write a review—tomorrow.

During the night, the artist died. Jimmy organized a sale of paintings by colleagues to aid his friend's family, and contributed the first two canvases himself.

Something had happened during that twilight conversation with the dying Holloway; Jimmy wanted to paint again. "I realize it now," he told Mallarmé. "One must work or die—like the old cart horse that was able to keep going in the traces, but if set free would instantly drop." But he would do only what gave him pleasure, and was not too taxing. He took a spacious studio in Fitzroy Square, not far from William Heinemann's flat, and started painting the waifs of Soho.

Jimmy felt at home with children. Like the poodle he brought back from Venice, and the kitten that was to be the companion of his last days, they touched off no tremors in his suspicious nature. As Walter Sickert said, "To men he was a coxcomb; to women, a witty enigma. But to children, to whom almost alone he showed his heart, he was a beloved friend."

He painted charming innocents: sad-eyed, long-haired Lily Pamington of *The Little Green Cap*, and Croal Thompson's daughter Evelyn, who always came flying down the path at Highgate to meet him, face uplifted to be kissed.

Then he found Eva Carrington, a cheeky fifteen-year-old, sipping whisky in a Soho alley, and embarked on a far more sophisticated series. Here his models were adolescents, his medium lithography or colored pastels, and his manner a throwback to the lightly draped neo-Greek maidens of Albert Moore.

Jimmy had never shared the English distaste for the unclad human body. Once asked at the Grosvenor whether he did not consider a nude there "indecent," he shot back, "No, but your question is!" The child-women of his new pastels were not naked, but disported their slender figures under flimsy draperies or carelessly flung veils . . . and were all the more provocative for it. Like the terra cotta figurines of ancient Athens, his London street girls and Quartier models were delicious nymphs. At once chaste and seductive, they had a perverse sensuality.

What drew him back to a last fling at big canvases was a handful of wealthy Americans. With the passing years, his nostalgia for his homeland had increased, quickened by the realization that Sargent and Abbey—but not Whistler—were busy executing their murals at the Boston Library. He sought out word of West Point, shuddering appropriately at news that football had been introduced there—"Imagine, a U. S. Army officer being rolled in the mud by a Harvard junior!"; and although he put up a show of annoyance at shipping a Chicagoan's portrait to "Hog Town," his heart wasn't in it. If he could not return to the land of his origins himself, he wanted his pictures to.

Charles L. Freer heartily agreed. Freer was a Detroit manufacturer of railroad cars, a fastidious bachelor in his early forties who after discovering Whistler and the art of the Orient invested his millions in little else. Starting in 1894 and gradually increasing his purchases, he wound up collecting some nine hundred of Jimmy's works in all media, and topped things off by bringing over the Peacock Room to America intact.

Another patron-friend was George Vanderbilt, from whose yacht Jimmy watched the Diamond Jubilee Naval Review in 1897. But Jimmy Whistler could never subsist on tycoons and Vanderbilts. Americans were titillated to read that the famous painter was dining regularly with the notorious Richard Canfield, scourge of moralists along the Eastern seaboard, semi-fugitive from New York District Attorney William Travers Jerome. Canfield, suave and clean-shaven, with ruddy good looks, ran the most prosperous faro and roulette house in Manhattan, and had been accused of questionable friendships with other people's wives.

Because his American backers wanted him to, Jimmy painted them. His somber full-length of Vanderbilt in particular, a "modern Philip" in riding habit, started out brilliantly. But he no longer had the emotional resilience for these drawn-out, exacting tasks; in every case, worried and inconfident, he fussed too long and ruined the canvas. Only with two self-portraits, where he had no outsider to please, was he more successful.

Re-Americanization brought two literary countrymen across Jimmy's path. Henry James, the Bostonian novelist-critic, was an imposing specimen of human architecture, stately as a club in the Pall Mall. A fancier of nuances, James was, after some early reservations, now firmly in the Whistler camp.

Jimmy, however, had only half a foot in the author's. Admittedly, Henry James turned a fine phrase. The trouble was, he kept turning it and turning it, wearing out listener and reader alike. As Jimmy complained to William Heinemann, "He'll drag a delicate little episode through his pages till it collapses of exhaustion."

"Quite. The best of wine loses its flavor if it's poured through too small a spigot."

"You're right. And it's James to a—drop."

If Henry James was the quintessential paleface of American letters, the lively redskin was Mark Twain. This most picturesque of mavericks, having accumulated mighty debts through horrendous investments, was making a weary turn-of-the-century circuit of the world's lecture platforms. Soon after he arrived in London, Jimmy met him at dinner and invited him to the Fitzroy Square studio. They were Southerners and wits together, celebrities, only a year apart in age.

Twain shuffled through the door and headed straight for the portrait of George Vanderbilt on the easel, index finger extended.

"Don't touch it!" Jimmy screamed. "It's still wet!"

The great white mane turned toward him. "That's all right—I'm wearing gloves."

Twain, accepting a cigar and a nip of Bourbon, allowed in his hoarse whisky-vat voice that as a "visiting yokel" he would like the grand tour. A famous scoffer at serious painting, he lingered only before Jimmy's two self-portraits. The larger depicted a slender wraith-like figure, monocle gleaming in the dim face, floating in the shadows as if undecided whether to materialize more fully or vanish altogether.

The humorist stood longer before the second, half-length canvas. It was quite as unsparing as the portrait of Jimmy done by Boldini, but much more complex, sliding sinuously beneath the surface to capture the oscillation between anger and compassion, sorrow and mocking laughter. The ironic tilt of the head, with its Cheshire-cat ghost of a smile; the scraggly wheelbarrow mustache—one could almost see the hand pass over it, ruefully stroking; the Oriental squint of the eyes, half-closed and inscrutable; all conspired to a portrait that conveyed the mature perspective of a much-lived life, and many stages experienced en route.

"Remarkable," said the writer at last. "You have caught me to a T."

"A Mark T., I trust."

"But I don't recall sitting to you."

There was logic to the humorist's fancy. The Twain-Whistler resemblance was not so much in detail—although the thin agile figure, tumbled locks, drooping mustache and virile neck offered a case there—as in the steel-edged sharpness of the glance: knowing, sardonic, beyond illusion or disillusion.

The combination of Holloway's misfortune, his own need to work and the stimulus of the American contingent overseas had brought Jimmy at least half way out of his shell. That was enough to put him within reach of the school and the art fraternity that were the last formal associations of his life.

The Académie Carmen came into being in 1898 because the anti-sentimentalist Whistler was sentimental. Three decades earlier, Carmen Rossi had sat to him often as a round-eyed, ragged street gamin of Montparnasse. Now she was a young woman with serious responsibilities. As Jimmy saw it, "Poor little Carmen, who is a mere child and has no money, is saddled with the usual Italian burden of a large, disreputable family: banditti brothers, a trifling husband, and all the rest of it." That "poor little Carmen" had grown to just under six feet, weighed 190 opulent pounds, and had a Howellian habit of "borrowing" canvases from his studio, was irrelevant.

Carmen wanted to open a painting school with Jimmy as visiting maestro. His name, she declared, would be her salvation. Jimmy hesitated. He believed in the Renaissance tradition of apprenticeships; and he preferred "rash youth," as he once said, to "timid senility." But all his life he had jeered at art professors and academic painting. "My dear Carmen, if it were anybody but you—"

Before he could change his mind, she rushed out and rented a large duplex studio in the Passage Stanislas, a paved-over meandering country lane that swung in a buttonhook curve between the Boulevard Raspail and Notre Dame des Champs. Jimmy installed a superb carved-oak staircase salvaged from a château in Provence, and his protégée announced she was open for business.

Although her tuition fees were twice the average, Carmen was flooded with applications. As the special idol of lady *artistes* from Boston and Philadelphia, Jimmy had a trail of admirers on his every stroll through the *Quartier*. Carmen accepted forty pupils of assorted background and slammed her doors.

Jimmy came once or twice a week, as the impulse moved him; and every visit had the excitement of a royal review. First intimation of Jimmy's approach would come from the Italian attendant, Tordo, posted at the head of the Passage. At his frantic hand signal, Carmen would pull in her head from the window. Her wooden shoes clattered up the stairs. "Ladies! Gentlemen! The Master is coming!"

Coiffures and palettes were hastily tidied; Jimmy always went to the ladies' floor first. The men waited, stiff as tin soldiers, for the dainty tap of the Master's feet ascending. A nervous monitor appeared: "Gentlemen, Mr. Whistler."

Curtains were brushed aside, and the small spare figure appeared on the landing, covered head to foot in black: towering straight-brimmed topper, long fur-lined coat buttoned down to the ankles, black gloves, and cane. The only notes of color came from the red Legion rosette and the slight flush of withered cheeks.

After a ceremonial exchange of greetings, Jimmy began his rounds. Usually his comments were brief: "Too dark, there"—"Try a bit more green." Occasionally he touched in a stroke, commenting, "Have you noticed how tenderly a musician cares for his violin? Your instrument is the palette. Its colors are your notes; on it you play your symphonies." He made no attempt to teach the rudiments of drawing. Those who had a personal vision would acquire technique; with the others it didn't matter.

One of his star pupils was Gwen John, later Rodin's model. Gwen's brother Augustus, himself destined for fame as an artist, commented to Jimmy on his sister's fine grasp of character.

"Character? What's that? It's the tone that matters. Your sister has a fine sense of tone."

He was Whistler, so he could be harsh with the bumptious. A cocky student from Stuttgart, grinning his self-satisfaction, stepped back from his canvas. "What do you think, Mr. Whistler?"

Jimmy adjusted his monocle. "I find nothing in it to remind me of the model."

"I paint things as I see them. Is that wrong?"

"I know of no statute. The dreadful moment will come when you *see* things as you have painted them."

But because he was Whistler, there were moments of unexpected gentleness. Standing behind a youth gazing wretchedly at a botched-up portrait, he murmured only "It's a long, long road." And a French girl, shivering in the drafty studio, found a shawl and a pair of warm gloves waiting for her at home. Jimmy's note to Carmen said he had "chanced upon these in the house, and I thought they would suit her."

With impoverished male students he was more direct. He never dropped in at a studio without leaving a 100-franc note on the table: "This is for paints."

Even before his R.S.B.A. days, Jimmy had preached that art should be international, and artists present their own public exhibitions. Both principles were embodied in the International Society of Sculptors, Painters and Engravers, founded in 1898 by a group of latter-day Followers from the New English Art Club and the Glasgow School. Jimmy was, without debate, elected president. Prime movers in the new body were John Lavery, Sir James Guthrie, Willie Rothenstein (some Whistler storms passed quickly, like tropical hurricanes), and the master-sculptor Auguste Rodin.

The first Society exhibition, spread out over five galleries in the mammoth skating rink at Knightsbridge, included paintings by Renoir, Cézanne, Whistler, Alfred Stevens, Pissarro, Sisley, Manet, Monet, and Toulouse-Lautrec, along with considerable sculpture and a memorial section devoted to Aubrey Beardsley. Although no bonanza financially, it was followed by showings in Paris, Budapest, Munich, and several American cities.

Jimmy kept a tight rein on proceedings: "Napoleon and I do these things." His first meeting with his fellow-autocrat Rodin, who succeeded him as president in 1903, was typically touchy on both sides. They breakfasted together at Notre Dame des Champs: blunt earnest peasant-artist with his thick-tufted head and square, powerful hands, and nimble-tongued Butterfly. Rodin was offended by the gramophone that Jimmy kept going at full blast through their talk; Jimmy was miffed by the sculptor's failure to ask for a look at the paintings neatly stacked facing the wall: "Not that I *wanted* to show him anything— but it seemed a lack of, well, what West Point would have demanded under the circumstances."

Luncheon at the home of their mutual friend, the sculptor Drouet, went better. Rodin expounded on the "justness and truth" of Jimmy's work, traceable in part, he felt, to the painter's study of Greek statuary. "You are also," he added, "an absolute inventor in the realm of color."

The three then repaired to Rodin's studio in the Rue de l'Université, where a group marble just executed for the Argentine Republic drew equally gratifying praise from the Society president.

Although the Society was making important gains all over Europe, Jimmy had not yet been able to enlist the one man he wanted most, his nominee for the greatest and truly great French painter of the century: Degas. Never too approachable, Degas had not been cordial since their last meeting at Maxim's.

The Frenchman was in a crisis of his own, over the Dreyfus affair. Arch-Catholic, royalist, militarist in his sympathies, Degas had taken a violently hostile position toward the Alsatian-Jewish captain on the General Staff accused of betraying secret documents to the Germans. Although evidence exonerating Alfred Dreyfus had been piling up since the case began in 1894, and the government had retreated to the point of issuing a pardon, Degas's attitude had merely hardened. He had broken with Claude Monet and then with Émile Zola, who went to jail for his pro-Dreyfus pamphlet *J'accuse.*

Jimmy, as a foreigner in a country that was being split in half by the dispute, tried to stay out of it. He was essentially indifferent both to politics and to religious dogma. His experience of Jews was limited: Whitechapel bill-collectors had irritated him in the White House days, but Murray Marks and the critic Malcolm Salaman had been among his earliest and strongest supporters; Willie Rothenstein was still protégé and intimate. On the other hand, as a West Pointer from a family of soldiers, his instinct was to close ranks with the officer class. He agreed with his artist friends that persecution of a man on anti-Semitic grounds was indefensible; but he felt that the French Army should not be driven relentlessly to the wall lest confidence in the nation's protectors be undermined. It was an equivocal position that he felt would not satisfy Degas.

He consulted Mallarmé. "Edgar is a man suffering two blindnesses," the poet told him. "And the spiritual one is more crippling than his failing eyesight. But he is still a great painter; his work rises above his prejudices. And he is very fond of you." Mallarmé saw the thick eyebrows go up. "Ah, I wish you could have heard him at dinner last year, swooning over the *Mother*. Yes, Degas. And when George Moore tried to tone him down with tales of Whistler 'arrogance,' the way he replied: *'Rien ne peut me débrouiller avec Whistler.'* Yes, you must get in touch with him by all means. When he returns from the sea-shore, I shall arrange something."

A month later, in September 1898, Mallarmé was dead at Fontaine-bleau. His sudden passing shook Jimmy deeply; Paris without Trixie or Stéphane was a city of ghosts. He forgot about Degas until the following year, when Madame Mallarmé held a memorial evening for her late husband. The first person he saw on entering, huddled by the fire-place, was Degas. In response to his greeting, Degas blinked feebly. "Ah, Whistler—it's you!" A pause, then, truculently: "I hear you've been defending that Jew!"

Jimmy remembered Mallarmé's warning. "Too busy for politics, my dear Degas. Our International Society is organizing a brilliant new show."

"Ha! One more brothel for the public edification!"

"I would agree many shows have been just that. But for the first time in history the artists themselves are in control. No meddling middle-men."

"Bah. You talk in visions. Joan of Arc with a brush."

"We are *creating* visions. But we need you, Degas. We are incomplete without you."

Grumbling, Degas agreed to talk about it further the next morning at his studio. "But no promises, mind you!"

At 9 o'clock, Jimmy was at his door on the Rue Victor Massé opposite the Bal Tabarin. Degas, shuffling about in an old robe, was in better humor. He agreed they should have been seeing more of each other. "But with people who understand, a look, a grunt is enough . . ."

He took Jimmy up to the studio on the third floor, where two canvases were displayed on easels. "I entrust these to your exhibition," he said abruptly. "And myself to you. Now come below, and I will show you what I have saved from the hands of the millionaire tourists."

Jimmy followed him down one flight into a huge room crowded with easels. On every one sat a superb painting, the personal choice of his host. Ingres was solidly represented, along with Daumier, Delacroix, and Corot. There were prints by Hiroshige and Hokusai, flanked by Pissarros, a Monet, a Gauguin.

Jimmy raised his monocle at a trio of small, exquisite seascapes. "Bless me, these are very nice!" He bent over the nearest, and confirmed the presence in a corner of a tiny pink signature Butterfly. Quite speechless, he turned to Degas.

"What did you expect to find here?" demanded the Frenchman gruffly. "Bougereau and the Salon clowns? I collect nothing but Masters."

At the Paris Universal Exposition in 1900, Jimmy was awarded Grand Prix gold medals in both painting and etching, read out to great applause at the head of the list. He might be sagging and weary at 66, bothered by colds and rheumatism; his white oriflamme and black curls might be merged into a nondescript gray; but he wasn't finished yet. With a burst of energy, he packed his paints and went to Dieppe. For three glorious weeks he painted sea and sky, hunted out remembered storefronts, drank *vin ordinaire*. Local boatmen, rowing him out beyond the breakers, marveled at the fragile old gentleman who sat calmly in the bow of the dancing skiff wielding his brushes. Walter Sickert, encountered on the *quai*, fell on his neck in a warm embrace; they sat up smoking and talking about Tite Street days till 2:00 A.M.

Then, one morning, Jimmy woke and had no voice. His bedclothes were soaked with sweat. A doctor, hastily summoned, pronounced emphatic judgment. It was a bad case of flu. He could pull Jimmy out this time: "But, m'sieu, if you ever go outdoors to paint again, it will be at the risk of your life!"

There was no longer any steadfast brother to restore and reassure him; Doctor Willie, risen to eminence and universal affection, had died a few months before. What Jimmy faced now was not a problem of mood or personal will; this was physical, irreversible.

He was terrified. Death was closing in everywhere: Ruskin had been found lifeless in bed after grappling through the night with an imagined emissary of Satan; Toulouse, alcohol-drenched and helpless, was on his way to the grave.

For several months Jimmy drifted back and forth joylessly across the Channel, fearful of every sneeze, a shriveled little man with pink cheeks and feverish darting eyes. He had a conglomeration of homes—the Rue du Bac, Heinemann's flat, Garlant's Hotel, Tallant's, the Chatham—and none. Frantic to find an escape from his worries, he seized upon the imperial "follies" of the despised British. With the anti-Western Boxer rebellion sweeping China, English troops were leading the siege of Peking. "All the Englishmen in the world," cried Jimmy, "are not worth one blue china vase!"

Half the globe away, Her Majesty's regiments were being chopped up by Boer irregulars in South Africa. Jimmy, chortling grimly over British announcements of "planned retreats," insisted that their commanding general, Sir Redvers Buller, had been picked because there was no one under eighty in the War Office's file of "A" names. "They ran down the list, you know, and here was this chap who at Eton had fought and licked a butcher boy." When the inept Buller boasted that he had pulled out of a Boer trap at the Tugela River "without losing a man or a gun," Jimmy added drily: "Or a minute."

But contemplating the Queen's headaches did not really relieve his own. In 1899, on the excuse of Heinemann's wedding, he had traveled to Rome, where he reported after a visit to St. Peter's: "You had only to go inside to know where Christopher Wren got his ideas—how he, well, you know, robbed Peter's to build Paul's!" Now he went south again in search of health and distraction, setting out alone for Tangiers by way of Gibraltar. The weather was bad, and he wound up in bed for two weeks in Marseilles. The doctor there recommended Corsica.

At Ajaccio, the sunshine helped. Jimmy amused himself mimicking fellow guests from Germany. He even got out his paints and did some near-abstract, pre-Kandinsky landscapes. But a "perfect Velázquez" of an equestrian portrait subject—a giant black-bearded shepherd clambering down the hillside with a long pole over his shoulder—was more than he felt able to manage.

Returning to Paris before the end of 1901, he found his house too damp and his studio stairs too steep to climb. He gave up both, slashing a score of unfinished canvases with a curved pruning knife from the Rue du Bac garden. Closing down the Académie Carmen—in three years "poor little Carmen" had made enough to retire—he said farewell to France.

Footloose again, he wandered to Bath and Brighton, where a waiter surmised that the gingery old chap in white ducks and jaunty straw was a "player from the 'alls."

In the spring of 1902, he returned to the banks of the Thames. The house he took at 74 Cheyne Walk in Chelsea overlooked the river, but its window panes were so badly placed as to kill the view. The street approach was marred by an ornate entrance door of beaten copper—"the disastrous effect," observed Jimmy, "of art on the British middle classes." And on the way in from the seashore he had caught a cold—"If it isn't the shocking British boat, it's the freezing British train." Swathed in heavy flannels, inhaling eucalyptus fumes from a steaming jug, he poured out his complaints to Walter Sickert: "The doctor says I am lowered in tone—the result, no doubt, of living among English pictures. I can't stand the climate, the people—what am I doing here, anyhow?"

He was there because he felt the end approaching, and the river held so many memories. The house was within a hundred yards of the old Lindsey Row mansions where he had first lived in London. It had a huge ground-floor studio, and enough bedrooms to accommodate the various Philips ladies—sisters and mother of Trixie—who looked after him.

His landlord promptly and wickedly began construction on the empty lot next door. Jimmy, furious at the daylong clatter but enjoined to avoid excitement, pulled himself to his feet and went to Holland with Charles Freer. At the Hôtel des Indes in The Hague, he was severely stricken with his old nemesis, rheumatic fever. Heinemann rushed to his bedside; Queen Wilhelmina of Holland sent her personal physician.

A reporter for the London *Morning Post*, noting that the doctor had referred to Jimmy's "advanced age," filed a gloomy account of the presumed last days of Whistler. His editor tagged on a semi-obituary summation of the Whistler career, asserting among other things that the *Little White Girl* had been inspired by Swinburne's poem.

Jimmy, insulated by round-the-clock nurses, did not see the story until several weeks later, when his fever had dropped. He had few gestures left to him, but those few he managed with style. He rang for pen, ink, and paper.

"Sirs: May I acknowledge the tender little glow of health induced by reading, as I sat here in the morning sun, the flattering attention paid me by your gentleman of ready wreath and quick biography? It is with almost sorrow that I must beg you to put it back into its pigeonhole . . .

"It is my marvelous privilege to come back, as who should say, while the air is still warm with appreciation, affection and regret, and to learn in how little I had offended. The continuing to wear my own hair and eyebrows, after distinguished *confrères* and eminent persons had long ceased their habit, has clearly given pain . . . I would make my apology, containing also promise, in years to come, to lose these signs of vexing presumption."

Jimmy offered one mild correction: the *Little White Girl* was not based on verses by Swinburne, "for the simple reason that those lines were only written, in my studio, after the picture was painted. And the writing of them was a rare and graceful tribute from the poet to the painter—a noble recognition of one work by the production of a nobler one."

Concluding, he requested that the *Post's* "unmerited eulogy" be withdrawn: "I appeal to your own kind sense of sympathy when I tell you I learn that I have, lurking in London, still 'a friend'—though for the life of me I cannot remember his name."

The old fires flared up again when George Sauter, a young Follower from Munich, stopped in to see Jimmy at The Hague. Sauter, a talented portrait painter, was Secretary of the International Society. Strong-chinned and forthright, with close-cropped black hair, he had an air of military briskness utterly belied by his sensitive canvases. He mentioned that he and his wife were on their way to the Frans Hals Museum in Haarlem.

"Ah, Hals!" cried Jimmy. "How I would love to go with you!" In Jimmy's eyes, the Dutch virtuoso ranked close to Velázquez and Hiroshige. A photo of the Hals canvas depicting the painter and his wife was a fixture of every Whistler studio.

Sauter, aware of Jimmy's precarious condition, pointed out that the 45-minute ride in a crowded express train would be wearing. "Besides, we shall have very little time." Jimmy looked chagrined, but dropped the subject.

Sauter was therefore astonished, on arriving with his wife at the museum in Haarlem Town Hall the next morning, to find Jimmy at the head of the staircase looking spruce if wispy. "Oh, this Hals is a swagger fellow," Jimmy chirped. "Elegant, *soigné*, a real cavalier!"

"Something like Whistler, eh?"

Jimmy beamed.

"But," Sauter went on, "Hals hardly ever set foot outside of Haarlem."

"Art has nothing to do with geography. He didn't have to—Descartes came here to him."

Mrs. Sauter, plump and timorous, fingered a guidebook. "The poor man was constantly in debt, though."

"What real artist isn't?"

"With a dozen children, and a woman who became a mother nine days after she became his wife. He was in his eighties before the town gave him a pension."

"Ah, but he had other rewards—and in this museum you can see them. The Louvre, the Rijksmuseum give you a glimpse of Hals; here you get the full grand sweep of his career. You can actually see on the walls how a master grows in his art, from picture to picture, to the very end." Jimmy's eyes grew brighter; Sauter felt a flicker of concern. But perhaps this kind of excitement would be considered salutary?

"Come," said Jimmy, leading them into the small side-gallery. "We shall start where Hals did. Zaffius, painted in 1611 when the painter was thirty-one. Sound, with a hint of the wonderful fabric-textures to come; but essentially academic. Now let us go to the group portraits, the great banquets of the Civic Guards."

Back in the main hall, they stood before the dozen revelers of the 1616 *Company of St. George*. "See how they are arranged according to status; in these early days he is still concerned with middle-class vanity. Yet notice the movement he creates, with just four diagonal figures and a flag!"

Jimmy pointed out how, in later groups, Hals had ceased tipping his hat to the hierarchy. "He put his interesting people where he wanted them. But what pains he took to make each one interesting! Look at that brushwork—how he makes the dullest face bloom with personality! It's ridiculous to prattle of Hals's 'drunkenness'—such a brush stroke couldn't be learned in a saloon. Of course, he must have been a gusty fellow who liked to gibe at the plodding burghers. So in their envy they built up the fable of an idler.

"Now we come to the finale." Jimmy stopped before a canvas of suddenly crushing power, *The Regents of the Old Men's Almshouse in Haarlem*. Six faces stared out of the canvas: a sot, a madman, an austere treasurer . . .

"Oh, I must touch them!" Jimmy cried out. Before Sauter could stop him, he was creeping under the railing that separated spectators from canvases.

An attendant jumped forward to scold him back. Sauter explained the identity of the visitor.

"*Ach!*" the guard exclaimed. "*De groote Schilder?*" In ten minutes the room was cleared. Jimmy and the Sauters were alone with Hals.

Jimmy scrambled back under the railing, this time before the somber, pitiless study of the almshouse Regentesses, five congealed old women. "Do get me a chair, Sauter . . . and now, do help me up on top of it. Ah, magnificent, magnificent. Those colors, how the palette has been cut down to a few perfect harmonious tones." His voice dropped to a whisper. "Such a white . . . black . . . flesh . . ." He let out a scream of joy: "Oh, I must touch it—just for the fun of it!" and ran his fingers gently over one of the stony faces.

He swayed a little and Sauter ran forward. "The man says we must go now, Jimmy. They have to close for lunch."

"Lunch? Pshaw!" But he let himself be led down. "Hals was eighty-four when he painted those women, Sauter. Imagine, eighty-four! A true painter never stops."

But Jimmy Whistler would have to stop soon, and he knew it. Soon after returning to Cheyne Walk in September he slipped out quite early in the morning, while "the ladies" were still occupied with their toilettes. Walking a block westward to the old pier, he stepped aboard the Thames steamer and, as the little boat hauled around for the long swing downstream, slid into a seat by the railing. By some quirk of circumstance—perhaps the glowering sky—he was the only passenger.

A good omen, because this was his river. It had flowed through his London life like a sweet mournful melody. There to his left were the orderly housefronts of Chelsea: 21 Cheyne Walk, where he had strolled and dreamed with Trixie; Tudor House a few doors east, silent now, with no Rossetti roaring epigrams, no elfish Swinburne sliding down the banisters. And in the surrounding side streets, the ghosts of Carlyle, Maud Franklin, Howell, Wilde.

Beyond Pimlico, the river curved northward toward Westminster.

Jimmy at his western rail caught a glimpse of St. James's Park, where he had taken his mother strolling on the day he finished her portrait. The Houses of Parliament, monumental and incredible as ever, rose to fill his mental canvas. Was it a quarter-century since he had tilted from the witness chair in the Court of Exchequer against the berobed majesty of the British Bar?

The steamer stopped briefly at Charing Cross, and two country couples got aboard. They looked over at the frail top-hatted stranger at the rail and scurried nervously to the other side of the boat.

Jimmy's voyage resumed: eastward in space, backward in time. They crossed under Blackfriars Bridge, where the Greaves boys had always stopped for a cigarette, and soon were threading through the noisy, cargo-jammed Pool of London. Just ahead, beyond the great round Tower of London and its bridge, was the salty pungent world of the East End.

Limehouse, Rotherhithe, Wapping . . . little had changed in forty years. The docks and warehouses lay under the sullen sky just as he had etched them. Among the weed-covered hawsers and bright-painted sails, the same bellowing voices echoed across the water, the same dirty urchins waited on the sloping gravelly bank for the five-hour tide to reach lowest ebb.

Jimmy got up stiffly and walked to the bow, so he could look for the Angel on the starboard side . . .

McGovern's Wharf, Elephant Lane, the herring cannery—and there it was! The overhanging balcony with its familiar rafters seemed a little more bleached, weary, crumbling than he remembered—but oh, how welcome to the eye! Just there he had sketched many an incipient Nocturne; and in the hall inside he had first seen Jo Heffernan dance. Over the boat whistles he heard again the fiery rat-a-tat of her heels.

He stayed at the bow through the slow turning, oblivious to the curious attention of his fellow passengers. The boat did not linger long in the East End, but it was long enough (his doctors, he knew, would have said too long). On the way back a squall came up, and the handful of passengers huddled in the cabin. That kept out the rain, but not the chill.

It was a worn-out Whistler who stumbled through the gaudy copper door in early afternoon. He was docile under Rosalind Birnie Philip's reproof. Quite right, he agreed; there would be no more solo outings.

He had, in fact, reached the point where it was difficult for him to get up the stairs to his bedroom; so just before New Year's of 1903 the model's chamber adjoining the studio on the ground floor was converted for his use. Very soon it was littered with the paraphernalia of the sickroom: medicine bottles, trays, hot water bags.

Jimmy resisted the hospital atmosphere. Wrapped in the fur-lined greatcoat that had been the most impressive feature of his costume at the Académie Carmen—he rejected dressing gowns as "unmanly" and "slovenly"—he dragged about the small room, railing at the nurse who brought him medicines, pushing aside the hot bouillon prescribed for his raw throat: "Take the damned thing away!"

He went out very little now, only when a trusted friend like Heinemann or Charles Freer took him for a drive. Often he was dozing after ten minutes in the crisp winter air.

Even in receiving visitors, his resources were painfully limited. The sparkle had gone from his eyes. After a few words of gossip, he usually fell silent. To Elizabeth Pennell he murmured, "Oh, I wish I felt as well as you look." Some days he scarcely stirred except to get fresh milk for the little alley cat, brown and white and gold, that had become the companion of his sleepless nights: "Beautiful creature, who will look after you when I am gone? You are spoiled, but you are beautiful and deserve to be spoiled."

Yet he had occasional spurts of animation, when he was able to sketch and even fumble among his oils. Each morning, in accordance with instructions, one or two models reported for work; and although they were almost always sent away with a ten-shilling note and a thank you, the fiction that Jimmy was only temporarily indisposed was carefully maintained.

For Richard Canfield he picked up his brush a few times. The gambler was scheduled to return to America in mid-May. From Jimmy's viewpoint, the public furor over their association was ridiculous. Canfield, although all but innocent of formal education, was enormously cultivated, largely through midnight-to-dawn studies during his years as a hotel clerk. Like Howell, he was perceptive, audacious and amusing; and Jimmy had always professed a "taste for low company."

Canfield had bought up some 34 Whistlers, including the portrait of the Comte de Montesquiou and five other major oils. According to Jimmy, Canfield was the "only man who never made a mistake in my studio"—or outside it, either, except perhaps in inducing Montesquiou to part with a painting that Jimmy had hoped would be donated to the Louvre.

The gambler came nearly every afternoon of his final month in London. Usually the two merely exchanged banter. Jimmy always addressed his visitor as "Your Reverence," in tribute to Canfield's immaculate white wing collar, the neat down-the-middle-part in his brown hair, and the paunchy dignity of his figure. In early May, Jimmy reported cheerfully that since Glasgow University had just awarded him an honorary LL.D., he could now, as "Dr. Whistler," meet with "His Reverence" on an equal footing.

The day before Canfield's departure, Jimmy managed to put in an hour at the easel. He suggested that, although the portrait could use a final touch or two, Canfield take it home. "His Reverence will really do very well as he is; and I suspect there may not be any work in me when you come back in autumn. People who observe these matters tell me I am approaching the Biblical three-score and ten."

"Nonsense. I want to see you apply those last touches. After which we shall celebrate in Madrid: Velázquez in the morning, bullfights in the afternoon."

"So be it. Now, Your Reverence, we shall say au revoir with a couple of mint juleps."

Canfield cocked an eyebrow. "Is that what your doctor is prescribing these days? Bourbon?"

"You forget—I am now *myself* a doctor!"

June came, and Jimmy was very feeble. Theodore Duret, crossing the Channel to see him, found a tottering old man who could only stare dumbly, unable to speak; overcome with emotion, Duret fled. The second week in July brought Jimmy's sixty-ninth birthday; it was studiously ignored. On that afternoon of the tenth he signed a few prints, eyes stuporous; but when he tried to draw up a letter exposing the latest critical gaffe of Frederick Wedmore, the pen fell from his fingers.

Not quite the brush. A few mornings later, dozing on his studio couch, Jimmy heard female voices in the hall. He caught the word "model," and a reference to Willie Rothenstein. He struggled into his slippers: "Send her in," he croaked.

A slender, red-haired girl in her twenties skipped through the door. Her wide mouth framed a cheery smile; bright eyes met the world with ingenuous gallantry. Jimmy felt a thrill of recognition. Even before he heard the Irish lilt of her voice, he knew whom she recalled: Hogarth's *Shrimp Girl*, fresh from hawking her wares in Covent Garden.

But the girl had something more than the portrait in the National Gallery. Beneath her sauciness was an ancient wisdom, a wordless compassion. A title flashed through his mind: *Daughter of Eve.*

Her name, she said, was Dorothy Seaton. She had sat to Mr. Rothenstein, who said she must go around to Mr. Whistler.

Jimmy nodded. Surely it was the Fates, acting through Willie, who had sent him the girl as a sign that he was not yet finished; otherwise they would not have put such a subject in his path.

To the model he said, "I must prepare my paints; please come tomorrow at ten." He had been faithful to his Muse, and had on the whole demanded little; now he asked only the strength for this last portrait.

When Dorothy arrived the next morning, he had a vertical 30 × 20 inch canvas on the easel. He posed her for a half-length, luxuriant red hair encircling the oval face, an apple cradled between right thumb and forefinger.

But his hand would not execute what his mind's eye saw. The folds of her black dress eluded him, and the slight curve of her upper lip. Squinting through his double pair of glasses, he lost balance and his brush clattered to the floor.

Jimmy shuffled back toward the window, muttering to himself. "You cannot do it, your day is done." He remained so for a moment, then threw back the bowed shoulders. "You *can* do it, you must try for as long as you live." Returning to the easel, he saw the expression of alarm on the model's face. "Take no notice of me, child." He patted her head lightly. "Old men talk to themselves."

After a few minutes, he put down his brushes. It wasn't going to happen today. "Tomorrow, eh? We'll make a fresh start."

As Dorothy reached the street, she encountered Rosalind Birnie Philip. Jimmy's ward held out a pound note. "Miss Seaton, I suggest you arrange to be ill tomorrow."

The girl paused, turned her head back toward the house. A thin hand waved at the window. She walked on.

The next day she came back—and with her, miraculously, the errant Whistler Muse. Jimmy's eye was clear, his hand steady; the painting unfolded swiftly, as if thirty years had fallen away overnight and he was back at Lindsey Row doing the portrait of his mother. Strange joyous noises hissed through his teeth, and quavery fragments of off-pitch Offenbach. Joseph Pennell came at noon, and was stunned. Jimmy faced him proudly: "How long do you think it took me to paint that? It was done in a couple of hours, this very morning!"

Suddenly, after lunch, his whole body screamed with exhaustion. He stretched out on the bed. Like Hals, he had painted to the end; now he was content to rest.

He opened his eyes to darkness; he did not know how long he had been asleep. The oil lamp that burned through the night beside his bed was on a low flame.

He felt faint. There was a bell cord over the bed for summoning aid; he strained upward, but his arm would not move. No matter. He fell back and stared at the lamp.

By just such a pale, mysterious light he had painted Trixie: *Harmony in Red, Lamplight.* He saw her again in that great barn of a Fulham studio, face sweetly uplifted, patient, accepting . . .

The light dimmed. Someone must have forgotten to replenish the lamp. Damned carelessness . . .

The glow was receding, slipping away from him. With a desperate effort of will, he held onto it.

The light snapped off for an instant, then returned. Now it was a gas jet, in an ancient brass fixture against a dark, grimy wall. He breathed in the smells of whisky, burning logs, pipe tobacco.

Something moved in the shadows. It was the head of a girl: green eyes, coppery hair. He knew those quick poignant features. It was . . . of course! Hadn't he just painted her? The *Daughter of Eve*.

No—that wasn't right. It was, it was . . . how annoying to have a thought just around the bend of one's mind . . .

Heels tapped suddenly on the worn plank floor. The red-haired girl was dancing. She whirled wildly across the smoke-blurred room, skirts flying, pursued by a pounding piano and hoarse excited voices: "*Togha*, Colleen!"; "*Wisha*, Jo! Her likes we'll not see again!"

The girl reached the door—or was it a wall?—and danced right through, onto the Angel balcony overlooking the Thames.

It was twilight along the river. The sky throbbed with pale shafts of orange and deep quiet blues. Behind the Tower of London to the west, a dying sun melted into the horizon.

Splendid, if a trifle obvious. The gathering dusk would mute down the tones to the soft, shimmering film that he wanted. A few moments more, and he would have a superb subject, a Nocturne in Blue-Black and Gold.

He was in no hurry. Lights twinkled a deliberate trail across the Tower Bridge. The shadows deepened. Slowly, a veil descended over the water . . .

# Present Locations of Whistler's Major Works

PARIS, *The Louvre:* *Arrangement in Grey and Black No. 1* (The Artist's Mother); *Head of an Old Man Smoking.*

LONDON, *Tate Gallery:* *The Little White Girl* (Jo Heffernan); *Miss Cicely Alexander; Crepuscule in Flesh Colour and Green* (*Valparaiso*); *Nocturnes: in Black and Gold* (*The Fire Wheel*); *in Blue and Gold* (*Old Battersea Bridge*); *in Blue and Silver* (*Cremorne Lights*).

GLASGOW, *City Art Gallery and Museum:* *Arrangement in Grey and Black No. 2* (Thomas Carlyle).

    *Glasgow University:* *Harmony in Red: Lamplight* (Trixie Whistler); *Gold and Brown: Self-Portrait* (full length).

AMSTERDAM, *Rijksmuseum:* *Arrangement in Yellow and Grey* (Effie Deans).

NEW YORK, *Metropolitan Museum:* *Portraits of Henry Irving; Theodore Duret; Connie Gilchrist. Cremorne Gardens No. 2.*

    *Frick Collection:* *Portraits of Rosa Corder, Lady Meux, Mrs. Leyland and Comte Robert de Montesquiou; Symphony in Grey and Green* (*The Ocean*).

    *New York Public Library:* Avery Collection (Whistler Etchings and some Lithographs)

    (The Brooklyn Museum owns the Boldini portrait of Whistler)

WASHINGTON, D.C. *Freer Gallery:* *The Peacock Room,* with *The Princess from the Land of Porcelain; Nocturne in Blue and Gold*

(*Valparaiso*); *The Thames in Ice; Caprice in Purple and Gold* (*the Golden Screen*); *the Music Room; Arrangement in Black and White: The Young American* (Maud Franklin); *Grey and Silver* (*The Angry Sea*).

*National Gallery: The White Girl*, later called *Symphony in White No. 1* (Jo Heffernan); *Self-Portrait, Gold and Brown* (half length); *George Vanderbilt*.

*Corcoran Gallery: Battersea Reach.*

BOSTON, MASS. *Boston Museum of Fine Arts: Little Rose of Lyme Regis; The Last of Old Westminster; Nocturne in Blue and Silver* (*Venice Lagoon*).

*Isabelle Steward Gardner Museum: Harmony in Blue and Silver* (*Trouville*); *Nocturne in Blue and Silver* (*Battersea Reach*).

CAMBRIDGE, MASS. *Fogg Art Museum: Nocturnes in Grey and Gold and Brown and Gold* (*Chelsea Snow, Chelsea Rags*); Venice pastels of *An Alley, Stormy Sunset*, and *Riva degli Schiavoni*.

WORCESTER, MASS. *Art Museum: The Fur Jacket* (Maud Franklin)

ANDOVER, MASS. *Addison Gallery of American Art: Brown and Silver* (*Old Battersea Bridge*).

HARTFORD, CONN. *Wadsworth Atheneum: The Coast of Brittany.*

FARMINGTON, CONN. *Hill-Stead Museum: The Blue Wave* (*Biarritz*).

PHILDELPHIA, PA. *Philadelphia Museum of Art: The Yellow Buskin* (Lady Archie Campbell); *Purple and Rose* (*The Lange Lijzen*); *Nocturne, Westminster Palace.*

PITTSBURGH, PA. *Carnegie Institute: Portrait of Sarasate.*

DETROIT, MICH. *Institute of Arts: Nocturne in Black and Gold* (*The Falling Rocket*); *Arrangement in Grey* (*Self-Portrait*).

CINCINNATI, OHIO, *Art Museum: At the Piano.*

CHICAGO, ILL. *Art Institute: The Artist's Studio; Southampton Waters.*

BALTIMORE, MD. *Walters Art Gallery:* Water color, *Maud Reading in Bed.*

BIRMINGHAM, ALA. *Barber Institute of Fine Arts: Symphony in White No. 3.*

There are good color reproductions of Whistler works in Denys Sutton's *James McNeill Whistler,* published by Phaidon Press, London, 1966.

www.ingramcontent.com/pod-product-compliance
Lightning Source LLC
Chambersburg PA
CBHW020927020726
47495CB00002B/376